100 GREATEST SHORT STORIES

James Wilde (b. 3 March 1972) is a British writer, editor, and lifelong lover of literature. With a deep appreciation for timeless storytelling, he has dedicated his career to curating and celebrating the written word. Wilde has edited numerous anthologies and is known for making classic fiction accessible to modern readers. *100 Greatest Short Stories* reflects his passion for preserving literary heritage while introducing new generations to the world's finest tales.

100 GREATEST SHORT STORIES

RUPA

Published by
Rupa Publications India Pvt. Ltd 2025
7/16, Ansari Road, Daryaganj
New Delhi 110002

Sales centres:
Bengaluru Chennai Hyderabad
Jaipur Kathmandu Kolkata
Mumbai Prayagraj

P-ISBN: 978-93-7003-248-4
E-ISBN: 978-93-7003-947-6

First impression 2025

10 9 8 7 6 5 4 3 2 1

Printed in India

Contents

1

The Gift of the Magi

O. Henry

One dollar and eighty-seven cents. That was all. And sixty cents of it was in pennies. Pennies saved one and two at a time by bulldozing the grocer and the vegetable man and the butcher until one's cheeks burned with the silent imputation of parsimony that such close dealing implied. Three times Della counted it. One dollar and eighty-seven cents. And the next day would be Christmas.

There was clearly nothing left to do but flop down on the shabby little couch and howl. So Della did it. Which instigates the moral reflection that life is made up of sobs, sniffles, and smiles, with sniffles predominating.

While the mistress of the home is gradually subsiding from the first stage to the second, take a look at the home. A furnished flat at $8 per week. It did not exactly beggar description, but it certainly had that word on the look-out for the mendicancy squad.

In the vestibule below was a letter-box into which no letter would go, and an electric button from which no mortal finger could coax a ring. Also appertaining thereunto was a card bearing the name "Mr. James Dillingham Young."

The "Dillingham" had been flung to the breeze during a former period of prosperity when its possessor was being paid $30 per week. Now, when the income was shrunk to $20, the letters of "Dillingham" looked blurred, as though they were thinking seriously of contracting to a modest and unassuming D. But whenever Mr. James Dillingham Young came home and reached his flat above he was called "Jim" and greatly hugged by Mrs. James Dillingham Young, already introduced to you as Della. Which is all very good.

Della finished her cry and attended to her cheeks with the powder rag. She stood by the window and looked out dully at a grey cat walking a grey fence in a grey backyard. To-morrow would be Christmas Day, and she had only $1.87 with which to buy Jim a present. She had been saving every penny she could for months, with this result. Twenty dollars a week doesn't go far. Expenses had been greater than she had calculated. They always are. Only $1.87 to buy a present for Jim. Her Jim. Many a happy hour she had spent planning for something nice for him. Something fine and rare and sterling—something just a little bit near to being worthy of the honour of being owned by Jim.

There was a pier-glass between the windows of the room. Perhaps you have seen a pier-glass in an $8 flat. A very thin and very agile person may, by observing his reflection in a rapid sequence of longitudinal strips, obtain a fairly accurate conception of his looks. Della, being slender, had mastered the art.

Suddenly she whirled from the window and stood before the glass. Her eyes were shining brilliantly, but her face had lost its colour within twenty seconds. Rapidly she pulled down her hair and let it fall to its full length.

Now, there were two possessions of the James Dillingham Youngs in which they both took a mighty pride. One was Jim's gold watch that had been his father's and his grandfather's. The other was Della's hair. Had the Queen of Sheba lived in the flat across the airshaft, Della would have let her hair hang out of the window some day to dry just to depreciate Her Majesty's jewels and gifts. Had King Solomon been the janitor, with all his treasures piled up in the basement, Jim would have pulled out his watch every time he passed, just to see him pluck at his beard from envy.

So now Della's beautiful hair fell about her, rippling and shining like a cascade of brown waters. It reached below her knee and made itself almost a garment for her. And then she did it up again nervously and quickly. Once she faltered for a minute and stood still while a tear or two splashed on the worn red carpet.

On went her old brown jacket; on went her old brown hat. With a whirl of skirts and with the brilliant sparkle still in her eyes, she cluttered out of the door and down the stairs to the street.

Where she stopped the sign read: "Mme Sofronie. Hair Goods of All Kinds." One Eight up Della ran, and collected herself, panting. Madame, large, too white, chilly, hardly looked the "Sofronie."

"Will you buy my hair?" asked Della.

"I buy hair," said Madame. "Take yer hat off and let's have a sight at the looks of it."

Down rippled the brown cascade.

"Twenty dollars," said Madame, lifting the mass with a practised hand.

"Give it to me quick," said Della.

Oh, and the next two hours tripped by on rosy wings. Forget the hashed metaphor. She was ransacking the stores for Jim's present.

She found it at last. It surely had been made for Jim and no one else. There was no other like it in any of the stores, and she had turned all of them inside out. It was a platinum fob chain simple and chaste in design, properly proclaiming its value by substance alone and not by meretricious ornamentation—as all good things should do. It was even worthy of The Watch. As soon as she saw it she knew that it must be Jim's. It was like him. Quietness and value—the description applied to both. Twenty-one dollars they took from her for it, and she hurried home with the 87 cents. With that chain on his watch Jim might be properly anxious about the time in any company. Grand as the watch was, he sometimes looked at it on the sly on account of the old leather strap that he used in place of a chain.

When Della reached home her intoxication gave way a little to prudence and reason. She got out her curling irons and lighted the gas and went to work repairing the ravages made by generosity added to love. Which is always a tremendous task dear friends—a mammoth task.

Within forty minutes her head was covered with tiny, close-lying curls that made her look wonderfully like a truant schoolboy. She looked at her reflection in the mirror long, carefully, and critically.

"If Jim doesn't kill me," she said to herself, "before he takes a second look at me, he'll say I look like a Coney Island chorus girl. But what could I do—oh! what could I do with a dollar and eighty-seven cents?"

At 7 o'clock the coffee was made and the frying-pan was on the back of the stove hot and ready to cook the chops.

Jim was never late. Della doubled the fob chain in her hand and sat on the corner of the table near the door that he always entered. Then she heard his step on the stair away down on the first flight, and she turned white for just a moment. She had a habit of saying little silent prayers about the simplest everyday things, and now she whispered:

"Please, God, make him think I am still pretty."

The door opened and Jim stepped in and closed it. He looked thin and very serious. Poor fellow, he was only twenty-two—and to be burdened with a family! He needed a new overcoat and he was without gloves.

Jim stepped inside the door, as immovable as a setter at the scent of quail. His eyes were fixed upon Della, and there was an expression in them that she could not read, and it terrified her. It was not anger, nor surprise, nor disapproval, nor horror, nor any of the sentiments that she had been prepared for. He simply stared at her fixedly with that peculiar expression on his face.

Della wriggled off the table and went for him.

"Jim, darling," she cried, "don't look at me that way. I had my hair cut off and sold it because I couldn't have lived through Christmas without giving you a present. It'll grow out again—you won't mind, will you? I just had to do it. My hair grows awfully fast. Say 'Merry Christmas!' Jim, and let's be happy. You don't know what a nice-what a beautiful, nice gift I've got for you."

"You've cut off your hair?" asked Jim, laboriously, as if he had not arrived at that patent fact yet, even after the hardest mental labour.

"Cut it off and sold it," said Della. "Don't you like me just as well, anyhow? I'm me without my hair, ain't I?"

Jim looked about the room curiously.

"You say your hair is gone?" he said, with an air almost of idiocy.

"You needn't look for it," said Della. "It's sold, I tell you—sold and gone, too. It's Christmas Eve, boy. Be good to me, for it went for you. Maybe the hairs of my head were numbered," she went on with a sudden serious sweetness, "but nobody could ever count my love for you. Shall I put the chops on, Jim?"

Out of his trance Jim seemed quickly to wake. He enfolded his Della. For ten seconds let us regard with discreet scrutiny some inconsequential object in the other direction. Eight dollars a week or a million a year—what is the difference? A mathematician or a wit would give you the wrong answer. The magi brought valuable gifts, but that was not among them. This dark assertion will be illuminated later on.

Jim drew a package from his overcoat pocket and threw it upon the table.

"Don't make any mistake, Dell," he said, "about me. I don't think there's anything in the way of a haircut or a shave or a shampoo that could make me like my girl any less. But if you'll unwrap that package you may see why you had me going a while at first."

White fingers and nimble tore at the string and paper. And then an ecstatic scream of joy; and then, alas! a quick feminine change to hysterical tears and wails, necessitating the immediate employment of all the comforting powers of the lord of the flat.

For there lay The Combs—the set of combs, side and back, that Della had worshipped for long in a Broadway window. Beautiful combs, pure tortoise-shell, with jewelled rims—just the shade to wear in the beautiful vanished hair. They were expensive combs, she knew, and her heart had simply craved and yearned over them without the least hope of possession. And now, they were hers, but the tresses that should have adorned the coveted adornments were gone.

But she hugged them to her bosom, and at length she was able to look up with dim eyes and a smile and say: "My hair grows so fast, Jim!"

And then Della leaped up like a little singed cat and cried, "Oh, oh!"

Jim had not yet seen his beautiful present. She held it out to him eagerly upon her open palm. The dull precious metal seemed to flash with a reflection of her bright and ardent spirit.

"Isn't it a dandy, Jim? I hunted all over town to find it. You'll have to look at the time a hundred times a day now. Give me your watch. I want to see how it looks on it."

Instead of obeying, Jim tumbled down on the couch and put his hands under the back of his head and smiled.

"Dell," said he, "let's put our Christmas presents away and keep 'em a while. They're too nice to use just at present. I sold the watch to get the money to buy your combs. And now suppose you put the chops on."

The magi, as you know, were wise men—wonderfully wise men—who brought gifts to the Babe in the manger. They invented the art of giving Christmas presents. Being wise, their gifts were no doubt wise ones, possibly bearing the privilege of exchange in case of duplication. And here I have lamely related to you the uneventful chronicle of two foolish children in a flat who most unwisely sacrificed for each other the greatest treasures of their house. But in a last word to the wise of these days let it be said that of all who give gifts these two were the wisest. Of all who give and receive gifts, such as they are wisest. Everywhere they are wisest. They are the magi.

2

The Last Leaf

O. Henry

In a little district west of Washington Square the streets have run crazy and broken themselves into small strips called "places." These "places" make strange angles and curves. One street crosses itself a time or two. An artist once discovered a valuable possibility in this street. Suppose a collector with a bill for paints, paper and canvas should, in traversing this route, suddenly meet himself coming back, without a cent having been paid on account!

So, to quaint old Greenwich Village the art people soon came prowling, hunting for north windows and eighteenth-century gables and Dutch attics and low rents. Then they imported some pewter mugs and a chafing dish or two from Sixth Avenue, and became a "colony."

At the top of a squatty, three-story brick Sue and Johnsy had their studio. "Johnsy" was familiar for Joanna. One was from Maine; the other from California. They had met at the *table d'hôte* of an Eighth Street "Delmonico's," and found their tastes in art, chicory salad and bishop sleeves so congenial that the joint studio resulted.

That was in May. In November a cold, unseen stranger, whom the doctors called Pneumonia, stalked about the colony, touching one here and there with his icy fingers. Over on the east side this ravager strode boldly, smiting his victims by scores, but his feet trod slowly through the maze of the narrow and moss-grown "places."

Mr. Pneumonia was not what you would call a chivalric old gentleman. A mite of a little woman with blood thinned by California zephyrs was hardly fair game for the red-fisted, short-breathed old duffer. But Johnsy he smote; and she lay, scarcely moving, on her painted iron bedstead, looking through the small Dutch window-panes at the blank side of the next brick house.

One morning the busy doctor invited Sue into the hallway with a shaggy, gray eyebrow.

"She has one chance in—let us say, ten," he said, as he shook down the mercury in his clinical thermometer. "And that chance is for her to want to live. This way people have of lining-up on the side of the undertaker makes the entire pharmacopoeia look silly. Your little lady has made up her mind that she's not going to get well. Has she anything on her mind?"

"She—-she wanted to paint the Bay of Naples some day." said Sue.

"Paint?—bosh! Has she anything on her mind worth thinking twice—a man for instance?"

"A man?" said Sue, with a jew's-harp twang in her voice. "Is a man worth—but, no, doctor; there is nothing of the kind."

"Well, it is the weakness, then," said the doctor. "I will do all that science, so far as it may filter through my efforts, can accomplish. But whenever my patient begins to count the carriages in her funeral procession I subtract 50 per cent from the curative power of medicines. If you will get her to ask one question about the new winter styles in cloak sleeves I will promise you a one-in-five chance for her, instead of one in ten."

After the doctor had gone Sue went into the workroom and cried a Japanese napkin to a pulp. Then she swaggered into Johnsy's room with her drawing board, whistling ragtime.

Johnsy lay, scarcely making a ripple under the bedclothes, with her face toward the window. Sue stopped whistling, thinking she was asleep.

She arranged her board and began a pen-and-ink drawing to illustrate a magazine story. Young artists must pave their way to Art by drawing pictures for magazine stories that young authors write to pave their way to Literature.

As Sue was sketching a pair of elegant horseshow riding trousers and a monocle of the figure of the hero, an Idaho cowboy, she heard a low sound, several times repeated. She went quickly to the bedside.

Johnsy's eyes were open wide. She was looking out the window and counting—counting backward.

"Twelve," she said, and little later "eleven"; and then "ten," and "nine"; and then "eight" and "seven", almost together.

Sue looked solicitously out of the window. What was there to count? There was only a bare, dreary yard to be seen, and the blank side of the brick house twenty feet away. An old, old ivy vine, gnarled and decayed at the roots, climbed half way up the brick wall. The cold breath of autumn had stricken its leaves from the vine until its skeleton branches clung, almost bare, to the crumbling bricks.

"What is it, dear?" asked Sue.

"Six," said Johnsy, in almost a whisper. "They're falling faster now. Three days ago there were almost a hundred. It made my head ache to count them. But now it's easy. There goes another one. There are only five left now."

"Five what, dear? Tell your Sudie."

"Leaves. On the ivy vine. When the last one falls I must go, too. I've known that for three days. Didn't the doctor tell you?"

"Oh, I never heard of such nonsense," complained Sue, with magnificent scorn. "What have old ivy leaves to do with your getting well? And you used to love that vine so, you naughty girl. Don't be a goosey. Why, the doctor told me this morning that your chances for getting well real soon were—let's see exactly what he said—he said the chances were ten to one! Why, that's almost as good a chance as we have in New York when we ride on the street cars or walk past a new building. Try to take some broth now, and let Sudie go back to her drawing, so she can sell the editor man with it, and buy port wine for her sick child, and pork chops for her greedy self."

"You needn't get any more wine," said Johnsy, keeping her eyes fixed out the window. "There goes another. No, I don't want any broth. That leaves just four. I want to see the last one fall before it gets dark. Then I'll go, too."

"Johnsy, dear," said Sue, bending over her, "will you promise me to keep your eyes closed, and not look out the window until I am done working? I must hand those drawings in by to-morrow. I need the light, or I would draw the shade down."

"Couldn't you draw in the other room?" asked Johnsy, coldly.

"I'd rather be here by you," said Sue. "Besides, I don't want you to keep looking at those silly ivy leaves."

"Tell me as soon as you have finished," said Johnsy, closing her eyes, and lying white and still as a fallen statue, "because I want to see the last one fall. I'm tired of waiting. I'm tired of thinking. I want to turn loose my hold on everything, and go sailing down, down, just like one of those poor, tired leaves."

"Try to sleep," said Sue. "I must call Behrman up to be my model for the old hermit miner. I'll not be gone a minute. Don't try to move 'til I come back."

Old Behrman was a painter who lived on the ground floor beneath them. He was past sixty and had a Michael Angelo's Moses beard curling down from the head of a satyr along with the body of an imp. Behrman was a failure in art. Forty years he had wielded the brush without getting near enough to touch the hem of his Mistress's robe. He had been always about to paint a masterpiece, but had never yet begun it. For several years he had painted nothing except now and then a daub in the line of commerce or advertising. He earned a little by serving as a model to those young artists in the colony who could not pay the price of a professional. He drank gin to excess, and still talked of his coming masterpiece. For the rest he was a fierce little old man, who scoffed terribly at softness in any one, and who regarded himself as especial mastiff-in-waiting to protect the two young artists in the studio above.

Sue found Behrman smelling strongly of juniper berries in his dimly lighted den below. In one corner was a blank canvas on an easel that had been waiting there for twenty-five years to receive the first line of the masterpiece. She told him of Johnsy's fancy, and how she feared she would, indeed, light and fragile as a leaf herself, float away, when her slight hold upon the world grew weaker.

Old Behrman, with his red eyes plainly streaming, shouted his contempt and derision for such idiotic imaginings.

"Vass!" he cried. "Is dere people in de world mit der foolishness to die because leafs dey drop off from a confounded vine? I haf not heard of such a thing. No, I will not bose as a model for your fool hermit-dunderhead. Vy do you allow dot silly pusiness to come in der brain of her? Ach, dot poor leetle Miss Yohnsy."

"She is very ill and weak," said Sue, "and the fever has left her mind morbid and full of strange fancies. Very well, Mr. Behrman, if you do not care to pose for me, you needn't. But I think you are a horrid old—old flibbertigibbet."

"You are just like a woman!" yelled Behrman. "Who said I will not bose? Go on. I come mit you. For half an hour I haf peen trying to say dot I am ready to bose. Gott! dis is not any blace in which one so goot as Miss Yohnsy shall lie sick. Some day I vill baint a masterpiece, and ve shall all go away. Gott! yes."

Johnsy was sleeping when they went upstairs. Sue pulled the shade down to the window-sill, and motioned Behrman into the other room. In there they peered out the window fearfully at the ivy vine. Then they looked at each other for a moment without speaking. A persistent, cold rain was falling, mingled with snow. Behrman, in his old blue shirt, took his seat as the hermit miner on an upturned kettle for a rock.

When Sue awoke from an hour's sleep the next morning she found Johnsy with dull, wide-open eyes staring at the drawn green shade.

"Pull it up; I want to see," she ordered, in a whisper.

Wearily Sue obeyed.

But, lo! after the beating rain and fierce gusts of wind that had endured through the livelong night, there yet stood out against the brick wall one ivy leaf. It was the last one on the vine. Still dark green near its stem, with its serrated edges tinted with the yellow of dissolution and decay, it hung bravely from the branch some twenty feet above the ground.

"It is the last one," said Johnsy. "I thought it would surely fall during the night. I heard the wind. It will fall to-day, and I shall die at the same time."

"Dear, dear!" said Sue, leaning her worn face down to the pillow, "think of me, if you won't think of yourself. What would I do?"

But Johnsy did not answer. The lonesomest thing in all the world is a soul when it is making ready to go on its mysterious, far journey. The fancy seemed to possess her more strongly as one by one the ties that bound her to friendship and to earth were loosed.

The day wore away, and even through the twilight they could see the lone ivy leaf clinging to its stem against the wall. And then, with the coming of the night the north wind was again loosed, while the rain still beat against the windows and pattered down from the low Dutch eaves.

When it was light enough Johnsy, the merciless, commanded that the shade be raised.

The ivy leaf was still there.

Johnsy lay for a long time looking at it. And then she called to Sue, who was stirring her chicken broth over the gas stove.

"I've been a bad girl, Sudie," said Johnsy. "Something has made that last leaf stay there to show me how wicked I was. It is a sin to want to die. You may bring a me a little broth now, and some milk with a little port in it, and—no; bring me a hand-mirror first, and then pack some pillows about me, and I will sit up and watch you cook."

And hour later she said:

"Sudie, some day I hope to paint the Bay of Naples."

The doctor came in the afternoon, and Sue had an excuse to go into the hallway as he left.

"Even chances," said the doctor, taking Sue's thin, shaking hand in his. "With good nursing you'll win." And now I must see another case I have downstairs. Behrman, his name is—some kind of an artist, I believe. Pneumonia, too. He is an old, weak man, and the attack is acute. There is no hope for him; but he goes to the hospital to-day to be made more comfortable."

The next day the doctor said to Sue: "She's out of danger. You won. Nutrition and care now—that's all."

And that afternoon Sue came to the bed where Johnsy lay, contentedly knitting a very blue and very useless woollen shoulder scarf, and put one arm around her, pillows and all.

"I have something to tell you, white mouse," she said. "Mr. Behrman died of pneumonia to-day in the hospital. He was ill only two days. The janitor found him the morning of the first day in his room downstairs helpless with pain. His shoes and clothing were wet through and icy cold. They couldn't imagine where he had been on such a dreadful night. And then they found a lantern, still lighted, and a ladder that had been dragged from its place, and some scattered brushes, and a palette with green and yellow colors mixed on it, and—look out the window, dear, at the last ivy leaf on the wall. Didn't you wonder why it never fluttered or moved when the wind blew? Ah, darling, it's Behrman's masterpiece—he painted it there the night that the last leaf fell."

3

The Cop and the Anthem

O. Henry

On his bench in Madison Square Soapy moved uneasily. When wild geese honk high of nights, and when women without sealskin coats grow kind to their husbands, and when Soapy moves uneasily on his bench in the park, you may know that winter is near at hand.

A dead leaf fell in Soapy's lap. That was Jack Frost's card. Jack is kind to the regular denizens of Madison Square, and gives fair warning of his annual call. At the corners of four streets he hands his pasteboard to the North Wind, footman of the mansion of All Outdoors, so that the inhabitants thereof may make ready.

Soapy's mind became cognisant of the fact that the time had come for him to resolve himself into a singular Committee of Ways and Means to provide against the coming rigour. And therefore he moved uneasily on his bench.

The hibernatorial ambitions of Soapy were not of the highest. In them there were no considerations of Mediterranean cruises, of soporific Southern skies drifting in the Vesuvian Bay. Three months on the Island was what his soul craved. Three months of assured board and bed and congenial company, safe from Boreas and bluecoats, seemed to Soapy the essence of things desirable.

For years the hospitable Blackwell's had been his winter quarters. Just as his more fortunate fellow New Yorkers had bought their tickets to Palm Beach and the Riviera each winter, so Soapy had made his humble arrangements for his annual hegira to the Island. And now the time was come. On the previous night three Sabbath newspapers, distributed beneath his coat, about his ankles and over his lap, had failed to repulse the cold as he slept on his bench near the spurting fountain in the ancient square. So the Island loomed big and timely in Soapy's mind. He scorned the provisions made in the name of charity for the city's dependents. In Soapy's opinion the Law was more benign than Philanthropy. There was an endless round of institutions, municipal and eleemosynary, on which he might set out and receive lodging and food accordant with the simple life. But to one of Soapy's proud spirit the gifts of charity are encumbered. If not in coin you must pay in humiliation of spirit for every benefit received at the hands of philanthropy. As Caesar had his Brutus, every bed of charity must have its toll of a bath, every loaf of bread its compensation of a private and personal inquisition. Wherefore it is better to be a guest of the law, which though conducted by rules, does not meddle unduly with a gentleman's private affairs.

Soapy, having decided to go to the Island, at once set about accomplishing his desire. There were many easy ways of doing this. The pleasantest was to dine luxuriously at some expensive restaurant; and then, after declaring insolvency, be handed over quietly and without uproar to a policeman. An accommodating magistrate would do the rest.

Soapy left his bench and strolled out of the square and across the level sea of asphalt, where Broadway and Fifth Avenue flow together. Up Broadway he turned, and halted at a glittering cafe, where are gathered together nightly the choicest products of the grape, the silkworm and the protoplasm.

Soapy had confidence in himself from the lowest button of his vest upward. He was shaven, and his coat was decent and his neat black, ready-tied four-in-hand had been presented to him by a lady missionary on Thanksgiving Day. If he could reach a table in the restaurant unsuspected success would be his. The portion of him that would show above the table would raise no doubt in the waiter's mind. A roasted mallard duck, thought Soapy, would be about the thing—with a bottle of Chablis, and then Camembert, a demi-tasse and a cigar. One dollar for the cigar would be enough. The total would not be so high as to call forth any supreme manifestation of revenge from the cafe management; and yet the meat would leave him filled and happy for the journey to his winter refuge.

But as Soapy set foot inside the restaurant door the head waiter's eye fell upon his frayed trousers and decadent shoes. Strong and ready hands turned him about and conveyed him in silence and haste to the sidewalk and averted the ignoble fate of the menaced mallard.

Soapy turned off Broadway. It seemed that his route to the coveted island was not to be an epicurean one. Some other way of entering limbo must be thought of.

At a corner of Sixth Avenue electric lights and cunningly displayed wares behind plate-glass made a shop window conspicuous. Soapy took a cobblestone and dashed it through the glass. People came running around the corner, a policeman in the lead. Soapy stood still, with his hands in his pockets, and smiled at the sight of brass buttons.

"Where's the man that done that?" inquired the officer excitedly.

"Don't you figure out that I might have had something to do with it?" said Soapy, not without sarcasm, but friendly, as one greets good fortune.

The policeman's mind refused to accept Soapy even as a clue. Men who smash windows do not remain to parley with the law's minions. They take to their heels. The policeman saw a man half way down the block running to catch a car. With drawn club he joined in the pursuit. Soapy, with disgust in his heart, loafed along, twice unsuccessful.

On the opposite side of the street was a restaurant of no great pretensions. It catered to large appetites and modest purses. Its crockery and atmosphere were thick; its soup and napery thin. Into this place Soapy took his accusive shoes and telltale trousers without challenge. At a table he sat and consumed beefsteak, flapjacks, doughnuts and pie. And then to the waiter be betrayed the fact that the minutest coin and himself were strangers.

"Now, get busy and call a cop," said Soapy. "And don't keep a gentleman waiting."

"No cop for youse," said the waiter, with a voice like butter cakes and an eye like the cherry in a Manhattan cocktail. "Hey, Con!"

Neatly upon his left ear on the callous pavement two waiters pitched Soapy. He arose, joint by joint, as a carpenter's rule opens, and beat the dust from his clothes. Arrest seemed but a rosy dream. The Island seemed very far away. A policeman who stood before a drug store two doors away laughed and walked down the street.

Five blocks Soapy travelled before his courage permitted him to woo capture again. This time the opportunity presented what he fatuously termed to himself a "cinch." A young woman of a modest and pleasing guise was standing before a show window gazing with sprightly interest at its display of shaving mugs and inkstands, and two yards from the window a large policeman of severe demeanour leaned against a water plug.

It was Soapy's design to assume the role of the despicable and execrated "masher." The refined and elegant appearance of his victim and the contiguity of the conscientious cop encouraged him to believe that he would soon feel the pleasant official clutch upon his arm that would insure his winter quarters on the right little, tight little isle.

Soapy straightened the lady missionary's readymade tie, dragged his shrinking cuffs into the open, set his hat at a killing cant and sidled toward the young woman. He made eyes at her, was taken with sudden coughs and "hems," smiled, smirked and went brazenly through the impudent and contemptible litany of the "masher." With half an eye Soapy saw that the policeman was watching him fixedly. The young woman moved away a few steps, and again bestowed her absorbed attention upon the shaving mugs. Soapy followed, boldly stepping to her side, raised his hat and said:

"Ah there, Bedelia! Don't you want to come and play in my yard?"

The policeman was still looking. The persecuted young woman had but to beckon a finger and Soapy would be practically en route for his insular haven. Already he imagined he could feel the cozy warmth of the station-house. The young woman faced him and, stretching out a hand, caught Soapy's coat sleeve.

"Sure, Mike," she said joyfully, "if you'll blow me to a pail of suds. I'd have spoke to you sooner, but the cop was watching."

With the young woman playing the clinging ivy to his oak Soapy walked past the policeman overcome with gloom. He seemed doomed to liberty.

At the next corner he shook off his companion and ran. He halted in the district where by night are found the lightest streets, hearts, vows and librettos.

Women in furs and men in greatcoats moved gaily in the wintry air. A sudden fear seized Soapy that some dreadful enchantment had rendered him immune to arrest. The thought brought a little of panic upon it, and when he came upon another policeman lounging grandly in front of a transplendent theatre he caught at the immediate straw of "disorderly conduct."

On the sidewalk Soapy began to yell drunken gibberish at the top of his harsh voice. He danced, howled, raved and otherwise disturbed the welkin.

The policeman twirled his club, turned his back to Soapy and remarked to a citizen.

"'Tis one of them Yale lads celebratin' the goose egg they give to the Hartford College. Noisy; but no harm. We've instructions to lave them be."

Disconsolate, Soapy ceased his unavailing racket. Would never a policeman lay hands on him? In his fancy the Island seemed an unattainable Arcadia. He buttoned his thin coat against the chilling wind.

In a cigar store he saw a well-dressed man lighting a cigar at a swinging light. His silk umbrella he had set by the door on entering. Soapy stepped inside, secured the umbrella and sauntered off with it slowly. The man at the cigar light followed hastily.

"My umbrella," he said, sternly.

"Oh, is it?" sneered Soapy, adding insult to petit larceny. "Well, why don't you call a policeman? I took it. Your umbrella! Why don't you call a cop? There stands one on the corner."

The umbrella owner slowed his steps. Soapy did likewise, with a presentiment that luck would again run against him. The policeman looked at the two curiously.

"Of course," said the umbrella man—"that is—well, you know how these mistakes occur—I—if it's your umbrella I hope you'll excuse me—I picked it up this morning in a restaurant—If you recognise it as yours, why—I hope you'll—"

"Of course it's mine," said Soapy, viciously.

The ex-umbrella man retreated. The policeman hurried to assist a tall blonde in an opera cloak across the street in front of a street car that was approaching two blocks away.

Soapy walked eastward through a street damaged by improvements. He hurled the umbrella wrathfully into an excavation. He muttered against the men who wear helmets and carry clubs. Because he wanted to fall into their clutches, they seemed to regard him as a king who could do no wrong.

At length Soapy reached one of the avenues to the east where the glitter and turmoil was but faint. He set his face down this toward

Madison Square, for the homing instinct survives even when the home is a park bench.

But on an unusually quiet corner Soapy came to a standstill. Here was an old church, quaint and rambling and gabled. Through one violet-stained window a soft light glowed, where, no doubt, the organist loitered over the keys, making sure of his mastery of the coming Sabbath anthem. For there drifted out to Soapy's ears sweet music that caught and held him transfixed against the convolutions of the iron fence.

The moon was above, lustrous and serene; vehicles and pedestrians were few; sparrows twittered sleepily in the eaves—for a little while the scene might have been a country churchyard. And the anthem that the organist played cemented Soapy to the iron fence, for he had known it well in the days when his life contained such things as mothers and roses and ambitions and friends and immaculate thoughts and collars.

The conjunction of Soapy's receptive state of mind and the influences about the old church wrought a sudden and wonderful change in his soul. He viewed with swift horror the pit into which he had tumbled, the degraded days, unworthy desires, dead hopes, wrecked faculties and base motives that made up his existence.

And also in a moment his heart responded thrillingly to this novel mood. An instantaneous and strong impulse moved him to battle with his desperate fate. He would pull himself out of the mire; he would make a man of himself again; he would conquer the evil that had taken possession of him. There was time; he was comparatively young yet; he would resurrect his old eager ambitions and pursue them without faltering. Those solemn but sweet organ notes had set up a revolution in him. To-morrow he would go into the roaring downtown district and find work. A fur importer had once offered him a place as driver. He would find him to-morrow and ask for the position. He would be somebody in the world. He would—

Soapy felt a hand laid on his arm. He looked quickly around into the broad face of a policeman.

"What are you doin' here?" asked the officer.

"Nothin'," said Soapy.

"Then come along," said the policeman.

"Three months on the Island," said the Magistrate in the Police Court the next morning.

4

A Retrieved Reformation

O. Henry

A guard came to the prison shoe-shop, where Jimmy Valentine was assiduously stitching uppers, and escorted him to the front office. There the warden handed Jimmy his pardon, which had been signed that morning by the governor. Jimmy took it in a tired kind of way. He had served nearly ten months of a four year sentence. He had expected to stay only about three months, at the longest. When a man with as many friends on the outside as Jimmy Valentine had is received in the "stir" it is hardly worth while to cut his hair.

"Now, Valentine," said the warden, "you'll go out in the morning. Brace up, and make a man of yourself. You're not a bad fellow at heart. Stop cracking safes, and live straight."

"Me?" said Jimmy, in surprise. "Why, I never cracked a safe in my life."

"Oh, no," laughed the warden. "Of course not. Let's see, now. How was it you happened to get sent up on that Springfield job? Was it because you wouldn't prove an alibi for fear of compromising somebody in extremely high-toned society? Or was it simply a case of a mean old jury that had it in for you? It's always one or the other with you innocent victims."

"Me?" said Jimmy, still blankly virtuous. "Why, warden, I never was in Springfield in my life!"

"Take him back, Cronin!" said the warden, "and fix him up with outgoing clothes. Unlock him at seven in the morning, and let him come to the bull-pen. Better think over my advice, Valentine."

At a quarter past seven on the next morning Jimmy stood in the warden's outer office. He had on a suit of the villainously fitting, ready-made clothes and a pair of the stiff, squeaky shoes that the state furnishes to its discharged compulsory guests.

The clerk handed him a railroad ticket and the five-dollar bill with which the law expected him to rehabilitate himself into good citizenship and prosperity. The warden gave him a cigar, and shook hands. Valentine, 9762, was chronicled on the books, "Pardoned by Governor," and Mr. James Valentine walked out into the sunshine.

Disregarding the song of the birds, the waving green trees, and the smell of the flowers, Jimmy headed straight for a restaurant. There he tasted the first sweet joys of liberty in the shape of a broiled chicken and a bottle of white wine—followed by a cigar a grade better than the one the warden had given him. From there he proceeded leisurely to the depot. He tossed a quarter into the hat of a blind man sitting by the door, and boarded his train. Three hours set him down in a little town near the state line. He went to the cafe of one Mike Dolan and shook hands with Mike, who was alone behind the bar.

"Sorry we couldn't make it sooner, Jimmy, me boy," said Mike. "But we had that protest from Springfield to buck against, and the governor nearly balked. Feeling all right?"

"Fine," said Jimmy. "Got my key?"

He got his key and went upstairs, unlocking the door of a room at the rear. Everything was just as he had left it. There on the floor was still Ben Price's collar-button that had been torn from that eminent detective's shirt-band when they had overpowered Jimmy to arrest him.

Pulling out from the wall a folding-bed, Jimmy slid back a panel in the wall and dragged out a dust-covered suit-case. He opened this and gazed fondly at the finest set of burglar's tools in the East. It was a complete set, made of specially tempered steel, the latest designs in drills, punches, braces and bits, jimmies, clamps, and augers, with two or three novelties, invented by Jimmy himself, in which he took pride. Over nine hundred dollars they had cost him to have made at ——, a place where they make such things for the profession.

In half an hour Jimmy went down stairs and through the cafe. He was now dressed in tasteful and well-fitting clothes, and carried his dusted and cleaned suit-case in his hand.

"Got anything on?" asked Mike Dolan, genially.

"Me?" said Jimmy, in a puzzled tone. "I don't understand. I'm representing the New York Amalgamated Short Snap Biscuit Cracker and Frazzled Wheat Company."

This statement delighted Mike to such an extent that Jimmy had to take a seltzer-and-milk on the spot. He never touched "hard" drinks.

A week after the release of Valentine, 9762, there was a neat job of safe-burglary done in Richmond, Indiana, with no clue to the author. A scant eight hundred dollars was all that was secured. Two weeks after that a patented, improved, burglar-proof safe in Logansport was opened like a cheese to the tune of fifteen hundred dollars, currency; securities and silver untouched. That began to interest the rogue-catchers. Then an old-fashioned bank-safe in Jefferson City became active and threw out of its crater an eruption of bank-notes amounting to five thousand dollars. The losses were now high enough to bring the matter up into Ben Price's class of work. By comparing notes, a remarkable similarity in the methods of the burglaries was noticed. Ben Price investigated the scenes of the robberies, and was heard to remark:

"That's Dandy Jim Valentine's autograph. He's resumed business. Look at that combination knob—jerked out as easy as pulling up a radish in wet weather. He's got the only clamps that can do it. And look how clean those tumblers were punched out! Jimmy never has to drill but one hole. Yes, I guess I want Mr. Valentine. He'll do his bit next time without any short-time or clemency foolishness."

Ben Price knew Jimmy's habits. He had learned them while working on the Springfield case. Long jumps, quick get-aways, no confederates, and a taste for good society—these ways had helped Mr. Valentine to become noted as a successful dodger of retribution. It was given out that Ben Price had taken up the trail of the elusive cracksman, and other people with burglar-proof safes felt more at ease.

One afternoon Jimmy Valentine and his suit-case climbed out of the mail-hack in Elmore, a little town five miles off the railroad down in the black-jack country of Arkansas. Jimmy, looking like an athletic young senior just home from college, went down the board side-walk toward the hotel.

A young lady crossed the street, passed him at the corner and entered a door over which was the sign, "The Elmore Bank." Jimmy Valentine looked into her eyes, forgot what he was, and became another man. She lowered her eyes and coloured slightly. Young men of Jimmy's style and looks were scarce in Elmore.

Jimmy collared a boy that was loafing on the steps of the bank as if he were one of the stockholders, and began to ask him questions about the town, feeding him dimes at intervals. By and by the young lady came out, looking royally unconscious of the young man with the suit- case, and went her way.

"Isn't that young lady Polly Simpson?" asked Jimmy, with specious guile.

"Naw," said the boy. "She's Annabel Adams. Her pa owns this bank. Why'd you come to Elmore for? Is that a gold watch-chain? I'm going to get a bulldog. Got any more dimes?"

Jimmy went to the Planters' Hotel, registered as Ralph D. Spencer, and engaged a room. He leaned on the desk and declared his platform to the clerk. He said he had come to Elmore to look for a location to go into business. How was the shoe business, now, in the town? He had thought of the shoe business. Was there an opening?

The clerk was impressed by the clothes and manner of Jimmy. He, himself, was something of a pattern of fashion to the thinly gilded youth of Elmore, but he now perceived his shortcomings. While trying to figure out Jimmy's manner of tying his four-in-hand he cordially gave information.

Yes, there ought to be a good opening in the shoe line. There wasn't an exclusive shoe-store in the place. The dry-goods and general stores handled them. Business in all lines was fairly good. Hoped Mr. Spencer would decide to locate in Elmore. He would find it a pleasant town to live in, and the people very sociable.

Mr. Spencer thought he would stop over in the town a few days and look over the situation. No, the clerk needn't call the boy. He would carry up his suit-case, himself; it was rather heavy.

Mr. Ralph Spencer, the phoenix that arose from Jimmy Valentine's ashes—ashes left by the flame of a sudden and alterative attack of love—remained in Elmore, and prospered. He opened a shoe-store and secured a good run of trade.

Socially he was also a success, and made many friends. And he accomplished the wish of his heart. He met Miss Annabel Adams, and became more and more captivated by her charms.

At the end of a year the situation of Mr. Ralph Spencer was this: he had won the respect of the community, his shoe-store was flourishing, and he and Annabel were engaged to be married in two weeks. Mr. Adams, the typical, plodding, country banker, approved of Spencer.

Annabel's pride in him almost equalled her affection. He was as much at home in the family of Mr. Adams and that of Annabel's married sister as if he were already a member.

One day Jimmy sat down in his room and wrote this letter, which he mailed to the safe address of one of his old friends in St. Louis:

Dear Old Pal:

I want you to be at Sullivan's place, in Little Rock, next Wednesday night, at nine o'clock. I want you to wind up some little matters for me. And, also, I want to make you a present of my kit of tools. I know you'll be glad to get them—you couldn't duplicate the lot for a thousand dollars. Say, Billy, I've quit the old business—a year ago. I've got a nice store. I'm making an honest living, and I'm going to marry the finest girl on earth two weeks from now. It's the only life, Billy—the straight one. I wouldn't touch a dollar of another man's money now for a million. After I get married I'm going to sell out and go West, where there won't be so much danger of having old scores brought up against me. I tell you, Billy, she's an angel. She believes in me; and I wouldn't do another crooked thing for the whole world. Be sure to be at Sully's, for I must see you. I'll bring along the tools with me.

Your old friend,
Jimmy.

On the Monday night after Jimmy wrote this letter, Ben Price jogged unobtrusively into Elmore in a livery buggy. He lounged about town in his quiet way until he found out what he wanted to know. From the drug-store across the street from Spencer's shoe-store he got a good look at Ralph D. Spencer.

"Going to marry the banker's daughter are you, Jimmy?" said Ben to himself, softly. "Well, I don't know!"

The next morning Jimmy took breakfast at the Adamses. He was going to Little Rock that day to order his wedding-suit and buy something nice for Annabel. That would be the first time he had left town since he came to Elmore. It had been more than a year now since those last professional "jobs," and he thought he could safely venture out.

After breakfast quite a family party went downtown together—Mr. Adams, Annabel, Jimmy, and Annabel's married sister with her two little girls, aged five and nine. They came by the hotel where Jimmy still boarded, and he ran up to his room and brought along his suit-case. Then they went on to the bank. There stood Jimmy's horse and buggy and Dolph Gibson, who was going to drive him over to the railroad station.

All went inside the high, carved oak railings into the banking-room—Jimmy included, for Mr. Adams's future son-in-law was welcome anywhere. The clerks were pleased to be greeted by the good-looking, agreeable young man who was going to marry Miss Annabel. Jimmy set his suit-case down. Annabel, whose heart was bubbling with happiness and lively youth, put on Jimmy's hat, and picked up the suit-case. "Wouldn't I make a nice drummer?" said Annabel. "My! Ralph, how heavy it is? Feels like it was full of gold bricks."

"Lot of nickel-plated shoe-horns in there," said Jimmy, coolly, "that I'm going to return. Thought I'd save express charges by taking them up. I'm getting awfully economical."

The Elmore Bank had just put in a new safe and vault. Mr. Adams was very proud of it, and insisted on an inspection by every one. The vault was a small one, but it had a new, patented door. It fastened with three solid steel bolts thrown simultaneously with a single handle, and had a time-lock. Mr. Adams beamingly explained its workings to Mr. Spencer, who showed a courteous but not too intelligent interest. The two children, May and Agatha, were delighted by the shining metal and funny clock and knobs.

While they were thus engaged Ben Price sauntered in and leaned on his elbow, looking casually inside between the railings. He told the teller that he didn't want anything; he was just waiting for a man he knew.

Suddenly there was a scream or two from the women, and a commotion. Unperceived by the elders, May, the nine-year-old girl, in a spirit of play, had shut Agatha in the vault. She had then shot the bolts and turned the knob of the combination as she had seen Mr. Adams do.

The old banker sprang to the handle and tugged at it for a moment. "The door can't be opened," he groaned. "The clock hasn't been wound nor the combination set."

Agatha's mother screamed again, hysterically.

"Hush!" said Mr. Adams, raising his trembling hand. "All be quite for a moment. Agatha!" he called as loudly as he could. "Listen to me." During the following silence they could just hear the faint sound of the child wildly shrieking in the dark vault in a panic of terror.

"My precious darling!" wailed the mother. "She will die of fright! Open the door! Oh, break it open! Can't you men do something?"

"There isn't a man nearer than Little Rock who can open that door," said Mr. Adams, in a shaky voice. "My God! Spencer, what shall we do? That child—she can't stand it long in there. There isn't enough air, and, besides, she'll go into convulsions from fright."

Agatha's mother, frantic now, beat the door of the vault with her hands. Somebody wildly suggested dynamite. Annabel turned to Jimmy, her large eyes full of anguish, but not yet despairing. To a woman nothing seems quite impossible to the powers of the man she worships.

"Can't you do something, Ralph—*try*, won't you?"

He looked at her with a queer, soft smile on his lips and in his keen eyes.

"Annabel," he said, "give me that rose you are wearing, will you?"

Hardly believing that she heard him aright, she unpinned the bud from the bosom of her dress, and placed it in his hand. Jimmy stuffed it into his vest-pocket, threw off his coat and pulled up his shirt- sleeves. With that act Ralph D. Spencer passed away and Jimmy Valentine took his place.

"Get away from the door, all of you," he commanded, shortly.

He set his suit-case on the table, and opened it out flat. From that time on he seemed to be unconscious of the presence of any one else. He laid out the shining, queer implements swiftly and orderly, whistling softly to himself as he always did when at work. In a deep silence and immovable, the others watched him as if under a spell.

In a minute Jimmy's pet drill was biting smoothly into the steel door. In ten minutes—breaking his own burglarious record—he threw back the bolts and opened the door.

Agatha, almost collapsed, but safe, was gathered into her mother's arms.

Jimmy Valentine put on his coat, and walked outside the railings towards the front door. As he went he thought he heard a far-away voice that he once knew call "Ralph!" But he never hesitated.

At the door a big man stood somewhat in his way.

"Hello, Ben!" said Jimmy, still with his strange smile. "Got around at last, have you? Well, let's go. I don't know that it makes much difference, now."

And then Ben Price acted rather strangely.

"Guess you're mistaken, Mr. Spencer," he said. "Don't believe I recognize you. Your buggy's waiting for you, ain't it?"

And Ben Price turned and strolled down the street.

5

The Tell-Tale Heart

Edgar Allen Poe

True!—nervous—very, very dreadfully nervous I had been and am; but why will you say that I am mad? The disease had sharpened my senses—not destroyed—not dulled them. Above all was the sense of hearing acute. I heard all things in the heaven and in the earth. I heard many things in hell. How, then, am I mad? Hearken! and observe how healthily—how calmly I can tell you the whole story.

It is impossible to say how first the idea entered my brain; but once conceived, it haunted me day and night. Object there was none. Passion there was none. I loved the old man. He had never wronged me. He had never given me insult. For his gold I had no desire. I think it was his eye! yes, it was this! One of his eyes resembled that of a vulture—a pale blue eye, with a film over it. Whenever it fell upon me, my blood ran cold; and so by degrees—very gradually—I made up my mind to take the life of the old man, and thus rid myself of the eye forever.

Now this is the point. You fancy me mad. Madmen know nothing. But you should have seen me. You should have seen how wisely I proceeded—with what caution—with what foresight—with what dissimulation I went to work! I was never kinder to the old man than during the whole week before I killed him. And every night, about midnight, I turned the latch of his door and opened it—oh, so gently! And then, when I had made an opening sufficient for my head, I put in a dark lantern, all closed, closed, so that no light shone out, and then I thrust in my head. Oh, you would have laughed to see how cunningly I thrust it in! I moved it slowly—very, very slowly, so that I might not disturb the old man's sleep. It took me an hour to place my whole head within the opening so far that I could see him as he lay upon his bed. Ha!—would a madman have been so wise as this? And then, when my head was well in the room, I undid the lantern cautiously—oh, so cautiously—cautiously (for the hinges creaked)—I undid it just so much that a single thin ray fell upon the vulture eye. And this I did for seven long nights—every night just at midnight—but I found the eye always closed; and so it was impossible to do the work; for it was not the old man who vexed me, but his Evil Eye. And every morning, when the day broke, I went boldly into the chamber, and spoke courageously to him, calling him by name in a hearty tone, and inquiring how he had passed the night. So you see he would have been a very profound old man, indeed, to suspect that every night, just at twelve, I looked in upon him while he slept.

Upon the eighth night I was more than usually cautious in opening the door. A watch's minute hand moves more quickly than did mine. Never before that night had I felt the extent of my own powers—of my sagacity. I could scarcely contain my feelings of triumph. To think that there I was, opening the door, little by little, and he not even to dream of my secret deeds or thoughts. I fairly chuckled at the idea; and perhaps he heard me; for he moved on the bed suddenly, as if startled. Now you may think that I drew back—but no. His room was as black as pitch with the thick darkness, (for the shutters were close fastened, through fear of robbers,) and so I knew that he could not see the opening of the door, and I kept pushing it on steadily, steadily.

I had my head in, and was about to open the lantern, when my thumb slipped upon the tin fastening, and the old man sprang up in the bed, crying out—"Who's there?"

I kept quite still and said nothing. For a whole hour I did not move a muscle, and in the meantime I did not hear him lie down. He was still sitting up in the bed listening;—just as I have done, night after night, hearkening to the death watches in the wall.

Presently I heard a slight groan, and I knew it was the groan of mortal terror. It was not a groan of pain or of grief—oh, no!—it was the low stifled sound that arises from the bottom of the soul when overcharged with awe. I knew the sound well. Many a night, just at midnight, when all the world slept, it has welled up from my own bosom, deepening, with its dreadful echo, the terrors that distracted me. I say I knew it well. I knew what the old man felt, and pitied him, although I chuckled at heart. I knew that he had been lying awake ever since the first slight noise, when he had turned in the bed. His fears had been ever since growing upon him. He had been trying to fancy them causeless, but could not. He had been saying to himself—"It is nothing but the wind in the chimney—it is only a mouse crossing the floor," or "it is merely a cricket which has made a single chirp." Yes, he has been trying to comfort himself with these suppositions: but he had found all in vain. All in vain; because Death, in approaching him had stalked with his black shadow before him, and enveloped the victim. And it was the mournful influence of the unperceived shadow that caused him to feel—although he neither saw nor heard—to feel the presence of my head within the room.

When I had waited a long time, very patiently, without hearing him lie down, I resolved to open a little—a very, very little crevice in the lantern. So I opened it—you cannot imagine how stealthily, stealthily—until, at length a single dim ray, like the thread of the spider, shot from out the crevice and fell upon the vulture eye.

It was open—wide, wide open—and I grew furious as I gazed upon it. I saw it with perfect distinctness—all a dull blue, with a hideous veil over it that chilled the very marrow in my bones; but I could see nothing else of the old man's face or person: for I had directed the ray as if by instinct, precisely upon the damned spot.

And have I not told you that what you mistake for madness is but over acuteness of the senses?—now, I say, there came to my ears a low, dull, quick sound, such as a watch makes when enveloped in cotton. I knew that sound well, too. It was the beating of the old man's heart. It increased my fury, as the beating of a drum stimulates the soldier into courage.

But even yet I refrained and kept still. I scarcely breathed. I held the lantern motionless. I tried how steadily I could maintain the ray upon the eye. Meantime the hellish tattoo of the heart increased. It grew quicker and quicker, and louder and louder every instant. The old man's terror must have been extreme! It grew louder, I say, louder every moment!—do you mark me well? I have told you that I am nervous: so I am. And now at the dead hour of the night, amid the dreadful silence of that old house, so strange a noise as this excited me to uncontrollable terror. Yet, for some minutes longer I refrained and stood still. But the beating grew louder, louder! I thought the heart must burst. And now a new anxiety seized me—the sound would be heard by a neighbor! The old man's hour had come! With a loud yell, I threw open the lantern and leaped into the room. He shrieked once—once only. In an instant I dragged him to the floor, and pulled the heavy bed over him. I then smiled gaily, to find the deed so far done. But, for many minutes, the heart beat on with a muffled sound. This, however, did not vex me; it would not be heard through the wall. At length it ceased. The old man was dead. I removed the bed and examined the corpse. Yes, he was stone, stone dead. I placed my hand upon the heart and held it there many minutes. There was no pulsation. He was stone dead. His eye would trouble me no more.

If still you think me mad, you will think so no longer when I describe the wise precautions I took for the concealment of the body. The night waned, and I worked hastily, but in silence. First of all I dismembered the corpse. I cut off the head and the arms and the legs.

I then took up three planks from the flooring of the chamber, and deposited all between the scantlings. I then replaced the boards so cleverly, so cunningly, that no human eye—not even his—could have detected any thing wrong. There was nothing to wash out—no stain of any kind—no blood-spot whatever. I had been too wary for that. A tub had caught all—ha! ha!

When I had made an end of these labors, it was four o'clock—still dark as midnight. As the bell sounded the hour, there came a knocking at the street door. I went down to open it with a light heart, — for what had I now to fear? There entered three men, who introduced themselves, with perfect suavity, as officers of the police. A shriek had been heard by a neighbor during the night; suspicion of foul play had been aroused; information had been lodged at the police office, and they (the officers) had been deputed to search the premises.

I smiled,—for what had I to fear? I bade the gentlemen welcome. The shriek, I said, was my own in a dream. The old man, I mentioned, was absent in the country. I took my visitors all over the house. I bade them search—search well. I led them, at length, to his chamber. I showed them his treasures, secure, undisturbed. In the enthusiasm of my confidence, I brought chairs into the room, and desired them here to rest from their fatigues, while I myself, in the wild audacity of my perfect triumph, placed my own seat upon the very spot beneath which reposed the corpse of the victim.

The officers were satisfied. My manner had convinced them. I was singularly at ease. They sat, and while I answered cheerily, they chatted of familiar things. But, ere long, I felt myself getting pale and wished them gone. My head ached, and I fancied a ringing in my ears: but still they sat and still chatted. The ringing became more distinct: — it continued and became more distinct: I talked more freely to get rid of the feeling: but it continued and gained definitiveness—until, at length, I found that the noise was not within my ears.

No doubt I now grew *very* pale; — but I talked more fluently, and with a heightened voice. Yet the sound increased—and what could I do? It was a low, dull, quick sound—much such a sound as a watch makes when enveloped in cotton. I gasped for breath—and yet the officers heard it not. I talked more quickly—more vehemently; but the noise steadily increased. I arose and argued about trifles, in a high key and with violent gesticulations; but the noise steadily increased. Why would they not be gone? I paced the floor to and fro with heavy strides, as if excited to fury by the observations of the men—but the noise steadily increased. Oh God! what could I do? I foamed—I raved—I swore! I swung the chair upon which I had been sitting, and grated it upon the boards, but the noise arose over all and continually increased. It grew louder—louder—louder! And still the men chatted pleasantly, and smiled. Was it possible they heard not? Almighty God!— no, no! They heard!—they suspected!—they knew!—they were making a mockery of my horror!—this I thought, and this I think. But anything was better than this agony! Anything was more tolerable than this derision! I could bear those hypocritical smiles no longer! I felt that I must scream or die!—and now—again!—hark! louder! louder! louder! *louder*!—

"Villains!" I shrieked, "dissemble no more! I admit the deed!—tear up the planks!—here, here!—it is the beating of his hideous heart!"

6

The Masque of the Red Death

Edgar Allen Poe

The "Red Death" had long devastated the country. No pestilence had been ever so fatal, or so hideous. Blood was its Avator and its seal—the redness and the horror of blood. There were sharp pains, and sudden dizziness, and then profuse bleedings at the pores, with dissolution. The scarlet stains upon the body and especially upon the face of the victim, were the pest-ban which shut him out from the aid and from the sympathy of his fellow-men. And the whole seizure, progress and termination of the disease were the incidents of half an hour.

But the Prince Prospero was happy and dauntless, and sagacious. When his dominions were half depopulated, he summoned to his presence a thousand hale and light-hearted friends from among the knights and dames of his court, and with these retired to the deep seclusion of one of his castellated abbeys. This was an extensive and magnificent structure, the creation of the prince's own eccentric yet august taste. A strong and lofty wall girdled it in. This wall had gates of iron. The courtiers, having entered, brought furnaces and massy hammers and welded the bolts. They resolved to leave means neither of ingress or egress to the sudden impulses of despair from without or of frenzy from within. The abbey was amply provisioned. With such precautions the courtiers might bid defiance to contagion. The external world could take care of itself. In the meantime it was folly to grieve, or to think. The prince had provided all the appliances of pleasure. There were buffoons, there were improvisatori, there were ballêt-dancers, there were musicians, there were cards, there was Beauty, there was wine. All these and security were within. Without was the "Red Death."

It was towards the close of the fifth or sixth month of his seclusion, and while the pestilence raged most furiously abroad, that the Prince Prospero entertained his thousand friends at a masked ball of the most unusual magnificence. It was a voluptuous scene that masquerade.

But first let me tell of the rooms in which it was held. There were seven—an imperial suite. In many palaces, however, such suites form a long and straight vista, while the folding doors slide back nearly to the walls on either hand, so that the view of the whole extent is scarcely impeded. Here the case was very different; as might have been expected from the duke's love of the *bizarre*. The apartments were so irregularly disposed that the vision embraced but little more than one at a time. There was a sharp turn at every twenty or thirty yards, and at each turn a novel effect. To the right and left, in the middle of each wall, a tall and narrow Gothic window looked out upon a closed corridor which pursued the windings of the suite. These windows were of stained glass whose color varied in accordance with the prevailing hue of the decorations of the chamber into which it opened. That at the eastern extremity was hung, for example, in blue—and vividly blue were its windows. The second chamber was purple in its ornaments and tapestries, and here the panes were purple. The third was green throughout, and so were the casements. The fourth was furnished and litten with orange—the fifth with white—the sixth with violet. The seventh apartment was closely shrouded in black velvet tapestries that hung all over the ceiling and down the walls, falling in heavy folds upon a carpet of the same material and hue. But, in this chamber only, the color of the windows failed to correspond with the decorations. The panes here were scarlet—a deep blood color. Now in no one of the seven apartments was there any lamp or candelabrum, amid the profusion of golden ornaments that lay scattered to and fro or depended from the roof. There was no light of any kind emanating from lamp or candle within the suite of chambers. But in the corridors that followed the suite, there stood, opposite to each window, a heavy tripod, bearing a brazier of fire that projected its rays through the tinted glass and so glaringly illumined the room. And thus were produced a multitude of gaudy and fantastic appearances. But in the western or black chamber the effect of the fire-light that streamed upon the dark hangings through the blood-tinted panes, was ghastly in the extreme, and produced so wild a look upon the countenances of those who entered, that there were few of the company bold enough to set foot within its precincts at all.

It was in this apartment, also, that there stood against the western wall, a gigantic clock of ebony. Its pendulum swung to and fro with a dull, heavy, monotonous clang; and when its minute-hand made the circuit of the face, and the hour was to be stricken, there came forth from the brazen lungs of the clock a sound which was clear and loud and deep and exceedingly musical, but of so peculiar a note and emphasis that, at each lapse of an hour, the musicians in the orchestra were constrained to pause, momently, in their performance, to harken to the sound; and thus the waltzers perforce ceased their evolutions; and there was a brief disconcert of the whole gay company; and, while the chimes of the clock yet rang, it was observed that the giddiest grew pale, and that the more aged and sedate passed their hands over their brows as if in confused reverie or meditation. But when the echoes had fully ceased, a light laughter at once pervaded the assembly; the musicians looked at each other and smiled as if at their own nervousness and folly, and made whispering vows, each to the other, that the next chiming of the clock should produce in them no similar emotion; and then, after the lapse of sixty minutes, (which embrace three thousand and six hundred seconds of the Time that flies,) there came yet another chiming of the clock, and then were the same disconcert and tremulousness and meditation as before.

But, in spite of these things, it was a gay and magnificent revel. The tastes of the duke were peculiar. He had a fine eye for colors and effects. He disregarded the *decora* of mere fashion. His plans were bold and fiery, and his conceptions glowed with barbaric lustre. There are some who would have thought him mad. His followers felt that he was not. It was necessary to hear and see and touch him to be *sure* that he was not.

He had directed, in great part, the moveable embellishments of the seven chambers, upon occasion of this great *fête*, and it was his own guiding taste which had given character to the costumes of the masqueraders. Be sure they were grotesque. There were much glare and glitter and piquancy and phantasm—much of what has been since seen in "Hernani." There were arabesque figures with unsuited limbs and appointments. There were delirious fancies such as the madman fashions. There was much of the beautiful, much of the wanton, much of the *bizarre*, something of the terrible, and not a little of that which might have excited disgust. To and fro in the seven chambers there stalked, in fact, a multitude of dreams. And these, the dreams—writhed in and about, taking hue from the rooms, and causing the wild music of the orchestra to seem as the echo of their steps. And, anon, there strikes the ebony clock which stands in the hall of the velvet. And then, for a moment, all is still, and all is silent save the voice of the clock. The dreams are stiff-frozen as they stand. But the echoes of the chime die away—they have endured but an instant—and a light, half-subdued laughter floats after them as they depart. And now again the music swells, and the dreams live, and writhe to and fro more merrily than ever, taking hue from the many-tinted windows through which stream the rays from the tripods. But to the chamber which lies most westwardly of the seven there are now none of the maskers who venture; for the night is waning away; and there flows a ruddier light through the blood-colored panes; and the blackness of the sable drapery appals; and to him whose foot falls upon the sable carpet, there comes from the near clock of ebony a muffled peal more solemnly emphatic than any which reaches *their* ears who indulge in the more remote gaieties of the other apartments.

But these other apartments were densely crowded, and in them beat feverishly the heart of life. And the revel went whirlingly on, until at length was sounded the twelfth hour upon the clock. And then the music ceased, as I have told; and the evolutions of the waltzers were quieted; and there was an uneasy cessation of all things as before. But now there were twelve strokes to be sounded by the bell of the clock; and thus it happened, perhaps, that more of thought crept, with more of time, into the meditations of the thoughtful among those who revelled. And thus, again, it happened, perhaps, that before the last echoes of the last chime had utterly sunk into silence, there were many individuals in the crowd who had found leisure to become aware of the presence of a masked figure which had arrested the attention of no single individual before. And the rumor of this new presence having spread itself whisperingly around, there arose at length from the whole company a buzz, or murmur, expressive at first of disapprobation and surprise—then, finally, of terror, of horror, and of disgust.

In an assembly of phantasms such as I have painted, it may well be supposed that no ordinary appearance could have excited such sensation. In truth the masquerade license of the night was nearly unlimited; but the figure in question had out-Heroded Herod, and gone beyond the bounds of even the prince's indefinite decorum. There are chords in the hearts of the most reckless which cannot be touched without emotion. Even with the utterly lost, to whom life and death are equally jests, there are matters of which no jest can be properly made. The whole company, indeed, seemed now deeply to feel that in the costume and bearing of the stranger neither wit nor propriety existed. The figure was tall and gaunt, and shrouded from head to foot in the habiliments of the grave. The mask which concealed the visage was made so nearly to resemble the countenance of a stiffened corpse that the closest scrutiny must have had difficulty in detecting the cheat. And yet all this might have been endured, if not approved, by the mad revellers around. But the mummer had gone so far as to assume the type of the Red Death. His vesture was dabbled in *blood*—and his broad brow, with all the features of the face, was besprinkled with the scarlet horror.

When the eyes of the Prince Prospero fell upon this spectral image (which with a slow and solemn movement, as if more fully to sustain its role, stalked to and fro among the waltzers) he was seen to be convulsed, in the first moment, with a strong shudder either of terror or distaste; but, in the next, his brow reddened with rage.

"Who dares?" he demanded hoarsely of the group that stood around him, "who dares thus to make mockery of our woes? Uncase the varlet that we may know whom we have to hang to-morrow at sunrise from the battlements. Will no one stir at my bidding?—stop him and strip him, I say, of those reddened vestures of sacrilege!"

It was in the eastern or blue chamber in which stood the Prince Prospero as he uttered these words. They rang throughout the seven rooms loudly and clearly—for the prince was a bold and robust man, and the music had become hushed at the waving of his hand.

It was in the blue room where stood the prince, with a group of pale courtiers by his side. At first, as he spoke, there was a slight rushing movement of this group in the direction of the intruder, who at the moment was also near at hand, and now, with deliberate and stately step, made closer approach to the speaker. But from a certain nameless awe with which the mad assumptions of the mummer had inspired the whole party, there were found none who put forth hand to seize him; so that, unimpeded, he passed within a yard of the prince's person; and, while the vast assembly, as if with one impulse, shrank from the centres of the rooms to the walls, he made his way uninterruptedly, but with the same solemn and measured step which had distinguished him from the first, through the blue chamber to the purple—through the purple to the green—through the green to the orange—through this again to the white—and even thence to the violet, ere a decided movement had been made to arrest him. It was then, however, that the Prince Prospero, maddening with rage and the shame of his own momentary cowardice, rushed hurriedly through the six chambers—while none followed him on account of a deadly terror that had seized upon all. He bore aloft a drawn dagger, and had approached, in rapid impetuosity, to within three or four feet of the retreating figure, when the latter, having attained the extremity of the velvet apartment, turned suddenly round and confronted his pursuer. There was a sharp cry—and the dagger dropped gleaming upon the sable carpet, upon which instantly afterwards, fell prostrate in death the Prince Prospero. Then, summoning the wild courage of despair, a throng of the revellers at once threw themselves into the black apartment, and, seizing the mummer, whose tall figure stood erect and motionless within the shadow of the ebony clock, gasped in unutterable horror at finding the grave-cerements and corpse-like mask which they handled with so violent a rudeness, untenanted by any tangible form.

And now was acknowledged the presence of the Red Death. He had come like a thief in the night. And one by one dropped the revellers in the blood-bedewed halls of their revel, and died each in the despairing posture of his fall. And the life of the ebony clock went out with that of the last of the gay. And the flames of the tripods expired. And Darkness and Decay and the Red Death held illimitable dominion over all.

7

Make Westing

Jack London

Whatever you do, make westing! make westing!

—Sailing directions for Cape Horn.

For seven weeks the *Mary Rogers* had been between 50° south in the Atlantic and 50° south in the Pacific, which meant that for seven weeks she had been struggling to round Cape Horn. For seven weeks she had been either in dirt, or close to dirt, save once, and then, following upon six days of excessive dirt, which she had ridden out under the shelter of the redoubtable Terra Del Fuego coast, she had almost gone ashore during a heavy swell in the dead calm that had suddenly fallen. For seven weeks she had wrestled with the Cape Horn gray-beards, and in return been buffeted and smashed by them. She was a wooden ship, and her ceaseless straining had opened her seams, so that twice a day the watch took its turn at the pumps.

The *Mary Rogers* was strained, the crew was strained, and big Dan Cullen, master, was likewise strained. Perhaps he was strained most of all, for upon him rested the responsibility of that titanic struggle. He slept most of the time in his clothes, though he rarely slept. He haunted the deck at night, a great, burly, robust ghost, black with the sunburn of thirty years of sea and hairy as an orang-utan. He, in turn, was haunted by one thought of action, a sailing direction for the Horn: *Whatever you do, make westing! make westing!* It was an obsession. He thought of nothing else, except, at times, to blaspheme God for sending such bitter weather.

Make westing! He hugged the Horn, and a dozen times lay hove to with the iron Cape bearing east-by-north, or north-north-east, a score of miles away. And each time the eternal west wind smote him back and he made easting. He fought gale after gale, south to 64°, inside the antarctic drift-ice, and pledged his immortal soul to the Powers of Darkness for a bit of westing, for a slant to take him around. And he made easting. In despair, he had tried to make the passage through the Straits of Le Maire. Halfway through, the wind hauled to the north 'ard of northwest, the glass dropped to 28.88, and he turned and ran before a gale of cyclonic fury, missing, by a hair's breadth, piling up the *Mary Rogers* on the black-toothed rocks. Twice he had made west to the Diego Ramirez Rocks, one of the times saved between two snow-squalls by sighting the gravestones of ships a quarter of a mile dead ahead.

Blow! Captain Dan Cullen instanced all his thirty years at sea to prove that never had it blown so before. The *Mary Rogers* was hove to at the time he gave the evidence, and, to clinch it, inside half an hour the *Mary Rogers* was hove down to the hatches. Her new main-topsail and brand new spencer were blown away like tissue paper; and five sails, furled and fast under double gaskets, were blown loose and stripped from the yards. And before morning the *Mary Rogers* was hove down twice again, and holes were knocked in her bulwarks to ease her decks from the weight of ocean that pressed her down.

On an average of once a week Captain Dan Cullen caught glimpses of the sun. Once, for ten minutes, the sun shone at midday, and ten minutes afterward a new gale was piping up, both watches were shortening sail, and all was buried in the obscurity of a driving snow-squall. For a fortnight, once, Captain Dan Cullen was without a meridian or a chronometer sight. Rarely did he know his position within half a degree, except when in sight of land; for sun and stars remained hidden behind the sky, and it was so gloomy that even at the best the horizons were poor for accurate observations. A gray gloom shrouded the world. The clouds were gray; the great driving seas were leaden gray gloom shrouded the world. The clouds were gray; the great driving seas were leadening; even the occasional albatrosses were gray, while the snow-flurries were not white, but gray, under the sombre pall of the heavens.

Life on board the *Mary Rogers* was gray,—gray and gloomy. The faces of the sailors were blue-gray; they were afflicted with sea-cuts and sea-boils, and suffered exquisitely. They were shadows of men. For seven weeks, in the forecastle or on deck, they had not known what it was to be dry. They had forgotten what it was to sleep out a watch, and all watches it was, "All hands on deck!" They caught snatches of agonized sleep, and they slept in their oilskins ready for the everlasting call. So weak and worn were they that it took both watches to do the work of one. That was why both watches were on deck so much of the time. And no shadow of a man could shirk duty. Nothing less than a broken leg could enable a man to knock off work; and there were two such, who had been mauled and pulped by the seas that broke aboard.

One other man who was the shadow of a man was George Dorety. He was the only passenger on board, a friend of the firm, and he had elected to make the voyage for his health. But seven weeks of Cape Horn had not bettered his health. He gasped and panted in his bunk through the long, heaving nights; and when on deck he was so bundled up for warmth that he resembled a peripatetic old-clothes shop. At midday, eating at the cabin table in a gloom so deep that the swinging sea-lamps burned always, he looked as blue-gray as the sickest, saddest man for'ard. Nor did gazing across the table at Captain Dan Cullen have any cheering effect upon him. Captain Cullen chewed and scowled and kept silent. The scowls were for God, and with every chew he reiterated the sole thought of his existence, which was *make westing.* He was a big, hairy brute, and the sight of him was not stimulating to the other's appetite. He looked upon George Dorety as a Jonah, and told him so, once each meal, savagely transferring the scowl from God to the passenger and back again.

Nor did the mate prove a first aid to a languid appetite. Joshua Higgins by name, a seaman by profession and pull, but a pot-wolloper by capacity, he was a loose-jointed, sniffling creature, heartless and selfish and cowardly, without a soul, in fear of his life of Dan Cullen, and a bully over the sailors, who knew that behind the mate was Captain Cullen, the lawgiver and compeller, the driver and the destroyer, the incarnation of a dozen bucko mates. In that wild weather at the southern end of the earth, Joshua Higgins ceased washing. His grimy face usually robbed George Dorety of what little appetite he managed to accumulate. Ordinarily this lavatorial dereliction would have caught Captain Cullen's eye and vocabulary, but in the present his mind was filled with making westing, to the exclusion of all other things not contributory thereto. Whether the mate's face was clean or dirty had no bearing upon westing. Later on, when 50° south in the Pacific had been reached, Joshua Higgins would wash his face very abruptly. In the meantime, at the cabin table, where gray twilight alternated with lamplight while the lamps were being filled, George Dorety sat between the two men, one a tiger and the other a hyena, and wondered why God had made them. The second mate, Matthew Turner, was a true sailor and a man, but George Dorety did not have the solace of his company, for he ate by himself, solitary, when they had finished.

On Saturday morning, July 24, George Dorety awoke to a feeling of life and headlong movement. On deck he found the *Mary Rogers* running off before a howling southeaster. Nothing was set but the lower topsails and the foresail. It was all she could stand, yet she was making fourteen knots, as Mr. Turner shouted in Dorety's ear when he came on deck. And it was all westing. She was going around the Horn at last... if the wind held. Mr. Turner looked happy. The end of the struggle was in sight. But Captain Cullen did not look happy. He scowled at Dorety in passing. Captain Cullen did not want God to know that he was pleased with that wind. He had a conception of a malicious God, and believed in his secret soul that if God knew it was a desirable wind, God would promptly efface it and send a snorter from the west. So he walked softly before God, smothering his joy down under scowls and muttered curses, and, so, fooling God, for God was the only thing in the universe of which Dan Cullen was afraid.

All Saturday and Saturday night the *Mary Rogers* raced her westing. Persistently she logged her fourteen knots, so that by Sunday morning she had covered three hundred and fifty miles. If the wind held, she would make around. If it failed, and the snorter came from anywhere between southwest and north, back the *Mary Rogers* would be hurled and be no better off than she had been seven weeks before. And on Sunday morning the wind *was* failing. The big sea was going down and running smooth. Both watches were on deck setting sail after sail as fast as the ship could stand it. And now Captain Cullen went around brazenly before God, smoking a big cigar, smiling jubilantly, as if the failing wind delighted him, while down underneath he was raging against God for taking the life out of the blessed wind. *Make westing*! So he would, if God would only leave him alone. Secretly, he pledged himself anew to the Powers of Darkness, if they would let him make westing. He pledged himself so easily because he did not believe in the Powers of Darkness. He really believed only in God, though he did not know it. And in his inverted theology God was really the Prince of Darkness. Captain Cullen was a devil-worshipper, but he called the devil by another name, that was all.

At midday, after calling eight bells, Captain Cullen ordered the royals on. The men went aloft faster than they had gone in weeks. Not alone were they nimble because of the westing, but a benignant sun was shining down and limbering their stiff bodies. George Dorety stood aft, near Captain Cullen, less bundled in clothes than usual, soaking in the grateful warmth as he watched the scene. Swiftly and abruptly the incident occurred. There was a cry from the foreroyal-yard of "Man overboard!" Somebody threw a life buoy over the side, and at the same instant the second mate's voice came aft, ringing and peremptory:—

"Hard down your helm!"

The man at the wheel never moved a spoke. He knew better, for Captain Dan Cullen was standing alongside of him. He wanted to move a spoke, to move all the spokes, to grind the wheel down, hard down, for his comrade drowning in the sea. He glanced at Captain Dan Cullen, and Captain Dan Cullen gave no sign.

"Down! Hard down!" the second mate roared, as he sprang aft.

But he ceased springing and commanding, and stood still, when he saw Dan Cullen by the wheel. And big Dan Cullen puffed at his cigar and said nothing. Astern, and going astern fast, could be seen the sailor. He had caught the life buoy and was clinging to it. Nobody spoke. Nobody moved. The men aloft clung to the royal yards and watched with terror stricken faces. And the *Mary Rogers* raced on, making her westing. A long, silent minute passed.

"Who was it!" Captain Cullen demanded.

"Mops, sir," eagerly answered the sailor at the wheel.

Mops topped a wave astern and disappeared temporarily in the trough. It was a large wave, but it was no graybeard. A small boat could live easily in such a sea, and in such a sea the *Mary Rogers* could easily come to. But she could not come to and make westing at the same time.

For the first time in all his years, George Dorety was seeing a real drama of life and death—a sordid little drama in which the scales balanced an unknown sailor named Mops against a few miles of longitude. At first he had watched the man astern, but now he watched big Dan Cullen, hairy and black, vested with power of life and death, smoking a cigar.

Captain Dan Cullen smoked another long, silent minute. Then he removed the cigar from his mouth. He glanced aloft at the spars of the *Mary Rogers*, and overside at the sea.

"Sheet home the royals!" he cried.

Fifteen minutes later they sat at table, in the cabin, with food served before them. On one side of George Dorety sat Dan Cullen, the tiger, on the other side, Joshua Higgins, the hyena. Nobody spoke. On deck the men were sheeting home the skysails. George Dorety could hear their cries, while a persistent vision haunted him of a man called Mops, alive and well, clinging to a life buoy miles astern in that lonely ocean. He glanced at Captain Cullen, and experienced a feeling of nausea, for the man was eating his food with relish, almost bolting it.

"Captain Cullen," Dorety said, "you are in command of this ship, and it is not proper for me to comment now upon what you do. But I wish to say one thing. There is a hereafter, and yours will be a hot one."

Captain Cullen did not even scowl. In his voice was regret as he said:—"It was blowing a living gale. It was impossible to save the man."

"He fell from the royal-yard," Dorety cried hotly. "You were setting the royals at the time. Fifteen minutes afterward you were setting the skysails."

"It was a living gale, wasn't it, Mr. Higgins?" Captain Cullen said, turning to the mate.

"If you'd brought her to, it'd have taken the sticks out of her," was the mate's answer. "You did the proper thing, Captain Cullen. The man hadn't a ghost of a show."

George Dorety made no answer, and to the meal's end no one spoke. After that, Dorety had his meals served in his stateroom. Captain Cullen scowled at him no longer, though no speech was exchanged between them, while the *Mary Rogers* sped north toward warmer latitudes. At the end of the week, Dan Cullen cornered Dorety on deck.

"What are you going to do when we get to Frisco?" he demanded bluntly.

"I am going to swear out a warrant for your arrest," Dorety answered quietly. "I am going to charge you with murder, and I am going to see you hanged for it."

"You're almighty sure of yourself," Captain Cullen sneered, turning on his heel.

A second week passed, and one morning found George Dorety standing in the coach-house companionway at the for'ard end of the long poop, taking his first gaze around the deck. The *Mary Rogers* was reaching full-and-by, in a stiff breeze. Every sail was set and drawing, including the staysails. Captain Cullen strolled for'ard along the poop. He strolled carelessly, glancing at the passenger out of the corner of his eye. Dorety was looking the other way, standing with head and shoulders outside the companionway, and only the back of his head was to be seen. Captain Cullen, with swift eye, embraced the mainstay-sail-block and the head and estimated the distance. He glanced about him. Nobody was looking. Aft, Joshua Higgins, pacing up and down, had just turned his back and was going the other way. Captain Cullen bent over suddenly and cast the staysail-sheet off from its pin. The heavy block hurtled through the air, smashing Dorety's head like an egg-shell and hurtling on and back and forth as the staysail whipped and slatted in the wind. Joshua Higgins turned around to see what had carried away, and met the full blast of the vilest portion of Captain Cullen's profanity.

"I made the sheet fast myself," whimpered the mate in the first lull, "with an extra turn to make sure. I remember it distinctly."

"Made fast?" the captain snarled back, for the benefit of the watch as it struggled to capture the flying sail before it tore to ribbons. "You couldn't make your grandmother fast, you useless scullion. If you made that sheet fast with an extra turn, why didn't it stay fast? That's what I want to know. Why didn't it stay fast?"

The mate whined inarticulately.

"Oh, shut up!" was the final word of Captain Cullen.

Half an hour later he was as surprised as any when the body of George Dorety was found inside the companionway on the floor. In the afternoon, alone in his room, he doctored up the log.

"*Ordinary seaman, Karl Brun,*" he wrote, "*lost overboard from foreroyal-yard in a gale of wind. Was running at the time, and for the safety of the ship did not dare come up to the wind. Nor could a boat have lived in the sea that was running.*"

On another page, he wrote:—

"*Had often warned Mr. Dorety about the danger he ran because of his carelessness on deck. I told him, once, that some day he would get his head knocked off by a block. A carelessly fastened mainstaysail sheet was the cause of the accident, which was deeply to be regretted because Mr. Dorety was a favorite with all of us."*

Captain Dan Cullen read over his literary effort with admiration, blotted the page, and closed the log. He lighted a cigar and stared before him. He felt the *Mary Rogers* lift, and heel, and surge along, and knew that she was making nine knots. A smile of satisfaction slowly dawned on his black and hairy face. Well, anyway, he had made his westing and fooled God.

8

The Giant Wistaria

Charlotte Perkins Gilman

"Meddle not with my new vine, child! See! Thou hast already broken the tender shoot! Never needle or distaff for thee, and yet thou wilt not be quiet!"

The nervous fingers wavered, clutched at a small carnelian cross that hung from her neck, then fell despairingly.

"Give me my child, mother, and then I will be quiet!"

"Hush! hush! thou fool—some one might be near! See—there is thy father coming, even now! Get in quickly!"

She raised her eyes to her mother's face, weary eyes that yet had a flickering, uncertain blaze in their shaded depths.

"Art thou a mother and hast no pity on me, a mother? Give me my child!"

Her voice rose in a strange, low cry, broken by her father's hand upon her mouth.

"Shameless!" said he, with set teeth. "Get to thy chamber, and be not seen again to-night, or I will have thee bound!"

She went at that, and a hard-faced serving woman followed, and presently returned, bringing a key to her mistress.

"Is all well with her—and the child also?"

"She is quiet, Mistress Dwining, well for the night, be sure. The child fretteth endlessly, but save for that it thriveth with me."

The parents were left alone together on the high square porch with its great pillars, and the rising moon began to make faint shadows of the young vine leaves that shot up luxuriantly around them; moving shadows, like little stretching fingers, on the broad and heavy planks of the oaken floor.

"It groweth well, this vine thou broughtest me in the ship, my husband."

"Aye," he broke in bitterly, "and so doth the shame I brought thee!

Had I known of it I would sooner have had the ship founder beneath us, and have seen our child cleanly drowned, than live to this end!"

"Thou art very hard, Samuel, art thou not afeard for her life? She grieveth sore for the child, aye, and for the green fields to walk in!"

"Nay," said he grimly, "I fear not. She hath lost already what is more than life; and she shall have air enough soon. To-morrow the ship is ready, and we return to England. None knoweth of our stain here, not one, and if the town hath a child unaccounted for to rear in decent ways—why, it is not the first, even here. It will be well enough cared for! And truly we have matter for thankfulness, that her cousin is yet willing to marry her."

"Hast thou told him?"

"Aye! Thinkest thou I would cast shame into another man's house, unknowing it? He hath always desired her, but she would none of him, the stubborn! She hath small choice now!"

"Will he be kind, Samuel? Can he—"

"Kind? What call'st thou it to take such as she to wife? Kind! How many men would take her, an' she had double the fortune? And being of the family already, he is glad to hide the blot forever."

"An' if she would not? He is but a coarse fellow, and she ever shunned him."

"Art thou mad, woman? She weddeth him ere we sail to-morrow, or she stayeth ever in that chamber. The girl is not so sheer a fool! He maketh an honest woman of her, and saveth our house from open shame. What other hope for her than a new life to cover the old? Let her have an honest child, an' she so longeth for one!"

He strode heavily across the porch, till the loose planks creaked again, strode back and forth, with his arms folded and his brows fiercely knit above his iron mouth.

Overhead the shadows flickered mockingly across a white face among the leaves, with eyes of wasted fire.

"O, George, what a house! What a lovely house! I am sure it's haunted! Let us get that house to live in this summer! We will have Kate and Jack and Susy and Jim of course, and a splendid time of it!"

Young husbands are indulgent, but still they have to recognize facts.

"My dear, the house may not be to rent; and it may also not be habitable."

"There is surely somebody in it. I am going to inquire!"

The great central gate was rusted off its hinges, and the long drive had trees in it, but a little footpath showed signs of steady usage, and up that Mrs. Jenny went, followed by her obedient George. The front windows of the old mansion were blank, but in a wing at the back they found white curtains and open doors. Outside, in the clear May sunshine, a woman was washing. She was polite and friendly, and evidently glad of visitors in that lonely place.

She "guessed it could be rented—didn't know." The heirs were in Europe, but "there was a lawyer in New York had the lettin' of it." There had been folks there years ago, but not in her time. She and her husband had the rent of their part for taking care of the place. Not that they took much care on't either, "but keepin' robbers out." It was furnished throughout, old-fashioned enough, but good; and "if they took it she could do the work for 'em herself, she guessed—if he was willin'!"

Never was a crazy scheme more easily arranged. George knew that lawyer in New York; the rent was not alarming; and the nearness to a rising sea-shore resort made it a still pleasanter place to spend the summer.

Kate and Jack and Susy and Jim cheerfully accepted, and the June moon found them all sitting on the high front porch.

They had explored the house from top to bottom, from the great room in the garret, with nothing in it but a rickety cradle, to the well in the cellar without a curb and with a rusty chain going down to unknown blackness below. They had explored the grounds, once beautiful with rare trees and shrubs, but now a gloomy wilderness of tangled shade.

The old lilacs and laburnums, the spirea and syringa, nodded against the second-story windows. What garden plants survived were great ragged bushes or great shapeless beds. A huge wistaria vine covered the whole front of the house. The trunk, it was too large to call a stem, rose at the corner of the porch by the high steps, and had once climbed its pillars; but now the pillars were wrenched from their places and held rigid and helpless by the tightly wound and knotted arms.

It fenced in all the upper story of the porch with a knitted wall of stem and leaf; it ran along the eaves, holding up the gutter that had once supported it; it shaded every window with heavy green; and the drooping, fragrant blossoms made a waving sheet of purple from roof to ground.

"Did you ever see such a wistaria!" cried ecstatic Mrs. Jenny. "It is worth the rent just to sit under such a vine—a fig tree beside it would be sheer superfluity and wicked extravagance!"

"Jenny makes much of her wistaria," said George, "because she's so disappointed about the ghosts. She made up her mind at first sight to have ghosts in the house, and she can't find even a ghost story!"

"No," Jenny assented mournfully; "I pumped poor Mrs. Pepperill for three days, but could get nothing out of her. But I'm convinced there is a story, if we could only find it. You need not tell me that a house like this, with a garden like this, and a cellar like this, isn't haunted!"

"I agree with you," said Jack. Jack was a reporter on a New York daily, and engaged to Mrs. Jenny's pretty sister. "And if we don't find a real ghost, you may be very sure I shall make one. It's too good an opportunity to lose!"

The pretty sister, who sat next him, resented. "You shan't do anything of the sort, Jack! This is a real ghostly place, and I won't have you make fun of it! Look at that group of trees out there in the long grass—it looks for all the world like a crouching, hunted figure!"

"It looks to me like a woman picking huckleberries," said Jim, who was married to George's pretty sister.

"Be still, Jim!" said that fair young woman. "I believe in Jenny's ghost as much as she does. Such a place! Just look at this great wistaria trunk crawling up by the steps here! It looks for all the world like a writhing body—cringing—beseeching!"

"Yes," answered the subdued Jim, "it does, Susy. See its waist,—about two yards of it, and twisted at that! A waste of good material!"

"Don't be so horrid, boys! Go off and smoke somewhere if you can't be congenial!"

"We can! We will! We'll be as ghostly as you please." And forthwith they began to see bloodstains and crouching figures so plentifully that the most delightful shivers multiplied, and the fair enthusiasts started for bed, declaring they should never sleep a wink.

"We shall all surely dream," cried Mrs. Jenny, "and we must all tell our dreams in the morning!"

"There's another thing certain," said George, catching Susy as she tripped over a loose plank; "and that is that you frisky creatures must use the side door till I get this Eiffel tower of a portico fixed, or we shall have some fresh ghosts on our hands! We found a plank here that yawns like a trap-door—big enough to swallow you—and I believe the bottom of the thing is in China!"

The next morning found them all alive, and eating a substantial New England breakfast, to the accompaniment of saws and hammers on the porch, where carpenters of quite miraculous promptness were tearing things to pieces generally.

"It's got to come down mostly," they had said. "These timbers are clean rotted through, what ain't pulled out o' line by this great creeper. That's about all that holds the thing up."

There was clear reason in what they said, and with a caution from anxious Mrs. Jenny not to hurt the wistaria, they were left to demolish and repair at leisure.

"How about ghosts?" asked Jack after a fourth griddle cake. "I had one, and it's taken away my appetite!"

Mrs. Jenny gave a little shriek and dropped her knife and fork.

"Oh, so had I! I had the most awful—well, not dream exactly, but feeling. I had forgotten all about it!"

"Must have been awful," said Jack, taking another cake. "Do tell us about the feeling. My ghost will wait."

"It makes me creep to think of it even now," she said. "I woke up, all at once, with that dreadful feeling as if something were going to happen, you know! I was wide awake, and hearing every little sound for miles around, it seemed to me. There are so many strange little noises in the country for all it is so still.

Millions of crickets and things outside, and all kinds of rustles in the trees! There wasn't much wind, and the moonlight came through in my three great windows in three white squares on the black old floor, and those fingery wistaria leaves we were talking of last night just seemed to crawl all over them. And—O, girls, you know that dreadful well in the cellar?"

A most gratifying impression was made by this, and Jenny proceeded cheerfully:

"Well, while it was so horridly still, and I lay there trying not to wake George, I heard as plainly as if it were right in the room, that old chain down there rattle and creak over the stones!"

"Bravo!" cried Jack. "That's fine! I'll put it in the Sunday edition!"

"Be still!" said Kate. "What was it, Jenny? Did you really see anything?"

"No, I didn't, I'm sorry to say. But just then I didn't want to. I woke George, and made such a fuss that he gave me bromide, and said he'd go and look, and that's the last I thought of it till Jack reminded me,—the bromide worked so well."

"Now, Jack, give us yours," said Jim. "Maybe, it will dovetail in somehow. Thirsty ghost, I imagine; maybe they had prohibition here even then!"

Jack folded his napkin, and leaned back in his most impressive manner.

"It was striking twelve by the great hall clock—" he began.

"There isn't any hall clock!"

"O hush, Jim, you spoil the current! It was just one o'clock then, by my old-fashioned repeater."

"Waterbury! Never mind what time it was!"

"Well, honestly, I woke up sharp, like our beloved hostess, and tried to go to sleep again, but couldn't. I experienced all those moonlight and grasshopper sensations, just like Jenny, and was wondering what could have been the matter with the supper, when in came my ghost, and I knew it was all a dream! It was a female ghost, and I imagine she was young and handsome, but all those crouching, hunted figures of last evening ran riot in my brain, and this poor creature looked just like them.

She was all wrapped up in a shawl, and had a big bundle under her arm,—dear me, I am spoiling the story! With the air and gait of one in frantic haste and terror, the muffled figure glided to a dark old bureau, and seemed taking things from the drawers. As she turned, the moonlight shone full on a little red cross that hung from her neck by a thin gold chain—I saw it glitter as she crept noiselessly from the room! That's all."

"O Jack, don't be so horrid! Did you really? Is that all? What do you think it was?"

"I am not horrid by nature, only professionally. I really did. That was all. And I am fully convinced it was the genuine, legitimate ghost of an eloping chambermaid with kleptomania!"

"You are too bad, Jack!" cried Jenny. "You take all the horror out of it. There isn't a 'creep' left among us."

"It's no time for creeps at nine-thirty A.M., with sunlight and carpenters outside! However, if you can't wait till twilight for your creeps, I think I can furnish one or two," said George. "I went down cellar after Jenny's ghost!"

There was a delighted chorus of female voices, and Jenny cast upon her lord a glance of genuine gratitude.

"It's all very well to lie in bed and see ghosts, or hear them," he went on. "But the young householder suspecteth burglars, even though as a medical man he knoweth nerves, and after Jenny dropped off I started on a voyage of discovery. I never will again, I promise you!"

"Why, what was it?"

"Oh, George!"

"I got a candle—"

"Good mark for the burglars," murmured Jack.

"And went all over the house, gradually working down to the cellar and the well."

"Well?" said Jack.

"Now you can laugh; but that cellar is no joke by daylight, and a candle there at night is about as inspiring as a lightning-bug in the Mammoth Cave. I went along with the light, trying not to fall into the well prematurely; got to it all at once; held the light down and then I saw, right under my feet—(I nearly fell over her, or walked through her, perhaps),—a woman, hunched up under a shawl!

She had hold of the chain, and the candle shone on her hands—white, thin hands,—on a little red cross that hung from her neck—*vide* Jack! I'm no believer in ghosts, and I firmly object to unknown parties in the house at night; so I spoke to her rather fiercely. She didn't seem to notice that, and I reached down to take hold of her,—then I came upstairs!"

"What for?"

"What happened?"

"What was the matter?"

"Well, nothing happened. Only she wasn't there! May have been indigestion, of course, but as a physician I don't advise any one to court indigestion alone at midnight in a cellar!"

"This is the most interesting and peripatetic and evasive ghost I ever heard of!" said Jack. "It's my belief she has no end of silver tankards, and jewels galore, at the bottom of that well, and I move we go and see!"

"To the bottom of the well, Jack?"

"To the bottom of the mystery. Come on!"

There was unanimous assent, and the fresh cambrics and pretty boots were gallantly escorted below by gentlemen whose jokes were so frequent that many of them were a little forced.

The deep old cellar was so dark that they had to bring lights, and the well so gloomy in its blackness that the ladies recoiled.

"That well is enough to scare even a ghost. It's my opinion you'd better let well enough alone!" quoth Jim.

"Truth lies hid in a well, and we must get her out," said George. "Bear a hand with the chain?"

Jim pulled away on the chain, George turned the creaking windlass, and Jack was chorus.

"A wet sheet for this ghost, if not a flowing sea," said he. "Seems to be hard work raising spirits! I suppose he kicked the bucket when he went down!"

As the chain lightened and shortened there grew a strained silence among them; and when at length the bucket appeared, rising slowly through the dark water, there was an eager, half reluctant peering, and a natural drawing back. They poked the gloomy contents. "Only water."

"Nothing but mud."

"Something—"

They emptied the bucket up on the dark earth, and then the girls all went out into the air, into the bright warm sunshine in front of the house, where was the sound of saw and hammer, and the smell of new wood. There was nothing said until the men joined them, and then Jenny timidly asked:

"How old should you think it was, George?"

"All of a century," he answered. "That water is a preservative,—lime in it. Oh!—you mean?—Not more than a month; a very little baby!"

There was another silence at this, broken by a cry from the workmen. They had removed the floor and the side walls of the old porch, so that the sunshine poured down to the dark stones of the cellar bottom. And there, in the strangling grasp of the roots of the great wistaria, lay the bones of a woman, from whose neck still hung a tiny scarlet cross on a thin chain of gold.

9

The Student

Anton Chekhov

At first the weather was fine and still. The thrushes were calling, and in the swamps close by something alive droned pitifully with a sound like blowing into an empty bottle. A snipe flew by, and the shot aimed at it rang out with a gay, resounding note in the spring air. But when it began to get dark in the forest a cold, penetrating wind blew inappropriately from the east, and everything sank into silence. Needles of ice stretched across the pools, and it felt cheerless, remote, and lonely in the forest. There was a whiff of winter.

Ivan Velikopolsky, the son of a sacristan, and a student of the clerical academy, returning home from shooting, kept walking on the path by the water-logged meadows. His fingers were numb and his face was burning with the wind. It seemed to him that the cold that had suddenly come on had destroyed the order and harmony of things, that nature itself felt ill at ease, and that was why the evening darkness was falling more rapidly than usual. All around it was deserted and peculiarly gloomy. The only light was one gleaming in the widows' gardens near the river; the village, over three miles away, and everything in the distance all round was plunged in the cold evening mist. The student remembered that, as he had left the house, his mother was sitting barefoot on the floor in the entryway, cleaning the samovar, while his father lay on the stove coughing; as it was Good Friday nothing had been cooked, and the student was terribly hungry. And now, shrinking from the cold, he thought that just such a wind had blown in the days of Rurik and in the time of Ivan the Terrible and Peter, and in their time there had been just the same desperate poverty and hunger, the same thatched roofs with holes in them, ignorance, misery, the same desolation around, the same darkness, the same feeling of oppression—all these had existed, did exist, and would exist, and the lapse of a thousand years would make life no better. And he did not want to go home.

The gardens were called the widows' because they were kept by two widows, mother and daughter. A campfire was burning brightly with a crackling sound, throwing out light far around on the ploughed earth. The widow Vasilisa, a tall, fat old woman in a man's coat, was standing by and looking thoughtfully into the fire; her daughter Lukerya, a little pockmarked woman with a stupid-looking face, was sitting on the ground, washing a cauldron and spoons. Apparently they had just had supper. There was a sound of men's voices; it was the laborers watering their horses at the river.

"Here you have winter back again," said the student, going up to the campfire. "Good evening."

Vasilisa started, but at once recognized him and smiled cordially.

"I did not know you; God bless you," she said. "You'll be rich."

They talked. Vasilisa, a woman of experience who had been in service with the gentry, first as a wet-nurse, afterwards as a children's nurse expressed herself with refinement, and a soft, sedate smile never left her face; her daughter Lukerya, a village peasant woman who had been beaten by her husband, simply screwed up her eyes at the student and said nothing, and she had a strange expression like that of a deaf mute.

"At just such a fire the Apostle Peter warmed himself," said the student, stretching out his hands to the fire, "so it must have been cold then, too. Ah, what a terrible night it must have been, granny! An utterly dismal long night!"

He looked round at the darkness, shook his head abruptly and asked:

"No doubt you have heard the reading of the Twelve Gospels?"

"Yes, I have," answered Vasilisa.

"If you remember, at the Last Supper Peter said to Jesus, 'I am ready to go with Thee into darkness and unto death.' And our Lord answered him thus: 'I say unto thee, Peter, before the cock croweth thou wilt have denied Me thrice.' After the supper Jesus went through the agony of death in the garden and prayed, and poor Peter was weary in spirit and faint, his eyelids were heavy and he could not struggle against sleep. He fell asleep. Then you heard how Judas the same night kissed Jesus and betrayed Him to His tormentors. They took Him bound to the high priest and beat Him, while Peter, exhausted, worn out with misery and alarm, hardly awake, you know, feeling that something awful was just going to happen on earth, followed behind... He loved Jesus passionately, intensely, and now he saw from far off how He was beaten..."

Lukerya left the spoons and fixed an immovable stare upon the student.

"They came to the high priest's," he went on; "they began to question Jesus, and meantime the laborers made a fire in the yard as it was cold, and warmed themselves. Peter, too, stood with them near the fire and warmed himself as I am doing. A woman, seeing him, said: 'He was with Jesus, too'—that is as much as to say that he, too, should be taken to be questioned. And all the laborers that were standing near the fire must have looked sourly and suspiciously at him, because he was confused and said: 'I don't know Him.' A little while after again someone recognized him as one of Jesus' disciples and said: 'Thou, too, art one of them,' but again he denied it. And for the third time someone turned to him: 'Why, did I not see thee with Him in the garden today?' For the third time he denied it. And immediately after that time the cock crowed, and Peter, looking from afar off at Jesus, remembered the words He had said to him in the evening... He remembered, he came to himself, went out of the yard and wept bitterly—bitterly. In the Gospel it is written: 'He went out and wept bitterly.' I imagine it: the still, still, dark, dark garden, and in the stillness, faintly audible, smothered sobbing..."

The student sighed and sank into thought. Still smiling, Vasilisa suddenly gave a gulp, big tears flowed freely down her cheeks, and she screened her face from the fire with her sleeve as though ashamed of her tears, and Lukerya, staring immovably at the student, flushed crimson, and her expression became strained and heavy like that of someone enduring intense pain.

The laborers came back from the river, and one of them riding a horse was quite near, and the light from the fire quivered upon him. The student said good-night to the widows and went on. And again the darkness was about him and his fingers began to be numb. A cruel wind was blowing, winter really had come back and it did not feel as though Easter would be the day after tomorrow.

Now the student was thinking about Vasilisa: since she had shed tears all that had happened to Peter the night before the Crucifixion must have some relation to her...

He looked round. The solitary light was still gleaming in the darkness and no figures could be seen near it now. The student thought again that if Vasilisa had shed tears, and her daughter had been troubled, it was evident that what he had just been telling them about, which had happened nineteen centuries ago, had a relation to the present—to both women, to the desolate village, to himself, to all people. The old woman had wept, not because he could tell the story touchingly, but because Peter was near to her, because her whole being was interested in what was passing in Peter's soul.

And joy suddenly stirred in his soul, and he even stopped for a minute to take breath. "The past," he thought, "is linked with the present by an unbroken chain of events flowing one out of another." And it seemed to him that he had just seen both ends of that chain; that when he touched one end the other quivered.

When he crossed the river by the ferryboat and afterwards, mounting the hill, looked at his village and towards the west where the cold crimson sunset lay a narrow streak of light, he thought that truth and beauty which had guided human life there in the garden and in the yard of the high priest had continued without interruption to this day, and had evidently always been the chief thing in human life and in all earthly life, indeed; and the feeling of youth, health, vigor—he was only twenty-two—and the inexpressible sweet expectation of happiness, of unknown mysterious happiness, took possession of him little by little, and life seemed to him enchanting, marvellous, and full of lofty meaning.

The pallid prominent personage almost died of fright. Brave as he was in the office and in the presence of inferiors generally, and although, at the sight of his manly form and appearance, every one said, "Ugh! how much character he had!" at this crisis, he, like many possessed of an heroic exterior, experienced such terror, that, not without cause, he began to fear an attack of illness. He flung his cloak hastily from his shoulders and shouted to his coachman in an unnatural voice, "Home at full speed!" The coachman, hearing the tone which is generally employed at critical moments and even accompanied by something much more tangible, drew his head down between his shoulders in case of an emergency, flourished his whip, and flew on like an arrow. In a little more than six minutes the prominent personage was at the entrance of his own house. Pale, thoroughly scared, and cloakless, he went home instead of to Karolina Ivanovna's, reached his room somehow or other, and passed the night in the direst distress; so that the next morning over their tea his daughter said, "You are very pale to-day, papa." But papa remained silent, and said not a word to any one of what had happened to him, where he had been, or where he had intended to go.

10

Araby

James Joyce

North Richmond Street, being blind, was a quiet street except at the hour when the Christian Brothers' School set the boys free. An uninhabited house of two storeys stood at the blind end, detached from its neighbours in a square ground. The other houses of the street, conscious of decent lives within them, gazed at one another with brown imperturbable faces.

The former tenant of our house, a priest, had died in the back drawing-room. Air, musty from having been long enclosed, hung in all the rooms, and the waste room behind the kitchen was littered with old useless papers. Among these I found a few paper-covered books, the pages of which were curled and damp: *The Abbot*, by Walter Scott, *The Devout Communicant* and *The Memoirs of Vidocq*. I liked the last best because its leaves were yellow. The wild garden behind the house contained a central apple-tree and a few straggling bushes under one of which I found the late tenant's rusty bicycle-pump. He had been a very charitable priest; in his will he had left all his money to institutions and the furniture of his house to his sister.

When the short days of winter came dusk fell before we had well eaten our dinners. When we met in the street the houses had grown sombre. The space of sky above us was the colour of ever-changing violet and towards it the lamps of the street lifted their feeble lanterns. The cold air stung us and we played till our bodies glowed. Our shouts echoed in the silent street. The career of our play brought us through the dark muddy lanes behind the houses where we ran the gauntlet of the rough tribes from the cottages, to the back doors of the dark dripping gardens where odours arose from the ashpits, to the dark odorous stables where a coachman smoothed and combed the horse or shook music from the buckled harness. When we returned to the street light from the kitchen windows had filled the areas. If my uncle was seen turning the corner we hid in the shadow until we had seen him safely housed. Or if Mangan's sister came out on the doorstep to call her brother in to his tea we watched her from our shadow peer up and down the street. We waited to see whether she would remain or go in and, if she remained, we left our shadow and walked up to Mangan's steps resignedly. She was waiting for us, her figure defined by the light from the half-opened door. Her brother always teased her before he obeyed and I stood by the railings looking at her. Her dress swung as she moved her body and the soft rope of her hair tossed from side to side.

Every morning I lay on the floor in the front parlour watching her door. The blind was pulled down to within an inch of the sash so that I could not be seen. When she came out on the doorstep my heart leaped. I ran to the hall, seized my books and followed her. I kept her brown figure always in my eye and, when we came near the point at which our ways diverged, I quickened my pace and passed her. This happened morning after morning. I had never spoken to her, except for a few casual words, and yet her name was like a summons to all my foolish blood.

Her image accompanied me even in places the most hostile to romance. On Saturday evenings when my aunt went marketing I had to go to carry some of the parcels. We walked through the flaring streets, jostled by drunken men and bargaining women, amid the curses of labourers, the shrill litanies of shop-boys who stood on guard by the barrels of pigs' cheeks, the nasal chanting of street-singers, who sang a *come-all-you* about O'Donovan Rossa, or a ballad about the troubles in our native land. These noises converged in a single sensation of life for me: I imagined that I bore my chalice safely through a throng of foes. Her name sprang to my lips at moments in strange prayers and praises which I myself did not understand. My eyes were often full of tears (I could not tell why) and at times a flood from my heart seemed to pour itself out into my bosom. I thought little of the future. I did not know whether I would ever speak to her or not or, if I spoke to her, how I could tell her of my confused adoration. But my body was like a harp and her words and gestures were like fingers running upon the wires.

One evening I went into the back drawing-room in which the priest had died. It was a dark rainy evening and there was no sound in the house. Through one of the broken panes I heard the rain impinge upon the earth, the fine incessant needles of water playing in the sodden beds. Some distant lamp or lighted window gleamed below me. I was thankful that I could see so little. All my senses seemed to desire to veil themselves and, feeling that I was about to slip from them, I pressed the palms of my hands together until they trembled, murmuring: *"O love! O love!"* many times.

At last she spoke to me. When she addressed the first words to me I was so confused that I did not know what to answer. She asked me was I going to *Araby*. I forgot whether I answered yes or no. It would be a splendid bazaar, she said; she would love to go.

"And why can't you?" I asked.

While she spoke she turned a silver bracelet round and round her wrist. She could not go, she said, because there would be a retreat that week in her convent. Her brother and two other boys were fighting for their caps and I was alone at the railings. She held one of the spikes, bowing her head towards me. The light from the lamp opposite our door caught the white curve of her neck, lit up her hair that rested there and, falling, lit up the hand upon the railing. It fell over one side of her dress and caught the white border of a petticoat, just visible as she stood at ease.

"It's well for you," she said.

"If I go," I said, "I will bring you something."

What innumerable follies laid waste my waking and sleeping thoughts after that evening! I wished to annihilate the tedious intervening days. I chafed against the work of school. At night in my bedroom and by day in the classroom her image came between me and the page I strove to read. The syllables of the word *Araby* were called to me through the silence in which my soul luxuriated and cast an Eastern enchantment over me. I asked for leave to go to the bazaar on Saturday night. My aunt was surprised and hoped it was not some Freemason affair. I answered few questions in class. I watched my master's face pass from amiability to sternness; he hoped I was not beginning to idle. I could not call my wandering thoughts together. I had hardly any patience with the serious work of life which, now that it stood between me and my desire, seemed to me child's play, ugly monotonous child's play.

On Saturday morning I reminded my uncle that I wished to go

to the bazaar in the evening. He was fussing at the hallstand, looking for the hat-brush, and answered me curtly:

"Yes, boy, I know."

As he was in the hall I could not go into the front parlour and lie at the window. I left the house in bad humour and walked slowly towards the school. The air was pitilessly raw and already my heart misgave me.

When I came home to dinner my uncle had not yet been home. Still it was early. I sat staring at the clock for some time and, when its ticking began to irritate me, I left the room. I mounted the staircase and gained the upper part of the house. The high cold empty gloomy rooms liberated me and I went from room to room singing. From the front window I saw my companions playing below in the street. Their cries reached me weakened and indistinct and, leaning my forehead against the cool glass, I looked over at the dark house where she lived. I may have stood there for an hour, seeing nothing but the brown-clad figure cast by my imagination, touched discreetly by the lamplight at the curved neck, at the hand upon the railings and at the border below the dress.

When I came downstairs again I found Mrs Mercer sitting at the fire. She was an old garrulous woman, a pawnbroker's widow, who collected used stamps for some pious purpose. I had to endure the gossip of the tea-table. The meal was prolonged beyond an hour and still my uncle did not come. Mrs Mercer stood up to go: she was sorry she couldn't wait any longer, but it was after eight o'clock and she did not like to be out late as the night air was bad for her. When she had gone I began to walk up and down the room, clenching my fists. My aunt said:

"I'm afraid you may put off your bazaar for this night of Our Lord."

At nine o'clock I heard my uncle's latchkey in the halldoor. I heard him talking to himself and heard the hallstand rocking when it had received the weight of his overcoat. I could interpret these signs. When he was midway through his dinner I asked him to give me the money to go to the bazaar. He had forgotten.

"The people are in bed and after their first sleep now," he said.

I did not smile. My aunt said to him energetically:

"Can't you give him the money and let him go? You've kept him late enough as it is."

My uncle said he was very sorry he had forgotten. He said he believed in the old saying: "All work and no play makes Jack a dull boy." He asked me where I was going and, when I had told him a second time he asked me did I know *The Arab's Farewell to his Steed.* When I left the kitchen he was about to recite the opening lines of the piece to my aunt.

I held a florin tightly in my hand as I strode down Buckingham Street towards the station. The sight of the streets thronged with buyers and glaring with gas recalled to me the purpose of my journey. I took my seat in a third-class carriage of a deserted train. After an intolerable delay the train moved out of the station slowly. It crept onward among ruinous houses and over the twinkling river. At Westland Row Station a crowd of people pressed to the carriage doors; but the porters moved them back, saying that it was a special train for the bazaar. I remained alone in the bare carriage. In a few minutes the train drew up beside an improvised wooden platform. I passed out on to the road and saw by the lighted dial of a clock that it was ten minutes to ten. In front of me was a large building which displayed the magical name.

I could not find any sixpenny entrance and, fearing that the bazaar would be closed, I passed in quickly through a turnstile, handing a shilling to a weary-looking man. I found myself in a big hall girdled at half its height by a gallery. Nearly all the stalls were closed and the greater part of the hall was in darkness. I recognised a silence like that which pervades a church after a service. I walked into the centre of the bazaar timidly. A few people were gathered about the stalls which were still open. Before a curtain, over which the words *Café Chantant* were written in coloured lamps, two men were counting money on a salver. I listened to the fall of the coins.

Remembering with difficulty why I had come I went over to one of the stalls and examined porcelain vases and flowered tea-sets. At the door of the stall a young lady was talking and laughing with two young gentlemen. I remarked their English accents and listened vaguely to their conversation.

"O, I never said such a thing!"

"O, but you did!"

"O, but I didn't!"

"Didn't she say that?"

"Yes. I heard her."

"O, there's a…fib!"

Observing me the young lady came over and asked me did I wish to buy anything. The tone of her voice was not encouraging; she seemed to have spoken to me out of a sense of duty. I looked humbly at the great jars that stood like eastern guards at either side of the dark entrance to the stall and murmured:

"No, thank you."

The young lady changed the position of one of the vases and went back to the two young men. They began to talk of the same subject. Once or twice the young lady glanced at me over her shoulder.

I lingered before her stall, though I knew my stay was useless, to make my interest in her wares seem the more real. Then I turned away slowly and walked down the middle of the bazaar. I allowed the two pennies to fall against the sixpence in my pocket. I heard a voice call from one end of the gallery that the light was out. The upper part of the hall was now completely dark.

Gazing up into the darkness I saw myself as a creature driven and derided by vanity; and my eyes burned with anguish and anger.

11

Eveline

James Joyce

She sat at the window watching the evening invade the avenue. Her head was leaned against the window curtains and in her nostrils was the odour of dusty cretonne. She was tired.

Few people passed. The man out of the last house passed on his way home; she heard his footsteps clacking along the concrete pavement and afterwards crunching on the cinder path before the new red houses. One time there used to be a field there in which they used to play every evening with other people's children. Then a man from Belfast bought the field and built houses in it—not like their little brown houses but bright brick houses with shining roofs. The children of the avenue used to play together in that field—the Devines, the Waters, the Dunns, little Keogh the cripple, she and her brothers and sisters. Ernest, however, never played: he was too grown up. Her father used often to hunt them in out of the field with his blackthorn stick; but usually little Keogh used to keep *nix* and call out when he saw her father coming. Still they seemed to have been rather happy then. Her father was not so bad then; and besides, her mother was alive. That was a long time ago; she and her brothers and sisters were all grown up; her mother was dead. Tizzie Dunn was dead, too, and the Waters had gone back to England. Everything changes. Now she was going to go away like the others, to leave her home.

Home! She looked round the room, reviewing all its familiar objects which she had dusted once a week for so many years, wondering where on earth all the dust came from. Perhaps she would never see again those familiar objects from which she had never dreamed of being divided. And yet during all those years she had never found out the name of the priest whose yellowing photograph hung on the wall above the broken harmonium beside the coloured print of the promises made to Blessed Margaret Mary Alacoque. He had been a school friend of her father.

Whenever he showed the photograph to a visitor her father used to pass it with a casual word:

"He is in Melbourne now."

She had consented to go away, to leave her home. Was that wise? She tried to weigh each side of the question. In her home anyway she had shelter and food; she had those whom she had known all her life about her. Of course she had to work hard, both in the house and at business. What would they say of her in the Stores when they found out that she had run away with a fellow? Say she was a fool, perhaps; and her place would be filled up by advertisement. Miss Gavan would be glad. She had always had an edge on her, especially whenever there were people listening.

"Miss Hill, don't you see these ladies are waiting?"

"Look lively, Miss Hill, please."

She would not cry many tears at leaving the Stores.

But in her new home, in a distant unknown country, it would not be like that. Then she would be married—she, Eveline. People would treat her with respect then. She would not be treated as her mother had been. Even now, though she was over nineteen, she sometimes felt herself in danger of her father's violence. She knew it was that that had given her the palpitations. When they were growing up he had never gone for her like he used to go for Harry and Ernest, because she was a girl; but latterly he had begun to threaten her and say what he would do to her only for her dead mother's sake. And now she had nobody to protect her. Ernest was dead and Harry, who was in the church decorating business, was nearly always down somewhere in the country. Besides, the invariable squabble for money on Saturday nights had begun to weary her unspeakably. She always gave her entire wages—seven shillings—and Harry always sent up what he could but the trouble was to get any money from her father. He said she used to squander the money, that she had no head, that he wasn't going to give her his hard-earned money to throw about the streets, and much more, for he was usually fairly bad of a Saturday night. In the end he would give her the money and ask her had she any intention of buying Sunday's dinner. Then she had to rush out as quickly as she could and do her marketing, holding her black leather purse tightly in her hand as she elbowed her way through the crowds and returning home late under her load of provisions. She had hard work to keep the house together and to see that the two young children who had been left to her charge went to school regularly and got their meals regularly. It was hard work—a hard life—but now that she was about to leave it she did not find it a wholly undesirable life.

She was about to explore another life with Frank. Frank was very kind, manly, open-hearted. She was to go away with him by the night-boat to be his wife and to live with him in Buenos Ayres where he had a home waiting for her. How well she remembered the first time she had seen him; he was lodging in a house on the main road where she used to visit. It seemed a few weeks ago. He was standing at the gate, his peaked cap pushed back on his head and his hair tumbled forward over a face of bronze. Then they had come to know each other. He used to meet her outside the Stores every evening and see her home. He took her to see *The Bohemian Girl* and she felt elated as she sat in an unaccustomed part of the theatre with him. He was awfully fond of music and sang a little. People knew that they were courting and, when he sang about the lass that loves a sailor, she always felt pleasantly confused. He used to call her Poppens out of fun. First of all it had been an excitement for her to have a fellow and then she had begun to like him. He had tales of distant countries. He had started as a deck boy at a pound a month on a ship of the Allan Line going out to Canada. He told her the names of the ships he had been on and the names of the different services. He had sailed through the Straits of Magellan and he told her stories of the terrible Patagonians. He had fallen on his feet in Buenos Ayres, he said, and had come over to the old country just for a holiday. Of course, her father had found out the affair and had forbidden her to have anything to say to him.

"I know these sailor chaps," he said.

One day he had quarrelled with Frank and after that she had to meet her lover secretly.

The evening deepened in the avenue. The white of two letters in her lap grew indistinct. One was to Harry; the other was to her father. Ernest had been her favourite but she liked Harry too. Her father was becoming old lately, she noticed; he would miss her. Sometimes he could be very nice. Not long before, when she had been laid up for a day, he had read her out a ghost story and made toast for her at the fire. Another day, when their mother was alive, they had all gone for a picnic to the Hill of Howth. She remembered her father putting on her mother's bonnet to make the children laugh.

Her time was running out but she continued to sit by the window, leaning her head against the window curtain, inhaling the odour of dusty cretonne. Down far in the avenue she could hear a street organ playing. She knew the air. Strange that it should come that very night to remind her of the promise to her mother, her promise to keep the home together as long as she could. She remembered the last night of her mother's illness; she was again in the close dark room at the other side of the hall and outside she heard a melancholy air of Italy. The organ-player had been ordered to go away and given sixpence. She remembered her father strutting back into the sickroom saying:

"Damned Italians! coming over here!"

As she mused the pitiful vision of her mother's life laid its spell on the very quick of her being—that life of commonplace sacrifices closing in final craziness. She trembled as she heard again her mother's voice saying constantly with foolish insistence:

"Derevaun Seraun! Derevaun Seraun!"

She stood up in a sudden impulse of terror. Escape! She must escape! Frank would save her. He would give her life, perhaps love, too. But she wanted to live. Why should she be unhappy? She had a right to happiness. Frank would take her in his arms, fold her in his arms. He would save her.

She stood among the swaying crowd in the station at the North Wall. He held her hand and she knew that he was speaking to her, saying something about the passage over and over again. The station was full of soldiers with brown baggages. Through the wide doors of the sheds she caught a glimpse of the black mass of the boat, lying in beside the quay wall, with illumined portholes. She answered nothing. She felt her cheek pale and cold and, out of a maze of distress, she prayed to God to direct her, to show her what was her duty. The boat blew a long mournful whistle into the mist. If she went, tomorrow she would be on the sea with Frank, steaming towards Buenos Ayres. Their passage had been booked. Could she still draw back after all he had done for her? Her distress awoke a nausea in her body and she kept moving her lips in silent fervent prayer.

A bell clanged upon her heart. She felt him seize her hand:

"Come!"

All the seas of the world tumbled about her heart. He was drawing her into them: he would drown her. She gripped with both hands at the iron railing.

"Come!"

No! No! No! It was impossible. Her hands clutched the iron in frenzy. Amid the seas she sent a cry of anguish!

"Eveline! Evvy!"

He rushed beyond the barrier and called to her to follow. He was shouted at to go on but he still called to her. She set her white face to him, passive, like a helpless animal. Her eyes gave him no sign of love or farewell or recognition.

12

Hills Like White Elephants

Ernest Hemingway

The hills across the valley of the Ebro were long and white. On this side there was no shade and no trees and the station was between two lines of rails in the sun. Close against the side of the station there was the warm shadow of the building and a curtain, made of strings of bamboo beads, hung across the open door into the bar, to keep out flies. The American and the girl with him sat at a table in the shade, outside the building. It was very hot and the express from Barcelona would come in forty minutes. It stopped at this junction for two minutes and went on to Madrid.

"What should we drink?" the girl asked. She had taken off her hat and put it on the table.

"It's pretty hot," the man said.

"Let's drink beer."

"Dos cervezas," the man said into the curtain.

"Big ones?" a woman asked from the doorway.

"Yes. Two big ones."

The woman brought two glasses of beer and two felt pads. She put the felt pads and the beer glasses on the table and looked at the man and the girl. The girl was looking off at the line of hills. They were white in the sun and the country was brown and dry.

"They look like white elephants," she said.

"I've never seen one," the man drank his beer.

"No, you wouldn't have."

"I might have," the man said. "Just because you say I wouldn't have doesn't prove anything."

The girl looked at the bead curtain. "They've painted something on it," she said. "What does it say?"

"Anis del Toro. It's a drink."

"Could we try it?"

The man called "Listen" through the curtain. The woman came out from the bar.

"Four reales."

"We want two Anis del Toro."

"With water?"

"Do you want it with water?"

"I don't know," the girl said. "Is it good with water?"

"It's all right."

"You want them with water?" asked the woman.

"Yes, with water."

"It tastes like licorice," the girl said and put the glass down.

"That's the way with everything."

"Yes," said the girl. "Everything tastes of licorice. Especially all the things you've waited so long for, like absinthe."

"Oh, cut it out."

"You started it," the girl said. "I was being amused. I was having a fine time."

"Well, let's try and have a fine time."

"All right. I was trying. I said the mountains looked like white elephants. Wasn't that bright?"

"That was bright."

"I wanted to try this new drink. That's all we do, isn't it—look at things and try new drinks?"

"I guess so."

The girl looked across at the hills.

"They're lovely hills," she said. "They don't really look like white elephants. I just meant the coloring of their skin through the trees."

"Should we have another drink?"

"All right."

The warm wind blew the bead curtain against the table.

"The beer's nice and cool," the man said.

"It's lovely," the girl said.

"It's really an awfully simple operation, Jig," the man said. "It's not really an operation at all."

The girl looked at the ground the table legs rested on.

"I know you wouldn't mind it, Jig. It's really not anything. It's just to let the air in."

The girl did not say anything.

"I'll go with you and I'll stay with you all the time. They just let the air in and then it's all perfectly natural."

"Then what will we do afterward?"

"We'll be fine afterward. Just like we were before."

"What makes you think so?"

"That's the only thing that bothers us. It's the only thing that's made us unhappy."

The girl looked at the bead curtain, put her hand out and took hold of two of the strings of beads.

"And you think then we'll be all right and be happy."

"I know we will. You don't have to be afraid. I've known lots of people that have done it."

"So have I," said the girl. "And afterward they were all so happy."

"Well," the man said, "if you don't want to you don't have to. I wouldn't have you do it if you didn't want to. But I know it's perfectly simple."

"And you really want to?"

"I think it's the best thing to do. But I don't want you to do it if you don't really want to."

"And if I do it you'll be happy and things will be like they were and you'll love me?"

"I love you now. You know I love you."

"I know. But if I do it, then it will be nice again if I say things are like white elephants, and you'll like it?"

"I'll love it. I love it now but I just can't think about it. You know how I get when I worry."

"If I do it you won't ever worry?"

"I won't worry about that because it's perfectly simple."

"Then I'll do it. Because I don't care about me."

"What do you mean?"

"I don't care about me."

"Well, I care about you."

"Oh, yes. But I don't care about me. And I'll do it and then everything will be fine."

"I don't want you to do it if you feel that way."

The girl stood up and walked to the end of the station. Across, on the other side, were fields of grain and trees along the banks of the Ebro. Far away, beyond the river, were mountains. The shadow of a cloud moved across the field of grain and she saw the river through the trees.

"And we could have all this," she said. "And we could have everything and every day we make it more impossible."

"What did you say?"

"I said we could have everything."

"We can have everything."

"No, we can't."

"We can have the whole world."

"No, we can't."

"We can go everywhere."

"No, we can't. It isn't ours any more."

"It's ours."

"No, it isn't. And once they take it away, you never get it back."

"But they haven't taken it away."

"We'll wait and see."

"Come on back in the shade," he said. "You mustn't feel that way."

"I don't feel any way," the girl said. "I just know things."

"I don't want you to do anything that you don't want to do——"

"Nor that isn't good for me," she said. "I know. Could we have another beer?"

"All right. But you've got to realize——"

"I realize," the girl said. "Can't we maybe stop talking?"

They sat down at the table and the girl looked across at the hills on the dry side of the valley and the man looked at her and at the table.

"You've got to realize," he said, "that I don't want you to do it if you don't want to. I'm perfectly willing to go through with it if it means anything to you."

"Doesn't it mean anything to you? We could get along."

"Of course it does. But I don't want anybody but you. I don't want any one else. And I know it's perfectly simple."

"Yes, you know it's perfectly simple."

"It's all right for you to say that, but I do know it."

"Would you do something for me now?"

"I'd do anything for you."

"Would you please please please please please please please stop talking?"

He did not say anything but looked at the bags against the wall of the station. There were labels on them from all the hotels where they had spent nights.

"But I don't want you to," he said, "I don't care anything about it."

"I'll scream," the girl said.

The woman came out through the curtains with two glasses of beer and put them down on the damp felt pads. "The train comes in five minutes," she said.

"What did she say?" asked the girl.

"That the train is coming in five minutes."

The girl smiled brightly at the woman, to thank her.

"I'd better take the bags over to the other side of the station," the man said. She smiled at him.

"All right. Then come back and we'll finish the beer."

He picked up the two heavy bags and carried them around the station to the other tracks. He looked up the tracks but could not see the train. Coming back, he walked through the barroom, where people waiting for the train were drinking. He drank an Anis at the bar and looked at the people. They were all waiting reasonably for the train. He went out through the bead curtain. She was sitting at the table and smiled at him.

"Do you feel better?" he asked.

"I feel fine," she said. "There's nothing wrong with me. I feel fine."

13

In Another Country

Ernest Hemingway

In the fall the war was always there, but we did not go to it any more. It was cold in the fall in Milan and the dark came very early. Then the electric lights came on, and it was pleasant along the streets looking in the windows. There was much game hanging outside the shops, and the snow powdered in the fur of the foxes and the wind blew their tails. The deer hung stiff and heavy and empty, and small birds blew in the wind and the wind turned their feathers. It was a cold fall and the wind came down from the mountains.

We were all at the hospital every afternoon, and there were different ways of walking across the town through the dusk to the hospital. Two of the ways were alongside canals, but they were long. Always, though, you crossed a bridge across a canal to enter the hospital. There was a choice of three bridges. On one of them a woman sold roasted chestnuts. It was warm, standing in front of her charcoal fire, and the chestnuts were warm afterward in your pocket. The hospital was very old and very beautiful, and you entered through a gate and walked across a courtyard and out a gate on the other side. There were usually funerals starting from the courtyard. Beyond the old hospital were the new brick pavilions, and there we met every afternoon and were all very polite and interested in what was the matter, and sat in the machines that were to make so much difference.

The doctor came up to the machine where I was sitting and said: "What did you like best to do before the war? Did you practise a sport?"

I said: "Yes, football."

"Good," he said. "You will be able to play football again better than ever."

My knee did not bend and the leg dropped straight from the knee to the ankle without a calf, and the machine was to bend the knee and make it move as in riding a tricycle. But it did not bend yet, and instead the machine lurched when it came to the bending part. The doctor said: "That will all pass. You are a fortunate young man. You will play football again like a champion."

In the next machine was a major who had a little hand like a baby's. He winked at me when the doctor examined his hand, which was between two leather straps that bounced up and down and flapped the stiff fingers, and said: "And will I too play football, captain-doctor?" He had been a very great fencer, and before the war the greatest fencer in Italy.

The doctor went to his office in a back room and brought a photograph which showed a hand that had been withered almost as small as the major's, before it had taken a machine course, and after was a little larger. The major held the photograph with his good hand and looked at it very carefully. "A wound?" he asked.

"An industrial accident," the doctor said.

"Very interesting, very interesting," the major said, and handed it back to the doctor.

"You have confidence?"

"No," said the major.

There were three boys who came each day who were about the same age I was. They were all three from Milan, and one of them was to be a lawyer, and one was to be a painter, and one had intended to be a soldier, and after we were finished with the machines, sometimes we walked back together to the Café Cova, which was next door to the Scala. We walked the short way through the communist quarter because we were four together. The people hated us because we were officers, and from a wine-shop some one would call out, "A basso gli ufficiali!" as we passed. Another boy who walked with us sometimes and made us five wore a black silk handkerchief across his face because he had no nose then and his face was to be rebuilt. He had gone out to the front from the military academy and been wounded within an hour after he had gone into the front line for the first time. They rebuilt his face, but he came from a very old family and they could never get the nose exactly right. He went to South America and worked in a bank. But this was a long time ago, and then we did not any of us know how it was going to be afterward. We only knew then that there was always the war, but that we were not going to it any more.

We all had the same medals, except the boy with the black silk bandage across his face, and he had not been at the front long enough to get any medals. The tall boy with a very pale face who was to be a lawyer had been a lieutenant of Arditi and had three medals of the sort we each had only one of. He had lived a very long time with death and was a little detached. We were all a little detached, and there was nothing that held us together except that we met every afternoon at the hospital. Although, as we walked to the Cova through the tough part of town, walking in the dark, with light and singing coming out of the wine-shops, and sometimes having to walk into the street when the men and women would crowd together on the sidewalk so that we would have had to jostle them to get by, we felt held together by there being something that had happened that they, the people who disliked us, did not understand.

We ourselves all understood the Cova, where it was rich and warm and not too brightly lighted, and noisy and smoky at certain hours, and there were always girls at the tables and the illustrated papers on a rack on the wall. The girls at the Cova were very patriotic, and I found that the most patriotic people in Italy were the café girls—and I believe they are still patriotic.

The boys at first were very polite about my medals and asked me what I had done to get them. I showed them the papers, which were written in very beautiful language and full of *fratellanza* and *abnegazione*, but which really said, with the adjectives removed, that I had been given the medals because I was an American. After that their manner changed a little toward me, although I was their friend against outsiders. I was a friend, but I was never really one of them after they had read the citations, because it had been different with them and they had done very different things to get their medals. I had been wounded, it was true; but we all knew that being wounded, after all, was really an accident. I was never ashamed of the ribbons, though, and sometimes, after the cocktail hour, I would imagine myself having done all the things they had done to get their medals; but walking home at night through the empty streets with the cold wind and all the shops closed, trying to keep near the street lights, I knew that I would never have done such things, and I was very much afraid to die, and often lay in bed at night by myself, afraid to die and wondering how I would be when I went back to the front again.

The three with the medals were like hunting-hawks; and I was not a hawk, although I might seem a hawk to those who had never hunted; they, the three, knew better and so we drifted apart. But I stayed good friends with the boy who had been wounded his first day at the front, because he would never know now how he would have turned out; so he could never be accepted either, and I liked him because I thought perhaps he would not have turned out to be a hawk either.

The major, who had been the great fencer, did not believe in bravery, and spent much time while we sat in the machines correcting my grammar. He had complimented me on how I spoke Italian, and we talked together very easily. One day I had said that Italian seemed such an easy language to me that I could not take a great interest in it; everything was so easy to say. "Ah, yes," the major said. "Why, then, do you not take up the use of grammar?" So we took up the use of grammar, and soon Italian was such a difficult language that I was afraid to talk to him until I had the grammar straight in my mind.

The major came very regularly to the hospital. I do not think he ever missed a day, although I am sure he did not believe in the machines. There was a time when none of us believed in the machines, and one day the major said it was all nonsense. The machines were new then and it was we who were to prove them. It was an idiotic idea, he said, "a theory, like another." I had not learned my grammar, and he said I was a stupid impossible disgrace, and he was a fool to have bothered with me. He was a small man and he sat straight up in his chair with his right hand thrust into the machine and looked straight ahead at the wall while the straps thumped up and down with his fingers in them.

"What will you do when the war is over if it is over?" he asked me. "Speak grammatically!"

"I will go to the States."

"Are you married?"

"No, but I hope to be."

"The more of a fool you are," he said. He seemed very angry. "A man must not marry."

"Why, Signor Maggiore?"

"Don't call me 'Signor Maggiore.'"

"Why must not a man marry?"

"He cannot marry. He cannot marry," he said angrily. "If he is to lose everything, he should not place himself in a position to lose that. He should not place himself in a position to lose. He should find things he cannot lose."

He spoke very angrily and bitterly, and looked straight ahead while he talked.

"But why should he necessarily lose it?"

"He'll lose it," the major said. He was looking at the wall. Then he looked down at the machine and jerked his little hand out from between the straps and slapped it hard against his thigh. "He'll lose it," he almost shouted. "Don't argue with me!" Then he called to the attendant who ran the machines. "Come and turn this damned thing off."

He went back into the other room for the light treatment and the massage. Then I heard him ask the doctor if he might use his telephone and he shut the door. When he came back into the room, I was sitting in another machine. He was wearing his cape and had his cap on, and he came directly toward my machine and put his arm on my shoulder.

"I am so sorry," he said, and patted me on the shoulder with his good hand. "I would not be rude. My wife has just died. You must forgive me."

"Oh—" I said, feeling sick for him. "I am *so* sorry."

He stood there biting his lower lip. "It is very difficult," he said. "I cannot resign myself."

He looked straight past me and out through the window. Then he began to cry. "I am utterly unable to resign myself," he said and choked. And then crying, his head up looking at nothing, carrying himself straight and soldierly, with tears on both his cheeks and biting his lips, he walked past the machines and out the door.

The doctor told me that the major's wife, who was very young and whom he had not married until he was definitely invalided out of the war, had died of pneumonia. She had been sick only a few days. No one expected her to die. The major did not come to the hospital for three days. Then he came at the usual hour, wearing a black band on the sleeve of his uniform. When he came back, there were large framed photographs around the wall, of all sorts of wounds before and after they had been cured by the machines. In front of the machine the major used were three photographs of hands like his that were completely restored. I do not know where the doctor got them. I always understood we were the first to use the machines. The photographs did not make much difference to the major because he only looked out of the window.

14

How the Leopard Got His Spots

Rudyard Kipling

In the days when everybody started fair, Best Beloved, the Leopard lived in a place called the High Veldt. 'Member it wasn't the Low Veldt, or the Bush Veldt, or the Sour Veldt, but the 'sclusively bare, hot, shiny High Veldt, where there was sand and sandy-coloured rock and 'sclusively tufts of sandy-yellowish grass. The Giraffe and the Zebra and the Eland and the Koodoo and the Hartebeest lived there; and they were 'sclusively sandy-yellow-brownish all over; but the Leopard, he was the 'sclusivest sandiest-yellowish-brownest of them all—a greyish-yellowish catty-shaped kind of beast, and he matched the 'sclusively yellowish-greyish-brownish colour of the High Veldt to one hair. This was very bad for the Giraffe and the Zebra and the rest of them; for he would lie down by a 'sclusively yellowish-greyish-brownish stone or clump of grass, and when the Giraffe or the Zebra or the Eland or the Koodoo or the Bush-Buck or the Bonte-Buck came by he would surprise them out of their jumpsome lives. He would indeed! And, also, there was an Ethiopian with bows and arrows (a 'sclusively greyish-brownish-yellowish man he was then), who lived on the High Veldt with the Leopard; and the two used to hunt together—the Ethiopian with his bows and arrows, and the Leopard 'sclusively with his teeth and claws—till the Giraffe and the Eland and the Koodoo and the Quagga and all the rest of them didn't know which way to jump, Best Beloved. They didn't indeed!

After a long time—things lived for ever so long in those days—they learned to avoid anything that looked like a Leopard or an Ethiopian; and bit by bit—the Giraffe began it, because his legs were the longest—they went away from the High Veldt. They scuttled for days and days and days till they came to a great forest, 'sclusively full of trees and bushes and stripy, speckly, patchy-blatchy shadows, and there they hid: and after another long time, what with standing half in the shade and half out of it, and what with the slippery-slidy shadows of the trees falling on them, the Giraffe grew blotchy, and the Zebra grew stripy, and the Eland and the Koodoo grew darker, with little wavy grey lines on their backs like bark on a tree trunk; and so, though you could hear them and smell them, you could very seldom see them, and then only when you knew precisely where to look. They had a beautiful time in the 'sclusively speckly-spickly shadows of the forest, while the Leopard and the Ethiopian ran about over the 'sclusively greyish-yellowish-reddish High Veldt outside, wondering where all their breakfasts and their dinners and their teas had gone. At last they were so hungry that they ate rats and beetles and rock-rabbits, the Leopard and the Ethiopian, and then they had the Big Tummy-ache, both together; and then they met Baviaan—the dog-headed, barking Baboon, who is Quite the Wisest Animal in All South Africa.

Said Leopard to Baviaan (and it was a very hot day), 'Where has all the game gone?'

And Baviaan winked. He knew.

Said the Ethiopian to Baviaan, 'Can you tell me the present habitat of the aboriginal Fauna?' (That meant just the same thing, but the Ethiopian always used long words. He was a grown-up.)

And Baviaan winked. He knew.

Then said Baviaan, 'The game has gone into other spots; and my advice to you, Leopard, is to go into other spots as soon as you can.'

And the Ethiopian said, 'That is all very fine, but I wish to know whither the aboriginal Fauna has migrated.'

Then said Baviaan, 'The aboriginal Fauna has joined the aboriginal Flora because it was high time for a change; and my advice to you, Ethiopian, is to change as soon as you can.'

That puzzled the Leopard and the Ethiopian, but they set off to look for the aboriginal Flora, and presently, after ever so many days, they saw a great, high, tall forest full of tree trunks all 'sclusively speckled and sprottled and spottled, dotted and splashed and slashed and hatched and cross-hatched with shadows. (Say that quickly aloud, and you will see how very shadowy the forest must have been.)

'What is this,' said the Leopard, 'that is so 'sclusively dark, and yet so full of little pieces of light?'

'I don't know, said the Ethiopian, 'but it ought to be the aboriginal Flora. I can smell Giraffe, and I can hear Giraffe, but I can't see Giraffe.'

'That's curious,' said the Leopard. 'I suppose it is because we have just come in out of the sunshine. I can smell Zebra, and I can hear Zebra, but I can't see Zebra.'

'Wait a bit, said the Ethiopian. 'It's a long time since we've hunted 'em. Perhaps we've forgotten what they were like.'

'Fiddle!' said the Leopard. 'I remember them perfectly on the High Veldt, especially their marrow-bones. Giraffe is about seventeen feet high, of a 'sclusively fulvous golden-yellow from head to heel; and Zebra is about four and a half feet high, of a'sclusively grey-fawn colour from head to heel.'

'Umm, said the Ethiopian, looking into the speckly-spickly shadows of the aboriginal Flora-forest. 'Then they ought to show up in this dark place like ripe bananas in a smokehouse.'

But they didn't. The Leopard and the Ethiopian hunted all day; and though they could smell them and hear them, they never saw one of them.

'For goodness' sake,' said the Leopard at tea-time, 'let us wait till it gets dark. This daylight hunting is a perfect scandal.'

So they waited till dark, and then the Leopard heard something breathing sniffily in the starlight that fell all stripy through the branches, and he jumped at the noise, and it smelt like Zebra, and it felt like Zebra, and when he knocked it down it kicked like Zebra, but he couldn't see it. So he said, 'Be quiet, O you person without any form. I am going to sit on your head till morning, because there is something about you that I don't understand.'

Presently he heard a grunt and a crash and a scramble, and the Ethiopian called out, 'I've caught a thing that I can't see. It smells like Giraffe, and it kicks like Giraffe, but it hasn't any form.'

'Don't you trust it,' said the Leopard. 'Sit on its head till the morning—same as me. They haven't any form—any of 'em.'

So they sat down on them hard till bright morning-time, and then Leopard said, 'What have you at your end of the table, Brother?'

The Ethiopian scratched his head and said, 'It ought to be 'sclusively a rich fulvous orange-tawny from head to heel, and it ought to be Giraffe; but it is covered all over with chestnut blotches. What have you at your end of the table, Brother?'

And the Leopard scratched his head and said, 'It ought to be 'sclusively a delicate greyish-fawn, and it ought to be Zebra; but it is covered all over with black and purple stripes. What in the world have you been doing to yourself, Zebra? Don't you know that if you were on the High Veldt I could see you ten miles off? You haven't any form.'

'Yes,' said the Zebra, 'but this isn't the High Veldt. Can't you see?'

'I can now,' said the Leopard. 'But I couldn't all yesterday. How is it done?'

'Let us up,' said the Zebra, 'and we will show you.

They let the Zebra and the Giraffe get up; and Zebra moved away to some little thorn-bushes where the sunlight fell all stripy, and Giraffe moved off to some tallish trees where the shadows fell all blotchy.

'Now watch,' said the Zebra and the Giraffe. 'This is the way it's done. One—two—three! And where's your breakfast?'

Leopard stared, and Ethiopian stared, but all they could see were stripy shadows and blotched shadows in the forest, but never a sign of Zebra and Giraffe. They had just walked off and hidden themselves in the shadowy forest.

'Hi! Hi!' said the Ethiopian. 'That's a trick worth learning. Take a lesson by it, Leopard. You show up in this dark place like a bar of soap in a coal-scuttle.'

'Ho! Ho!' said the Leopard. 'Would it surprise you very much to know that you show up in this dark place like a mustard-plaster on a sack of coals?'

'Well, calling names won't catch dinner, said the Ethiopian. 'The long and the little of it is that we don't match our backgrounds. I'm going to take Baviaan's advice. He told me I ought to change; and as I've nothing to change except my skin I'm going to change that.'

'What to?' said the Leopard, tremendously excited.

'To a nice working blackish-brownish colour, with a little purple in it, and touches of slaty-blue. It will be the very thing for hiding in hollows and behind trees.'

So he changed his skin then and there, and the Leopard was more excited than ever; he had never seen a man change his skin before.

'But what about me?' he said, when the Ethiopian had worked his last little finger into his fine new black skin.

'You take Baviaan's advice too. He told you to go into spots.'

'So I did,' said the Leopard. I went into other spots as fast as I could. I went into this spot with you, and a lot of good it has done me.'

'Oh,' said the Ethiopian, 'Baviaan didn't mean spots in South Africa. He meant spots on your skin.'

'What's the use of that?' said the Leopard.

'Think of Giraffe,' said the Ethiopian. 'Or if you prefer stripes, think of Zebra. They find their spots and stripes give them per-feet satisfaction.'

'Umm,' said the Leopard. 'I wouldn't look like Zebra—not for ever so.'

'Well, make up your mind,' said the Ethiopian, 'because I'd hate to go hunting without you, but I must if you insist on looking like a sun-flower against a tarred fence.'

'I'll take spots, then,' said the Leopard; 'but don't make 'em too vulgar-big. I wouldn't look like Giraffe—not for ever so.'

'I'll make 'em with the tips of my fingers,' said the Ethiopian. 'There's plenty of black left on my skin still. Stand over!'

Then the Ethiopian put his five fingers close together (there was plenty of black left on his new skin still) and pressed them all over the Leopard, and wherever the five fingers touched they left five little black marks, all close together. You can see them on any Leopard's skin you like, Best Beloved. Sometimes the fingers slipped and the marks got a little blurred; but if you look closely at any Leopard now you will see that there are always five spots—off five fat black finger-tips.

'Now you are a beauty!' said the Ethiopian. 'You can lie out on the bare ground and look like a heap of pebbles. You can lie out on the naked rocks and look like a piece of pudding-stone. You can lie out on a leafy branch and look like sunshine sifting through the leaves; and you can lie right across the centre of a path and look like nothing in particular. Think of that and purr!'

'But if I'm all this,' said the Leopard, 'why didn't you go spotty too?'

'Oh, plain black's best for a nigger,' said the Ethiopian. 'Now come along and we'll see if we can't get even with Mr. One-Two-Three Where's your Breakfast!'

So they went away and lived happily ever afterward, Best Beloved. That is all.

Oh, now and then you will hear grown-ups say, 'Can the Ethiopian change his skin or the Leopard his spots?' I don't think even grown-ups would keep on saying such a silly thing if the Leopard and the Ethiopian hadn't done it once—do you? But they will never do it again, Best Beloved. They are quite contented as they are.

I AM the Most Wise Baviaan, saying in most wise tones,
'Let us melt into the landscape—just us two by our lones.'
People have come—in a carriage—calling. But Mummy is there....
Yes, I can go if you take me—Nurse says she don't care.
Let's go up to the pig-sties and sit on the farmyard rails!
Let's say things to the bunnies, and watch 'em skitter their tails!
Let's—oh, anything, daddy, so long as it's you and me,
And going truly exploring, and not being in till tea!
Here's your boots (I've brought 'em), and here's your cap and stick,
And here's your pipe and tobacco. Oh, come along out of it—quick.

15

In a Grove

Ryūnosuke Akutagawa

The Testimony of a Woodcutter Questioned by a High Police Commissioner

Yes, sir. Certainly, it was I who found the body. This morning, as usual, I went to cut my daily quota of cedars, when I found the body in a grove in a hollow in the mountains. The exact location? About 150 meters off the Yamashina stage road. It's an out-of-the-way grove of bamboo and cedars.

The body was lying flat on its back dressed in a bluish silk kimono and a wrinkled head-dress of the Kyoto style. A single sword-stroke had pierced the breast. The fallen bamboo-blades around it were stained with bloody blossoms. No, the blood was no longer running. The wound had dried up, I believe. And also, a gad-fly was stuck fast there, hardly noticing my footsteps.

You ask me if I saw a sword or any such thing?

No, nothing, sir. I found only a rope at the root of a cedar nearby. And… well, in addition to a rope, I found a comb. That was all. Apparently he must have made a battle of it before he was murdered, because the grass and fallen bamboo-blades had been trampled down all around.

"A horse was nearby?"

No, sir. It's hard enough for a man to enter, let alone a horse.

The Testimony of a Traveling Buddhist Priest Questioned by a High Police Commissioner

The time? Certainly, it was about noon yesterday, sir. The unfortunate man was on the road from Sekiyama to Yamashina. He was walking toward Sekiyama with a woman accompanying him on horse back, who I have since learned was his wife. A scarf hanging from her head hid her face from view. All I saw was the color of her clothes, a lilac-colored suit. Her horse was a sorrel with a fine mane. The lady's height? Oh, about four feet five inches. Since I am a Buddhist priest, I took little noice about her details. Well, the man was armed with a sword as well as a bow and arrows. And I remember that he carried some twenty odd arrows in his quiver.

Little did I expect that he would meet such a fate. Truly human life is as evanescent as the morning dew or a flash of lightning. My words are inadequate to express my sympathy for him.

The Testimony of a Policeman Questioned by a High Police Commissioner

The man that I arrested? He is a notorious brigand called Tajomaru. When I arrested him, he had fallen off his horse. He was groaning on the bridge at Awataguchi. The time? It was in the early hours of last night. For the record, I might say that the other day I tried to arrest him, but unfortunately he escaped. He was wearing a dark blue silk kimono and a large plain sword. And, as you see, he got a bow and arrows somewhere. You say that this bow and these arrows look like the ones owned by the dead man? Then Tajomaru must be the murderer. The bow wound with leather strips, the black lacquered quiver, the seventeen arrows with hawk feathers—these were all in his possession I believe. Yes, Sir, the horse is, as you say, a sorrel with a fine mane. A little beyond the stone bridge I found the horse grazing by the roadside, with his long rein dangling. Surely there is some providence in his having been thrown by the horse.

Of all the robbers prowling around Kyoto, this Tajomaru has given the most grief to the women in town. Last autumn a wife who came to the mountain back of the Pindora of the Toribe Temple, presumably to pay a visit, was murdered, along with a girl. It has been suspected that it was his doing. If this criminal murdered the man, you cannot tell what he may have done with the man's wife. May it please your honor to look in to this problem as well.

The Testimony of an Old Woman Questioned by a High Police Commissioner

Yes, sir, that corpse is the man who married my daughter. He does not come from Kyoto. He was a samurai in the town of Kokufu in the province of Wakasa. His name was Kanazawa no Takehiko, and his age was twenty-six. He was of a gentle disposition, so I am sure he did nothing to provoke the anger of others.

My daughter? Her name is Masago, and her age is nineteen. She is a spirited, fun-loving girl, but I am sure she has never known any man except Takehiko. She has a small, oval, dark-complected face with a mole at the corner of her left eye.

Yesterday Takehiko left for Wakasa with my daughter. What bad luck it is that things should have come to such a sad end! What has become of my daughter? I am resigned to giving up my son-in-law as lost, but the fate of my daughter worries me sick. For heaven's sake leave no stone unturned to find her. I hate that robber Tajomaru, or whatever his name is. Not only my son-in-law, but my daughter… (Her later words were drowned in tears.)

Tajomaru's Confession

I killed him, but not her. Where's she gone? I can't tell. Oh, wait a minute. No torture can make me confess what I don't know. Now things have come to such a head, I won't keep anything from you. Yesterday a little past noon I met that couple. Just then a puff of wind blew, and raised her hanging scarf, so that I caught a glimpse of her face. Instantly it was again covered from my view. That may have been one reason; she looked like a Bodhisattva. At that moment I made up my mind to capture her even if I had to kill her man.

Why? To me killing isn't a matter of such great consequence as you might think. When a woman is captured, her man has to be killed any way. In killing, I use the sword I wear at my side. Am I the only one who kills people? You, you don't use your swords. You kill people with your power, with your money. Sometimes you kill them on the pretext of working for their good. It's true they don't bleed. They are in the best of health, but all the same you've killed them. It's hard to say who is a greater sinner, you or me. (An ironical smile.)

But it would be good if I could capture a woman without killing her man. So, I made up my mind to capture her, and do my best not to kill him. But it's out of the question on the Yamashina stage road. So I managed to lure the couple into the mountains.

It was quite easy. I became their traveling companion, and I told them there was an old mound in the mountain over there, and that I had dug it open and found many mirrors and swords. I went on to tell them I'd buried the things in a grove behind the mountain, and that I'd like to sell them at a low price to anyone who would care to have them. Then… you see, isn't greed terrible? He was beginning to be moved by my talk before he knew it. In less than half an hour they were driving their horse toward the mountain with me.

When he came in front of the grove, I told them that the treasures were buried in it, and I asked them to come and see. The man had no objection—he was blinded by greed. The woman said she would wait on horseback. It was natural for her to say so, at the sight of a thick grove. To tell you the truth, my plan worked just as I wished, so I went into the grove with him, leaving her behind alone.

The grove is only bamboo for some distance. About fifty yards ahead there's a rather open clump of cedars. It was a convenient spot for my purpose. Pushing my way through the grove, I told him a plausible lie that the treasures were buried under the cedars. When I told him this, he pushed his laborious way toward the slender cedar visible through the grove. After a while the bamboo thinned out, and we came to where a number of cedars grew in a row. As soon as we got there, I seized him from behind. Because he was a trained, sword-bearing warrior, he was quite strong, but he was taken by surprise, so there was no help for him. I soon tied him up to the root of a cedar. Where did I get a rope? Thank heaven, being a robber, I had a rope with me, since I might have to scale a wall at any moment. Of course it was easy to stop him from calling out by gagging his mouth with fallen bamboo leaves.

When I disposed of him, I went to his woman and asked her to come and see him, because he seemed to have been suddenly taken sick. It's needless to say that this plan also worked well. The woman, her sedge hat off, came into the depths of the grove, where I led her by the hand. The instant she caught sight of her husband, she drew a small sword. I've never seen a woman of such violent temper. If I'd been off guard, I'd have got a thrust in my side. I dodged, but she kept on slashing at me. She might have wounded me deeply or killed me. But I'm Tajomaru. I managed to strike down her small sword without drawing my own. The most spirited woman is defenseless without a weapon. At least I could satisfy my desire for her without taking her husband's life.

Yes… without taking his life. I had no wish to kill him. I was about to run away from the grove, leaving the woman behind in tears, when she frantically clung to my arm. In broken fragments of words, she asked that either her husband or I die. She said it was more trying than death to have her shame known to two men. She gasped out that she wanted to be the wife of whichever survived. Then a furious desire to kill him seized me. (Gloomy excitement.)

Telling you in this way, no doubt I seem a crueler man than you. But that's because you didn't see her face. Especially her burning eyes at that moment. As I saw her eye to eye, I wanted to make her my wife even if I were to be struck by lightning. I wanted to make her my wife… this single desire filled my mind. This was not only lust, as you might think. At that time if I'd had no other desire than lust, I'd surely not have minded knocking her down and running away. Then I wouldn't have stained my sword with his blood. But the moment I gazed at her face in the dark grove, I decided not to leave there without killing him.

But I didn't like to resort to unfair means to kill him. I untied him and told him to cross swords with me. (The rope that was found at the root of the cedar is the rope I dropped at the time.) Furious with anger, he drew his thick sword. And quick as thought, he sprang at me ferociously, without speaking a word. I needn't tell you how our fight turned out. The twenty-third stroke… please remember this. I'm impressed with this fact still. Nobody under the sun has ever clashed swords with me twenty strokes. (A cheerful smile.)

When he fell, I turned toward her, lowering my blood-stained sword. But to my great astonishment she was gone. I wondered to where she had run away. I looked for her in the clump of cedars. I listened, but heard only a groaning sound from the throat of the dying man.

As soon as we started to cross swords, she may have run away through the grove to call for help. When I thought of that, I decided it was a matter of life and death to me. So, robbing him of his sword, and bow and arrows, I ran out to the mountain road. There I found her horse still grazing quietly. It would be a mere waste of words to tell you the later details, but before I entered town I had already parted with the sword. That's all my confession. I know that my head will be hung in chains anyway, so put me down for the maximum penalty. (A defiant attitude.)

The Repentance of a Woman Who Has Come to Kiyomizu Temple

That man in the blue silk kimono, after forcing me to yield to him, laughed mockingly as he looked at my bound husband. How horrified my husband must have been! But no matter how hard he struggled in agony, the rope cut into him all the more tightly. In spite of myself I ran stumblingly toward his side. Or rather I tried to run toward him, but the man instantly knocked me down. Just at that moment I saw an indescribable light in my husband's eyes. Something beyond expression… his eyes make me shudder even now. That instantaneous look of my husband, who couldn't speak a word, told me all his heart. The flash in his eyes was neither anger nor sorrow… only a cold light, a look of loathing. More struck by the look in his eyes than by the blow of the thief, I called out in spite of myself and fell unconscious.

In the course of time I came to, and found that the man in blue silk was gone. I saw only my husband still bound to the root of the cedar. I raised myself from the bamboo-blades with difficulty, and looked into his face; but the expression in his eyes was just the same as before.

Beneath the cold contempt in his eyes, there was hatred. Shame, grief, and anger… I don't know how to express my heart at that time. Reeling to my feet, I went up to my husband.

"Takejiro," I said to him, "since things have come to this pass, I cannot live with you. I'm determined to die… but you must die, too. You saw my shame. I can't leave you alive as you are."

This was all I could say. Still he went on gazing at me with loathing and contempt. My heart breaking, I looked for his sword. It must have been taken by the robber. Neither his sword nor his bow and arrows were to be seen in the grove. But fortunately my small sword was lying at my feet. Raising it over head, once more I said, "Now give me your life. I'll follow you right away."

When he heard these words, he moved his lips with difficulty. Since his mouth was stuffed with leaves, of course his voice could not be heard at all. But at a glance I understood his words. Despising me, his look said only, "Kill me." Neither conscious nor unconscious, I stabbed the small sword through the lilac-colored kimono into his breast.

Again at this time I must have fainted. By the time I managed to look up, he had already breathed his last—still in bonds. A streak of sinking sunlight streamed through the clump of cedars and bamboos, and shone on his pale face. Gulping down my sobs, I untied the rope from his dead body. And... and what has become of me? Only that, since I have no more strength to tell you. Anyway, I hadn't the strength to die. I stabbed my own throat with the small sword, I threw myself into a pond at the foot of the mountain, and I tried to kill myself in many ways. Unable to end my life, I am still living in dishonor. (A lonely smile.) Worthless as I am, I must have been forsaken even by the most merciful Kwannon. I killed my own husband. I was violated by the robber. Whatever can I do? Whatever can I... I... (Gradually, violent sobbing.)

The Story of the Murdered Man, as Told Through a Medium

After violating my wife, the robber, sitting there, began to speak comforting words to her. Of course I couldn't speak. My whole body was tied fast to the root of a cedar. But meanwhile I winked at her many times, as much as to say "Don't believe the robber." I wanted to convey some such meaning to her. But my wife, sitting dejectedly on the bamboo leaves, was looking hard at her lap. To all appearance, she was listening to his words. I was agonized by jealousy. In the meantime the robber went on with his clever talk, from one subject to another. The robber finally made his bold brazen proposal. "Once your virtue is stained, you won't get along well with your husband, so won't you be my wife instead? It's my love for you that made me be violent toward you."

While the criminal talked, my wife raised her face as if in a trance. She had never looked so beautiful as at that moment. What did my beautiful wife say in answer to him while I was sitting bound there? I am lost in space, but I have never thought of her answer without burning with anger and jealousy. Truly she said, "Then take me away with you wherever you go."

This is not the whole of her sin. If that were all, I would not be tormented so much in the dark. When she was going out of the grove as if in a dream, her hand in the robber's, she suddenly turned pale, and pointed at me tied to the root of the cedar, and said, "Kill him! I cannot marry you as long as he lives." "Kill him!" she cried many times, as if she had gone crazy. Even now these words threaten to blow me headlong into the bottomless abyss of darkness. Has such a hateful thing come out of a human mouth ever before? Have such cursed words ever struck a human ear, even once? Even once such a… (A sudden cry of scorn.) At these words the robber himself turned pale. "Kill him," she cried, clinging to his arms. Looking hard at her, he answered neither yes nor no… but hardly had I thought about his answer before she had been knocked down into the bamboo leaves. (Again a cry of scorn.) Quietly folding his arms, he looked at me and said, "What will you do with her? Kill her or save her? You have only to nod. Kill her?" For these words alone I would like to pardon his crime.

While I hesitated, she shrieked and ran into the depths of the grove. The robber instantly snatched at her, but he failed even to grasp her sleeve.

After she ran away, he took up my sword, and my bow and arrows. With a single stroke he cut one of my bonds. I remember his mumbling, "My fate is next." Then he disappeared from the grove. All was silent after that. No, I heard someone crying. Untying the rest of my bonds, I listened carefully, and I noticed that it was my own crying. (Long silence.)

I raised my exhausted body from the foot of the cedar. In front of me there was shining the small sword which my wife had dropped. I took it up and stabbed it into my breast. A bloody lump rose to my mouth, but I didn't feel any pain. When my breast grew cold, everything was as silent as the dead in their graves. What profound silence! Not a single bird note was heard in the sky over this grave in the hollow of the mountains. Only a lonely light lingered on the cedars and mountains.

By and by the light gradually grew fainter, till the cedars and bamboo were lost to view. Lying there, I was enveloped in deep silence.

Then someone crept up to me. I tried to see who it was. But darkness had already been gathering round me. Someone… that someone drew the small sword softly out of my breast in its invisible hand. At the same time once more blood flowed into my mouth. And once and for all I sank down into the darkness of space.

16

Hunting the Deceitful Turkey

Mark Twain

When I was a boy my uncle and his big boys hunted with the rifle, the youngest boy Fred and I with a shotgun—a small single-barrelled shotgun which was properly suited to our size and strength; it was not much heavier than a broom. We carried it turn about, half an hour at a time. I was not able to hit anything with it, but I liked to try. Fred and I hunted feathered small game, the others hunted deer, squirrels, wild turkeys, and such things. My uncle and the big boys were good shots. They killed hawks and wild geese and such like on the wing; and they didn't wound or kill squirrels, they stunned them. When the dogs treed a squirrel, the squirrel would scamper aloft and run out on a limb and flatten himself along it, hoping to make himself invisible in that way—and not quite succeeding. You could see his wee little ears sticking up. You couldn't see his nose, but you knew where it was. Then the hunter, despising a "rest" for his rifle, stood up and took offhand aim at the limb and sent a bullet into it immediately under the squirrel's nose, and down tumbled the animal, unwounded, but unconscious; the dogs gave him a shake and he was dead. Sometimes when the distance was great and the wind not accurately allowed for, the bullet would hit the squirrel's head; the dogs could do as they pleased with that one—the hunter's pride was hurt, and he wouldn't allow it to go into the gamebag.

In the first faint gray of the dawn the stately wild turkeys would be stalking around in great flocks, and ready to be sociable and answer invitations to come and converse with other excursionists of their kind. The hunter concealed himself and imitated the turkey-call by sucking the air through the leg-bone of a turkey which had previously answered a call like that and lived only just long enough to regret it. There is nothing that furnishes a perfect turkey-call except that bone. Another of Nature's treacheries, you see. She is full of them; half the time she doesn't know which she likes best—to betray her child or protect it. In the case of the turkey she is badly mixed: she gives it a bone to be used in getting it into trouble, and she also furnishes it with a trick for getting itself out of the trouble again. When a mamma-turkey answers an invitation and finds she has made a mistake in accepting it, she does as the mamma-partridge does—remembers a previous engagement—and goes limping and scrambling away, pretending to be very lame; and at the same time she is saying to her not-visible children, "Lie low, keep still, don't expose yourselves; I shall be back as soon as I have beguiled this shabby swindler out of the country."

When a person is ignorant and confiding, this immoral device can have tiresome results. I followed an ostensibly lame turkey over a considerable part of the United States one morning, because I believed in her and could not think she would deceive a mere boy, and one who was trusting her and considering her honest. I had the single-barrelled shotgun, but my idea was to catch her alive. I often got within rushing distance of her, and then made my rush; but always, just as I made my final plunge and put my hand down where her back had been, it wasn't there; it was only two or three inches from there and I brushed the tail-feathers as I landed on my stomach—a very close call, but still not quite close enough; that is, not close enough for success, but just close enough to convince me that I could do it next time. She always waited for me, a little piece away, and let on to be resting and greatly fatigued; which was a lie, but I believed it, for I still thought her honest long after I ought to have begun to doubt her, suspecting that this was no way for a high-minded bird to be acting. I followed, and followed, and followed, making my periodical rushes, and getting up and brushing the dust off, and resuming the voyage with patient confidence; indeed, with a confidence which grew, for I could see by the change of climate and vegetation that we were getting up into the high latitudes, and as she always looked a little tireder and a little more discouraged after each rush, I judged that I was safe to win, in the end, the competition being purely a matter of staying power and the advantage lying with me from the start because she was lame.

Along in the afternoon I began to feel fatigued myself. Neither of us had had any rest since we first started on the excursion, which was upwards of ten hours before, though latterly we had paused awhile after rushes, I letting on to be thinking about something else; but neither of us sincere, and both of us waiting for the other to call game but in no real hurry about it, for indeed those little evanescent snatches of rest were very grateful to the feelings of us both; it would naturally be so, skirmishing along like that ever since dawn and not a bite in the meantime; at least for me, though sometimes as she lay on her side fanning herself with a wing and praying for strength to get out of this difficulty a grasshopper happened along whose time had come, and that was well for her, and fortunate, but I had nothing—nothing the whole day.

More than once, after I was very tired, I gave up taking her alive, and was going to shoot her, but I never did it, although it was my right, for I did not believe I could hit her; and besides, she always stopped and posed, when I raised the gun, and this made me suspicious that she knew about me and my marksmanship, and so I did not care to expose myself to remarks.

I did not get her, at all. When she got tired of the game at last, she rose from almost under my hand and flew aloft with the rush and whir of a shell and lit on the highest limb of a great tree and sat down and crossed her legs and smiled down at me, and seemed gratified to see me so astonished.

I was ashamed, and also lost; and it was while wandering the woods hunting for myself that I found a deserted log cabin and had one of the best meals there that in my life-days I have eaten. The weed-grown garden was full of ripe tomatoes, and I ate them ravenously, though I had never liked them before. Not more than two or three times since have I tasted anything that was so delicious as those tomatoes. I surfeited myself with them, and did not taste another one until I was in middle life. I can eat them now, but I do not like the look of them. I suppose we have all experienced a surfeit at one time or another. Once, in stress of circumstances, I ate part of a barrel of sardines, there being nothing else at hand, but since then I have always been able to get along without sardines.

17

The Lumber Room

Saki

The children were to be driven, as a special treat, to the sands at Jagborough. Nicholas was not to be of the party; he was in disgrace. Only that morning he had refused to eat his wholesome bread-and-milk on the seemingly frivolous ground that there was a frog in it. Older and wiser and better people had told him that there could not possibly be a frog in his bread-and-milk and that he was not to talk nonsense; he continued, nevertheless, to talk what seemed the veriest nonsense, and described with much detail the coloration and markings of the alleged frog. The dramatic part of the incident was that there really was a frog in Nicholas's basin of bread-and-milk; he had put it there himself, so he felt entitled to know something about it. The sin of taking a frog from the garden and putting it into a bowl of wholesome bread-and-milk was enlarged on at great length, but the fact that stood out clearest in the whole affair, as it presented itself to the mind of Nicholas, was that the older, wiser, and better people had been proved to be profoundly in error in matters about which they had expressed the utmost assurance.

"You said there couldn't possibly be a frog in my bread-and-milk; there was a frog in my bread-and-milk," he repeated, with the insistence of a skilled tactician who does not intend to shift from favourable ground.

So his boy-cousin and girl-cousin and his quite uninteresting younger brother were to be taken to Jagborough sands that afternoon and he was to stay at home. His cousins' aunt, who insisted, by an unwarranted stretch of imagination, in styling herself his aunt also, had hastily invented the Jagborough expedition in order to impress on Nicholas the delights that he had justly forfeited by his disgraceful conduct at the breakfast-table. It was her habit, whenever one of the children fell from grace, to improvise something of a festival nature from which the offender would be rigorously debarred; if all the children sinned collectively they were suddenly informed of a circus in a neighbouring town, a circus of unrivalled merit and uncounted elephants, to which, but for their depravity, they would have been taken that very day.

A few decent tears were looked for on the part of Nicholas when the moment for the departure of the expedition arrived. As a matter of fact, however, all the crying was done by his girl-cousin, who scraped her knee rather painfully against the step of the carriage as she was scrambling in. "How she did howl," said Nicholas cheerfully, as the party drove off without any of the elation of high spirits that should have characterized it.

"She'll soon get over that," said the *soi-disant* aunt; "it will be a glorious afternoon for racing about over those beautiful sands. How they will enjoy themselves!"

"Bobby won't enjoy himself much, and he won't race much either," said Nicholas with a grim chuckle; "his boots are hurting him. They're too tight."

"Why didn't he tell me they were hurting?" asked the aunt with some asperity.

"He told you twice, but you weren't listening. You often don't listen when we tell you important things."

"You are not to go into the gooseberry garden," said the aunt, changing the subject.

"Why not?" demanded Nicholas.

"Because you are in disgrace," said the aunt loftily.

Nicholas did not admit the flawlessness of the reasoning; he felt perfectly capable of being in disgrace and in a gooseberry garden at the same moment. His face took on an expression of considerable obstinacy. It was clear to his aunt that he was determined to get into the gooseberry garden, "only," as she remarked to herself, "because I have told him he is not to."

Now the gooseberry garden had two doors by which it might be entered, and once a small person like Nicholas could slip in there he could effectually disappear from view amid the masking growth of artichokes, raspberry canes, and fruit bushes. The aunt had many other things to do that afternoon, but she spent an hour or two in trivial gardening operations among flower beds and shrubberies, whence she could watch the two doors that led to the forbidden paradise. She was a woman of few ideas, with immense powers of concentration.

Nicholas made one or two sorties into the front garden, wriggling his way with obvious stealth of purpose towards one or other of the doors, but never able for a moment to evade the aunt's watchful eye. As a matter of fact, he had no intention of trying to get into the gooseberry garden, but it was extremely convenient for him that his aunt should believe that he had; it was a belief that would keep her on self-imposed sentry-duty for the greater part of the afternoon. Having thoroughly confirmed and fortified her suspicions, Nicholas slipped back into the house and rapidly put into execution a plan of action that had long germinated in his brain. By standing on a chair in the library one could reach a shelf on which reposed a fat, important-looking key. The key was as important as it looked; it was the instrument which kept the mysteries of the lumber-room secure from unauthorized intrusion, which opened a way only for aunts and such-like privileged persons. Nicholas had not had much experience of the art of fitting keys into keyholes and turning locks, but for some days past he had practised with the key of the schoolroom door; he did not believe in trusting too much to luck and accident. The key turned stiffly in the lock, but it turned. The door opened, and Nicholas was in an unknown land, compared with which the gooseberry garden was a stale delight, a mere material pleasure.

Often and often Nicholas had pictured to himself what the lumber-room might be like, that region that was so carefully sealed from youthful eyes and concerning which no questions were ever answered. It came up to his expectations. In the first place it was large and dimly lit, one high window opening onto the forbidden garden being its only source of illumination. In the second place it was a storehouse of unimagined treasures. The aunt-by-assertion was one of those people who think that things spoil by use and consign them to dust and damp by way of preserving them. Such parts of the house as Nicholas knew best were rather bare and cheerless, but here there were wonderful things for the eye to feast on. First and foremost there was a piece of framed tapestry that was evidently meant to be a fire-screen. To Nicholas it was a living, breathing story; he sat down on a roll of Indian hangings, glowing in wonderful colours beneath a layer of dust, and took in all the details of the tapestry picture. A man, dressed in the hunting costume of some remote period, had just transfixed a stag with an arrow; it could not have been a difficult shot because the stag was only one or two paces away from him; in the thickly growing vegetation that the picture suggested it would not have been difficult to creep up to a feeding stag, and the two spotted dogs that were springing forward to join in the chase had evidently been trained to keep to heel till the arrow was discharged. That part of the picture was simple, if interesting, but did the huntsman see, what Nicholas saw, that four galloping wolves were coming in his direction through the wood? There might be more than four of them hidden behind the trees, and in any case would the man and his dogs be able to cope with the four wolves if they made an attack? The man had only two arrows left in his quiver, and he might miss with one or both of them; all one knew about his skill in shooting was that he could hit a large stag at a ridiculously short range. Nicholas sat for many golden minutes revolving the possibilities of the scene; he was inclined to think that there were more than four wolves and that the man and his dogs were in a tight corner.

But there were other objects of delight and interest claiming his instant attention; there were quaint twisted candlesticks in the shape of snakes, and a teapot fashioned like a china duck, out of whose open beak the tea was supposed to come. How dull and shapeless the nursery teapot seemed in comparison! And there was a carved sandalwood box packed tight with aromatic cotton-wool, and between the layers of cotton-wool were little brass figures, hump-necked bulls, and peacocks and goblins, delightful to see and to handle. Less promising in appearance was a large square book with plain black covers; Nicholas peeped into it, and, behold, it was full of coloured pictures of birds. And such birds! In the garden, and in the lanes when he went for a walk, Nicholas came across a few birds, of which the largest were an occasional magpie or wood-pigeons here were herons and bustards, kites, toucans, tiger-bitterns, brush turkeys, ibises, golden pheasants, a whole portrait gallery of undreamed-of creatures. And as he was admiring the colouring of the mandarin duck and assigning a life-history to it, the voice of his aunt in shrill vociferation of his name came from the gooseberry garden without. She had grown suspicious at his long disappearance, and had leapt to the conclusion that he had climbed over the wall behind the sheltering screen of the lilac bushes: she was now engaged in energetic and rather hopeless search for him among the artichokes and raspberry canes.

"Nicholas, Nicholas!" she screamed, "you are to come out of this at once. It's no use trying to hide there; I can see you all the time."

It was probably the first time for twenty years that anyone had smiled in that lumber-room.

Presently the angry repetitions of Nicholas's name gave way to a shriek, and a cry for somebody to come quickly. Nicholas shut the book, restored it carefully to its place in a corner, and shook some dust from a neighbouring pile of newspapers over it. Then he crept from the room, locked the door, and replaced the key exactly where he had found it. His aunt was still calling his name when he sauntered into the front garden.

"Who's calling?" he asked.

"Me," came the answer from the other side of the wall; "didn't you hear me? I've been looking for you in the gooseberry garden, and I've slipped into the rain-water tank. Luckily there's no water in it, but the sides are slippery and I can't get out. Fetch the little ladder from under the cherry tree—"

"I was told I wasn't to go into the gooseberry garden," said Nicholas promptly.

"I told you not to, and now I tell you that you may," came the voice from the rain-water tank, rather impatiently.

"Your voice doesn't sound like aunt's," objected Nicholas; "you may be the Evil One tempting me to be disobedient. Aunt often tells me that the Evil One tempts me and that I always yield. This time I'm not going to yield."

"Don't talk nonsense," said the prisoner in the tank; "go and fetch the ladder."

"Will there be strawberry jam for tea?" asked Nicholas innocently.

"Certainly there will be," said the aunt, privately resolving that Nicholas should have none of it.

"Now I know that you are the Evil One and not aunt," shouted Nicholas gleefully; "when we asked aunt for strawberry jam yesterday she said there wasn't any. I know there are four jars of it in the store cupboard, because I looked, and of course you know it's there, but she doesn't, because she said there wasn't any. Oh, Devil, you have sold yourself!"

There was an unusual sense of luxury in being able to talk to an aunt as though one was talking to the Evil One, but Nicholas knew, with childish discernment that such luxuries were not to be over-indulged in. He walked noisily away, and it was a kitchenmaid, in search of parsley, who eventually rescued the aunt from the rain-water tank. Tea that evening was partaken of in a fearsome silence. The tide had been at its highest when the children had arrived at Jagborough Cove, so there had been no sands to play on—a circumstance that the aunt had overlooked in the haste of organising her punitive expedition. The tightness of Bobby's boots had had a disastrous effect on his temper the whole of the afternoon, and altogether the children could not have been said to have enjoyed themselves. The aunt maintained the frozen muteness of one who has suffered undignified and unmerited detention in a rain-water tank for thirty-five minutes. As for Nicholas, he, too, was silent, in the absorption of one who has much to think about; it was just possible, he considered, that the huntsman would escape with his hounds while the wolves feasted on the stricken stag.

18

The Open Window

Saki

"My aunt will be down presently, Mr. Nuttel," said a very self-possessed young lady of fifteen; "in the meantime you must try and put up with me."

Framton Nuttel endeavoured to say the correct something which should duly flatter the niece of the moment without unduly discounting the aunt that was to come. Privately he doubted more than ever whether these formal visits on a succession of total strangers would do much towards helping the nerve cure which he was supposed to be undergoing.

"I know how it will be," his sister had said when he was preparing to migrate to this rural retreat; "you will bury yourself down there and not speak to a living soul, and your nerves will be worse than ever from moping. I shall just give you letters of introduction to all the people I know there. Some of them, as far as I can remember, were quite nice."

Framton wondered whether Mrs. Sappleton, the lady to whom he was presenting one of the letters of introduction came into the nice division.

"Do you know many of the people round here?" asked the niece, when she judged that they had had sufficient silent communion.

"Hardly a soul," said Framton. "My sister was staying here, at the rectory, you know, some four years ago, and she gave me letters of introduction to some of the people here."

He made the last statement in a tone of distinct regret.

"Then you know practically nothing about my aunt?" pursued the self-possessed young lady.

"Only her name and address," admitted the caller. He was wondering whether Mrs. Sappleton was in the married or widowed state. An undefinable something about the room seemed to suggest masculine habitation.

"Her great tragedy happened just three years ago," said the child;

"that would be since your sister's time."

"Her tragedy?" asked Framton; somehow in this restful country spot tragedies seemed out of place.

"You may wonder why we keep that window wide open on an October afternoon," said the niece, indicating a large French window that opened on to a lawn.

"It is quite warm for the time of the year," said Framton; "but has that window got anything to do with the tragedy?"

"Out through that window, three years ago to a day, her husband and her two young brothers went off for their day's shooting. They never came back. In crossing the moor to their favourite snipe-shooting ground they were all three engulfed in a treacherous piece of bog. It had been that dreadful wet summer, you know, and places that were safe in other years gave way suddenly without warning. Their bodies were never recovered. That was the dreadful part of it." Here the child's voice lost its self-possessed note and became falteringly human. "Poor aunt always thinks that they will come back someday, they and the little brown spaniel that was lost with them, and walk in at that window just as they used to do. That is why the window is kept open every evening till it is quite dusk. Poor dear aunt, she has often told me how they went out, her husband with his white waterproof coat over his arm, and Ronnie, her youngest brother, singing 'Bertie, why do you bound?' as he always did to tease her, because she said it got on her nerves. Do you know, sometimes on still, quiet evenings like this, I almost get a creepy feeling that they will all walk in through that window…"

She broke off with a little shudder. It was a relief to Framton when the aunt bustled into the room with a whirl of apologies for being late in making her appearance.

"I hope Vera has been amusing you?" she said.

"She has been very interesting," said Framton.

"I hope you don't mind the open window," said Mrs. Sappleton briskly; "my husband and brothers will be home directly from shooting, and they always come in this way. They've been out for snipe in the marshes today, so they'll make a fine mess over my poor carpets. So like you menfolk, isn't it?"

She rattled on cheerfully about the shooting and the scarcity of birds, and the prospects for duck in the winter. To Framton it was all purely horrible. He made a desperate but only partially successful effort to turn the talk on to a less ghastly topic, he was conscious that his hostess was giving him only a fragment of her attention, and her eyes were constantly straying past him to the open window and the lawn beyond. It was certainly an unfortunate coincidence that he should have paid his visit on this tragic anniversary.

"The doctors agree in ordering me complete rest, an absence of mental excitement, and avoidance of anything in the nature of violent physical exercise," announced Framton, who laboured under the tolerably widespread delusion that total strangers and chance acquaintances are hungry for the least detail of one's ailments and infirmities, their cause and cure. "On the matter of diet they are not so much in agreement," he continued.

"No?" said Mrs. Sappleton, in a voice which only replaced a yawn at the last moment. Then she suddenly brightened into alert attention—but not to what Framton was saying.

"Here they are at last!" she cried. "Just in time for tea, and don't they look as if they were muddy up to the eyes!"

Framton shivered slightly and turned towards the niece with a look intended to convey sympathetic comprehension. The child was staring out through the open window with a dazed horror in her eyes. In a chill shock of nameless fear Framton swung round in his seat and looked in the same direction.

In the deepening twilight three figures were walking across the lawn towards the window, they all carried guns under their arms, and one of them was additionally burdened with a white coat hung over his shoulders. A tired brown spaniel kept close at their heels. Noiselessly they neared the house, and then a hoarse young voice chanted out of the dusk: "I said, Bertie, why do you bound?"

Framton grabbed wildly at his stick and hat; the hall door, the gravel drive, and the front gate were dimly noted stages in his headlong retreat. A cyclist coming along the road had to run into the hedge to avoid imminent collision.

"Here we are, my dear," said the bearer of the white mackintosh, coming in through the window, "fairly muddy, but most of it's dry. Who was that who bolted out as we came up?"

"A most extraordinary man, a Mr. Nuttel," said Mrs. Sappleton;

"could only talk about his illnesses, and dashed off without a word of goodbye or apology when you arrived. One would think he had seen a ghost."

"I expect it was the spaniel," said the niece calmly; "he told me he had a horror of dogs. He was once hunted into a cemetery somewhere on the banks of the Ganges by a pack of pariah dogs, and had to spend the night in a newly dug grave with the creatures snarling and grinning and foaming just above him. Enough to make anyone lose their nerve."

Romance at short notice was her speciality.

19

Shock Tactics

Saki

On a late spring afternoon Ella McCarthy sat on a green-painted chair in Kensington Gardens, staring listlessly at an uninteresting stretch of park landscape, that blossomed suddenly into tropical radiance as an expected figure appeared in the middle distance.

"Hullo, Bertie!" she exclaimed sedately, when the figure arrived at the painted chair that was the nearest neighbour to her own, and dropped into it eagerly, yet with a certain due regard for the set of its trousers; "hasn't it been a perfect spring afternoon?"

The statement was a distinct untruth as far as Ella's own feelings were concerned; until the arrival of Bertie the afternoon had been anything but perfect.

Bertie made a suitable reply, in which a questioning note seemed to hover.

"Thank you ever so much for those lovely handkerchiefs," said Ella, answering the unspoken question; "they were just what I've been wanting. There's only one thing spoilt my pleasure in your gift," she added, with a pout.

"What was that?" asked Bertie anxiously, fearful that perhaps he had chosen a size of handkerchief that was not within the correct feminine limit.

"I should have liked to have written and thanked you for them as soon as I got them," said Ella, and Bertie's sky clouded at once.

"You know what mother is," he protested; "she opens all my letters, and if she found I'd been giving presents to any one there'd have been something to talk about for the next fortnight."

"Surely, at the age of twenty—" began Ella.

"I'm not twenty till September," interrupted Bertie.

"At the age of nineteen years and eight months," persisted Ella, "you might be allowed to keep your correspondence private to yourself."

"I ought to be, but things aren't always what they ought to be. Mother opens every letter that comes into the house, whoever it's for. My sisters and I have made rows about it time and again, but she goes on doing it."

"I'd find some way to stop her if I were in your place," said Ella valiantly, and Bertie felt that the glamour of his anxiously deliberated present had faded away in the disagreeable restriction that hedged round its acknowledgment.

"Is anything the matter?" asked Bertie's friend Clovis when they met that evening at the swimming-bath.

"Why do you ask?" said Bertie.

"When you wear a look of tragic gloom in a swimming-bath," said Clovis, "it's especially noticeable from the fact that you're wearing very little else. Didn't she like the handkerchiefs?"

Bertie explained the situation.

"It is rather galling, you know," he added, "when a girl has a lot of things she wants to write to you and can't send a letter except by some roundabout, underhand way."

"One never realises one's blessings while one enjoys them," said Clovis; "now I have to spend a considerable amount of ingenuity inventing excuses for not having written to people."

"It's not a joking matter," said Bertie resentfully: "you wouldn't find it funny if your mother opened all your letters."

"The funny thing to me is that you should let her do it."

"I can't stop it. I've argued about it—"

"You haven't used the right kind of argument, I expect. Now, if every time one of your letters was opened you lay on your back on the dining-table during dinner and had a fit, or roused the entire family in the middle of the night to hear you recite one of Blake's 'Poems of Innocence,' you would get a far more respectful hearing for future protests. People yield more consideration to a mutilated mealtime or a broken night's rest, than ever they would to a broken heart."

"Oh, dry up," said Bertie crossly, inconsistently splashing Clovis from head to foot as he plunged into the water.

It was a day or two after the conversation in the swimming-bath that a letter addressed to Bertie Heasant slid into the letter-box at his home, and thence into the hands of his mother. Mrs. Heasant was one of those empty-minded individuals to whom other people's affairs are perpetually interesting. The more private they are intended to be the more acute is the interest they arouse. She would have opened this particular letter in any case; the fact that it was marked "private," and diffused a delicate but penetrating aroma merely caused her to open it with headlong haste rather than matter-of-course deliberation. The harvest of sensation that rewarded her was beyond all expectations.

"Bertie, carissimo," it began, "I wonder if you will have the nerve to do it: it will take some nerve, too. Don't forget the jewels. They are a detail, but details interest me.

"Yours as ever,
"Clotilde.

"Your mother must not know of my existence. If questioned swear you never heard of me."

For years Mrs. Heasant had searched Bertie's correspondence diligently for traces of possible dissipation or youthful entanglements, and at last the suspicions that had stimulated her inquisitorial zeal were justified by this one splendid haul. That any one wearing the exotic name "Clotilde" should write to Bertie under the incriminating announcement "as ever" was sufficiently electrifying, without the astounding allusion to the jewels. Mrs. Heasant could recall novels and dramas wherein jewels played an exciting and commanding role, and here, under her own roof, before her very eyes as it were, her own son was carrying on an intrigue in which jewels were merely an interesting detail. Bertie was not due home for another hour, but his sisters were available for the immediate unburdening of a scandal-laden mind.

"Bertie is in the toils of an adventuress," she screamed; "her name is Clotilde," she added, as if she thought they had better know the worst at once. There are occasions when more harm than good is done by shielding young girls from a knowledge of the more deplorable realities of life.

By the time Bertie arrived his mother had discussed every possible and improbable conjecture as to his guilty secret; the girls limited themselves to the opinion that their brother had been weak rather than wicked.

"Who is Clotilde?" was the question that confronted Bertie almost before he had got into the hall. His denial of any knowledge of such a person was met with an outburst of bitter laughter.

"How well you have learned your lesson!" exclaimed Mrs. Heasant. But satire gave way to furious indignation when she realised that Bertie did not intend to throw any further light on her discovery.

"You shan't have any dinner till you've confessed everything," she stormed.

Bertie's reply took the form of hastily collecting material for an impromptu banquet from the larder and locking himself into his bedroom. His mother made frequent visits to the locked door and shouted a succession of interrogations with the persistence of one who thinks that if you ask a question often enough an answer will eventually result. Bertie did nothing to encourage the supposition. An hour had passed in fruitless one-sided palaver when another letter addressed to Bertie and marked "private" made its appearance in the letter-box. Mrs. Heasant pounced on it with the enthusiasm of a cat that has missed its mouse and to whom a second has been unexpectedly vouchsafed. If she hoped for further disclosures assuredly she was not disappointed.

> "So you have really done it!" the letter abruptly commenced; "Poor Dagmar. Now she is done for I almost pity her. You did it very well, you wicked boy, the servants all think it was suicide, and there will be no fuss. Better not touch the jewels till after the inquest.
>
> "Clotilde."

Anything that Mrs. Heasant had previously done in the way of outcry was easily surpassed as she raced upstairs and beat frantically at her son's door.

"Miserable boy, what have you done to Dagmar?"

"It's Dagmar now, is it?" he snapped; "it will be Geraldine next."

"That it should come to this, after all my efforts to keep you at home of an evening," sobbed Mrs. Heasant; "it's no use you trying to hide things from me; Clotilde's letter betrays everything."

"Does it betray who she is?" asked Bertie; "I've heard so much about her, I should like to know something about her home-life. Seriously, if you go on like this I shall fetch a doctor; I've often enough been preached at about nothing, but I've never had an imaginary harem dragged into the discussion."

"Are these letters imaginary?" screamed Mrs. Heasant; "what about the jewels, and Dagmar, and the theory of suicide?"

No solution of these problems was forthcoming through the bedroom door, but the last post of the evening produced another letter for Bertie, and its contents brought Mrs. Heasant that enlightenment which had already dawned on her son.

> "Dear Bertie," it ran; "I hope I haven't distracted your brain with the spoof letters I've been sending in the name of a fictitious Clotilde. You told me the other day that the servants, or somebody at your home, tampered with your letters, so I thought I would give any one that opened them something exciting to read. The shock might do them good.
>
> "Yours,
> "Clovis Sangrail."

Mrs. Heasant knew Clovis slightly, and was rather afraid of him. It was not difficult to read between the lines of his successful hoax. In a chastened mood she rapped once more at Bertie's door.

"A letter from Mr. Sangrail. It's all been a stupid hoax. He wrote those other letters. Why, where are you going?"

Bertie had opened the door; he had on his hat and overcoat.

"I'm going for a doctor to come and see if anything's the matter with you. Of course it was all a hoax, but no person in his right mind could have believed all that rubbish about murder and suicide and jewels. You've been making enough noise to bring the house down for the last hour or two."

"But what was I to think of those letters?" whimpered Mrs. Heasant.

"I should have known what to think of them," said Bertie; "if you choose to excite yourself over other people's correspondence it's your own fault. Anyhow, I'm going for a doctor."

It was Bertie's great opportunity, and he knew it. His mother was conscious of the fact that she would look rather ridiculous if the story got about. She was willing to pay hush-money.

"I'll never open your letters again," she promised. And Clovis has no more devoted slave than Bertie Heasant.

20

The Way to the Dairy

Saki

The Baroness and Clovis sat in a much-frequented corner of the Park exchanging biographical confidences about the long succession of passers-by.

"Who are those depressed-looking young women who have just gone by?" asked the Baroness; "they have the air of people who have bowed to destiny and are not quite sure whether the salute will be returned."

"Those," said Clovis, "are the Brimley Bomefields. I dare say you would look depressed if you had been through their experiences."

"I'm always having depressing experiences;" said the Baroness, "but I never give them outward expression. It's as bad as looking one's age. Tell me about the Brimley Bomefields."

"Well," said Clovis, "the beginning of their tragedy was that they found an aunt. The aunt had been there all the time, but they had very nearly forgotten her existence until a distant relative refreshed their memory by remembering her very distinctly in his will; it is wonderful what the force of example will accomplish. The aunt, who had been unobtrusively poor, became quite pleasantly rich, and the Brimley Bomefields grew suddenly concerned at the loneliness of her life and took her under their collective wings. She had as many wings around her at this time as one of those beast-things in Revelation."

"So far I don't see any tragedy from the Brimley Bomefields' point of view," said the Baroness.

"We haven't got to it yet," said Clovis. "The aunt had been used to living very simply, and had seen next to nothing of what we should consider life, and her nieces didn't encourage her to do much in the way of making a splash with her money. Quite a good deal of it would come to them at her death, and she was a fairly old woman, but there was one circumstance which cast a shadow of gloom over the satisfaction they felt in the discovery and acquisition of this desirable aunt: she openly acknowledged that a comfortable slice of her little fortune would go to a nephew on the other side of her family. He was rather a deplorable thing in rotters, and quite hopelessly top-hole in the way of getting through money, but he had been more or less decent to the old lady in her unremembered days, and she wouldn't hear anything against him. At least, she wouldn't pay any attention to what she did hear, but her nieces took care that she should have to listen to a good deal in that line. It seemed such a pity, they said among themselves, that good money should fall into such worthless hands. They habitually spoke of their aunt's money as 'good money,' as though other people's aunts dabbled for the most part in spurious currency.

"Regularly after the Derby, St. Leger, and other notable racing events they indulged in audible speculations as to how much money Roger had squandered in unfortunate betting transactions.

"'His travelling expenses must come to a big sum,' said the eldest Brimley Bomefield one day; 'they say he attends every race-meeting in England, besides others abroad. I shouldn't wonder if he went all the way to India to see the race for the Calcutta Sweepstake that one hears so much about.'

"'Travel enlarges the mind, my dear Christine,' said her aunt.

"'Yes, dear aunt, travel undertaken in the right spirit,' agreed Christine; 'but travel pursued merely as a means towards gambling and extravagant living is more likely to contract the purse than to enlarge the mind. However, as long as Roger enjoys himself, I suppose he doesn't care how fast or unprofitably the money goes, or where he is to find more. It seems a pity, that's all.'

"The aunt by that time had begun to talk of something else, and it was doubtful if Christine's moralizing had been even accorded a hearing. It was her remark, however—the aunt's remark, I mean—about travel enlarging the mind, that gave the youngest Brimley Bomefield her great idea for the showing-up of Roger.

"'If aunt could only be taken somewhere to see him gambling and throwing away money,' she said, 'it would open her eyes to his character more effectually than anything we can say.'

"'My dear Veronique,' said her sisters, 'we can't go following him to race-meetings.'

"'Certainly not to race-meetings,' said Veronique, 'but we might go to some place where one can look on at gambling without taking part in it.'

"'Do you mean Monte Carlo?' they asked her, beginning to jump rather at the idea.

"'Monte Carlo is a long way off, and has a dreadful reputation,' said Veronique; 'I shouldn't like to tell our friends that we were going to Monte Carlo. But I believe Roger usually goes to Dieppe about this time of year, and some quite respectable English people go there, and the journey wouldn't be expensive. If aunt could stand the Channel crossing the change of scene might do her a lot of good.'

"And that was how the fateful idea came to the Brimley Bomefields.

"From the very first set-off disaster hung over the expedition, as they afterwards remembered. To begin with, all the Brimley Bomefields were extremely unwell during the crossing, while the aunt enjoyed the sea air and made friends with all manner of strange travelling companions. Then, although it was many years since she had been on the Continent, she had served a very practical apprenticeship there as a paid companion, and her knowledge of colloquial French beat theirs to a standstill. It became increasingly difficult to keep under their collective wings a person who knew what she wanted and was able to ask for it and to see that she got it. Also, as far as Roger was concerned, they drew Dieppe blank; it turned out that he was staying at Pourville, a little watering-place a mile or two further west. The Brimley Bomefields discovered that Dieppe was too crowded and frivolous, and persuaded the old lady to migrate to the comparative seclusion of Pourville.

"'You won't find it dull, you know,' they assured her; 'there is a little casino attached to the hotel, and you can watch the people dancing and throwing away their money at PETITS CHEVAUX.'

"It was just before PETITS CHEVAUX had been supplanted by BOULE.

"Roger was not staying in the same hotel, but they knew that the casino would be certain of his patronage on most afternoons and evenings.

"On the first evening of their visit they wandered into the casino after a fairly early dinner, and hovered near the tables. Bertic van Tahn was staying there at the time, and he described the whole incident to me. The Brimley Bomefields kept a furtive watch on the doors as though they were expecting some one to turn up, and the aunt got more and more amused and interested watching the little horses whirl round and round the board.

"'Do you know, poor little number eight hasn't won for the last thirty-two times,' she said to Christine; 'I've been keeping count. I shall really have to put five francs on him to encourage him.'

"'Come and watch the dancing, dear,' said Christine nervously. It was scarcely a part of their strategy that Roger should come in and find the old lady backing her fancy at the PETITS CHEVAUX table.

"'Just wait while I put five francs on number eight,' said the aunt, and in another moment her money was lying on the table. The horses commenced to move round, it was a slow race this time, and number eight crept up at the finish like some crafty demon and placed his nose just a fraction in front of number three, who had seemed to be winning easily. Recourse had to be had to measurement, and the number eight was proclaimed the winner. The aunt picked up thirty-five francs. After that the Brimley Bomefields would have had to have used concerted force to get her away from the tables. When Roger appeared on the scene she was fifty-two francs to the good; her nieces were hovering forlornly in the background, like chickens that have been hatched out by a duck and are despairingly watching their parent disporting herself in a dangerous and uncongenial element. The supper-party which Roger insisted on standing that night in honour of his aunt and the three Miss Brimley Bomefields was remarkable for the unrestrained gaiety of two of the participants and the funereal mirthlessness of the remaining guests.

"'I do not think,' Christine confided afterwards to a friend, who re-confided it to Bertie van Tahn, 'that I shall ever be able to touch PATÉ DE FOIE GRAS again. It would bring back memories of that awful evening.'

"For the next two or three days the nieces made plans for returning to England or moving on to some other resort where there was no casino. The aunt was busy making a system for winning at PETITS CHEVAUX. Number eight, her first love, had been running rather unkindly for her, and a series of plunges on number five had turned out even worse.

"'Do you know, I dropped over seven hundred francs at the tables this afternoon,' she announced cheerfully at dinner on the fourth evening of their visit.

"'Aunt! Twenty-eight pounds! And you were losing last night too.'

"'Oh, I shall get it all back,' she said optimistically; 'but not here. These silly little horses are no good. I shall go somewhere where one can play comfortably at roulette. You needn't look so shocked. I've always felt that, given the opportunity, I should be an inveterate gambler, and now you darlings have put the opportunity in my way. I must drink your very good healths. Waiter, a bottle of PONTET CANET. Ah, it's number seven on the wine list; I shall plunge on number seven tonight. It won four times running this afternoon when I was backing that silly number five.'

"Number seven was not in a winning mood that evening. The Brimley Bomefields, tired of watching disaster from a distance, drew near to the table where their aunt was now an honoured habituée, and gazed mournfully at the successive victories of one and five and eight and four, which swept 'good money' out of the purse of seven's obstinate backer. The day's losses totalled something very near two thousand francs.

"'You incorrigible gamblers,' said Roger chaffingly to them, when he found them at the tables.

"'We are not gambling,' said Christine freezingly; 'we are looking on.'

"'I DON'T think,' said Roger knowingly; 'of course you're a syndicate and aunt is putting the stakes on for all of you. Anyone can tell by your looks when the wrong horse wins that you've got a stake on.'

"Aunt and nephew had supper alone that night, or at least they would have if Bertie hadn't joined them; all the Brimley Bomefields had headaches.

"The aunt carried them all off to Dieppe the next day and set cheerily about the task of winning back some of her losses. Her luck was variable; in fact, she had some fair streaks of good fortune, just enough to keep her thoroughly amused with her new distraction; but on the whole she was a loser. The Brimley Bomefields had a collective attack of nervous prostration on the day when she sold out a quantity of shares in Argentine rails. 'Nothing will ever bring that money back,' they remarked lugubriously to one another.

"'Veronique at last could bear it no longer, and went home; you see, it had been her idea to bring the aunt on this disastrous expedition, and though the others did not cast the fact verbally in her face, there was a certain lurking reproach in their eyes which was harder to meet than actual upbraidings. The other two remained behind, forlornly mounting guard over their aunt until such time as the waning of the Dieppe season should at last turn her in the direction of home and safety. They made anxious calculations as to how little 'good money' might, with reasonable luck, be squandered in the meantime. Here, however, their reckoning went far astray; the close of the Dieppe season merely turned their aunt's thoughts in search of some other convenient gambling resort. 'Show a cat the way to the dairy—' I forget how the proverb goes on, but it summed up the situation as far as the Brimley Bomefields' aunt was concerned. She had been introduced to unexplored pleasures, and found them greatly to her liking, and she was in no hurry to forgo the fruits of her newly acquired knowledge. You see, for the first time in her life the old thing was thoroughly enjoying herself; she was losing money, but she had plenty of fun and excitement over the process, and she had enough left to do very comfortably on. Indeed, she was only just learning to understand the art of doing oneself well. She was a popular hostess, and in return her fellow-gamblers were always ready to entertain her to dinners and suppers when their luck was in. Her nieces, who still remained in attendance on her, with the pathetic unwillingness of a crew to leave a foundering treasure ship which might yet be steered into port, found little pleasure in these Bohemian festivities; to see 'good money' lavished on good living for the entertainment of a nondescript circle of acquaintances who were not likely to be in any way socially useful to them, did not attune them to a spirit of revelry. They contrived, whenever possible, to excuse themselves from participation in their aunt's deplored gaieties; the Brimley Bomefield headaches became famous.

"And one day the nieces came to the conclusion that, as they would have expressed it, 'no useful purpose would be served' by their continued attendance on a relative who had so thoroughly emancipated herself from the sheltering protection of their wings. The aunt bore the announcement of their departure with a cheerfulness that was almost disconcerting.

"'It's time you went home and had those headaches seen to by a specialist,' was her comment on the situation.

"The homeward journey of the Brimley Bomefields was a veritable retreat from Moscow, and what made it the more bitter was the fact that the Moscow, in this case, was not overwhelmed with fire and ashes, but merely extravagantly over-illuminated.

"From mutual friends and acquaintances they sometimes get glimpses of their prodigal relative, who has settled down into a confirmed gambling maniac, living on such salvage of income as obliging moneylenders have left at her disposal.

"So you need not be surprised," concluded Clovis, "if they do wear a depressed look in public."

"Which is Veronique?" asked the Baroness.

"The most depressed-looking of the three," said Clovis.

21

Cousin Teresa

Saki

Basset Harrowcluff returned to the home of his fathers, after an absence of four years, distinctly well pleased with himself. He was only thirty-one, but he had put in some useful service in an out-of-the-way, though not unimportant, corner of the world. He had quieted a province, kept open a trade route, enforced the tradition of respect which is worth the ransom of many kings in out-of-the-way regions, and done the whole business on rather less expenditure than would be requisite for organising a charity in the home country. In Whitehall and places where they think, they doubtless thought well of him. It was not inconceivable, his father allowed himself to imagine, that Basset's name might figure in the next list of Honours.

Basset was inclined to be rather contemptuous of his half-brother, Lucas, whom he found feverishly engrossed in the same medley of elaborate futilities that had claimed his whole time and energies, such as they were, four years ago, and almost as far back before that as he could remember. It was the contempt of the man of action for the man of activities, and it was probably reciprocated. Lucas was an over-well nourished individual, some nine years Basset's senior, with a colouring that would have been accepted as a sign of intensive culture in an asparagus, but probably meant in this case mere abstention from exercise. His hair and forehead furnished a recessional note in a personality that was in all other respects obtrusive and assertive. There was certainly no Semitic blood in Lucas's parentage, but his appearance contrived to convey at least a suggestion of Jewish extraction. Clovis Sangrail, who knew most of his associates by sight, said it was undoubtedly a case of protective mimicry.

Two days after Basset's return, Lucas frisked in to lunch in a state of twittering excitement that could not be restrained even for the immediate consideration of soup, but had to be verbally discharged in spluttering competition with mouthfuls of vermicelli.

"I've got hold of an idea for something immense," he babbled, "something that is simply It."

Basset gave a short laugh that would have done equally well as a snort, if one had wanted to make the exchange. His half-brother was in the habit of discovering futilities that were "simply It" at frequently recurring intervals. The discovery generally meant that he flew up to town, preceded by glowingly-worded telegrams, to see some one connected with the stage or the publishing world, got together one or two momentous luncheon parties, flitted in and out of "Gambrinus" for one or two evenings, and returned home with an air of subdued importance and the asparagus tint slightly intensified. The great idea was generally forgotten a few weeks later in the excitement of some new discovery.

"The inspiration came to me whilst I was dressing," announced Lucas; "it will be *the* thing in the next music-hall *revue*. All London will go mad over it. It's just a couplet; of course there will be other words, but they won't matter. Listen:

Cousin Teresa takes out Cæsar,
Fido, Jock, and the big borzoi.

A lifting, catchy sort of refrain, you see, and big-drum business on the two syllables of bor-zoi. It's immense. And I've thought out all the business of it; the singer will sing the first verse alone, then during the second verse Cousin Teresa will walk through, followed by four wooden dogs on wheels; Cæsar will be an Irish terrier, Fido a black poodle, Jock a fox-terrier, and the borzoi, of course, will be a borzoi. During the third verse Cousin Teresa will come on alone, and the dogs will be drawn across by themselves from the opposite wing; then Cousin Teresa will catch on to the singer and go off-stage in one direction, while the dogs' procession goes off in the other, crossing en route, which is always very effective. There'll be a lot of applause there, and for the fourth verse Cousin Teresa will come on in sables and the dogs will all have coats on. Then I've got a great idea for the fifth verse; each of the dogs will be led on by a Nut, and Cousin Teresa will come on from the opposite side, crossing en route, always effective, and then she turns round and leads the whole lot of them off on a string, and all the time every one singing like mad:

Cousin Teresa takes out Cæsar
Fido, Jock, and the big borzoi.

Tum-Tum! Drum business on the two last syllables. I'm so excited, I shan't sleep a wink to-night. I'm off to-morrow by the ten-fifteen. I've wired to Hermanova to lunch with me."

If any of the rest of the family felt any excitement over the creation of Cousin Teresa, they were signally successful in concealing the fact.

"Poor Lucas does take his silly little ideas seriously," said Colonel Harrowcluff afterwards in the smoking-room.

"Yes," said his younger son, in a slightly less tolerant tone, "in a day or two he'll come back and tell us that his sensational masterpiece is above the heads of the public, and in about three weeks' time he'll be wild with enthusiasm over a scheme to dramatise the poems of Herrick or something equally promising."

And then an extraordinary thing befell. In defiance of all precedent Lucas's glowing anticipations were justified and endorsed by the course of events. If Cousin Teresa was above the heads of the public, the public heroically adapted itself to her altitude. Introduced as an experiment at a dull moment in a new *revue*, the success of the item was unmistakable; the calls were so insistent and uproarious that even Lucas' ample devisings of additional "business" scarcely sufficed to keep pace with the demand. Packed houses on successive evenings confirmed the verdict of the first night audience, stalls and boxes filled significantly just before the turn came on, and emptied significantly after the last *encore* had been given. The manager tearfully acknowledged that Cousin Teresa was It. Stage hands and supers and programme sellers acknowledged it to one another without the least reservation. The name of the *revue* dwindled to secondary importance, and vast letters of electric blue blazoned the words "Cousin Teresa" from the front of the great palace of pleasure. And, of course, the magic of the famous refrain laid its spell all over the Metropolis. Restaurant proprietors were obliged to provide the members of their orchestras with painted wooden dogs on wheels, in order that the much-demanded and always conceded melody should be rendered with the necessary spectacular effects, and the crash of bottles and forks on the tables at the mention of the big borzoi usually drowned the sincerest efforts of drum or cymbals. Nowhere and at no time could one get away from the double thump that brought up the rear of the refrain; revellers reeling home at night banged it on doors and hoardings, milkmen clashed their cans to its cadence, messenger boys hit smaller messenger boys resounding double smacks on the same principle. And the more thoughtful circles of the great city were not deaf to the claims and significance of the popular melody. An enterprising and emancipated preacher discoursed from his pulpit on the inner meaning of "Cousin Teresa," and Lucas Harrowcluff was invited to lecture on the subject of his great achievement to members of the Young Mens' Endeavour League, the Nine Arts Club, and other learned and willing-to-learn bodies. In Society it seemed to be the one thing people really cared to talk about; men and women of middle age and average education might be seen together in corners earnestly discussing, not the question whether Servia should have an outlet on the Adriatic, or the possibilities of a British success in international polo contests, but the more absorbing topic of the problematic Aztec or Nilotic origin of the Teresa *motiv*.

"Politics and patriotism are so boring and so out of date," said a revered lady who had some pretensions to oracular utterance; "we are too cosmopolitan nowadays to be really moved by them. That is why one welcomes an intelligible production like 'Cousin Teresa,' that has a genuine message for one. One can't understand the message all at once, of course, but one felt from the very first that it was there. I've been to see it eighteen times and I'm going again to-morrow and on Thursday. One can't see it often enough."

"It would be rather a popular move if we gave this Harrowcluff person a knighthood or something of the sort," said the Minister reflectively.

"Which Harrowcluff?" asked his secretary.

"Which? There is only one, isn't there?" said the Minister; "the 'Cousin Teresa' man, of course. I think every one would be pleased if we knighted him. Yes, you can put him down on the list of certainties—under the letter L."

"The letter L," said the secretary, who was new to his job; "does that stand for Liberalism or liberality?"

Most of the recipients of Ministerial favour were expected to qualify in both of those subjects.

"Literature," explained the Minister.

And thus, after a fashion, Colonel Harrowcluff's expectation of seeing his son's name in the list of Honours was gratified.

22

A Ghost Story

Mark Twain

I took a large room, far up Broadway, in a huge old building whose upper stories had been wholly unoccupied for years until I came. The place had long been given up to dust and cobwebs, to solitude and silence. I seemed groping among the tombs and invading the privacy of the dead, that first night I climbed up to my quarters. For the first time in my life a superstitious dread came over me; and as I turned a dark angle of the stairway and an invisible cobweb swung its slazy woof in my face and clung there, I shuddered as one who had encountered a phantom.

I was glad enough when I reached my room and locked out the mold and the darkness. A cheery fire was burning in the grate, and I sat down before it with a comforting sense of relief. For two hours I sat there, thinking of bygone times; recalling old scenes, and summoning half-forgotten faces out of the mists of the past; listening, in fancy, to voices that long ago grew silent for all time, and to once familiar songs that nobody sings now. And as my reverie softened down to a sadder and sadder pathos, the shrieking of the winds outside softened to a wail, the angry beating of the rain against the panes diminished to a tranquil patter, and one by one the noises in the street subsided, until the hurrying footsteps of the last belated straggler died away in the distance and left no sound behind.

The fire had burned low. A sense of loneliness crept over me. I arose and undressed, moving on tiptoe about the room, doing stealthily what I had to do, as if I were environed by sleeping enemies whose slumbers it would be fatal to break. I covered up in bed, and lay listening to the rain and wind and the faint creaking of distant shutters, till they lulled me to sleep.

I slept profoundly, but how long I do not know. All at once I found myself awake, and filled with a shuddering expectancy. All was still.

All but my own heart—I could hear it beat. Presently the bedclothes began to slip away slowly toward the foot of the bed, as if some one were pulling them! I could not stir; I could not speak. Still the blankets slipped deliberately away, till my breast was uncovered. Then with a great effort I seized them and drew them over my head. I waited, listened, waited. Once more that steady pull began, and once more I lay torpid a century of dragging seconds till my breast was naked again. At last I roused my energies and snatched the covers back to their place and held them with a strong grip. I waited. By and by I felt a faint tug, and took a fresh grip. The tug strengthened to a steady strain—it grew stronger and stronger. My hold parted, and for the third time the blankets slid away. I groaned. An answering groan came from the foot of the bed! Beaded drops of sweat stood upon my forehead. I was more dead than alive. Presently I heard a heavy footstep in my room—the step of an elephant, it seemed to me—it was not like anything human. But it was moving from me—there was relief in that. I heard it approach the door—pass out without moving bolt or lock—and wander away among the dismal corridors, straining the floors and joists till they creaked again as it passed—and then silence reigned once more.

When my excitement had calmed, I said to myself, "This is a dream—simply a hideous dream." And so I lay thinking it over until I convinced myself that it was a dream, and then a comforting laugh relaxed my lips and I was happy again. I got up and struck a light; and when I found that the locks and bolts were just as I had left them, another soothing laugh welled in my heart and rippled from my lips. I took my pipe and lit it, and was just sitting down before the fire, when-down went the pipe out of my nerveless fingers, the blood forsook my cheeks, and my placid breathing was cut short with a gasp! In the ashes on the hearth, side by side with my own bare footprint, was another, so vast that in comparison mine was but an infant's! Then I had had a visitor, and the elephant tread was explained.

I put out the light and returned to bed, palsied with fear. I lay a long time, peering into the darkness, and listening.—Then I heard a grating noise overhead, like the dragging of a heavy body across the floor; then the throwing down of the body, and the shaking of my windows in response to the concussion. In distant parts of the building I heard the muffled slamming of doors. I heard, at intervals, stealthy footsteps creeping in and out among the corridors, and up and down the stairs. Sometimes these noises approached my door, hesitated, and went away again. I heard the clanking of chains faintly, in remote passages, and listened while the clanking grew nearer—while it wearily climbed the stairways, marking each move by the loose surplus of chain that fell with an accented rattle upon each succeeding step as the goblin that bore it advanced. I heard muttered sentences; half-uttered screams that seemed smothered violently; and the swish of invisible garments, the rush of invisible wings. Then I became conscious that my chamber was invaded—that I was not alone. I heard sighs and breathings about my bed, and mysterious whisperings. Three little spheres of soft phosphorescent light appeared on the ceiling directly over my head, clung and glowed there a moment, and then dropped—two of them upon my face and one upon the pillow. They, spattered, liquidly, and felt warm. Intuition told me they had—turned to gouts of blood as they fell—I needed no light to satisfy myself of that. Then I saw pallid faces, dimly luminous, and white uplifted hands, floating bodiless in the air—floating a moment and then disappearing. The whispering ceased, and the voices and the sounds, anal a solemn stillness followed. I waited and listened. I felt that I must have light or die. I was weak with fear. I slowly raised myself toward a sitting posture, and my face came in contact with a clammy hand! All strength went from me apparently, and I fell back like a stricken invalid. Then I heard the rustle of a garment it seemed to pass to the door and go out.

When everything was still once more, I crept out of bed, sick and feeble, and lit the gas with a hand that trembled as if it were aged with a hundred years. The light brought some little cheer to my spirits. I sat down and fell into a dreamy contemplation of that great footprint in the ashes. By and by its outlines began to waver and grow dim. I glanced up and the broad gas-flame was slowly wilting away. In the same moment I heard that elephantine tread again. I noted its approach, nearer and nearer, along the musty halls, and dimmer and dimmer the light waned. The tread reached my very door and paused—the light had dwindled to a sickly blue, and all things about me lay in a spectral twilight. The door did not open, and yet I felt a faint gust of air fan my cheek, and presently was conscious of a huge, cloudy presence before me. I watched it with fascinated eyes. A pale glow stole over the Thing;

gradually its cloudy folds took shape—an arm appeared, then legs, then a body, and last a great sad face looked out of the vapor. Stripped of its filmy housings, naked, muscular and comely, the majestic Cardiff Giant loomed above me!

All my misery vanished—for a child might know that no harm could come with that benignant countenance. My cheerful spirits returned at once, and in sympathy with them the gas flamed up brightly again. Never a lonely outcast was so glad to welcome company as I was to greet the friendly giant. I said:

"Why, is it nobody but you? Do you know, I have been scared to death for the last two or three hours? I am most honestly glad to see you. I wish I had a chair—Here, here, don't try to sit down in that thing—"

But it was too late. He was in it before I could stop him and down he went—I never saw a chair shivered so in my life.

"Stop, stop, you'll ruin ev—"

Too late again. There was another crash, and another chair was resolved into its original elements.

"Confound it, haven't you got any judgment at all? Do you want to ruin all the furniture on the place? Here, here, you petrified fool—"

But it was no use. Before I could arrest him he had sat down on the bed, and it was a melancholy ruin.

"Now what sort of a way is that to do? First you come lumbering about the place bringing a legion of vagabond goblins along with you to worry me to death, and then when I overlook an indelicacy of costume which would not be tolerated anywhere by cultivated people except in a respectable theater, and not even there if the nudity were of your sex, you repay me by wrecking all the furniture you can find to sit down on. And why will you? You damage yourself as much as you do me. You have broken off the end of your spinal column, and littered up the floor with chips of your hams till the place looks like a marble yard. You ought to be ashamed of yourself—you are big enough to know better."

"Well, I will not break any more furniture. But what am I to do? I have not had a chance to sit down for a century." And the tears came into his eyes.

"Poor devil," I said, "I should not have been so harsh with you. And you are an orphan, too, no doubt. But sit down on the floor here—nothing else can stand your weight—and besides, we cannot be sociable with you away up there above me; I want you down where I can perch on this high counting-house stool and gossip with you face to face."

So he sat down on the floor, and lit a pipe which I gave him, threw one of my red blankets over his shoulders, inverted my sitz-bath on his head, helmet fashion, and made himself picturesque and comfortable. Then he crossed his ankles, while I renewed the fire, and exposed the flat, honeycombed bottoms of his prodigious feet to the grateful warmth.

"What is the matter with the bottom of your feet and the back of your legs, that they are gouged up so?"

"Infernal chilblains—I caught them clear up to the back of my head, roosting out there under Newell's farm. But I love the place; I love it as one loves his old home. There is no peace for me like the peace I feel when I am there."

We talked along for half an hour, and then I noticed that he looked tired, and spoke of it.

"Tired?" he said. "Well, I should think so. And now I will tell you all about it, since you have treated me so well. I am the spirit of the Petrified Man that lies across the street there in the museum. I am the ghost of the Cardiff Giant. I can have no rest, no peace, till they have given that poor body burial again. Now what was the most natural thing for me to do, to make men satisfy this wish? Terrify them into it!—haunt the place where the body lay! So I haunted the museum night after night. I even got other spirits to help me. But it did no good, for nobody ever came to the museum at midnight. Then it occurred to me to come over the way and haunt this place a little. I felt that if I ever got a hearing I must succeed, for I had the most efficient company that perdition could furnish. Night after night we have shivered around through these mildewed halls, dragging chains, groaning, whispering, tramping up and down stairs, till, to tell you the truth, I am almost worn out. But when I saw a light in your room to-night I roused my energies again and went at it with a deal of the old freshness. But I am tired out—entirely fagged out. Give me, I beseech you, give me some hope!" I lit off my perch in a burst of excitement, and exclaimed:

"This transcends everything! everything that ever did occur! Why you poor blundering old fossil, you have had all your trouble for nothing—

you have been haunting a plaster cast of yourself—the real Cardiff Giant is in Albany!—[A fact. The original fraud was ingeniously and fraudfully duplicated, and exhibited in New York as the "only genuine" Cardiff Giant (to the unspeakable disgust of the owners of the real colossus) at the very same time that the latter was drawing crowds at a museum is Albany,]—Confound it, don't you know your own remains?"

I never saw such an eloquent look of shame, of pitiable humiliation, overspread a countenance before.

The Petrified Man rose slowly to his feet, and said:

"Honestly, is that true?"

"As true as I am sitting here."

He took the pipe from his mouth and laid it on the mantel, then stood irresolute a moment (unconsciously, from old habit, thrusting his hands where his pantaloons pockets should have been, and meditatively dropping his chin on his breast); and finally said:

"Well—I never felt so absurd before. The Petrified Man has sold everybody else, and now the mean fraud has ended by selling its own ghost! My son, if there is any charity left in your heart for a poor friendless phantom like me, don't let this get out. Think how you would feel if you had made such an ass of yourself."

I heard his stately tramp die away, step by step down the stairs and out into the deserted street, and felt sorry that he was gone, poor fellow—and sorrier still that he had carried off my red blanket and my bath-tub.

23

The Model Millionaire

Oscar Wilde

Unless one is wealthy there is no use in being a charming fellow. Romance is the privilege of the rich, not the profession of the unemployed. The poor should be practical and prosaic. It is better to have a permanent income than to be fascinating. These are the great truths of modern life which Hughie Erskine never realised. Poor Hughie! Intellectually, we must admit, he was not of much importance. He never said a brilliant or even an ill-natured thing in his life. But then he was wonderfully good-looking, with his crisp brown hair, his clear-cut profile, and his grey eyes. He was as popular with men as he was with women, and he had every accomplishment except that of making money. His father had bequeathed him his cavalry sword, and a *History of the Peninsular War* in fifteen volumes. Hughie hung the first over his looking-glass, put the second on a shelf between *Ruff's Guide* and Bailey's *Magazine*, and lived on two hundred a year that an old aunt allowed him. He had tried everything. He had gone on the Stock Exchange for six months; but what was a butterfly to do among bulls and bears? He had been a tea-merchant for a little longer, but had soon tired of pekoe and souchong. Then he had tried selling dry sherry. That did not answer; the sherry was a little too dry. Ultimately he became nothing, a delightful, ineffectual young man with a perfect profile and no profession.

To make matters worse, he was in love. The girl he loved was Laura Merton, the daughter of a retired Colonel who had lost his temper and his digestion in India, and had never found either of them again. Laura adored him, and he was ready to kiss her shoe-strings. They were the handsomest couple in London, and had not a penny-piece between them. The Colonel was very fond of Hughie, but would not hear of any engagement.

'Come to me, my boy, when you have got ten thousand pounds

of your own, and we will see about it,' he used to say; and Hughie looked very glum on those days, and had to go to Laura for consolation.

One morning, as he was on his way to Holland Park, where the Mertons lived, he dropped in to see a great friend of his, Alan Trevor. Trevor was a painter. Indeed, few people escape that nowadays. But he was also an artist, and artists are rather rare. Personally he was a strange rough fellow, with a freckled face and a red ragged beard. However, when he took up the brush he was a real master, and his pictures were eagerly sought after. He had been very much attracted by Hughie at first, it must be acknowledged, entirely on account of his personal charm. 'The only people a painter should know,' he used to say, 'are people who are *bête* and beautiful, people who are an artistic pleasure to look at and an intellectual repose to talk to. Men who are dandies and women who are darlings rule the world, at least they should do so.' However, after he got to know Hughie better, he liked him quite as much for his bright buoyant spirits and his generous reckless nature, and had given him the permanent *entrée* to his studio.

When Hughie came in he found Trevor putting the finishing touches to a wonderful life-size picture of a beggar-man. The beggar himself was standing on a raised platform in a corner of the studio. He was a wizened old man, with a face like wrinkled parchment, and a most piteous expression. Over his shoulders was flung a coarse brown cloak, all tears and tatters; his thick boots were patched and cobbled, and with one hand he leant on a rough stick, while with the other he held out his battered hat for alms.

'What an amazing model!' whispered Hughie, as he shook hands with his friend.

'An amazing model?' shouted Trevor at the top of his voice; 'I should think so! Such beggars as he are not to be met with every day. A *trouvaille, mon cher*; a living Velasquez! My stars! what an etching Rembrandt would have made of him!'

'Poor old chap!' said Hughie, 'how miserable he looks! But I suppose, to you painters, his face is his fortune?'

'Certainly,' replied Trevor, 'you don't want a beggar to look happy, do you?'

'How much does a model get for sitting?' asked Hughie, as he found himself a comfortable seat on a divan.

'A shilling an hour.'

'And how much do you get for your picture, Alan?'

'Oh, for this I get two thousand!'

'Pounds?'

'Guineas. Painters, poets, and physicians always get guineas.'

'Well, I think the model should have a percentage,' cried Hughie, laughing; 'they work quite as hard as you do.'

'Nonsense, nonsense! Why, look at the trouble of laying on the paint alone, and standing all day long at one's easel! It's all very well, Hughie, for you to talk, but I assure you that there are moments when Art almost attains to the dignity of manual labour. But you mustn't chatter; I'm very busy. Smoke a cigarette, and keep quiet.'

After some time the servant came in, and told Trevor that the frame-maker wanted to speak to him.

'Don't run away, Hughie,' he said, as he went out, 'I will be back in a moment.'

The old beggar-man took advantage of Trevor's absence to rest for a moment on a wooden bench that was behind him. He looked so forlorn and wretched that Hughie could not help pitying him, and felt in his pockets to see what money he had. All he could find was a sovereign and some coppers. 'Poor old fellow,' he thought to himself, 'he wants it more than I do, but it means no hansoms for a fortnight'; and he walked across the studio and slipped the sovereign into the beggar's hand.

The old man started, and a faint smile flitted across his withered lips. 'Thank you, sir,' he said, 'thank you.'

Then Trevor arrived, and Hughie took his leave, blushing a little at what he had done. He spent the day with Laura, got a charming scolding for his extravagance, and had to walk home.

That night he strolled into the Palette Club about eleven o'clock, and found Trevor sitting by himself in the smoking-room drinking hock and seltzer.

'Well, Alan, did you get the picture finished all right?' he said, as he lit his cigarette.

'Finished and framed, my boy!' answered Trevor; 'and, by-the-bye, you have made a conquest. That old model you saw is quite devoted to you. I had to tell him all about you—who you are, where you live, what your income is, what prospects you have—'

'My dear Alan,' cried Hughie, 'I shall probably find him waiting for me when I go home. But of course you are only joking. Poor old wretch! I wish I could do something for him. I think it is dreadful that any one should be so miserable. I have got heaps of old clothes at home—do you think he would care for any of them? Why, his rags were falling to bits.'

'But he looks splendid in them,' said Trevor. 'I wouldn't paint him in a frock-coat for anything. What you call rags I call romance. What seems poverty to you is picturesqueness to me. However, I'll tell him of your offer.'

'Alan,' said Hughie seriously, 'you painters are a heartless lot.'

'An artist's heart is his head,' replied Trevor; 'and besides, our business is to realise the world as we see it, not to reform it as we know it. À chacun son métier. And now tell me how Laura is. The old model was quite interested in her.'

'You don't mean to say you talked to him about her?' said Hughie.

'Certainly I did. He knows all about the relentless colonel, the lovely Laura, and the £10,000.'

'You told that old beggar all my private affairs?' cried Hughie, looking very red and angry.

'My dear boy,' said Trevor, smiling, 'that old beggar, as you call him, is one of the richest men in Europe. He could buy all London to-morrow without overdrawing his account. He has a house in every capital, dines off gold plate, and can prevent Russia going to war when he chooses.'

'What on earth do you mean?' exclaimed Hughie.

'What I say,' said Trevor. 'The old man you saw to-day in the studio was Baron Hausberg. He is a great friend of mine, buys all my pictures and that sort of thing, and gave me a commission a month ago to paint him as a beggar. *Que voulez-vous? La fantaisie d'un millionnaire*! And I must say he made a magnificent figure in his rags, or perhaps I should say in my rags; they are an old suit I got in Spain.'

'Baron Hausberg!' cried Hughie. 'Good heavens! I gave him a sovereign!' and he sank into an armchair the picture of dismay.

'Gave him a sovereign!' shouted Trevor, and he burst into a roar of laughter. 'My dear boy, you'll never see it again. *Son affaire c'est l'argent des autres.*'

'I think you might have told me, Alan,' said Hughie sulkily, 'and not have let me make such a fool of myself.'

'Well, to begin with, Hughie,' said Trevor, 'it never entered my mind that you went about distributing alms in that reckless way. I can understand your kissing a pretty model, but your giving a sovereign to an ugly one—by Jove, no! Besides, the fact is that I really was not at home to-day to any one; and when you came in I didn't know whether Hausberg would like his name mentioned. You know he wasn't in full dress.'

'What a duffer he must think me!' said Hughie.

'Not at all. He was in the highest spirits after you left; kept chuckling to himself and rubbing his old wrinkled hands together. I couldn't make out why he was so interested to know all about you; but I see it all now. He'll invest your sovereign for you, Hughie, pay you the interest every six months, and have a capital story to tell after dinner.'

'I am an unlucky devil,' growled Hughie. 'The best thing I can do is to go to bed; and, my dear Alan, you mustn't tell any one. I shouldn't dare show my face in the Row.'

'Nonsense! It reflects the highest credit on your philanthropic spirit, Hughie. And don't run away. Have another cigarette, and you can talk about Laura as much as you like.'

However, Hughie wouldn't stop, but walked home, feeling very unhappy, and leaving Alan Trevor in fits of laughter.

The next morning, as he was at breakfast, the servant brought him up a card on which was written, 'Monsieur Gustave Naudin, *de la part de* M. le Baron Hausberg.'

'I suppose he has come for an apology,' said Hughie to himself; and he told the servant to show the visitor up.

An old gentleman with gold spectacles and grey hair came into the room, and said, in a slight French accent, 'Have I the honour of addressing Monsieur Erskine?'

Hughie bowed.

'I have come from Baron Hausberg,' he continued. 'The Baron—'

'I beg, sir, that you will offer him my sincerest apologies,' stammered Hughie.

'The Baron,' said the old gentleman, with a smile, 'has commissioned me to bring you this letter;' and he extended a sealed envelope.

On the outside was written, 'A wedding present to Hugh Erskine and Laura Merton, from an old beggar,' and inside was a cheque for £10,000.

When they were married Alan Trevor was the best-man, and the Baron made a speech at the wedding-breakfast.

'Millionaire models,' remarked Alan, 'are rare enough; but, by Jove, model millionaires are rarer still!'

24

The Sphinx without a Secret

Oscar Wilde

One afternoon I was sitting outside the Cafe de la Paix, watching the splendour and shabbiness of Parisian life, and wondering over my vermouth at the strange panorama of pride and poverty that was passing before me, when I heard some one call my name. I turned round, and saw Lord Murchison. We had not met since we had been at college together, nearly ten years before, so I was delighted to come across him again, and we shook hands warmly. At Oxford we had been great friends. I had liked him immensely, he was so handsome, so high-spirited, and so honourable. We used to say of him that he would be the best of fellows, if he did not always speak the truth, but I think we really admired him all the more for his frankness. I found him a good deal changed. He looked anxious and puzzled, and seemed to be in doubt about something. I felt it could not be modern scepticism, for Murchison was the stoutest of Tories, and believed in the Pentateuch as firmly as he believed in the House of Peers; so I concluded that it was a woman, and asked him if he was married yet.

'I don't understand women well enough,' he answered.

'My dear Gerald,' I said, 'women are meant to be loved, not to be understood.'

'I cannot love where I cannot trust,' he replied.

'I believe you have a mystery in your life, Gerald,' I exclaimed; 'tell me about it.'

'Let us go for a drive,' he answered, 'it is too crowded here. No, not a yellow carriage, any other colour—there, that dark-green one will do'; and in a few moments we were trotting down the boulevard in the direction of the Madeleine.

'Where shall we go to?' I said.

'Oh, anywhere you like!' he answered—'to the restaurant in the Bois; we will dine there, and you shall tell me all about yourself.'

'I want to hear about you first,' I said. 'Tell me your mystery.'

He took from his pocket a little silver-clasped morocco case, and handed it to me. I opened it. Inside there was the photograph of a woman. She was tall and slight, and strangely picturesque with her large vague eyes and loosened hair. She looked like a *clairvoyante*, and was wrapped in rich furs.

'What do you think of that face?' he said; 'is it truthful?'

I examined it carefully. It seemed to me the face of some one who had a secret, but whether that secret was good or evil I could not say. Its beauty was a beauty moulded out of many mysteries—the beauty, in face, which is psychological, not plastic—and the faint smile that just played across the lips was far too subtle to be really sweet.

'Well,' he cried impatiently, 'what do you say?'

'She is the Gioconda in sables,' I answered. 'Let me know all about her.'

'Not now,' he said; 'after dinner;' and began to talk of other things.

When the waiter brought us our coffee and cigarettes I reminded Gerald of his promise. He rose from his seat, walked two or three times up and down the room, and, sinking into an armchair, told me the following story:—

'One evening,' he said, 'I was walking down Bond Street about five o'clock. There was a terrific crush of carriages, and the traffic was almost stopped. Close to the pavement was standing a little yellow brougham, which, for some reason or other, attracted my attention. As I passed by there looked out from it the face I showed you this afternoon. I fascinated me immediately. All that night I kept thinking of it, and all the next day. I wandered up and down that wretched Row, peering into every carriage, and waiting for the yellow brougham; but I could not find *ma belle inconnue*, and at last I began to think she was merely a dream. About a week afterwards I was dining with Madame de Rastail. Dinner was for eight o'clock; but at half-past eight we were still waiting in the drawing-room. Finally the servant threw open the door, and announced Lady Alroy. It was the woman I had been looking for. She came in very slowly, looking like a moonbeam in grey lace, and, to my intense delight, I was asked to take her in to dinner. After we had sat down I remarked quite innocently, "I think I caught sight of you in Bond Street some time ago, Lady Alroy." She grew very pale, and said to me in a low voice, "Pray do not talk so loud; you may be overheard." I felt miserable at having made such a bad beginning, and plunged recklessly into the subject of French plays. She spoke very little, always in the same low musical voice, and seemed as if she was afraid of some one listening. I fell passionately, stupidly in love, and the indefinable atmosphere of mystery that surrounded her excited my most ardent curiosity. When she was going away, which she did very soon after dinner, I asked her if I might call and see her. She hesitated for a moment, glanced round to see if any one was near us, and then said, "Yes; to-morrow at a quarter to five." I begged Madame de Rastail to tell me about her; but all that I could learn was that she was a window with a beautiful house in Park Lane, and as some scientific bore began a dissertation of widows, as exemplifying the survival of the matrimonially fittest, I left and went home.

'The next day I arrived at Park Lane punctual to the moment, but was told by the butler that Lady Alroy had just gone out. I went down to the club quite unhappy and very much puzzled, and after long consideration wrote her a letter, asking if I might be allowed to try my chance some other afternoon. I had no answer for several days, but at last I got a little note saying she would be at home on Sunday at four, and with this extraordinary postscript: "Please do not write to me here again; I will explain when I see you." On Sunday she received me, and was perfectly charming; but when I was going away she begged of me, if I ever had occasion to write to her again, to address my letter to "Mrs. Knox, care of Whittaker's Library, Green Street." "There are reasons," she said, "why I cannot receive letters in my own house."

'All through the season I saw a great deal of her, and the atmosphere of mystery never left her. Sometimes I thought that she was in the power of some man, but she looked so unapproachable that I could not believe it. It was really very difficult for me to come to any conclusion, for she was like one of those strange crystals that one sees in museums, which are at one moment clear, and at another clouded. At last I determined to ask her to be my wife: I was sick and tired of the incessant secrecy that she imposed on all my visits, and on the few letters I sent her. I wrote to her at the library to ask her if she could see me the following Monday at six. She answered yes, and I was in the seventh heaven of delight. I was infatuated with her: in spite of the mystery, I thought then—in consequence of it, I see now. No; it was the woman herself I loved. The mystery troubled me, maddened me. Why did chance put me in its track?'

'You discovered it, then?' I cried.

'I fear so,' he answered. 'You can judge for yourself.'

'When Monday came round I went to lunch with my uncle, and about four o'clock found myself in the Marylebone Road. My uncle, you know, lives in Regent's Park. I wanted to get to Piccadilly, and took a short cut through a lot of shabby little streets. Suddenly I saw in front of me Lady Alroy, deeply veiled and walking very fast. On coming to the last house in the street, she went up the steps, took out a latch-key, and let herself in. "Here is the mystery," I said to myself; and I hurried on and examined the house. It seemed a sort of place for letting lodgings. On the doorstep lay her handkerchief, which she had dropped. I picked it up and put it in my pocket. Then I began to consider what I should do. I came to the conclusion that I had no right to spy on her, and I drove down to the club. At six I called to see her. She was lying on a sofa, in a tea-gown of silver tissue looped up by some strange moonstones that she always wore. She was looking quite lovely. "I am so glad to see you," she said; "I have not been out all day." I stared at her in amazement, and pulling the handkerchief out of my pocket, handed it to her. "You dropped this in Cumnor Street this afternoon, Lady Alroy," I said very calmly. She looked at me in terror, but made no attempt to take the handkerchief. "What were you doing there?" I asked. "What right have you to question me?" she answered. "The right of a man who loves you," I replied; "I came here to ask you to be my wife." She hid her face in her hands, and burst into floods of tears. "You must tell me," I continued. She stood up, and, looking me straight in the face, said, "Lord Murchison, there is nothing to tell you."—"You went to meet some one," I cried; "this is your mystery." She grew dreadfully white, and said, "I went to meet no one,"—"Can't you tell the truth?" I exclaimed. "I have told it," she replied. I was mad, frantic; I don't know what I said, but I said terrible things to her. Finally I rushed out of the house. She wrote me a letter the next day; I sent it back unopened, and started for Norway with Alan Colville. After a month I came back, and the first thing I saw in the *Morning Post* was the death of Lady Alroy. She had caught a chill at the Opera, and had died in five days of congestion of the lungs. I shut myself up and saw no one. I had loved her so much, I had loved her so madly. Good God! how I had loved that woman!'

'You went to the street, to the house in it?' I said.

'Yes,' he answered.

'One day I went to Cumnor Street. I could not help it; I was tortured with doubt. I knocked at the door, and a respectable-looking woman opened it to me. I asked her if she had any rooms to let. "Well, sir," she replied, "the drawing-rooms are supposed to be let; but I have not seen the lady for three months, and as rent is owing on them, you can have them."—"Is this the lady?" I said, showing the photograph. "That's her, sure enough," she exclaimed; "and when is she coming back, sir?"—"The lady is dead," I replied. "Oh, sir, I hope not!" said the woman; "she was my best lodger. She paid me three guineas a week merely to sit in my drawing-rooms now and then."—"She met some one here?" I said; but the woman assured me that it was not so, that she always came alone, and saw no one. "What on earth did she do here?" I cried. "She simply sat in the drawing-room, sir, reading books, and sometimes had tea," the woman answered. I did not know what to say, so I gave her a sovereign and went away. Now, what do you think it all meant? You don't believe the woman was telling the truth?'

'I do.'

'Then why did Lady Alroy go there?'

'My dear Gerald,' I answered, 'Lady Alroy was simply a woman with a mania for mystery. She took these rooms for the pleasure of going there with her veil down, and imagining she was a heroine. She had a passion for secrecy, but she herself was merely a Sphinx without a secret.'

'Do you really think so?'

'I am sure of it,' I replied.

He took out the morocco case, opened it, and looked at the photograph. 'I wonder?' he said at last.

25

The Nightingale and the Rose

Oscar Wilde

'She said that she would dance with me if I brought her red roses,' cried the young Student; 'but in all my garden there is no red rose.'

From her nest in the holm-oak tree the Nightingale heard him, and she looked out through the leaves, and wondered.

'No red rose in all my garden!' he cried, and his beautiful eyes filled with tears. 'Ah, on what little things does happiness depend! I have read all that the wise men have written, and all the secrets of philosophy are mine, yet for want of a red rose is my life made wretched.'

'Here at last is a true lover,' said the Nightingale. 'Night after night have I sung of him, though I knew him not: night after night have I told his story to the stars, and now I see him. His hair is dark as the hyacinth-blossom, and his lips are red as the rose of his desire; but passion has made his lace like pale Ivory, and sorrow has set her seal upon his brow.'

'The Prince gives a ball to-morrow night,' murmured the young Student, 'and my love will be of the company. If I bring her a red rose she will dance with me till dawn. If I bring her a red rose, I shall hold her in my arms, and she will lean her head upon my shoulder, and her hand will be clasped in mine. But there is no red rose in my garden, so I shall sit lonely, and she will pass me by. She will have no heed of me, and my heart will break.'

'Here indeed is the true lover,' said the Nightingale. 'What I sing of he suffers—what is joy to me, to him is pain. Surely Love is a wonderful thing. It is more precious than emeralds, and dearer than fine opals. Pearls and pomegranates cannot buy it, nor is it set forth in the market-place. It may not be purchased of the merchants, nor can it be weighed out in the balance for gold.'

'The musicians will sit in their gallery,' said the young Student, 'and play upon their stringed instruments, and my love will dance to the sound of the harp and the violin. She will dance so lightly that her feet will not touch the floor, and the courtiers in their gay dresses will throng round her. But with me she will not dance, for I have no red rose to give her;' and he flung himself down on the grass, and buried his face in his hands, and wept.

'Why is he weeping?' asked a little Green Lizard, as he ran past him with his tail in the air.

'Why, indeed?' said a Butterfly, who was fluttering about after a sunbeam.

'Why, indeed?' whispered a Daisy to his neighbour, in a soft, low voice.

'He is weeping for a red rose,' said the Nightingale.

'For a red rose!' they cried; 'how very ridiculous!' and the little Lizard, who was something of a cynic, laughed outright.

But the Nightingale understood the secret of the Student's sorrow, and she sat silent in the oak-tree, and thought about the mystery of Love.

Suddenly she spread her brown wings for flight, and soared into the air. She passed through the grove like a shadow, and like a shadow she sailed across the garden.

In the centre of the grass-plot was standing a beautiful Rose-tree, and when she saw it, she flew over to it, and lit upon a spray.

'Give me a red rose,' she cried, 'and I will sing you my sweetest song.'

But the Tree shook its head.

'My roses are white,' it answered; 'as white as the foam of the sea, and whiter than the snow upon the mountain. But go to my brother who grows round the old sun-dial, and perhaps he will give you what you want.'

So the Nightingale flew over to the Rose-tree that was growing round the old sun-dial.

'Give me a red rose,' she cried, 'and I will sing you my sweetest song.'

But the Tree shook its head.

'My roses are yellow,' it answered; 'as yellow as the hair of the mermaiden who sits upon an amber throne, and yellower than the daffodil that blooms in the meadow before the mower comes with his scythe. But go to my brother who grows beneath the Student's window, and perhaps he will give you what you want.'

So the Nightingale flew over to the Rose-tree that was growing beneath the Student's window.

'Give me a red rose,' she cried, 'and I will sing you my sweetest song.'

But the Tree shook its head.

'My roses are red,' it answered, 'as red as the feet of the dove, and redder than the great fans of coral that wave and wave in the ocean-cavern. But the winter has chilled my veins, and the frost has nipped my buds, and the storm has broken my branches, and I shall have no roses at all this year.'

'One red rose is all I want,' cried the Nightingale, 'only one red rose! Is there no way by which I can get it?'

'There is a way,' answered the Tree; 'but it is so terrible that I dare not tell it to you.'

'Tell it to me,' said the Nightingale, 'I am not afraid.'

'If you want a red rose,' said the Tree, 'you must build it out of music by moonlight, and stain it with your own heart's-blood. You must sing to me with your breast against a thorn. All night long you must sing to me, and the thorn must pierce your heart, and your life-blood must flow into my veins, and become mine.'

'Death is a great price to pay for a red rose,' cried the Nightingale, 'and Life is very dear to all. It is pleasant to sit in the green wood, and to watch the Sun in his chariot of gold, and the Moon in her chariot of pearl. Sweet is the scent of the hawthorn, and sweet are the bluebells that hide in the valley, and the heather that blows on the hill. Yet Love is better than Life, and what is the heart of a bird compared to the heart of a man?'

So she spread her brown wings for flight, and soared into the air. She swept over the garden like a shadow, and like a shadow she sailed through the grove.

The young Student was still lying on the grass, where she had left him, and the tears were not yet dry in his beautiful eyes.

'Be happy,' cried the Nightingale, 'be happy; you shall have your red rose. I will build it out of music by moonlight, and stain it with my own heart's-blood. All that I ask of you in return is that you will be a true lover, for Love is wiser than Philosophy, though she is wise, and mightier than Power, though he is mighty. Flame-coloured are his wings, and coloured like flame is his body. His lips are sweet as honey, and his breath is like frankincense.'

The Student looked up from the grass, and listened, but he could not understand what the Nightingale was saying to him, for he only knew the things that are written down in books.

But the Oak-tree understood, and felt sad, for he was very fond of the little Nightingale who had built her nest in his branches.

'Sing me one last song,' he whispered; 'I shall feel very lonely when you are gone.'

So the Nightingale sang to the Oak-tree, and her voice was like water bubbling from a silver jar.

When she had finished her song the Student got up, and pulled a note-book and a lead-pencil out of his pocket.

'She has form,' he said to himself, as he walked away through the grove—'that cannot be denied to her; but has she got feeling? I am afraid not. In fact, she is like most artists; she is all style, without any sincerity. She would not sacrifice herself for others. She thinks merely of music, and everybody knows that the arts are selfish. Still, it must be admitted that she has some beautiful notes in her voice. What a pity it is that they do not mean anything, or do any practical good.' And he went into his room, and lay down on his little pallet-bed, and began to think of his love; and, after a time, he fell asleep.

And when the Moon shone in the heavens the Nightingale flew to the Rose-tree, and set her breast against the thorn. All night long she sang with her breast against the thorn, and the cold crystal Moon leaned down and listened. All night long she sang, and the thorn went deeper and deeper into her breast, and her life-blood ebbed away from her.

She sang first of the birth of love in the heart of a boy and a girl. And on the topmost spray of the Rose-tree there blossomed a marvellous rose, petal following petal, as song followed song. Pale was it, at first, as the mist that hangs over the river—pale as the feet of the morning, and silver as the wings of the dawn. As the shadow of a rose in a mirror of silver, as the shadow of a rose in a water-pool, so was the rose that blossomed on the topmost spray of the Tree.

But the Tree cried to the Nightingale to press closer against the thorn. 'Press closer, little Nightingale,' cried the Tree, 'or the Day will come before the rose is finished.'

So the Nightingale pressed closer against the thorn, and louder and louder grew her song, for she sang of the birth of passion in the soul of a man and a maid.

And a delicate flush of pink came into the leaves of the rose, like the flush in the face of the bridegroom when he kisses the lips of the bride. But the thorn had not yet reached her heart, so the rose's heart remained white, for only a Nightingale's heart's-blood can crimson the heart of a rose.

And the Tree cried to the Nightingale to press closer against the thorn. 'Press closer, little Nightingale,' cried the Tree, 'or the Day will come before the rose is finished.'

So the Nightingale pressed closer against the thorn, and the thorn touched her heart, and a fierce pang of pain shot through her. Bitter, bitter was the pain, and wilder and wilder grew her song, for she sang of the Love that is perfected by Death, of the Love that dies not in the tomb.

And the marvellous rose became crimson, like the rose of the eastern sky. Crimson was the girdle of petals, and crimson as a ruby was the heart.

But the Nightingale's voice grew fainter, and her little wings began to beat, and a film came over her eyes. Fainter and fainter grew her song, and she felt something choking her in her throat.

Then she gave one last burst of music. The white Moon heard it, and she forgot the dawn, and lingered on in the sky. The red rose heard it, and it trembled all over with ecstasy, and opened its petals to the cold morning air. Echo bore it to her purple cavern in the hills, and woke the sleeping shepherds from their dreams. It floated through the reeds of the river, and they carried its message to the sea.

'Look, look!' cried the Tree, 'the rose is finished now;' but the Nightingale made no answer, for she was lying dead in the long grass, with the thorn in her heart.

And at noon the Student opened his window and looked out.

'Why, what a wonderful piece of luck! he cried; 'here is a red rose! I have never seen any rose like it in all my life. It is so beautiful that I am sure it has a long Latin name;' and he leaned down and plucked it.

Then he put on his hat, and ran up to the Professor's house with the rose in his hand.

The daughter of the Professor was sitting in the doorway winding blue silk on a reel, and her little dog was lying at her feet.

'You said that you would dance with me if I brought you a red rose,' cried the Student. Here is the reddest rose in all the world. You will wear it to-night next your heart, and as we dance together it will tell you how I love you.'

But the girl frowned.

'I am afraid it will not go with my dress,' she answered; 'and, besides, the Chamberlain's nephew has sent me some real jewels, and everybody knows that jewels cost far more than flowers.'

'Well, upon my word, you are very ungrateful,' said the Student angrily; and he threw the rose into the street, where it fell into the gutter, and a cart-wheel went over it.

'Ungrateful!' said the girl. 'I tell you what, you are very rude; and, after all, who are you? Only a Student. Why, I don't believe you have even got silver buckles to your shoes as the Chamberlain's nephew has;' and she got up from her chair and went into the house.

'What a silly thing Love is,' said the Student as he walked away. 'It is not half as useful as Logic, for it does not prove anything, and it is always telling one of things that are not going to happen, and making one believe things that are not true. In fact, it is quite unpractical, and, as in this age to be practical is everything, I shall go back to Philosophy and study Metaphysics.'

So he returned to his room and pulled out a great dusty book, and began to read.

26

The Happy Prince

Oscar Wilde

High above the city, on a tall column, stood the statue of the Happy Prince. He was gilded all over with thin leaves of fine gold, for eyes he had two bright sapphires, and a large red ruby glowed on his sword-hilt.

He was very much admired indeed. "He is as beautiful as a weathercock," remarked one of the Town Councillors who wished to gain a reputation for having artistic tastes; "only not quite so useful," he added, fearing lest people should think him unpractical, which he really was not.

"Why can't you be like the Happy Prince?" asked a sensible mother of her little boy who was crying for the moon. "The Happy Prince never dreams of crying for anything."

"I am glad there is some one in the world who is quite happy," muttered a disappointed man as he gazed at the wonderful statue.

"He looks just like an angel," said the Charity Children as they came out of the cathedral in their bright scarlet cloaks and their clean white pinafores.

"How do you know?" said the Mathematical Master, "you have never seen one."

"Ah! but we have, in our dreams," answered the children; and the Mathematical Master frowned and looked very severe, for he did not approve of children dreaming.

One night there flew over the city a little Swallow. His friends had gone away to Egypt six weeks before, but he had stayed behind, for he was in love with the most beautiful Reed. He had met her early in the spring as he was flying down the river after a big yellow moth, and had been so attracted by her slender waist that he had stopped to talk to her.

"Shall I love you?" said the Swallow, who liked to come to the point at once, and the Reed made him a low bow. So he flew round and round her, touching the water with his wings, and making silver ripples. This was his courtship, and it lasted all through the summer.

"It is a ridiculous attachment," twittered the other Swallows; "she has no money, and far too many relations"; and indeed the river was quite full of Reeds. Then, when the autumn came they all flew away.

After they had gone he felt lonely, and began to tire of his lady-love. "She has no conversation," he said, "and I am afraid that she is a coquette, for she is always flirting with the wind." And certainly, whenever the wind blew, the Reed made the most graceful curtseys. "I admit that she is domestic," he continued, "but I love travelling, and my wife, consequently, should love travelling also."

"Will you come away with me?" he said finally to her; but the Reed shook her head, she was so attached to her home.

"You have been trifling with me," he cried. "I am off to the Pyramids. Good-bye!" and he flew away.

All day long he flew, and at night-time he arrived at the city. "Where shall I put up?" he said; "I hope the town has made preparations."

Then he saw the statue on the tall column.

"I will put up there," he cried; "it is a fine position, with plenty of fresh air." So he alighted just between the feet of the Happy Prince.

"I have a golden bedroom," he said softly to himself as he looked round, and he prepared to go to sleep; but just as he was putting his head under his wing a large drop of water fell on him. "What a curious thing!" he cried; "there is not a single cloud in the sky, the stars are quite clear and bright, and yet it is raining. The climate in the north of Europe is really dreadful. The Reed used to like the rain, but that was merely her selfishness."

Then another drop fell.

"What is the use of a statue if it cannot keep the rain off?" he said; "I must look for a good chimney-pot," and he determined to fly away.

But before he had opened his wings, a third drop fell, and he looked up, and saw—Ah! what did he see?

The eyes of the Happy Prince were filled with tears, and tears were running down his golden cheeks. His face was so beautiful in the moonlight that the little Swallow was filled with pity.

"Who are you?" he said.

"I am the Happy Prince."

"Why are you weeping then?" asked the Swallow; "you have quite drenched me."

"When I was alive and had a human heart," answered the statue, "I did not know what tears were, for I lived in the Palace of Sans-Souci, where sorrow is not allowed to enter. In the daytime I played with my companions in the garden, and in the evening I led the dance in the Great Hall. Round the garden ran a very lofty wall, but I never cared to ask what lay beyond it, everything about me was so beautiful. My courtiers called me the Happy Prince, and happy indeed I was, if pleasure be happiness. So I lived, and so I died. And now that I am dead they have set me up here so high that I can see all the ugliness and all the misery of my city, and though my heart is made of lead yet I cannot chose but weep."

"What! is he not solid gold?" said the Swallow to himself. He was too polite to make any personal remarks out loud.

"Far away," continued the statue in a low musical voice, "far away in a little street there is a poor house. One of the windows is open, and through it I can see a woman seated at a table. Her face is thin and worn, and she has coarse, red hands, all pricked by the needle, for she is a seamstress. She is embroidering passion-flowers on a satin gown for the loveliest of the Queen's maids-of-honour to wear at the next Court-ball. In a bed in the corner of the room her little boy is lying ill. He has a fever, and is asking for oranges. His mother has nothing to give him but river water, so he is crying. Swallow, Swallow, little Swallow, will you not bring her the ruby out of my sword-hilt? My feet are fastened to this pedestal and I cannot move."

"I am waited for in Egypt," said the Swallow. "My friends are flying up and down the Nile, and talking to the large lotus-flowers. Soon they will go to sleep in the tomb of the great King. The King is there himself in his painted coffin. He is wrapped in yellow linen, and embalmed with spices. Round his neck is a chain of pale green jade, and his hands are like withered leaves."

"Swallow, Swallow, little Swallow," said the Prince, "will you not stay with me for one night, and be my messenger? The boy is so thirsty, and the mother so sad."

"I don't think I like boys," answered the Swallow. "Last summer, when I was staying on the river, there were two rude boys, the miller's sons, who were always throwing stones at me. They never hit me, of course; we swallows fly far too well for that, and besides, I come of a family famous for its agility; but still, it was a mark of disrespect."

But the Happy Prince looked so sad that the little Swallow was sorry. "It is very cold here," he said; "but I will stay with you for one night, and be your messenger."

"Thank you, little Swallow," said the Prince.

So the Swallow picked out the great ruby from the Prince's sword, and flew away with it in his beak over the roofs of the town.

He passed by the cathedral tower, where the white marble angels were sculptured. He passed by the palace and heard the sound of dancing. A beautiful girl came out on the balcony with her lover. "How wonderful the stars are," he said to her, "and how wonderful is the power of love!"

"I hope my dress will be ready in time for the State-ball," she answered; "I have ordered passion-flowers to be embroidered on it; but the seamstresses are so lazy."

He passed over the river, and saw the lanterns hanging to the masts of the ships. He passed over the Ghetto, and saw the old Jews bargaining with each other, and weighing out money in copper scales. At last he came to the poor house and looked in. The boy was tossing feverishly on his bed, and the mother had fallen asleep, she was so tired. In he hopped, and laid the great ruby on the table beside the woman's thimble. Then he flew gently round the bed, fanning the boy's forehead with his wings. "How cool I feel," said the boy, "I must be getting better"; and he sank into a delicious slumber.

Then the Swallow flew back to the Happy Prince, and told him what he had done. "It is curious," he remarked, "but I feel quite warm now, although it is so cold."

"That is because you have done a good action," said the Prince. And the little Swallow began to think, and then he fell asleep. Thinking always made him sleepy.

When day broke he flew down to the river and had a bath. "What a remarkable phenomenon," said the Professor of Ornithology as he was passing over the bridge. "A swallow in winter!" And he wrote a long letter about it to the local newspaper. Every one quoted it, it was full of so many words that they could not understand.

"To-night I go to Egypt," said the Swallow, and he was in high spirits at the prospect. He visited all the public monuments, and sat a long time on top of the church steeple. Wherever he went the Sparrows chirruped, and said to each other, "What a distinguished stranger!" so he enjoyed himself very much.

When the moon rose he flew back to the Happy Prince. "Have you any commissions for Egypt?" he cried; "I am just starting."

"Swallow, Swallow, little Swallow," said the Prince, "will you not stay with me one night longer?"

"I am waited for in Egypt," answered the Swallow. "To-morrow my friends will fly up to the Second Cataract. The river-horse couches there among the bulrushes, and on a great granite throne sits the God Memnon. All night long he watches the stars, and when the morning star shines he utters one cry of joy, and then he is silent. At noon the yellow lions come down to the water's edge to drink. They have eyes like green beryls, and their roar is louder than the roar of the cataract."

"Swallow, Swallow, little Swallow," said the Prince, "far away across the city I see a young man in a garret. He is leaning over a desk covered with papers, and in a tumbler by his side there is a bunch of withered violets. His hair is brown and crisp, and his lips are red as a pomegranate, and he has large and dreamy eyes. He is trying to finish a play for the Director of the Theatre, but he is too cold to write any more. There is no fire in the grate, and hunger has made him faint."

"I will wait with you one night longer," said the Swallow, who really had a good heart. "Shall I take him another ruby?"

"Alas! I have no ruby now," said the Prince; "my eyes are all that I have left. They are made of rare sapphires, which were brought out of India a thousand years ago. Pluck out one of them and take it to him. He will sell it to the jeweller, and buy food and firewood, and finish his play."

"Dear Prince," said the Swallow, "I cannot do that"; and he began to weep.

"Swallow, Swallow, little Swallow," said the Prince, "do as I command you."

So the Swallow plucked out the Prince's eye, and flew away to the student's garret. It was easy enough to get in, as there was a hole in the roof. Through this he darted, and came into the room. The young man had his head buried in his hands, so he did not hear the flutter of the bird's wings, and when he looked up he found the beautiful sapphire lying on the withered violets.

"I am beginning to be appreciated," he cried; "this is from some great admirer. Now I can finish my play," and he looked quite happy.

The next day the Swallow flew down to the harbour. He sat on the mast of a large vessel and watched the sailors hauling big chests out of the hold with ropes. "Heave a-hoy!" they shouted as each chest came up. "I am going to Egypt"! cried the Swallow, but nobody minded, and when the moon rose he flew back to the Happy Prince.

"I am come to bid you good-bye," he cried.

"Swallow, Swallow, little Swallow," said the Prince, "will you not stay with me one night longer?"

"It is winter," answered the Swallow, "and the chill snow will soon be here. In Egypt the sun is warm on the green palm-trees, and the crocodiles lie in the mud and look lazily about them. My companions are building a nest in the Temple of Baalbec, and the pink and white doves are watching them, and cooing to each other. Dear Prince, I must leave you, but I will never forget you, and next spring I will bring you back two beautiful jewels in place of those you have given away. The ruby shall be redder than a red rose, and the sapphire shall be as blue as the great sea."

"In the square below," said the Happy Prince, "there stands a little match-girl. She has let her matches fall in the gutter, and they are all spoiled. Her father will beat her if she does not bring home some money, and she is crying. She has no shoes or stockings, and her little head is bare. Pluck out my other eye, and give it to her, and her father will not beat her."

"I will stay with you one night longer," said the Swallow, "but I cannot pluck out your eye. You would be quite blind then."

"Swallow, Swallow, little Swallow," said the Prince, "do as I command you."

So he plucked out the Prince's other eye, and darted down with it. He swooped past the match-girl, and slipped the jewel into the palm of her hand. "What a lovely bit of glass," cried the little girl; and she ran home, laughing.

Then the Swallow came back to the Prince. "You are blind now," he said, "so I will stay with you always."

"No, little Swallow," said the poor Prince, "you must go away to Egypt."

"I will stay with you always," said the Swallow, and he slept at the Prince's feet.

All the next day he sat on the Prince's shoulder, and told him stories of what he had seen in strange lands. He told him of the red ibises, who stand in long rows on the banks of the Nile, and catch gold-fish in their beaks; of the Sphinx, who is as old as the world itself, and lives in the desert, and knows everything; of the merchants, who walk slowly by the side of their camels, and carry amber beads in their hands; of the King of the Mountains of the Moon, who is as black as ebony, and worships a large crystal; of the great green snake that sleeps in a palm-tree, and has twenty priests to feed it with honey-cakes; and of the pygmies who sail over a big lake on large flat leaves, and are always at war with the butterflies.

"Dear little Swallow," said the Prince, "you tell me of marvellous things, but more marvellous than anything is the suffering of men and of women. There is no Mystery so great as Misery. Fly over my city, little Swallow, and tell me what you see there."

So the Swallow flew over the great city, and saw the rich making merry in their beautiful houses, while the beggars were sitting at the gates. He flew into dark lanes, and saw the white faces of starving children looking out listlessly at the black streets. Under the archway of a bridge two little boys were lying in one another's arms to try and keep themselves warm. "How hungry we are!" they said. "You must not lie here," shouted the Watchman, and they wandered out into the rain.

Then he flew back and told the Prince what he had seen.

"I am covered with fine gold," said the Prince, "you must take it off, leaf by leaf, and give it to my poor; the living always think that gold can make them happy."

Leaf after leaf of the fine gold the Swallow picked off, till the Happy Prince looked quite dull and grey. Leaf after leaf of the fine gold he brought to the poor, and the children's faces grew rosier, and they laughed and played games in the street. "We have bread now!" they cried.

Then the snow came, and after the snow came the frost. The streets looked as if they were made of silver, they were so bright and glistening; long icicles like crystal daggers hung down from the eaves of the houses, everybody went about in furs, and the little boys wore scarlet caps and skated on the ice.

The poor little Swallow grew colder and colder, but he would not leave the Prince, he loved him too well. He picked up crumbs outside the baker's door when the baker was not looking and tried to keep himself warm by flapping his wings.

But at last he knew that he was going to die. He had just strength to fly up to the Prince's shoulder once more. "Good-bye, dear Prince!" he murmured, "will you let me kiss your hand?"

"I am glad that you are going to Egypt at last, little Swallow," said the Prince, "you have stayed too long here; but you must kiss me on the lips, for I love you."

"It is not to Egypt that I am going," said the Swallow. "I am going to the House of Death. Death is the brother of Sleep, is he not?"

And he kissed the Happy Prince on the lips, and fell down dead at his feet.

At that moment a curious crack sounded inside the statue, as if something had broken. The fact is that the leaden heart had snapped right in two. It certainly was a dreadfully hard frost.

Early the next morning the Mayor was walking in the square below in company with the Town Councillors. As they passed the column he looked up at the statue: "Dear me! how shabby the Happy Prince looks!" he said.

"How shabby indeed!" cried the Town Councillors, who always agreed with the Mayor; and they went up to look at it.

"The ruby has fallen out of his sword, his eyes are gone, and he is golden no longer," said the Mayor in fact, "he is little better than a beggar!"

"Little better than a beggar," said the Town Councillors.

"And here is actually a dead bird at his feet!" continued the Mayor. "We must really issue a proclamation that birds are not to be allowed to die here." And the Town Clerk made a note of the suggestion.

So they pulled down the statue of the Happy Prince. "As he is no longer beautiful he is no longer useful," said the Art Professor at the University.

Then they melted the statue in a furnace, and the Mayor held a meeting of the Corporation to decide what was to be done with the metal. “We must have another statue, of course,” he said, “and it shall be a statue of myself.”

“Of myself,” said each of the Town Councillors, and they quarrelled. When I last heard of them they were quarrelling still.

“What a strange thing!” said the overseer of the workmen at the foundry. “This broken lead heart will not melt in the furnace. We must throw it away.” So they threw it on a dust-heap where the dead Swallow was also lying.

“Bring me the two most precious things in the city,” said God to one of His Angels; and the Angel brought Him the leaden heart and the dead bird.

“You have rightly chosen,” said God, “for in my garden of Paradise this little bird shall sing for evermore, and in my city of gold the Happy Prince shall praise me.”

27

The Postmaster

Rabindranath Tagore

The first posting that the Postmaster got was in the newly established Post Office at the tiny village of Ulapur. There was an indigo plantation nearby and its Englishman planter had got this Post Office set up after a lot of effort.

The Postmaster hailed from the city of Kolkata and felt like a fish out of water in this village. His office was in a huge and dark mud hut near a pond that had jungle all around it and was itself green with vegetation. The employees at the plantation were very busy and anyway, not fit company for the city-bred young man. Nor did he know the art of mixing with village people. On the other hand, he did not have too much work to handle. He tried his hand at writing poetry. Although he sang the praise of nature in his poems, he would have been much relieved to find buildings rather than trees all around him.

His salary was very meager. He had to cook for himself and had an orphan girl doing other tasks for him in exchange for a few frugal meals. Ratan, as she was called, was about ten or twelve years in age, but hardly had any prospects of marriage.

In the evenings, when the smoke of mosquito repellents coiled up from the cow-sheds of the village, crickets sang in the bushes, and mendicant groups sang drunken music in their shelters, the Postmaster felt somewhat scared to sit alone in the darkness of his hut, watching the trembling trees. Lighting a small lamp in a corner of his room, he used to call out: "Ratan!"

"What is it, Babu (gentleman/master)", Ratan did not come immediately. "Why do you call me?"

"What are you at?"

"I am just going to light the kitchen fire—there is work in the kitchen—"

"Let the kitchen work be—you get me my tobacco."

Ratan used to come in soon, her cheeks puffed out, blowing at the fire at the end of the Postmaster's country-made pipe.

Snatching it from her, Postmaster started off a conversation with her. "Well, Ratan, do you remember your mother?"

Yes and no, Ratan used to say. She remembered her father ore. He had been more affectionate towards her. She also remembered a little brother whom she had played with. One memory came back to her more than the others—the memory of playing the game of fishing, sitting by a pond with her brother and pretending that a stick was their fishing rod.

Chatting like this, sometimes it grew late and then the Postmaster did not feel like cooking any more. Ratan quickly lit the fire, made a few chapattis. Left-over sabzi and chapatti served as dinner for both of them. On some other days, sitting on a wooden bed in that huge mud hut, the Postmaster began to talk of his own home. He talked of his mother, elder sister and younger brother—whom he missed so much in his village posting—but could not mention to the plantation employees. He found no problem in discussing them freely with this small, illiterate village girl. It came about that Ratan began referring to them as Ma (mother), Didi (elder sister) and Bhai (younger brother)—as if she had known them all her life. She even drew up sketches of them in the small canvass of her heart. From Babu, the postmaster too became Dada (elder brother)-babu.

One rainy afternoon the Postmaster had nothing to do and felt particularly like having some one of his own near him.

Sighing, he called out: "Ratan!"

Ratan was sitting under a nearby guava tree, legs outstretched, guava in hand.

She rushed up to her master. "Did you call me, Dada-babu?"

"I am going to teach you to read and write", said the Postmaster.

The whole afternoon passed by in introducing Ratan to the letters of the Bengali alphabet. Within a few days, Ratan mastered them and began to read and write complete words.

It was the month of Shravana. Monsoon was in full force.

One rainy day, Ratan waited for long at the door for a call from her teacher the Postmaster, but the call never came. She finally went in with her books and stuff, only to find the Postmaster huddled in his wooden bed. "Ratan, I am not feeling too well"', he called in a suffering tone. "Will you put your hand on my forehead and check if I have got fever?"

Ratan responded to this forlorn cry for family affection. She no longer remained just a small girl. From that instant she took up the position of a mother. She called the village doctor, administered the medicines to the Postmaster at the right hours, sat by the bedside all night, and of her own accord, cooked him his recommended diet. Every now and then she would ask: "Are you feeling a little better, Dada-babu?"

After a long spell of illness, the Postmaster recovered. He decided inwardly that enough was enough, and he had to get himself a different posting. Mentioning the local conditions, he immediately applied to the postal authority at Kolkata for a transfer.

Being relieved from her duties as a nurse, Ratan once again came out and occupied her old position by the door. But there were no calls for her as before. She peeped in some times, and found the Postmaster sitting or lying down most absentmindedly. Ratan waited for her call and the Postmaster waited for his transfer order. Sitting by the door, Ratan went over her old lessons a hundred times. She had the fear that she might mix up her spellings the day there was a sudden call for her.

After a week or so, indeed there was a call.

Ratan went in and asked, "Dada-babu, were you calling me?"

"Ratan, I am going away tomorrow itself", said the Postmaster.

"Where are you going, Dada-babu?" asked Ratan.

"I am going home"

"When will you be coming back?"

"I won't be coming back".

Ratan did not ask anything further. The Postmaster himself told her that he had applied for a transfer. The application had been rejected. So he was resigning his post and going home.

For a long time nobody said a word. In the flickering lamplight, rain dropped down through a hole in the roof and collected in a bowl kept right under the hole.

After a while Ratan got up and went to the kitchen to make the chapattis. The task took longer than usual. After the Postmaster had eaten, the girl asked her: "Dada-babu, will you take me to your home?"

"How can that be!" said the Postmaster with a laugh. He did not even feel it necessary to explain to the girl why it was impossible.

All night through her sleep and wakeful hours, the girl heard his laughing words: 'How can that be!'

The Postmaster, like most people from Kolkata, had the habit of bathing not in the pond or river directly but in water that had been collected in a bucket.

Next morning as soon as he got up, he found the water ready and waiting for him. For some reason Ratan had not been able to ask him exactly when he would be going. So she had gone right in the night and fetched the water, and kept it ready for him.

Once the Postmaster had taken his bath, he called for Ratan. Ratan entered silently and looked at her master, awaiting his instruction.

"Ratan", said her master, "I'll talk to the man who will come in my stead. He will care for you just as I used to. You don't have to worry at all."

These words might have been kind but Ratan burst out crying: "No, no, you don't have to talk to anyone. I don't want to stay on." The Postmaster had never seen Ratan behave like this and was surprised.

The new Postmaster arrived. The old Postmaster handed over the charge to him and began to take his leave. He called Ratan and offered her some money. "Ratan, I have never been able to give you anything. Now, while leaving, I am giving you something. It will take care of you for a few days."

Keeping only the travel expenses with him, he took his whole salary out of his pocket. Ratan fell to the ground and caught hold of his feet.

"Dada-babu, please, you don't have to give me anything. Please, nobody has to think of me—"

With this, she ran away from there.

The ex-Postmaster sighed, and started off, with his tin box and umbrella.

As he mounted the boat, and as the boat started along the river swollen in monsoon, he felt a deep twinge of pain. Let me go back and get that orphaned child along with me, he thought for a moment. But the boat was already on the move, and the Postmaster comforted himself with the theory: "Life is full of partings. What is the point of going back?"

But Ratan had no theories to comfort her. She just hung around the Post Office, tears flooding her face. A faint hope kept her tied to it: perhaps Dada-babu will come back?

28

The Cabuliwalah

Rabindranath Tagore

My five years' old daughter Mini cannot live without chattering. I really believe that in all her life she has not wasted a minute in silence. Her mother is often vexed at this, and would stop her prattle, but I would not. To see Mini quiet is unnatural, and I cannot bear it long. And so my own talk with her is always lively.

One morning, for instance, when I was in the midst of the seventeenth chapter of my new novel, my little Mini stole into the room, and putting her hand into mine, said: "Father! Ramdayal the door-keeper calls a crow a krow! He doesn't know anything, does he?"

Before I could explain to her the differences of language in this world, she was embarked on the full tide of another subject. "What do you think, Father? Bhola says there is an elephant in the clouds, blowing water out of his trunk, and that is why it rains!"

And then, darting off anew, while I sat still making ready some reply to this last saying: "Father! what relation is Mother to you?"

With a grave face I contrived to say: "Go and play with Bhola, Mini! I am busy!"

The window of my room overlooks the road. The child had seated herself at my feet near my table, and was playing softly, drumming on her knees. I was hard at work on my seventeenth chapter, where Pratap Singh, the hero, had just caught Kanchanlata, the heroine, in his arms, and was about to escape with her by the third-story window of the castle, when all of a sudden Mini left her play, and ran to the window, crying: "A Cabuliwallah! a Cabuliwallah!" Sure enough in the street below was a Cabuliwallah, passing slowly along. He wore the loose, soiled clothing of his people, with a tall turban; there was a bag on his back, and he carried boxes of grapes in his hand.

I cannot tell what were my daughter's feelings at the sight of this man, but she began to call him loudly. "Ah!" I thought, "he will come in, and my seventeenth chapter will never be finished!" At which exact moment the Cabuliwallah turned, and looked up at the child. When she saw this, overcome by terror, she fled to her mother's protection and disappeared. She had a blind belief that inside the bag, which the big man carried, there were perhaps two or three other children like herself. The pedlar meanwhile entered my doorway and greeted me with a smiling face.

So precarious was the position of my hero and my heroine, that my first impulse was to stop and buy something, since the man had been called. I made some small purchases, and a conversation began about Abdurrahman, the Russians, the English, and the Frontier Policy.

As he was about to leave, he asked: "And where is the little girl, sir?"

And I, thinking that Mini must get rid of her false fear, had her brought out.

She stood by my chair, and looked at the Cabuliwallah and his bag. He offered her nuts and raisins, but she would not be tempted, and only clung the closer to me, with all her doubts increased.

This was their first meeting.

One morning, however, not many days later, as I was leaving the house, I was startled to find Mini, seated on a bench near the door, laughing and talking, with the great Cabuliwallah at her feet. In all her life, it appeared, my small daughter had never found so patient a listener, save her father. And already the corner of her little *sari* was stuffed with almonds and raisins, the gift of her visitor. "Why did you give her those?" I said, and taking out an eight-anna bit, I handed it to him. The man accepted the money without demur, and slipped it into his pocket.

Alas, on my return an hour later, I found the unfortunate coin had made twice its own worth of trouble! For the Cabuliwallah had given it to Mini; and her mother, catching sight of the bright round object, had pounced on the child with: "Where did you get that eight-anna bit?"

"The Cabuliwallah gave it me," said Mini cheerfully.

"The Cabuliwallah gave it you!" cried her mother much shocked. "O Mini! how could you take it from him?"

I, entering at the moment, saved her from impending disaster, and proceeded to make my own inquiries.

It was not the first or second time, I found, that the two had met.

The Cabuliwallah had overcome the child's first terror by a judicious bribery of nuts and almonds, and the two were now great friends.

They had many quaint jokes, which afforded them much amusement. Seated in front of him, looking down on his gigantic frame in all her tiny dignity, Mini would ripple her face with laughter and begin: "O Cabuliwallah! Cabuliwallah! what have you got in your bag?"

And he would reply, in the nasal accents of the mountaineer: "An elephant!" Not much cause for merriment, perhaps; but how they both enjoyed the fun! And for me, this child's talk with a grown-up man had always in it something strangely fascinating.

Then the Cabuliwallah, not to be behindhand, would take his turn: "Well, little one, and when are you going to the father-in-law's house?"

Now most small Bengali maidens have heard long ago about the father-in-law's house; but we, being a little new-fangled, had kept these things from our child, and Mini at this question must have been a trifle bewildered. But she would not show it, and with ready tact replied: "Are *you* going there?»

Amongst men of the Cabuliwallah's class, however, it is well known that the words *father-in-law's house* have a double meaning. It is a euphemism for *jail*, the place where we are well cared for, at no expense to ourselves. In this sense would the sturdy pedlar take my daughter's question. "Ah," he would say, shaking his fist at an invisible policeman, "I will thrash my father-in-law!" Hearing this, and picturing the poor discomfited relative, Mini would go off into peals of laughter, in which her formidable friend would join.

These were autumn mornings, the very time of year when kings of old went forth to conquest; and I, never stirring from my little corner in Calcutta, would let my mind wander over the whole world. At the very name of another country, my heart would go out to it, and at the sight of a foreigner in the streets, I would fall to weaving a network of dreams,—the mountains, the glens, and the forests of his distant home, with his cottage in its setting, and the free and independent life of far-away wilds. Perhaps the scenes of travel conjure themselves up before me and pass and repass in my imagination all the more vividly, because I lead such a vegetable existence that a call to travel would fall upon me like a thunder-bolt. In the presence of this Cabuliwallah I was immediately transported to the foot of arid mountain peaks, with narrow little defiles twisting in and out amongst their towering heights. I could see the string of camels bearing the merchandise, and the company of turbanned merchants carrying some their queer old firearms, and some their spears, journeying downward towards the plains. I could see—. But at some such point Mini›s mother would intervene, imploring me to "beware of that man."

Mini's mother is unfortunately a very timid lady. Whenever she hears a noise in the street, or sees people coming towards the house, she always jumps to the conclusion that they are either thieves, or drunkards, or snakes, or tigers, or malaria, or cockroaches, or caterpillars. Even after all these years of experience, she is not able to overcome her terror. So she was full of doubts about the Cabuliwallah, and used to beg me to keep a watchful eye on him.

I tried to laugh her fear gently away, but then she would turn round on me seriously, and ask me solemn questions:—

Were children never kidnapped?

Was it, then, not true that there was slavery in Cabul?

Was it so very absurd that this big man should be able to carry off a tiny child?

I urged that, though not impossible, it was highly improbable. But this was not enough, and her dread persisted. As it was indefinite, however, it did not seem right to forbid the man the house, and the intimacy went on unchecked.

Once a year in the middle of January Rahmun, the Cabuliwallah, was in the habit of returning to his country, and as the time approached he would be very busy, going from house to house collecting his debts. This year, however, he could always find time to come and see Mini. It would have seemed to an outsider that there was some conspiracy between the two, for when he could not come in the morning, he would appear in the evening.

Even to me it was a little startling now and then, in the corner of a dark room, suddenly to surprise this tall, loose-garmented, much bebagged man; but when Mini would run in smiling, with her "O Cabuliwallah! Cabuliwallah!" and the two friends, so far apart in age, would subside into their old laughter and their old jokes, I felt reassured.

One morning, a few days before he had made up his mind to go, I was correcting my proof sheets in my study. It was chilly weather.

Through the window the rays of the sun touched my feet, and the slight warmth was very welcome. It was almost eight o'clock, and the early pedestrians were returning home with their heads covered. All at once I heard an uproar in the street, and, looking out, saw Rahmun being led away bound between two policemen, and behind them a crowd of curious boys. There were blood-stains on the clothes of the Cabuliwallah, and one of the policemen carried a knife. Hurrying out, I stopped them, and inquired what it all meant. Partly from one, partly from another, I gathered that a certain neighbour had owed the pedlar something for a Rampuri shawl, but had falsely denied having bought it, and that in the course of the quarrel Rahmun had struck him. Now, in the heat of his excitement, the prisoner began calling his enemy all sorts of names, when suddenly in a verandah of my house appeared my little Mini, with her usual exclamation: "O Cabuliwallah! Cabuliwallah!" Rahmun's face lighted up as he turned to her. He had no bag under his arm to-day, so she could not discuss the elephant with him. She at once therefore proceeded to the next question: "Are you going to the father-in-law's house?" Rahmun laughed and said: "Just where I am going, little one!" Then, seeing that the reply did not amuse the child, he held up his fettered hands. "Ah!" he said, "I would have thrashed that old father-in-law, but my hands are bound!"

On a charge of murderous assault, Rahmun was sentenced to some years' imprisonment.

Time passed away and he was not remembered. The accustomed work in the accustomed place was ours, and the thought of the once free mountaineer spending his years in prison seldom or never occurred to us. Even my light-hearted Mini, I am ashamed to say, forgot her old friend. New companions filled her life. As she grew older, she spent more of her time with girls. So much time indeed did she spend with them that she came no more, as she used to do, to her father's room. I was scarcely on speaking terms with her.

Years had passed away. It was once more autumn and we had made arrangements for our Mini's marriage. It was to take place during the Puja Holidays. With Durga returning to Kailas, the light of our home also was to depart to her husband's house, and leave her father's in the shadow.

The morning was bright. After the rains, there was a sense of ablution in the air, and the sun-rays looked like pure gold. So bright were they, that they gave a beautiful radiance even to the sordid brick walls of our Calcutta lanes. Since early dawn that day the wedding-pipes had been sounding, and at each beat my own heart throbbed. The wail of the tune, Bhairavi, seemed to intensify my pain at the approaching separation. My Mini was to be married that night.

From early morning noise and bustle had pervaded the house. In the courtyard the canopy had to be slung on its bamboo poles; the chandeliers with their tinkling sound must be hung in each room and verandah. There was no end of hurry and excitement. I was sitting in my study, looking through the accounts, when some one entered, saluting respectfully, and stood before me. It was Rahmun the Cabuliwallah. At first I did not recognise him. He had no bag, nor the long hair, nor the same vigour that he used to have. But he smiled, and I knew him again.

"When did you come, Rahmun?" I asked him.

"Last evening," he said, "I was released from jail."

The words struck harsh upon my ears. I had never before talked with one who had wounded his fellow, and my heart shrank within itself when I realised this; for I felt that the day would have been better-omened had he not turned up.

"There are ceremonies going on," I said, "and I am busy. Could you perhaps come another day?"

At once he turned to go; but as he reached the door he hesitated, and said: "May I not see the little one, sir, for a moment?" It was his belief that Mini was still the same. He had pictured her running to him as she used, calling "O Cabuliwallah! Cabuliwallah!" He had imagined too that they would laugh and talk together, just as of old. In fact, in memory of former days he had brought, carefully wrapped up in paper, a few almonds and raisins and grapes, obtained somehow from a countryman; for his own little fund was dispersed.

I said again: "There is a ceremony in the house, and you will not be able to see any one to-day."

The man's face fell. He looked wistfully at me for a moment, then said "Good morning," and went out.

I felt a little sorry, and would have called him back, but I found he was returning of his own accord. He came close up to me holding out his offerings with the words: "I brought these few things, sir, for the little one. Will you give them to her?"

I took them and was going to pay him, but he caught my hand and said: "You are very kind, sir! Keep me in your recollection. Do not offer me money!—You have a little girl: I too have one like her in my own home. I think of her, and bring fruits to your child—not to make a profit for myself."

Saying this, he put his hand inside his big loose robe, and brought out a small and dirty piece of paper. With great care he unfolded this, and smoothed it out with both hands on my table. It bore the impression of a little hand. Not a photograph. Not a drawing. The impression of an ink-smeared hand laid flat on the paper. This touch of his own little daughter had been always on his heart, as he had come year after year to Calcutta to sell his wares in the streets.

Tears came to my eyes. I forgot that he was a poor Cabuli fruit-seller, while I was—. But no, what was I more than he? He also was a father.

That impression of the hand of his little *Pārbati* in her distant mountain home reminded me of my own little Mini.

I sent for Mini immediately from the inner apartment. Many difficulties were raised, but I would not listen. Clad in the red silk of her wedding-day, with the sandal paste on her forehead, and adorned as a young bride, Mini came, and stood bashfully before me.

The Cabuliwallah looked a little staggered at the apparition. He could not revive their old friendship. At last he smiled and said: "Little one, are you going to your father-in-law's house?"

But Mini now understood the meaning of the word "father-in-law," and she could not reply to him as of old. She flushed up at the question, and stood before him with her bride-like face turned down.

I remembered the day when the Cabuliwallah and my Mini had first met, and I felt sad. When she had gone, Rahmun heaved a deep sigh, and sat down on the floor. The idea had suddenly come to him that his daughter too must have grown in this long time, and that he would have to make friends with her anew. Assuredly he would not find her as he used to know her. And besides, what might not have happened to her in these eight years?

The marriage-pipes sounded, and the mild autumn sun streamed round us. But Rahmun sat in the little Calcutta lane, and saw before him the barren mountains of Afghanistan.

I took out a bank-note and gave it to him, saying: "Go back to your own daughter, Rahmun, in your own country, and may the happiness of your meeting bring good fortune to my child!"

Having made this present, I had to curtail some of the festivities. I could not have the electric lights I had intended, nor the military band, and the ladies of the house were despondent at it. But to me the wedding-feast was all the brighter for the thought that in a distant land a long-lost father met again with his only child.

29

The Victory

Rabindranath Tagore

She was the Princess Ajita. And the court poet of King Narayan had never seen her. On the day he recited a new poem to the king he would raise his voice just to that pitch which could be heard by unseen hearers in the screened balcony high above the hall. He sent up his song towards the star-land out of his reach, where, circled with light, the planet who ruled his destiny shone unknown and out of ken.

He would espy some shadow moving behind the veil. A tinkling sound would come to his ear from afar, and would set him dreaming of the ankles whose tiny golden bells sang at each step. Ah, the rosy red tender feet that walked the dust of the earth like God's mercy on the fallen! The poet had placed them on the altar of his heart, where he wove his songs to the tune of those golden bells. Doubt never arose in his mind as to whose shadow it was that moved behind the screen, and whose anklets they were that sang to the time of his beating heart.

Manjari, the maid of the princess, passed by the poet's house on her way to the river, and she never missed a day to have a few words with him on the sly. When she found the road deserted, and the shadow of dusk on the land, she would boldly enter his room, and sit at the corner of his carpet. There was a suspicion of an added care in the choice of the colour of her veil, in the setting of the flower in her hair.

People smiled and whispered at this, and they were not to blame. For Shekhar the poet never took the trouble to hide the fact that these meetings were a pure joy to him.

The meaning of her name was the *spray of flowers*. One must confess that for an ordinary mortal it was sufficient in its sweetness. But Shekhar made his own addition to this name, and called her the Spray of Spring Flowers. And ordinary mortals shook their heads and said, Ah, me!

In the spring songs that the poet sang the praise of the spray of spring flowers was conspicuously reiterated; and the king winked and smiled at him when he heard it, and the poet smiled in answer.

The king would put him the question; "Is it the business of the bee merely to hum in the court of the spring?"

The poet would answer; "No, but also to sip the honey of the spray of spring flowers."

And they all laughed in the king's hall. And it was rumoured that the Princess Ajita also laughed at her maid's accepting the poet's name for her, and Manjari felt glad in her heart.

Thus truth and falsehood mingle in life—and to what God builds man adds his own decoration.

Only those were pure truths which were sung by the poet. The theme was Krishna, the lover god, and Radha, the beloved, the Eternal Man and the Eternal Woman, the sorrow that comes from the beginning of time, and the joy without end. The truth of these songs was tested in his inmost heart by everybody from the beggar to the king himself. The poet's songs were on the lips of all. At the merest glimmer of the moon and the faintest whisper of the summer breeze his songs would break forth in the land from windows and courtyards, from sailing-boats, from shadows of the wayside trees, in numberless voices.

Thus passed the days happily. The poet recited, the king listened, the hearers applauded, Manjari passed and repassed by the poet's room on her way to the river—the shadow flitted behind the screened balcony, and the tiny golden bells tinkled from afar.

Just then set forth from his home in the south a poet on his path of conquest. He came to King Narayan, in the kingdom of Amarapur. He stood before the throne, and uttered a verse in praise of the king. He had challenged all the court poets on his way, and his career of victory had been unbroken.

The king received him with honour, and said: "Poet, I offer you welcome."

Pundarik, the poet, proudly replied: "Sire, I ask for war."

Shekhar, the court poet of the king did not know how the battle of the muse was to be waged. He had no sleep at night. The mighty figure of the famous Pundarik, his sharp nose curved like a scimitar, and his proud head tilted on one side, haunted the poet's vision in the dark.

With a trembling heart Shekhar entered the arena in the morning. The theatre was filled with the crowd.

The poet greeted his rival with a smile and a bow. Pundarik returned it with a slight toss of his head, and turned his face towards his circle of adoring followers with a meaning smile. Shekhar cast his glance towards the screened balcony high above, and saluted his lady in his mind, saying! "If I am the winner at the combat to-day, my lady, thy victorious name shall be glorified."

The trumpet sounded. The great crowd stood up, shouting victory to the king. The king, dressed in an ample robe of white, slowly came into the hall like a floating cloud of autumn, and sat on his throne.

Pundarik stood up, and the vast hall became still. With his head raised high and chest expanded, he began in his thundering voice to recite the praise of King Narayan. His words burst upon the walls of the hall like breakers of the sea, and seemed to rattle against the ribs of the listening crowd. The skill with which he gave varied meanings to the name Narayan, and wove each letter of it through the web of his verses in all mariner of combinations, took away the breath of his amazed hearers.

For some minutes after he took his seat his voice continued to vibrate among the numberless pillars of the king's court and in thousands of speechless hearts. The learned professors who had come from distant lands raised their right hands, and cried, Bravo!

The king threw a glance on Shekhar's face, and Shekhar in answer raised for a moment his eyes full of pain towards his master, and then stood up like a stricken deer at bay. His face was pale, his bashfulness was almost that of a woman, his slight youthful figure, delicate in its outline, seemed like a tensely strung *vina* ready to break out in music at the least touch.

His head was bent, his voice was low, when he began. The first few verses were almost inaudible. Then he slowly raised his head, and his clear sweet voice rose into the sky like a quivering flame of fire. He began with the ancient legend of the kingly line lost in the haze of the past, and brought it down through its long course of heroism and matchless generosity to the present age. He fixed his gaze on the king's face, and all the vast and unexpressed love of the people for the royal house rose like incense in his song, and enwreathed the throne on all sides. These were his last words when, trembling, he took his seat: "My master, I may be beaten in play of words, but not in my love for thee."

Tears filled the eyes of the hearers, and the stone walls shook with cries of victory.

Mocking this popular outburst of feeling, with an august shake of his head and a contemptuous sneer, Pundarik stood up, and flung this question to the assembly; "What is there superior to words?" In a moment the hall lapsed into silence again.

Then with a marvellous display of learning, he proved that the Word was in the beginning, that the Word was God. He piled up quotations from scriptures, and built a high altar for the Word to be seated above all that there is in heaven and in earth. He repeated that question in his mighty voice: "What is there superior to words?"

Proudly he looked around him. None dared to accept his challenge, and he slowly took his seat like a lion who had just made a full meal of its victim. The pandits shouted, Bravo! The king remained silent with wonder, and the poet Shekhar felt himself of no account by the side of this stupendous learning. The assembly broke up for that day.

Next day Shekhar began his song. It was of that day when the pipings of love's flute startled for the first time the hushed air of the Vrinda forest. The shepherd women did not know who was the player or whence came the music. Sometimes it seemed to come from the heart of the south wind, and sometimes from the straying clouds of the hilltops. It came with a message of tryst from the land of the sunrise, and it floated from the verge of sunset with its sigh of sorrow. The stars seemed to be the stops of the instrument that flooded the dreams of the night with melody. The music seemed to burst all at once from all sides, from fields and groves, from the shady lanes and lonely roads, from the melting blue of the sky, from the shimmering green of the grass. They neither knew its meaning nor could they find words to give utterance to the desire of their hearts. Tears filled their eyes, and their life seemed to long for a death that would be its consummation.

Shekhar forgot his audience, forgot the trial of his strength with a rival. He stood alone amid his thoughts that rustled and quivered round him like leaves in a summer breeze, and sang the Song of the Flute. He had in his mind the vision of an image that had taken its shape from a shadow, and the echo of a faint tinkling sound of a distant footstep.

He took his seat. His hearers trembled with the sadness of an indefinable delight, immense and vague, and they forgot to applaud him. As this feeling died away Pundarik stood up before the throne and challenged his rival to define who was this Lover and who was the Beloved. He arrogantly looked around him, he smiled at his followers and then put the question again: "Who is Krishna, the lover, and who is Radha, the beloved?"

Then he began to analyse the roots of those names,—and various interpretations of their meanings. He brought before the bewildered audience all the intricacies of the different schools of metaphysics with consummate skill. Each letter of those names he divided from its fellow, and then pursued them with a relentless logic till they fell to the dust in confusion, to be caught up again and restored to a meaning never before imagined by the subtlest of word-mongers.

The pandits were in ecstasy; they applauded vociferously; and the crowd followed them, deluded into the certainty that they had witnessed, that day, the last shred of the curtains of Truth torn to pieces before their eyes by a prodigy of intellect. The performance of his tremendous feat so delighted them that they forgot to ask themselves if there was any truth behind it after all.

The king's mind was overwhelmed with wonder. The atmosphere was completely cleared of all illusion of music, and the vision of the world around seemed to be changed from its freshness of tender green to the solidity of a high road levelled and made hard with crushed stones.

To the people assembled their own poet appeared a mere boy in comparison with this giant, who walked with such case, knocking down difficulties at each step in the world of words and thoughts. It became evident to them for the first time that the poems Shekhar wrote were absurdly simple, and it must be a mere accident that they did not write them themselves. They were neither new, nor difficult, nor instructive, nor necessary.

The king tried to goad his poet with keen glances, silently inciting him to make a final effort. But Shekhar took no notice, and remained fixed to his seat.

The king in anger came down from his throne—took off his pearl chain and put it on Pundarik's head. Everybody in the hall cheered. From the upper balcony came a slight sound of the movements of rustling robes and waist-chains hung with golden bells. Shekhar rose from his seat and left the hall.

It was a dark night of waning moon. The poet Shekhar took down his MSS. from his shelves and heaped them on the floor. Some of them contained his earliest writings, which he had almost forgotten. He turned over the pages, reading passages here and there. They all seemed to him poor and trivial—mere words and childish rhymes!

One by one he tore his books to fragments, and threw them into a vessel containing fire, and said: "To thee, to thee, O my beauty, my fire! Thou hast been burning in my heart all these futile years. If my life were a piece of gold it would come out of its trial brighter, but it is a trodden turf of grass, and nothing remains of it but this handful of ashes."

The night wore on. Shekhar opened wide his windows. He spread upon his bed the white flowers that he loved, the jasmines, tuberoses and chrysanthemums, and brought into his bedroom all the lamps he had in his house and lighted them. Then mixing with honey the juice of some poisonous root he drank it and lay down on his bed.

Golden anklets tinkled in the passage outside the door, and a subtle perfume came into the room with the breeze.

The poet, with his eyes shut, said; "My lady, have you taken pity upon your servant at last and come to see him?"

The answer came in a sweet voice "My poet, I have come."

Shekhar opened his eyes—and saw before his bed the figure of a woman.

His sight was dim and blurred. And it seemed to him that the image made of a shadow that he had ever kept throned in the secret shrine of his heart had come into the outer world in his last moment to gaze upon his face.

The woman said; "I am the Princess Ajita."

The poet with a great effort sat up on his bed.

The princess whispered into his ear: "The king has not done you justice. It was you who won at the combat, my poet, and I have come to crown you with the crown of victory."

She took the garland of flowers from her own neck, and put it on his hair, and the poet fell down upon his bed stricken by death.

30

The Homecoming

Rabindranath Tagore

Phatik Chakravorti was ringleader among the boys of the village. A new mischief got into his head. There was a heavy log lying on the mud-flat of the river waiting to be shaped into a mast for a boat. He decided that they should all work together to shift the log by main force from its place and roll it away. The owner of the log would be angry and surprised, and they would all enjoy the fun. Every one seconded the proposal, and it was carried unanimously.

But just as the fun was about to begin, Mākhan, Phatik's younger brother, sauntered up and sat down on the log in front of them all without a word. The boys were puzzled for a moment. He was pushed, rather timidly, by one of the boys and told to get up; but he remained quite unconcerned. He appeared like a young philosopher meditating on the futility of games. Phatik was furious. "Mākhan," he cried, "if you don't get down this minute I'll thrash you!".

Mākhan only moved to a more comfortable position.

Now, if Phatik was to keep his regal dignity before the public, it was clear he ought to carry out his threat. But his courage failed him at the crisis. His fertile brain, however, rapidly seized upon a new manœuvre which would discomfit his brother and afford his followers an added amusement. He gave the word of command to roll the log and Mākhan over together. Mākhan heard the order and made it a point of honour to stick on. But he overlooked the fact, like those who attempt earthly fame in other matters, that there was peril in it.

The boys began to heave at the log with all their might, calling out, "One, two, three, go!" At the word "go" the log went; and with it went Mākhan's philosophy, glory and all.

The other boys shouted themselves hoarse with delight. But Phatik was a little frightened. He knew what was coming. And, sure enough, Mākhan rose from Mother Earth blind as Fate and screaming like the

Furies. He rushed at Phatik and scratched his face and beat him and kicked him, and then went crying home. The first act of the drama was over.

Phatik wiped his face, and sat down on the edge of a sunken barge by the river bank, and began to chew a piece of grass. A boat came up to the landing and a middle-aged man, with grey hair and dark moustache, stepped on shore. He saw the boy sitting there doing nothing and asked him where the Chakravortis lived. Phatik went on chewing the grass and said: "Over there," but it was quite impossible to tell where he pointed. The stranger asked him again. He swung his legs to and fro on the side of the barge and said: "Go and find out," and continued to chew the grass as before.

But now a servant came down from the house and told Phatik his mother wanted him. Phatik refused to move. But the servant was the master on this occasion. He took Phatik up roughly and carried him, kicking and struggling in impotent rage.

When Phatik came into the house, his mother saw him. She called out angrily: "So you have been hitting Mākhan again?"

Phatik answered indignantly: "No, I haven't! Who told you that?"

His mother shouted: "Don't tell lies! You have."

Phatik said sullenly: "I tell you, I haven't. You ask Mākhan!" But Mākhan thought it best to stick to his previous statement. He said: "Yes, mother. Phatik did hit me."

Phatik's patience was already exhausted. He could not bear this injustice. He rushed at Mākhan and hammered him with blows: "Take that," he cried, "and that, and that, for telling lies."

His mother took Mākhan's side in a moment, and pulled Phatik away, beating him with her hands. When Phatik pushed her aside, she shouted out: "What! you little villain! Would you hit your own mother?"

It was just at this critical juncture that the grey-haired stranger arrived. He asked what was the matter. Phatik looked sheepish and ashamed.

But when his mother stepped back and looked at the stranger, her anger was changed to surprise. For she recognized her brother and cried: "Why, Dada! Where have you come from?"

As she said these words, she bowed to the ground and touched his feet. Her brother had gone away soon after she had married; and he had started business in Bombay. His sister had lost her husband while he was there. Bishamber had now come back to Calcutta and had at once made enquiries about his sister. He had then hastened to see her as soon as he found out where she was.

The next few days were full of rejoicing. The brother asked after the education of the two boys. He was told by his sister that Phatik was a perpetual nuisance. He was lazy, disobedient, and wild. But Mākhan was as good as gold, as quiet as a lamb, and very fond of reading. Bishamber kindly offered to take Phatik off his sister's hands and educate him with his own children in Calcutta. The widowed mother readily agreed. When his uncle asked Phatik if he would like to go to Calcutta with him, his joy knew no bounds and he said: "Oh, yes, uncle!" in a way that made it quite clear that he meant it.

It was an immense relief to the mother to get rid of Phatik. She had a prejudice against the boy, and no love was lost between the two brothers. She was in daily fear that he would either drown Mākhan some day in the river, or break his head in a fight, or run him into some danger. At the same time she was a little distressed to see Phatik's extreme eagerness to get away.

Phatik, as soon as all was settled, kept asking his uncle every minute when they were to start. He was on pins and needles all day long with excitement and lay awake most of the night. He bequeathed to Mākhan, in perpetuity, his fishing-rod, his big kite, and his marbles. Indeed, at this time of departure, his generosity towards Mākhan was unbounded.

When they reached Calcutta, Phatik made the acquaintance of his aunt for the first time. She was by no means pleased with this unnecessary addition to her family. She found her own three boys quite enough to manage without taking any one else. And to bring a village lad of fourteen into their midst was terribly upsetting. Bishamber should really have thought twice before committing such an indiscretion.

In this world of human affairs there is no worse nuisance than a boy at the age of fourteen. He is neither ornamental nor useful. It is impossible to shower affection on him as on a little boy; and he is always getting in the way. If he talks with a childish lisp he is called a baby, and if he answers in a grown-up way he is called impertinent. In fact any talk at all from him is resented. Then he is at the unattractive, growing age. He grows out of his clothes with indecent haste; his voice grows hoarse and breaks and quavers; his face grows suddenly angular and unsightly. It is easy to excuse the shortcomings of early childhood, but it is hard to tolerate even unavoidable lapses in a boy of fourteen. The lad himself becomes painfully self-conscious. When he talks with elderly people he is either unduly forward, or else so unduly shy that he appears ashamed of his very existence.

Yet it is at this very age when, in his heart of hearts, a young lad most craves for recognition and love; and he becomes the devoted slave of any one who shows him consideration. But none dare openly love him, for that would be regarded as undue indulgence and therefore bad for the boy. So, what with scolding and chiding, he becomes very much like a stray dog that has lost his master.

For a boy of fourteen his own home is the only Paradise. To live in a strange house with strange people is little short of torture, while the height of bliss is to receive the kind looks of women and never to be slighted by them.

It was anguish to Phatik to be the unwelcome guest in his aunt's house, despised by this elderly woman and slighted on every occasion. If ever she asked him to do anything for her, he would be so overjoyed that he would overdo it; and then she would tell him not to be so stupid, but to get on with his lessons.

The cramped atmosphere of neglect oppressed Phatik so much that he felt that he could hardly breathe. He wanted to go out into the open country and fill his lungs with fresh air. But there was no open country to go to. Surrounded on all sides by Calcutta houses and walls, he would dream night after night of his village home and long to be back there. He remembered the glorious meadow where he used to fly his kite all day long; the broad river-banks where he would wander about the live-long day singing and shouting for joy; the narrow brook where he could go and dive and swim at any time he liked. He thought of his band of boy companions over whom he was despot; and, above all, the memory of that tyrant mother of his, who had such a prejudice against him, occupied him day and night. A kind of physical love like that of animals, a longing to be in the presencc of the one who is loved, an inexpressible wistfulness during absence, a silent cry of the inmost heart for the mother, like the lowing of a calf in the twilight,—this love, which was almost an animal instinct, agitated the shy, nervous, lean, uncouth and ugly boy. No one could understand it, but it preyed upon his mind continually.

There was no more backward boy in the whole school than Phatik. He gaped and remained silent when the teacher asked him a question, and like an overladen ass patiently suffered all the blows that came down on his back. When other boys were out at play, he stood wistfully by the window and gazed at the roofs of the distant houses. And if by chance he espied children playing on the open terrace of any roof, his heart would ache with longing.

One day he summoned up all his courage and asked his uncle: "Uncle, when can I go home?"

His uncle answered: "Wait till the holidays come."

But the holidays would not come till October and there was a long time still to wait.

One day Phatik lost his lesson book. Even with the help of books he had found it very difficult indeed to prepare his lesson. Now it was impossible. Day after day the teacher would cane him unmercifully. His condition became so abjectly miserable that even his cousins were ashamed to own him. They began to jeer and insult him more than the other boys. He went to his aunt at last and told her that he had lost his book.

His aunt pursed her lips in contempt and said: "You great clumsy, country lout! How can I afford, with all my family, to buy you new books five times a month?"

That night, on his way back from school, Phatik had a bad headache with a fit of shivering. He felt he was going to have an attack of malarial fever. His one great fear was that he would be a nuisance to his aunt.

The next morning Phatik was nowhere to be seen. All searches in the neighbourhood proved futile. The rain had been pouring in torrents all night, and those who went out in search of the boy got drenched through to the skin. At last Bishamber asked help from the police.

At the end of the day a police van stopped at the door before the house. It was still raining and the streets were all flooded. Two constables brought out Phatik in their arms and placed him before Bishamber. He was wet through from head to foot, muddy all over, his face and eyes flushed red with fever and his limbs trembling. Bishamber carried him in his arms and took him into the inner apartments. When his wife saw him she exclaimed: "What a heap of trouble this boy has given us! Hadn't you better send him home?"

Phatik heard her words and sobbed out loud: "Uncle, I was just going home; but they dragged me back again."

The fever rose very high, and all that night the boy was delirious. Bishamber brought in a doctor. Phatik opened his eyes, flushed with fever, and looked up to the ceiling and said vacantly: "Uncle, have the holidays come yet?"

Bishamber wiped the tears from his own eyes and took Phatik's lean and burning hands in his own and sat by him through the night. The boy began again to mutter. At last his voice became excited: "Mother!" he cried, "don't beat me like that.... Mother! I *am* telling the truth!"

The next day Phatik became conscious for a short time. He turned his eyes about the room, as if expecting some one to come. At last, with an air of disappointment, his head sank back on the pillow. He turned his face to the wall with a deep sigh.

Bishamber knew his thoughts and bending down his head whispered: "Phatik, I have sent for your mother."

The day went by. The doctor said in a troubled voice that the boy's condition was very critical.

Phatik began to cry out: "By the mark—three fathoms. By the mark—four fathoms. By the mark——." He had heard the sailor on the river-steamer calling out the mark on the plumb-line. Now he was himself plumbing an unfathomable sea.

Later in the day Phatik's mother burst into the room, like a whirlwind, and began to toss from side to side and moan and cry in a loud voice.

Bishamber tried to calm her agitation, but she flung herself on the bed, and cried: "Phatik, my darling, my darling."

Phatik stopped his restless movements for a moment. His hands ceased beating up and down. He said: "Eh?"

The mother cried again: "Phatik, my darling, my darling."

Phatik very slowly turned his head and without seeing anybody said: "Mother, the holidays have come."

31

The Piece of String

Guy de Maupassant

It was market-day, and from all the country round Goderville the peasants and their wives were coming toward the town. The men walked slowly, throwing the whole body forward at every step of their long, crooked legs. They were deformed from pushing the plough which makes the left-shoulder higher, and bends their figures side-ways; from reaping the grain, when they have to spread their legs so as to keep on their feet. Their starched blue blouses, glossy as though varnished, ornamented at collar and cuffs with a little embroidered design and blown out around their bony bodies, looked very much like balloons about to soar, whence issued two arms and two feet.

Some of these fellows dragged a cow or a calf at the end of a rope. And just behind the animal followed their wives beating it over the back with a leaf-covered branch to hasten its pace, and carrying large baskets out of which protruded the heads of chickens or ducks. These women walked more quickly and energetically than the men, with their erect, dried-up figures, adorned with scanty little shawls pinned over their flat bosoms, and their heads wrapped round with a white cloth, enclosing the hair and surmounted by a cap.

Now a char-à-banc passed by, jogging along behind a nag and shaking up strangely the two men on the seat, and the woman at the bottom of the cart who held fast to its sides to lessen the hard jolting.

In the market-place at Goderville was a great crowd, a mingled multitude of men and beasts. The horns of cattle, the high, long-napped hats of wealthy peasants, the head-dresses of the women came to the surface of that sea. And the sharp, shrill, barking voices made a continuous, wild din, while above it occasionally rose a huge burst of laughter from the sturdy lungs of a merry peasant or a prolonged bellow from a cow tied fast to the wall of a house.

It all smelled of the stable, of milk, of hay and of perspiration, giving off that half-human, half-animal odor which is peculiar to country folks.

Maître Hauchecorne, of Bréauté, had just arrived at Goderville and was making his way toward the square when he perceived on the ground a little piece of string. Maître Hauchecorne, economical as are all true Normans, reflected that everything was worth picking up which could be of any use, and he stooped down, but painfully, because he suffered from rheumatism. He took the bit of thin string from the ground and was carefully preparing to roll it up when he saw Maître Malandain, the harness maker, on his doorstep staring at him. They had once had a quarrel about a halter, and they had borne each other malice ever since. Maître Hauchecorne was overcome with a sort of shame at being seen by his enemy picking up a bit of string in the road. He quickly hid it beneath his blouse and then slipped it into his breeches, pocket, then pretended to be still looking for something on the ground which he did not discover and finally went off toward the market-place, his head bent forward and his body almost doubled in two by rheumatic pains.

He was at once lost in the crowd, which kept moving about slowly and noisily as it chaffered and bargained. The peasants examined the cows, went off, came back, always in doubt for fear of being cheated, never quite daring to decide, looking the seller square in the eye in the effort to discover the tricks of the man and the defect in the beast.

The women, having placed their great baskets at their feet, had taken out the poultry, which lay upon the ground, their legs tied together, with terrified eyes and scarlet combs.

They listened to propositions, maintaining their prices in a decided manner with an impassive face or perhaps deciding to accept the smaller price offered, suddenly calling out to the customer who was starting to go away:

"All right, I'll let you have them, Mait' Anthime."

Then, little by little, the square became empty, and when the Angelus struck midday those who lived at a distance poured into the inns.

At Jourdain's the great room was filled with eaters, just as the vast court was filled with vehicles of every sort—wagons, gigs, chars- à-bancs, tilburies, innumerable vehicles which have no name, yellow with mud, misshapen, pieced together, raising their shafts to heaven like two arms, or it may be with their nose on the ground and their rear in the air.

Just opposite to where the diners were at table the huge fireplace, with its bright flame, gave out a burning heat on the backs of those who sat at the right. Three spits were turning, loaded with chickens, with pigeons and with joints of mutton, and a delectable odor of roast meat and of gravy flowing over crisp brown skin arose from the hearth, kindled merriment, caused mouths to water.

All the aristocracy of the plough were eating there at Maît' Jourdain's, the innkeeper's, a dealer in horses also and a sharp fellow who had made a great deal of money in his day.

The dishes were passed round, were emptied, as were the jugs of yellow cider. Every one told of his affairs, of his purchases and his sales. They exchanged news about the crops. The weather was good for greens, but too wet for grain.

Suddenly the drum began to beat in the courtyard before the house. Every one, except some of the most indifferent, was on their feet at once and ran to the door, to the windows, their mouths full and napkins in their hand.

When the public crier had finished his tattoo he called forth in a jerky voice, pausing in the wrong places:

"Be it known to the inhabitants of Goderville and in general to all persons present at the market that there has been lost this morning on the Beuzeville road, between nine and ten o'clock, a black leather pocketbook containing five hundred francs and business papers. You are requested to return it to the mayor's office at once or to Maître Fortune Houlbreque, of Manneville. There will be twenty francs reward."

Then the man went away. They heard once more at a distance the dull beating of the drum and the faint voice of the crier. Then they all began to talk of this incident, reckoning up the chances which Maître Houlbreque had of finding or of not finding his pocketbook again.

The meal went on. They were finishing their coffee when the corporal of gendarmes appeared on the threshold.

He asked:

"Is Maître Hauchecorne, of Bréauté, here?"

Maître Hauchecorne, seated at the other end of the table answered:

"Here I am, here I am."

And he followed the corporal.

The mayor was waiting for him, seated in an armchair. He was the notary of the place, a tall, grave man of pompous speech.

"Maître Hauchecorne," said he, "this morning on the Beuzeville road, you were seen to pick up the pocketbook lost by Maître Houlbreque, of Manneville."

The countryman looked at the mayor in amazement frightened already at this suspicion which rested on him, he knew not why.

"I—I picked up that pocketbook?"

"Yes, YOU."

"I swear I don't even know anything about it."

"You were seen."

"I was seen—I? Who saw me?"

"M. Malandain, the harness-maker."

Then the old man remembered, understood, and, reddening with anger, said:

"Ah! he saw me, did he, the rascal? He saw me picking up this string here, M'sieu le Maire."

And fumbling at the bottom of his pocket, he pulled out of it the little end of string.

But the mayor incredulously shook his head:

"You will not make me believe, Maître Hauchecorne, that M. Malandain, who is a man whose word can be relied on, has mistaken this string for a pocketbook."

The peasant, furious, raised his hand and spat on the ground beside him as if to attest his good faith, repeating:

"For all that, it is God's truth, M'sieu le Maire. There! On my soul's salvation, I repeat it."

The mayor continued:

"After you picked up the object in question, you even looked about for some time in the mud to see if a piece of money had not dropped out of it."

The good man was choking with indignation and fear.

"How can they tell—how can they tell such lies as that to slander an honest man! How can they?"

His protestations were in vain; he was not believed.

He was confronted with M. Malandain, who repeated and sustained his testimony. They railed at one another for an hour. At his own request Maitre Hauchecorne was searched. Nothing was found on him.

At last the mayor, much perplexed, sent him away, warning him that he would inform the public prosecutor and ask for orders.

The news had spread. When he left the mayor's office the old man was surrounded, interrogated with a curiosity which was serious or mocking, as the case might be, but into which no indignation entered. And he began to tell the story of the string. They did not believe him. They laughed.

He passed on, buttonholed by every one, himself buttonholing his acquaintances, beginning over and over again his tale and his protestations, showing his pockets turned inside out to prove that he had nothing in them.

They said to him:

"You old rogue!"

He grew more and more angry, feverish, in despair at not being believed, and kept on telling his story.

The night came. It was time to go home. He left with three of his neighbors, to whom he pointed out the place where he had picked up the string, and all the way he talked of his adventure.

That evening he made the round of the village of Bréauté for the purpose of telling every one. He met only unbelievers.

He brooded over it all night long.

The next day, about one in the afternoon, Marius Paumelle, a farm hand of MaîtreBreton, the market gardener at Ymauville, returned the pocketbook and its contents to MaîtreHoulbrèque, of Manneville.

This man said, indeed, that he had found it on the road, but not knowing how to read, he had carried it home and given it to his master.

The news spread to the environs. Maitre Hauchecorne was informed. He started off at once and began to relate his story with the denouement. He was triumphant.

"What grieved me," said he, "was not the thing itself, do you understand, but it was being accused of lying. Nothing does you so much harm as being in disgrace for lying."

All day he talked of his adventure. He told it on the roads to the people who passed, at the cabaret to the people who drank and next Sunday when they came out of church. He even stopped strangers to tell them about it. He was easy now, and yet something worried him without his knowing exactly what it was. People had a joking manner while they listened. They did not seem convinced. He seemed to feel their remarks behind his back.

On Tuesday of the following week he went to market at Goderville, prompted solely by the need of telling his story.

Malandain, standing on his doorstep, began to laugh as he saw him pass. Why?

He accosted a farmer of Criquetot, who did not let him finish, and giving him a punch in the pit of the stomach cried in his face: "Oh, you great rogue!" Then he turned his heel upon him.

Maître Hauchecorne remained speechless and grew more and more uneasy. Why had they called him "great rogue"?

When seated at table in Jourdain's tavern he began again to explain the whole affair.

A horse dealer of Montivilliers shouted at him:

"Get out, get out, you old scamp! I know all about your old string."

Hauchecorne stammered:

"But since they found it again, the pocketbook!"

But the other continued:

"Hold your tongue, daddy; there's one who finds it and there's another who returns it. And no one the wiser."

The farmer was speechless. He understood at last. They accused him of having had the pocketbook brought back by an accomplice, by a confederate.

He tried to protest. The whole table began to laugh.

He could not finish his dinner, and went away amid a chorus of jeers.

He went home indignant, choking with rage, with confusion, the more cast down since with his Norman craftiness he was, perhaps, capable of having done what they accused him of and even of boasting of it as a good trick. He was dimly conscious that it was impossible to prove his innocence, his craftiness being so well known. He felt himself struck to the heart by the injustice of the suspicion.

He began anew to tell his tale, lengthening his recital every day, each day adding new proofs, more energetic declarations and more sacred oaths, which he thought of, which he prepared in his hours of solitude, for his mind was entirely occupied with the story of thc string. The more he denied it, the more artful his arguments, the less he was believed.

"Those are liars proofs," they said behind his back.

He felt this. It preyed upon him and he exhausted himself in useless efforts.

He was visibly wasting away.

Jokers would make him tell the story of "the piece of string" to amuse them, just as you make a soldier who has been on a campaign tell his story of the battle. His mind kept growing weaker and about the end of December he took to his bed.

He passed away early in January, and, in the ravings of death agony, he protested his innocence, repeating:

"A little bit of string—a little bit of string. See, here it is, M'sieu le Maire."

32

The Devil

Guy de Maupassant

The peasant and the doctor stood on opposite sides of the bed, beside the old, dying woman. She was calm and resigned and her mind quite clear as she looked at them and listened to their conversation. She was going to die, and she did not rebel at it, for her time was come, as she was ninety-two.

The July sun streamed in at the window and the open door and cast its hot flames on the uneven brown clay floor, which had been stamped down by four generations of clodhoppers. The smell of the fields came in also, driven by the sharp wind and parched by the noontide heat. The grass-hoppers chirped themselves hoarse, and filled the country with their shrill noise, which was like that of the wooden toys which are sold to children at fair time.

The doctor raised his voice and said: "Honore, you cannot leave your mother in this state; she may die at any moment." And the peasant, in great distress, replied: "But I must get in my wheat, for it has been lying on the ground a long time, and the weather is just right for it; what do you say about it, mother?" And the dying old woman, still tormented by her Norman avariciousness, replied yes with her eyes and her forehead, and thus urged her son to get in his wheat, and to leave her to die alone.

But the doctor got angry, and, stamping his foot, he said: "You are no better than a brute, do you hear, and I will not allow you to do it, do you understand? And if you must get in your wheat today, go and fetch Rapet's wife and make her look after your mother; I will have it, do you understand me? And if you do not obey me, I will let you die like a dog, when you are ill in your turn; do you hear?"

The peasant, a tall, thin fellow with slow movements, who was tormented by indecision, by his fear of the doctor and his fierce love of saving, hesitated, calculated, and stammered out: "How much does

La Rapet charge for attending sick people?" "How should I know?" the doctor cried. "That depends upon how long she is needed. Settle it with her, by Heaven! But I want her to be here within an hour, do you hear?"

So the man decided. "I will go for her," he replied; "don't get angry, doctor." And the latter left, calling out as he went: "Be careful, be very careful, you know, for I do not joke when I am angry!" As soon as they were alone the peasant turned to his mother and said in a resigned voice: "I will go and fetch La Rapet, as the man will have it. Don't worry till I get back."

And he went out in his turn.

La Rapet, old was an old washerwoman, watched the dead and the dying of the neighborhood, and then, as soon as she had sewn her customers into that linen cloth from which they would emerge no more, she went and took up her iron to smooth out the linen of the living. Wrinkled like a last year's apple, spiteful, envious, avaricious with a phenomenal avarice, bent double, as if she had been broken in half across the loins by the constant motion of passing the iron over the linen, one might have said that she had a kind of abnormal and cynical love of a death struggle. She never spoke of anything but of the people she had seen die, of the various kinds of deaths at which she had been present, and she related with the greatest minuteness details which were always similar, just as a sportsman recounts his luck.

When Honore Bontemps entered her cottage, he found her preparing the starch for the collars of the women villagers, and he said: "Good-evening; I hope you are pretty well, Mother Rapet?"

She turned her head round to look at him, and said: "As usual, as usual, and you?" "Oh! as for me, I am as well as I could wish, but my mother is not well." "Your mother?" "Yes, my mother!" "What is the matter with her?" "She is going to turn up her toes, that's what's the matter with her!"

The old woman took her hands out of the water and asked with sudden sympathy: "Is she as bad as all that?" "The doctor says she will not last till morning." "Then she certainly is very bad!" Honore hesitated, for he wanted to make a few preparatory remarks before coming to his proposition; but as he could hit upon nothing, he made up his mind suddenly.

"How much will you ask to stay with her till the end? You know that I am not rich, and I can not even afford to keep a servant girl. It is just that which has brought my poor mother to this state—too much worry and fatigue! She did the work of ten, in spite of her ninety-two years. You don't find any made of that stuff nowadays!"

La Rapet answered gravely: "There are two prices: Forty sous by day and three francs by night for the rich, and twenty sous by day and forty by night for the others. You shall pay me the twenty and forty." But the, peasant reflected, for he knew his mother well. He knew how tenacious of life, how vigorous and unyielding she was, and she might last another week, in spite of the doctor's opinion; and so he said resolutely: "No, I would rather you would fix a price for the whole time until the end. I will take my chance, one way or the other. The doctor says she will die very soon. If that happens, so much the better for you, and so much the worse for her, but if she holds out till to-morrow or longer, so much the better for her and so much the worse for you!"

The nurse looked at the man in astonishment, for she had never treated a death as a speculation, and she hesitated, tempted by the idea of the possible gain, but she suspected that he wanted to play her a trick. "I can say nothing until I have seen your mother," she replied.

"Then come with me and see her."

She washed her hands, and went with him immediately.

They did not speak on the road; she walked with short, hasty steps, while he strode on with his long legs, as if he were crossing a brook at every step.

The cows lying down in the fields, overcome by the heat, raised their heads heavily and lowed feebly at the two passers-by, as if to ask them for some green grass.

When they got near the house, Honore Bontemps murmured: "Suppose it is all over?" And his unconscious wish that it might be so showed itself in the sound of his voice.

But the old woman was not dead. She was lying on her back, on her wretched bed, her hands covered with a purple cotton counterpane, horribly thin, knotty hands, like the claws of strange animals, like crabs, half closed by rheumatism, fatigue and the work of nearly a century which she had accomplished.

La Rapet went up to the bed and looked at the dying woman, felt her pulse, tapped her on the chest, listened to her breathing, and asked her questions, so as to hear her speak; and then, having looked at her for some time, she went out of the room, followed by Honore. Her decided opinion was that the old woman would not last till night. He asked: "Well?" And the sick-nurse replied: "Well, she may last two days, perhaps three. You will have to give me six francs, everything included."

"Six francs! six francs!" he shouted. "Are you out of your mind? I tell you she cannot last more than five or six hours!" And they disputed angrily for some time, but as the nurse said she must go home, as the time was going by, and as his wheat would not come to the farmyard of its own accord, he finally agreed to her terms.

"Very well, then, that is settled; six francs, including everything, until the corpse is taken out."

And he went away, with long strides, to his wheat which was lying on the ground under the hot sun which ripens the grain, while the sick-nurse went in again to the house.

She had brought some work with her, for she worked without ceasing by the side of the dead and dying, sometimes for herself, sometimes for the family which employed her as seamstress and paid her rather more in that capacity. Suddenly, she asked: "Have you received the last sacraments, Mother Bontemps?"

The old peasant woman shook her head, and La Rapet, who was very devout, got up quickly:

"Good heavens, is it possible? I will go and fetch the cure"; and she rushed off to the parsonage so quickly that the urchins in the street thought some accident had happened, when they saw her running.

The priest came immediately in his surplice, preceded by a choir boy who rang a bell to announce the passage of the Host through the parched and quiet country. Some men who were working at a distance took off their large hats and remained motionless until the white vestment had disappeared behind some farm buildings; the women who were making up the sheaves stood up to make the sign of the cross; the frightened black hens ran away along the ditch until they reached a well-known hole, through which they suddenly disappeared, while a foal which was tied in a meadow took fright at the sight of the surplice and began to gallop round and round, kicking cut every now and then. The acolyte, in his red cassock, walked quickly, and the priest, with his head inclined toward one shoulder and his square biretta on his head, followed him, muttering some prayers; while last of all came La Rapet, bent almost double as if she wished to prostrate herself, as she walked with folded hands as they do in church.

Honore saw them pass in the distance, and he asked: "Where is our priest going?" His man, who was more intelligent, replied: "He is taking the sacrament to your mother, of course!"

The peasant was not surprised, and said: "That may be," and went on with his work.

Mother Bontemps confessed, received absolution and communion, and the priest took his departure, leaving the two women alone in the suffocating room, while La Rapet began to look at the dying woman, and to ask herself whether it could last much longer.

The day was on the wane, and gusts of cooler air began to blow, causing a view of Epinal, which was fastened to the wall by two pins, to flap up and down; the scanty window curtains, which had formerly been white, but were now yellow and covered with fly-specks, looked as if they were going to fly off, as if they were struggling to get away, like the old woman's soul.

Lying motionless, with her eyes open, she seemed to await with indifference that death which was so near and which yet delayed its coming. Her short breathing whistled in her constricted throat. It would stop altogether soon, and there would be one woman less in the world; no one would regret her.

At nightfall Honore returned, and when he went up to the bed and saw that his mother was still alive, he asked: "How is she?" just as he had done formerly when she had been ailing, and then he sent La Rapet away, saying to her: "To-morrow morning at five o'clock, without fail." And she replied: "To-morrow, at five o'clock."

She came at daybreak, and found Honore eating his soup, which he had made himself before going to work, and the sick-nurse asked him: "Well, is your mother dead?" "She is rather better, on the contrary," he replied, with a sly look out of the corner of his eyes. And he went out.

La Rapet, seized with anxiety, went up to the dying woman, who remained in the same state, lethargic and impassive, with her eyes open and her hands clutching the counterpane. The nurse perceived that this might go on thus for two days, four days, eight days, and her avaricious mind was seized with fear, while she was furious at the sly fellow who had tricked her, and at the woman who would not die.

Nevertheless, she began to work, and waited, looking intently at the wrinkled face of Mother Bontemps. When Honore returned to breakfast he seemed quite satisfied and even in a bantering humor. He was decidedly getting in his wheat under very favorable circumstances.

La Rapet was becoming exasperated; every minute now seemed to her so much time and money stolen from her. She felt a mad inclination to take this old woman, this, headstrong old fool, this obstinate old wretch, and to stop that short, rapid breath, which was robbing her of her time and money, by squeezing her throat a little. But then she reflected on the danger of doing so, and other thoughts came into her head; so she went up to the bed and said: "Have you ever seen the Devil?" Mother Bontemps murmured: "No."

Then the sick-nurse began to talk and to tell her tales which were likely to terrify the weak mind of the dying woman. Some minutes before one dies the Devil appears, she said, to all who are in the death throes. He has a broom in his hand, a saucepan on his head, and he utters loud cries. When anybody sees him, all is over, and that person has only a few moments longer to live. She then enumerated all those to whom the Devil had appeared that year: Josephine Loisel, Eulalie Ratier, Sophie Padaknau, Seraphine Grospied.

Mother Bontemps, who had at last become disturbed in mind, moved about, wrung her hands, and tried to turn her head to look toward the end of the room. Suddenly La Rapet disappeared at the foot of the bed. She took a sheet out of the cupboard and wrapped herself up in it; she put the iron saucepan on her head, so that its three short bent feet rose up like horns, and she took a broom in her right hand and a tin pail in her left, which she threw up suddenly, so that it might fall to the ground noisily.

When it came down, it certainly made a terrible noise. Then, climbing upon a chair, the nurse lifted up the curtain which hung at the bottom of the bed, and showed herself, gesticulating and uttering shrill cries into the iron saucepan which covered her face, while she menaced the old peasant woman, who was nearly dead, with her broom.

Terrified, with an insane expression on her face, the dying woman made a superhuman effort to get up and escape; she even got her shoulders and chest out of bed; then she fell back with a deep sigh.

All was over, and La Rapet calmly put everything back into its place; the broom into the corner by the cupboard the sheet inside it, the saucepan on the hearth, the pail on the floor, and the chair against the wall. Then, with professional movements, she closed the dead woman's large eyes, put a plate on the bed and poured some holy water into it, placing in it the twig of boxwood that had been nailed to the chest of drawers, and kneeling down, she fervently repeated the prayers for the dead, which she knew by heart, as a matter of business.

And when Honore returned in the evening he found her praying, and he calculated immediately that she had made twenty sows out of him, for she had only spent three days and one night there, which made five francs altogether, instead of the six which he owed her.

33

The Terrible Old Man

H.P. Lovecraft

It was the design of Angelo Ricci and Joe Czanek and Manuel Silva to call on the Terrible Old Man. This old man dwells all alone in a very ancient house on Water Street near the sea, and is reputed to be both exceedingly rich and exceedingly feeble; which forms a situation very attractive to men of the profession of Messrs. Ricci, Czanek, and Silva, for that profession was nothing less dignified than robbery.

The inhabitants of Kingsport say and think many things about the Terrible Old Man which generally keep him safe from the attention of gentlemen like Mr. Ricci and his colleagues, despite the almost certain fact that he hides a fortune of indefinite magnitude somewhere about his musty and venerable abode. He is, in truth, a very strange person, believed to have been a captain of East India clipper ships in his day; so old that no one can remember when he was young, and so taciturn that few know his real name. Among the gnarled trees in the front yard of his aged and neglected place he maintains a strange collection of large stones, oddly grouped and painted so that they resemble the idols in some obscure Eastern temple. This collection frightens away most of the small boys who love to taunt the Terrible Old Man about his long white hair and beard, or to break the small-paned windows of his dwelling with wicked missiles; but there are other things which frighten the older and more curious folk who sometimes steal up to the house to peer in through the dusty panes. These folk say that on a table in a bare room on the ground floor are many peculiar bottles, in each a small piece of lead suspended pendulum-wise from a string. And they say that the Terrible Old Man talks to these bottles, addressing them by such names as Jack, Scar-Face, Long Tom, Spanish Joe, Peters, and Mate Ellis, and that whenever he speaks to a bottle the little lead pendulum within makes certain definite vibrations as if in answer. Those who have watched the tall, lean, Terrible Old Man in these peculiar conversations, do not watch him again. But Angelo Ricci and Joe Czanek and Manuel Silva were not of Kingsport blood; they were of that new and heterogeneous alien stock which lies outside the charmed circle of New England life and traditions, and they saw in the Terrible Old Man merely a tottering, almost helpless greybeard, who could not walk without the aid of his knotted cane, and whose thin, weak hands shook pitifully. They were really quite sorry in their way for the lonely, unpopular old fellow, whom everybody shunned, and at whom all the dogs barked singularly. But business is business, and to a robber whose soul is in his profession, there is a lure and a challenge about a very old and very feeble man who has no account at the bank, and who pays for his few necessities at the village store with Spanish gold and silver minted two centuries ago.

Messrs. Ricci, Czanek, and Silva selected the night of April 11th for their call. Mr. Ricci and Mr. Silva were to interview the poor old gentleman, whilst Mr. Czanek waited for them and their presumable metallic burden with a covered motor-car in Ship Street, by the gate in the tall rear wall of their host's grounds. Desire to avoid needless explanations in case of unexpected police intrusions prompted these plans for a quiet and unostentatious departure.

As prearranged, the three adventurers started out separately in order to prevent any evil-minded suspicions afterward. Messrs. Ricci and Silva met in Water Street by the old man's front gate, and although they did not like the way the moon shone down upon the painted stones through the budding branches of the gnarled trees, they had more important things to think about than mere idle superstition. They feared it might be unpleasant work making the Terrible Old Man loquacious concerning his hoarded gold and silver, for aged sea-captains are notably stubborn and perverse. Still, he was very old and very feeble, and there were two visitors. Messrs. Ricci and Silva were experienced in the art of making unwilling persons voluble, and the screams of a weak and exceptionally venerable man can be easily muffled. So they moved up to the one lighted window and heard the Terrible Old Man talking childishly to his bottles with pendulums. Then they donned masks and knocked politely at the weather-stained oaken door.

Waiting seemed very long to Mr. Czanek as he fidgeted restlessly in the covered motor-car by the Terrible Old Man's back gate in Ship

Street. He was more than ordinarily tender-hearted, and he did not like the hideous screams he had heard in the ancient house just after the hour appointed for the deed. Had he not told his colleagues to be as gentle as possible with the pathetic old sea-captain? Very nervously he watched that narrow oaken gate in the high and ivy-clad stone wall. Frequently he consulted his watch, and wondered at the delay. Had the old man died before revealing where his treasure was hidden, and had a thorough search become necessary? Mr. Czanek did not like to wait so long in the dark in such a place. Then he sensed a soft tread or tapping on the walk inside the gate, heard a gentle fumbling at the rusty latch, and saw the narrow, heavy door swing inward. And in the pallid glow of the single dim street-lamp he strained his eyes to see what his colleagues had brought out of that sinister house which loomed so close behind. But when he looked, he did not see what he had expected; for his colleagues were not there at all, but only the Terrible Old Man leaning quietly on his knotted cane and smiling hideously. Mr. Czanek had never before noticed the colour of that man's eyes; now he saw that they were yellow.

Little things make considerable excitement in little towns, which is the reason that Kingsport people talked all that spring and summer about the three unidentifiable bodies, horribly slashed as with many cutlasses, and horribly mangled as by the tread of many cruel boot-heels, which the tide washed in. And some people even spoke of things as trivial as the deserted motor-car found in Ship Street, or certain especially inhuman cries, probably of a stray animal or migratory bird, heard in the night by wakeful citizens. But in this idle village gossip the Terrible Old Man took no interest at all. He was by nature reserved, and when one is aged and feeble one's reserve is doubly strong. Besides, so ancient a sea-captain must have witnessed scores of things much more stirring in the far-off days of his unremembered youth.

34

The Bread of Discontent

Mary De Morgan

Once there was a baker who had a very bad, violent temper, and whenever a batch of bread was spoiled he flew into such a rage, that his wife and daughters dared not go near him. One day it happened that all his bread was burnt, and on this he stamped and raved with anger. He threw the loaves all about the floor, when one, burnt blacker than the rest, broke in half, and out of it crept a tiny thin black man, no thicker than an eel, with long arms and legs.

"What are you making all this fuss about, Master Baker?" said he. "If you will give me a home in your oven I will see to the baking of your bread, and will answer for it that you shall never have so much as a loaf spoiled."

"And pray what sort of bread would it be, if you were in the oven, and helped to bake it?" said the baker; " I think my customers might not like to eat it."

"On the contrary," said the imp, "they would like it exceedingly. It is true that it would make them rather unhappy, but that will not hurt you, as you need not eat it yourself."

"Why should it make them unhappy?" said the baker. "If it is good bread it won't do any one harm, and if it is bad they won't buy it."

"It will taste very good," replied the imp, "but it will make all who eat it discontented, and they will think themselves very unfortunate whether they are so or no; but this will not do you any harm, and I promise you that you shall sell as much as you wish."

"Agreed!" said the baker. So the little imp crept into the oven and curled himself into the darkness behind, and the baker saw no more of him.

But next day he made a great batch of bread, and though he took no heed of the time when he put it in, and drew it out, just as he wanted it, it was done quite right—neither too dark nor too light—and the baker was in high good humour.

The first person who tasted the bread was the chief justice. He came down to breakfast in high spirits, for he had just heard that an old aunt was dead, and had left him a great deal of money. So he kissed his wife and chucked his daughters under the chin, and told them that he had good news for them. His old aunt had left him twenty thousand pounds in her will. On this his wife clapped her hands for joy, and his daughters ran to him and kissed him, and begged him to let them have some of it. So they all sat down to breakfast in great glee, but no sooner had the justice tasted the bread than his face fell.

"This is excellent bread," he said, taking a large slice; "I wish everything else were as good;" and he heaved a deep sigh.

"Why?" cried his wife, who had not yet begun to eat. "This morning, I am sure, there is nothing for you to complain of."

"Nay!" said the mayor; "it is very nice to have twenty thousand pounds, but think how much nicer it would have been if it had been thirty. How much more one could have done with that! Or even if it had been twenty-five thousand pounds, or even twenty-one. Twenty-one thousand pounds is a very nice sum of money, but twenty thousand pounds is no good at all. I am not sure that it would not be better not to have had any."

"Nonsense!" cried his wife, who was now eating her breakfast also; "you are very wicked to be so discontented; but one thing I do say. It would have been much nicer if we had had it when we were young and better able to enjoy it. Money is very little use to people at our time of life. It would have been really nice if we had had it fifteen years ago. As it is, I can't say I care much for it, and it makes me sad to think we did not get it before."

"Nay," cried the daughters; "in that case how much better it would have been for us to have it instead of you; we are young, and able to enjoy ourselves, and we could have given you a little of it if you'd liked, but we could have been very happy with the rest; as it is, it is no pleasure to us."

So they fell to quarrelling about the money, and by the time breakfast was done, they all had tears in their eyes, and felt discontented and unhappy.

The next person to eat the bread was the village doctor. All night long he had been sitting up with a man who had broken his leg, and he had feared lest he should die, but as morning came he saw he would live, so he returned home to his wife in very good spirits, although he was sadly tired. The wife had already had her breakfast, but she had made all ready for her husband, with a loaf of the baker's new bread.

"See, dear husband," she said, "here is your breakfast, and some nice bread quite new, because I know you like it. How glad we ought to be, that this poor man is likely to live."

"Yes, indeed," said the doctor; "being up all night is tiring work, but I don't grudge it when I know that it does some good," and then he began to eat. "I am not sure, after all, that I have done such a good thing in curing this man. It is true that his broken leg hurt him very much, but perhaps when he is well again, he may break his back, and that would be much worse. Perhaps I had better have left him to die. I daresay when he is quite well, all kinds of misfortunes will befall him; I had much better have let him alone."

"Why," cried his wife in surprise, "what are you saying, husband? Are you not a doctor, and is it not your business to cure people? And when you succeed ought you not to be glad?"

"I wish I were not a doctor," said the husband, sighing. "It would be much better if there were no doctors at all;" and he sat and lamented, and nothing his wife could say, could cheer him.

In a pretty little cottage near the doctor's house lived a young couple, who were newly married, and were as happy as the day was long. Their cottage was covered with roses, and filled with pretty things, and they had everything their hearts could desire. This morning they both came down smiling and happy, and the young wife kissed her husband, and sang for joy. So they sat down to breakfast, chattering like two birds in a nest; but no sooner had the husband tasted the bread than his face fell, and he was silent for a time; then he said,

"It is a very terrible thing to think how happy we are, for it cannot last. Something melancholy is sure to happen to us, and till it comes we shall live in dread of it; for we know happiness never lasts, and this is a thought that makes me very sad."

The wife had now also taken some bread.

"What is this you are saying?" she said. "How can you think such dreadful things? I do not like you when you talk like that; and I think it is very hard for me to be married to a man who wants to be unhappy."

"The best thing we can hope for," said the husband, sighing, "is for some great misfortune to befall us; then we should be all right, for we should know then, that we knew the worst that could come. As it is we shall live in suspense all our days."

"Now," cried his wife, "I am indeed unfortunate. What could be worse than to have a husband who does not like being happy? I wish I had married some one else; or indeed had no husband at all."

So both began to grumble, and at last to quarrel, and finally both were crying with anger.

Not far out of the village was a large pleasant farmhouse, standing amongst fields, and the farmer was a hale, bright man, with a good wife and pretty children. He was very busy just now getting in the corn, for it was autumn, and he stood among his men, directing them as they worked in the fields. He had not had time to have a proper breakfast before going to work, but his wife sent some out to him with some of the baker's new bread, and he sat down under a tree to eat it. As he did so he looked up at the farmhouse, and thought, with pride, that it was the largest farm in all the country round, and that it had belonged to his father, and his grandfather, and his great-grandfather, before him.

"'Tis a fine old house, for sure," thought he, as he took a large piece of bread, "'Tis so well built and strong;" but no sooner had he swallowed a mouthful than his thoughts changed.

"What should I do if it were to fall down and crush me some day," he said to himself. "After all, 'tis only built of brick, and might tumble any day. How much stronger it would have been if it had been built of stone. Then it would not have been nearly so likely to give way. Really when my great-grandfather built it he should have thought of this. How selfish all men are;" and he became quite unhappy lest his house should fall, and lamented while he ate.

In the kitchen the farmer's wife was very busy cooking and cleaning, and scarcely stopped to eat till near mid-day. Then she took up a piece of bread and cheese, and leant against the window as she ate it, that she might watch for her eldest girl and boy, Janey and Jimmy, who would now be returning from school.

"Our baker really bakes very decent bread," said she; "'tis almost as good as my own;" and she went on eating till she saw her two children coming through the fields together.

"Here they come," said she; "How bonny they look. Really I ought to be very proud of them. I don't know which is the prettier, Janey or Jimmy, but 'tis a pity, for sure, that Janey is the eldest. It would be much better if Jimmy were older than she. 'Tis a bad thing for the sister to be older than the brother. Now, if he were her age, and she were his, that would be really nice, for then he could take care of her and see after her; but, as it is, she will try to direct him, and boys never like to obey their sisters; I really almost think I had better not have had any children at all," and the tears filled her eyes, and when her girl and boy ran in to her, her face was very sad, and she seemed to be scarcely glad to see them.

So things went on all over the village. Each one as he tasted the bread grew discontented and angry, till at last all the people went about grumbling and complaining, or else shedding tears outright. Only the baker himself was cheerful and merry, and sang as he kneaded his dough, and sold it to his customers with a light heart, for his trade had never been so good. Every atom of bread he made was sold at once, so he cared not one whit for the trouble of the other people, and laughed to himself when he heard them complaining, and thought of the words of the dark little elf.

One day as he stood kneading at the door and whistling to himself, the doctor walked past and looked angrily at him.

"What on earth are you making that whistling for?" he asked. "I declare one would think that you were as happy as a man could be."

"And so I am," said the baker, "And so I should think were you too, for you have nothing to trouble you."

"Nothing to trouble me, forsooth!" cried the doctor in a rage. "How dare you insult me in this way? I tell you what it is, my fine fellow, I think you are very impertinent, and if I have any more of your impudence I will take my stick and thrash you soundly. It really is not to be borne, that one man should be allowed to tell another that he has nothing to complain of."

"Nay, you can have as much to complain of as you like, so long as I have not," cried the baker, and he laughed loudly. This only made the doctor angrier still, and he was just going to seize the baker when up came the farmer.

"Was there ever such a village as this?" he cried. "It is not fit for any one to live in, there is always such fighting and quarrelling going on. What is the matter here?"

"Matter enough," cried the doctor. "Here is a fellow dares to tell me I have nothing to complain of, nor he either."

"This is monstrous!" said the farmer; "he deserves to be hung. How dares he say such a thing on such a wretched day as this, with such a blue sky and such a bright sun?"

"Why, Master Farmer," cried the baker, "yesterday you grumbled because it was raining, and now you grumble because it is fine."

"And I tell you that it is enough to make one grumble," said the farmer. "It should have been fair yesterday, and should have rained to-day. You ought to be ashamed of such talk, Master Baker, and I think it would serve you justly right if we took you before the Justice and let us see what he thinks of your conduct."

"Nay!" cried the baker, beginning to be frightened, "what have I done that I am to be taken before the Justice?"

"What have you done, indeed!" said the doctor. "We will see if the Justice cannot find that out pretty quickly." So they seized the baker and dragged him away in spite of himself, and as they pulled him through the village the people thronged about them, and followed till there was quite a large crowd.

The Justice sat at his door smoking a pipe, with tears in his eyes.

"Now what is all this uproar for?" cried he. "Am I never to be left in peace? How hard is the life of a Justice!" but he got up and came out on the steps to meet them.

"See here," cried the doctor; "here is a man who says he has nothing to complain of, and we have brought him to you, to know if he is to be punished, or to be allowed to go on talking like this."

"Certainly not," cried the Justice, "or we shall soon have the whole village in an uproar. Let him be taken to the market-place, and I will order that he be publicly flogged by the soldiers."

At this the poor baker burst out crying, and entreated to be let off, saying that now indeed he had plenty to complain of, but at this the justice was angrier still. "Then," said he, "you certainly deserve to be flogged for having told an untruth before, when you said you had not. Take him away, and do as I bid."

So they dragged the baker off to the market-place, and made a ring round him, so that he could not escape, and then there came down two or three soldiers with ropes in their hands, and they seized him, and began to beat him before all the crowd.

But by this time all the people were so enraged against him, that a number of them cried, "Let us go to his house and pull it down." So off they ran to the baker's house, and broke the windows and knocked about the furniture, and then some of them fell on the oven, and wrenched off the door, and others seized the pokers and tongs, and smashed in its sides, and in the hurry and scuffle, the little dark man crept out of the oven and scuttled away unseen by any one. But no sooner had he gone than a great change came across the people.

The soldiers on the green stopped beating the baker, and looked at each other aghast, and the Justice called out,

"Stop! What is all this uproar about? And what has this man done that you are beating him without my orders?" and the people in the crowd whispered to each other; "It is true,—what has he done?" and they slunk away, looking ashamed.

The Justice also at first looked somewhat ashamed of himself, but he drew himself up, and looking very important, said,

"There, my man, you are forgiven for this once, and now go your way, and see that you behave better in future;" and then he walked away with much dignity.

So the baker was left alone in the market-place, and he cried for rage and pain.

"This all comes of the oven imp," cried he, as he limped home. "Directly I get home I will drive him out of my oven, and away from my house. Better to have a hundred batches of bread spoiled than to be flogged for saying one is happy." But when he reached his house the little dark man was nowhere to be found; there was nought but the broken oven with its sides battered in.

The baker mended the oven, and from that time forth his bread was just like other people's; but for all that he had learnt to be quite contented, for now he knew that there were worse things than having his loaves burnt black, and he was only too well pleased to take his chance with other people, without the help of fairy folk. As for the little black imp, he was never heard of more, and the people in the village soon recovered their good humour, and were just as happy and contented as they had been before they tasted the bread of discontent.

35

The Boarded Window

Ambrose Bierce

In 1830, only a few miles away from what is now the great city of Cincinnati, lay an immense and almost unbroken forest. The whole region was sparsely settled by people of the frontier—restless souls who no sooner had hewn fairly habitable homes out of the wilderness and attained to that degree of prosperity which to-day we should call indigence than impelled by some mysterious impulse of their nature they abandoned all and pushed farther westward, to encounter new perils and privations in the effort to regain the meagre comforts which they had voluntarily renounced. Many of them had already forsaken that region for the remoter settlements, but among those remaining was one who had been of those first arriving. He lived alone in a house of logs surrounded on all sides by the great forest, of whose gloom and silence he seemed a part, for no one had ever known him to smile nor speak a needless word. His simple wants were supplied by the sale or barter of skins of wild animals in the river town, for not a thing did he grow upon the land which, if needful, he might have claimed by right of undisturbed possession. There were evidences of "improvement"—a few acres of ground immediately about the house had once been cleared of its trees, the decayed stumps of which were half concealed by the new growth that had been suffered to repair the ravage wrought by the ax. Apparently the man's zeal for agriculture had burned with a failing flame, expiring in penitential ashes.

The little log house, with its chimney of sticks, its roof of warping clapboards weighted with traversing poles and its "chinking" of clay, had a single door and, directly opposite, a window. The latter, however, was boarded up—nobody could remember a time when it was not. And none knew why it was so closed; certainly not because of the occupant's dislike of light and air, for on those rare occasions when a hunter had passed that lonely spot the recluse had commonly been seen sunning himself on his doorstep if heaven had provided sunshine for his need. I fancy there are few persons living to-day who ever knew the secret of that window, but I am one, as you shall see.

The man's name was said to be Murlock. He was apparently seventy years old, actually about fifty. Something besides years had had a hand in his aging. His hair and long, full beard were white, his gray, lustreless eyes sunken, his face singularly seamed with wrinkles which appeared to belong to two intersecting systems. In figure he was tall and spare, with a stoop of the shoulders—a burden bearer. I never saw him; these particulars I learned from my grandfather, from whom also I got the man's story when I was a lad. He had known him when living near by in that early day.

One day Murlock was found in his cabin, dead. It was not a time and place for coroners and newspapers, and I suppose it was agreed that he had died from natural causes or I should have been told, and should remember. I know only that with what was probably a sense of the fitness of things the body was buried near the cabin, alongside the grave of his wife, who had preceded him by so many years that local tradition had retained hardly a hint of her existence. That closes the final chapter of this true story—excepting, indeed, the circumstance that many years afterward, in company with an equally intrepid spirit, I penetrated to the place and ventured near enough to the ruined cabin to throw a stone against it, and ran away to avoid the ghost which every well-informed boy thereabout knew haunted the spot. But there is an earlier chapter—that supplied by my grandfather.

When Murlock built his cabin and began laying sturdily about with his ax to hew out a farm—the rifle, meanwhile, his means of support—he was young, strong and full of hope. In that eastern country whence he came he had married, as was the fashion, a young woman in all ways worthy of his honest devotion, who shared the dangers and privations of his lot with a willing spirit and light heart. There is no known record of her name; of her charms of mind and person tradition is silent and the doubter is at liberty to entertain his doubt; but God forbid that I should share it! Of their affection and happiness there is abundant assurance in every added day of the man's widowed life; for what but the magnetism of a blessed memory could have chained that venturesome spirit to a lot like that?

One day Murlock returned from gunning in a distant part of the forest to find his wife prostrate with fever, and delirious. There was no physician within miles, no neighbor; nor was she in a condition to be left, to summon help. So he set about the task of nursing her back to health, but at the end of the third day she fell into unconsciousness and so passed away, apparently, with never a gleam of returning reason.

From what we know of a nature like his we may venture to sketch in some of the details of the outline picture drawn by my grandfather. When convinced that she was dead, Murlock had sense enough to remember that the dead must be prepared for burial. In performance of this sacred duty he blundered now and again, did certain things incorrectly, and others which he did correctly were done over and over. His occasional failures to accomplish some simple and ordinary act filled him with astonishment, like that of a drunken man who wonders at the suspension of familiar natural laws. He was surprised, too, that he did not weep—surprised and a little ashamed; surely it is unkind not to weep for the dead. "To-morrow," he said aloud, "I shall have to make the coffin and dig the grave; and then I shall miss her, when she is no longer in sight; but now—she is dead, of course, but it is all right—it must be all right, somehow. Things cannot be so bad as they seem."

He stood over the body in the fading light, adjusting the hair and putting the finishing touches to the simple toilet, doing all mechanically, with soulless care. And still through his consciousness ran an undersense of conviction that all was right—that he should have her again as before, and everything explained. He had had no experience in grief; his capacity had not been enlarged by use. His heart could not contain it all, nor his imagination rightly conceive it. He did not know he was so hard struck; *that* knowledge would come later, and never go. Grief is an artist of powers as various as the instruments upon which he plays his dirges for the dead, evoking from some the sharpest, shrillest notes, from others the low, grave chords that throb recurrent like the slow beating of a distant drum. Some natures it startles; some it stupefies. To one it comes like the stroke of an arrow, stinging all the sensibilities to a keener life; to another as the blow of a bludgeon, which in crushing benumbs. We may conceive Murlock to have been that way affected, for (and here we are upon surer ground than that of conjecture) no sooner had he finished his pious work than, sinking into a chair by the side of the table upon which the body lay, and noting how white the profile showed in the deepening gloom, he laid his arms upon the table's edge, and dropped his face into them, tearless yet and unutterably weary. At that moment came in through the open window a long, wailing sound like the cry of a lost child in the far deeps of the darkening wood! But the man did not move. Again, and nearer than before, sounded that unearthly cry upon his failing sense. Perhaps it was a wild beast; perhaps it was a dream. For Murlock was asleep.

Some hours later, as it afterward appeared, this unfaithful watcher awoke and lifting his head from his arms intently listened—he knew not why. There in the black darkness by the side of the dead, recalling all without a shock, he strained his eyes to see—he knew not what. His senses were all alert, his breath was suspended, his blood had stilled its tides as if to assist the silence. Who—what had waked him, and where was it?

Suddenly the table shook beneath his arms, and at the same moment he heard, or fancied that he heard, a light, soft step—another—sounds as of bare feet upon the floor!

He was terrified beyond the power to cry out or move. Perforce he waited—waited there in the darkness through seeming centuries of such dread as one may know, yet live to tell. He tried vainly to speak the dead woman's name, vainly to stretch forth his hand across the table to learn if she were there. His throat was powerless, his arms and hands were like lead. Then occurred something most frightful. Some heavy body seemed hurled against the table with an impetus that pushed it against his breast so sharply as nearly to overthrow him, and at the same instant he heard and felt the fall of something upon the floor with so violent a thump that the whole house was shaken by the impact. A scuffling ensued, and a confusion of sounds impossible to describe. Murlock had risen to his feet. Fear had by excess forfeited control of his faculties. He flung his hands upon the table. Nothing was there!

There is a point at which terror may turn to madness; and madness incites to action. With no definite intent, from no motive but the wayward impulse of a madman, Murlock sprang to the wall, with a little groping seized his loaded rifle, and without aim discharged it. By the flash which lit up the room with a vivid illumination, he saw an enormous panther dragging the dead woman toward the window, its teeth fixed in her throat! Then there were darkness blacker than before, and silence; and when he returned to consciousness the sun was high and the wood vocal with songs of birds.

The body lay near the window, where the beast had left it when frightened away by the flash and report of the rifle. The clothing was deranged, the long hair in disorder, the limbs lay anyhow. From the throat, dreadfully lacerated, had issued a pool of blood not yet entirely coagulated. The ribbon with which he had bound the wrists was broken; the hands were tightly clenched. Between the teeth was a fragment of the animal's ear.

36

The Verdict

Edith Wharton

I had always thought Jack Gisburn rather a cheap genius—though a good fellow enough—so it was no great surprise to me to hear that, in the height of his glory, he had dropped his painting, married a rich widow, and established himself in a villa on the Riviera. (Though I rather thought it would have been Rome or Florence.)

"The height of his glory"—that was what the women called it. I can hear Mrs. Gideon Thwing—his last Chicago sitter—deploring his unaccountable abdication. "Of course it's going to send the value of my picture 'way up; but I don't think of that, Mr. Rickham—the loss to Arrt is all I think of." The word, on Mrs. Thwing's lips, multiplied its *rs* as though they were reflected in an endless vista of mirrors. And it was not only the Mrs. Thwings who mourned. Had not the exquisite Hermia Croft, at the last Grafton Gallery show, stopped me before Gisburn's "Moon-dancers" to say, with tears in her eyes: "We shall not look upon its like again"?

Well!—even through the prism of Hermia's tears I felt able to face the fact with equanimity. Poor Jack Gisburn! The women had made him—it was fitting that they should mourn him. Among his own sex fewer regrets were heard, and in his own trade hardly a murmur. Professional jealousy? Perhaps. If it were, the honour of the craft was vindicated by little Claude Nutley, who, in all good faith, brought out in the Burlington a very handsome "obituary" on Jack—one of those showy articles stocked with random technicalities that I have heard (I won't say by whom) compared to Gisburn's painting. And so—his resolve being apparently irrevocable—the discussion gradually died out, and, as Mrs. Thwing had predicted, the price of "Gisburns" went up.

It was not till three years later that, in the course of a few weeks' idling on the Riviera, it suddenly occurred to me to wonder why Gisburn had given up his painting. On reflection, it really was a tempting problem.

To accuse his wife would have been too easy—his fair sitters had been denied the solace of saying that Mrs. Gisburn had "dragged him down." For Mrs. Gisburn—as such—had not existed till nearly a year after Jack's resolve had been taken. It might be that he had married her—since he liked his ease—because he didn't want to go on painting; but it would have been hard to prove that he had given up his painting because he had married her.

Of course, if she had not dragged him down, she had equally, as Miss Croft contended, failed to "lift him up"—she had not led him back to the easel. To put the brush into his hand again—what a vocation for a wife! But Mrs. Gisburn appeared to have disdained it—and I felt it might be interesting to find out why.

The desultory life of the Riviera lends itself to such purely academic speculations; and having, on my way to Monte Carlo, caught a glimpse of Jack's balustraded terraces between the pines, I had myself borne thither the next day.

I found the couple at tea beneath their palm-trees; and Mrs. Gisburn's welcome was so genial that, in the ensuing weeks, I claimed it frequently. It was not that my hostess was "interesting": on that point I could have given Miss Croft the fullest reassurance. It was just because she was *not* interesting—if I may be pardoned the bull—that I found her so. For Jack, all his life, had been surrounded by interesting women: they had fostered his art, it had been reared in the hot-house of their adulation. And it was therefore instructive to note what effect the "deadening atmosphere of mediocrity" (I quote Miss Croft) was having on him.

I have mentioned that Mrs. Gisburn was rich; and it was immediately perceptible that her husband was extracting from this circumstance a delicate but substantial satisfaction. It is, as a rule, the people who scorn money who get most out of it; and Jack's elegant disdain of his wife's big balance enabled him, with an appearance of perfect good-breeding, to transmute it into objects of art and luxury. To the latter, I must add, he remained relatively indifferent; but he was buying Renaissance bronzes and eighteenth-century pictures with a discrimination that bespoke the amplest resources.

"Money's only excuse is to put beauty into circulation," was one of the axioms he laid down across the Sevres and silver of an exquisitely appointed luncheon-table, when, on a later day, I had again run over from Monte Carlo; and Mrs. Gisburn, beaming on him, added for my enlightenment: "Jack is so morbidly sensitive to every form of beauty."

Poor Jack! It had always been his fate to have women say such things of him: the fact should be set down in extenuation. What struck me now was that, for the first time, he resented the tone. I had seen him, so often, basking under similar tributes—was it the conjugal note that robbed them of their savour? No—for, oddly enough, it became apparent that he was fond of Mrs. Gisburn—fond enough not to see her absurdity. It was his own absurdity he seemed to be wincing under—his own attitude as an object for garlands and incense.

"My dear, since I've chucked painting people don't say that stuff about me—they say it about Victor Grindle," was his only protest, as he rose from the table and strolled out onto the sunlit terrace.

I glanced after him, struck by his last word. Victor Grindle was, in fact, becoming the man of the moment—as Jack himself, one might put it, had been the man of the hour. The younger artist was said to have formed himself at my friend's feet, and I wondered if a tinge of jealousy underlay the latter's mysterious abdication. But no—for it was not till after that event that the rose Dubarry drawing-rooms had begun to display their "Grindles."

I turned to Mrs. Gisburn, who had lingered to give a lump of sugar to her spaniel in the dining-room.

"Why *has* he chucked painting?" I asked abruptly.

She raised her eyebrows with a hint of good-humoured surprise.

"Oh, he doesn't *have* to now, you know; and I want him to enjoy himself," she said quite simply.

I looked about the spacious white-panelled room, with its *famille-verte* vases repeating the tones of the pale damask curtains, and its eighteenth-century pastels in delicate faded frames.

"Has he chucked his pictures too? I haven't seen a single one in the house."

A slight shade of constraint crossed Mrs. Gisburn's open countenance. "It's his ridiculous modesty, you know. He says they're not fit to have about; he's sent them all away except one—my portrait—and that I have to keep upstairs."

His ridiculous modesty—Jack's modesty about his pictures? My curiosity was growing like the bean-stalk. I said persuasively to my hostess: "I must really see your portrait, you know."

She glanced out almost timorously at the terrace where her husband, lounging in a hooded chair, had lit a cigar and drawn the Russian deerhound's head between his knees.

"Well, come while he's not looking," she said, with a laugh that tried to hide her nervousness; and I followed her between the marble Emperors of the hall, and up the wide stairs with terracotta nymphs poised among flowers at each landing.

In the dimmest corner of her boudoir, amid a profusion of delicate and distinguished objects, hung one of the familiar oval canvases, in the inevitable garlanded frame. The mere outline of the frame called up all Gisburn's past!

Mrs. Gisburn drew back the window-curtains, moved aside a *jardiniere* full of pink azaleas, pushed an arm-chair away, and said: "If you stand here you can just manage to see it. I had it over the mantel-piece, but he wouldn't let it stay."

Yes—I could just manage to see it—the first portrait of Jack's I had ever had to strain my eyes over! Usually they had the place of honour—say the central panel in a pale yellow or rose Dubarry drawing-room, or a monumental easel placed so that it took the light through curtains of old Venetian point. The more modest place became the picture better; yet, as my eyes grew accustomed to the half-light, all the characteristic qualities came out—all the hesitations disguised as audacities, the tricks of prestidigitation by which, with such consummate skill, he managed to divert attention from the real business of the picture to some pretty irrelevance of detail. Mrs. Gisburn, presenting a neutral surface to work on—forming, as it were, so inevitably the background of her own picture—had lent herself in an unusual degree to the display of this false virtuosity. The picture was one of Jack's "strongest," as his admirers would have put it—it represented, on his part, a swelling of muscles, a congesting of veins, a balancing, straddling and straining, that reminded one of the circus-clown's ironic efforts to lift a feather. It met, in short, at every point the demand of lovely woman to be painted "strongly" because she was tired of being painted "sweetly"—and yet not to lose an atom of the sweetness.

"It's the last he painted, you know," Mrs. Gisburn said with pardonable pride. "The last but one," she corrected herself—"but the other doesn't count, because he destroyed it."

"Destroyed it?" I was about to follow up this clue when I heard a footstep and saw Jack himself on the threshold.

As he stood there, his hands in the pockets of his velveteen coat, the thin brown waves of hair pushed back from his white forehead, his lean sunburnt cheeks furrowed by a smile that lifted the tips of a self-confident moustache, I felt to what a degree he had the same quality as his pictures—the quality of looking cleverer than he was.

His wife glanced at him deprecatingly, but his eyes travelled past her to the portrait.

"Mr. Rickham wanted to see it," she began, as if excusing herself. He shrugged his shoulders, still smiling.

"Oh, Rickham found me out long ago," he said lightly; then, passing his arm through mine: "Come and see the rest of the house."

He showed it to me with a kind of naive suburban pride: the bath-rooms, the speaking-tubes, the dress-closets, the trouser-presses—all the complex simplifications of the millionaire's domestic economy. And whenever my wonder paid the expected tribute he said, throwing out his chest a little: "Yes, I really don't see how people manage to live without that."

Well—it was just the end one might have foreseen for him. Only he was, through it all and in spite of it all—as he had been through, and in spite of, his pictures—so handsome, so charming, so disarming, that one longed to cry out: "Be dissatisfied with your leisure!" as once one had longed to say: "Be dissatisfied with your work!"

But, with the cry on my lips, my diagnosis suffered an unexpected check.

"This is my own lair," he said, leading me into a dark plain room at the end of the florid vista. It was square and brown and leathery: no "effects"; no bric-a-brac, none of the air of posing for reproduction in a picture weekly—above all, no least sign of ever having been used as a studio.

The fact brought home to me the absolute finality of Jack's break with his old life.

"Don't you ever dabble with paint any more?" I asked, still looking about for a trace of such activity.

"Never," he said briefly.

"Or water-colour—or etching?"

His confident eyes grew dim, and his cheeks paled a little under their handsome sunburn.

"Never think of it, my dear fellow—any more than if I'd never touched a brush."

And his tone told me in a flash that he never thought of anything else.

I moved away, instinctively embarrassed by my unexpected discovery; and as I turned, my eye fell on a small picture above the mantel-piece—the only object breaking the plain oak panelling of the room.

"Oh, by Jove!" I said.

It was a sketch of a donkey—an old tired donkey, standing in the rain under a wall.

"By Jove—a Stroud!" I cried.

He was silent; but I felt him close behind me, breathing a little quickly.

"What a wonder! Made with a dozen lines—but on everlasting foundations. You lucky chap, where did you get it?"

He answered slowly: "Mrs. Stroud gave it to me."

"Ah—I didn't know you even knew the Strouds. He was such an inflexible hermit."

"I didn't—till after… She sent for me to paint him when he was dead."

"When he was dead? You?"

I must have let a little too much amazement escape through my surprise, for he answered with a deprecating laugh: "Yes—she's an awful simpleton, you know, Mrs. Stroud. Her only idea was to have him done by a fashionable painter—ah, poor Stroud! She thought it the surest way of proclaiming his greatness—of forcing it on a purblind public. And at the moment I was the fashionable painter."

"Ah, poor Stroud—as you say. Was *that* his history?"

"That was his history. She believed in him, gloried in him—or thought she did. But she couldn't bear not to have all the drawing-rooms with her. She couldn't bear the fact that, on varnishing days, one could always get near enough to see his pictures. Poor woman! She's just a fragment groping for other fragments. Stroud is the only whole I ever knew."

"You ever knew? But you just said—"

Gisburn had a curious smile in his eyes.

"Oh, I knew him, and he knew me—only it happened after he was dead."

I dropped my voice instinctively. "When she sent for you?"

"Yes—quite insensible to the irony. She wanted him vindicated—and by me!"

He laughed again, and threw back his head to look up at the sketch of the donkey. "There were days when I couldn't look at that thing—couldn't face it. But I forced myself to put it here; and now it's cured me—cured me. That's the reason why I don't dabble any more, my dear Rickham; or rather Stroud himself is the reason."

For the first time my idle curiosity about my companion turned into a serious desire to understand him better.

"I wish you'd tell me how it happened," I said.

He stood looking up at the sketch, and twirling between his fingers a cigarette he had forgotten to light. Suddenly he turned toward me.

"I'd rather like to tell you—because I've always suspected you of loathing my work."

I made a deprecating gesture, which he negatived with a goodhumoured shrug.

"Oh, I didn't care a straw when I believed in myself—and now it's an added tie between us!"

He laughed slightly, without bitterness, and pushed one of the deep arm-chairs forward. "There: make yourself comfortable—and here are the cigars you like."

He placed them at my elbow and continued to wander up and down the room, stopping now and then beneath the picture.

"How it happened? I can tell you in five minutes—and it didn't take much longer to happen… I can remember now how surprised and pleased I was when I got Mrs. Stroud's note. Of course, deep down, I had always *felt* there was no one like him—only I had gone with the stream, echoed the usual platitudes about him, till I half got to think he was a failure, one of the kind that are left behind. By Jove, and he *was* left behind-because he had come to stay! The rest of us had to let ourselves be swept along or go under, but he was high above the current—on everlasting foundations, as you say.

"Well, I went off to the house in my most egregious mood—rather moved, Lord forgive me, at the pathos of poor Stroud's career of failure being crowned by the glory of my painting him! Of course I meant to do the picture for nothing—I told Mrs. Stroud so when she began to stammer something about her poverty. I remember getting off a prodigious phrase about the honour being *mine*—oh, I was princely, my dear Rickham! I was posing to myself like one of my own sitters.

"Then I was taken up and left alone with him. I had sent all my traps in advance, and I had only to set up the easel and get to work. He had been dead only twenty-four hours, and he died suddenly, of heart disease, so that there had been no preliminary work of destruction—his face was clear and untouched. I had met him once or twice, years before, and thought him insignificant and dingy. Now I saw that he was superb.

"I was glad at first, with a merely aesthetic satisfaction: glad to have my hand on such a 'subject.' Then his strange lifelikeness began to affect me queerly—as I blocked the head in I felt as if he were watching me do it. The sensation was followed by the thought: if he *were* watching me, what would he say to my way of working? My strokes began to go a little wild—I felt nervous and uncertain.

"Once, when I looked up, I seemed to see a smile behind his close grayish beard—as if he had the secret, and were amusing himself by holding it back from me. That exasperated me still more. The secret? Why, I had a secret worth twenty of his! I dashed at the canvas furiously, and tried some of my bravura tricks. But they failed me, they crumbled. I saw that he wasn't watching the showy bits—I couldn't distract his attention; he just kept his eyes on the hard passages between. Those were the ones I had always shirked, or covered up with some lying paint. And how he saw through my lies!

"I looked up again, and caught sight of that sketch of the donkey hanging on the wall near his bed. His wife told me afterward it was the last thing he had done—just a note taken with a shaking hand, when he was down in Devonshire recovering from a previous heart attack. Just a note! But it tells his whole history. There are years of patient scornful persistence in every line. A man who had swum with the current could never have learned that mighty up-stream stroke…

"I turned back to my work, and went on groping and muddling; then I looked at the donkey again. I saw that, when Stroud laid in the first stroke, he knew just what the end would be. He had possessed his subject, absorbed it, recreated it. When had I done that with any of my things? They hadn't been born of me—I had just adopted them…

"Hang it, Rickham, with that face watching me I couldn't do another stroke. The plain truth was, I didn't know where to put it—I *had never known*. Only, with my sitters and my public, a showy splash of colour covered up the fact—I just threw paint into their faces… Well, paint was the one medium those dead eyes could see through—see straight to the tottering foundations underneath. Don't you know how, in talking a foreign language, even fluently, one says half the time not what one wants to but what one can? Well—that was the way I painted; and as he lay there and watched me, the thing they called my 'technique' collapsed like a house of cards. He didn't sneer, you understand, poor Stroud—he just lay there quietly watching, and on his lips, through the gray beard, I seemed to hear the question: 'Are you sure you know where you're coming out?'

"If I could have painted that face, with that question on it, I should have done a great thing. The next greatest thing was to see that I couldn't—and that grace was given me. But, oh, at that minute, Rickham, was there anything on earth I wouldn't have given to have Stroud alive before me, and to hear him say: 'It's not too late—I'll show you how'?

"It *was* too late—it would have been, even if he'd been alive. I packed up my traps, and went down and told Mrs. Stroud. Of course I didn't tell her *that*—it would have been Greek to her. I simply said I couldn't paint him, that I was too moved. She rather liked the idea—she's so romantic! It was that that made her give me the donkey. But she was terribly upset at not getting the portrait—she did so want him 'done' by some one showy! At first I was afraid she wouldn't let me off—and at my wits' end I suggested Grindle. Yes, it was I who started Grindle: I told Mrs. Stroud he was the 'coming' man, and she told somebody else, and so it got to be true… And he painted Stroud without wincing; and she hung the picture among her husband's things… "

He flung himself down in the arm-chair near mine, laid back his head, and clasping his arms beneath it, looked up at the picture above the chimney-piece.

"I like to fancy that Stroud himself would have given it to me, if he'd been able to say what he thought that day."

And, in answer to a question I put half-mechanically—"Begin again?" he flashed out. "When the one thing that brings me anywhere near him is that I knew enough to leave off?"

He stood up and laid his hand on my shoulder with a laugh. "Only the irony of it is that I am still painting—since Grindle's doing it for me! The Strouds stand alone, and happen once—but there's no exterminating our kind of art."

37

The Fulness of Life

Edith Wharton

I

For hours she had lain in a kind of gentle torpor, not unlike that sweet lassitude which masters one in the hush of a midsummer noon, when the heat seems to have silenced the very birds and insects, and, lying sunk in the tasselled meadow-grasses, one looks up through a level roofing of maple-leaves at the vast shadowless, and unsuggestive blue. Now and then, at ever-lengthening intervals, a flash of pain darted through her, like the ripple of sheet-lightning across such a midsummer sky; but it was too transitory to shake her stupor, that calm, delicious, bottomless stupor into which she felt herself sinking more and more deeply, without a disturbing impulse of resistance, an effort of reattachment to the vanishing edges of consciousness.

The resistance, the effort, had known their hour of violence; but now they were at an end. Through her mind, long harried by grotesque visions, fragmentary images of the life that she was leaving, tormenting lines of verse, obstinate presentments of pictures once beheld, indistinct impressions of rivers, towers, and cupolas, gathered in the length of journeys half forgotten—through her mind there now only moved a few primal sensations of colorless well-being; a vague satisfaction in the thought that she had swallowed her noxious last draught of medicine... and that she should never again hear the creaking of her husband's boots—those horrible boots—and that no one would come to bother her about the next day's dinner...or the butcher's book...

At last even these dim sensations spent themselves in the thickening obscurity which enveloped her; a dusk now filled with pale geometric roses, circling softly, interminably before her, now darkened to a uniform blue-blackness, the hue of a summer night without stars. And into this darkness she felt herself sinking, sinking, with the gentle sense of security of one upheld from beneath. Like a tepid tide it rose around her, gliding ever higher and higher, folding in its velvety embrace her relaxed and tired body, now submerging her breast and shoulders, now creeping gradually, with soft inexorableness, over her throat to her chin, to her ears, to her mouth... Ah, now it was rising too high; the impulse to struggle was renewed;... her mouth was full;... she was choking... Help!

"It is all over," said the nurse, drawing down the eyelids with official composure.

The clock struck three. They remembered it afterward. Someone opened the window and let in a blast of that strange, neutral air which walks the earth between darkness and dawn; someone else led the husband into another room. He walked vaguely, like a blind man, on his creaking boots.

II

She stood, as it seemed, on a threshold, yet no tangible gateway was in front of her. Only a wide vista of light, mild yet penetrating as the gathered glimmer of innumerable stars, expanded gradually before her eyes, in blissful contrast to the cavernous darkness from which she had of late emerged.

She stepped forward, not frightened, but hesitating, and as her eyes began to grow more familiar with the melting depths of light about her, she distinguished the outlines of a landscape, at first swimming in the opaline uncertainty of Shelley's vaporous creations, then gradually resolved into distincter shape—the vast unrolling of a sunlit plain, aerial forms of mountains, and presently the silver crescent of a river in the valley, and a blue stencilling of trees along its curve—something suggestive in its ineffable hue of an azure background of Leonardo's, strange, enchanting, mysterious, leading on the eye and the imagination into regions of fabulous delight. As she gazed, her heart beat with a soft and rapturous surprise; so exquisite a promise she read in the summons of that hyaline distance.

"And so death is not the end after all," in sheer gladness she heard herself exclaiming aloud. "I always knew that it couldn't be. I believed in Darwin, of course. I do still; but then Darwin himself said that he wasn't sure about the soul—at least, I think he did—and Wallace was a spiritualist; and then there was St. George Mivart—"

Her gaze lost itself in the ethereal remoteness of the mountains.

"How beautiful! How satisfying!" she murmured. "Perhaps now I shall really know what it is to live."

As she spoke she felt a sudden thickening of her heart-beats, and looking up she was aware that before her stood the Spirit of Life.

"Have you never really known what it is to live?" the Spirit of Life asked her.

"I have never known," she replied, "that fulness of life which we all feel ourselves capable of knowing; though my life has not been without scattered hints of it, like the scent of earth which comes to one sometimes far out at sea."

"And what do you call the fulness of life?" the Spirit asked again.

"Oh, I can't tell you, if you don't know," she said, almost reproachfully. "Many words are supposed to define it—love and sympathy are those in commonest use, but I am not even sure that they are the right ones, and so few people really know what they mean."

"You were married," said the Spirit, "yet you did not find the fulness of life in your marriage?"

"Oh, dear, no," she replied, with an indulgent scorn, "my marriage was a very incomplete affair."

"And yet you were fond of your husband?"

"You have hit upon the exact word; I was fond of him, yes, just as I was fond of my grandmother, and the house that I was born in, and my old nurse. Oh, I was fond of him, and we were counted a very happy couple. But I have sometimes thought that a woman's nature is like a great house full of rooms: there is the hall, through which everyone passes in going in and out; the drawing-room, where one receives formal visits; the sitting-room, where the members of the family come and go as they list; but beyond that, far beyond, are other rooms, the handles of whose doors perhaps are never turned; no one knows the way to them, no one knows whither they lead; and in the innermost room, the holy of holies, the soul sits alone and waits for a footstep that never comes."

"And your husband," asked the Spirit, after a pause, "never got beyond the family sitting-room?"

"Never," she returned, impatiently; "and the worst of it was that he was quite content to remain there. He thought it perfectly beautiful, and sometimes, when he was admiring its commonplace furniture, insignificant as the chairs and tables of a hotel parlor, I felt like crying out to him: 'Fool, will you never guess that close at hand are rooms full of treasures and wonders, such as the eye of man hath not seen, rooms that no step has crossed, but that might be yours to live in, could you but find the handle of the door?'"

"Then," the Spirit continued, "those moments of which you lately spoke, which seemed to come to you like scattered hints of the fulness of life, were not shared with your husband?"

"Oh, no—never. He was different. His boots creaked, and he always slammed the door when he went out, and he never read anything but railway novels and the sporting advertisements in the papers—and—and, in short, we never understood each other in the least."

"To what influence, then, did you owe those exquisite sensations?"

"I can hardly tell. Sometimes to the perfume of a flower; sometimes to a verse of Dante or of Shakespeare; sometimes to a picture or a sunset, or to one of those calm days at sea, when one seems to be lying in the hollow of a blue pearl; sometimes, but rarely, to a word spoken by someone who chanced to give utterance, at the right moment, to what I felt but could not express."

"Someone whom you loved?" asked the Spirit.

"I never loved anyone, in that way," she said, rather sadly, "nor was I thinking of any one person when I spoke, but of two or three who, by touching for an instant upon a certain chord of my being, had called forth a single note of that strange melody which seemed sleeping in my soul. It has seldom happened, however, that I have owed such feelings to people; and no one ever gave me a moment of such happiness as it was my lot to feel one evening in the Church of Or San Michele, in Florence."

"Tell me about it," said the Spirit.

"It was near sunset on a rainy spring afternoon in Easter week. The clouds had vanished, dispersed by a sudden wind, and as we entered the church the fiery panes of the high windows shone out like lamps through the dusk. A priest was at the high altar, his white cope a livid spot in the incense-laden obscurity, the light of the candles flickering up and down like fireflies about his head; a few people knelt near by. We stole behind them and sat down on a bench close to the tabernacle of Orcagna.

"Strange to say, though Florence was not new to me, I had never been in the church before; and in that magical light I saw for the first time the inlaid steps, the fluted columns, the sculptured bas-reliefs and canopy of the marvellous shrine. The marble, worn and mellowed by the subtle hand of time, took on an unspeakable rosy hue, suggestive in some remote way of the honeycolored columns of the Parthenon, but more mystic, more complex, a color not born of the sun's inveterate kiss, but made up of cryptal twilight, and the flame of candles upon martyrs' tombs, and gleams of sunset through symbolic panes of chrysoprase and ruby; such a light as illumines the missals in the library of Siena, or burns like a hidden fire through the Madonna of Gian Bellini in the Church of the Redeemer, at Venice; the light of the Middle Ages, richer, more solemn, more significant than the limpid sunshine of Greece.

"The church was silent, but for the wail of the priest and the occasional scraping of a chair against the floor, and as I sat there, bathed in that light, absorbed in rapt contemplation of the marble miracle which rose before me, cunningly wrought as a casket of ivory and enriched with jewel-like incrustations and tarnished gleams of gold, I felt myself borne onward along a mighty current, whose source seemed to be in the very beginning of things, and whose tremendous waters gathered as they went all the mingled streams of human passion and endeavor. Life in all its varied manifestations of beauty and strangeness seemed weaving a rhythmical dance around me as I moved, and wherever the spirit of man had passed I knew that my foot had once been familiar.

"As I gazed the mediaeval bosses of the tabernacle of Orcagna seemed to melt and flow into their primal forms so that the folded lotus of the Nile and the Greek acanthus were braided with the runic knots and fish-tailed monsters of the North, and all the plastic terror and beauty born of man's hand from the Ganges to the Baltic quivered and mingled in Orcagna's apotheosis of Mary. And so the river bore me on, past the alien face of antique civilizations and the familiar wonders of Greece, till I swam upon the fiercely rushing tide of the Middle Ages, with its swirling eddies of passion, its heaven-reflecting pools of poetry and art; I heard the rhythmic blow of the craftsmen's hammers in the goldsmiths' workshops and on the walls of churches, the party-cries of armed factions in the narrow streets, the organ-roll of Dante's verse, the crackle of the fagots around Arnold of Brescia, the twitter of the swallows to which St. Francis preached, the laughter of the ladies listening on the hillside to the quips of the Decameron, while plague-struck Florence howled beneath them—all this and much more I heard, joined in strange unison with voices earlier and more remote, fierce, passionate, or tender, yet subdued to such awful harmony that I thought of the song that the morning stars sang together and felt as though it were sounding in my ears. My heart beat to suffocation, the tears burned my lids, the joy, the mystery of it seemed too intolerable to be borne. I could not understand even then the words of the song; but I knew that if there had been someone at my side who could have heard it with me, we might have found the key to it together.

"I turned to my husband, who was sitting beside me in an attitude of patient dejection, gazing into the bottom of his hat; but at that moment he rose, and stretching his stiffened legs, said, mildly: 'Hadn't we better be going? There doesn't seem to be much to see here, and you know the table d'hote dinner is at half-past six o'clock."

Her recital ended, there was an interval of silence; then the Spirit of Life said: "There is a compensation in store for such needs as you have expressed."

"Oh, then you *do* understand?" she exclaimed. "Tell me what compensation, I entreat you!"

"It is ordained," the Spirit answered, "that every soul which seeks in vain on earth for a kindred soul to whom it can lay bare its inmost being shall find that soul here and be united to it for eternity."

A glad cry broke from her lips. "Ah, shall I find him at last?" she cried, exultant.

"He is here," said the Spirit of Life.

She looked up and saw that a man stood near whose soul (for in that unwonted light she seemed to see his soul more clearly than his face) drew her toward him with an invincible force.

"Are you really he?" she murmured.

"I am he," he answered.

She laid her hand in his and drew him toward the parapet which overhung the valley.

"Shall we go down together," she asked him, "into that marvellous country; shall we see it together, as if with the self-same eyes, and tell each other in the same words all that we think and feel?"

"So," he replied, "have I hoped and dreamed."

"What?" she asked, with rising joy. "Then you, too, have looked for me?"

"All my life."

"How wonderful! And did you never, never find anyone in the other world who understood you?"

"Not wholly—not as you and I understand each other."

"Then you feel it, too? Oh, I am happy," she sighed.

They stood, hand in hand, looking down over the parapet upon the shimmering landscape which stretched forth beneath them into sapphirine space, and the Spirit of Life, who kept watch near the threshold, heard now and then a floating fragment of their talk blown backward like the stray swallows which the wind sometimes separates from their migratory tribe.

"Did you never feel at sunset—"

"Ah, yes; but I never heard anyone else say so. Did you?"

"Do you remember that line in the third canto of the 'Inferno?'"

"Ah, that line—my favorite always. Is it possible—"

"You know the stooping Victory in the frieze of the Nike Apteros?"

"You mean the one who is tying her sandal? Then you have noticed, too, that all Botticelli and Mantegna are dormant in those flying folds of her drapery?"

"After a storm in autumn have you never seen—"

"Yes, it is curious how certain flowers suggest certain painters-the perfume of the incarnation, Leonardo; that of the rose, Titian; the tuberose, Crivelli—"

"I never supposed that anyone else had noticed it."

"Have you never thought—"

"Oh, yes, often and often; but I never dreamed that anyone else had."

"But surely you must have felt—"

"Oh, yes, yes; and you, too—"

"How beautiful! How strange—"

Their voices rose and fell, like the murmur of two fountains answering each other across a garden full of flowers. At length, with a certain tender impatience, he turned to her and said: "Love, why should we linger here? All eternity lies before us. Let us go down into that beautiful country together and make a home for ourselves on some blue hill above the shining river."

As he spoke, the hand she had forgotten in his was suddenly withdrawn, and he felt that a cloud was passing over the radiance of her soul.

"A home," she repeated, slowly, "a home for you and me to live in for all eternity?"

"Why not, love? Am I not the soul that yours has sought?"

"Y-yes—yes, I know—but, don't you see, home would not be like home to me, unless—"

"Unless?" he wonderingly repeated.

She did not answer, but she thought to herself, with an impulse of whimsical inconsistency, "Unless you slammed the door and wore creaking boots."

But he had recovered his hold upon her hand, and by imperceptible degrees was leading her toward the shining steps which descended to the valley.

"Come, O my soul's soul," he passionately implored; "why delay a moment? Surely you feel, as I do, that eternity itself is too short to hold such bliss as ours. It seems to me that I can see our home already. Have I not always seem it in my dreams? It is white, love, is it not, with polished columns, and a sculptured cornice against the blue? Groves of laurel and oleander and thickets of roses surround it; but from the terrace where we walk at sunset, the eye looks out over woodlands and cool meadows where, deep-bowered under ancient boughs, a stream goes delicately toward the river. Indoors our favorite pictures hang upon the walls and the rooms are lined with books. Think, dear, at last we shall have time to read them all. With which shall we begin? Come, help me to choose. Shall it be 'Faust' or the 'Vita Nuova,' the 'Tempest' or 'Les Caprices de Marianne,' or the thirty-first canto of the 'Paradise,' or 'Epipsychidion' or "Lycidas'? Tell me, dear, which one?"

As he spoke he saw the answer trembling joyously upon her lips; but it died in the ensuing silence, and she stood motionless, resisting the persuasion of his hand.

"What is it?" he entreated.

"Wait a moment," she said, with a strange hesitation in her voice.

"Tell me first, are you quite sure of yourself? Is there no one on earth whom you sometimes remember?"

"Not since I have seen you," he replied; for, being a man, he had indeed forgotten.

Still she stood motionless, and he saw that the shadow deepened on her soul.

"Surely, love," he rebuked her, "it was not that which troubled you? For my part I have walked through Lethe. The past has melted like a cloud before the moon. I never lived until I saw you."

She made no answer to his pleadings, but at length, rousing herself with a visible effort, she turned away from him and moved toward the Spirit of Life, who still stood near the threshold.

"I want to ask you a question," she said, in a troubled voice.

"Ask," said the Spirit.

"A little while ago," she began, slowly, "you told me that every soul which has not found a kindred soul on earth is destined to find one here."

"And have you not found one?" asked the Spirit.

"Yes; but will it be so with my husband's soul also?"

"No," answered the Spirit of Life, "for your husband imagined that he had found his soul's mate on earth in you; and for such delusions eternity itself contains no cure."

She gave a little cry. Was it of disappointment or triumph?

"Then—then what will happen to him when he comes here?"

"That I cannot tell you. Some field of activity and happiness he will doubtless find, in due measure to his capacity for being active and happy."

She interrupted, almost angrily: "He will never be happy without me."

"Do not be too sure of that," said the Spirit.

She took no notice of this, and the Spirit continued: "He will not understand you here any better than he did on earth."

"No matter," she said; "I shall be the only sufferer, for he always thought that he understood me."

"His boots will creak just as much as ever—"

"No matter."

"And he will slam the door—"

"Very likely."

"And continue to read railway novels—"

She interposed, impatiently: "Many men do worse than that."

"But you said just now," said the Spirit, "that you did not love him."

"True," she answered, simply; "but don't you understand that I shouldn't feel at home without him? It is all very well for a week or two—but for eternity! After all, I never minded the creaking of his boots, except when my head ached, and I don't suppose it will ache here; and he was always so sorry when he had slammed the door, only he never could remember not to. Besides, no one else would know how to look after him, he is so helpless. His inkstand would never be filled, and he would always be out of stamps and visiting-cards. He would never remember to have his umbrella re-covered, or to ask the price of anything before he bought it. Why, he wouldn't even know what novels to read. I always had to choose the kind he liked, with a murder or a forgery and a successful detective."

She turned abruptly to her kindred soul, who stood listening with a mien of wonder and dismay.

"Don't you see," she said, "that I can't possibly go with you?"

"But what do you intend to do?" asked the Spirit of Life.

"What do I intend to do?" she returned, indignantly. "Why, I mean to wait for my husband, of course. If he had come here first he would have waited for me for years and years; and it would break his heart not to find me here when he comes." She pointed with a contemptuous gesture to the magic vision of hill and vale sloping away to the translucent mountains. "He wouldn't give a fig for all that," she said, "if he didn't find me here."

"But consider," warned the Spirit, "that you are now choosing for eternity. It is a solemn moment."

"Choosing!" she said, with a half-sad smile. "Do you still keep up here that old fiction about choosing? I should have thought that you knew better than that. How can I help myself? He will expect to find me here when he comes, and he would never believe you if you told him that I had gone away with someone else—never, never."

"So be it," said the Spirit. "Here, as on earth, each one must decide for himself."

She turned to her kindred soul and looked at him gently, almost wistfully. "I am sorry," she said. "I should have liked to talk with you again; but you will understand, I know, and I dare say you will find someone else a great deal cleverer—"

And without pausing to hear his answer she waved him a swift farewell and turned back toward the threshold.

"Will my husband come soon?" she asked the Spirit of Life.

"That you are not destined to know," the Spirit replied.

"No matter," she said, cheerfully; "I have all eternity to wait in."

And still seated alone on the threshold, she listens for the creaking of his boots.

38

Little Girls Wiser than Men

Leo Tolstoy

It was an early Easter. Sledging was just over. Snow still lay in the yards, and water ran in streams across the village. Between two yards, out of manure, a big puddle filled up. And two girls from different houses came to the puddle one smaller, another a little older. Their mothers had dressed them both in new frocks. Blue one—on little girl, and yellow—on the elder. Both had red scarfs on their heads. After Mass, girls came to the puddle, showed each other their dresses and began to play. And they wanted to splash in the water. The little one went in the puddle with her shoes, and the elder one said:

— Don't go in, Malasha, your mother will scold you. Let me take the shoes off, and you do the same.

The girls took their shoes off, lifted their skirts, and went through the puddle toward each other. Malasha went in, up to her ankles, and says:

— It's deep, Akuljushka, I'm afraid.

— That's OK, the other one said—it won't get any deeper. Go right at me.

They came closer to each other. And Akulka says:—You, Malasha, be sure not to splash, but walk carefully.

She just said that, but Malasha plopped her foot over the water—and it splashed right on Akulka's dress. Dress got spattered, and some went on her nose and eyes. Akulka saw stains on her dress, got angry at Malashka, scolded, ran after her, wanted to slap her. Malasha scared, saw that she caused trouble, jumped out of the puddle, ran home. Akulka's mother walked past, saw—her daughter's frock was spattered and shirt was dirty.

— Where did you, naughty girl, soil yourself?

— Malasha spattered me, on purpose.

Akulka's mother grabbed Malasha, and slapped her on the back of her head. Malasha wailed so she was heard across the street. Malasha's mother came out.

— What do you hit my daughter for? —She started scolding her neighbor. Word after word, women quarreled. Men jumped out, gathered on the street in a large bunch. All shout, nobody is listening to each other. Quarreled, quarreled, one pushed the other, a fight almost started, but an old woman, Akulka's grandmother, stepped in. She came in the middle of the men and began to coax:

— What are you, dear, doing, it such days? We should rejoice, but you started such a sin.

They didn't listen to the old woman, nearly knocked her off her feet. And the old woman wouldn't persuade them, if it weren't for Akulka with Malasha.

While the women cursed each other, Akulka had wiped the mud off her frock, and came out again to the pathway with the puddle. Picked up a stone and began to scrape the ground to let the water out into the street. While she was scraping, Malasha came up and began to help her, also digging a channel with a tiny chip of wood.

Guys just began to fight, when the girls' water ran by the groove, by the street, and into the creek. Girls put the wooden chip into the water. The stream carried the chip across the street, right to the place where the old woman was taking the men apart. The girls are running—one from one side, another from the other side of the stream.

— Catch it, Malasha, catch it!—shouts Akulka. Malasha also wants to say something, but can't help laughing.

So the girls are running, laughing at the chip as it dives in the stream. And they ran straight in between the men. The old woman saw them and said to the men:

— Fear God, you guys, dragged yourself into a fight because of these girls, and they have long time ago forgotten everything—again are in love together, blessed, playing. They are wiser than you!

The men looked at the girls, and got embarrassed. But then they laughed at themselves, and went to back to their homes.

"Unless ye become as little children, ye shall not enter into the Kingdom of God."

39

Half a Sheet of Foolscap

August Strindberg

The last furniture van had left; the tenant, a young man with a crape band round his hat, walked for the last time through the empty rooms to make sure that nothing had been left behind. No, nothing had been forgotten, nothing at all. He went out into the front hall, firmly determined never to think again of all that had happened to him in these rooms. And all at once his eyes fell on half a sheet of foolscap, which somehow had got wedged between the wall and the telephone; the paper was covered with writing, evidently the writing of more persons than one. Some of the entries were written quite legibly with pen and ink, while others were scribbled with a lead-pencil; here and there even a red pencil had been used. It was a record of everything that had happened to him in the short period of two years; all these things, which he had made up his mind to forget, were noted down. It was a slice of a human life on half a sheet of foolscap.

He detached the paper; it was a piece of scribbling paper, yellow and shining like the sun. He put it on the mantelpiece in the drawing-room and glanced at it. Heading the list was a woman's name: "Alice," the most beautiful name in the world, as it had seemed to him then, for it was the name of his fiancée. Next to the name was a number, "15,11." It looked like the number of a hymn, on the hymn-board. Underneath was written "Bank." That was where his work lay, his sacred work to which he owed bread, home, and wife—the foundations of life. But a pen had been drawn through the word, for the Bank had failed, and although he had eventually found another berth, it was not until after a short period of anxiety and uneasiness.

The next entries were: "Flower-shop and livery-stable." They related to his betrothal, when he had plenty of money in his pockets.

Then came "furniture dealer and paper-hanger"—they were furnishing their house. "Forwarding agents"—they were moving into it. The "Box-office of the Opera-house, No. 50,50"—they were newly married, and went to the opera on Sunday evenings; the most enjoyable hours of their lives were spent there, for they had to sit quite still, while their souls met in the beauty and harmony of the fairyland on the other side of the curtain.

Then followed the name of a man, crossed out. He had been a friend of his youth, a man who had risen high in the social scale, but who fell, spoilt by success, fell irremediably, and had to leave the country.

So unstable was fortune!

Now, something new entered the lives of husband and wife. The next entry was in a lady's hand: "Nurse." What nurse? Well, of course, the kindly woman with the big cloak and the sympathetic face, who walked with a soft footfall, and never went into the drawing-room, but walked straight down the passage to the bedroom.

Underneath her name was written "Dr. L."

And now, for the first time, a relative appeared on the list: "Mama." That was his mother-in-law, who had kept away discreetly, so as not to disturb their newly found happiness, but was glad to come now, when she was needed.

A great number of entries in red and blue pencil followed: "Servants' Registry Office"—the maid had left and a new one had to be engaged. "The chemist's"—hm! life was growing dark. "The dairy"—milk had been ordered—sterilised milk!

"Butcher, grocer, etc." The affairs of the house were being conducted by telephone; it argued that the mistress was not at her post. No, she wasn't, for she was laid up.

He could not read what followed, for it grew dark before his eyes; he might have been a drowning man trying to see through salt water. And yet, there it was written, plainly enough: "undertaker—a large coffin and a small one." And the word "dust" was added in parenthesis.

It was the last word of the whole record. It ended with "dust"! and that is exactly what happens in life.

He took the yellow paper, kissed it, folded it carefully, and put it in his pocket.

In two minutes he had lived again through two years of his life.

But he was not bowed down as he left the house. On the contrary, he carried his head high, like a happy and proud man, for he knew that the best things life has to bestow had been given to him. And he pitied all those from whom they are withheld.

40

Memory

H.P. Lovecraft

In the valley of Nis the accursed waning moon shines thinly, tearing a path for its light with feeble horns through the lethal foliage of a great upas-tree. And within the depths of the valley, where the light reaches not, move forms not meet to be beheld. Rank is the herbage on each slope, where evil vines and creeping plants crawl amidst the stones of ruined palaces, twining tightly about broken columns and strange monoliths, and heaving up marble pavements laid by forgotten hands. And in trees that grow gigantic in crumbling courtyards leap little apes, while in and out of deep treasure-vaults writhe poison serpents and scaly things without a name.

Vast are the stones which sleep beneath coverlets of dank moss, and mighty were the walls from which they fell. For all time did their builders erect them, and in sooth they yet serve nobly, for beneath them the grey toad makes his habitation.

At the very bottom of the valley lies the river Than, whose waters are slimy and filled with weeds. From hidden springs it rises, and to subterranean grottoes it flows, so that the Daemon of the Valley knows not why its waters are red, nor whither they are bound.

The Genie that haunts the moonbeams spake to the Daemon of the Valley, saying, "I am old, and forget much. Tell me the deeds and aspect and name of them who built these things of stone." And the Daemon replied, "I am Memory, and am wise in lore of the past, but I too am old. These beings were like the waters of the river Than, not to be understood. Their deeds I recall not, for they were but of the moment. Their aspect I recall dimly, for it was like to that of the little apes in the trees. Their name I recall clearly, for it rhymed with that of the river. These beings of yesterday were called Man."

So the Genie flew back to the thin horned moon, and the Daemon looked intently at a little ape in a tree that grew in a crumbling courtyard.

41

A Haunted House

Virginia Woolf

Whatever hour you woke there was a door shutting. From room to room they went, hand in hand, lifting here, opening there, making sure—a ghostly couple.

"Here we left it," she said. And he added, "Oh, but here too!" "It's upstairs," she murmured. "And in the garden," he whispered "Quietly," they said, "or we shall wake them."

But it wasn't that you woke us. Oh, no. "They're looking for it; they're drawing the curtain," one might say, and so read on a page or two. "Now they've found it," one would be certain, stopping the pencil on the margin. And then, tired of reading, one might rise and see for oneself, the house all empty, the doors standing open, only the wood pigeons bubbling with content and the hum of the threshing machine sounding from the farm. "What did I come in here for? What did I want to find?" My hands were empty. "Perhaps it's upstairs then?" The apples were in the loft. And so down again, the garden still as ever, only the book had slipped into the grass.

But they had found it in the drawing room. Not that one could ever see them. The window panes reflected apples, reflected roses; all the leaves were green in the glass. If they moved in the drawing room, the apple only turned its yellow side. Yet, the moment after, if the door was opened, spread about the floor, hung upon the walls, pendant from the ceiling—what? My hands were empty. The shadow of a thrush crossed the carpet; from the deepest wells of silence the wood pigeon drew its bubble of sound. "Safe, safe, safe," the pulse of the house beat softly. "The treasure buried; the room..." the pulse stopped short. Oh, was that the buried treasure?

A moment later the light had faded. Out in the garden then? But the trees spun darkness for a wandering beam of sun. So fine, so rare, coolly sunk beneath the surface the beam I sought always burnt behind the glass. Death was the glass; death was between us; coming to the woman first, hundreds of years ago, leaving the house, sealing all the windows; the rooms were darkened. He left it, left her, went North, went East, saw the stars turned in the Southern sky; sought the house, found it dropped beneath the Downs. "Safe, safe, safe," the pulse of the house beat gladly. "The Treasure yours."

The wind roars up the avenue. Trees stoop and bend this way and that. Moonbeams splash and spill wildly in the rain. But the beam of the lamp falls straight from the window. The candle burns stiff and still. Wandering through the house, opening the windows, whispering not to wake us, the ghostly couple seek their joy.

"Here we slept," she says. And he adds, "Kisses without number." "Waking in the morning—" "Silver between the trees—" "Upstairs—" "In the garden—" "When summer came—" "In winter snowtime—" The doors go shutting far in the distance, gently knocking like the pulse of a heart.

Nearer they come; cease at the doorway. The wind falls, the rain slides silver down the glass. Our eyes darken; we hear no steps beside us; we see no lady spread her ghostly cloak. His hands shield the lantern. "Look," he breathes. "Sound asleep. Love upon their lips."

Stooping, holding their silver lamp above us, long they look and deeply. Long they pause. The wind drives straightly; the flame stoops slightly. Wild beams of moonlight cross both floor and wall, and, meeting, stain the faces bent; the faces pondering; the faces that search the sleepers and seek their hidden joy.

"Safe, safe, safe," the heart of the house beats proudly. "Long years—" he sighs. "Again you found me." "Here," she murmurs, "sleeping; in the garden reading; laughing, rolling apples in the loft. Here we left our treasure—" Stooping, their light lifts the lids upon my eyes. "Safe! safe! safe!" the pulse of the house beats wildly. Waking, I cry "Oh, is this your buried treasure? The light in the heart."

42

The Oval Portrait

Edgar Allan Poe

The château into which my valet had ventured to make forcible entrance, rather than permit me, in my desperately wounded condition, to pass a night in the open air, was one of those piles of commingled gloom and grandeur which have so long frowned among the Appennines, not less in fact than in the fancy of Mrs. Radcliffe. To all appearance it had been temporarily and very lately abandoned. We established ourselves in one of the smallest and least sumptuously furnished apartments. It lay in a remote turret of the building. Its decorations were rich, yet tattered and antique. Its walls were hung with tapestry and bedecked with manifold and multiform armorial trophies, together with an unusually great number of very spirited modern paintings in frames of rich golden arabesque. In these paintings, which depended from the walls not only in their main surfaces, but in very many nooks which the bizarre architecture of the château rendered necessary—in these paintings my incipient delirium, perhaps, had caused me to take deep interest; so that I bade Pedro to close the heavy shutters of the room—since it was already night—to light the tongues of a tall candelabrum which stood by the head of my bed—and to throw open far and wide the fringed curtains of black velvet which enveloped the bed itself. I wished all this done that I might resign myself, if not to sleep, at least alternately to the contemplation of these pictures, and the perusal of a small volume which had been found upon the pillow, and which purported to criticise and describe them.

Long—long I read—and devoutly, devotedly I gazed. Rapidly and gloriously the hours flew by and the deep midnight came. The position of the candelabrum displeased me, and outreaching my hand with difficulty, rather than disturb my slumbering valet, I placed it so as to throw its rays more fully upon the book.

But the action produced an effect altogether unanticipated. The rays of the numerous candles (for there were many) now fell within a niche of the room which had hitherto been thrown into deep shade by one of the bed-posts. I thus saw in vivid light a picture all unnoticed before. It was the portrait of a young girl just ripening into womanhood. I glanced at the painting hurriedly, and then closed my eyes. Why I did this was not at first apparent even to my own perception. But while my lids remained thus shut, I ran over in my mind my reason for so shutting them. It was an impulsive movement to gain time for thought—to make sure that my vision had not deceived me—to calm and subdue my fancy for a more sober and more certain gaze. In a very few moments I again looked fixedly at the painting.

That I now saw aright I could not and would not doubt; for the first flashing of the candles upon that canvas had seemed to dissipate the dreamy stupor which was stealing over my senses, and to startle me at once into waking life.

The portrait, I have already said, was that of a young girl. It was a mere head and shoulders, done in what is technically termed a vignette manner; much in the style of the favourite heads of Sully. The arms, the bosom, and even the ends of the radiant hair melted imperceptibly into the vague yet deep shadow which formed the back-ground of the whole. The frame was oval, richly gilded and filigreed in Moresque. As a thing of art nothing could be more admirable than the painting itself. But it could have been neither the execution of the work, nor the immortal beauty of the countenance, which had so suddenly and so vehemently moved me. Least of all, could it have been that my fancy, shaken from its half slumber, had mistaken the head for that of a living person. I saw at once that the peculiarities of the design, of the vignetting, and of the frame, must have instantly dispelled such idea—must have prevented even its momentary entertainment. Thinking earnestly upon these points, I remained, for an hour perhaps, half sitting, half reclining, with my vision riveted upon the portrait. At length, satisfied with the true secret of its effect, I fell back within the bed. I had found the spell of the picture in an absolute life-likeliness of expression, which, at first startling, finally confounded, subdued, and appalled me. With deep and reverent awe I replaced the candelabrum in its former position. The cause of my deep agitation being thus shut from view, I sought eagerly the volume which discussed the paintings and their histories. Turning to the number which designated the oval portrait, I there read the vague and quaint words which follow:

"She was a maiden of rarest beauty, and not more lovely than full of glee. And evil was the hour when she saw, and loved, and wedded the painter. He, passionate, studious, austere, and having already a bride in his Art; she a maiden of rarest beauty, and not more lovely than full of glee; all light and smiles, and frolicsome as the young fawn; loving and cherishing all things; hating only the Art which was her rival; dreading only the pallet and brushes and other untoward instruments which deprived her of the countenance of her lover. It was thus a terrible thing for this lady to hear the painter speak of his desire to portray even his young bride. But she was humble and obedient, and sat meekly for many weeks in the dark, high turret-chamber where the light dripped upon the pale canvas only from overhead. But he, the painter, took glory in his work, which went on from hour to hour, and from day to day. And he was a passionate, and wild, and moody man, who became lost in reveries; so that he would not see that the light which fell so ghastly in that lone turret withered the health and the spirits of his bride, who pined visibly to all but him. Yet she smiled on and still on, uncomplainingly, because she saw that the painter (who had high renown) took a fervid and burning pleasure in his task, and wrought day and night to depict her who so loved him, yet who grew daily more dispirited and weak. And in sooth some who beheld the portrait spoke of its resemblance in low words, as of a mighty marvel, and a proof not less of the power of the painter than of his deep love for her whom he depicted so surpassingly well. But at length, as the labour drew nearer to its conclusion, there were admitted none into the turret; for the painter had grown wild with the ardour of his work, and turned his eyes from canvas merely, even to regard the countenance of his wife. And he would not see that the tints which he spread upon the canvas were drawn from the cheeks of her who sat beside him. And when many weeks had passed, and but little remained to do, save one brush upon the mouth and one tint upon the eye, the spirit of the lady again flickered up as the flame within the socket of the lamp. And then the brush was given, and then the tint was placed; and, for one moment, the painter stood entranced before the work which he had wrought; but in the next, while he yet gazed, he grew tremulous and very pallid, and aghast, and crying with a loud voice, 'This is indeed Life itself!' turned suddenly to regard his beloved:—She was dead!"

43

The Child's Story

Charles Dickens

Once upon a time, a good many years ago, there was a traveller, and he set out upon a journey. It was a magic journey, and was to seem very long when he began it, and very short when he got half way through.

He travelled along a rather dark path for some little time, without meeting anything, until at last he came to a beautiful child. So he said to the child, "What do you do here?" And the child said, "I am always at play. Come and play with me!"

So, he played with that child, the whole day long, and they were very merry. The sky was so blue, the sun was so bright, the water was so sparkling, the leaves were so green, the flowers were so lovely, and they heard such singing-birds and saw so many butterflies, that everything was beautiful. This was in fine weather. When it rained, they loved to watch the falling drops, and to smell the fresh scents. When it blew, it was delightful to listen to the wind, and fancy what it said, as it came rushing from its home—where was that, they wondered!—whistling and howling, driving the clouds before it, bending the trees, rumbling in the chimneys, shaking the house, and making the sea roar in fury. But, when it snowed, that was best of all; for, they liked nothing so well as to look up at the white flakes falling fast and thick, like down from the breasts of millions of white birds; and to see how smooth and deep the drift was; and to listen to the hush upon the paths and roads.

They had plenty of the finest toys in the world, and the most astonishing picture-books: all about scimitars and slippers and turbans, and dwarfs and giants and genii and fairies, and blue-beards and bean-stalks and riches and caverns and forests and Valentines and Orsons: and all new and all true.

But, one day, of a sudden, the traveller lost the child. He called to him over and over again, but got no answer. So, he went upon his road, and went on for a little while without meeting anything, until at last he came to a handsome boy. So, he said to the boy, "What do you do here?" And the boy said, "I am always learning. Come and learn with me."

So he learned with that boy about Jupiter and Juno, and the Greeks and the Romans, and I don't know what, and learned more than I could tell—or he either, for he soon forgot a great deal of it. But, they were not always learning; they had the merriest games that ever were played. They rowed upon the river in summer, and skated on the ice in winter; they were active afoot, and active on horseback; at cricket, and all games at ball; at prisoners' base, hare and hounds, follow my leader, and more sports than I can think of; nobody could beat them. They had holidays too, and Twelfth cakes, and parties where they danced till midnight, and real Theatres where they saw palaces of real gold and silver rise out of the real earth, and saw all the wonders of the world at once. As to friends, they had such dear friends and so many of them, that I want the time to reckon them up. They were all young, like the handsome boy, and were never to be strange to one another all their lives through.

Still, one day, in the midst of all these pleasures, the traveller lost the boy as he had lost the child, and, after calling to him in vain, went on upon his journey. So he went on for a little while without seeing anything, until at last he came to a young man. So, he said to the young man, "What do you do here?" And the young man said, "I am always in love. Come and love with me."

So, he went away with that young man, and presently they came to one of the prettiest girls that ever was seen—just like Fanny in the corner there—and she had eyes like Fanny, and hair like Fanny, and dimples like Fanny's, and she laughed and coloured just as Fanny does while I am talking about her. So, the young man fell in love directly—just as Somebody I won't mention, the first time he came here, did with Fanny. Well! he was teased sometimes—just as Somebody used to be by Fanny; and they quarrelled sometimes—just as Somebody and Fanny used to quarrel; and they made it up, and sat in the dark, and wrote letters every day, and never were happy asunder, and were always looking out for one another and pretending not to, and were engaged at Christmas-time, and sat close to one another by the fire, and were going to be married very soon—all exactly like Somebody I won't mention, and Fanny!

But, the traveller lost them one day, as he had lost the rest of his friends, and, after calling to them to come back, which they never did, went on upon his journey. So, he went on for a little while without seeing anything, until at last he came to a middle-aged gentleman. So, he said to the gentleman, "What are you doing here?" And his answer was, "I am always busy. Come and be busy with me!"

So, he began to be very busy with that gentleman, and they went on through the wood together. The whole journey was through a wood, only it had been open and green at first, like a wood in spring; and now began to be thick and dark, like a wood in summer; some of the little trees that had come out earliest, were even turning brown. The gentleman was not alone, but had a lady of about the same age with him, who was his Wife; and they had children, who were with them too. So, they all went on together through the wood, cutting down the trees, and making a path through the branches and the fallen leaves, and carrying burdens, and working hard.

Sometimes, they came to a long green avenue that opened into deeper woods. Then they would hear a very little, distant voice crying, "Father, father, I am another child! Stop for me!" And presently they would see a very little figure, growing larger as it came along, running to join them. When it came up, they all crowded round it, and kissed and welcomed it; and then they all went on together.

Sometimes, they came to several avenues at once, and then they all stood still, and one of the children said, "Father, I am going to sea," and another said, "Father, I am going to India," and another, "Father, I am going to seek my fortune where I can," and another, "Father, I am going to Heaven!" So, with many tears at parting, they went, solitary, down those avenues, each child upon its way; and the child who went to Heaven, rose into the golden air and vanished.

Whenever these partings happened, the traveller looked at the gentleman, and saw him glance up at the sky above the trees, where the day was beginning to decline, and the sunset to come on. He saw, too, that his hair was turning grey. But, they never could rest long, for they had their journey to perform, and it was necessary for them to be always busy.

At last, there had been so many partings that there were no children left, and only the traveller, the gentleman, and the lady, went upon their way in company. And now the wood was yellow; and now brown; and the leaves, even of the forest trees, began to fall.

So, they came to an avenue that was darker than the rest, and were pressing forward on their journey without looking down it when the lady stopped.

"My husband," said the lady. "I am called."

They listened, and they heard a voice a long way down the avenue, say, "Mother, mother!"

It was the voice of the first child who had said, "I am going to Heaven!" and the father said, "I pray not yet. The sunset is very near. I pray not yet!"

But, the voice cried, "Mother, mother!" without minding him, though his hair was now quite white, and tears were on his face.

Then, the mother, who was already drawn into the shade of the dark avenue and moving away with her arms still round his neck, kissed him, and said, "My dearest, I am summoned, and I go!" And she was gone. And the traveller and he were left alone together.

And they went on and on together, until they came to very near the end of the wood: so near, that they could see the sunset shining red before them through the trees.

Yet, once more, while he broke his way among the branches, the traveller lost his friend. He called and called, but there was no reply, and when he passed out of the wood, and saw the peaceful sun going down upon a wide purple prospect, he came to an old man sitting on a fallen tree. So, he said to the old man, "What do you do here?" And the old man said with a calm smile, "I am always remembering. Come and remember with me!"

So the traveller sat down by the side of that old man, face to face with the serene sunset; and all his friends came softly back and stood around him. The beautiful child, the handsome boy, the young man in love, the father, mother, and children: every one of them was there, and he had lost nothing. So, he loved them all, and was kind and forbearing with them all, and was always pleased to watch them all, and they all honoured and loved him. And I think the traveller must be yourself, dear Grandfather, because this is what you do to us, and what we do to you.

44

The Story of an Hour

Kate Chopin

Knowing that Mrs. Mallard was afflicted with a heart trouble, great care was taken to break to her as gently as possible the news of her husband's death.

It was her sister Josephine who told her, in broken sentences; veiled hints that revealed in half concealing. Her husband's friend Richards was there, too, near her. It was he who had been in the newspaper office when intelligence of the railroad disaster was received, with Brently Mallard's name leading the list of "killed." He had only taken the time to assure himself of its truth by a second telegram, and had hastened to forestall any less careful, less tender friend in bearing the sad message.

She did not hear the story as many women have heard the same, with a paralyzed inability to accept its significance. She wept at once, with sudden, wild abandonment, in her sister's arms. When the storm of grief had spent itself she went away to her room alone. She would have no one follow her.

There stood, facing the open window, a comfortable, roomy armchair. Into this she sank, pressed down by a physical exhaustion that haunted her body and seemed to reach into her soul.

She could see in the open square before her house the tops of trees that were all aquiver with the new spring life. The delicious breath of rain was in the air. In the street below a peddler was crying his wares. The notes of a distant song which some one was singing reached her faintly, and countless sparrows were twittering in the eaves. There were patches of blue sky showing here and there through the clouds that had met and piled one above the other in the west facing her window.

She sat with her head thrown back upon the cushion of the chair, quite motionless, except when a sob came up into her throat and shook her, as a child who has cried itself to sleep continues to sob in its dreams.

She was young, with a fair, calm face, whose lines bespoke repression and even a certain strength. But now there was a dull stare in her eyes, whose gaze was fixed away off yonder on one of those patches of blue sky. It was not a glance of reflection, but rather indicated a suspension of intelligent thought.

There was something coming to her and she was waiting for it, fearfully. What was it? She did not know; it was too subtle and elusive to name. But she felt it, creeping out of the sky, reaching toward her through the sounds, the scents, the color that filled the air.

Now her bosom rose and fell tumultuously. She was beginning to recognize this thing that was approaching to possess her, and she was striving to beat it back with her will—as powerless as her two white slender hands would have been. When she abandoned herself a little whispered word escaped her slightly parted lips. She said it over and over under her breath: "free, free, free!" The vacant stare and the look of terror that had followed it went from her eyes. They stayed keen and bright. Her pulses beat fast, and the coursing blood warmed and relaxed every inch of her body. She did not stop to ask if it were or were not a monstrous joy that held her. A clear and exalted perception enabled her to dismiss the suggestion as trivial.

She knew that she would weep again when she saw the kind, tender hands folded in death; the face that had never looked save with love upon her, fixed and gray and dead. But she saw beyond that bitter moment a long procession of years to come that would belong to her absolutely. And she opened and spread her arms out to them in welcome. There would be no one to live for her during those coming years; she would live for herself. There would be no powerful will bending hers in that blind persistence with which men and women believe they have a right to impose a private will upon a fellow-creature. A kind intention or a cruel intention made the act seem no less a crime as she looked upon it in that brief moment of illumination.

And yet she had loved him—sometimes. Often she had not. What did it matter! What could love, the unsolved mystery, count for in face of this possession of self-assertion which she suddenly recognized as the strongest impulse of her being!

"Free! Body and soul free!" she kept whispering.

Josephine was kneeling before the closed door with her lips to the keyhole, imploring for admission. "Louise, open the door! I beg, open the door—you will make yourself ill. What are you doing, Louise? For heaven's sake open the door."

"Go away. I am not making myself ill." No; she was drinking in a very elixir of life through that open window. Her fancy was running riot along those days ahead of her. Spring days, and summer days, and all sorts of days that would be her own. She breathed a quick prayer that life might be long. It was only yesterday she had thought with a shudder that life might be long.

She arose at length and opened the door to her sister's importunities. There was a feverish triumph in her eyes, and she carried herself unwittingly like a goddess of Victory. She clasped her sister's waist, and together they descended the stairs. Richards stood waiting for them at the bottom.

Someone was opening the front door with a latchkey. It was Brently Mallard who entered, a little travel-stained, composedly carrying his grip-sack and umbrella. He had been far from the scene of the accident, and did not even know there had been one. He stood amazed at Josephine's piercing cry; at Richards' quick motion to screen him from the view of his wife.

But Richards was too late.

When the doctors came they said she had died of heart disease—of the joy that kills.

45

The Death of a Government Clerk

Anton Chekhov

One fine evening, a no less fine government clerk called Ivan Dmitritch Tchervyakov was sitting in the second row of the stalls, gazing through an opera glass at the Cloches de Corneville. He gazed and felt at the acme of bliss. But suddenly… In stories one so often meets with this "But suddenly." The authors are right: life is so full of surprises! But suddenly his face puckered up, his eyes disappeared, his breathing was arrested…he took the opera glass from his eyes, bent over and…"Aptchee!!" he sneezed as you perceive. It is not reprehensible for anyone to sneeze anywhere. Peasants sneeze and so do police superintendents, and sometimes even privy councillors. All men sneeze. Tchervyakov was not in the least confused, he wiped his face with his handkerchief, and like a polite man, looked round to see whether he had disturbed any one by his sneezing. But then he was overcome with confusion. He saw that an old gentleman sitting in front of him in the first row of the stalls was carefully wiping his bald head and his neck with his glove and muttering something to himself. In the old gentleman, Tchervyakov recognised Brizzhalov, a civilian general serving in the Department of Transport.

"I have spattered him," thought Tchervyakov, "he is not the head of my department, but still it is awkward. I must apologise."

Tchervyakov gave a cough, bent his whole person forward, and whispered in the general's ear.

"Pardon, your Excellency, I spattered you accidentally… "

"Never mind, never mind."

"For goodness sake excuse me, I…I did not mean to."

"Oh, please, sit down! let me listen!"

Tchervyakov was embarrassed, he smiled stupidly and fell to gazing at the stage. He gazed at it but was no longer feeling bliss. He began to be troubled by uneasiness. In the interval, he went up to Brizzhalov, walked beside him, and overcoming his shyness, muttered:

"I spattered you, your Excellency, forgive me…you see…I didn't do it to … "

"Oh, that's enough…I'd forgotten it, and you keep on about it!" said the general, moving his lower lip impatiently.

"He has forgotten, but there is a fiendish light in his eye," thought Tchervyakov, looking suspiciously at the general. "And he doesn't want to talk. I ought to explain to him…that I really didn't intend…that it is the law of nature or else he will think I meant to spit on him. He doesn't think so now, but he will think so later!"

On getting home, Tchervyakov told his wife of his breach of good manners. It struck him that his wife took too frivolous a view of the incident; she was a little frightened, but when she learned that Brizzhalov was in a different department, she was reassured.

"Still, you had better go and apologise," she said, "or he will think you don't know how to behave in public."

"That's just it! I did apologise, but he took it somehow queerly… he didn't say a word of sense. There wasn't time to talk properly."

Next day Tchervyakov put on a new uniform, had his hair cut and went to Brizzhalov's to explain; going into the general's reception room he saw there a number of petitioners and among them the general himself, who was beginning to interview them. After questioning several petitioners the general raised his eyes and looked at Tchervyakov.

"Yesterday at the Arcadia, if you recollect, your Excellency," the latter began, "I sneezed and…accidentally spattered…Exc… "

"What nonsense… It's beyond anything! What can I do for you," said the general addressing the next petitioner.

"He won't speak," thought Tchervyakov, turning pale; "that means that he is angry… No, it can't be left like this… I will explain to him."

When the general had finished his conversation with the last of the petitioners and was turning towards his inner apartments, Tchervyakov took a step towards him and muttered:

"Your Excellency! If I venture to trouble your Excellency, it is simply from a feeling I may say of regret!…It was not intentional if you will graciously believe me."

The general made a lachrymose face, and waved his hand.

"Why, you are simply making fun of me, sir," he said as he closed the door behind him.

"Where's the making fun in it?" thought Tchervyakov, "there is nothing of the sort! He is a general, but he can't understand. If that is how it is I am not going to apologise to that fanfaron any more! The devil take him. I'll write a letter to him, but I won't go. By Jove, I won't."

So thought Tchervyakov as he walked home; he did not write a letter to the general, he pondered and pondered and could not make up that letter. He had to go next day to explain in person.

"I ventured to disturb your Excellency yesterday," he muttered, when the general lifted enquiring eyes upon him, "not to make fun as you were pleased to say. I was apologising for having spattered you in sneezing… And I did not dream of making fun of you. Should I dare to make fun of you, if we should take to making fun, then there would be no respect for persons, there would be… "

"Be off!" yelled the general, turning suddenly purple, and shaking all over.

"What?" asked Tchervyakov, in a whisper turning numb with horror.

"Be off!" repeated the general, stamping.

Something seemed to give way in Tchervyakov's stomach. Seeing nothing and hearing nothing he reeled to the door, went out into the street, and went staggering along… Reaching home mechanically, without taking off his uniform, he lay down on the sofa and died.

46

The Mockingbird

Ambrose Bierce

The time, a pleasant Sunday afternoon in the early autumn of 1861. The place, a forest's heart in the mountain region of southwestern Virginia. Private Grayrock of the Federal Army is discovered seated comfortably at the root of a great pine tree, against which he leans, his legs extended straight along the ground, his rifle lying across his thighs, his hands (clasped in order that they may not fall away to his sides) resting upon the barrel of the weapon. The contact of the back of his head with the tree has pushed his cap downward over his eyes, almost concealing them; one seeing him would say that he slept.

Private Grayrock did not sleep; to have done so would have imperiled the interests of the United States, for he was a long way outside the lines and subject to capture or death at the hands of the enemy. Moreover, he was in a frame of mind unfavorable to repose. The cause of his perturbation of spirit was this: during the previous night he had served on the picket-guard, and had been posted as a sentinel in this very forest. The night was clear, though moonless, but in the gloom of the wood the darkness was deep. Grayrock's post was at a considerable distance from those to right and left, for the pickets had been thrown out a needless distance from the camp, making the line too long for the force detailed to occupy it. The war was young, and military camps entertained the error that while sleeping they were better protected by thin lines a long way out toward the enemy than by thicker ones close in. And surely they needed as long notice as possible of an enemy's approach, for they were at that time addicted to the practice of undressing—than which nothing could be more unsoldierly. On the morning of the memorable 6th of April, at Shiloh, many of Grant's men when spitted on Confederate bayonets were as naked as civilians; but it should be allowed that this was not because of any defect in their picket line. Their error was of another sort: they had no pickets. This is perhaps a vain digression. I should not care to undertake to interest the reader in the fate of an army; what we have here to consider is that of Private Grayrock.

For two hours after he had been left at his lonely post that Saturday night he stood stock-still, leaning against the trunk of a large tree, staring into the darkness in his front and trying to recognize known objects; for he had been posted at the same spot during the day. But all was now different; he saw nothing in detail, but only groups of things, whose shapes, not observed when there was something more of them to observe, were now unfamiliar. They seemed not to have been there before. A landscape that is all trees and undergrowth, moreover, lacks definition, is confused and without accentuated points upon which attention can gain a foothold. Add the gloom of a moonless night, and something more than great natural intelligence and a city education is required to preserve one's knowledge of direction. And that is how it occurred that Private Grayrock, after vigilantly watching the spaces in his front and then imprudently executing a circumspection of his whole dimly visible environment (silently walking around his tree to accomplish it) lost his bearings and seriously impaired his usefulness as a sentinel. Lost at his post—unable to say in which direction to look for an enemy's approach, and in which lay the sleeping camp for whose security he was accountable with his life—conscious, too, of many another awkward feature of the situation and of considerations affecting his own safety, Private Grayrock was profoundly disquieted. Nor was he given time to recover his tranquillity, for almost at the moment that he realized his awkward predicament he heard a stir of leaves and a snap of fallen twigs, and turning with a stilled heart in the direction whence it came, saw in the gloom the indistinct outlines of a human figure.

"Halt!" shouted Private Grayrock, peremptorily as in duty bound, backing up the command with the sharp metallic snap of his cocking rifle—"who goes there?"

There was no answer; at least there was an instant's hesitation, and the answer, if it came, was lost in the report of the sentinel's rifle. In the silence of the night and the forest the sound was deafening, and hardly had it died away when it was repeated by the pieces of the pickets to right and left, a sympathetic fusillade. For two hours every unconverted civilian of them had been evolving enemies from his imagination, and peopling the woods in his front with them, and Grayrock's shot had started the whole encroaching host into visible existence. Having fired, all retreated, breathless, to the reserves—all but Grayrock, who did not know in what direction to retreat. When, no enemy appearing, the roused camp two miles away had undressed and got itself into bed again, and the picket line was cautiously re-established, he was discovered bravely holding his ground, and was complimented by the officer of the guard as the one soldier of that devoted band who could rightly be considered the moral equivalent of that uncommon unit of value, "a whoop in hell."

In the mean time, however, Grayrock had made a close but unavailing search for the mortal part of the intruder at whom he had fired, and whom he had a marksman's intuitive sense of having hit; for he was one of those born experts who shoot without aim by an instinctive sense of direction, and are nearly as dangerous by night as by day. During a full half of his twenty-four years he had been a terror to the targets of all the shooting-galleries in three cities. Unable now to produce his dead game he had the discretion to hold his tongue, and was glad to observe in his officer and comrades the natural assumption that not having run away he had seen nothing hostile. His "honorable mention" had been earned by not running away anyhow.

Nevertheless, Private Grayrock was far from satisfied with the night's adventure, and when the next day he made some fair enough pretext to apply for a pass to go outside the lines, and the general commanding promptly granted it in recognition of his bravery the night before, he passed out at the point where that had been displayed. Telling the sentinel then on duty there that he had lost something,—which was true enough—he renewed the search for the person whom he supposed himself to have shot, and whom if only wounded he hoped to trail by the blood. He was no more successful by daylight than he had been in the darkness, and after covering a wide area and boldly penetrating a long distance into "the Confederacy" he gave up the search, somewhat fatigued, seated himself at the root of the great pine tree, where we have seen him, and indulged his disappointment.

It is not to be inferred that Grayrock's was the chagrin of a cruel nature balked of its bloody deed. In the clear large eyes, finely wrought lips, and broad forehead of that young man one could read quite another story, and in point of fact his character was a singularly felicitous compound of boldness and sensibility, courage and conscience.

"I find myself disappointed," he said to himself, sitting there at the bottom of the golden haze submerging the forest like a subtler sea—"disappointed in failing to discover a fellow-man dead by my hand! Do I then really wish that I had taken life in the performance of a duty as well performed without? What more could I wish? If any danger threatened, my shot averted it; that is what I was there to do. No, I am glad indeed if no human life was needlessly extinguished by me. But I am in a false position. I have suffered myself to be complimented by my officers and envied by my comrades. The camp is ringing with praise of my courage. That is not just; I know myself courageous, but this praise is for specific acts which I did not perform, or performed—otherwise. It is believed that I remained at my post bravely, without firing, whereas it was I who began the fusillade, and I did not retreat in the general alarm because bewildered. What, then, shall I do? Explain that I saw an enemy and fired? They have all said that of themselves, yet none believes it. Shall I tell a truth which, discrediting my courage, will have the effect of a lie? Ugh! it is an ugly business altogether. I wish to God I could find my man!"

And so wishing, Private Grayrock, overcome at last by the languor of the afternoon and lulled by the stilly sounds of insects droning and prosing in certain fragrant shrubs, so far forgot the interests of the United States as to fall asleep and expose himself to capture. And sleeping he dreamed.

He thought himself a boy, living in a far, fair land by the border of a great river upon which the tall steamboats moved grandly up and down beneath their towering evolutions of black smoke, which announced them long before they had rounded the bends and marked their movements when miles out of sight. With him always, at his side as he watched them, was one to whom he gave his heart and soul in love—a twin brother. Together they strolled along the banks of the stream; together explored the fields lying farther away from it, and gathered pungent mints and sticks of fragrant sassafras in the hills overlooking all—beyond which lay the Realm of Conjecture, and from which, looking southward across the great river, they caught glimpses of the Enchanted Land. Hand in hand and heart in heart they two, the only children of a widowed mother, walked in paths of light through valleys of peace, seeing new things under a new sun. And through all the golden days floated one unceasing sound—the rich, thrilling melody of a mocking-bird in a cage by the cottage door. It pervaded and possessed all the spiritual intervals of the dream, like a musical benediction. The joyous bird was always in song; its infinitely various notes seemed to flow from its throat, effortless, in bubbles and rills at each heart-beat, like the waters of a pulsing spring. That fresh, clear melody seemed, indeed, the spirit of the scene, the meaning and interpretation to sense of the mysteries of life and love.

But there came a time when the days of the dream grew dark with sorrow in a rain of tears. The good mother was dead, the meadowside home by the great river was broken up, and the brothers were parted between two of their kinsmen. William (the dreamer) went to live in a populous city in the Realm of Conjecture, and John, crossing the river into the Enchanted Land, was taken to a distant region whose people in their lives and ways were said to be strange and wicked. To him, in the distribution of the dead mother's estate, had fallen all that they deemed of value—the mocking-bird. They could be divided, but it could not, so it was carried away into the strange country, and the world of William knew it no more forever. Yet still through the aftertime of his loneliness its song filled all the dream, and seemed always sounding in his ear and in his heart.

The kinsmen who had adopted the boys were enemies, holding no communication. For a time letters full of boyish bravado and boastful narratives of the new and larger experience—grotesque descriptions of their widening lives and the new worlds they had conquered—passed between them; but these gradually became less frequent, and with William's removal to another and greater city ceased altogether. But ever through it all ran the song of the mocking-bird, and when the dreamer opened his eyes and stared through the vistas of the pine forest the cessation of its music first apprised him that he was awake.

The sun was low and red in the west; the level rays projected from the trunk of each giant pine a wall of shadow traversing the golden haze to eastward until light and shade were blended in undistinguishable blue.

Private Grayrock rose to his feet, looked cautiously about him, shouldered his rifle and set off toward camp. He had gone perhaps a half-mile, and was passing a thicket of laurel, when a bird rose from the midst of it and perching on the branch of a tree above, poured from its joyous breast so inexhaustible floods of song as but one of all God's creatures can utter in His praise. There was little in that—it was only to open the bill and breathe; yet the man stopped as if struck—stopped and let fall his rifle, looked upward at the bird, covered his eyes with his hands and wept like a child! For the moment he was, indeed, a child, in spirit and in memory, dwelling again by the great river, over-against the Enchanted Land! Then with an effort of the will he pulled himself together, picked up his weapon and audibly damning himself for an idiot strode on. Passing an opening that reached into the heart of the little thicket he looked in, and there, supine upon the earth, its arms all abroad, its gray uniform stained with a single spot of blood upon the breast, its white face turned sharply upward and backward, lay the image of himself!—the body of John Grayrock, dead of a gunshot wound, and still warm! He had found his man.

As the unfortunate soldier knelt beside that masterwork of civil war the shrilling bird upon the bough overhead stilled her song and, flushed with sunset's crimson glory, glided silently away through the solemn spaces of the wood. At roll-call that evening in the Federal camp the name William Grayrock brought no response, nor ever again there-after.

47

A Horseman in the Sky

Ambrose Bierce

I

One sunny afternoon in the autumn of the year 1861, a soldier lay in a clump of laurel by the side of a road in Western Virginia. He lay at full length, upon his stomach, his feet resting upon the toes, his head upon the left forearm. His extended right hand loosely grasped his rifle. But for the somewhat methodical disposition of his limbs and a slight rhythmic movement of the cartridge-box at the back of his belt, he might have been thought to be dead. He was asleep at his post of duty. But if detected he would be dead shortly afterward, that being the just and legal penalty of his crime.

The clump of laurel in which the criminal lay was in the angle of a road which, after, ascending, southward, a steep acclivity to that point, turned sharply to the west, running along the summit for perhaps one hundred yards. There it turned southward again and went zigzagging downward through the forest. At the salient of that second angle was a large flat rock, jutting out northward, overlooking the deep valley from which the road ascended. The rock capped a high cliff; a stone dropped from its outer edge would have fallen sheer downward one thousand feet to the tops of the pines. The angle where the soldier lay was on another spur of the same cliff. Had he been awake, he would have commanded a view, not only of the short arm of the road and the jutting rock, but of the entire profile of the cliff below it. It might well have made him giddy to look.

The country was wooded everywhere except at the bottom of the valley to the northward, where there was a small natural meadow, through which flowed a stream scarcely visible from the valley's rim. This open ground looked hardly larger than an ordinary dooryard, but was really several acres in extent. Its green was more vivid than that of the inclosing forest. Away beyond it rose a line of giant cliffs similar to those upon which we are supposed to stand in our survey of the savage scene, and through which the road had some how made its climb to the summit. The configuration of the valley, indeed, was such that from this point of observation it seemed entirely shut in, and one could not but have wondered how the road which found a way out of it had found a way into it, and whence came and whither went the waters of the stream that parted the meadow two thousand feet below.

No country is so wild and difficult but men will make it a theater of war; concealed in the forest at the bottom of that military rat-trap, in which half a hundred men in possession of the exits might have starved an army to submission, lay five regiments of Federal infantry. They had marched all the previous day and night, and were resting. At nightfall they would take to the road again, climb to the place where their unfaithful sentinel now slept, and, descending the other slope of the ridge, fall upon a camp of the enemy at about midnight. Their hope was to surprise it, for the road led to the rear of it. In case of failure, their position would be perilous in the extreme; and fail they surely would, should accident or vigilance apprise the enemy of the movement.

II

The sleeping sentinel in the clump of laurel was a young Virginian named Carter Druse. He was the son of wealthy parents, an only child, and had known such ease and cultivation and high living as wealth and taste were able to command in the mountain country of Western Virginia. His home was but a few miles from where he now lay. One morning he had risen from the breakfast table and said, quietly but gravely: "Father, a Union regiment has arrived at Grafton. I am going to join it."

The father lifted his leonine head, looked at the son a moment in silence, and replied: "Well, go, sir, and, whatever may occur, do what you conceive to be your duty. Virginia, to which you are a traitor, must get on without you. Should we both live to the end of the war, we will speak further of the matter. Your mother, as the physician has informed you, is in a most critical condition; at the best, she cannot be with us longer than a few weeks, but that time is precious. It would be better not to disturb her."

So Carter Druse, bowing reverently to his father, who returned the salute with a stately courtesy which masked a breaking heart, left the home of his childhood to go soldiering. By conscience and courage, by deeds of devotion and daring, he soon commended himself to his fellows and his officers; and it was to these qualities and to some knowledge of the country that he owed his selection for his present perilous duty at the extreme outpost. Nevertheless, fatigue had been stronger than resolution, and he had fallen asleep. What good or bad angel came in a dream to rouse him from his state of crime, who shall say? Without a movement, without a sound, in the profound silence and the languor of the late afternoon, some invisible messenger of fate touched with unsealing finger the eyes of his consciousness—whispered into the ear of his spirit the mysterious awakening word which no human lips ever have spoken, no human memory ever has recalled. He quietly raised his forehead from his arm and looked between the masking stems of the laurels, instinctively closing his right hand about the stock of his rifle.

His first feeling was a keen artistic delight. On a colossal pedestal, the cliff,—motionless at the extreme edge of the capping rock and sharply outlined against the sky,—was an equestrian statue of impressive dignity. The figure of the man sat the figure of the horse, straight and soldierly, but with the repose of a Grecian god carved in the marble which limits the suggestion of activity. The gray costume harmonized with its aerial background; the metal of accoutrement and caparison was softened and subdued by the shadow; the animal's skin had no points of high light. A carbine, strikingly foreshortened, lay across the pommel of the saddle, kept in place by the right hand grasping it at the "grip"; the left hand, holding the bridle rein, was invisible. In silhouette against the sky, the profile of the horse was cut with the sharpness of a cameo; it looked across the heights of air to the confronting cliffs beyond. The face of the rider, turned slightly away, showed only an outline of temple and beard; he was looking downward to the bottom of the valley. Magnified by its lift against the sky and by the soldier's testifying sense of the formidableness of a near enemy, the group appeared of heroic, almost colossal, size.

For an instant Druse had a strange, half-defined feeling that he had slept to the end of the war and was looking upon a noble work of art reared upon that commanding eminence to commemorate the deeds of an heroic past of which he had been an inglorious part. The feeling was dispelled by a slight movement of the group: the horse, without moving its feet, had drawn its body slightly backward from the verge; the man remained immobile as before. Broad awake and keenly alive to the significance of the situation, Druse now brought the butt of his rifle against his cheek by cautiously pushing the barrel forward through the bushes, cocked the piece, and, glancing through the sights, covered a vital spot of the horseman's breast. A touch upon the trigger and all would have been well with Carter Druse. At that instant the horseman turned his head and looked in the direction of his concealed foeman—seemed to look into his very face, into his eyes, into his brave, compassionate heart.

Is it, then, so terrible to kill an enemy in war—an enemy who has surprised a secret vital to the safety of one's self and comrades—an enemy more formidable for his knowledge than all his army for its numbers? Carter Druse grew pale; he shook in every limb, turned faint, and saw the statuesque group before him as black figures, rising, falling, moving unsteadily in arcs of circles in a fiery sky. His hand fell away from his weapon, his head slowly dropped until his face rested on the leaves in which he lay. This courageous gentleman and hardy soldier was near swooning from intensity of emotion.

It was not for long; in another moment his face was raised from earth, his hands resumed their places on the rifle, his forefinger sought the trigger; mind, heart and eyes were clear, conscience and reason sound. He could not hope to capture that enemy; to alarm him would but send him dashing to his camp with his fatal news. The duty of the soldier was plain: the man must be shot dead from ambush—without warning, without a moment's spiritual preparation, with never so much as an unspoken prayer, he must be sent to his account. But no—there is a hope; he may have discovered nothing; perhaps he is but admiring the sublimity of the landscape. If permitted, he may turn and ride carelessly away in the direction whence he came. Surely it will be possible to judge at the instant of his withdrawing whether he knows. It may well be that his fixity of attention—Druse turned his head and looked through the deeps of air downward as from the surface of the bottom of a translucent sea. He saw creeping across the green meadow a sinuous line of figures of men and horses—some foolish commander was permitting the soldiers of his escort to water their beasts in the open, in plain view from a hundred summits!

Druse withdrew his eyes from the valley and fixed them again upon the group of man and horse in the sky, and again it was through the sights of his rifle. But this time his aim was at the horse. In his memory, as if they were a divine mandate, rang the words of his father at their parting: "Whatever may occur, do what you conceive to be your duty." He was calm now. His teeth were firmly but not rigidly closed; his nerves were as tranquil as a sleeping babe's—not a tremor affected any muscle of his body; his breathing, until suspended in the act of taking aim, was regular and slow. Duty had conquered; the spirit had said to the body: "Peace, be still." He fired.

III

An officer of the Federal force, who, in a spirit of adventure or in quest of knowledge, had left the hidden bivouac in the valley, and, with aimless feet, had made his way to the lower edge of a small open space near the foot of the cliff, was considering what he had to gain by pushing his exploration further. At a distance of a quarter-mile before him, but apparently at a stone's throw, rose from its fringe of pines the gigantic face of rock, towering to so great a height above him that it made him giddy to look up to where its edge cut a sharp, rugged line against the sky. At some distance away to his right it presented a clean, vertical profile against a background of blue sky to a point half the way down, and of distant hills hardly less blue, thence to the tops of the trees at its base. Lifting his eyes to the dizzy altitude of its summit, the officer saw an astonishing sight—a man on horseback riding down into the valley through the air!

Straight upright sat the rider, in military fashion, with a firm seat in the saddle, a strong clutch upon the rein to hold his charger from too impetuous a plunge. From his bare head his long hair streamed upward, waving like a plume. His hands were concealed in the cloud of the horse's lifted mane. The animal's body was as level as if every hoof-stroke encountered the resistant earth. Its motions were those of a wild gallop, but even as the officer looked they ceased, with all the legs thrown sharply forward as in the act of alighting from a leap. But this was a flight!

Filled with amazement and terror by this apparition of a horseman in the sky-half believing himself the chosen scribe of some new apocalypse, the officer was overcome by the intensity of his emotions; his legs failed him and he fell. Almost at the same instant he heard a crashing sound in the trees—a sound that died without an echo—and all was still.

The officer rose to his feet, trembling. The familiar sensation of an abraded shin recalled his dazed faculties. Pulling himself together, he ran obliquely away from the cliff to a point distant from its foot; thereabout he expected to find his man; and thereabout he naturally failed. In the fleeting instant of his vision his imagination had been so wrought upon by the apparent grace and ease and intention of the marvelous performance that it did not occur to him that the line of march of aerial cavalry is directly downward, and that he could find the objects of his search at the very foot of the cliff. A half-hour later he returned to camp.

This officer was a wise man; he knew better than to tell an incredible truth. He said nothing of what he had seen. But when the commander asked him if in his scout he had learned anything of advantage to the expedition, he answered:

"Yes, sir; there is no road leading down into this valley from the southward."

The commander, knowing better, smiled.

IV

After firing his shot, Private Carter Druse reloaded his rifle and resumed his watch. Ten minutes had hardly passed when a Federal sergeant crept cautiously to him on hands and knees. Druse neither turned his head nor looked at him, but lay without motion or sign of recognition.

"Did you fire?" the sergeant whispered.

"Yes."

"At what?"

"A horse. It was standing on yonder rock-pretty far out. You see it is no longer there. It went over the cliff."

The man's face was white, but he showed no other sign of emotion. Having answered, he turned away his eyes and said no more. The sergeant did not understand.

"See here, Druse," he said, after a moment's silence, "it's no use making a mystery. I order you to report. Was there anybody on the horse?"

"Yes."

"Well?"

"My father."

The sergeant rose to his feet and walked away. "Good God!" he said.

48

My Financial Career

Stephen Leacock

When I go into a bank I get rattled. The clerks rattle me; the wickets rattle me; the sight of the money rattles me; everything rattles me.

The moment I cross the threshold of a bank and attempt to transact business there, I become an irresponsible idiot.

I knew this beforehand, but my salary had been raised to fifty dollars a month and I felt that the bank was the only place for it.

So I shambled in and looked timidly round at the clerks. I had an idea that a person about to open an account must needs consult the manager.

I went up to a wicket marked "Accountant." The accountant was a tall, cool devil. The very sight of him rattled me. My voice was sepulchral.

"Can I see the manager?" I said, and added solemnly, "alone." I don't know why I said "alone."

"Certainly," said the accountant, and fetched him.

The manager was a grave, calm man. I held my fifty-six dollars clutched in a crumpled ball in my pocket.

"Are you the manager?" I said. God knows I didn't doubt it.

"Yes," he said.

"Can I see you," I asked, "alone?" I didn't want to say "alone" again, but without it the thing seemed self-evident.

The manager looked at me in some alarm. He felt that I had an awful secret to reveal.

"Come in here," he said, and led the way to a private room. He turned the key in the lock.

"We are safe from interruption here," he said; "sit down."

We both sat down and looked at each other. I found no voice to speak.

"You are one of Pinkerton's men, I presume," he said.

He had gathered from my mysterious manner that I was a detective. I knew what he was thinking, and it made me worse.

"No, not from Pinkerton's," I said, seeming to imply that I came from a rival agency.

"To tell the truth," I went on, as if I had been prompted to lie about it, "I am not a detective at all. I have come to open an account. I intend to keep all my money in this bank."

The manager looked relieved but still serious; he concluded now that I was a son of Baron Rothschild or a young Gould.

"A large account, I suppose," he said.

"Fairly large," I whispered. "I propose to deposit fifty-six dollars now and fifty dollars a month regularly."

The manager got up and opened the door. He called to the accountant.

"Mr. Montgomery," he said unkindly loud, "this gentleman is opening an account, he will deposit fifty-six dollars. Good morning."

I rose.

A big iron door stood open at the side of the room.

"Good morning," I said, and stepped into the safe.

"Come out," said the manager coldly, and showed me the other way.

I went up to the accountant's wicket and poked the ball of money at him with a quick convulsive movement as if I were doing a conjuring trick.

My face was ghastly pale.

"Here," I said, "deposit it." The tone of the words seemed to mean, "Let us do this painful thing while the fit is on us."

He took the money and gave it to another clerk.

He made me write the sum on a slip and sign my name in a book. I no longer knew what I was doing. The bank swam before my eyes.

"Is it deposited?" I asked in a hollow, vibrating voice.

"It is," said the accountant.

"Then I want to draw a cheque."

My idea was to draw out six dollars of it for present use. Someone gave me a chequebook through a wicket and someone else began telling me how to write it out. The people in the bank had the impression that I was an invalid millionaire. I wrote something on the cheque and thrust it in at the clerk. He looked at it.

"What! are you drawing it all out again?" he asked in surprise. Then I realized that I had written fifty-six instead of six. I was too far gone to reason now. I had a feeling that it was impossible to explain the thing. All the clerks had stopped writing to look at me.

Reckless with misery, I made a plunge.

"Yes, the whole thing."

"You withdraw your money from the bank?"

"Every cent of it."

"Are you not going to deposit any more?" said the clerk, astonished.

"Never."

An idiot hope struck me that they might think something had insulted me while I was writing the cheque and that I had changed my mind. I made a wretched attempt to look like a man with a fearfully quick temper.

The clerk prepared to pay the money.

"How will you have it?" he said.

"What?"

"How will you have it?"

"Oh"—I caught his meaning and answered without even trying to think—"in fifties."

He gave me a fifty-dollar bill.

"And the six?" he asked dryly.

"In sixes," I said.

He gave it me and I rushed out.

As the big door swung behind me I caught the echo of a roar of laughter that went up to the ceiling of the bank. Since then I bank no more. I keep my money in cash in my trousers pocket and my savings in silver dollars in a sock.

49

The Pot of Gold

Mary Eleanor Wilkins Freeman

The Flower family lived in a little house in a broad grassy meadow, which sloped a few rods from their front door down to a gentle, silvery river. Right across the river rose a lovely dark green mountain, and when there was a rainbow, as there frequently was, nothing could have looked more enchanting than it did rising from the opposite bank of the stream with the wet, shadowy mountain for a background. All the Flower family would invariably run to their front windows and their door to see it.

The Flower family numbered nine: Father and Mother Flower and seven children. Father Flower was an unappreciated poet, Mother Flower was very much like all mothers, and the seven children were very sweet and interesting. Their first names all matched beautifully with their last name, and with their personal appearance. For instance, the oldest girl, who had soft blue eyes and flaxen curls, was called Flax Flower; the little boy, who came next, and had very red cheeks and loved to sleep late in the morning, was called Poppy Flower, and so on. This charming suitableness of their names was owing to Father Flower. He had a theory that a great deal of the misery and discord in the world comes from things not matching properly as they should; and he thought there ought to be a certain correspondence between all things that were in juxtaposition to each other, just as there ought to be between the last two words of a couplet of poetry. But he found, very often, there was no correspondence at all, just as words in poetry do not always rhyme when they should. However, he did his best to remedy it. He saw that every one of his children's names were suitable and accorded with their personal characteristics; and in his flower-garden—for he raised flowers for the market—only those of complementary colors were allowed to grow in adjoining beds, and, as often as possible, they rhymed in their names. But that was a more difficult matter to manage, and very few flowers were rhymed, or, if they were, none rhymed correctly. He had a bed of box next to one of phlox, and a trellis of woodbine grew next to one of eglantine, and a thicket of elder-blows was next to one of rose; but he was forced to let his violets and honeysuckles and many others go entirely unrhymed—this disturbed him considerably, but he reflected that it was not his fault, but that of the man who made the language and named the different flowers—he should have looked to it that those of complementary colors had names to rhyme with each other, then all would have been harmonious and as it should have been.

Father Flower had chosen this way of earning his livelihood when he realized that he was doomed to be an unappreciated poet, because it suited so well with his name; and if the flowers had only rhymed a little better he would have been very well contented. As it was, he never grumbled. He also saw to it that the furniture in his little house and the cooking utensils rhymed as nearly as possible, though that too was oftentimes a difficult matter to bring about, and required a vast deal of thought and hard study. The table always stood under the gable end of the roof, the foot-stool always stood where it was cool, and the big rocking-chair in a glare of sunlight; the lamp, too, he kept down cellar where it was damp. But all these were rather far-fetched, and sometimes quite inconvenient. Occasionally there would be an article that he could not rhyme until he had spent years of thought over it, and when he did it would disturb the comfort of the family greatly. There was the spider. He puzzled over that exceedingly, and when he rhymed it at last, Mother Flower or one of the little girls had always to take the spider beside her, when she sat down, which was of course quite troublesome. The kettle he rhymed first with nettle, and hung a bunch of nettle over it, till all the children got dreadfully stung. Then he tried settle, and hung the kettle over the settle. But that was no place for it; they had to go without their tea, and everybody who sat on the settle bumped his head against the kettle. At last it occurred to Father Flower that if he should make a slight change in the language the kettle could rhyme with the skillet, and sit beside it on the stove, as it ought, leaving harmony out of the question, to do. Accordingly all the children were instructed to call the skillet a skettle, and the kettle stood by its side on the stove ever afterward.

The house was a very pretty one, although it was quite rude and very simple. It was built of logs and had a thatched roof, which projected far out over the walls. But it was all overrun with the loveliest flowering vines imaginable, and, inside, nothing could have been more exquisitely neat and homelike; although there was only one room and a little garret over it. All around the house were the flower-beds and the vine-trellises and the blooming shrubs, and they were always in the most beautiful order. Now, although all this was very pretty to see, and seemingly very simple to bring to pass, yet there was a vast deal of labor in it for some one; for flowers do not look so trim and thriving without tending, and houses do not look so spotlessly clean without constant care. All the Flower family worked hard; even the littlest children had their daily tasks set them. The oldest girl, especially, little Flax Flower, was kept busy from morning till night taking care of her younger brothers and sisters, and weeding flowers. But for all that she was a very happy little girl, as indeed were the whole family, as they did not mind working, and loved each other dearly.

Father Flower, to be sure, felt a little sad sometimes; for, although his lot in life was a pleasant one, it was not exactly what he would have chosen. Once in a while he had a great longing for something different. He confided a great many of his feelings to Flax Flower; she was more like him than any of the other children, and could understand him even better than his wife, he thought.

One day, when there had been a heavy shower and a beautiful rainbow, he and Flax were out in the garden tying up some rose-bushes, which the rain had beaten down, and he said to her how he wished he could find the Pot of Gold at the end of the rainbow. Flax, if you will believe me, had never heard of it; so he had to tell her all about it, and also say a little poem he had made about it to her.

The poem ran something in this way:

O what is it shineth so golden-clear
        At the rainbow's foot on the dark green hill?
'Tis the Pot of Gold, that for many a year
        Has shone, and is shining and dazzling still.
And whom is it for, O Pilgrim, pray?
For thee, Sweetheart, should'st thou go that way.

Flax listened with her soft blue eyes very wide open. "I suppose if we should find that pot of gold it would make us very rich, wouldn't it, father?" said she.

"Yes," replied her father; "we could then have a grand house, and keep a gardener, and a maid to take care of the children, and we should no longer have to work so hard." He sighed as he spoke, and tears stood in his gentle blue eyes, which were very much like Flax's. "However, we shall never find it," he added.

"Why couldn't we run ever so fast when we saw the rainbow," inquired Flax, "and get the Pot of Gold?"

"Don't be foolish, child!" said her father; "you could not possibly reach it before the rainbow was quite faded away!"

"True," said Flax, but she fell to thinking as she tied up the dripping roses.

The next rainbow they had she eyed very closely, standing out on the front door-step in the rain, and she saw that one end of it seemed to touch the ground at the foot of a pine-tree on the side of the mountain, which was quite conspicuous amongst its fellows, it was so tall. The other end had nothing especial to mark it.

"I will try the end where the tall pine-tree is first," said Flax to herself, "because that will be the easiest to find—if the Pot of Gold isn't there I will try to find the other end."

A few days after that it was very hot and sultry, and at noon the thunder heads were piled high all around the horizon.

"I don't doubt but we shall have showers this afternoon," said Father Flower, when he came in from the garden for his dinner.

After the dinner-dishes were washed up, and the baby rocked to sleep, Flax came to her mother with a petition.

"Mother," said she, "won't you give me a holiday this afternoon?"

"Why, where do you want to go, Flax?" said her mother.

"I want to go over on the mountain and hunt for wild flowers," replied Flax.

"But I think it is going to rain, child, and you will get wet."

"That won't hurt me any, mother," said Flax, laughing.

"Well, I don't know as I care," said her mother, hesitatingly. "You have been a very good industrious girl, and deserve a little holiday. Only don't go so far that you cannot soon run home if a shower should come up."

So Flax curled her flaxen hair and tied it up with a blue ribbon, and put on her blue and white checked dress. By the time she was ready to go the clouds over in the northwest were piled up very high and black, and it was quite late in the afternoon. Very likely her mother would not have let her gone if she had been at home, but she had taken the baby, who had waked from his nap, and gone to call on her nearest neighbor, half a mile away. As for her father, he was busy in the garden, and all the other children were with him, and they did not notice Flax when she stole out of the front door. She crossed the river on a pretty arched stone bridge nearly opposite the house, and went directly into the woods on the side of the mountain.

Everything was very still and dark and solemn in the woods. They knew about the storm that was coming. Now and then Flax heard the leaves talking in queer little rustling voices. She inherited the ability to understand what they said from her father. They were talking to each other now in the words of her father's song. Very likely he had heard them saying it sometime, and that was how he happened to know it,

> "O what is it shineth so golden-clear
> At the rainbow's foot on the dark green hill?"

Flax heard the maple leaves inquire. And the pine-leaves answered back:

> "'Tis the Pot of Gold, that for many a year
> Has shone, and is shining and dazzling still."

Then the maple-leaves asked:

> "And whom is it for, O Pilgrim, pray?"

And the pine-leaves answered:

> "For thee, Sweetheart, should'st thou go that way."

Flax did not exactly understand the sense of the last question and answer between maple and pine-leaves. But they kept on saying it over and over as she ran along. She was going straight to the tall pine-tree. She knew just where it was, for she had often been there. Now the rain-drops began to splash through the green boughs, and the thunder rolled along the sky. The leaves all tossed about in a strong wind and their soft rustles grew into a roar, and the branches and the whole tree caught it up and called out so loud as they writhed and twisted about that Flax was almost deafened, the words of the song:

"O what is it shineth so golden-clear?"

Flax sped along through the wind and the rain and the thunder. She was very much afraid that she should not reach the tall pine which was quite a way distant before the sun shone out, and the rainbow came.

The sun was already breaking through the clouds when she came in sight of it, way up above her on a rock. The rain-drops on the trees began to shine like diamonds, and the words of the song rushed out from their midst, louder and sweeter:

"O what is it shineth so golden-clear?"

Flax climbed for dear life. Red and green and golden rays were already falling thick around her, and at the foot of the pine-tree something was shining wonderfully clear and bright.

At last she reached it, and just at that instant the rainbow became a perfect one, and there at the foot of the wonderful arch of glory was the Pot of Gold. Flax could see it brighter than all the brightness of the rainbow. She sank down beside it and put her hand on it, then she closed her eyes and sat still, bathed in red and green and violet light—that, and the golden light from the Pot, made her blind and dizzy. As she sat there with her hand on the Pot of Gold at the foot of the rainbow, she could hear the leaves over her singing louder and louder, till the tones fairly rushed like a wind through her ears. But this time they only sang the last words of the song:

"And whom is it for, O Pilgrim, pray?
For thee, Sweetheart, should'st thou go that way."

At last she ventured to open her eyes. The rainbow had faded almost entirely away, only a few tender rose and green shades were arching over her; but the Pot of Gold under her hand was still there, and shining brighter than ever. All the pine needles with which the ground around it was thickly spread, were turned to needles of gold, and some stray couplets of leaves which were springing up through them were all gilded.

Flax bent over it trembling and lifted the lid off the pot. She expected, of course, to find it full of gold pieces that would buy the grand house and the gardener and the maid that her father had spoken about. But to her astonishment, when she had lifted the lid off and bent over the Pot to look into it, the first thing she saw was the face of her mother looking out of it at her. It was smaller of course, but just the same loving, kindly face she had left at home. Then, as she looked longer, she saw her father smiling gently up at her, then came Poppy and the baby and all the rest of her dear little brothers and sisters smiling up at her out of the golden gloom inside the Pot. At last she actually saw the garden and her father in it tying up the roses, and the pretty little vine-covered house, and, finally, she could see right into the dear little room where her mother sat with the baby in her lap, and all the others around her.

Flax jumped up. "I will run home," said she, "it is late, and I do want to see them all dreadfully."

So she left the Golden Pot shining all alone under the pine-tree, and ran home as fast as she could.

When she reached the house it was almost twilight, but her father was still in the garden. Every rose and lily had to be tied up after the shower, and he was but just finishing. He had the tin milk pan hung on him like a shield, because it rhymed with man. It certainly was a beautiful rhyme, but it was very inconvenient. Poor Mother Flower was at her wits' end to know what to do without it, and it was very awkward for Father Flower to work with it fastened to him.

Flax ran breathlessly into the garden, and threw her arms around her father's neck and kissed him. She bumped her nose against the milk pan, but she did not mind that; she was so glad to see him again. Somehow, she never remembered being so glad to see him as she was now since she had seen his face in the Pot of Gold.

"Dear father," cried she, "how glad I am to see you! I found the Pot of Gold at the end of the rainbow!"

Her father stared at her in amazement.

"Yes, I did, truly, father," said she. "But it was not full of gold, after all. You was in it, and mother and the children and the house and garden and—everything."

"You were mistaken, dear," said her father, looking at her with his gentle, sorrowful eyes. "You could not have found the true end of the rainbow, nor the true Pot of Gold—that is surely full of the most beautiful gold pieces, with an angel stamped on every one."

"But I did, father," persisted Flax.

"You had better go into your mother, Flax," said her father; "she will be anxious to see you. I know better than you about the Pot of Gold at the end of the rainbow."

So Flax went sorrowfully into the house. There was the tea-kettle singing beside the "skettle," which had some nice smelling soup in it, the table was laid for supper, and there sat her mother with the baby in her lap and the others all around her—just as they had looked in the Pot of Gold.

Flax had never been so glad to see them before—and if she didn't hug and kiss them all!

"I found the Pot of Gold at the end of the rainbow, mother," cried she, "and it was not full of gold, at all; but you and father and the children looked out of it at me, and I saw the house and garden and everything in it."

Her mother looked at her lovingly. "Yes, Flax dear," said she.

"But father said I was mistaken," said Flax, "and did not find it."

"Well, dear," said her mother, "your father is a poet, and very wise; we will say no more about it. You can sit down here and hold the baby now, while I make the tea."

Flax was perfectly ready to do that; and, as she sat there with her darling little baby brother crowing in her lap, and watched her pretty little brothers and sisters and her dear mother, she felt so happy that she did not care any longer whether she had found the true Pot of Gold at the end of the rainbow or not.

But, after all, do you know, I think her father was mistaken, and that she had.

50

An Arrow in a Sunbeam

Sarah Orne Jewett

The minister of a fashionable church had noticed Sunday after Sunday a little old lady with a sad, patient face, dressed in very shabby mourning, sitting in the strangers' pew.

Like Job this good man could say, "The cause that I knew not, I sought out." He soon learned from the sexton her name and residence, and was surprised to find her in the very topmost room of a house, amid evidences of real poverty.

In the one little window bloomed a monthly rose and a vigorous heliotrope, and beside the pots lay half-a-dozen books, such as are rarely seen in the homes of the very poor. On the wall hung two fine engravings, and an old fashioned gold watch was suspended from a faded velvet case over the mantel piece.

Her story, when she was induced to tell it, was neither new nor startling. She had long been a widow. Her children had been called from her, till now she had but one, and he, being a cripple, could do little more than supply his own absolute wants by his work as a repairer of watches.

The pastor was charmed with her patient endurance of what others would call the hard discipline of life, and when he left her he felt that he had been a learner instead of a teacher in that poor room.

Being too delicate to allude to her apparent poverty, he said at parting, "As you are a stranger among us, I will send some of the visitors of the church to cheer and comfort you."

He selected two bright, rosy girls, full of life and happiness, of whose visits among the poor he had often heard.

They came to the widow like sunbeams through a storm. They talked cheerily, and did not appear to notice the bareness of the room. They asked something of her history, and told of their grandmothers, who also had seen much sorrow; and in this way drew her out till she told of her former competency, of her early advantages in England, and of all the misfortunes which had brought her to her present position. "And yet," she said, "I have little to complain of while I have the love and tender care of such a son as Walter."

Little by little, without a complaint from her, they found that the old lady lacked many things for her comfort. Their sympathies were aroused. It would be a delight to make her happy by gifts that would be of service to her.

Lucy Grey, a girl full of fun as well as of kindness, said, "I wish you would let me make you a bonnet; I make lovely ones. Grandma won't wear a milliner's bonnet, she likes mine so much better."

Grace Wheeler volunteered to make a dress and caps, adding, playfully, "As my dear grandma is gone, you must let me adopt you and do all I can for you. There are four of us girls always looking round for somebody to help. You can call on us for anything you want."

Four young girls, who laughingly styled themselves "The Quartette of Mercy," met at Grace Wheeler's house with materials for a dress, and a bonnet and caps. The old lady was coming two hours afterward to be fitted, having being measured before they left her house.

The girls were in a perfect gala of joy that bright afternoon. They chatted merrily while working, and one would have thought they were making costumes for comic tableaux rather than the garb of a sorrowful widow.

"I'll tell you, girls," said Lucy Grey, "the old dowager will shine when she gets my bonnet on!" and trying it on over her chestnut curls, she added, "I half-wish I was a downfallen lady myself,—a haberdasher's daughter from England! Oh, I hope I shall be a widow some time! Widows' caps are so becoming!"

"Well," replied Grace, laughing, "do your best for Goody Horn, and maybe she'll let you have 'dear Walter.' Then you'll be a widow soon,—he's so feeble."

"Oh, I wish I had the dressing of her! 'She'd surprise herself,' as the Dutchman said. I'd put a canary-coloured pompon and a white aigrette in that bonnet, and"—here she slipped a scarlet bird out of her own hat and stuck it into a fold of the crape Lucy was laying on to the old fashioned close frame—"I'd make her an upper skirt with a tie-back, get scarlet stockings and low shoes, and"——

"Pho! you'd make the dear old soul look like Mother Hubbard!" cried another.

"No," said Grace; "but she looks now like

"Little Dame Crump, with her brand-new broom;"

and no doubt Walter looks either like Mother Hubbard's dog, or—or I don't know what."

"Oh, by-the-way, did you notice a violin on the bureau? Whoever gets 'dear Walter' will have a chance to do all the family dancing. The dowager's too old, and Walter's too lame; but there, what stuff I'm talking; it's well mother isn't within hearing. She won't let me have any sport. But I do think old folks are so comical! I'll do anything in the world to help them, though."

They worked on some time, and in the real kindness which was hidden under this nonsense they laid plans for the dear old stranger's future comfort.

"Why, girls, it's time she was here now!"

"Nora," called Grace, as a girl passed the door, "when an old lady comes, send her right up stairs."

"There was an old person here an hour ago, and as you told me not to let any one in who asked for you for an hour, I told her to sit down in the hall. I suppose she's there now. I forgot all about her," was the reply.

Grace flew down, but there was no one there.

"That was some old beggar who got tired of waiting. I'm sure she'll be here soon," said Lucy.

But she did not come, and they grew tired of waiting to try on the dress and hat. So they resolved to go, all four together, the next day, to the "opening at Madam Horn's," and carry the things themselves.

They did so; but when the "dowager" opened the door at their knock, they hardly knew her. She looked straight, and solemn, and cold. She did not even ask them in; but they went in and seated themselves.

Grace said, "You didn't come yesterday to try on the dress, and thinking you might be ill, we brought it here."

"But I did go, ladies. I went an hour earlier than you asked me, to beg that the dress might be cut perfectly plain, without upper skirt or flounce. The girl seated me in the hall, and while I sat there, I was forced to hear myself and my son ridiculed and turned to scorn in a way I could not believe possible.

"I have done nothing to merit this. I never begged of you, nor sought your sympathy in my sorrows, and I cannot understand why I am made the butt of your scorn."

"Oh, Mrs. Horn," cried Lucy, "we were only in sport! I hope you will forgive us."

"Is it sport to cast contempt on an aged woman who has been walking for years in a fiery furnace upheld and comforted by God? Is it sport to ridicule an unfortunate boy who has a continual warfare with pain to keep up this poor home?"

"Oh, don't speak of it again!" said Grace blushing deeply and half-ready to cry, as she untied the package in her hand, while Lucy unpinned the paper that held the bonnet.

"Put them up, please, young ladies. I cannot look on them, and I never could wear them. When you first came, I told Walter that I felt as if a sunbeam had come into the house and remained behind you. Last night I told him that my new sunbeam had an arrow concealed in it."

"But you *will* take the things, after all our trouble?" implored Grace, with tears dropping from her eyes.

"No, never; I can hear the Gospel in my old clothes. I should take no pleasure in these; they are associated with too painful thoughts. I hope God will bless you, children, and save you from an old age of poverty, and give you what He has given me,—a full trust in His love and tenderness. Good-by."

You can imagine the feelings of those young girls when they left that poor room in tears.

Respectful treatment is more to the sensitive poor than gifts of food, garments or money; and nothing is so likely to harden the hearts of the young as the habit of getting sport out of the sorrows and infirmities of others.

51

Uncle Abraham's Romance

Edith Nesbit

"No, my dear," my Uncle Abraham answered me, "no—nothing romantic ever happened to me—unless—but no: that wasn't romantic either——"

I was. To me, I being eighteen, romance was the world. My Uncle Abraham was old and lame. I followed the gaze of his faded eyes, and my own rested on a miniature that hung at his elbow-chair's right hand, a portrait of a woman, whose loveliness even the miniature-painter's art had been powerless to disguise—a woman with large lustrous eyes and perfect oval face.

I rose to look at it. I had looked at it a hundred times. Often enough in my baby days I had asked, "Who's that, uncle?" always receiving the same answer: "A lady who died long ago, my dear."

As I looked again at the picture, I asked, "Was she like this?"

"Who?"

"Your—your romance!"

Uncle Abraham looked hard at me. "Yes," he said at last. "Very—very like."

I sat down on the floor by him. "Won't you tell me about her?"

"There's nothing to tell," he said. "I think it was fancy, mostly, and folly; but it's the realest thing in my long life, my dear."

A long pause. I kept silence. "Hurry no man's cattle" is a good motto, especially with old people.

"I remember," he said in the dreamy tone always promising so well to the ear that a story delighteth—"I remember, when I was a young man, I was very lonely indeed. I never had a sweetheart. I was always lame, my dear, from quite a boy; and the girls used to laugh at me."

He sighed. Presently he went on—

"And so I got into the way of mooning off by myself in lonely places, and one of my favourite walks was up through our churchyard, which was set high on a hill in the middle of the marsh country. I liked that because I never met any one there. It's all over, years ago. I was a silly lad; but I couldn't bear of a summer evening to hear a rustle and a whisper from the other side of the hedge, or maybe a kiss as I went by.

"Well, I used to go and sit all by myself in the churchyard, which was always sweet with thyme, and quite light (on account of its being so high) long after the marshes were dark. I used to watch the bats flitting about in the red light, and wonder why God didn't make every one's legs straight and strong, and wicked follies like that. But by the time the light was gone I had always worked it off, so to speak, and could go home quietly and say my prayers without any bitterness.

"Well, one hot night in August, when I had watched the sunset fade and the crescent moon grow golden, I was just stepping over the low stone wall of the churchyard when I heard a rustle behind me. I turned round, expecting it to be a rabbit or a bird. It was a woman."

He looked at the portrait. So did I.

"Yes," he said, "that was her very face. I was a bit scared and said something—I don't know what—and she laughed and said, 'Did I think she was a ghost?' and I answered back, and I stayed talking to her over the churchyard wall till 'twas quite dark, and the glowworms were out in the wet grass all along the way home.

"Next night I saw her again; and the next night and the next. Always at twilight time; and if I passed any lovers leaning on the stiles in the marshes it was nothing to me now."

Again my uncle paused. "It's very long ago," he said slowly, "and I'm an old man; but I know what youth means, and happiness, though I was always lame, and the girls used to laugh at me. I don't know how long it went on—you don't measure time in dreams—but at last your grandfather said I looked as if I had one foot in the grave, and he would be sending me to stay with our kin at Bath and take the waters. I had to go. I could not tell my father why I would rather had died than go."

"What was her name, uncle?" I asked.

"She never would tell me her name, and why should she? I had names enough in my heart to call her by. Marriage? My dear, even then I knew marriage was not for me. But I met her night after night, always in our churchyard where the yew-trees were and the lichened gravestones. It was there we always met and always parted. The last time was the night before I went away. She was very sad, and dearer than life itself. And she said—

"'If you come back before the new moon I shall meet you here just as usual. But if the new moon shines on this grave and you are not here—you will never see me again any more.'

"She laid her hand on the yellow lichened tomb against which we had been leaning. It was an old weather-worn stone, and bore on it the inscription—

'Susannah Kingsnorth,
Ob. 1713.'

"'I shall be here.' I said.

"'I mean it,' she said, with deep and sudden seriousness, 'it is no fancy. You will be here when the new moon shines?'

"I promised, and after a while we parted.

"I had been with my kinsfolk at Bath nearly a month. I was to go home on the next day, when, turning over a case in the parlour, I came upon that miniature. I could not speak for a minute. At last I said, with dry tongue, and heart beating to the tune of heaven and hell—

"'Who is this?'

"'That?' said my aunt. 'Oh! she was betrothed to one of our family many years ago, but she died before the wedding. They say she was a bit of a witch. A handsome one, wasn't she?'

"I looked again at the face, the lips, the eyes of my dear and lovely love, whom I was to meet to-morrow night when the new moon shone on that tomb in our churchyard.

"'Did you say she was dead?' I asked, and I hardly knew my own voice.

"'Years and years ago! Her name's on the back and her date——'

"I took the portrait from its faded red-velvet bed, and read on the back—'Susannah Kingsnorth, *Ob.* 1713.'

"That was in 1813." My uncle stopped short.

"What happened?" I asked breathlessly.

"I believe I had a fit," my uncle answered slowly; "at any rate, I was very ill."

"And you missed the new moon on the grave?"

"I missed the new moon on the grave."

"And you never saw her again?"

"I never saw her again——"

"But, uncle, do you really believe?—Can the dead?—was she—did you——"

My uncle took out his pipe and filled it.

"It's a long time ago," he said, "a many, many years. Old man's tales, my dear! Old man's tales! Don't you take any notice of them."

He lighted the pipe, puffed silently a moment or two, and then added: "But I know what youth means, and happiness, though I was lame, and the girls used to laugh at me."

52

The Mystery of the Semi-Detached

Edith Nesbit

He was waiting for her; he had been waiting an hour and a half in a dusty suburban lane, with a row of big elms on one side and some eligible building sites on the other—and far away to the south-west the twinkling yellow lights of the Crystal Palace. It was not quite like a country lane, for it had a pavement and lamp-posts, but it was not a bad place for a meeting all the same; and farther up, towards the cemetery, it was really quite rural, and almost pretty, especially in twilight. But twilight had long deepened into night, and still he waited. He loved her, and he was engaged to be married to her, with the complete disapproval of every reasonable person who had been consulted. And this half-clandestine meeting was to-night to take the place of the grudgingly sanctioned weekly interview—because a certain rich uncle was visiting at her house, and her mother was not the woman to acknowledge to a moneyed uncle, who might "go off" any day, a match so deeply ineligible as hers with him.

So he waited for her, and the chill of an unusually severe May evening entered into his bones.

The policeman passed him with but a surly response to his "Good night." The bicyclists went by him like grey ghosts with fog-horns; and it was nearly ten o'clock, and she had not come.

He shrugged his shoulders and turned towards his lodgings. His road led him by her house—desirable, commodious, semi-detached—and he walked slowly as he neared it. She might, even now, be coming out. But she was not. There was no sign of movement about the house, no sign of life, no lights even in the windows. And her people were not early people.

He paused by the gate, wondering.

Then he noticed that the front door was open—wide open—and the street lamp shone a little way into the dark hall. There was something about all this that did not please him—that scared him a little, indeed. The house had a gloomy and deserted air. It was obviously impossible that it harboured a rich uncle. The old man must have left early. In which case——

He walked up the path of patent-glazed tiles, and listened. No sign of life. He passed into the hall. There was no light anywhere. Where was everybody, and why was the front door open? There was no one in the drawing-room, the dining-room and the study (nine feet by seven) were equally blank. Every one was out, evidently. But the unpleasant sense that he was, perhaps, not the first casual visitor to walk through that open door impelled him to look through the house before he went away and closed it after him. So he went upstairs, and at the door of the first bedroom he came to he struck a wax match, as he had done in the sitting-rooms. Even as he did so he felt that he was not alone. And he was prepared to see *something*; but for what he saw he was not prepared. For what he saw lay on the bed, in a white loose gown—and it was his sweetheart, and its throat was cut from ear to ear. He doesn't know what happened then, nor how he got downstairs and into the street; but he got out somehow, and the policeman found him in a fit, under the lamp-post at the corner of the street. He couldn't speak when they picked him up, and he passed the night in the police-cells, because the policeman had seen plenty of drunken men before, but never one in a fit.

The next morning he was better, though still very white and shaky. But the tale he told the magistrate was convincing, and they sent a couple of constables with him to her house.

There was no crowd about it as he had fancied there would be, and the blinds were not down.

As he stood, dazed, in front of the door, it opened, and she came out.

He held on to the door-post for support.

"*She's* all right, you see," said the constable, who had found him under the lamp. "I told you you was drunk, but you *would* know best——"

When he was alone with her he told her—not all—for that would not bear telling—but how he had come into the commodious semi-detached, and how he had found the door open and the lights out, and that he had been into that long back room facing the stairs, and had seen something—in even trying to hint at which he turned sick and broke down and had to have brandy given him.

"But, my dearest," she said, "I dare say the house was dark, for we were all at the Crystal Palace with my uncle, and no doubt the door was open, for the maids *will* run out if they're left. But you could not have been in that room, because I locked it when I came away, and the key was in my pocket. I dressed in a hurry and I left all my odds and ends lying about."

"I know," he said; "I saw a green scarf on a chair, and some long brown gloves, and a lot of hairpins and ribbons, and a prayer-book, and a lace handkerchief on the dressing-table. Why, I even noticed the almanack on the mantelpiece—October 21. At least it couldn't be that, because this is May. And yet it was. Your almanac is at October 21, isn't it?"

"No, of course it isn't," she said, smiling rather anxiously; "but all the other things were just as you say. You must have had a dream, or a vision, or something."

He was a very ordinary, commonplace, City young man, and he didn't believe in visions, but he never rested day or night till he got his sweetheart and her mother away from that commodious semi-detached, and settled them in a quite distant suburb. In the course of the removal he incidentally married her, and the mother went on living with them.

His nerves must have been a good bit shaken, because he was very queer for a long time, and was always inquiring if any one had taken the desirable semi-detached; and when an old stockbroker with a family took it, he went the length of calling on the old gentleman and imploring him by all that he held dear, not to live in that fatal house.

"Why?" said the stockbroker, not unnaturally.

And then he got so vague and confused, between trying to tell why and trying not to tell why, that the stockbroker showed him out, and thanked his God he was not such a fool as to allow a lunatic to stand in the way of his taking that really remarkably cheap and desirable semi-detached residence.

Now the curious and quite inexplicable part of this story is that when she came down to breakfast on the morning of the 22nd of October she found him looking like death, with the morning paper in his hand. He caught hers—he couldn't speak, and pointed to the paper. And there she read that on the night of the 21st a young lady, the stockbroker's daughter, had been found, with her throat cut from ear to ear, on the bed in the long back bedroom facing the stairs of that desirable semi-detached.

53

A Midsummer Night's Dream

Edith Nesbit and William Shakespeare

Hermia and Lysander were lovers; but Hermia's father wished her to marry another man, named Demetrius.

Now, in Athens, where they lived, there was a wicked law, by which any girl who refused to marry according to her father's wishes, might be put to death. Hermia's father was so angry with her for refusing to do as he wished, that he actually brought her before the Duke of Athens to ask that she might be killed, if she still refused to obey him. The Duke gave her four days to think about it, and, at the end of that time, if she still refused to marry Demetrius, she would have to die.

Lysander of course was nearly mad with grief, and the best thing to do seemed to him for Hermia to run away to his aunt's house at a place beyond the reach of that cruel law; and there he would come to her and marry her. But before she started, she told her friend, Helena, what she was going to do.

Helena had been Demetrius' sweetheart long before his marriage with Hermia had been thought of, and being very silly, like all jealous people, she could not see that it was not poor Hermia's fault that Demetrius wished to marry her instead of his own lady, Helena. She knew that if she told Demetrius that Hermia was going, as she was, to the wood outside Athens, he would follow her, "and I can follow him, and at least I shall see him," she said to herself. So she went to him, and betrayed her friend's secret.

Now this wood where Lysander was to meet Hermia, and where the other two had decided to follow them, was full of fairies, as most woods are, if one only had the eyes to see them, and in this wood on this night were the King and Queen of the fairies, Oberon and Titania. Now fairies are very wise people, but now and then they can be quite as foolish as mortal folk. Oberon and Titania, who might have been as happy as the days were long, had thrown away all their joy in a foolish quarrel. They never met without saying disagreeable things to each other, and scolded each other so dreadfully that all their little fairy followers, for fear, would creep into acorn cups and hide them there.

So, instead of keeping one happy Court and dancing all night through in the moonlight as is fairies' use, the King with his attendants wandered through one part of the wood, while the Queen with hers kept state in another. And the cause of all this trouble was a little Indian boy whom Titania had taken to be one of her followers. Oberon wanted the child to follow him and be one of his fairy knights; but the Queen would not give him up.

On this night, in a mossy moonlit glade, the King and Queen of the fairies met.

"Ill met by moonlight, proud Titania," said the King.

"What! jealous, Oberon?" answered the Queen. "You spoil everything with your quarreling. Come, fairies, let us leave him. I am not friends with him now."

"It rests with you to make up the quarrel," said the King.

"Give me that little Indian boy, and I will again be your humble servant and suitor."

"Set your mind at rest," said the Queen. "Your whole fairy kingdom buys not that boy from me. Come, fairies."

And she and her train rode off down the moonbeams.

"Well, go your ways," said Oberon. "But I'll be even with you before you leave this wood."

Then Oberon called his favorite fairy, Puck. Puck was the spirit of mischief. He used to slip into the dairies and take the cream away, and get into the churn so that the butter would not come, and turn the beer sour, and lead people out of their way on dark nights and then laugh at them, and tumble people's stools from under them when they were going to sit down, and upset their hot ale over their chins when they were going to drink.

"Now," said Oberon to this little sprite, "fetch me the flower called Love-in-idleness. The juice of that little purple flower laid on the eyes of those who sleep will make them, when they wake, to love the first thing they see. I will put some of the juice of that flower on my Titania's eyes, and when she wakes she will love the first thing she sees, were it lion, bear, or wolf, or bull, or meddling monkey, or a busy ape."

While Puck was gone, Demetrius passed through the glade followed by poor Helena, and still she told him how she loved him and reminded him of all his promises, and still he told her that he did not and could not love her, and that his promises were nothing. Oberon was sorry for poor Helena, and when Puck returned with the flower, he bade him follow Demetrius and put some of the juice on his eyes, so that he might love Helena when he woke and looked on her, as much as she loved him. So Puck set off, and wandering through the wood found, not Demetrius, but Lysander, on whose eyes he put the juice; but when Lysander woke, he saw not his own Hermia, but Helena, who was walking through the wood looking for the cruel Demetrius; and directly he saw her he loved her and left his own lady, under the spell of the purple flower.

When Hermia woke she found Lysander gone, and wandered about the wood trying to find him. Puck went back and told Oberon what he had done, and Oberon soon found that he had made a mistake, and set about looking for Demetrius, and having found him, put some of the juice on his eyes. And the first thing Demetrius saw when he woke was also Helena. So now Demetrius and Lysander were both following her through the wood, and it was Hermia's turn to follow her lover as Helena had done before. The end of it was that Helena and Hermia began to quarrel, and Demetrius and Lysander went off to fight. Oberon was very sorry to see his kind scheme to help these lovers turn out so badly. So he said to Puck—

"These two young men are going to fight. You must overhang the night with drooping fog, and lead them so astray, that one will never find the other. When they are tired out, they will fall asleep. Then drop this other herb on Lysander's eyes. That will give him his old sight and his old love. Then each man will have the lady who loves him, and they will all think that this has been only a Midsummer Night's Dream. Then when this is done, all will be well with them."

So Puck went and did as he was told, and when the two had fallen asleep without meeting each other, Puck poured the juice on Lysander's eyes, and said:—

"When thou wakest,
Thou takest

True delight
In the sight
Of thy former lady's eye:
Jack shall have Jill;
Nought shall go ill."

Meanwhile Oberon found Titania asleep on a bank where grew wild thyme, oxlips, and violets, and woodbine, musk-roses and eglantine. There Titania always slept a part of the night, wrapped in the enameled skin of a snake. Oberon stooped over her and laid the juice on her eyes, saying:—

"What thou seest when thou wake,
Do it for thy true love take."

Now, it happened that when Titania woke the first thing she saw was a stupid clown, one of a party of players who had come out into the wood to rehearse their play. This clown had met with Puck, who had clapped an ass's head on his shoulders so that it looked as if it grew there. Directly Titania woke and saw this dreadful monster, she said, "What angel is this? Are you as wise as you are beautiful?"

"If I am wise enough to find my way out of this wood, that's enough for me," said the foolish clown.

"Do not desire to go out of the wood," said Titania. The spell of the love-juice was on her, and to her the clown seemed the most beautiful and delightful creature on all the earth. "I love you," she went on. "Come with me, and I will give you fairies to attend on you."

So she called four fairies, whose names were Peaseblossom, Cobweb, Moth, and Mustardseed.

"You must attend this gentleman," said the Queen. "Feed him with apricots and dewberries, purple grapes, green figs, and mulberries. Steal honey-bags for him from the bumble-bees, and with the wings of painted butterflies fan the moonbeams from his sleeping eyes."

"I will," said one of the fairies, and all the others said, "I will."

"Now, sit down with me," said the Queen to the clown, "and let me stroke your dear cheeks, and stick musk-roses in your smooth, sleek head, and kiss your fair large ears, my gentle joy."

"Where's Peaseblossom?" asked the clown with the ass's head. He did not care much about the Queen's affection, but he was very proud of having fairies to wait on him. "Ready," said Peaseblossom.

"Scratch my head, Peaseblossom," said the clown. "Where's Cobweb?" "Ready," said Cobweb.

"Kill me," said the clown, "the red bumble-bee on the top of the thistle yonder, and bring me the honey-bag. Where's Mustardseed?"

"Ready," said Mustardseed.

"Oh, I want nothing," said the clown. "Only just help Cobweb to scratch. I must go to the barber's, for methinks I am marvelous hairy about the face."

"Would you like anything to eat?" said the fairy Queen.

"I should like some good dry oats," said the clown—for his donkey's head made him desire donkey's food—"and some hay to follow."

"Shall some of my fairies fetch you new nuts from the squirrel's house?" asked the Queen.

"I'd rather have a handful or two of good dried peas," said the clown. "But please don't let any of your people disturb me; I am going to sleep."

Then said the Queen, "And I will wind thee in my arms."

And so when Oberon came along he found his beautiful Queen lavishing kisses and endearments on a clown with a donkey's head.

And before he released her from the enchantment, he persuaded her to give him the little Indian boy he so much desired to have. Then he took pity on her, and threw some juice of the disenchanting flower on her pretty eyes; and then in a moment she saw plainly the donkey-headed clown she had been loving, and knew how foolish she had been.

Oberon took off the ass's head from the clown, and left him to finish his sleep with his own silly head lying on the thyme and violets.

Thus all was made plain and straight again. Oberon and Titania loved each other more than ever. Demetrius thought of no one but Helena, and Helena had never had any thought of anyone but Demetrius.

As for Hermia and Lysander, they were as loving a couple as you could meet in a day's march, even through a fairy wood.

So the four mortal lovers went back to Athens and were married; and the fairy King and Queen live happily together in that very wood at this very day.

54

The Tempest

Edith Nesbit and William Shakespeare

Prospero, the Duke of Milan, was a learned and studious man, who lived among his books, leaving the management of his dukedom to his brother Antonio, in whom indeed he had complete trust. But that trust was ill-rewarded, for Antonio wanted to wear the duke's crown himself, and, to gain his ends, would have killed his brother but for the love the people bore him. However, with the help of Prospero's great enemy, Alonso, King of Naples, he managed to get into his hands the dukedom with all its honor, power, and riches. For they took Prospero to sea, and when they were far away from land, forced him into a little boat with no tackle, mast, or sail. In their cruelty and hatred they put his little daughter, Miranda (not yet three years old), into the boat with him, and sailed away, leaving them to their fate.

But one among the courtiers with Antonio was true to his rightful master, Prospero. To save the duke from his enemies was impossible, but much could be done to remind him of a subject's love. So this worthy lord, whose name was Gonzalo, secretly placed in the boat some fresh water, provisions, and clothes, and what Prospero valued most of all, some of his precious books.

The boat was cast on an island, and Prospero and his little one landed in safety. Now this island was enchanted, and for years had lain under the spell of a fell witch, Sycorax, who had imprisoned in the trunks of trees all the good spirits she found there. She died shortly before Prospero was cast on those shores, but the spirits, of whom Ariel was the chief, still remained in their prisons.

Prospero was a great magician, for he had devoted himself almost entirely to the study of magic during the years in which he allowed his brother to manage the affairs of Milan. By his art he set free the imprisoned spirits, yet kept them obedient to his will, and they were more truly his subjects than his people in Milan had been. For he treated them kindly as long as they did his bidding, and he exercised his power over them wisely and well. One creature alone he found it necessary to treat with harshness: this was Caliban, the son of the wicked old witch, a hideous, deformed monster, horrible to look on, and vicious and brutal in all his habits.

When Miranda was grown up into a maiden, sweet and fair to see, it chanced that Antonio and Alonso, with Sebastian, his brother, and Ferdinand, his son, were at sea together with old Gonzalo, and their ship came near Prospero's island. Prospero, knowing they were there, raised by his art a great storm, so that even the sailors on board gave themselves up for lost; and first among them all Prince Ferdinand leaped into the sea, and, as his father thought in his grief, was drowned. But Ariel brought him safe ashore; and all the rest of the crew, although they were washed overboard, were landed unhurt in different parts of the island, and the good ship herself, which they all thought had been wrecked, lay at anchor in the harbor whither Ariel had brought her. Such wonders could Prospero and his spirits perform.

While yet the tempest was raging, Prospero showed his daughter the brave ship laboring in the trough of the sea, and told her that it was filled with living human beings like themselves. She, in pity of their lives, prayed him who had raised this storm to quell it. Then her father bade her to have no fear, for he intended to save every one of them.

Then, for the first time, he told her the story of his life and hers, and that he had caused this storm to rise in order that his enemies, Antonio and Alonso, who were on board, might be delivered into his hands.

When he had made an end of his story he charmed her into sleep, for Ariel was at hand, and he had work for him to do. Ariel, who longed for his complete freedom, grumbled to be kept in drudgery, but on being threateningly reminded of all the sufferings he had undergone when Sycorax ruled in the land, and of the debt of gratitude he owed to the master who had made those sufferings to end, he ceased to complain, and promised faithfully to do whatever Prospero might command.

"Do so," said Prospero, "and in two days I will discharge thee."

Then he bade Ariel take the form of a water nymph and sent him in search of the young prince. And Ariel, invisible to Ferdinand, hovered near him, singing the while—

"Come unto these yellow sands
And then take hands:
Court'sied when you have, and kiss'd
(The wild waves whist),
Foot it featly here and there;
And, sweet sprites, the burden bear!"

And Ferdinand followed the magic singing, as the song changed to a solemn air, and the words brought grief to his heart, and tears to his eyes, for thus they ran—

"Full fathom five thy father lies;
Of his bones are coral made.
Those are pearls that were his eyes,
Nothing of him that doth fade,
But doth suffer a sea-change
Into something rich and strange.
Sea-nymphs hourly ring his knell.
Hark! now I hear them,—ding dong bell!"

And so singing, Ariel led the spell-bound prince into the presence of Prospero and Miranda. Then, behold! all happened as Prospero desired. For Miranda, who had never, since she could first remember, seen any human being save her father, looked on the youthful prince with reverence in her eyes, and love in her secret heart.

"I might call him," she said, "a thing divine, for nothing natural I ever saw so noble!"

And Ferdinand, beholding her beauty with wonder and delight, exclaimed—

"Most sure the goddess on whom these airs attend!"

Nor did he attempt to hide the passion which she inspired in him, for scarcely had they exchanged half a dozen sentences, before he vowed to make her his queen if she were willing. But Prospero, though secretly delighted, pretended wrath.

"You come here as a spy," he said to Ferdinand. "I will manacle your neck and feet together, and you shall feed on fresh water mussels, withered roots and husk, and have sea-water to drink. Follow."

"No," said Ferdinand, and drew his sword. But on the instant Prospero charmed him so that he stood there like a statue, still as stone;

and Miranda in terror prayed her father to have mercy on her lover. But he harshly refused her, and made Ferdinand follow him to his cell. There he set the Prince to work, making him remove thousands of heavy logs of timber and pile them up; and Ferdinand patiently obeyed, and thought his toil all too well repaid by the sympathy of the sweet Miranda.

She in very pity would have helped him in his hard work, but he would not let her, yet he could not keep from her the secret of his love, and she, hearing it, rejoiced and promised to be his wife.

Then Prospero released him from his servitude, and glad at heart, he gave his consent to their marriage.

"Take her," he said, "she is thine own."

In the meantime, Antonio and Sebastian in another part of the island were plotting the murder of Alonso, the King of Naples, for Ferdinand being dead, as they thought, Sebastian would succeed to the throne on Alonso's death. And they would have carried out their wicked purpose while their victim was asleep, but that Ariel woke him in good time.

Many tricks did Ariel play them. Once he set a banquet before them, and just as they were going to fall to, he appeared to them amid thunder and lightning in the form of a harpy, and immediately the banquet disappeared. Then Ariel upbraided them with their sins and vanished too.

Prospero by his enchantments drew them all to the grove without his cell, where they waited, trembling and afraid, and now at last bitterly repenting them of their sins.

Prospero determined to make one last use of his magic power, "And then," said he, "I'll break my staff and deeper than did ever plummet sound I'll drown my book."

So he made heavenly music to sound in the air, and appeared to them in his proper shape as the Duke of Milan. Because they repented, he forgave them and told them the story of his life since they had cruelly committed him and his baby daughter to the mercy of wind and waves. Alonso, who seemed sorriest of them all for his past crimes, lamented the loss of his heir. But Prospero drew back a curtain and showed them Ferdinand and Miranda playing at chess. Great was Alonso's joy to greet his loved son again, and when he heard that the fair maid with whom Ferdinand was playing was Prospero's daughter, and that the young folks had plighted their troth, he said—

"Give me your hands, let grief and sorrow still embrace his heart that doth not wish you joy."

So all ended happily. The ship was safe in the harbor, and next day they all set sail for Naples, where Ferdinand and Miranda were to be married. Ariel gave them calm seas and auspicious gales; and many were the rejoicings at the wedding.

Then Prospero, after many years of absence, went back to his own dukedom, where he was welcomed with great joy by his faithful subjects. He practiced the arts of magic no more, but his life was happy, and not only because he had found his own again, but chiefly because, when his bitterest foes who had done him deadly wrong lay at his mercy, he took no vengeance on them, but nobly forgave them.

As for Ariel, Prospero made him free as air, so that he could wander where he would, and sing with a light heart his sweet song—

"Where the bee sucks, there suck I:
In a cowslip's bell I lie;
There I couch when owls do cry.
On the bat's back I do fly
After summer, merrily:
Merrily, merrily, shall I live now,
Under the blossom that hangs on the bough."

55

As You Like It

Edith Nesbit and William Shakespeare

There was once a wicked Duke named Frederick, who took the dukedom that should have belonged to his brother, sending him into exile. His brother went into the Forest of Arden, where he lived the life of a bold forester, as Robin Hood did in Sherwood Forest in merry England.

The banished Duke's daughter, Rosalind, remained with Celia, Frederick's daughter, and the two loved each other more than most sisters. One day there was a wrestling match at Court, and Rosalind and Celia went to see it. Charles, a celebrated wrestler, was there, who had killed many men in contests of this kind. Orlando, the young man he was to wrestle with, was so slender and youthful, that Rosalind and Celia thought he would surely be killed, as others had been; so they spoke to him, and asked him not to attempt so dangerous an adventure; but the only effect of their words was to make him wish more to come off well in the encounter, so as to win praise from such sweet ladies.

Orlando, like Rosalind's father, was being kept out of his inheritance by his brother, and was so sad at his brother's unkindness that, until he saw Rosalind, he did not care much whether he lived or died. But now the sight of the fair Rosalind gave him strength and courage, so that he did marvelously, and at last, threw Charles to such a tune, that the wrestler had to be carried off the ground. Duke Frederick was pleased with his courage, and asked his name.

"My name is Orlando, and I am the youngest son of Sir Rowland de Boys," said the young man.

Now Sir Rowland de Boys, when he was alive, had been a good friend to the banished Duke, so that Frederick heard with regret whose son Orlando was, and would not befriend him. But Rosalind was delighted to hear that this handsome young stranger was the son of her father's old friend, and as they were going away, she turned back more than once to say another kind word to the brave young man.

"Gentleman," she said, giving him a chain from her neck, "wear this for me. I could give more, but that my hand lacks means."

Rosalind and Celia, when they were alone, began to talk about the handsome wrestler, and Rosalind confessed that she loved him at first sight.

"Come, come," said Celia, "wrestle with thy affections."

"Oh," answered Rosalind, "they take the part of a better wrestler than myself. Look, here comes the Duke."

"With his eyes full of anger," said Celia.

"You must leave the Court at once," he said to Rosalind. "Why?" she asked.

"Never mind why," answered the Duke, "you are banished. If within ten days you are found within twenty miles of my Court, you die."

So Rosalind set out to seek her father, the banished Duke, in the Forest of Arden. Celia loved her too much to let her go alone, and as it was rather a dangerous journey, Rosalind, being the taller, dressed up as a young countryman, and her cousin as a country girl, and Rosalind said that she would be called Ganymede, and Celia, Aliena. They were very tired when at last they came to the Forest of Arden, and as they were sitting on the grass a countryman passed that way, and Ganymede asked him if he could get them food. He did so, and told them that a shepherd's flocks and house were to be sold. They bought these and settled down as shepherd and shepherdess in the forest.

In the meantime, Oliver having sought to take his brother Orlando's life, Orlando also wandered into the forest, and there met with the rightful Duke, and being kindly received, stayed with him. Now, Orlando could think of nothing but Rosalind, and he went about the forest carving her name on trees, and writing love sonnets and hanging them on the bushes, and there Rosalind and Celia found them. One day Orlando met them, but he did not know Rosalind in her boy's clothes, though he liked the pretty shepherd youth, because he fancied a likeness in him to her he loved.

"There is a foolish lover," said Rosalind, "who haunts these woods and hangs sonnets on the trees. If I could find him, I would soon cure him of his folly."

Orlando confessed that he was the foolish lover, and Rosalind said—"If you will come and see me every day, I will pretend to be Rosalind, and I will take her part, and be wayward and contrary, as is the way of women, till I make you ashamed of your folly in loving her."

And so every day he went to her house, and took a pleasure in saying to her all the pretty things he would have said to Rosalind; and she had the fine and secret joy of knowing that all his love-words came to the right ears. Thus many days passed pleasantly away.

One morning, as Orlando was going to visit Ganymede, he saw a man asleep on the ground, and that there was a lioness crouching near, waiting for the man who was asleep to wake: for they say that lions will not prey on anything that is dead or sleeping. Then Orlando looked at the man, and saw that it was his wicked brother, Oliver, who had tried to take his life. He fought with the lioness and killed her, and saved his brother's life.

While Orlando was fighting the lioness, Oliver woke to see his brother, whom he had treated so badly, saving him from a wild beast at the risk of his own life. This made him repent of his wickedness, and he begged Orlando's pardon, and from thenceforth they were dear brothers. The lioness had wounded Orlando's arm so much, that he could not go on to see the shepherd, so he sent his brother to ask Ganymede to come to him.

Oliver went and told the whole story to Ganymede and Aliena, and Aliena was so charmed with his manly way of confessing his faults, that she fell in love with him at once. But when Ganymede heard of the danger Orlando had been in she fainted; and when she came to herself, said truly enough, "I should have been a woman by right."

Oliver went back to his brother and told him all this, saying, "I love Aliena so well that I will give up my estates to you and marry her, and live here as a shepherd."

"Let your wedding be to-morrow," said Orlando, "and I will ask the Duke and his friends."

When Orlando told Ganymede how his brother was to be married on the morrow, he added: "Oh, how bitter a thing it is to look into happiness through another man's eyes."

Then answered Rosalind, still in Ganymede's dress and speaking with his voice—"If you do love Rosalind so near the heart, then when your brother marries Aliena, shall you marry her."

Now the next day the Duke and his followers, and Orlando, and Oliver, and Aliena, were all gathered together for the wedding.

Then Ganymede came in and said to the Duke, "If I bring in your daughter Rosalind, will you give her to Orlando here?" "That I would," said the Duke, "if I had all kingdoms to give with her."

"And you say you will have her when I bring her?" she said to Orlando. "That would I," he answered, "were I king of all kingdoms."

Then Rosalind and Celia went out, and Rosalind put on her pretty woman's clothes again, and after a while came back.

She turned to her father—"I give myself to you, for I am yours." "If there be truth in sight," he said, "you are my daughter."

Then she said to Orlando, "I give myself to you, for I am yours." "If there be truth in sight," he said, "you are my Rosalind."

"I will have no father if you be not he," she said to the Duke, and to Orlando, "I will have no husband if you be not he."

So Orlando and Rosalind were married, and Oliver and Celia, and they lived happy ever after, returning with the Duke to the kingdom. For Frederick had been shown by a holy hermit the wickedness of his ways, and so gave back the dukedom of his brother, and himself went into a monastery to pray for forgiveness.

The wedding was a merry one, in the mossy glades of the forest. A shepherd and shepherdess who had been friends with Rosalind, when she was herself disguised as a shepherd, were married on the same day, and all with such pretty feastings and merrymakings as could be nowhere within four walls, but only in the beautiful green wood.

56

The Winter's Tale

Edith Nesbit and William Shakespeare

Leontes was the King of Sicily, and his dearest friend was Polixenes, King of Bohemia. They had been brought up together, and only separated when they reached man's estate and each had to go and rule over his kingdom. After many years, when each was married and had a son, Polixenes came to stay with Leontes in Sicily.

Leontes was a violent-tempered man and rather silly, and he took it into his stupid head that his wife, Hermione, liked Polixenes better than she did him, her own husband. When once he had got this into his head, nothing could put it out; and he ordered one of his lords, Camillo, to put a poison in Polixenes' wine. Camillo tried to dissuade him from this wicked action, but finding he was not to be moved, pretended to consent. He then told Polixenes what was proposed against him, and they fled from the Court of Sicily that night, and returned to Bohemia, where Camillo lived on as Polixenes' friend and counselor.

Leontes threw the Queen into prison; and her son, the heir to the throne, died of sorrow to see his mother so unjustly and cruelly treated.

While the Queen was in prison she had a little baby, and a friend of hers, named Paulina, had the baby dressed in its best, and took it to show the King, thinking that the sight of his helpless little daughter would soften his heart towards his dear Queen, who had never done him any wrong, and who loved him a great deal more than he deserved; but the King would not look at the baby, and ordered Paulina's husband to take it away in a ship, and leave it in the most desert and dreadful place he could find, which Paulina's husband, very much against his will, was obliged to do.

Then the poor Queen was brought up to be tried for treason in preferring Polixenes to her King; but really she had never thought of anyone except Leontes, her husband. Leontes had sent some messengers to ask the god, Apollo, whether he was not right in his cruel thoughts of the Queen. But he had not patience to wait till they came back, and so it happened that they arrived in the middle of the trial. The Oracle said—

"Hermione is innocent, Polixenes blameless, Camillo a true subject, Leontes a jealous tyrant, and the King shall live without an heir, if that which is lost be not found."

Then a man came and told them that the little Prince was dead. The poor Queen, hearing this, fell down in a fit; and then the King saw how wicked and wrong he had been. He ordered Paulina and the ladies who were with the Queen to take her away, and try to restore her. But Paulina came back in a few moments, and told the King that Hermione was dead.

Now Leontes' eyes were at last opened to his folly. His Queen was dead, and the little daughter who might have been a comfort to him he had sent away to be the prey of wolves and kites. Life had nothing left for him now. He gave himself up to his grief, and passed many sad years in prayer and remorse.

The baby Princess was left on the seacoast of Bohemia, the very kingdom where Polixenes reigned. Paulina's husband never went home to tell Leontes where he had left the baby; for as he was going back to the ship, he met a bear and was torn to pieces. So there was an end of him.

But the poor deserted little baby was found by a shepherd. She was richly dressed, and had with her some jewels, and a paper was pinned to her cloak, saying that her name was Perdita, and that she came of noble parents.

The shepherd, being a kind-hearted man, took home the little baby to his wife, and they brought it up as their own child. She had no more teaching than a shepherd's child generally has, but she inherited from her royal mother many graces and charms, so that she was quite different from the other maidens in the village where she lived.

One day Prince Florizel, the son of the good King of Bohemia, was bunting near the shepherd's house and saw Perdita, now grown up to a charming woman. He made friends with the shepherd, not telling him that he was the Prince, but saying that his name was Doricles, and that he was a private gentleman; and then, being deeply in love with the pretty Perdita, he came almost daily to see her.

The King could not understand what it was that took his son nearly every day from home; so he set people to watch him, and then found out that the heir of the King of Bohemia was in love with Perdita, the pretty shepherd girl. Polixenes, wishing to see whether this was true, disguised himself, and went with the faithful Camillo, in disguise too, to the old shepherd's house. They arrived at the feast of sheep-shearing, and, though strangers, they were made very welcome. There was dancing going on, and a peddler was selling ribbons and laces and gloves, which the young men bought for their sweethearts.

Florizel and Perdita, however, were taking no part in this gay scene, but sat quietly together talking. The King noticed the charming manners and great beauty of Perdita, never guessing that she was the daughter of his old friend, Leontes. He said to Camillo—

"This is the prettiest low-born lass that ever ran on the green sward. Nothing she does or seems but smacks of something greater than herself—too noble for this place."

And Camillo answered, "In truth she is the Queen of curds and cream."

But when Florizel, who did not recognize his father, called upon the strangers to witness his betrothal with the pretty shepherdess, the King made himself known and forbade the marriage, adding that if ever she saw Florizel again, he would kill her and her old father, the shepherd; and with that he left them. But Camillo remained behind, for he was charmed with Perdita, and wished to befriend her.

Camillo had long known how sorry Leontes was for that foolish madness of his, and he longed to go back to Sicily to see his old master. He now proposed that the young people should go there and claim the protection of Leontes. So they went, and the shepherd went with them, taking Perdita's jewels, her baby clothes, and the paper he had found pinned to her cloak.

Leontes received them with great kindness. He was very polite to Prince Florizel, but all his looks were for Perdita. He saw how much she was like the Queen Hermione, and said again and again—

"Such a sweet creature my daughter might have been, if I had not cruelly sent her from me."

When the old shepherd heard that the King had lost a baby daughter, who had been left upon the coast of Bohemia, he felt sure that Perdita, the child he had reared, must be the King's daughter, and when he told his tale and showed the jewels and the paper, the King perceived that Perdita was indeed his long-lost child. He welcomed her with joy, and rewarded the good shepherd.

Polixenes had hastened after his son to prevent his marriage with Perdita, but when he found that she was the daughter of his old friend, he was only too glad to give his consent.

Yet Leontes could not be happy. He remembered how his fair Queen, who should have been at his side to share his joy in his daughter's happiness, was dead through his unkindness, and he could say nothing for a long time but—

"Oh, thy mother! thy mother!" and ask forgiveness of the King of Bohemia, and then kiss his daughter again, and then the Prince Florizel, and then thank the old shepherd for all his goodness.

Then Paulina, who had been high all these years in the King's favor, because of her kindness to the dead Queen Hermione, said—"I have a statue made in the likeness of the dead Queen, a piece many years in doing, and performed by the rare Italian master, Giulio Romano. I keep it in a private house apart, and there, ever since you lost your Queen, I have gone twice or thrice a day. Will it please your Majesty to go and see the statue?"

So Leontes and Polixenes, and Florizel and Perdita, with Camillo and their attendants, went to Paulina's house where there was a heavy purple curtain screening off an alcove; and Paulina, with her hand on the curtain, said—

"She was peerless when she was alive, and I do believe that her dead likeness excels whatever yet you have looked upon, or that the hand of man hath done. Therefore I keep it lonely, apart. But here it is—behold, and say, 'tis well."

And with that she drew back the curtain and showed them the statue. The King gazed and gazed on the beautiful statue of his dead wife, but said nothing.

"I like your silence," said Paulina; "it the more shows off your wonder. But speak, is it not like her?"

"It is almost herself," said the King, "and yet, Paulina, Hermione was not so much wrinkled, nothing so old as this seems."

"Oh, not by much," said Polixenes.

"Ah," said Paulina, "that is the cleverness of the carver, who shows her to us as she would have been had she lived till now."

And still Leontes looked at the statue and could not take his eyes away.

"If I had known," said Paulina, "that this poor image would so have stirred your grief, and love, I would not have shown it to you."

But he only answered, "Do not draw the curtain."

"No, you must not look any longer," said Paulina, "or you will think it moves."

"Let be! let be!" said the King. "Would you not think it breathed?"

"I will draw the curtain," said Paulina; "you will think it lives presently."

"Ah, sweet Paulina," said Leontes, "make me to think so twenty years together."

"If you can bear it," said Paulina, "I can make the statue move, make it come down and take you by the hand. Only you would think it was by wicked magic."

"Whatever you can make her do, I am content to look on," said the King.

And then, all folks there admiring and beholding, the statue moved from its pedestal, and came down the steps and put its arms round the King's neck, and he held her face and kissed her many times, for this was no statue, but the real living Queen Hermione herself. She had lived hidden, by Paulina's kindness, all these years, and would not discover herself to her husband, though she knew he had repented, because she could not quite forgive him till she knew what had become of her little baby.

Now that Perdita was found, she forgave her husband everything, and it was like a new and beautiful marriage to them, to be together once more.

Florizel and Perdita were married and lived long and happily.

To Leontes his many years of suffering were well paid for in the moment when, after long grief and pain, he felt the arms of his true love around him once again.

57

King Lear

Edith Nesbit and William Shakespeare

King Lear was old and tired. He was aweary of the business of his kingdom, and wished only to end his days quietly near his three daughters. Two of his daughters were married to the Dukes of Albany and Cornwall; and the Duke of Burgundy and the King of France were both suitors for the hand of Cordelia, his youngest daughter.

Lear called his three daughters together, and told them that he proposed to divide his kingdom between them. "But first," said he, "I should like to know how much you love me."

Goneril, who was really a very wicked woman, and did not love her father at all, said she loved him more than words could say; she loved him dearer than eyesight, space or liberty, more than life, grace, health, beauty, and honor.

"I love you as much as my sister and more," professed Regan, "since I care for nothing but my father's love."

Lear was very much pleased with Regan's professions, and turned to his youngest daughter, Cordelia. "Now, our joy, though last not least," he said, "the best part of my kingdom have I kept for you. What can you say?"

"Nothing, my lord," answered Cordelia.

"Nothing can come of nothing. Speak again," said the King.

And Cordelia answered, "I love your Majesty according to my duty—no more, no less."

And this she said, because she was disgusted with the way in which her sisters professed love, when really they had not even a right sense of duty to their old father.

"I am your daughter," she went on, "and you have brought me up and loved me, and I return you those duties back as are right and fit, obey you, love you, and most honor you."

Lear, who loved Cordelia best, had wished her to make more

extravagant professions of love than her sisters. "Go," he said, "be for ever a stranger to my heart and me."

The Earl of Kent, one of Lear's favorite courtiers and captains, tried to say a word for Cordelia's sake, but Lear would not listen. He divided the kingdom between Goneril and Regan, and told them that he should only keep a hundred knights at arms, and would live with his daughters by turns.

When the Duke of Burgundy knew that Cordelia would have no share of the kingdom, he gave up his courtship of her. But the King of France was wiser, and said, "Thy dowerless daughter, King, is Queen of us—of ours, and our fair France."

"Take her, take her," said the King; "for I will never see that face of hers again."

So Cordelia became Queen of France, and the Earl of Kent, for having ventured to take her part, was banished from the kingdom. The King now went to stay with his daughter Goneril, who had got everything from her father that he had to give, and now began to grudge even the hundred knights that he had reserved for himself. She was harsh and undutiful to him, and her servants either refused to obey his orders or pretended that they did not hear them.

Now the Earl of Kent, when he was banished, made as though he would go into another country, but instead he came back in the disguise of a servingman and took service with the King. The King had now two friends—the Earl of Kent, whom he only knew as his servant, and his Fool, who was faithful to him. Goneril told her father plainly that his knights only served to fill her Court with riot and feasting; and so she begged him only to keep a few old men about him such as himself.

"My train are men who know all parts of duty," said Lear. "Goneril, I will not trouble you further—yet I have left another daughter."

And his horses being saddled, he set out with his followers for the castle of Regan. But she, who had formerly outdone her sister in professions of attachment to the King, now seemed to outdo her in undutiful conduct, saying that fifty knights were too many to wait on him, and Goneril (who had hurried thither to prevent Regan showing any kindness to the old King) said five were too many, since her servants could wait on him.

Then when Lear saw that what they really wanted was to drive him away, he left them. It was a wild and stormy night, and he wandered about the heath half mad with misery, and with no companion but the poor Fool. But presently his servant, the good Earl of Kent, met him, and at last persuaded him to lie down in a wretched little hovel. At daybreak the Earl of Kent removed his royal master to Dover, and hurried to the Court of France to tell Cordelia what had happened.

Cordelia's husband gave her an army and with it she landed at Dover. Here she found poor King Lear, wandering about the fields, wearing a crown of nettles and weeds. They brought him back and fed and clothed him, and Cordelia came to him and kissed him.

"You must bear with me," said Lear; "forget and forgive. I am old and foolish."

And now he knew at last which of his children it was that had loved him best, and who was worthy of his love.

Goneril and Regan joined their armies to fight Cordelia's army, and were successful; and Cordelia and her father were thrown into prison. Then Goneril's husband, the Duke of Albany, who was a good man, and had not known how wicked his wife was, heard the truth of the whole story; and when Goneril found that her husband knew her for the wicked woman she was, she killed herself, having a little time before given a deadly poison to her sister, Regan, out of a spirit of jealousy.

But they had arranged that Cordelia should be hanged in prison, and though the Duke of Albany sent messengers at once, it was too late. The old King came staggering into the tent of the Duke of Albany, carrying the body of his dear daughter Cordelia, in his arms.

And soon after, with words of love for her upon his lips, he fell with her still in his arms, and died.

58

Twelfth Night

Edith Nesbit and William Shakespeare

Orsino, the Duke of Illyria, was deeply in love with a beautiful Countess named Olivia. Yet was all his love in vain, for she disdained his suit; and when her brother died, she sent back a messenger from the Duke, bidding him tell his master that for seven years she would not let the very air behold her face, but that, like a nun, she would walk veiled; and all this for the sake of a dead brother's love, which she would keep fresh and lasting in her sad remembrance.

The Duke longed for someone to whom he could tell his sorrow, and repeat over and over again the story of his love. And chance brought him such a companion. For about this time a goodly ship was wrecked on the Illyrian coast, and among those who reached land in safety were the captain and a fair young maid, named Viola. But she was little grateful for being rescued from the perils of the sea, since she feared that her twin brother was drowned, Sebastian, as dear to her as the heart in her bosom, and so like her that, but for the difference in their manner of dress, one could hardly be told from the other. The captain, for her comfort, told her that he had seen her brother bind himself "to a strong mast that lived upon the sea," and that thus there was hope that he might be saved.

Viola now asked in whose country she was, and learning that the young Duke Orsino ruled there, and was as noble in his nature as in his name, she decided to disguise herself in male attire, and seek for employment with him as a page.

In this she succeeded, and now from day to day she had to listen to the story of Orsino's love. At first she sympathized very truly with him, but soon her sympathy grew to love. At last it occurred to Orsino that his hopeless love-suit might prosper better if he sent this pretty lad to woo Olivia for him. Viola unwillingly went on this errand, but when she came to the house, Malvolio, Olivia's steward, a vain, officious man, sick, as his mistress told him, of self-love, forbade the messenger admittance.

Viola, however (who was now called Cesario), refused to take any denial, and vowed to have speech with the Countess. Olivia, hearing how her instructions were defied and curious to see this daring youth, said, "We'll once more hear Orsino's embassy."

When Viola was admitted to her presence and the servants had been sent away, she listened patiently to the reproaches which this bold messenger from the Duke poured upon her, and listening she fell in love with the supposed Cesario; and when Cesario had gone, Olivia longed to send some love-token after him. So, calling Malvolio, she bade him follow the boy.

"He left this ring behind him," she said, taking one from her finger. "Tell him I will none of it."

Malvolio did as he was bid, and then Viola, who of course knew perfectly well that she had left no ring behind her, saw with a woman's quickness that Olivia loved her. Then she went back to the Duke, very sad at heart for her lover, and for Olivia, and for herself.

It was but cold comfort she could give Orsino, who now sought to ease the pangs of despised love by listening to sweet music, while Cesario stood by his side.

"Ah," said the Duke to his page that night, "you too have been in love."

"A little," answered Viola.

"What kind of woman is it?" he asked.

"Of your complexion," she answered.

"What years, i' faith?" was his next question.

To this came the pretty answer, "About your years, my lord."

"Too old, by Heaven!" cried the Duke. "Let still the woman take an elder than herself."

And Viola very meekly said, "I think it well, my lord."

By and by Orsino begged Cesario once more to visit Olivia and to plead his love-suit. But she, thinking to dissuade him, said—

"If some lady loved you as you love Olivia?"

"Ah! that cannot be," said the Duke.

"But I know," Viola went on, "what love woman may have for a man. My father had a daughter loved a man, as it might be," she added blushing, "perhaps, were I a woman, I should love your lordship."

"And what is her history?" he asked.

"A blank, my lord," Viola answered. "She never told her love, but let concealment like a worm in the bud feed on her damask cheek: she pined in thought, and with a green and yellow melancholy she sat, like Patience on a monument, smiling at grief. Was not this love indeed?"

"But died thy sister of her love, my boy?" the Duke asked; and Viola, who had all the time been telling her own love for him in this pretty fashion, said—

"I am all the daughters my father has and all the brothers—Sir, shall I go to the lady?"

"To her in haste," said the Duke, at once forgetting all about the story, "and give her this jewel."

So Viola went, and this time poor Olivia was unable to hide her love, and openly confessed it with such passionate truth, that Viola left her hastily, saying—

"Nevermore will I deplore my master's tears to you."

But in vowing this, Viola did not know the tender pity she would feel for other's suffering. So when Olivia, in the violence of her love, sent a messenger, praying Cesario to visit her once more, Cesario had no heart to refuse the request.

But the favors which Olivia bestowed upon this mere page aroused the jealousy of Sir Andrew Aguecheek, a foolish, rejected lover of hers, who at that time was staying at her house with her merry old uncle Sir Toby. This same Sir Toby dearly loved a practical joke, and knowing Sir Andrew to be an arrant coward, he thought that if he could bring off a duel between him and Cesario, there would be rare sport indeed. So he induced Sir Andrew to send a challenge, which he himself took to Cesario. The poor page, in great terror, said—

"I will return again to the house, I am no fighter."

"Back you shall not to the house," said Sir Toby, "unless you fight me first."

And as he looked a very fierce old gentleman, Viola thought it best to await Sir Andrew's coming; and when he at last made his appearance, in a great fright, if the truth had been known, she tremblingly drew her sword, and Sir Andrew in like fear followed her example. Happily for them both, at this moment some officers of the Court came on the scene, and stopped the intended duel. Viola gladly made off with what speed she might, while Sir Toby called after her—

"A very paltry boy, and more a coward than a hare!"

Now, while these things were happening, Sebastian had escaped all the dangers of the deep, and had landed safely in Illyria, where he determined to make his way to the Duke's Court. On his way thither he passed Olivia's house just as Viola had left it in such a hurry, and whom should he meet but Sir Andrew and Sir Toby. Sir Andrew, mistaking Sebastian for the cowardly Cesario, took his courage in both hands, and walking up to him struck him, saying, "There's for you."

"Why, there's for you; and there, and there!" said Sebastian, bitting back a great deal harder, and again and again, till Sir Toby came to the rescue of his friend. Sebastian, however, tore himself free from Sir Toby's clutches, and drawing his sword would have fought them both, but that Olivia herself, having heard of the quarrel, came running in, and with many reproaches sent Sir Toby and his friend away. Then turning to Sebastian, whom she too thought to be Cesario, she besought him with many a pretty speech to come into the house with her.

Sebastian, half dazed and all delighted with her beauty and grace, readily consented, and that very day, so great was Olivia's baste, they were married before she had discovered that he was not Cesario, or Sebastian was quite certain whether or not he was in a dream.

Meanwhile Orsino, hearing how ill Cesario sped with Olivia, visited her himself, taking Cesario with him. Olivia met them both before her door, and seeing, as she thought, her husband there, reproached him for leaving her, while to the Duke she said that his suit was as fat and wholesome to her as howling after music.

"Still so cruel?" said Orsino.

"Still so constant," she answered.

Then Orsino's anger growing to cruelty, he vowed that, to be revenged on her, he would kill Cesario, whom he knew she loved. "Come, boy," he said to the page.

And Viola, following him as he moved away, said, "I, to do you rest, a thousand deaths would die."

A great fear took hold on Olivia, and she cried aloud, "Cesario, husband, stay!"

"Her husband?" asked the Duke angrily.

"No, my lord, not I," said Viola.

"Call forth the holy father," cried Olivia.

And the priest who had married Sebastian and Olivia, coming in, declared Cesario to be the bridegroom.

"O thou dissembling cub!" the Duke exclaimed. "Farewell, and take her, but go where thou and I henceforth may never meet."

At this moment Sir Andrew came up with bleeding crown, complaining that Cesario had broken his head, and Sir Toby's as well.

"I never hurt you," said Viola, very positively; "you drew your sword on me, but I bespoke you fair, and hurt you not."

Yet, for all her protesting, no one there believed her; but all their thoughts were on a sudden changed to wonder, when Sebastian came in.

"I am sorry, madam," he said to his wife, "I have hurt your kinsman. Pardon me, sweet, even for the vows we made each other so late ago."

"One face, one voice, one habit, and two persons!" cried the Duke, looking first at Viola, and then at Sebastian.

"An apple cleft in two," said one who knew Sebastian, "is not more twin than these two creatures. Which is Sebastian?"

"I never had a brother," said Sebastian. "I had a sister, whom the blind waves and surges have devoured." "Were you a woman," he said to Viola, "I should let my tears fall upon your cheek, and say, 'Thrice welcome, drowned Viola!'"

Then Viola, rejoicing to see her dear brother alive, confessed that she was indeed his sister, Viola. As she spoke, Orsino felt the pity that is akin to love.

"Boy," he said, "thou hast said to me a thousand times thou never shouldst love woman like to me."

"And all those sayings will I overswear," Viola replied, "and all those swearings keep true."

"Give me thy hand," Orsino cried in gladness. "Thou shalt be my wife, and my fancy's queen."

Thus was the gentle Viola made happy, while Olivia found in Sebastian a constant lover, and a good husband, and he in her a true and loving wife.

59

Much Ado about Nothing

Edith Nesbit and William Shakespeare

In Sicily is a town called Messina, which is the scene of a curious storm in a teacup that raged several hundred years ago.

It began with sunshine. Don Pedro, Prince of Arragon, in Spain, had gained so complete a victory over his foes that the very land whence they came is forgotten. Feeling happy and playful after the fatigues of war, Don Pedro came for a holiday to Messina, and in his suite were his stepbrother Don John and two young Italian lords, Benedick and Claudio.

Benedick was a merry chatterbox, who had determined to live a bachelor. Claudio, on the other hand, no sooner arrived at Messina than he fell in love with Hero, the daughter of Leonato, Governor of Messina.

One July day, a perfumer called Borachio was burning dried lavender in a musty room in Leonato's house, when the sound of conversation floated through the open window.

"Give me your candid opinion of Hero," Claudio, asked, and Borachio settled himself for comfortable listening.

"Too short and brown for praise," was Benedick's reply; "but alter her color or height, and you spoil her."

"In my eyes she is the sweetest of women," said Claudio.

"Not in mine," retorted Benedick, "and I have no need for glasses. She is like the last day of December compared with the first of May if you set her beside her cousin. Unfortunately, the Lady Beatrice is a fury."

Beatrice was Leonato's niece. She amused herself by saying witty and severe things about Benedick, who called her Dear Lady Disdain. She was wont to say that she was born under a dancing star, and could not therefore be dull.

Claudio and Benedick were still talking when Don Pedro came up and said good-humoredly, "Well, gentlemen, what's the secret?"

"I am longing," answered Benedick, "for your Grace to command me to tell."

"I charge you, then, on your allegiance to tell me," said Don Pedro, falling in with his humor.

"I can be as dumb as a mute," apologized Benedick to Claudio, "but his Grace commands my speech." To Don Pedro he said, "Claudio is in love with Hero, Leonato's short daughter."

Don Pedro was pleased, for he admired Hero and was fond of Claudio. When Benedick had departed, he said to Claudio, "Be steadfast in your love for Hero, and I will help you to win her. To-night her father gives a masquerade, and I will pretend I am Claudio, and tell her how Claudio loves her, and if she be pleased, I will go to her father and ask his consent to your union."

Most men like to do their own wooing, but if you fall in love with a Governor's only daughter, you are fortunate if you can trust a prince to plead for you.

Claudio then was fortunate, but he was unfortunate as well, for he had an enemy who was outwardly a friend. This enemy was Don Pedro's stepbrother Don John, who was jealous of Claudio because Don Pedro preferred him to Don John.

It was to Don John that Borachio came with the interesting conversation which he had overheard.

"I shall have some fun at that masquerade myself," said Don John when Borachio ceased speaking.

On the night of the masquerade, Don Pedro, masked and pretending he was Claudio, asked Hero if he might walk with her.

They moved away together, and Don John went up to Claudio and said, "Signor Benedick, I believe?" "The same," fibbed Claudio.

"I should be much obliged then," said Don John, "if you would use your influence with my brother to cure him of his love for Hero. She is beneath him in rank."

"How do you know he loves her?" inquired Claudio.

"I heard him swear his affection," was the reply, and Borachio chimed in with, "So did I too."

Claudio was then left to himself, and his thought was that his Prince had betrayed him. "Farewell, Hero," he muttered; "I was a fool to trust to an agent."

Meanwhile Beatrice and Benedick (who was masked) were having a brisk exchange of opinions.

"Did Benedick ever make you laugh?" asked she.

"Who is Benedick?" he inquired.

"A Prince's jester," replied Beatrice, and she spoke so sharply that "I would not marry her," he declared afterwards, "if her estate were the Garden of Eden."

But the principal speaker at the masquerade was neither Beatrice nor Benedick. It was Don Pedro, who carried out his plan to the letter, and brought the light back to Claudio's face in a twinkling, by appearing before him with Leonato and Hero, and saying, "Claudio, when would you like to go to church?"

"To-morrow," was the prompt answer. "Time goes on crutches till I marry Hero."

"Give her a week, my dear son," said Leonato, and Claudio's heart thumped with joy.

"And now," said the amiable Don Pedro, "we must find a wife for Signor Benedick. It is a task for Hercules."

"I will help you," said Leonato, "if I have to sit up ten nights."

Then Hero spoke. "I will do what I can, my lord, to find a good husband for Beatrice."

Thus, with happy laughter, ended the masquerade which had given Claudio a lesson for nothing.

Borachio cheered up Don John by laying a plan before him with which he was confident he could persuade both Claudio and Don Pedro that Hero was a fickle girl who had two strings to her bow. Don John agreed to this plan of hate.

Don Pedro, on the other hand, had devised a cunning plan of love. "If," he said to Leonato, "we pretend, when Beatrice is near enough to overhear us, that Benedick is pining for her love, she will pity him, see his good qualities, and love him. And if, when Benedick thinks we don't know he is listening, we say how sad it is that the beautiful Beatrice should be in love with a heartless scoffer like Benedick, he will certainly be on his knees before her in a week or less."

So one day, when Benedick was reading in a summer-house, Claudio sat down outside it with Leonato, and said, "Your daughter told me something about a letter she wrote."

"Letter!" exclaimed Leonato. "She will get up twenty times in the night and write goodness knows what. But once Hero peeped, and saw the words 'Benedick and Beatrice' on the sheet, and then Beatrice tore it up."

"Hero told me," said Claudio, "that she cried, 'O sweet Benedick!'"

Benedick was touched to the core by this improbable story, which he was vain enough to believe. "She is fair and good," he said to himself. "I must not seem proud. I feel that I love her. People will laugh, of course; but their paper bullets will do me no harm."

At this moment Beatrice came to the summerhouse, and said, "Against my will, I have come to tell you that dinner is ready."

"Fair Beatrice, I thank you," said Benedick.

"I took no more pains to come than you take pains to thank me," was the rejoinder, intended to freeze him.

But it did not freeze him. It warmed him. The meaning he squeezed out of her rude speech was that she was delighted to come to him.

Hero, who had undertaken the task of melting the heart of Beatrice, took no trouble to seek an occasion. She simply said to her maid Margaret one day, "Run into the parlor and whisper to Beatrice that Ursula and I are talking about her in the orchard."

Having said this, she felt as sure that Beatrice would overhear what was meant for her ears as if she had made an appointment with her cousin.

In the orchard was a bower, screened from the sun by honeysuckles, and Beatrice entered it a few minutes after Margaret had gone on her errand.

"But are you sure," asked Ursula, who was one of Hero's attendants, "that Benedick loves Beatrice so devotedly?"

"So say the Prince and my betrothed," replied Hero, "and they wished me to tell her, but I said, 'No! Let Benedick get over it.'"

"Why did you say that?"

"Because Beatrice is unbearably proud. Her eyes sparkle with disdain and scorn. She is too conceited to love. I should not like to see her making game of poor Benedick's love. I would rather see Benedick waste away like a covered fire."

"I don't agree with you," said Ursula. "I think your cousin is too clear-sighted not to see the merits of Benedick." "He is the one man in Italy, except Claudio," said Hero.

The talkers then left the orchard, and Beatrice, excited and tender, stepped out of the summer-house, saying to herself, "Poor dear Benedick, be true to me, and your love shall tame this wild heart of mine."

We now return to the plan of hate.

The night before the day fixed for Claudio's wedding, Don John entered a room in which Don Pedro and Claudio were conversing, and asked Claudio if he intended to be married to-morrow.

"You know he does!" said Don Pedro.

"He may know differently," said Don John, "when he has seen what I will show him if he will follow me."

They followed him into the garden; and they saw a lady leaning out of Hero's window talking love to Borachio.

Claudio thought the lady was Hero, and said, "I will shame her for it to-morrow!" Don Pedro thought she was Hero, too; but she was not Hero; she was Margaret.

Don John chuckled noiselessly when Claudio and Don Pedro quitted the garden; he gave Borachio a purse containing a thousand ducats.

The money made Borachio feel very gay, and when he was walking in the street with his friend Conrade, he boasted of his wealth and the giver, and told what he had done.

A watchman overheard them, and thought that a man who had been paid a thousand ducats for villainy was worth taking in charge. He therefore arrested Borachio and Conrade, who spent the rest of the night in prison.

Before noon of the next day half the aristocrats in Messina were at church. Hero thought it was her wedding day, and she was there in her wedding dress, no cloud on her pretty face or in her frank and shining eyes.

The priest was Friar Francis.

Turning to Claudio, he said, "You come hither, my lord, to marry this lady?" "No!" contradicted Claudio.

Leonato thought he was quibbling over grammar. "You should have said, Friar," said he, "'You come to be married to her.'"

Friar Francis turned to Hero. "Lady," he said, "you come hither to be married to this Count?" "I do," replied Hero.

"If either of you know any impediment to this marriage, I charge you to utter it," said the Friar.

"Do you know of any, Hero?" asked Claudio. "None," said she.

"Know you of any, Count?" demanded the Friar. "I dare reply for him, 'None,'" said Leonato.

Claudio exclaimed bitterly, "O! what will not men dare say! Father," he continued, "will you give me your daughter?" "As freely," replied Leonato, "as God gave her to me."

"And what can I give you," asked Claudio, "which is worthy of this gift?" "Nothing," said Don Pedro, "unless you give the gift back to the giver."

"Sweet Prince, you teach me," said Claudio. "There, Leonato, take her back."

These brutal words were followed by others which flew from Claudio, Don Pedro and Don John.

The church seemed no longer sacred. Hero took her own part as long as she could, then she swooned. All her persecutors left the church, except her father, who was befooled by the accusations against her, and cried, "Hence from her! Let her die!"

But Friar Francis saw Hero blameless with his clear eyes that probed the soul. "She is innocent," he said; "a thousand signs have told me so."

Hero revived under his kind gaze. Her father, flurried and angry, knew not what to think, and the Friar said, "They have left her as one dead with shame. Let us pretend that she is dead until the truth is declared, and slander turns to remorse."

"The Friar advises well," said Benedick. Then Hero was led away into a retreat, and Beatrice and Benedick remained alone in the church.

Benedick knew she had been weeping bitterly and long. "Surely I do believe your fair cousin is wronged," he said. She still wept.

"Is it not strange," asked Benedick, gently, "that I love nothing in the world as well as you?"

"It were as possible for me to say I loved nothing as well as you," said Beatrice, "but I do not say it. I am sorry for my cousin."

"Tell me what to do for her," said Benedick. "Kill Claudio."

"Ha! not for the wide world," said Benedick. "Your refusal kills me," said Beatrice. "Farewell."

"Enough! I will challenge him," cried Benedick.

During this scene Borachio and Conrade were in prison. There they were examined by a constable called Dogberry.

The watchman gave evidence to the effect that Borachio had said that he had received a thousand ducats for conspiring against Hero.

Leonato was not present at this examination, but he was nevertheless now thoroughly convinced Of Hero's innocence. He played the part of bereaved father very well, and when Don Pedro and Claudio called on him in a friendly way, he said to the Italian, "You have slandered my child to death, and I challenge you to combat."

"I cannot fight an old man," said Claudio.

"You could kill a girl," sneered Leonato, and Claudio crimsoned.

Hot words grew from hot words, and both Don Pedro and Claudio were feeling scorched when Leonato left the room and Benedick entered.

"The old man," said Claudio, "was like to have snapped my nose off."

"You are a villain!" said Benedick, shortly. "Fight me when and with what weapon you please, or I call you a coward."

Claudio was astounded, but said, "I'll meet you. Nobody shall say I can't carve a calf's head."

Benedick smiled, and as it was time for Don Pedro to receive officials, the Prince sat down in a chair of state and prepared his mind for justice.

The door soon opened to admit Dogberry and his prisoners.

"What offence," said Don Pedro, "are these men charged with?"

Borachio thought the moment a happy one for making a clean breast of it. He laid the whole blame on Don John, who had disappeared. "The lady Hero being dead," he said, "I desire nothing but the reward of a murderer."

Claudio heard with anguish and deep repentance.

Upon the re-entrance of Leonato be said to him, "This slave makes clear your daughter's innocence. Choose your revenge.

"Leonato," said Don Pedro, humbly, "I am ready for any penance you may impose."

"I ask you both, then," said Leonato, "to proclaim my daughter's innocence, and to honor her tomb by singing her praise before it. As for you, Claudio, I have this to say: my brother has a daughter so like Hero that she might be a copy of her. Marry her, and my vengeful feelings die."

"Noble sir," said Claudio, "I am yours." Claudio then went to his room and composed a solemn song. Going to the church with Don Pedro and his attendants, he sang it before the monument of Leonato's family.

When he had ended he said, "Good night, Hero. Yearly will I do this."

He then gravely, as became a gentleman whose heart was Hero's, made ready to marry a girl whom he did not love. He was told to meet her in Leonato's house, and was faithful to his appointment.

He was shown into a room where Antonio (Leonato's brother) and several masked ladies entered after him. Friar Francis, Leonato, and Benedick were present.

Antonio led one of the ladies towards Claudio.

"Sweet," said the young man, "let me see your face."

"Swear first to marry her," said Leonato.

"Give me your hand," said Claudio to the lady; "before this holy friar I swear to marry you if you will be my wife."

"Alive I was your wife," said the lady, as she drew off her mask.

"Another Hero!" exclaimed Claudio.

"Hero died," explained Leonato, "only while slander lived."

The Friar was then going to marry the reconciled pair, but Benedick interrupted him with, "Softly, Friar; which of these ladies is Beatrice?"

Hereat Beatrice unmasked, and Benedick said, "You love me, don't you?"

"Only moderately," was the reply. "Do you love me?"

"Moderately," answered Benedick.

"I was told you were well-nigh dead for me," remarked Beatrice.

"Of you I was told the same," said Benedick.

"Here's your own hand in evidence of your love," said Claudio, producing a feeble sonnet which Benedick had written to his sweetheart. "And here," said Hero, "is a tribute to Benedick, which I picked out of the pocket of Beatrice."

"A miracle!" exclaimed Benedick. "Our hands are against our hearts! Come, I will marry you, Beatrice."

"You shall be my husband to save your life," was the rejoinder.

Benedick kissed her on the mouth; and the Friar married them after he had married Claudio and Hero.

"How is Benedick the married man?" asked Don Pedro.

"Too happy to be made unhappy," replied Benedick. "Crack what jokes you will. As for you, Claudio, I had hoped to run you through the body, but as you are now my kinsman, live whole and love my cousin."

"My cudgel was in love with you, Benedick, until to-day," said Claudio; but, "Come, come, let's dance," said Benedick.

And dance they did. Not even the news of the capture of Don John was able to stop the flying feet of the happy lovers, for revenge is not sweet against an evil man who has failed to do harm.

60

Romeo and Juliet

Edith Nesbit and William Shakespeare

Once upon a time there lived in Verona two great families named Montagu and Capulet. They were both rich, and I suppose they were as sensible, in most things, as other rich people. But in one thing they were extremely silly. There was an old, old quarrel between the two families, and instead of making it up like reasonable folks, they made a sort of pet of their quarrel, and would not let it die out. So that a Montagu wouldn't speak to a Capulet if he met one in the street—nor a Capulet to a Montagu—or if they did speak, it was to say rude and unpleasant things, which often ended in a fight. And their relations and servants were just as foolish, so that street fights and duels and uncomfortablenesses of that kind were always growing out of the Montagu-and-Capulet quarrel.

Now Lord Capulet, the head of that family, gave a party—a grand supper and a dance—and he was so hospitable that he said anyone might come to it except (of course) the Montagues. But there was a young Montagu named Romeo, who very much wanted to be there, because Rosaline, the lady he loved, had been asked. This lady had never been at all kind to him, and he had no reason to love her; but the fact was that he wanted to love somebody, and as he hadn't seen the right lady, he was obliged to love the wrong one. So to the Capulet's grand party he came, with his friends Mercutio and Benvolio.

Old Capulet welcomed him and his two friends very kindly—and young Romeo moved about among the crowd of courtly folk dressed in their velvets and satins, the men with jeweled sword hilts and collars, and the ladies with brilliant gems on breast and arms, and stones of price set in their bright girdles. Romeo was in his best too, and though he wore a black mask over his eyes and nose, everyone could see by his mouth and his hair, and the way he held his head, that he was twelve times handsomer than anyone else in the room.

Presently amid the dancers he saw a lady so beautiful and so lovable that from that moment he never again gave one thought to that Rosaline whom he had thought he loved. And he looked at this other fair lady, as she moved in the dance in her white satin and pearls, and all the world seemed vain and worthless to him compared with her. And he was saying this, or something like it, when Tybalt, Lady Capulet's nephew, hearing his voice, knew him to be Romeo. Tybalt, being very angry, went at once to his uncle, and told him how a Montagu had come uninvited to the feast; but old Capulet was too fine a gentleman to be discourteous to any man under his own roof, and he bade Tybalt be quiet. But this young man only waited for a chance to quarrel with Romeo.

In the meantime Romeo made his way to the fair lady, and told her in sweet words that he loved her, and kissed her. Just then her mother sent for her, and then Romeo found out that the lady on whom he had set his heart's hopes was Juliet, the daughter of Lord Capulet, his sworn foe. So he went away, sorrowing indeed, but loving her none the less.

Then Juliet said to her nurse:

"Who is that gentleman that would not dance?"

"His name is Romeo, and a Montagu, the only son of your great enemy," answered the nurse.

Then Juliet went to her room, and looked out of her window, over the beautiful green-grey garden, where the moon was shining. And Romeo was hidden in that garden among the trees—because he could not bear to go right away without trying to see her again. So she—not knowing him to be there—spoke her secret thought aloud, and told the quiet garden how she loved Romeo.

And Romeo heard and was glad beyond measure. Hidden below, he looked up and saw her fair face in the moonlight, framed in the blossoming creepers that grew round her window, and as he looked and listened, he felt as though he had been carried away in a dream, and set down by some magician in that beautiful and enchanted garden.

"Ah—why are you called Romeo?" said Juliet. "Since I love you, what does it matter what you are called?"

"Call me but love, and I'll be new baptized—henceforth I never will be Romeo," he cried, stepping into the full white moonlight from the shade of the cypresses and oleanders that had hidden him.

She was frightened at first, but when she saw that it was Romeo himself, and no stranger, she too was glad, and, he standing in the garden below and she leaning from the window, they spoke long together, each one trying to find the sweetest words in the world, to make that pleasant talk that lovers use. And the tale of all they said, and the sweet music their voices made together, is all set down in a golden book, where you children may read it for yourselves some day.

And the time passed so quickly, as it does for folk who love each other and are together, that when the time came to part, it seemed as though they had met but that moment—and indeed they hardly knew how to part.

"I will send to you to-morrow," said Juliet.

And so at last, with lingering and longing, they said good-bye.

Juliet went into her room, and a dark curtain bid her bright window. Romeo went away through the still and dewy garden like a man in a dream.

The next morning, very early, Romeo went to Friar Laurence, a priest, and, telling him all the story, begged him to marry him to Juliet without delay. And this, after some talk, the priest consented to do.

So when Juliet sent her old nurse to Romeo that day to know what he purposed to do, the old woman took back a message that all was well, and all things ready for the marriage of Juliet and Romeo on the next morning.

The young lovers were afraid to ask their parents' consent to their marriage, as young people should do, because of this foolish old quarrel between the Capulets and the Montagues.

And Friar Laurence was willing to help the young lovers secretly, because he thought that when they were once married their parents might soon be told, and that the match might put a happy end to the old quarrel.

So the next morning early, Romeo and Juliet were married at Friar Laurence's cell, and parted with tears and kisses. And Romeo promised to come into the garden that evening, and the nurse got ready a rope-ladder to let down from the window, so that Romeo could climb up and talk to his dear wife quietly and alone.

But that very day a dreadful thing happened.

Tybalt, the young man who had been so vexed at Romeo's going to the Capulet's feast, met him and his two friends, Mercutio and Benvolio, in the street, called Romeo a villain, and asked him to fight. Romeo had no wish to fight with Juliet's cousin, but Mercutio drew his sword, and he and Tybalt fought. And Mercutio was killed. When Romeo saw that this friend was dead, he forgot everything except anger at the man who had killed him, and he and Tybalt fought till Tybalt fell dead.

So, on the very day of his wedding, Romeo killed his dear Juliet's cousin, and was sentenced to be banished. Poor Juliet and her young husband met that night indeed; he climbed the rope-ladder among the flowers, and found her window, but their meeting was a sad one, and they parted with bitter tears and hearts heavy, because they could not know when they should meet again.

Now Juliet's father, who, of course, had no idea that she was married, wished her to wed a gentleman named Paris, and was so angry when she refused, that she hurried away to ask Friar Laurence what she should do. He advised her to pretend to consent, and then he said:

"I will give you a draught that will make you seem to be dead for two days, and then when they take you to church it will be to bury you, and not to marry you. They will put you in the vault thinking you are dead, and before you wake up Romeo and I will be there to take care of you. Will you do this, or are you afraid?"

"I will do it; talk not to me of fear!" said Juliet. And she went home and told her father she would marry Paris. If she had spoken out and told her father the truth…well, then this would have been a different story.

Lord Capulet was very much pleased to get his own way, and set about inviting his friends and getting the wedding feast ready. Everyone stayed up all night, for there was a great deal to do, and very little time to do it in. Lord Capulet was anxious to get Juliet married because he saw she was very unhappy. Of course she was really fretting about her husband Romeo, but her father thought she was grieving for the death of her cousin Tybalt, and he thought marriage would give her something else to think about.

Early in the morning the nurse came to call Juliet, and to dress her for her wedding; but she would not wake, and at last the nurse cried out suddenly—

"Alas! alas! help! help! my lady's dead! Oh, well-a-day that ever I was born!"

Lady Capulet came running in, and then Lord Capulet, and Lord Paris, the bridegroom. There lay Juliet cold and white and lifeless, and all their weeping could not wake her. So it was a burying that day instead of a marrying. Meantime Friar Laurence had sent a messenger to Mantua with a letter to Romeo telling him of all these things; and all would have been well, only the messenger was delayed, and could not go.

But ill news travels fast. Romeo's servant who knew the secret of the marriage, but not of Juliet's pretended death, heard of her funeral, and hurried to Mantua to tell Romeo how his young wife was dead and lying in the grave.

"Is it so?" cried Romeo, heart-broken. "Then I will lie by Juliet's side to-night."

And he bought himself a poison, and went straight back to Verona. He hastened to the tomb where Juliet was lying. It was not a grave, but a vault. He broke open the door, and was just going down the stone steps that led to the vault where all the dead Capulets lay, when he heard a voice behind him calling on him to stop.

It was the Count Paris, who was to have married Juliet that very day.

"How dare you come here and disturb the dead bodies of the Capulets, you vile Montagu?" cried Paris.

Poor Romeo, half mad with sorrow, yet tried to answer gently.

"You were told," said Paris, "that if you returned to Verona you must die."

"I must indeed," said Romeo. "I came here for nothing else. Good, gentle youth—leave me! Oh, go—before I do you any harm! I love you better than myself—go—leave me here—"

Then Paris said, "I defy you, and I arrest you as a felon," and Romeo, in his anger and despair, drew his sword. They fought, and Paris was killed.

As Romeo's sword pierced him, Paris cried—

"Oh, I am slain! If thou be merciful, open the tomb, and lay me with Juliet!"

And Romeo said, "In faith I will."

And he carried the dead man into the tomb and laid him by the dear Juliet's side. Then he kneeled by Juliet and spoke to her, and held her in his arms, and kissed her cold lips, believing that she was dead, while all the while she was coming nearer and nearer to the time of her awakening. Then he drank the poison, and died beside his sweetheart and wife.

Now came Friar Laurence when it was too late, and saw all that had happened—and then poor Juliet woke out of her sleep to find her husband and her friend both dead beside her.

The noise of the fight had brought other folks to the place too, and Friar Laurence, hearing them, ran away, and Juliet was left alone. She saw the cup that had held the poison, and knew how all had happened, and since no poison was left for her, she drew her Romeo's dagger and thrust it through her heart—and so, falling with her head on her Romeo's breast, she died. And here ends the story of these faithful and most unhappy lovers.

And when the old folks knew from Friar Laurence of all that had befallen, they sorrowed exceedingly, and now, seeing all the mischief their wicked quarrel had wrought, they repented them of it, and over the bodies of their dead children they clasped hands at last, in friendship and forgiveness.

61

Pericles

Edith Nesbit and William Shakespeare

Pericles, the Prince of Tyre, was unfortunate enough to make an enemy of Antiochus, the powerful and wicked King of Antioch; and so great was the danger in which he stood that, on the advice of his trusty counselor, Lord Helicanus, he determined to travel about the world for a time. He came to this decision despite the fact that, by the death of his father, he was now King of Tyre. So he set sail for Tarsus, appointing Helicanus Regent during his absence. That he did wisely in thus leaving his kingdom was soon made clear.

Hardly had he sailed on his voyage, when Lord Thaliard arrived from Antioch with instructions from his royal master to kill Pericles. The faithful Helicanus soon discovered the deadly purpose of this wicked lord, and at once sent messengers to Tarsus to warn the King of the danger which threatened him.

The people of Tarsus were in such poverty and distress that Pericles, feeling that he could find no safe refuge there, put to sea again. But a dreadful storm overtook the ship in which he was, and the good vessel was wrecked, while of all on board only Pericles was saved. Bruised and wet and faint, he was flung upon the cruel rocks on the coast of Pentapolis, the country of the good King Simonides. Worn out as he was, he looked for nothing but death, and that speedily. But some fishermen, coming down to the beach, found him there, and gave him clothes and bade him be of good cheer.

"Thou shalt come home with me," said one of them, "and we will have flesh for holidays, fish for fasting days, and moreo'er, puddings and flapjacks, and thou shalt be welcome."

They told him that on the morrow many princes and knights were going to the King's Court, there to joust and tourney for the love of his daughter, the beautiful Princess Thaisa.

"Did but my fortunes equal my desires," said Pericles, "I'd wish to make one there."

As he spoke, some of the fishermen came by, drawing their net, and it dragged heavily, resisting all their efforts, but at last they hauled it in, to find that it contained a suit of rusty armor; and looking at it, he blessed Fortune for her kindness, for he saw that it was his own, which had been given to him by his dead father. He begged the fishermen to let him have it that he might go to Court and take part in the tournament, promising that if ever his ill fortunes bettered, he would reward them well. The fishermen readily consented, and being thus fully equipped, Pericles set off in his rusty armor to the King's Court.

In the tournament none bore himself so well as Pericles, and he won the wreath of victory, which the fair Princess herself placed on his brows. Then at her father's command she asked him who he was, and whence he came; and he answered that he was a knight of Tyre, by name Pericles, but he did not tell her that he was the King of that country, for he knew that if once his whereabouts became known to Antiochus, his life would not be worth a pin's purchase.

Nevertheless Thaisa loved him dearly, and the King was so pleased with his courage and graceful bearing that he gladly permitted his daughter to have her own way, when she told him she would marry the stranger knight or die.

Thus Pericles became the husband of the fair lady for whose sake he had striven with the knights who came in all their bravery to joust and tourney for her love.

Meanwhile the wicked King Antiochus had died, and the people in Tyre, hearing no news of their King, urged Lord Helicanus to ascend the vacant throne. But they could only get him to promise that he would become their King, if at the end of a year Pericles did not come back. Moreover, he sent forth messengers far and wide in search of the missing Pericles.

Some of these made their way to Pentapolis, and finding their King there, told him how discontented his people were at his long absence, and that, Antiochus being dead, there was nothing now to hinder him from returning to his kingdom. Then Pericles told his wife and father-in-law who he really was, and they and all the subjects of Simonides greatly rejoiced to know that the gallant husband of Thaisa was a King in his own right. So Pericles set sail with his dear wife for his native land. But once more the sea was cruel to him, for again a dreadful storm broke out, and while it was at its height, a servant came to tell him that a little daughter was born to him. This news would have made his heart glad indeed, but that the servant went on to add that his wife—his dear, dear Thaisa—was dead.

While he was praying the gods to be good to his little baby girl, the sailors came to him, declaring that the dead Queen must be thrown overboard, for they believed that the storm would never cease so long as a dead body remained in the vessel. So Thaisa was laid in a big chest with spices and jewels, and a scroll on which the sorrowful King wrote these lines:

"Here I give to understand
(If e'er this coffin drive a-land),
I, King Pericles, have lost
This Queen worth all our mundane cost.
Who finds her, give her burying;
She was the daughter of a King;
Besides this treasure for a fee,
The gods requite his charity!"

Then the chest was cast into the sea, and the waves taking it, by and by washed it ashore at Ephesus, where it was found by the servants of a lord named Cerimon. He at once ordered it to be opened, and when he saw how lovely Thaisa looked, he doubted if she were dead, and took immediate steps to restore her. Then a great wonder happened, for she, who had been thrown into the sea as dead, came back to life. But feeling sure that she would never see her husband again, Thaisa retired from the world, and became a priestess of the Goddess Diana.

While these things were happening, Pericles went on to Tarsus with his little daughter, whom he called Marina, because she had been born at sea. Leaving her in the hands of his old friend the Governor of Tarsus, the King sailed for his own dominions.

Now Dionyza, the wife of the Governor of Tarsus, was a jealous and wicked woman, and finding that the young Princess grew up a more accomplished and charming girl than her own daughter, she determined to take Marina's life. So when Marina was fourteen, Dionyza ordered one of her servants to take her away and kill her. This villain would have done so, but that he was interrupted by some pirates who came in and carried Marina off to sea with them, and took her to Mitylene, where they sold her as a slave. Yet such was her goodness, her grace, and her beauty, that she soon became honored there, and Lysimachus, the young Governor, fell deep in love with her, and would have married her, but that he thought she must be of too humble parentage to become the wife of one in his high position.

The wicked Dionyza believed, from her servant's report, that Marina was really dead, and so she put up a monument to her memory, and showed it to King Pericles, when after long years of absence he came to see his much-loved child. When he heard that she was dead, his grief was terrible to see. He set sail once more, and putting on sackcloth, vowed never to wash his face or cut his hair again. There was a pavilion erected on deck, and there he lay alone, and for three months he spoke word to none.

At last it chanced that his ship came into the port of Mitylene, and Lysimachus, the Governor, went on board to enquire whence the vessel came. When he heard the story of Pericles' sorrow and silence, he bethought him of Marina, and believing that she could rouse the King from his stupor, sent for her and bade her try her utmost to persuade the King to speak, promising whatever reward she would, if she succeeded. Marina gladly obeyed, and sending the rest away, she sat and sang to her poor grief-laden father, yet, sweet as was her voice, he made no sign. So presently she spoke to him, saying that her grief might equal his, for, though she was a slave, she came from ancestors that stood equal to mighty kings.

Something in her voice and story touched the King's heart, and he looked up at her, and as he looked, he saw with wonder how like she was to his lost wife, so with a great hope springing up in his heart, he bade her tell her story.

Then, with many interruptions from the King, she told him who she was and how she had escaped from the cruel Dionyza. So Pericles knew that this was indeed his daughter, and he kissed her again and again, crying that his great seas of joy drowned him with their sweetness. "Give me my robes," he said: "O Heaven, bless my girl!"

Then there came to him, though none else could hear it, the sound of heavenly music, and falling asleep, he beheld the goddess Diana, in a vision.

"Go," she said to him, "to my temple at Ephesus, and when my maiden priests are met together, reveal how thou at sea didst lose thy wife."

Pericles obeyed the goddess and told his tale before her altar. Hardly had he made an end, when the chief priestess, crying out, "You are—you are—O royal Pericles!" fell fainting to the ground, and presently recovering, she spoke again to him, "O my lord, are you not Pericles?" "The voice of dead Thaisa!" exclaimed the King in wonder. "That Thaisa am I," she said, and looking at her he saw that she spoke the very truth.

Thus Pericles and Thaisa, after long and bitter suffering, found happiness once more, and in the joy of their meeting they forgot the pain of the past. To Marina great happiness was given, and not only in being restored to her dear parents; for she married Lysimachus, and became a princess in the land where she had been sold as a slave.

62

Hamlet

Edith Nesbit and William Shakespeare

Hamlet was the only son of the King of Denmark. He loved his father and mother dearly—and was happy in the love of a sweet lady named Ophelia. Her father, Polonius, was the King's Chamberlain.

While Hamlet was away studying at Wittenberg, his father died. Young Hamlet hastened home in great grief to hear that a serpent had stung the King, and that he was dead. The young Prince had loved his father so tenderly that you may judge what he felt when he found that the Queen, before yet the King had been laid in the ground a month, had determined to marry again—and to marry the dead King's brother.

Hamlet refused to put off mourning for the wedding.

"It is not only the black I wear on my body," he said, "that proves my loss. I wear mourning in my heart for my dead father. His son at least remembers him, and grieves still."

Then said Claudius the King's brother, "This grief is unreasonable. Of course you must sorrow at the loss of your father, but—"

"Ah," said Hamlet, bitterly, "I cannot in one little month forget those I love."

With that the Queen and Claudius left him, to make merry over their wedding, forgetting the poor good King who had been so kind to them both.

And Hamlet, left alone, began to wonder and to question as to what he ought to do. For he could not believe the story about the snake-bite. It seemed to him all too plain that the wicked Claudius had killed the King, so as to get the crown and marry the Queen. Yet he had no proof, and could not accuse Claudius.

And while he was thus thinking came Horatio, a fellow student of his, from Wittenberg.

"What brought you here?" asked Hamlet, when he had greeted his friend kindly.

"I came, my lord, to see your father's funeral."

"I think it was to see my mother's wedding," said Hamlet, bitterly. "My father! We shall not look upon his like again."

"My lord," answered Horatio, "I think I saw him yesternight."

Then, while Hamlet listened in surprise, Horatio told how he, with two gentlemen of the guard, had seen the King›s ghost on the battlements. Hamlet went that night, and true enough, at midnight, the ghost of the King, in the armor he had been wont to wear, appeared on the battlements in the chill moonlight. Hamlet was a brave youth. Instead of running away from the ghost he spoke to it—and when it beckoned him he followed it to a quiet place, and there the ghost told him that what he had suspected was true. The wicked Claudius had indeed killed his good brother the King, by dropping poison into his ear as he slept in his orchard in the afternoon.

"And you," said the ghost, "must avenge this cruel murder—on my wicked brother. But do nothing against the Queen—for I have loved her, and she is your mother. Remember me."

Then seeing the morning approach, the ghost vanished.

"Now," said Hamlet, "there is nothing left but revenge. Remember thee—I will remember nothing else—books, pleasure, youth—let all go—and your commands alone live on my brain."

So when his friends came back he made them swear to keep the secret of the ghost, and then went in from the battlements, now gray with mingled dawn and moonlight, to think how he might best avenge his murdered father.

The shock of seeing and hearing his father's ghost made him feel almost mad, and for fear that his uncle might notice that he was not himself, he determined to hide his mad longing for revenge under a pretended madness in other matters.

And when he met Ophelia, who loved him—and to whom he had given gifts, and letters, and many loving words—he behaved so wildly to her, that she could not but think him mad. For she loved him so that she could not believe he would be as cruel as this, unless he were quite mad. So she told her father, and showed him a pretty letter from Hamlet. And in the letter was much folly, and this pretty verse—

"Doubt that the stars are fire;
Doubt that the sun doth move;
Doubt truth to be a liar;
But never doubt I love."

And from that time everyone believed that the cause of Hamlet's supposed madness was love.

Poor Hamlet was very unhappy. He longed to obey his father's ghost—and yet he was too gentle and kindly to wish to kill another man, even his father's murderer. And sometimes he wondered whether, after all, the ghost spoke truly.

Just at this time some actors came to the Court, and Hamlet ordered them to perform a certain play before the King and Queen. Now, this play was the story of a man *who had been murdered in his garden by a near relation, who afterwards married the dead man's wife.*

You may imagine the feelings of the wicked King, as he sat on his throne, with the Queen beside him and all his Court around, and saw, acted on the stage, the very wickedness that he had himself done. And when, in the play, the wicked relation poured poison into the ear of the sleeping man, the wicked Claudius suddenly rose, and staggered from the room—the Queen and others following.

Then said Hamlet to his friends—

"Now I am sure the ghost spoke true. For if Claudius had not done this murder, he could not have been so distressed to see it in a play."

Now the Queen sent for Hamlet, by the King's desire, to scold him for his conduct during the play, and for other matters; and Claudius, wishing to know exactly what happened, told old Polonius to hide himself behind the hangings in the Queen's room. And as they talked, the Queen got frightened at Hamlet's rough, strange words, and cried for help, and Polonius behind the curtain cried out too. Hamlet, thinking it was the King who was hidden there, thrust with his sword at the hangings, and killed, not the King, but poor old Polonius.

So now Hamlet had offended his uncle and his mother, and by bad hap killed his true love's father.

"Oh! what a rash and bloody deed is this," cried the Queen.

And Hamlet answered bitterly, "Almost as bad as to kill a king, and marry his brother." Then Hamlet told the Queen plainly all his thoughts and how he knew of the murder, and begged her, at least, to have no more friendship or kindness of the base Claudius, who had killed the good King. And as they spoke the King's ghost again appeared before Hamlet, but the Queen could not see it. So when the ghost had gone, they parted.

When the Queen told Claudius what had passed, and how Polonius was dead, he said, "This shows plainly that Hamlet is mad, and since he has killed the Chancellor, it is for his own safety that we must carry out our plan, and send him away to England."

So Hamlet was sent, under charge of two courtiers who served the King, and these bore letters to the English Court, requiring that Hamlet should be put to death. But Hamlet had the good sense to get at these letters, and put in others instead, with the names of the two courtiers who were so ready to betray him. Then, as the vessel went to England, Hamlet escaped on board a pirate ship, and the two wicked courtiers left him to his fate, and went on to meet theirs.

Hamlet hurried home, but in the meantime a dreadful thing had happened. Poor pretty Ophelia, having lost her lover and her father, lost her wits too, and went in sad madness about the Court, with straws, and weeds, and flowers in her hair, singing strange scraps of songs, and talking poor, foolish, pretty talk with no heart of meaning to it. And one day, coming to a stream where willows grew, she tried to bang a flowery garland on a willow, and fell into the water with all her flowers, and so died.

And Hamlet had loved her, though his plan of seeming madness had made him hide it; and when he came back, he found the King and Queen, and the Court, weeping at the funeral of his dear love and lady.

Ophelia's brother, Laertes, had also just come to Court to ask justice for the death of his father, old Polonius; and now, wild with grief, he leaped into his sister's grave, to clasp her in his arms once more.

"I loved her more than forty thousand brothers," cried Hamlet, and leapt into the grave after him, and they fought till they were parted.

Afterwards Hamlet begged Laertes to forgive him.

"I could not bear," he said, "that any, even a brother, should seem to love her more than I."

But the wicked Claudius would not let them be friends. He told Laertes how Hamlet had killed old Polonius, and between them they made a plot to slay Hamlet by treachery.

Laertes challenged him to a fencing match, and all the Court were present. Hamlet had the blunt foil always used in fencing, but Laertes had prepared for himself a sword, sharp, and tipped with poison. And the wicked King had made ready a bowl of poisoned wine, which he meant to give poor Hamlet when he should grow warm with the sword play, and should call for drink.

So Laertes and Hamlet fought, and Laertes, after some fencing, gave Hamlet a sharp sword thrust. Hamlet, angry at this treachery—for they had been fencing, not as men fight, but as they play—closed with Laertes in a struggle; both dropped their swords, and when they picked them up again, Hamlet, without noticing it, had exchanged his own blunt sword for Laertes' sharp and poisoned one. And with one thrust of it he pierced Laertes, who fell dead by his own treachery.

At this moment the Queen cried out, "The drink, the drink! Oh, my dear Hamlet! I am poisoned!"

She had drunk of the poisoned bowl the King had prepared for Hamlet, and the King saw the Queen, whom, wicked as he was, he really loved, fall dead by his means.

Then Ophelia being dead, and Polonius, and the Queen, and Laertes, and the two courtiers who had been sent to England, Hamlet at last found courage to do the ghost's bidding and avenge his father's murder—which, if he had braced up his heart to do long before, all these lives had been spared, and none had suffered but the wicked King, who well deserved to die.

Hamlet, his heart at last being great enough to do the deed he ought, turned the poisoned sword on the false King.

"Then—venom—do thy work!" he cried, and the King died.

So Hamlet in the end kept the promise he had made his father. And all being now accomplished, he himself died. And those who stood by saw him die, with prayers and tears, for his friends and his people loved him with their whole hearts. Thus ends the tragic tale of Hamlet, Prince of Denmark.

63

Cymbeline

Edith Nesbit and William Shakespeare

Cymbeline was the King of Britain. He had three children. The two sons were stolen away from him when they were quite little children, and he was left with only one daughter, Imogen. The King married a second time, and brought up Leonatus, the son of a dear friend, as Imogen's playfellow; and when Leonatus was old enough, Imogen secretly married him. This made the King and Queen very angry, and the King, to punish Leonatus, banished him from Britain.

Poor Imogen was nearly heart-broken at parting from Leonatus, and he was not less unhappy. For they were not only lovers and husband and wife, but they had been friends and comrades ever since they were quite little children. With many tears and kisses they said "Good-bye." They promised never to forget each other, and that they would never care for anyone else as long as they lived.

"This diamond was my mother's, love," said Imogen; "take it, my heart, and keep it as long as you love me."

"Sweetest, fairest," answered Leonatus, "wear this bracelet for my sake."

"Ah!" cried Imogen, weeping, "when shall we meet again?"

And while they were still in each other's arms, the King came in, and Leonatus had to leave without more farewell.

When he was come to Rome, where he had gone to stay with an old friend of his father's, he spent his days still in thinking of his dear Imogen, and his nights in dreaming of her. One day at a feast some Italian and French noblemen were talking of their sweethearts, and swearing that they were the most faithful and honorable and beautiful ladies in the world. And a Frenchman reminded Leonatus how he had said many times that his wife Imogen was more fair, wise, and constant than any of the ladies in France.

"I say so still," said Leonatus.

"She is not so good but that she would deceive," said Iachimo, one of the Italian nobles.

"She never would deceive," said Leonatus.

"I wager," said Iachimo, "that, if I go to Britain, I can persuade your wife to do whatever I wish, even if it should be against your wishes."

"That you will never do," said Leonatus. "I wager this ring upon my finger," which was the very ring Imogen had given him at parting, "that my wife will keep all her vows to me, and that you will never persuade her to do otherwise."

So Iachimo wagered half his estate against the ring on Leonatus's finger, and started forthwith for Britain, with a letter of introduction to Leonatus's wife. When he reached there he was received with all kindness; but he was still determined to win his wager.

He told Imogen that her husband thought no more of her, and went on to tell many cruel lies about him. Imogen listened at first, but presently perceived what a wicked person Iachimo was, and ordered him to leave her. Then he said—

"Pardon me, fair lady, all that I have said is untrue. I only told you this to see whether you would believe me, or whether you were as much to be trusted as your husband thinks. Will you forgive me?"

"I forgive you freely," said Imogen.

"Then," went on Iachimo, "perhaps you will prove it by taking charge of a trunk, containing a number of jewels which your husband and I and some other gentlemen have bought as a present for the Emperor of Rome."

"I will indeed," said Imogen, "do anything for my husband and a friend of my husband's. Have the jewels sent into my room, and I will take care of them."

"It is only for one night," said Iachimo, "for I leave Britain again to-morrow."

So the trunk was carried into Imogen's room, and that night she went to bed and to sleep. When she was fast asleep, the lid of the trunk opened and a man got out. It was Iachimo. The story about the jewels was as untrue as the rest of the things he had said. He had only wished to get into her room to win his wicked wager. He looked about him and noticed the furniture, and then crept to the side of the bed where Imogen was asleep and took from her arm the gold bracelet which had been the parting gift of her husband. Then he crept back to the trunk, and next morning sailed for Rome.

When he met Leonatus, he said—

"I have been to Britain and I have won the wager, for your wife no longer thinks about you. She stayed talking with me all one night in her room, which is hung with tapestry and has a carved chimney-piece, and silver andirons in the shape of two winking Cupids."

"I do not believe she has forgotten me; I do not believe she stayed talking with you in her room. You have heard her room described by the servants."

"Ah!" said Iachimo, "but she gave me this bracelet. She took it from her arm. I see her yet. Her pretty action did outsell her gift, and yet enriched it too. She gave it me, and said she prized it once."

"Take the ring," cried Leonatus, "you have won; and you might have won my life as well, for I care nothing for it now I know my lady has forgotten me."

And mad with anger, he wrote letters to Britain to his old servant, Pisanio, ordering him to take Imogen to Milford Haven, and to murder her, because she had forgotten him and given away his gift. At the same time he wrote to Imogen herself, telling her to go with Pisanio, his old servant, to Milford Haven, and that he, her husband, would be there to meet her.

Now when Pisanio got this letter he was too good to carry out its orders, and too wise to let them alone altogether. So he gave Imogen the letter from her husband, and started with her for Milford Haven. Before he left, the wicked Queen gave him a drink which, she said, would be useful in sickness. She hoped he would give it to Imogen, and that Imogen would die, and the wicked Queen's son could be King. For the Queen thought this drink was a poison, but really and truly it was only a sleeping-draft.

When Pisanio and Imogen came near to Milford Haven, he told her what was really in the letter he had had from her husband.

"I must go on to Rome, and see him myself," said Imogen.

And then Pisanio helped her to dress in boy's clothes, and sent her on her way, and went back to the Court. Before he went he gave her the drink he had had from the Queen.

Imogen went on, getting more and more tired, and at last came to a cave. Someone seemed to live there, but no one was in just then. So she went in, and as she was almost dying of hunger, she took some food she saw there, and had just done so, when an old man and two boys came into the cave. She was very much frightened when she saw them, for she thought that they would be angry with her for taking their food, though she had meant to leave money for it on the table. But to her surprise they welcomed her kindly. She looked very pretty in her boy's clothes and her face was good, as well as pretty.

"You shall be our brother," said both the boys; and so she stayed with them, and helped to cook the food, and make things comfortable. But one day when the old man, whose name was Bellarius, was out hunting with the two boys, Imogen felt ill, and thought she would try the medicine Pisanio had given her. So she took it, and at once became like a dead creature, so that when Bellarius and the boys came back from hunting, they thought she was dead, and with many tears and funeral songs, they carried her away and laid her in the wood, covered with flowers.

They sang sweet songs to her, and strewed flowers on her, pale primroses, and the azure harebell, and eglantine, and furred moss, and went away sorrowful. No sooner had they gone than Imogen awoke, and not knowing how she came there, nor where she was, went wandering through the wood.

Now while Imogen had been living in the cave, the Romans had decided to attack Britain, and their army had come over, and with them Leonatus, who had grown sorry for his wickedness against Imogen, so had come back, not to fight with the Romans against Britain, but with the Britons against Rome. So as Imogen wandered alone, she met with Lucius, the Roman General, and took service with him as his page.

When the battle was fought between the Romans and Britons, Bellarius and his two boys fought for their own country, and Leonatus, disguised as a British peasant, fought beside them. The Romans had taken Cymbeline prisoner, and old Bellarius, with his sons and Leonatus, bravely rescued the King. Then the Britons won the battle, and among the prisoners brought before the King were Lucius, with Imogen, Iachimo, and Leonatus, who had put on the uniform of a Roman soldier. He was tired of his life since he had cruelly ordered his wife to be killed, and he hoped that, as a Roman soldier, he would be put to death.

When they were brought before the King, Lucius spoke out—

"A Roman with a Roman's heart can suffer," he said. "If I must die, so be it. This one thing only will I entreat. My boy, a Briton born, let him be ransomed. Never master had a page so kind, so duteous, diligent, true. He has done no Briton harm, though he has served a Roman. Save him, Sir."

Then Cymbeline looked on the page, who was his own daughter, Imogen, in disguise, and though he did not recognize her, he felt such a kindness that he not only spared the boy's life, but he said—

"He shall have any boon he likes to ask of me, even though he ask a prisoner, the noblest taken."

Then Imogen said, "The boon I ask is that this gentleman shall say from whom he got the ring he has on his finger," and she pointed to Iachimo.

"Speak," said Cymbeline, "how did you get that diamond?"

Then Iachimo told the whole truth of his villainy. At this, Leonatus was unable to contain himself, and casting aside all thought of disguise, he came forward, cursing himself for his folly in having believed Iachimo's lying story, and calling again and again on his wife whom he believed dead.

"Oh, Imogen, my love, my life!" he cried. "Oh, Imogen!

Then Imogen, forgetting she was disguised, cried out, "Peace, my lord—here, here!"

Leonatus turned to strike the forward page who thus interfered in his great trouble, and then he saw that it was his wife, Imogen, and they fell into each other's arms.

The King was so glad to see his dear daughter again, and so grateful to the man who had rescued him (whom he now found to be Leonatus), that he gave his blessing on their marriage, and then he turned to Bellarius, and the two boys. Now Bellarius spoke—

"I am your old servant, Bellarius. You accused me of treason when I had only been loyal to you, and to be doubted, made me disloyal. So I stole your two sons, and see,—they are here!" And he brought forward the two boys, who had sworn to be brothers to Imogen when they thought she was a boy like themselves.

The wicked Queen was dead of some of her own poisons, and the King, with his three children about him, lived to a happy old age.

So the wicked were punished, and the good and true lived happy ever after. So may the wicked suffer, and honest folk prosper till the world's end.

64

Macbeth

Edith Nesbit and William Shakespeare

When a person is asked to tell the story of Macbeth, he can tell two stories. One is of a man called Macbeth who came to the throne of Scotland by a crime in the year of our Lord 1039, and reigned justly and well, on the whole, for fifteen years or more. This story is part of Scottish history. The other story issues from a place called Imagination; it is gloomy and wonderful, and you shall hear it.

A year or two before Edward the Confessor began to rule England, a battle was won in Scotland against a Norwegian King by two generals named Macbeth and Banquo. After the battle, the generals walked together towards Forres, in Elginshire, where Duncan, King of Scotland, was awaiting them.

While they were crossing a lonely heath, they saw three bearded women, sisters, hand in hand, withered in appearance and wild in their attire.

"Speak, who are you?" demanded Macbeth.

"Hail, Macbeth, chieftain of Glamis," said the first woman.

"Hail, Macbeth, chieftain of Cawdor," said the second woman.

"Hail, Macbeth, King that is to be," said the third woman.

Then Banquo asked, "What of me?" and the third woman replied, "Thou shalt be the father of kings."

"Tell me more," said Macbeth. "By my father's death I am chieftain of Glamis, but the chieftain of Cawdor lives, and the King lives, and his children live. Speak, I charge you!"

The women replied only by vanishing, as though suddenly mixed with the air.

Banquo and Macbeth knew then that they had been addressed by witches, and were discussing their prophecies when two nobles approached. One of them thanked Macbeth, in the King's name, for his military services, and the other said, "He bade me call you chieftain of Cawdor."

Macbeth then learned that the man who had yesterday borne that title was to die for treason, and he could not help thinking, "The third witch called me, 'King that is to be.'"

"Banquo," he said, "you see that the witches spoke truth concerning me. Do you not believe, therefore, that your child and grandchild will be kings?"

Banquo frowned. Duncan had two sons, Malcolm and Donalbain, and he deemed it disloyal to hope that his son Fleance should rule Scotland. He told Macbeth that the witches might have intended to tempt them both into villainy by their prophecies concerning the throne. Macbeth, however, thought the prophecy that he should be King too pleasant to keep to himself, and he mentioned it to his wife in a letter.

Lady Macbeth was the grand-daughter of a King of Scotland who had died in defending his crown against the King who preceded Duncan, and by whose order her only brother was slain. To her, Duncan was a reminder of bitter wrongs. Her husband had royal blood in his veins, and when she read his letter, she was determined that he should be King.

When a messenger arrived to inform her that Duncan would pass a night in Macbeth's castle, she nerved herself for a very base action.

She told Macbeth almost as soon as she saw him that Duncan must spend a sunless morrow. She meant that Duncan must die, and that the dead are blind. "We will speak further," said Macbeth uneasily, and at night, with his memory full of Duncan's kind words, he would fain have spared his guest.

"Would you live a coward?" demanded Lady Macbeth, who seems to have thought that morality and cowardice were the same.

"I dare do all that may become a man," replied Macbeth; "who dare do more is none."

"Why did you write that letter to me?" she inquired fiercely, and with bitter words she egged him on to murder, and with cunning words she showed him how to do it.

After supper Duncan went to bed, and two grooms were placed on guard at his bedroom door. Lady Macbeth caused them to drink wine till they were stupefied. She then took their daggers and would have killed the King herself if his sleeping face had not looked like her father's.

Macbeth came later, and found the daggers lying by the grooms; and soon with red hands he appeared before his wife, saying, "Methought I heard a voice cry, 'Sleep no more! Macbeth destroys the sleeping.'"

"Wash your hands," said she. "Why did you not leave the daggers by the grooms? Take them back, and smear the grooms with blood."

"I dare not," said Macbeth.

His wife dared, and she returned to him with hands red as his own, but a heart less white, she proudly told him, for she scorned his fear.

The murderers heard a knocking, and Macbeth wished it was a knocking which could wake the dead. It was the knocking of Macduff, the chieftain of Fife, who had been told by Duncan to visit him early. Macbeth went to him, and showed him the door of the King's room.

Macduff entered, and came out again crying, "O horror! horror! horror!"

Macbeth appeared as horror-stricken as Macduff, and pretending that he could not bear to see life in Duncan's murderers, he slew the two grooms with their own daggers before they could proclaim their innocence.

These murders did not shriek out, and Macbeth was crowned at Scone. One of Duncan's sons went to Ireland, the other to England. Macbeth was King. But he was discontented. The prophecy concerning Banquo oppressed his mind. If Fleance were to rule, a son of Macbeth would not rule. Macbeth determined, therefore, to murder both Banquo and his son. He hired two ruffians, who slew Banquo one night when he was on his way with Fleance to a banquet which Macbeth was giving to his nobles. Fleance escaped.

Meanwhile Macbeth and his Queen received their guests very graciously, and he expressed a wish for them which has been uttered thousands of times since his day—"Now good digestion wait on appetite, and health on both."

"We pray your Majesty to sit with us," said Lennox, a Scotch noble; but ere Macbeth could reply, the ghost of Banquo entered the banqueting hall and sat in Macbeth's place.

Not noticing the ghost, Macbeth observed that, if Banquo were present, he could say that he had collected under his roof the choicest chivalry of Scotland. Macduff, however, had curtly declined his invitation.

The King was again pressed to take a seat, and Lennox, to whom Banquo's ghost was invisible, showed him the chair where it sat.

But Macbeth, with his eyes of genius, saw the ghost. He saw it like a form of mist and blood, and he demanded passionately, "Which of you have done this?"

Still none saw the ghost but he, and to the ghost Macbeth said, "Thou canst not say I did it."

The ghost glided out, and Macbeth was impudent enough to raise a glass of wine "to the general joy of the whole table, and to our dear friend Banquo, whom we miss."

The toast was drunk as the ghost of Banquo entered for the second time.

"Begone!" cried Macbeth. "You are senseless, mindless! Hide in the earth, thou horrible shadow."

Again none saw the ghost but he.

"What is it your Majesty sees?" asked one of the nobles.

The Queen dared not permit an answer to be given to this question. She hurriedly begged her guests to quit a sick man who was likely to grow worse if he was obliged to talk.

Macbeth, however, was well enough next day to converse with the witches whose prophecies had so depraved him.

He found them in a cavern on a thunderous day. They were revolving round a cauldron in which were boiling particles of many strange and horrible creatures, and they knew he was coming before he arrived.

"Answer me what I ask you," said the King.

"Would you rather hear it from us or our masters?" asked the first witch.

"Call them," replied Macbeth.

Thereupon the witches poured blood into the cauldron and grease into the flame that licked it, and a helmeted head appeared with the visor on, so that Macbeth could only see its eyes.

He was speaking to the head, when the first witch said gravely, "He knows thy thought," and a voice in the head said, "Macbeth, beware Macduff, the chieftain of Fife." The head then descended Into the cauldron till it disappeared.

"One word more," pleaded Macbeth.

"He will not be commanded," said the first witch, and then a crowned child ascended from the cauldron bearing a tree in his hand The child said—

"Macbeth shall be unconquerable till
The Wood of Birnam climbs Dunsinane Hill."

"That will never be," said Macbeth; and he asked to be told if Banquo's descendants would ever rule Scotland.

The cauldron sank into the earth; music was heard, and a procession of phantom kings filed past Macbeth; behind them was Banquo's ghost. In each king, Macbeth saw a likeness to Banquo, and he counted eight kings.

Then he was suddenly left alone.

His next proceeding was to send murderers to Macduff's castle. They did not find Macduff, and asked Lady Macduff where he was. She gave a stinging answer, and her questioner called Macduff a traitor. "Thou liest!" shouted Macduff's little son, who was immediately stabbed, and with his last breath entreated his mother to fly. The murderers did not leave the castle while one of its inmates remained alive.

Macduff was in England listening, with Malcolm, to a doctor's tale of cures wrought by Edward the Confessor when his friend Ross came to tell him that his wife and children were no more. At first Ross dared not speak the truth, and turn Macduff's bright sympathy with sufferers relieved by royal virtue into sorrow and hatred. But when Malcolm said that England was sending an army into Scotland against Macbeth, Ross blurted out his news, and Macduff cried, "*All* dead, did you say? *All* my pretty ones and their mother? Did you say *all*?"

His sorry hope was in revenge, but if he could have looked into Macbeth's castle on Dunsinane Hill, he would have seen at work a force more solemn than revenge. Retribution was working, for Lady Macbeth was mad. She walked in her sleep amid ghastly dreams. She was wont to wash her hands for a quarter of an hour at a time; but after all her washing, would still see a red spot of blood upon her skin. It was pitiful to hear her cry that all the perfumes of Arabia could not sweeten her little hand.

"Canst thou not minister to a mind diseased?" inquired Macbeth of the doctor, but the doctor replied that his patient must minister to her own mind. This reply gave Macbeth a scorn of medicine. "Throw physic to the dogs," he said; "I'll none of it."

One day he heard a sound of women crying. An officer approached him and said, "The Queen, your Majesty, is dead." "Out, brief candle," muttered Macbeth, meaning that life was like a candle, at the mercy of a puff of air. He did not weep; he was too familiar with death.

Presently a messenger told him that he saw Birnam Wood on the march. Macbeth called him a liar and a slave, and threatened to hang him if he had made a mistake. "If you are right you can hang me," he said.

From the turret windows of Dunsinane Castle, Birnam Wood did indeed appear to be marching. Every soldier of the English army held aloft a bough which he had cut from a tree in that wood, and like human trees they climbed Dunsinane Hill.

Macbeth had still his courage. He went to battle to conquer or die, and the first thing he did was to kill the English general's son in single combat. Macbeth then felt that no man could fight him and live, and when Macduff came to him blazing for revenge, Macbeth said to him, "Go back; I have spilt too much of your blood already."

"My voice is in my sword," replied Macduff, and hacked at him and bade him yield.

"I will not yield!" said Macbeth, but his last hour had struck. He fell.

Macbeth's men were in retreat when Macduff came before Malcolm holding a King's head by the hair.

"Hail, King!" he said; and the new King looked at the old.

So Malcolm reigned after Macbeth; but in years that came afterwards the descendants of Banquo were kings.

65

The Comedy of Errors

Edith Nesbit and William Shakespeare

Ægeon was a merchant of Syracuse, which is a seaport in Sicily. His wife was Æmilia, and they were very happy until Ægeon's manager died, and he was obliged to go by himself to a place called Epidamnum on the Adriatic. As soon as she could Æmilia followed him, and after they had been together some time two baby boys were born to them. The babies were exactly alike; even when they were dressed differently they looked the same.

And now you must believe a very strange thing. At the same inn where these children were born, and on the same day, two baby boys were born to a much poorer couple than Æmilia and Ægeon; so poor, indeed, were the parents of these twins that they sold them to the parents of the other twins.

Æmilia was eager to show her children to her friends in Syracuse, and in treacherous weather she and Ægeon and the four babies sailed homewards.

They were still far from Syracuse when their ship sprang a leak, and the crew left it in a body by the only boat, caring little what became of their passengers.

Æmilia fastened one of her children to a mast and tied one of the slave-children to him; Ægeon followed her example with the remaining children. Then the parents secured themselves to the same masts, and hoped for safety.

The ship, however, suddenly struck a rock and was split in two, and Æmilia, and the two children whom she had tied, floated away from Ægeon and the other children. Æmilia and her charges were picked up by some people of Epidamnum, but some fishermen of Corinth took the babies from her by force, and she returned to Epidanmum alone, and very miserable. Afterwards she settled in Ephesus, a famous town in Asia Minor.

Ægeon and his charges were also saved; and, more fortunate than Æmilia, he was able to return to Syracuse and keep them till they were eighteen. His own child he called Antipholus, and the slavechild he called Dromio; and, strangely enough, these were the names given to the children who floated away from him.

At the age of eighteen the son who was with Ægeon grew restless with a desire to find his brother. Ægeon let him depart with his servant, and the young men are henceforth known as Antipholus of Syracuse and Dromio of Syracuse.

Let alone, Ægeon found his home too dreary to dwell in, and traveled for five years. He did not, during his absence, learn all the news of Syracuse, or he would never have gone to Ephesus.

As it was, his melancholy wandering ceased in that town, where he was arrested almost as soon as he arrived. He then found that the Duke of Syracuse had been acting in so tyrannical a manner to Ephesians unlucky enough to fall into his hands, that the Government of Ephesus had angrily passed a law which punished by death or a fine of a thousand pounds any Syracusan who should come to Ephesus. Ægeon was brought before Solinus, Duke of Ephesus, who told him that he must die or pay a thousand pounds before the end of the day.

You will think there was fate in this when I tell you that the children who were kidnapped by the fishermen of Corinth were now citizens of Ephesus, whither they had been brought by Duke Menaphon, an uncle of Duke Solinus. They will henceforth be called Antipholus of Ephesus and Dromio of Ephesus.

Moreover, on the very day when Ægeon was arrested, Antipholus of Syracuse landed in Ephesus and pretended that he came from Epidamnum in order to avoid a penalty. He handed his money to his servant Dromio of Syracuse, and bade him take it to the Centaur Inn and remain there till he came.

In less than ten minutes he was met on the Mart by Dromio of Ephesus, his brother's slave, and immediately mistook him for his own Dromio. "Why are you back so soon? Where did you leave the money?" asked Antipholus of Syracuse.

This Drornio knew of no money except sixpence, which he had received on the previous Wednesday and given to the saddler; but he did know that his mistress was annoyed because his master was not in to dinner, and he asked Antipholus of Syracuse to go to a house called The Phoenix without delay. His speech angered the hearer, who would have beaten him if he had not fled. Antipholus of Syracuse them went to The Centaur, found that his gold had been deposited there, and walked out of the inn.

He was wandering about Ephesus when two beautiful ladies signaled to him with their hands. They were sisters, and their names were Adriana and Luciana. Adriana was the wife of his brother Antipholus of Ephesus, and she had made up her mind, from the strange account given her by Dromio of Ephesus, that her husband preferred another woman to his wife. "Ay, you may look as if you did not know me," she said to the man who was really her brother-in-law, "but I can remember when no words were sweet unless I said them, no meat flavorsome unless I carved it."

"Is it I you address?" said Antipholus of Syracuse stiffly. "I do not know you."

"Fie, brother," said Luciana. "You know perfectly well that she sent Dromio to you to bid you come to dinner;" and Adriana said, "Come, come; I have been made a fool of long enough. My truant husband shall dine with me and confess his silly pranks and be forgiven."

They were determined ladies, and Antipholus of Syracuse grew weary of disputing with them, and followed them obediently to The Phoenix, where a very late "mid-day" dinner awaited them.

They were at dinner when Antipholus of Ephesus and his slave Dromio demanded admittance. "Maud, Bridget, Marian, Cecily, Gillian, Ginn!" shouted Dromio of Ephesus, who knew all his fellow-servants' names by heart.

From within came the reply, "Fool, dray-horse, coxcomb, idiot!" It was Dromio of Syracuse unconsciously insulting his brother.

Master and man did their best to get in, short of using a crowbar, and finally went away; but Antipholus of Ephesus felt so annoyed with his wife that he decided to give a gold chain which he had promised her, to another woman.

Inside The Phoenix, Luciana, who believed Antipholus of Syracuse to be her sister's husband, attempted, by a discourse in rhyme, when alone with him, to make him kinder to Adriana. In reply he told her that he was not married, but that he loved her so much that, if Luciana were a mermaid, he would gladly lie on the sea if he might feel beneath him her floating golden hair.

Luciana was shocked and left him, and reported his lovemaking to Adriana, who said that her husband was old and ugly, and not fit to be seen or heard, though secretly she was very fond of him.

Antipholus of Syracuse soon received a visitor in the shape of Angelo the goldsmith, of whom Antipholus of Ephesus had ordered the chain which he had promised his wife and intended to give to another woman. The goldsmith handed the chain to Antipholus of Syracuse, and treated his "I bespoke it not" as mere fun, so that the puzzled merchant took the chain as good-humoredly as he had partaken of Adriana's dinner. He offered payment, but Angelo foolishly said he would call again.

The consequence was that Angelo was without money when a creditor of the sort that stands no nonsense, threatened him with arrest unless he paid his debt immediately. This creditor had brought a police officer with him, and Angelo was relieved to see Antipholus of Ephesus coming out of the house where he had been dining because he had been locked out of The Phoenix. Bitter was Angelo's dismay when Antipholus denied receipt of the chain. Angelo could have sent his mother to prison if she had said that, and he gave Antipholus of Ephesus in charge.

At this moment up came Dromio of Syracuse and told the wrong Antipholus that he had shipped his goods, and that a favorable wind was blowing. To the ears of Antipholus of Ephesus this talk was simple nonsense. He would gladly have beaten the slave, but contented himself with crossly telling him to hurry to Adriana and bid her send to her arrested husband a purse of money which she would find in his desk.

Though Adriana was furious with her husband because she thought he had been making love to her sister, she did not prevent Luciana from getting the purse, and she bade Dromio of Syracuse bring home his master immediately.

Unfortunately, before Dromio could reach the police station he met his real master, who had never been arrested, and did not understand what he meant by offering him a purse. Antipholus of Syracuse was further surprised when a lady whom he did not know asked him for a chain that he had promised her. She was, of course, the lady with whom Antipholus of Ephesus had dined when his brother was occupying his place at table. "Avaunt, thou witch!" was the answer which, to her astonishment, she received.

Meanwhile Antipholus of Ephesus waited vainly for the money which was to have released him. Never a good-tempered man, he was crazy with anger when Dromio of Ephesus, who, of course, had not been instructed to fetch a purse, appeared with nothing more useful than a rope. He beat the slave in the street despite the remonstrance of the police officer; and his temper did not mend when Adriana, Luciana, and a doctor arrived under the impression that he was mad and must have his pulse felt. He raged so much that men came forward to bind him. But the kindness of Adriana spared him this shame. She promised to pay the sum demanded of him, and asked the doctor to lead him to The Phoenix.

Angelo's merchant creditor being paid, the two were friendly again, and might soon have been seen chatting before an abbey about the odd behavior of Antipholus of Ephesus. "Softly," said the merchant at last, "that's he, I think."

It was not; it was Antipholus of Syracuse with his servant Dromio, and he wore Angelo's chain round his neck! The reconciled pair fairly pounced upon him to know what he meant by denying the receipt of the chain he had the impudence to wear. Antipholus of Syracuse lost his temper, and drew his sword, and at that moment Adriana and several others appeared. "Hold!" shouted the careful wife. "Hurt him not; he is mad. Take his sword away. Bind him—and Dromio too."

Dromio of Syracuse did not wish to be bound, and he said to his master, "Run, master! Into that abbey, quick, or we shall be robbed!"

They accordingly retreated into the abbey.

Adriana, Luciana, and a crowd remained outside, and the Abbess came out, and said, "People, why do you gather here?"

"To fetch my poor distracted husband," replied Adriana.

Angelo and the merchant remarked that they had not known that he was mad.

Adriana then told the Abbess rather too much about her wifely worries, for the Abbess received the idea that Adriana was a shrew, and that if her husband was distracted he had better not return to her for the present.

Adriana determined, therefore, to complain to Duke Solinus, and, lo and behold! a minute afterwards the great man appeared with officers and two others. The others were Ægeon and the headsman. The thousand marks had not been found, and Ægeon's fate seemed sealed.

Ere the Duke could pass the abbey Adriana knelt before him, and told a woeful tale of a mad husband rushing about stealing jewelry and drawing his sword, adding that the Abbess refused to allow her to lead him home.

The Duke bade the Abbess be summoned, and no sooner had he given the order than a servant from The Phoenix ran to Adriana with the tale that his master had singed off the doctor's beard.

"Nonsense!" said Adriana, "he's in the abbey."

"As sure as I live I speak the truth," said the servant.

Antipholus of Syracuse had not come out of the abbey, before his brother of Ephesus prostrated himself in front of the Duke, exclaiming, "Justice, most gracious Duke, against that woman." He pointed to Adriana. "She has treated another man like her husband in my own house."

Even while he was speaking Ægeon said, "Unless I am delirious, I see my son Antipholus."

No one noticed him, and Antipholus of Ephesus went on to say how the doctor, whom he called "a threadbare juggler," had been one of a gang who tied him to his slave Dromio, and thrust them into a vault whence he had escaped by gnawing through his bonds.

The Duke could not understand how the same man who spoke to him was seen to go into the abbey, and he was still wondering when Ægeon asked Antipholus of Ephesus if he was not his son. He replied, "I never saw my father in my life;" but so deceived was Ægeon by his likeness to the brother whom he had brought up, that he said, "Thou art ashamed to acknowledge me in misery."

Soon, however, the Abbess advanced with Antipholus of Syracuse and Dromio of Syracuse.

Then cried Adriana, "I see two husbands or mine eyes deceive me;" and Antipholus, espying his father, said, "Thou art Ægeon or his ghost."

It was a day of surprises, for the Abbess said, "I will free that man by paying his fine, and gain my husband whom I lost. Speak, Ægeon, for I am thy wife Æmilia."

The Duke was touched. "He is free without a fine," he said.

So Ægeon and Æmilia were reunited, and Adriana and her husband reconciled; but no one was happier than Antipholus of Syracuse, who, in the Duke's presence, went to Luciana and said, "I told you I loved you. Will you be my wife?"

Her answer was given by a look, and therefore is not written.

The two Dromios were glad to think they would receive no more beatings.

66

The Merchant of Venice

Edith Nesbit and William Shakespeare

Antonio was a rich and prosperous merchant of Venice. His ships were on nearly every sea, and he traded with Portugal, with Mexico, with England, and with India. Although proud of his riches, he was very generous with them, and delighted to use them in relieving the wants of his friends, among whom his relation, Bassanio, held the first place.

Now Bassanio, like many another gay and gallant gentleman, was reckless and extravagant, and finding that he had not only come to the end of his fortune, but was also unable to pay his creditors, he went to Antonio for further help.

"To you, Antonio," he said, "I owe the most in money and in love: and I have thought of a plan to pay everything I owe if you will but help me."

"Say what I can do, and it shall be done," answered his friend.

Then said Bassanio, "In Belmont is a lady richly left, and from all quarters of the globe renowned suitors come to woo her, not only because she is rich, but because she is beautiful and good as well. She looked on me with such favor when last we met, that I feel sure that I should win her away from all rivals for her love had I but the means to go to Belmont, where she lives."

"All my fortunes," said Antonio, "are at sea, and so I have no ready money; but luckily my credit is good in Venice, and I will borrow for you what you need."

There was living in Venice at this time a rich money-lender, named Shylock. Antonio despised and disliked this man very much, and treated him with the greatest harshness and scorn. He would thrust him, like a cur, over his threshold, and would even spit on him. Shylock submitted to all these indignities with a patient shrug; but deep in his heart he cherished a desire for revenge on the rich, smug merchant. For Antonio both hurt his pride and injured his business. "But for him," thought

Shylock, "I should be richer by half a million ducats. On the market place, and wherever he can, he denounces the rate of interest I charge, and—worse than that—he lends out money freely."

So when Bassanio came to him to ask for a loan of three thousand ducats to Antonio for three months, Shylock hid his hatred, and turning to Antonio, said—"Harshly as you have treated me, I would be friends with you and have your love. So I will lend you the money and charge you no interest. But, just for fun, you shall sign a bond in which it shall be agreed that if you do not repay me in three months' time, then I shall have the right to a pound of your flesh, to be cut from what part of your body I choose."

"No," cried Bassanio to his friend, "you shall run no such risk for me."

"Why, fear not," said Antonio, "my ships will be home a month before the time. I will sign the bond."

Thus Bassanio was furnished with the means to go to Belmont, there to woo the lovely Portia. The very night he started, the money-lender's pretty daughter, Jessica, ran away from her father's house with her lover, and she took with her from her father's hoards some bags of ducats and precious stones. Shylock's grief and anger were terrible to see. His love for her changed to hate. "I would she were dead at my feet and the jewels in her ear," he cried. His only comfort now was in hearing of the serious losses which had befallen Antonio, some of whose ships were wrecked. "Let him look to his bond," said Shylock, "let him look to his bond."

Meanwhile Bassanio had reached Belmont, and had visited the fair Portia. He found, as he had told Antonio, that the rumor of her wealth and beauty had drawn to her suitors from far and near. But to all of them Portia had but one reply. She would only accept that suitor who would pledge himself to abide by the terms of her father's will. These were conditions that frightened away many an ardent wooer. For he who would win Portia's heart and hand, had to guess which of three caskets held her portrait. If he guessed aright, then Portia would be his bride; if wrong, then he was bound by oath never to reveal which casket he chose, never to marry, and to go away at once.

The caskets were of gold, silver, and lead. The gold one bore this inscription:—"Who chooseth me shall gain what many men desire;"

the silver one had this:—"Who chooseth me shall get as much as he deserves;" while on the lead one were these words:—"Who chooseth me must give and hazard all he hath." The Prince of Morocco, as brave as he was black, was among the first to submit to this test. He chose the gold casket, for he said neither base lead nor silver could contain her picture. So be chose the gold casket, and found inside the likeness of what many men desire—death.

After him came the haughty Prince of Arragon, and saying, "Let me have what I deserve—surely I deserve the lady," he chose the silver one, and found inside a fool's head. "Did I deserve no more than a fool's head?" he cried.

Then at last came Bassanio, and Portia would have delayed him from making his choice from very fear of his choosing wrong. For she loved him dearly, even as he loved her. "But," said Bassanio, "let me choose at once, for, as I am, I live upon the rack."

Then Portia bade her servants to bring music and play while her gallant lover made his choice. And Bassanio took the oath and walked up to the caskets—the musicians playing softly the while. "Mere outward show," he said, "is to be despised. The world is still deceived with ornament, and so no gaudy gold or shining silver for me. I choose the lead casket; joy be the consequence!" And opening it, he found fair Portia's portrait inside, and he turned to her and asked if it were true that she was his.

"Yes," said Portia, "I am yours, and this house is yours, and with them I give you this ring, from which you must never part."

And Bassanio, saying that he could hardly speak for joy, found words to swear that he would never part with the ring while he lived.

Then suddenly all his happiness was dashed with sorrow, for messengers came from Venice to tell him that Antonio was ruined, and that Shylock demanded from the Duke the fulfilment of the bond, under which he was entitled to a pound of the merchant's flesh. Portia was as grieved as Bassanio to hear of the danger which threatened his friend.

"First," she said, "take me to church and make me your wife, and then go to Venice at once to help your friend. You shall take with you money enough to pay his debt twenty times over."

But when her newly-made husband had gone, Portia went after him, and arrived in Venice disguised as a lawyer, and with an introduction from a celebrated lawyer Bellario, whom the Duke of Venice had called in to decide the legal questions raised by Shylock's claim to a pound of Antonio's flesh. When the Court met, Bassanio offered Shylock twice the money borrowed, if he would withdraw his claim. But the money-lender's only answer was—

"If every ducat in six thousand ducats,
Were in six parts, and every part a ducat,
I would not draw them,—I would have my bond."

It was then that Portia arrived in her disguise, and not even her own husband knew her. The Duke gave her welcome on account of the great Bellario's introduction, and left the settlement of the case to her. Then in noble words she bade Shylock have mercy. But he was deaf to her entreaties. "I will have the pound of flesh," was his reply.

"What have you to say?" asked Portia of the merchant.

"But little," he answered; "I am armed and well prepared."

"The Court awards you a pound of Antonio's flesh," said Portia to the money-lender.

"Most righteous judge!" cried Shylock. "A sentence: come, prepare."

"Tarry a little. This bond gives you no right to Antonio's blood, only to his flesh. If, then, you spill a drop of his blood, all your property will be forfeited to the State. Such is the Law."

And Shylock, in his fear, said, "Then I will take Bassanio's offer."

"No," said Portia sternly, "you shall have nothing but your bond. Take your pound of flesh, but remember, that if you take more or less, even by the weight of a hair, you will lose your property and your life."

Shylock now grew very much frightened. "Give me my three thousand ducats that I lent him, and let him go."

Bassanio would have paid it to him, but said Portia, "No! He shall have nothing but his bond."

"You, a foreigner," she added, "have sought to take the life of a Venetian citizen, and thus by the Venetian law, your life and goods are forfeited. Down, therefore, and beg mercy of the Duke."

Thus were the tables turned, and no mercy would have been shown to Shylock had it not been for Antonio. As it was, the money-lender forfeited half his fortune to the State, and he had to settle the other half on his daughter's husband, and with this he had to be content.

Bassanio, in his gratitude to the clever lawyer, was induced to part with the ring his wife had given him, and with which he had promised never to part, and when on his return to Belmont he confessed as much to Portia, she seemed very angry, and vowed she would not be friends with him until she had her ring again. But at last she told him that it was she who, in the disguise of the lawyer, had saved his friend's life, and got the ring from him. So Bassanio was forgiven, and made happier than ever, to know how rich a prize he had drawn in the lottery of the caskets.

67

Timon of Athens

Edith Nesbit and William Shakespeare

Four hundred years before the birth of Christ, a man lived in Athens whose generosity was not only great, but absurd. He was very rich, but no worldly wealth was enough for a man who spent and gave like Timon. If anybody gave Timon a horse, he received from Timon twenty better horses. If anybody borrowed money of Timon and offered to repay it, Timon was offended. If a poet had written a poem and Timon had time to read it, he would be sure to buy it; and a painter had only to hold up his canvas in front of Timon to receive double its market price.

Flavius, his steward, looked with dismay at his reckless mode of life. When Timon's house was full of noisy lords drinking and spilling costly wine, Flavius would sit in a cellar and cry. He would say to himself, "There are ten thousand candles burning in this house, and each of those singers braying in the concert-room costs a poor man's yearly income a night;" and he would remember a terrible thing said by Apemantus, one of his master's friends, "O what a number of men eat Timon, and Timon sees them not!"

Of course, Timon was much praised.

A jeweler who sold him a diamond pretended that it was not quite perfect till Timon wore it. "You mend the jewel by wearing it," he said. Timon gave the diamond to a lord called Sempronius, and the lord exclaimed, "O, he's the very soul of bounty." "Timon is infinitely dear to me," said another lord, called Lucullus, to whom he gave a beautiful horse; and other Athenians paid him compliments as sweet.

But when Apemantus had listened to some of them, he said, "I'm going to knock out an honest Athenian's brains."

"You will die for that," said Timon.

"Then I shall die for doing nothing," said Apemantus. And now you know what a joke was like four hundred years before Christ.

This Apernantus was a frank despiser of mankind, but a healthy one, because he was not unhappy. In this mixed world anyone with a number of acquaintances knows a person who talks bitterly of men, but does not shun them, and boasts that he is never deceived by their fine speeches, and is inwardly cheerful and proud. Apemantus was a man like that.

Timon, you will be surprised to hear, became much worse than Apemantus, after the dawning of a day which we call Quarter Day.

Quarter Day is the day when bills pour in. The grocer, the butcher, and the baker are all thinking of their debtors on that day, and the wise man has saved enough money to be ready for them. But Timon had not; and he did not only owe money for food. He owed it for jewels and horses and furniture; and, worst of all, he owed it to money-lenders, who expected him to pay twice as much as he had borrowed.

Quarter Day is a day when promises to pay are scorned, and on that day Timon was asked for a large sum of money. "Sell some land," he said to his steward. "You have no land," was the reply. "Nonsense! I had a hundred, thousand acres," said Timon. "You could have spent the price of the world if you had possessed it," said Flavius.

"Borrow some then," said Timon; "try Ventidius." He thought of Ventidius because he had once got Ventidius out of prison by paying a creditor of this young man. Ventidius was now rich. Timon trusted in his gratitude. But not for all; so much did he owe! Servants were despatched with requests for loans of money to several friends:

One servant (Flaminius) went to Lucullus. When he was announced Lucullus said, "A gift, I warrant. I dreamt of a silver jug and basin last night." Then, changing his tone, "How is that honorable, free-hearted, perfect gentleman, your master, eh?"

"Well in health, sir," replied Flaminius.

"And what have you got there under your cloak?" asked Lucullus, jovially.

"Faith, sir, nothing but an empty box, which, on my master's behalf, I beg you to fill with money, sir."

"La! la! la!" said Lucullus, who could not pretend to mean, "Ha! ha! ha!" "Your master's one fault is that he is too fond of giving parties. I've warned him that it was expensive. Now, look here, Flaminius, you know this is no time to lend money without security, so suppose you act like a good boy and tell him that I was not at home. Here's three solidares for yourself."

"Back, wretched money," cried Flaminius, "to him who worships you!"

Others of Timon's friends were tried and found stingy. Amongst them was Sempronius.

"Hum," he said to Timon's servant, "has he asked Ventidius? Ventidius is beholden to him."

"He refused."

"Well, have you asked Lucullus?"

"He refused."

"A poor compliment to apply to me last of all," said Sempronius, in affected anger. "If he had sent to me at first, I would gladly have lent him money, but I'm not going to be such a fool as to lend him any now."

"Your lordship makes a good villain," said the servant.

When Timon found that his friends were so mean, he took advantage of a lull in his storm of creditors to invite Ventidius and Company to a banquet. Flavius was horrified, but Ventidius and Company, were not in the least ashamed, and they assembled accordingly in Timon's house, and said to one another that their princely host had been jesting with them.

"I had to put off an important engagement in order to come here," said Lucullus; "but who could refuse Timon?"

"It was a real grief to me to be without ready money when he asked for some," said Sempronius.

"The same here," chimed in a third lord.

Timon now appeared, and his guests vied with one another in apologies and compliments. Inwardly sneering, Timon was gracious to them all.

In the banqueting ball was a table resplendent with covered dishes. Mouths watered. These summer-friends loved good food.

"Be seated, worthy friends," said Timon. He then prayed aloud to the gods of Greece. "Give each man enough," he said, "for if you, who are our gods, were to borrow of men they would cease to adore you. Let men love the joint more than the host. Let every score of guests contain twenty villains. Bless my friends as much as they have blessed me. Uncover the dishes, dogs, and lap!"

The hungry lords were too much surprised by this speech to resent it. They thought Timon was unwell, and, although he had called them dogs, they uncovered the dishes.

There was nothing in them but warm water.

"May you never see a better feast," wished Timon "I wash off the flatteries with which you plastered me and sprinkle you with your villainy." With these words he threw the water into his guests' faces, and then he pelted them with the dishes. Having thus ended the banquet, he went into an outhouse, seized a spade, and quitted Athens for ever.

His next dwelling was a cave near the sea.

Of all his friends, the only one who had not refused him aid was a handsome soldier named Alcibiades, and he had not been asked because, having quarreled with the Government of Athens, he had left that town. The thought that Alcibiades might have proved a true friend did not soften Timon's bitter feeling. He was too weak-minded to discern the fact that good cannot be far from evil in this mixed world. He determined to see nothing better in all mankind than the ingratitude of Ventidius and the meanness of Lucullus.

He became a vegetarian, and talked pages to himself as he dug in the earth for food.

One day, when he was digging for roots near the shore, his spade struck gold. If he had been a wise man he would have enriched himself quickly, and returned to Athens to live in comfort. But the sight of the gold vein gave no joy but only scorn to Timon. "This yellow slave," he said, "will make and break religions. It will make black white and foul fair. It will buy murder and bless the accursed."

He was still ranting when Alcibiades, now an enemy of Athens, approached with his soldiers and two beautiful women who cared for nothing but pleasure.

Timon was so changed by his bad thoughts and rough life that Alcibiades did not recognize him at first.

"Who are you?" he asked.

"A beast, as you are," was the reply.

Alcibiades knew his voice, and offered him help and money. But Timon would none of it, and began to insult the women. They, however, when they found he had discovered a gold mine, cared not a jot for his opinion of them, but said, "Give us some gold, good Timon. Have you more?"

With further insults, Timon filled their aprons with gold ore.

"Farewell," said Alcibiades, who deemed that Timon's wits were lost; and then his disciplined soldiers left without profit the mine which could have paid their wages, and marched towards Athens.

Timon continued to dig and curse, and affected great delight when he dug up a root and discovered that it was not a grape.

Just then Apemantus appeared. "I am told that you imitate me," said Apemantus.

"Only," said Timon, "because you haven't a dog which I can imitate."

"You are revenging yourself on your friends by punishing yourself," said Apemantus. "That is very silly, for they live just as comfortably as they ever did. I am sorry that a fool should imitate me."

"If I were like you," said Timon, "I should throw myself away."

"You have done so," sneered Apemantus. "Will the cold brook make you a good morning drink, or an east wind warm your clothes as a valet would?"

"Off with you!" said Timon; but Apemantus stayed a while longer and told him he had a passion for extremes, which was true. Apemantus even made a pun, but there was no good laughter to be got out of Timon.

Finally, they lost their temper like two schoolboys, and Timon said he was sorry to lose the stone which he flung at Apemantus, who left him with an evil wish.

This was almost an "at home" day for Timon, for when Apemantus had departed, he was visited by some robbers. They wanted gold.

"You want too much," said Timon. "Here are water, roots and berries."

"We are not birds and pigs," said a robber.

"No, you are cannibals," said Timon. "Take the gold, then, and may it poison you! Henceforth rob one another."

He spoke so frightfully to them that, though they went away with full pockets, they almost repented of their trade. His last visitor on that day of visits was his good steward Flavius. "My dearest master!" cried he.

"Away! What are you?" said Timon.

"Have you forgotten me, sir?" asked Flavius, mournfully.

"I have forgotten all men," was the reply; "and if you'll allow that you are a man, I have forgotten you."

"I was your honest servant," said Flavius.

"Nonsense! I never had an honest man about me," retorted Timon.

Flavius began to cry.

"What! shedding tears?" said Timon. "Come nearer, then. I will love you because you are a woman, and unlike men, who only weep when they laugh or beg."

They talked awhile; then Timon said, "Yon gold is mine. I will make you rich, Flavius, if you promise me to live by yourself and hate mankind. I will make you very rich if you promise me that you will see the flesh slide off the beggar's bones before you feed him, and let the debtor die in jail before you pay his debt."

Flavius simply said, "Let me stay to comfort you, my master."

"If you dislike cursing, leave me," replied Timon, and he turned his back on Flavius, who went sadly back to Athens, too much accustomed to obedience to force his services upon his ailing master.

The steward had accepted nothing, but a report got about that a mighty nugget of gold had been given him by his former master, and Timon therefore received more visitors. They were a painter and a poet, whom he had patronized in his prosperity.

"Hail, worthy Timon!" said the poet. "We heard with astonishment how your friends deserted you. No whip's large enough for their backs!"

"We have come," put in the painter, "to offer our services."

"You've heard that I have gold," said Timon.

"There was a report," said the painter, blushing; "but my friend and I did not come for that."

"Good honest men!" jeered Timon. "All the same, you shall have plenty of gold if you will rid me of two villains."

"Name them," said his two visitors in one breath. "Both of you!" answered Timon. Giving the painter a whack with a big stick, he said, "Put that into your palette and make money out of it." Then he gave a whack to the poet, and said, "Make a poem out of that and get paid for it. There's gold for you."

They hurriedly withdrew.

Finally Timon was visited by two senators who, now that Athens was threatened by Alcibiades, desired to have on their side this bitter noble whose gold might help the foe.

"Forget your injuries," said the first senator. "Athens offers you dignities whereby you may honorably live."

"Athens confesses that your merit was overlooked, and wishes to atone, and more than atone, for her forgetfulness," said the second senator.

"Worthy senators," replied Timon, in his grim way, "I am almost weeping; you touch me so! All I need are the eyes of a woman and the heart of a fool."

But the senators were patriots. They believed that this bitter man could save Athens, and they would not quarrel with him. "Be our captain," they said, "and lead Athens against Alcibiades, who threatens to destroy her."

"Let him destroy the Athenians too, for all I care," said Timon; and seeing an evil despair in his face, they left him.

The senators returned to Athens, and soon afterwards trumpets were blown before its walls. Upon the walls they stood and listened to Alcibiades, who told them that wrong-doers should quake in their easy chairs. They looked at his confident army, and were convinced that Athens must yield if he assaulted it, therefore they used the voice that strikes deeper than arrows.

"These walls of ours were built by the hands of men who never wronged you, Alcibiades," said the first senator.

"Enter," said the second senator, "and slay every tenth man, if your revenge needs human flesh."

"Spare the cradle," said the first senator.

"I ask only justice," said Alcibiades. "If you admit my army, I will inflict the penalty of your own laws upon any soldier who breaks them."

At that moment a soldier approached Alcibiades, and said, "My noble general, Timon is dead." He handed Alcibiades a sheet of wax, saying, "He is buried by the sea, on the beach, and over his grave is a stone with letters on it which I cannot read, and therefore I have impressed them on wax."

Alcibiades read from the sheet of wax this couplet—

"Here lie I, Timon, who, alive,
all living men did hate.
Pass by and say your worst; but pass,
and stay not here your gait."

"Dead, then, is noble Timon," said Alcibiades; and be entered Athens with an olive branch instead of a sword.

So it was one of Timon's friends who was generous in a greater matter than Timon's need; yet are the sorrow and rage of Timon remembered as a warning lest another ingratitude should arise to turn love into hate.

68

All's Well That Ends Well

Edith Nesbit and William Shakespeare

In the year thirteen hundred and something, the Countess of Rousillon was unhappy in her palace near the Pyrenees. She had lost her husband, and the King of France had summoned her son Bertram to Paris, hundreds of miles away.

Bertram was a pretty youth with curling hair, finely arched eyebrows, and eyes as keen as a hawk's. He was as proud as ignorance could make him, and would lie with a face like truth itself to gain a selfish end. But a pretty youth is a pretty youth, and Helena was in love with him.

Helena was the daughter of a great doctor who had died in the service of the Count of Rousillon. Her sole fortune consisted in a few of her father's prescriptions.

When Bertram had gone, Helena's forlorn look was noticed by the Countess, who told her that she was exactly the same to her as her own child. Tears then gathered in Helena's eyes, for she felt that the Countess made Bertram seem like a brother whom she could never marry. The Countess guessed her secret forthwith, and Helena confessed that Bertram was to her as the sun is to the day.

She hoped, however, to win this sun by earning the gratitude of the King of France, who suffered from a lingering illness, which made him lame. The great doctors attached to the Court despaired of curing him, but Helena had confidence in a prescription which her father had used with success.

Taking an affectionate leave of the Countess, she went to Paris, and was allowed to see the King.

He was very polite, but it was plain he thought her a quack. "It would not become me," he said, "to apply to a simple maiden for the relief which all the learned doctors cannot give me."

"Heaven uses weak instruments sometimes," said Helena, and she declared that she would forfeit her life if she failed to make him well.

"And if you succeed?" questioned the King.

"Then I will ask your Majesty to give me for a husband the man whom I choose!"

So earnest a young lady could not be resisted forever by a suffering king. Helena, therefore, became the King's doctor, and in two days the royal cripple could skip.

He summoned his courtiers, and they made a glittering throng in the throne room of his palace. Well might the country girl have been dazzled, and seen a dozen husbands worth dreaming of among the handsome young noblemen before her. But her eyes only wandered till they found Bertram. Then she went up to him, and said, "I dare not say I take you, but I am yours!" Raising her voice that the King might hear, she added, "This is the Man!"

"Bertram," said the King, "take her; she's your wife!"

"My wife, my liege?" said Bertram. "I beg your Majesty to permit me to choose a wife."

"Do you know, Bertram, what she has done for your King?" asked the monarch, who had treated Bertram like a son.

"Yes, your Majesty," replied Bertram; "but why should I marry a girl who owes her breeding to my father's charity?"

"You disdain her for lacking a title, but I can give her a title," said the King; and as he looked at the sulky youth a thought came to him, and he added, "Strange that you think so much of blood when you could not distinguish your own from a beggar's if you saw them mixed together in a bowl."

"I cannot love her," asserted Bertram; and Helena said gently, "Urge him not, your Majesty. I am glad to have cured my King for my country's sake."

"My honor requires that scornful boy's obedience," said the King. "Bertram, make up your mind to this. You marry this lady, of whom you are so unworthy, or you learn how a king can hate. Your answer?"

Bertram bowed low and said, "Your Majesty has ennobled the lady by your interest in her. I submit."

"Take her by the hand," said the King, "and tell her she is yours."

Bertram obeyed, and with little delay he was married to Helena.

Fear of the King, however, could not make him a lover. Ridicule helped to sour him. A base soldier named Parolles told him to his face that now he had a "kicky-wicky" his business was not to fight but to stay at home. "Kicky-wicky" was only a silly epithet for a wife, but it made Bertram feel he could not bear having a wife, and that he must go to the war in Italy, though the King had forbidden him.

Helena he ordered to take leave of the King and return to Rousillon, giving her letters for his mother and herself. He then rode off, bidding her a cold good-bye.

She opened the letter addressed to herself, and read, "When you can get the ring from my finger you can call me husband, but against that 'when' I write 'never.'"

Dry-eyed had Helena been when she entered the King's presence and said farewell, but he was uneasy on her account, and gave her a ring from his own finger, saying, "If you send this to me, I shall know you are in trouble, and help you."

She did not show him Bertram's letter to his wife; it would have made him wish to kill the truant Count; but she went back to Rousillon and handed her mother-in-law the second letter. It was short and bitter. "I have run away," it said. "If the world be broad enough, I will be always far away from her."

"Cheer up," said the noble widow to the deserted wife. "I wash his name out of my blood, and you alone are my child."

The Dowager Countess, however, was still mother enough to Bertram to lay the blame of his conduct on Parolles, whom she called "a very tainted fellow."

Helena did not stay long at Rousillon. She clad herself as a pilgrim, and, leaving a letter for her mother-in-law, secretly set out for Florence.

On entering that city she inquired of a woman the way to the Pilgrims' House of Rest, but the woman begged "the holy pilgrim" to lodge with her.

Helena found that her hostess was a widow, who had a beautiful daughter named Diana.

When Diana heard that Helena came from France, she said, "A countryman of yours, Count Rousillon, has done worthy service for Florence." But after a time, Diana had something to tell which was not at all worthy of Helena's husband. Bertram was making love to Diana. He did not hide the fact that he was married, but Diana heard from Parolles that his wife was not worth caring for.

The widow was anxious for Diana's sake, and Helena decided to inform her that she was the Countess Rousillon.

"He keeps asking Diana for a lock of her hair," said the widow.

Helena smiled mournfully, for her hair was as fine as Diana's and of the same color. Then an idea struck her, and she said, "Take this purse of gold for yourself. I will give Diana three thousand crowns if she will help me to carry out this plan. Let her promise to give a lock of her hair to my husband if he will give her the ring which he wears on his finger. It is an ancestral ring. Five Counts of Rousillon have worn it, yet he will yield it up for a lock of your daughter's hair. Let your daughter insist that he shall cut the lock of hair from her in a dark room, and agree in advance that she shall not speak a single word."

The widow listened attentively, with the purse of gold in her lap. She said at last, "I consent, if Diana is willing."

Diana was willing, and, strange to say, the prospect of cutting off a lock of hair from a silent girl in a dark room was so pleasing to Bertram that he handed Diana his ring, and was told when to follow her into the dark room. At the time appointed he came with a sharp knife, and felt a sweet face touch his as he cut off the lock of hair, and he left the room satisfied, like a man who is filled with renown, and on his finger was a ring which the girl in the dark room had given him.

The war was nearly over, but one of its concluding chapters taught Bertram that the soldier who had been impudent enough to call Helena his "kicky-wicky" was far less courageous than a wife. Parolles was such a boaster, and so fond of trimings to his clothes, that the French officers played him a trick to discover what he was made of. He had lost his drum, and had said that he would regain it unless he was killed in the attempt. His attempt was a very poor one, and he was inventing the story of a heroic failure, when he was surrounded and disarmed.

"Portotartarossa," said a French lord.

"What horrible lingo is this?" thought Parolles, who had been blindfolded.

"He's calling for the tortures," said a French man, affecting to act as interpreter. "What will you say without 'em?"

"As much," replied Parolles, "as I could possibly say if you pinched me like a pasty." He was as good as his word. He told them how many there were in each regiment of the Florentine army, and he refreshed them with spicy anecdotes of the officers commanding it.

Bertram was present, and heard a letter read, in which Parolles told Diana that he was a fool.

"This is your devoted friend," said a French lord.

"He is a cat to me now," said Bertram, who detested our hearthrug pets.

Parolles was finally let go, but henceforth he felt like a sneak, and was not addicted to boasting.

We now return to France with Helena, who had spread a report of her death, which was conveyed to the Dowager Countess at Rousillon by Lafeu, a lord who wished to marry his daughter Magdalen to Bertram.

The King mourned for Helena, but he approved of the marriage proposed for Bertram, and paid a visit to Rousillon in order to see it accomplished.

"His great offense is dead," he said. "Let Bertram approach me."

Then Bertram, scarred in the cheek, knelt before his Sovereign, and said that if he had not loved Lafeu's daughter before he married Helena, he would have prized his wife, whom he now loved when it was too late.

"Love that is late offends the Great Sender," said the King. "Forget sweet Helena, and give a ring to Magdalen."

Bertram immediately gave a ring to Lafeu, who said indignantly, "It's Helena's!"

"It's not!" said Bertram.

Hereupon the King asked to look at the ring, and said, "This is the ring I gave to Helena, and bade her send to me if ever she needed help. So you had the cunning to get from her what could help her most."

Bertram denied again that the ring was Helena's, but even his mother said it was.

"You lie!" exclaimed the King. "Seize him, guards!" but even while they were seizing him, Bertram wondered how the ring, which he thought Diana had given him, came to be so like Helena's. A gentleman now entered, craving permission to deliver a petition to the King. It was a petition signed Diana Capilet, and it begged that the King would order Bertram to marry her whom he had deserted after winning her love.

"I'd sooner buy a son-in-law at a fair than take Bertram now," said Lafeu.

"Admit the petitioner," said the King.

Bertram found himself confronted by Diana and her mother. He denied that Diana had any claim on him, and spoke of her as though her life was spent in the gutter. But she asked him what sort of gentlewoman it was to whom he gave, as to her he gave, the ring of his ancestors now missing from his finger?

Bertram was ready to sink into the earth, but fate had one crowning generosity reserved for him. Helena entered.

"Do I see reality?" asked the King.

"O pardon! pardon!" cried Bertram.

She held up his ancestral ring. "Now that I have this," said she, "will you love me, Bertram?"

"To the end of my life," cried he.

"My eyes smell onions," said Lafeu. Tears for Helena were twinkling in them.

The King praised Diana when he was fully informed by that not very shy young lady of the meaning of her conduct. For Helena's sake she had wished to expose Bertram's meanness, not only to the King, but to himself. His pride was now in shreds, and it is believed that he made a husband of some sort after all.

69

Frau Brechenmacher Attends a Wedding

Katherine Mansfield

Getting ready was a terrible business. After supper Frau Brechenmacher packed four of the five babies to bed, allowing Rosa to stay with her and help to polish the buttons of Herr Brechenmacher's uniform. Then she ran over his best shirt with a hot iron, polished his boots, and put a stitch or two into his black satin necktie.

"Rosa," she said, "fetch my dress and hang it in front of the stove to get the creases out. Now, mind, you must look after the children and not sit up later than half-past eight, and not touch the lamp—you know what will happen if you do."

"Yes, Mamma," said Rosa, who was nine and felt old enough to manage a thousand lamps. "But let me stay up—the 'Bub' may wake and want some milk."

"Half-past eight!" said the Frau. "I'll make the father tell you too."

Rosa drew down the corners of her mouth.

"But... but...."

"Here comes the father. You go into the bedroom and fetch my blue silk handkerchief. You can wear my black shawl while I'm out—there now!"

Rosa dragged it off her mother's shoulders and wound it carefully round her own, tying the two ends in a knot at the back. After all, she reflected, if she had to go to bed at half past eight she would keep the shawl on. Which resolution comforted her absolutely.

"Now, then, where are my clothes?" cried Herr Brechenmacher, hanging his empty letter-bag behind the door and stamping the snow out of his boots. "Nothing ready, of course, and everybody at the wedding by this time. I heard the music as I passed. What are you doing? You're not dressed. You can't go like that."

"Here they are—all ready for you on the table, and some warm water in the tin basin. Dip your head in. Rosa, give your father the towel. Everything ready except the trousers. I haven't had time to shorten them. You must tuck the ends into your boots until we get there."

"Nu," said the Herr, "there isn't room to turn. I want the light. You go and dress in the passage."

Dressing in the dark was nothing to Frau Brechenmacher. She hooked her skirt and bodice, fastened her handkerchief round her neck with a beautiful brooch that had four medals to the Virgin dangling from it, and then drew on her cloak and hood.

"Here, come and fasten this buckle," called Herr Brechenmacher. He stood in the kitchen puffing himself out, the buttons on his blue uniform shining with an enthusiasm which nothing but official buttons could possibly possess. "How do I look?"

"Wonderful," replied the little Frau, straining at the waist buckle and giving him a little pull here, a little tug there. "Rosa, come and look at your father."

Herr Brechenmacher strode up and down the kitchen, was helped on with his coat, then waited while the Frau lighted the lantern.

"Now, then—finished at last! Come along."

"The lamp, Rosa," warned the Frau, slamming the front door behind them.

Snow had not fallen all day; the frozen ground was slippery as an icepond. She had not been out of the house for weeks past, and the day had so flurried her that she felt muddled and stupid—felt that Rosa had pushed her out of the house and her man was running away from her.

"Wait, wait!" she cried.

"No. I'll get my feet damp—you hurry."

It was easier when they came into the village. There were fences to cling to, and leading from the railway station to the Gasthaus a little path of cinders had been strewn for the benefit of the wedding guests.

The Gasthaus was very festive. Lights shone out from every window, wreaths of fir twigs hung from the ledges. Branches decorated the front doors, which swung open, and in the hall the landlord voiced his superiority by bullying the waitresses, who ran about continually with glasses of beer, trays of cups and saucers, and bottles of wine.

"Up the stairs—up the stairs!" boomed the landlord. "Leave your coats on the landing."

Herr Brechenmacher, completely overawed by this grand manner, so far forgot his rights as a husband as to beg his wife's pardon for jostling her against the banisters in his efforts to get ahead of everybody else.

Herr Brechenmacher's colleagues greeted him with acclamation as he entered the door of the Festsaal, and the Frau straightened her brooch and folded her hands, assuming the air of dignity becoming to the wife of a postman and the mother of five children. Beautiful indeed was the Festsaal. Three long tables were grouped at one end, the remainder of the floor space cleared for dancing. Oil lamps, hanging from the ceiling, shed a warm, bright light on the walls decorated with paper flowers and garlands; shed a warmer, brighter light on the red faces of the guests in their best clothes.

At the head of the centre table sat the bride and bridegroom, she in a white dress trimmed with stripes and bows of coloured ribbon, giving her the appearance of an iced cake all ready to be cut and served in neat little pieces to the bridegroom beside her, who wore a suit of white clothes much too large for him and a white silk tie that rose halfway up his collar. Grouped about them, with a fine regard for dignity and precedence, sat their parents and relations; and perched on a stool at the bride's right hand a little girl in a crumpled muslin dress with a wreath of forget-me-nots hanging over one ear. Everybody was laughing and talking, shaking hands, clinking glasses, stamping on the floor—a stench of beer and perspiration filled the air.

Frau Brechenmacher, following her man down the room after greeting the bridal party, knew that she was going to enjoy herself. She seemed to fill out and become rosy and warm as she sniffed that familiar festive smell. Somebody pulled at her skirt, and, looking down, she saw Frau Rupp, the butcher's wife, who pulled out an empty chair and begged her to sit beside her.

"Fritz will get you some beer," she said. "My dear, your skirt is open at the back. We could not help laughing as you walked up the room with the white tape of your petticoat showing!"

"But how frightful!" said Frau Brechenmacher, collapsing into her chair and biting her lip.

"Na, it's over now," said Frau Rupp, stretching her fat hands over the table and regarding her three mourning rings with intense enjoyment;

"but one must be careful, especially at a wedding."

"And such a wedding as this," cried Frau Ledermann, who sat on the other side of Frau Brechenmacher. "Fancy Theresa bringing that child with her. It's her own child, you know, my dear, and it's going to live with them. That's what I call a sin against the Church for a free-born child to attend its own mother's wedding."

The three women sat and stared at the bride, who remained very still, with a little vacant smile on her lips, only her eyes shifting uneasily from side to side.

"Beer they've given it, too," whispered Frau Rupp, "and white wine and an ice. It never did have a stomach; she ought to have left it at home."

Frau Brechenmacher turned round and looked towards the bride's mother. She never took her eyes off her daughter, but wrinkled her brown forehead like an old monkey, and nodded now and again very solemnly. Her hands shook as she raised her beer mug, and when she had drunk she spat on the floor and savagely wiped her mouth with her sleeve. Then the music started and she followed Theresa with her eyes, looking suspiciously at each man who danced with her.

"Cheer up, old woman," shouted her husband, digging her in the ribs; "this isn't Theresa's funeral." He winked at the guests, who broke into loud laughter.

"I *am* cheerful," mumbled the old woman, and beat upon the table with her fist, keeping time to the music, proving she was not out of the festivities.

"She can't forget how wild Theresa has been," said Frau Ledermann. "Who could—with the child there? I heard that last Sunday evening Theresa had hysterics and said that she would not marry this man. They had to get the priest to her."

"Where is the other one?" asked Frau Brechenmacher. "Why didn't he marry her?"

The woman shrugged her shoulders.

"Gone—disappeared. He was a traveller, and only stayed at their house two nights. He was selling shirt buttons—I bought some myself, and they were beautiful shirt buttons—but what a pig of a fellow! I can't think what he saw in such a plain girl—but you never know. Her mother says she's been like fire ever since she was sixteen!"

Frau Brechenmacher looked down at her beer and blew a little hole in the froth.

"That's not how a wedding should be," she said; "it's not religion to love two men."

"Nice time she'll have with this one," Frau Rupp exclaimed. "He was lodging with me last summer and I had to get rid of him. He never changed his clothes once in two months, and when I spoke to him of the smell in his room he told me he was sure it floated up from the shop. Ah, every wife has her cross. Isn't that true, my dear?"

Frau Brechenmacher saw her husband among his colleagues at the next table. He was drinking far too much, she knew—gesticulating wildly, the saliva spluttering out of his mouth as he talked.

"Yes," she assented, "that's true. Girls have a lot to learn."

Wedged in between these two fat old women, the Frau had no hope of being asked to dance. She watched the couples going round and round; she forgot her five babies and her man and felt almost like a girl again. The music sounded sad and sweet. Her roughened hands clasped and unclasped themselves in the folds of her skirt. While the music went on she was afraid to look anybody in the face, and she smiled with a little nervous tremor round the mouth.

"But, my God," Frau Rupp cried, "they've given that child of Theresa's a piece of sausage. It's to keep her quiet. There's going to be a presentation now—your man has to speak."

Frau Brechenmacher sat up stiffly. The music ceased, and the dancers took their places again at the tables.

Herr Brechenmacher alone remained standing—he held in his hands a big silver coffee-pot. Everybody laughed at his speech, except the Frau; everybody roared at his grimaces, and at the way he carried the coffee-pot to the bridal pair, as if it were a baby he was holding.

She lifted the lid, peeped in, then shut it down with a little scream and sat biting her lips. The bridegroom wrenched the pot away from her and drew forth a baby's bottle and two little cradles holding china dolls. As he dandled these treasures before Theresa the hot room seemed to heave and sway with laughter.

Frau Brechenmacher did not think it funny. She stared round at the laughing faces, and suddenly they all seemed strange to her. She wanted to go home and never come out again. She imagined that all these people were laughing at her, more people than there were in the room even—all laughing at her because they were so much stronger than she was.

They walked home in silence. Herr Brechenmacher strode ahead, she stumbled after him. White and forsaken lay the road from the railway station to their house—a cold rush of wind blew her hood from her face, and suddenly she remembered how they had come home together the first night. Now they had five babies and twice as much money; *but—*

"Na, what is it all for?" she muttered, and not until she had reached home, and prepared a little supper of meat and bread for her man did she stop asking herself that silly question.

Herr Brechenmacher broke the bread into his plate, smeared it round with his fork and chewed greedily.

"Good?" she asked, leaning her arms on the table and pillowing her breast against them.

"But fine!"

He took a piece of the crumb, wiped it round his plate edge, and held it up to her mouth. She shook her head.

"Not hungry," she said.

"But it is one of the best pieces, and full of the fat."

He cleared the plate; then pulled off his boots and flung them into a corner.

"Not much of a wedding," he said, stretching out his feet and wriggling his toes in the worsted socks.

"N—no," she replied, taking up the discarded boots and placing them on the oven to dry.

Herr Brechenmacher yawned and stretched himself, and then looked up at her, grinning.

"Remember the night that we came home? You were an innocent one, you were."

"Get along! Such a time ago I forget." Well she remembered.

"Such a clout on the ear as you gave me.... But I soon taught you."

"Oh, don't start talking. You've too much beer. Come to bed."

He tilted back in his chair, chuckling with laughter.

"That's not what you said to me that night. God, the trouble you gave me!"

But the little Frau seized the candle and went into the next room.

The children were all soundly sleeping. She stripped the mattress off the baby's bed to see if he was still dry, then began unfastening her blouse and skirt.

"Always the same," she said—"all over the world the same; but, God in heaven—but *stupid*."

Then even the memory of the wedding faded quite. She lay down on the bed and put her arm across her face like a child who expected to be hurt as Herr Brechenmacher lurched in.

70

Frau Fischer

Katherine Mansfield

Frau Fischer was the fortunate possessor of a candle factory somewhere on the banks of the Eger, and once a year she ceased from her labours to make a "cure" in Dorschausen, arriving with a dress-basket neatly covered in a black tarpaulin and a hand-bag. The latter contained amongst her handkerchiefs, eau de Cologne, toothpicks, and a certain woollen muffler very comforting to the "magen," samples of her skill in candle-making, to be offered up as tokens of thanksgiving when her holiday time was over.

Four of the clock one July afternoon she appeared at the Pension Müller. I was sitting in the arbour and watched her bustling up the path followed by the red-bearded porter with her dress-basket in his arms and a sunflower between his teeth. The widow and her five innocent daughters stood tastefully grouped upon the steps in appropriate attitudes of welcome; and the greetings were so long and loud that I felt a sympathetic glow.

"What a journey!" cried the Frau Fischer. "And nothing to eat in the train—nothing solid. I assure you the sides of my stomach are flapping together. But I must not spoil my appetite for dinner—just a cup of coffee in my room. Bertha," turning to the youngest of the five, "how changed! What a bust! Frau Hartmann, I congratulate you."

Once again the Widow seized Frau Fischer's hands. "Kathi, too, a splendid woman; but a little pale. Perhaps the young man from Nürnberg is here again this year. How you keep them all I don't know. Each year I come expecting to find you with an empty nest. It's surprising."

Frau Hartmann, in an ashamed, apologetic voice: "We are such a happy family since my dear man died."

"But these marriages—one must have courage; and after all, give them time, they all make the happy family bigger—thank God for that.... Are there many people here just now?"

"Every room engaged."

Followed a detailed description in the hall, murmured on the stairs, continued in six parts as they entered the large room (windows opening upon the garden) which Frau Fischer occupied each successive year. I was reading the "Miracles of Lourdes," which a Catholic priest—fixing a gloomy eye upon my soul—had begged me to digest; but its wonders were completely routed by Frau Fischer's arrival. Not even the white roses upon the feet of the Virgin could flourish in that atmosphere.

"... It was a simple shepherd-child who pastured her flocks upon the barren fields...."

Voices from the room above: "The washstand has, of course, been scrubbed over with soda."

"... Poverty-stricken, her limbs with tattered rags half covered...."

"Every stick of the furniture has been sunning in the garden for three days. And the carpet we made ourselves out of old clothes. There is a piece of that beautiful flannel petticoat you left us last summer."

"... Deaf and dumb was the child; in fact, the population considered her half idiot...."

"Yes, that is a new picture of the Kaiser. We have moved the thorn-crowned one of Jesus Christ out into the passage. It was not cheerful to sleep with. Dear Frau Fischer, won't you take your coffee out in the garden?"

"That is a very nice idea. But first I must remove my corsets and my boots. Ah, what a relief to wear sandals again. I am needing the 'cure' very badly this year. My nerves! I am a mass of them. During the entire journey I sat with my handkerchief over my head, even while the guard collected the tickets. Exhausted!"

She came into the arbour wearing a black and white spotted dressing-gown, and a calico cap peaked with patent leather, followed by Kathi, carrying the little blue jugs of malt coffee. We were formally introduced. Frau Fischer sat down, produced a perfectly clean pocket handkerchief and polished her cup and saucer, then lifted the lid of the coffee-pot and peered in at the contents mournfully.

"Malt coffee," she said. "Ah, for the first few days I wonder how I can put up with it. Naturally, absent from home one must expect much discomfort and strange food. But as I used to say to my dear husband: with a clean sheet and a good cup of coffee I can find my happiness anywhere. But now, with nerves like mine, no sacrifice is too terrible for me to make. What complaint are you suffering from? You look exceedingly healthy!"

I smiled and shrugged my shoulders.

"Ah, that is so strange about you English. You do not seem to enjoy discussing the functions of the body. As well speak of a railway train and refuse to mention the engine. How can we hope to understand anybody, knowing nothing of their stomachs? In my husband's most severe illness—the poultices—"

She dipped a piece of sugar in her coffee and watched it dissolve.

"Yet a young friend of mine who travelled to England for the funeral of his brother told me that women wore bodices in public restaurants no waiter could help looking into as he handed the soup."

"But only German waiters," I said. "English ones look over the top of your head."

"There," she cried, "now you see your dependence on Germany. Not even an efficient waiter can you have by yourselves."

"But I prefer them to look over your head."

"And that proves that you must be ashamed of your bodice."

I looked out over the garden full of wall-flowers and standard rose-trees growing stiffly like German bouquets, feeling I did not care one way or the other. I rather wanted to ask her if the young friend had gone to England in the capacity of waiter to attend the funeral baked meats, but decided it was not worth it. The weather was too hot to be malicious, and who could be uncharitable, victimised by the flapping sensations which Frau Fischer was enduring until six-thirty? As a gift from heaven for my forbearance, down the path towards us came the Herr Rat, angelically clad in a white silk suit. He and Frau Fischer were old friends. She drew the folds of her dressing-gown together, and made room for him on the little green bench.

"How cool you are looking," she said; "and if I may make the remark—what a beautiful suit!"

"Surely I wore it last summer when you were here? I brought the silk from China—smuggled it through the Russian customs by swathing it round my body. And such a quantity: two dress lengths for my sister-in-law, three suits for myself, a cloak for the housekeeper of my flat in Munich. How I perspired! Every inch of it had to be washed afterwards."

"Surely you have had more adventures than any man in Germany. When I think of the time that you spent in Turkey with a drunken guide who was bitten by a mad dog and fell over a precipice into a field of attar of roses, I lament that you have not written a book."

"Time—time. I am getting a few notes together. And now that you are here we shall renew our quiet little talks after supper. Yes? It is necessary and pleasant for a man to find relaxation in the company of women occasionally."

"Indeed I realise that. Even here your life is too strenuous—you are so sought after—so admired. It was just the same with my dear husband. He was a tall, beautiful man, and sometimes in the evening he would come down into the kitchen and say: 'Wife, I would like to be stupid for two minutes.' Nothing rested him so much then as for me to stroke his head."

The Herr Rat's bald pate glistening in the sunlight seemed symbolical of the sad absence of a wife.

I began to wonder as to the nature of these quiet little after-supper talks. How could one play Delilah to so shorn a Samson?

"Herr Hoffmann from Berlin arrived yesterday," said the Herr Rat.

"That young man I refuse to converse with. He told me last year that he had stayed in France in an hotel where they did not have serviettes; what a place it must have been! In Austria even the cabmen have serviettes. Also I have heard that he discussed 'free love' with Bertha as she was sweeping his room. I am not accustomed to such company. I had suspected him for a long time."

"Young blood," answered the Herr Rat genially. "I have had several disputes with him—you have heard them—is it not so?" turning to me.

"A great many," I said, smiling.

"Doubtless you too consider me behind the times. I make no secret of my age; I am sixty-nine; but you must have surely observed how impossible it was for him to speak at all when I raised my voice."

I replied with the utmost conviction, and, catching Frau Fischer's eye, suddenly realised I had better go back to the house and write some letters.

It was dark and cool in my room. A chestnut-tree pushed green boughs against the window. I looked down at the horsehair sofa so openly flouting the idea of curling up as immoral, pulled the red pillow on to the floor and lay down. And barely had I got comfortable when the door opened and Frau Fischer entered.

"The Herr Rat had a bathing appointment," she said, shutting the door after her. "May I come in? Pray do not move. You look like a little Persian kitten. Now, tell me something really interesting about your life. When I meet new people I squeeze them dry like a sponge. To begin with—you are married."

I admitted the fact.

"Then, dear child, where is your husband?"

I said he was a sea-captain on a long and perilous voyage.

"What a position to leave you in—so young and so unprotected."

She sat down on the sofa and shook her finger at me playfully.

"Admit, now, that you keep your journeys secret from him. For what man would think of allowing a woman with such a wealth of hair to go wandering in foreign countries? Now, supposing that you lost your purse at midnight in a snowbound train in North Russia?"

"But I haven't the slightest intention—" I began.

"I don't say that you have. But when you said good-bye to your dear man I am positive that you had no intention of coming here. My dear, I am a woman of experience, and I know the world. While he is away you have a fever in your blood. Your sad heart flies for comfort to these foreign lands. At home you cannot bear the sight of that empty bed—it is like widowhood. Since the death of my dear husband I have never known an hour's peace."

"I like empty beds," I protested sleepily, thumping the pillow.

"That cannot be true because it is not natural. Every wife ought to feel that her place is by her husband's side—sleeping or waking. It is plain to see that the strongest tie of all does not yet bind you. Wait until a little pair of hands stretches across the water—wait until he comes into harbour and sees you with the child at your breast."

I sat up stiffly.

"But I consider child-bearing the most ignominious of all professions," I said.

For a moment there was silence. Then Frau Fischer reached down and caught my hand.

"So young and yet to suffer so cruelly," she murmured. "There is nothing that sours a woman so terribly as to be left alone without a man, especially if she is married, for then it is impossible for her to accept the attention of others—unless she is unfortunately a widow. Of course, I know that sea-captains are subject to terrible temptations, and they are as inflammable as tenor singers—that is why you must present a bright and energetic appearance, and try and make him proud of you when his ship reaches port."

This husband that I had created for the benefit of Frau Fischer became in her hands so substantial a figure that I could no longer see myself sitting on a rock with seaweed in my hair, awaiting that phantom ship for which all women love to suppose they hunger. Rather, I saw myself pushing a perambulator up the gangway, and counting up the missing buttons on my husband's uniform jacket.

"Handfuls of babies, that is what you are really in need of," mused Frau Fischer. "Then, as the father of a family he cannot leave you. Think of his delight and excitement when he saw you!"

The plan seemed to me something of a risk. To appear suddenly with handfuls of strange babies is not generally calculated to raise enthusiasm in the heart of the average British husband. I decided to wreck my virgin conception and send him down somewhere off Cape Horn.

Then the dinner-gong sounded.

"Come up to my room afterwards," said Frau Fischer. "There is still much that I must ask you."

She squeezed my hand, but I did not squeeze back.

71

Germans at Meat

Katherine Mansfield

Bread soup was placed upon the table.

"Ah," said the Herr Rat, leaning upon the table as he peered into the tureen, "that is what I need. My 'magen' has not been in order for several days. Bread soup, and just the right consistency. I am a good cook myself"—he turned to me.

"How interesting," I said, attempting to infuse just the right amount of enthusiasm into my voice.

"Oh yes—when one is not married it is necessary. As for me, I have had all I wanted from women without marriage." He tucked his napkin into his collar and blew upon his soup as he spoke. "Now at nine o'clock I make myself an English breakfast, but not much. Four slices of bread, two eggs, two slices of cold ham, one plate of soup, two cups of tea—that is nothing to you."

He asserted the fact so vehemently that I had not the courage to refute it.

All eyes were suddenly turned upon me. I felt I was bearing the burden of the nation's preposterous breakfast—I who drank a cup of coffee while buttoning my blouse in the morning.

"Nothing at all," cried Herr Hoffmann from Berlin. "Ach, when I was in England in the morning I used to eat."

He turned up his eyes and his moustache, wiping the soup drippings from his coat and waistcoat.

"Do they really eat so much?" asked Fräulein Stiegelauer. "Soup and baker's bread and pig's flesh, and tea and coffee and stewed fruit, and honey and eggs, and cold fish and kidneys, and hot fish and liver? All the ladies eat, too, especially the ladies."

"Certainly. I myself have noticed it, when I was living in a hotel in Leicester Square," cried the Herr Rat. "It was a good hotel, but they could not make tea—now—"

"Ah, that's one thing I *can* do," said I, laughing brightly. "I can make very good tea. The great secret is to warm the teapot."

"Warm the teapot," interrupted the Herr Rat, pushing away his soup plate. "What do you warm the teapot for? Ha! ha! that's very good! One does not eat the teapot, I suppose?"

He fixed his cold blue eyes upon me with an expression which suggested a thousand premeditated invasions.

"So that is the great secret of your English tea? All you do is to warm the teapot."

I wanted to say that was only the preliminary canter, but could not translate it, and so was silent.

The servant brought in veal, with "sauerkraut" and potatoes.

"I eat sauerkraut with great pleasure," said the Traveller from North Germany, "but now I have eaten so much of it that I cannot retain it. I am immediately forced to—"

"A beautiful day," I cried, turning to Fräulein Stiegelauer. "Did you get up early?"

"At five o'clock I walked for ten minutes in the wet grass. Again in bed. At half-past five I fell asleep, and woke at seven, when I made an 'overbody' washing! Again in bed. At eight o'clock I had a cold-water poultice, and at half past eight I drank a cup of mint tea. At nine I drank some malt coffee, and began my 'cure.' Pass me the sauerkraut, please. You do not eat it?"

"No, thank you. I still find it a little strong."

"Is it true," asked the Widow, picking her teeth with a hairpin as she spoke, "that you are a vegetarian?"

"Why, yes; I have not eaten meat for three years."

"Im—possible! Have you any family?"

"No."

"There now, you see, that's what you're coming to! Who ever heard of having children upon vegetables? It is not possible. But you never have large families in England now; I suppose you are too busy with your suffragetting. Now I have had nine children, and they are all alive, thank God. Fine, healthy babies—though after the first one was born I had to—"

"How *wonderful!*" I cried.

"Wonderful," said the Widow contemptuously, replacing the hairpin in the knob which was balanced on the top of her head. "Not at all! A friend of mine had four at the same time. Her husband was so pleased he gave a supper-party and had them placed on the table. Of course she was very proud."

"Germany," boomed the Traveller, biting round a potato which he had speared with his knife, "is the home of the Family."

Followed an appreciative silence.

The dishes were changed for beef, red currants and spinach. They wiped their forks upon black bread and started again.

"How long are you remaining here?" asked the Herr Rat.

"I do not know exactly. I must be back in London in September."

"Of course you will visit München?"

"I am afraid I shall not have time. You see, it is important not to break into my 'cure.'"

"But you *must* go to München. You have not seen Germany if you have not been to München. All the Exhibitions, all the Art and Soul life of Germany are in München. There is the Wagner Festival in August, and Mozart and a Japanese collection of pictures—and there is the beer! You do not know what good beer is until you have been to München. Why, I see fine ladies every afternoon, but fine ladies, I tell you, drinking glasses so high." He measured a good washstand pitcher in height, and I smiled.

"If I drink a great deal of München beer I sweat so," said Herr Hoffmann. "When I am here, in the fields or before my baths, I sweat, but I enjoy it; but in the town it is not at all the same thing."

Prompted by the thought, he wiped his neck and face with his dinner napkin and carefully cleaned his ears.

A glass dish of stewed apricots was placed upon the table.

"Ah, fruit!" said Fräulein Stiegelauer, "that is so necessary to health. The doctor told me this morning that the more fruit I could eat the better."

She very obviously followed the advice.

Said the Traveller: "I suppose you are frightened of an invasion, too, eh? Oh, that's good. I've been reading all about your English play in a newspaper. Did you see it?"

"Yes." I sat upright. "I assure you we are not afraid."

"Well, then, you ought to be," said the Herr Rat. "You have got no army at all—a few little boys with their veins full of nicotine poisoning."

"Don't be afraid," Herr Hoffmann said. "We don't want England. If we did we would have had her long ago. We really do not want you."

He waved his spoon airily, looking across at me as though I were a little child whom he would keep or dismiss as he pleased.

"We certainly do not want Germany," I said.

"This morning I took a half bath. Then this afternoon I must take a knee bath and an arm bath," volunteered the Herr Rat; "then I do my exercises for an hour, and my work is over. A glass of wine and a couple of rolls with some sardines—"

They were handed cherry cake with whipped cream.

"What is your husband's favourite meat?" asked the Widow.

"I really do not know," I answered.

"You really do not know? How long have you been married?"

"Three years."

"But you cannot be in earnest! You would not have kept house as his wife for a week without knowing that fact."

"I really never asked him; he is not at all particular about his food."

A pause. They all looked at me, shaking their heads, their mouths full of cherry stones.

"No wonder there is a repetition in England of that dreadful state of things in Paris," said the Widow, folding her dinner napkin. "How can a woman expect to keep her husband if she does not know his favourite food after three years?"

"Mahlzeit!"

"Mahlzeit!"

I closed the door after me.

72

The Baron

Katherine Mansfield

"Who is he?" I said. "And why does he sit always alone, with his back to us, too?"

"Ah!" whispered the Frau Oberregierungsrat, "he is a *Baron*."

She looked at me very solemnly, and yet with the slightest possible contempt—a "fancy-not-recognising-that-at-the-first-glance" expression.

"But, poor soul, he cannot help it," I said. "Surely that unfortunate fact ought not to debar him from the pleasures of intellectual intercourse."

If it had not been for her fork I think she would have crossed herself.

"Surely you cannot understand. He is one of the First Barons."

More than a little unnerved, she turned and spoke to the Frau Doktor on her left.

"My omelette is empty—*empty*," she protested, "and this is the third I have tried!"

I looked at the First of the Barons. He was eating salad—taking a whole lettuce leaf on his fork and absorbing it slowly, rabbit-wise—a fascinating process to watch.

Small and slight, with scanty black hair and beard and yellow-toned complexion, he invariably wore black serge clothes, a rough linen shirt, black sandals, and the largest black-rimmed spectacles that I had ever seen.

The Herr Oberlehrer, who sat opposite me, smiled benignantly.

"It must be very interesting for you, gnädige Frau, to be able to watch... of course this is a *very fine house*. There was a lady from the Spanish Court here in the summer; she had a liver. We often spoke together."

I looked gratified and humble.

"Now, in England, in your 'boarding 'ouse', one does not find the First Class, as in Germany."

"No, indeed," I replied, still hypnotised by the Baron, who looked like a little yellow silkworm.

"The Baron comes every year," went on the Herr Oberlehrer, "for his nerves. He has never spoken to any of the guests—*yet.*" A smile crossed his face. I seemed to see his visions of some splendid upheaval of that silence—a dazzling exchange of courtesies in a dim future, a splendid sacrifice of a newspaper to this Exalted One, a "danke schön" to be handed down to future generations.

At that moment the postman, looking like a German army officer, came in with the mail. He threw my letters into my milk pudding, and then turned to a waitress and whispered. She retired hastily. The manager of the pension came in with a little tray. A picture post card was deposited on it, and reverently bowing his head, the manager of the pension carried it to the Baron.

Myself, I felt disappointed that there was not a salute of twenty-five guns.

At the end of the meal we were served with coffee. I noticed the Baron took three lumps of sugar, putting two in his cup and wrapping up the third in a corner of his pocket-handkerchief. He was always the first to enter the dining-room and the last to leave; and in a vacant chair beside him he placed a little black leather bag.

In the afternoon, leaning from my window, I saw him pass down the street, walking tremulously and carrying the bag. Each time he passed a lamp-post he shrank a little, as though expecting it to strike him, or maybe the sense of plebeian contamination....

I wondered where he was going, and why he carried the bag. Never had I seen him at the Casino or the Bath Establishment. He looked forlorn, his feet slipped in his sandals. I found myself pitying the Baron.

That evening a party of us were gathered in the salon discussing the day's "kur" with feverish animation. The Frau Oberregierungsrat sat by me knitting a shawl for her youngest of nine daughters, who was in that very interesting, frail condition.... "But it is bound to be quite satisfactory," she said to me. "The dear married a banker—the desire of her life."

There must have been eight or ten of us gathered together, we who were married exchanging confidences as to the underclothing and peculiar characteristics of our husbands, the unmarried discussing the over-clothing and peculiar fascinations of Possible Ones.

"I knit them myself," I heard the Frau Lehrer cry, "of thick grey wool. He wears one a month, with two soft collars."

"And then," whispered Fräulein Lisa, "he said to me, 'Indeed you please me. I shall, perhaps, write to your mother.'"

Small wonder that we were a little violently excited, a little expostulatory.

Suddenly the door opened and admitted the Baron.

Followed a complete and deathlike silence.

He came in slowly, hesitated, took up a toothpick from a dish on the top of the piano, and went out again.

When the door was closed we raised a triumphant cry! It was the first time he had ever been known to enter the salon. Who could tell what the Future held?

Days lengthened into weeks. Still we were together, and still the solitary little figure, head bowed as though under the weight of the spectacles, haunted me. He entered with the black bag, he retired with the black bag—and that was all.

At last the manager of the pension told us the Baron was leaving the next day.

"Oh," I thought, "surely he cannot drift into obscurity—be lost without one word! Surely he will honour the Frau Oberregierungsrat or the Frau Feldleutnantswitwe *once* before he goes."

In the evening of that day it rained heavily. I went to the post office, and as I stood on the steps, umbrellaless, hesitating before plunging into the slushy road, a little, hesitating voice seemed to come from under my elbow.

I looked down. It was the First of the Barons with the black bag and an umbrella. Was I mad? Was I sane? He was asking me to share the latter. But I was exceedingly nice, a trifle diffident, appropriately reverential. Together we walked through the mud and slush.

Now, there is something peculiarly intimate in sharing an umbrella.

It is apt to put one on the same footing as brushing a man's coat for him—a little daring, naïve.

I longed to know why he sat alone, why he carried the bag, what he did all day. But he himself volunteered some information.

"I fear," he said, "that my luggage will be damp. I invariably carry it with me in this bag—one requires so little—for servants are untrustworthy."

"A wise idea," I answered. And then: "Why have you denied us the pleasure—"

"I sit alone that I may eat more," said the Baron, peering into the dusk; "my stomach requires a great deal of food. I order double portions, and eat them in peace."

Which sounded finely Baronial.

"And what do you do all day?"

"I imbibe nourishment in my room," he replied, in a voice that closed the conversation and almost repented of the umbrella.

When we arrived at the pension there was very nearly an open riot.

I ran half way up the stairs, and thanked the Baron audibly from the landing.

He distinctly replied: "Not at all!"

It was very friendly of the Herr Oberlehrer to have sent me a bouquet that evening, and the Frau Oberregierungsrat asked me for my pattern of a baby's bonnet!

Next day the Baron was gone.

Sic transit gloria German mundi.

73

The Sister of the Baroness

Katherine Mansfield

"There are two new guests arriving this afternoon," said the manager of the pension, placing a chair for me at the breakfast-table. "I have only received the letter acquainting me with the fact this morning. The Baroness von Gall is sending her little daughter—the poor child is dumb—to make the 'cure.' She is to stay with us a month, and then the Baroness herself is coming."

"Baroness von Gall," cried the Frau Doktor, coming into the room and positively scenting the name. "Coming here? There was a picture of her only last week in *Sport and Salon*. She is a friend of the Court: I have heard that the Kaiserin says 'du' to her. But this is delightful! I shall take my doctor's advice and spend an extra six weeks here. There is nothing like young society."

"But the child is dumb," ventured the manager apologetically.

"Bah! What does that matter? Afflicted children have such pretty ways."

Each guest who came into the breakfast-room was bombarded with the wonderful news. "The Baroness von Gall is sending her little daughter here; the Baroness herself is coming in a month's time." Coffee and rolls took on the nature of an orgy. We positively scintillated. Anecdotes of the High Born were poured out, sweetened and sipped: we gorged on scandals of High Birth generously buttered.

"They are to have the room next to yours," said the manager, addressing me. "I was wondering if you would permit me to take down the portrait of the Kaiserin Elizabeth from above your bed to hang over their sofa."

"Yes, indeed, something homelike"—the Frau Oberregierungsrat patted my hand—"and of no possible significance to you."

I felt a little crushed. Not at the prospect of losing that vision of diamonds and blue velvet bust, but at the tone—placing me outside the pale—branding me as a foreigner.

We dissipated the day in valid speculations. Decided it was too warm to walk in the afternoon, so lay down on our beds, mustering in great force for afternoon coffee. And a carriage drew up at the door. A tall young girl got out, leading a child by the hand. They entered the hall, were greeted and shown to their room. Ten minutes later she came down with the child to sign the visitors' book. She wore a black, closely fitting dress, touched at throat and wrists with white frilling. Her brown hair, braided, was tied with a black bow—unusually pale, with a small mole on her left cheek.

"I am the Baroness von Gall's sister," she said, trying the pen on a piece of blotting-paper, and smiling at us deprecatingly. Even for the most jaded of us life holds its thrilling moments. Two Baronesses in two months! The manager immediately left the room to find a new nib.

To my plebeian eyes that afflicted child was singularly unattractive. She had the air of having been perpetually washed with a blue bag, and hair like grey wool—dressed, too, in a pinafore so stiffly starched that she could only peer at us over the frill of it—a social barrier of a pinafore—and perhaps it was too much to expect a noble aunt to attend to the menial consideration of her niece's ears. But a dumb niece with unwashed ears struck me as a most depressing object.

They were given places at the head of the table. For a moment we all looked at one another with an eena-deena-dina-do expression. Then the Frau Oberregierungsrat:

"I hope you are not tired after your journey."

"No," said the sister of the Baroness, smiling into her cup.

"I hope the dear child is not tired," said the Frau Doktor.

"Not at all."

"I expect, I hope you will sleep well to-night," the Herr Oberlehrer said reverently.

"Yes."

The poet from Munich never took his eyes off the pair. He allowed his tie to absorb most of his coffee while he gazed at them exceedingly soulfully.

Unyoking Pegasus, thought I. Death spasms of his Odes to Solitude! There were possibilities in that young woman for an inspiration, not to mention a dedication, and from that moment his suffering temperament took up its bed and walked.

They retired after the meal, leaving us to discuss them at leisure.

"There is a likeness," mused the Frau Doktor. "Quite. What a manner she has. Such reserve, such a tender way with the child."

"Pity she has the child to attend to," exclaimed the student from Bonn. He had hitherto relied upon three scars and a ribbon to produce an effect, but the sister of a Baroness demanded more than these.

Absorbing days followed. Had she been one whit less beautifully born we could not have endured the continual conversation about her, the songs in her praise, the detailed account of her movements. But she graciously suffered our worship and we were more than content.

The poet she took into her confidence. He carried her books when we went walking, he jumped the afflicted one on his knee—poetic licence, this—and one morning brought his notebook into the salon and read to us.

"The sister of the Baroness has assured me she is going into a convent," he said. (That made the student from Bonn sit up.) "I have written these few lines last night from my window in the sweet night air—"

"Oh, your *delicate* chest," commented the Frau Doktor.

He fixed a stony eye on her, and she blushed.

"I have written these lines:

"'Ah, will you to a convent fly,
So young, so fresh, so fair?
Spring like a doe upon the fields
And find your beauty there.'"

Nine verses equally lovely commanded her to equally violent action. I am certain that had she followed his advice not even the remainder of her life in a convent would have given her time to recover her breath.

"I have presented her with a copy," he said. "And to-day we are going to look for wild flowers in the wood."

The student from Bonn got up and left the room. I begged the poet to repeat the verses once more. At the end of the sixth verse I saw from the window the sister of the Baroness and the scarred youth disappearing through the front gate, which enabled me to thank the poet so charmingly that he offered to write me out a copy.

But we were living at too high pressure in those days. Swinging from our humble pension to the high walls of palaces, how could we help but fall? Late one afternoon the Frau Doktor came upon me in the writing-room and took me to her bosom.

"She has been telling me all about her life," whispered the Frau Doktor. "She came to my bedroom and offered to massage my arm. You know, I am the greatest martyr to rheumatism. And, fancy now, she has already had six proposals of marriage. Such beautiful offers that I assure you I wept—and every one of noble birth. My dear, the most beautiful was in the wood. Not that I do not think a proposal should take place in a drawing-room—it is more fitting to have four walls—but this was a private wood. He said, the young officer, she was like a young tree whose branches had never been touched by the ruthless hand of man. Such delicacy!" She sighed and turned up her eyes.

"Of course it is difficult for you English to understand when you are always exposing your legs on cricket-fields, and breeding dogs in your back gardens. The pity of it! Youth should be like a wild rose. For myself I do not understand how your women ever get married at all."

She shook her head so violently that I shook mine too, and a gloom settled round my heart. It seemed we were really in a very bad way. Did the spirit of romance spread her rose wings only over aristocratic Germany?

I went to my room, bound a pink scarf about my hair, and took a volume of Mörike's lyrics into the garden. A great bush of purple lilac grew behind the summer-house. There I sat down, finding a sad significance in the delicate suggestion of half mourning. I began to write a poem myself.

"They sway and languish dreamily,
And we, close pressed, are kissing there."

It ended! "Close pressed" did not sound at all fascinating. Savoured of wardrobes. Did my wild rose then already trail in the dust? I chewed a leaf and hugged my knees. Then—magic moment—I heard voices from the summer-house, the sister of the Baroness and the student from Bonn.

Second-hand was better than nothing; I pricked up my ears.

"What small hands you have," said the student from Bonn. "They are like white lilies lying in the pool of your black dress." This certainly sounded the real thing. Her high-born reply was what interested me. Sympathetic murmur only.

"May I hold one?"

I heard two sighs—presumed they held—he had rifled those dark waters of a noble blossom.

"Look at my great fingers beside yours."

"But they are beautifully kept," said the sister of the Baroness shyly.

The minx! Was love then a question of manicure?

"How I should adore to kiss you," murmured the student. "But you know I am suffering from severe nasal catarrh, and I dare not risk giving it to you. Sixteen times last night did I count myself sneezing. And three different handkerchiefs."

I threw Mörike into the lilac bush, and went back to the house. A great automobile snorted at the front door. In the salon great commotion. The Baroness was paying a surprise visit to her little daughter. Clad in a yellow mackintosh she stood in the middle of the room questioning the manager. And every guest the pension contained was grouped about her, even the Frau Doktor, presumably examining a timetable, as near to the august skirts as possible.

"But where is my maid?" asked the Baroness.

"There was no maid," replied the manager, "save for your gracious sister and daughter."

"Sister!" she cried sharply. "Fool, I have no sister. My child travelled with the daughter of my dressmaker."

Tableau grandissimo!

74

The Luft Bad

Katherine Mansfield

I think it must be the umbrellas which make us look ridiculous. When I was admitted into the enclosure for the first time, and saw my fellow-bathers walking about very nearly "in their nakeds," it struck me that the umbrellas gave a distinctly "Little Black Sambo" touch.

Ridiculous dignity in holding over yourself a green cotton thing with a red parroquet handle when you are dressed in nothing larger than a handkerchief.

There are no trees in the "Luft Bad." It boasts a collection of plain, wooden cells, a bath shelter, two swings and two odd clubs—one, presumably the lost property of Hercules or the German army, and the other to be used with safety in the cradle.

And there in all weathers we take the air—walking, or sitting in little companies talking over each other's ailments and measurements and ills that flesh is heir to.

A high wooden wall compasses us all about; above it the pine-trees look down a little superciliously, nudging each other in a way that is peculiarly trying to a *débutante*. Over the wall, on the right side, is the men's section. We hear them chopping down trees and sawing through planks, dashing heavy weights to the ground, and singing part songs. Yes, they take it far more seriously.

On the first day I was conscious of my legs, and went back into my cell three times to look at my watch, but when a woman with whom I had played chess for three weeks cut me dead, I took heart and joined a circle.

We lay curled on the ground while a Hungarian lady of immense proportions told us what a beautiful tomb she had bought for her second husband.

"A vault it is," she said, "with nice black railings. And so large that I can go down there and walk about. Both their photographs are there, with two very handsome wreaths sent me by my first husband's brother. There is an enlargement of a family group photograph, too, and an illuminated address presented to my first husband on his marriage. I am often there; it makes such a pleasant excursion for a fine Saturday afternoon."

She suddenly lay down flat on her back, took in six long breaths, and sat up again.

"The death agony was dreadful," she said brightly; "of the second, I mean. The 'first' was run into by a furniture wagon, and had fifty marks stolen out of a new waistcoat pocket, but the 'second' was dying for sixty-seven hours. I never ceased crying once—not even to put the children to bed."

A young Russian, with a "bang" curl on her forehead, turned to me.

"Can you do the 'Salome' dance?" she asked. "I can."

"How delightful," I said.

"Shall I do it now? Would you like to see me?"

She sprang to her feet, executed a series of amazing contortions for the next ten minutes, and then paused, panting, twisting her long hair.

"Isn't that nice?" she said. "And now I am perspiring so splendidly. I shall go and take a bath."

Opposite to me was the brownest woman I have ever seen, lying on her back, her arms clasped over her head.

"How long have you been here to-day?" she was asked.

"Oh, I spend the day here now," she answered. "I am making my own 'cure,' and living entirely on raw vegetables and nuts, and each day I feel my spirit is stronger and purer. After all, what can you expect? The majority of us are walking about with pig corpuscles and oxen fragments in our brain. The wonder is the world is as good as it is. Now I live on the simple, provided food"—she pointed to a little bag beside her—"a lettuce, a carrot, a potato, and some nuts are ample, rational nourishment. I wash them under the tap and eat them raw, just as they come from the harmless earth—fresh and uncontaminated."

"Do you take nothing else all day?" I cried.

"Water. And perhaps a banana if I wake in the night." She turned round and leaned on one elbow. "You over-eat yourself dreadfully," she said; "shamelessly! How can you expect the Flame of the Spirit to burn brightly under layers of superfluous flesh?"

I wished she would not stare at me, and thought of going to look at my watch again when a little girl wearing a string of coral beads joined us.

"The poor Frau Hauptmann cannot join us to-day," she said; "she has come out in spots all over on account of her nerves. She was very excited yesterday after having written two post-cards."

"A delicate woman," volunteered the Hungarian, "but pleasant. Fancy, she has a separate plate for each of her front teeth! But she has no right to let her daughters wear such short sailor suits. They sit about on benches, crossing their legs in a most shameless manner. What are you going to do this afternoon, Fräulein Anna?"

"Oh," said the Coral Necklace, "the Herr Oberleutnant has asked me to go with him to Landsdorf. He must buy some eggs there to take home to his mother. He saves a penny on eight eggs by knowing the right peasants to bargain with."

"Are you an American?" said the Vegetable Lady, turning to me.

"No."

"Then you are an Englishwoman?"

"Well, hardly—"

"You must be one of the two; you cannot help it. I have seen you walking alone several times. You wear your—"

I got up and climbed on to the swing. The air was sweet and cool, rushing past my body. Above, white clouds trailed delicately through the blue sky. From the pine forest streamed a wild perfume, the branches swayed together, rhythmically, sonorously. I felt so light and free and happy—so childish! I wanted to poke my tongue out at the circle on the grass, who, drawing close together, were whispering meaningly.

"Perhaps you do not know," cried a voice from one of the cells, "to swing is very upsetting for the stomach? A friend of mine could keep nothing down for three weeks after exciting herself so."

I went to the bath shelter and was hosed.

As I dressed, someone tapped on the wall.

"Do you know," said a voice, "there is a man who *lives* in the Luft Bad next door? He buries himself up to the armpits in mud and refuses to believe in the Trinity."

The umbrellas are the saving grace of the Luft Bad. Now when I go, I take my husband's "storm gamp" and sit in a corner, hiding behind it.

Not that I am in the least ashamed of my legs.

75

The Child-Who-Was-Tired

Katherine Mansfield

She was just beginning to walk along a little white road with tall black trees on either side, a little road that led to nowhere, and where nobody walked at all, when a hand gripped her shoulder, shook her, slapped her ear.

"Oh, oh, don't stop me," cried the Child-Who-Was-Tired. "Let me go."

"Get up, you good-for-nothing brat," said a voice; "get up and light the oven or I'll shake every bone out of your body."

With an immense effort she opened her eyes, and saw the Frau standing by, the baby bundled under one arm. The three other children who shared the same bed with the Child-Who-Was-Tired, accustomed to brawls, slept on peacefully. In a corner of the room the Man was fastening his braces.

"What do you mean by sleeping like this the whole night through—like a sack of potatoes? You've let the baby wet his bed twice."

She did not answer, but tied her petticoat string, and buttoned on her plaid frock with cold, shaking fingers.

"There, that's enough. Take the baby into the kitchen with you, and heat that cold coffee on the spirit lamp for the master, and give him the loaf of black bread out of the table drawer. Don't guzzle it yourself or I'll know."

The Frau staggered across the room, flung herself on to her bed, drawing the pink bolster round her shoulders.

It was almost dark in the kitchen. She laid the baby on the wooden settle, covering him with a shawl, then poured the coffee from the earthenware jug into the saucepan, and set it on the spirit lamp to boil.

"I'm sleepy," nodded the Child-Who-Was-Tired, kneeling on the floor and splitting the damp pine logs into little chips. "That's why I'm not awake."

The oven took a long time to light. Perhaps it was cold, like herself, and sleepy.... Perhaps it had been dreaming of a little white road with black trees on either side, a little road that led to nowhere.

Then the door was pulled violently open and the Man strode in.

"Here, what are you doing, sitting on the floor?" he shouted. "Give me my coffee. I've got to be off. Ugh! You haven't even washed over the table."

She sprang to her feet, poured his coffee into an enamel cup, and gave him bread and a knife, then, taking a wash rag from the sink, smeared over the black linoleumed table.

"Swine of a day—swine's life," mumbled the Man, sitting by the table and staring out of the window at the bruised sky, which seemed to bulge heavily over the dull land. He stuffed his mouth with bread and then swilled it down with the coffee.

The Child drew a pail of water, turned up her sleeves, frowning the while at her arms, as if to scold them for being so thin, so much like little stunted twigs, and began to mop over the floor.

"Stop sousing about the water while I'm here," grumbled the Man. "Stop the baby snivelling; it's been going on like that all night."

The Child gathered the baby into her lap and sat rocking him.

"Ts—ts—ts," she said. "He's cutting his eye teeth, that's what makes him cry so. *And* dribble—I never seen a baby dribble like this one." She wiped his mouth and nose with a corner of her skirt. "Some babies get their teeth without you knowing it," she went on, "and some take on this way all the time. I once heard of a baby that died, and they found all its teeth in its stomach."

The Man got up, unhooked his cloak from the back of the door, and flung it round him.

"There's another coming," said he.

"What—a tooth!" exclaimed the Child, startled for the first time that morning out of her dreadful heaviness, and thrusting her finger into the baby's mouth.

"No," he said grimly, "another baby. Now, get on with your work; it's time the others got up for school." She stood a moment quite silently, hearing his heavy steps on the stone passage, then the gravel walk, and finally the slam of the front gate.

"Another baby! Hasn't she finished having them *yet?*" thought the

Child. "Two babies getting eye teeth—two babies to get up for in the night—two babies to carry about and wash their little piggy clothes!" She looked with horror at the one in her arms, who, seeming to understand the contemptuous loathing of her tired glance, doubled his fists, stiffened his body, and began violently screaming.

"Ts—ts—ts." She laid him on the settle and went back to her floor-washing. He never ceased crying for a moment, but she got quite used to it and kept time with her broom. Oh, how tired she was! Oh, the heavy broom handle and the burning spot just at the back of her neck that ached so, and a funny little fluttering feeling just at the back of her waistband, as though something were going to break.

The clock struck six. She set the pan of milk in the oven, and went into the next room to wake and dress the three children. Anton and Hans lay together in attitudes of mutual amity which certainly never existed out of their sleeping hours. Lena was curled up, her knees under her chin, only a straight, standing-up pigtail of hair showing above the bolster.

"Get up," cried the Child, speaking in a voice of immense authority, pulling off the bedclothes and giving the boys sundry pokes and digs. "I've been calling you this last half-hour. It's late, and I'll tell on you if you don't get dressed this minute."

Anton awoke sufficiently to turn over and kick Hans on a tender part, whereupon Hans pulled Lena's pigtail until she shrieked for her mother.

"Oh, do be quiet," whispered the Child. "Oh, do get up and dress. You know what will happen. There—I'll help you."

But the warning came too late. The Frau got out of bed, walked in a determined fashion into the kitchen, returning with a bundle of twigs in her hand fastened together with a strong cord. One by one she laid the children across her knee and severely beat them, expending a final burst of energy on the Child-Who-Was-Tired, then returned to bed, with a comfortable sense of her maternal duties in good working order for the day. Very subdued, the three allowed themselves to be dressed and washed by the Child, who even laced the boys' boots, having found through experience that if left to themselves they hopped about for at least five minutes to find a comfortable ledge for their foot, and then spat on their hands and broke the bootlaces.

While she gave them their breakfast they became uproarious, and the baby would not cease crying. When she filled the tin kettle with milk, tied on the rubber teat, and, first moistening it herself, tried with little coaxing words to make him drink, he threw the bottle on to the floor and trembled all over.

"Eye teeth!" shouted Hans, hitting Anton over the head with his empty cup; "he's getting the evil-eye teeth, I should say."

"Smarty!" retorted Lena, poking out her tongue at him, and then, when he promptly did the same, crying at the top of her voice, "Mother, Hans is making faces at me!"

"That's right," said Hans; "go on howling, and when you're in bed to-night I'll wait till you're asleep, and then I'll creep over and take a little tiny piece of your arm and twist and twist it until—" He leant over the table making the most horrible faces at Lena, not noticing that Anton was standing behind his chair until the little boy bent over and spat on his brother's shaven head.

"Oh, weh! oh, weh!"

The Child-Who-Was-Tired pushed and pulled them apart, muffled them into their coats, and drove them out of the house.

"Hurry, hurry! the second bell's rung," she urged, knowing perfectly well she was telling a story, and rather exulting in the fact. She washed up the breakfast things, then went down to the cellar to look out the potatoes and beetroot.

Such a funny, cold place the coal cellar! With potatoes banked on one corner, beetroot in an old candle box, two tubs of sauerkraut, and a twisted mass of dahlia roots—that looked as real as though they were fighting one another, thought the Child.

She gathered the potatoes into her skirt, choosing big ones with few eyes because they were easier to peel, and bending over the dull heap in the silent cellar, she began to nod.

"Here, you, what are you doing down there?" cried the Frau, from the top of the stairs. "The baby's fallen off the settle, and got a bump as big as an egg over his eye. Come up here, and I'll teach you!"

"It wasn't me—it wasn't me!" screamed the Child, beaten from one side of the hall to the other, so that the potatoes and beetroot rolled out of her skirt.

The Frau seemed to be as big as a giant, and there was a certain heaviness in all her movements that was terrifying to anyone so small.

"Sit in the corner, and peel and wash the vegetables, and keep the baby quiet while I do the washing."

Whimpering she obeyed, but as to keeping the baby quiet, that was impossible. His face was hot, little beads of sweat stood all over his head, and he stiffened his body and cried. She held him on her knees, with a pan of cold water beside her for the cleaned vegetables and the "ducks' bucket" for the peelings.

"Ts—ts—ts!" she crooned, scraping and boring; "there's going to be another soon, and you can't both keep on crying. Why don't you go to sleep, baby? I would, if I were you. I'll tell you a dream. Once upon a time there was a little white road—"

She shook back her head, a great lump ached in her throat and then the tears ran down her face on to the vegetables.

"That's no good," said the Child, shaking them away. "Just stop crying until I've finished this, baby, and I'll walk you up and down."

But by that time she had to peg out the washing for the Frau. A wind had sprung up. Standing on tiptoe in the yard, she almost felt she would be blown away. There was a bad smell coming from the ducks' coop, which was half full of manure water, but away in the meadow she saw the grass blowing like little green hairs. And she remembered having heard of a child who had once played for a whole day in just such a meadow with real sausages and beer for her dinner—and not a little bit of tiredness. Who had told her that story? She could not remember, and yet it was so plain.

The wet clothes flapped in her face as she pegged them; danced and jigged on the line, bulged out and twisted. She walked back to the house with lagging steps, looking longingly at the grass in the meadow.

"What must I do now, please?" she said.

"Make the beds and hang the baby's mattress out of the window, then get the wagon and take him for a little walk along the road. In front of the house, mind—where I can see you. Don't stand there, gaping! Then come in when I call you and help me cut up the salad."

When she had made the beds the Child stood and looked at them. Gently she stroked the pillow with her hand, and then, just for one moment, let her head rest there. Again the smarting lump in her throat, the stupid tears that fell and kept on falling as she dressed the baby and dragged the little wagon up and down the road.

A man passed, driving a bullock wagon. He wore a long, queer feather in his hat, and whistled as he passed. Two girls with bundles on their shoulders came walking out of the village—one wore a red handkerchief about her head and one a blue. They were laughing and holding each other by the hand. Then the sun pushed by a heavy fold of grey cloud and spread a warm yellow light over everything.

"Perhaps," thought the Child-Who-Was-Tired, "if I walked far enough up this road I might come to a little white one, with tall black trees on either side—a little road—"

"Salad, salad!" cried the Frau's voice from the house.

Soon the children came home from school, dinner was eaten, the Man took the Frau's share of pudding as well as his own, and the three children seemed to smear themselves all over with whatever they ate. Then more dish-washing and more cleaning and baby-minding. So the afternoon dragged coldly through.

Old Frau Grathwohl came in with a fresh piece of pig's flesh for the Frau, and the Child listened to them gossiping together.

"Frau Manda went on her 'journey to Rome' last night, and brought back a daughter. How are you feeling?"

"I was sick twice this morning," said the Frau. "My insides are all twisted up with having children too quickly."

"I see you've got a new help," commented old Mother Grathwohl.

"Oh, dear Lord"—the Frau lowered her voice—"don't you know her? She's the free-born one—daughter of the waitress at the railway station. They found her mother trying to squeeze her head in the wash-hand jug, and the child's half silly."

"Ts—ts—ts!" whispered the "free-born" one to the baby.

As the day drew in the Child-Who-Was-Tired did not know how to fight her sleepiness any longer. She was afraid to sit down or stand still. As she sat at supper the Man and the Frau seemed to swell to an immense size as she watched them, and then become smaller than dolls, with little voices that seemed to come from outside the window. Looking at the baby, it suddenly had two heads, and then no head. Even his crying made her feel worse. When she thought of the nearness of bedtime she shook all over with excited joy. But as eight o'clock approached there was the sound of wheels on the road, and presently in came a party of friends to spend the evening.

Then it was:

"Put on the coffee."

"Bring me the sugar tin."

"Carry the chairs out of the bedroom."

"Set the table."

And, finally, the Frau sent her into the next room to keep the baby quiet.

There was a little piece of candle burning in the enamel bracket. As she walked up and down she saw her great big shadow on the wall like a grown-up person with a grown-up baby. Whatever would it look like when she carried two babies so!

"Ts—ts—ts! Once upon a time she was walking along a little white road, with oh! such great big black trees on either side."

"Here you!" called the Frau's voice, "bring me my new jacket from behind the door." And as she took it into the warm room one of the women said, "She looks like an owl. Such children are seldom right in their heads."

"Why don't you keep that baby quiet?" said the Man, who had just drunk enough beer to make him feel very brave and master of his house.

"If you don't keep that baby quiet you'll know why later on."

They burst out laughing as she stumbled back into the bedroom.

"I don't believe Holy Mary could keep him quiet," she murmured. "Did Jesus cry like this when He was little? If I was not so tired perhaps I could do it; but the baby just knows that I want to go to sleep. And there is going to be another one."

She flung the baby on the bed, and stood looking at him with terror.

From the next room there came the jingle of glasses and the warm sound of laughter.

And she suddenly had a beautiful marvellous idea.

She laughed for the first time that day, and clapped her hands.

"Ts—ts—ts!" she said, "lie there, silly one; you *will* go to sleep. You'll not cry any more or wake up in the night. Funny, little, ugly baby."

He opened his eyes, and shrieked loudly at the sight of the Child-Who-Was-Tired. From the next room she heard the Frau call out to her.

"One moment—he is almost asleep," she cried.

And then gently, smiling, on tiptoe, she brought the pink bolster from the Frau's bed and covered the baby's face with it, pressed with all her might as he struggled, "like a duck with its head off, wriggling", she thought.

She heaved a long sigh, then fell back on to the floor, and was walking along a little white road with tall black trees on either side, a little road that led to nowhere, and where nobody walked at all—nobody at all.

76

A Blaze

Katherine Mansfield

"Max, you silly devil, you'll break your neck if you go careering down the slide that way. Drop it, and come to the Club House with me and get some coffee."

"I've had enough for to-day. I'm damp all through. There, give us a cigarette, Victor, old man. When are you going home?"

"Not for another hour. It's fine this afternoon, and I'm getting into decent shape. Look out, get off the track; here comes Fräulein Winkel. Damned elegant the way she manages her sleigh!"

"I'm cold all through. That's the worst of this place—the mists—it's a damp cold. Here, Forman, look after this sleigh—and stick it somewhere so that I can get it without looking through a hundred and fifty others to-morrow morning."

They sat down at a small round table near the stove and ordered coffee. Victor sprawled in his chair, patting his little brown dog Bobo and looking, half laughingly, at Max.

"What's the matter, my dear? Isn't the world being nice and pretty?"

"I want my coffee, and I want to put my feet into my pocket—they're like stones.... Nothing to eat, thanks—the cake is like underdone india-rubber here."

Fuchs and Wistuba came and sat at their table. Max half turned his back and stretched his feet out to the oven. The three other men all began talking at once—of the weather—of the record slide—of the fine condition of the Wald See for skating.

Suddenly Fuchs looked at Max, raised his eyebrows and nodded across to Victor, who shook his head.

"Baby doesn't feel well," he said, feeding the brown dog with broken lumps of sugar, "and nobody's to disturb him—I'm nurse."

"That's the first time I've ever known him off colour," said Wistuba. "I've always imagined he had the better part of this world that could not be taken away from him. I think he says his prayers to the dear Lord for having spared him being taken home in seven basketsful to-night. It's a fool's game to risk your all that way and leave the nation desolate."

"Dry up," said Max. "You ought to be wheeled about on the snow in a perambulator."

"Oh, no offence, I hope. Don't get nasty.... How's your wife, Victor?"

"She's not at all well. She hurt her head coming down the slide with Max on Sunday. I told her to stay at home all day."

"I'm sorry. Are you other fellows going back to the town or stopping on here?"

Fuchs and Victor said they were stopping—Max did not answer, but sat motionless while the men paid for their coffee and moved away. Victor came back a moment and put a hand on his shoulder.

"If you're going right back, my dear, I wish you'd look Elsa up and tell her I won't be in till late. And feed with us to-night at Limpold, will you? And take some hot grog when you get in."

"Thanks, old fellow, I'm all right. Going back now."

He rose, stretched himself, buttoned on his heavy coat and lighted another cigarette.

From the door Victor watched him plunging through the heavy snow—head bent—hands thrust in his pockets—he almost appeared to be running through the heavy snow towards the town.

Someone came stamping up the stairs—paused at the door of her sitting-room, and knocked.

"Is that you, Victor?" she called.

"No, it is I... can I come in?"

"Of course. Why, what a Santa Claus! Hang your coat on the landing and shake yourself over the banisters. Had a good time?"

The room was full of light and warmth. Elsa, in a white velvet tea-gown, lay curled up on the sofa—a book of fashions on her lap, a box of creams beside her.

The curtains were not yet drawn before the windows and a blue light shone through, and the white boughs of the trees sprayed across.

A woman's room—full of flowers and photographs and silk pillows—the floor smothered in rugs—an immense tiger-skin under the piano—just the head protruding—sleepily savage.

"It was good enough," said Max. "Victor can't be in till late. He told me to come up and tell you."

He started walking up and down—tore off his gloves and flung them on the table.

"Don't do that, Max," said Elsa, "you get on my nerves. And I've got a headache to-day; I'm feverish and quite flushed.... Don't I look flushed?"

He paused by the window and glanced at her a moment over his shoulder.

"No," he said; "I didn't notice it."

"Oh, you haven't looked at me properly, and I've got a new tea-gown on, too." She pulled her skirts together and patted a little place on the couch.

"Come along and sit by me and tell me why you're being naughty."

But, standing by the window, he suddenly flung his arm across his eyes.

"Oh," he said, "I can't. I'm done—I'm spent—I'm smashed."

Silence in the room. The fashion-book fell to the floor with a quick rustle of leaves. Elsa sat forward, her hands clasped in her lap; a strange light shone in her eyes, a red colour stained her mouth.

Then she spoke very quietly.

"Come over here and explain yourself. I don't know what on earth you are talking about."

"You do know—you know far better than I. You've simply played with Victor in my presence that I may feel worse. You've tormented me—you've led me on—offering me everything and nothing at all. It's been a spider-and-fly business from first to last—and I've never for one moment been ignorant of that—and I've never for one moment been able to withstand it."

He turned round deliberately.

"Do you suppose that when you asked me to pin your flowers into your evening gown—when you let me come into your bedroom when Victor was out while you did your hair—when you pretended to be a baby and let me feed you with grapes—when you have run to me and searched in all my pockets for a cigarette—knowing perfectly well where they were kept—going through every pocket just the same—I knowing too—I keeping up the farce—do you suppose that now you have finally lighted your bonfire you are going to find it a peaceful and pleasant thing—you are going to prevent the whole house from burning?"

She suddenly turned white and drew in her breath sharply.

"Don't talk to me like that. You have no right to talk to me like that. I am another man's wife."

"Hum," he sneered, throwing back his head, "that's rather late in the game, and that's been your trump card all along. You only love Victor on the cat-and-cream principle—you a poor little starved kitten that he's given everything to, that he's carried in his breast, never dreaming that those little pink claws could tear out a man's heart."

She stirred, looking at him with almost fear in her eyes.

"After all"—unsteadily—"this is my room; I'll have to ask you to go."

But he stumbled towards her, knelt down by the couch, burying his head in her lap, clasping his arms round her waist.

"And I *love* you—I love you; the humiliation of it—I adore you. Don't—don't—just a minute let me stay here—just a moment in a whole life—Elsa! Elsa!"

She leant back and pressed her head into the pillows.

Then his muffled voice: "I feel like a savage. I want your whole body. I want to carry you away to a cave and love you until I kill you—you can't understand how a man feels. I kill myself when I see you—I'm sick of my own strength that turns in upon itself, and dies, and rises new born like a Phœnix out of the ashes of that horrible death. Love me just this once, tell me a lie, *say* that you do—you are always lying."

Instead, she pushed him away—frightened.

"Get up," she said; "suppose the servant came in with the tea?"

"Oh, ye gods!" He stumbled to his feet and stood staring down at her.

"You're rotten to the core and so am I. But you're heathenishly beautiful."

The woman went over to the piano—stood there—striking one note—her brows drawn together. Then she shrugged her shoulders and smiled.

"I'll make a confession. Every word you have said is true. I can't help it. I can't help seeking admiration any more than a cat can help going to people to be stroked. It's my nature. I'm born out of my time. And yet, you know, I'm not a *common* woman. I like men to adore me—to flatter me—even to make love to me—but I would never give myself to any man. I would never let a man kiss me... even."

"It's immeasurably worse—you've no legitimate excuse. Why, even a prostitute has a greater sense of generosity!"

"I know," she said, "I know perfectly well—but I can't help the way I'm built.... Are you going?"

He put on his gloves.

"Well," he said, "what's going to happen to us now?"

Again she shrugged her shoulders.

"I haven't the slightest idea. I never have—just let things occur."

"All alone?" cried Victor. "Has Max been here?"

"He only stayed a moment, and wouldn't even have tea. I sent him home to change his clothes.... He was frightfully boring."

"You poor darling, your hair's coming down. I'll fix it, stand still a moment... so you were bored?"

"Um-m—frightfully.... Oh, you've run a hairpin right into your wife's head—you naughty boy!"

She flung her arms round his neck and looked up at him, half laughing, like a beautiful, loving child.

"God! What a woman you are," said the man. "You make me so infernally proud—dearest, that I... I tell you!"

77

A Man and His Dog

Katherine Mansfield

To look at Mr. Potts one would have thought that there at least went someone who had nothing to boast about. He was a little insignificant fellow with a crooked tie, a hat too small for him and a coat too large. The brown canvas portfolio that he carried to and from the Post Office every day was not like a business man's portfolio. It was like a child's school satchel; it did up even with a round-eyed button. One imagined there were crumbs and an apple core inside. And then there was something funny about his boots, wasn't there? Through the laces his coloured socks peeped out. What the dickens had the chap done with the tongues? "Fried 'em," suggested the wit of the Chesney bus. Poor old Potts! "More likely buried 'em in his garden." Under his arm he clasped an umbrella. And in wet weather when he put it up, he disappeared completely. He was not. He was a walking umbrella—no more—the umbrella became his shell.

Mr. Potts lived in a little bungalow on Chesney Flat. The bulge of the water tank to one side gave it a mournful air, like a little bungalow with the toothache. There was no garden. A path had been cut in the paddock turf from the gate to the front door, and two beds, one round, one oblong, had been cut in what was going to be the front lawn. Down that path went Potts every morning at half-past eight and was picked up by the Chesney bus; up that path walked Potts every evening while the great kettle of a bus droned on. In the late evening, when he crept as far as the gate, eager to smoke a pipe—he wasn't allowed to smoke any nearer to the house than that—so humble, so modest was his air, that the big, merrily-shining stars seemed to wink at each other, to laugh, to say, "Look at him! Let's throw something!"

When Potts got out of the tram at the Fire Station to change into the Chesney bus he saw that something was up. The car was there all right, but the driver was off his perch; he was flat on his face half under the engine, and the conductor, his cap off, sat on a step rolling a cigarette and looking dreamy. A little group of business men and a woman clerk or two stood staring at the empty car; there was something mournful, pitiful about the way it leaned to one side and shivered faintly when the driver shook something. It was like someone who'd had an accident and tries to say: "Don't touch me! Don't come near me! Don't hurt me!"

But all this was so familiar—the cars had only been running to Chesney the last few months—that nobody said anything, nobody asked anything. They just waited on the off chance. In fact, two or three decided to walk it as Potts came up. But Potts didn't want to walk unless he had to. He was tired. He'd been up half the night rubbing his wife's chest—she had one of her mysterious pains—and helping the sleepy servant girl heat compresses and hot-water bottles and make tea. The window was blue and the roosters had started crowing before he lay down finally with feet like ice. And all this was familiar, too.

Standing at the edge of the pavement and now and again changing his brown canvas portfolio from one hand to the other Potts began to live over the night before. But it was vague, shadowy. He saw himself moving like a crab, down the passage to the cold kitchen and back again. The two candles quivered on the dark chest of drawers, and as he bent over his wife her big eyes suddenly flashed and she cried:

"I get no sympathy—no sympathy. You only do it because you have to. Don't contradict me. I can see you grudge doing it."

Trying to soothe her only made matters worse. There had been an awful scene ending with her sitting up and saying solemnly with her hand raised: "Never mind, it will not be for long now." But the sound of these words frightened her so terribly that she flung back on the pillow and sobbed, "Robert! Robert!" Robert was the name of the young man to whom she had been engaged years ago, before she met Potts. And Potts was very glad to hear him invoked. He had come to know that meant the crisis was over and she'd begin to quieten down....

By this time Potts had wheeled round; he had walked across the pavement to the paling fence that ran beside. A piece of light grass pushed through the fence and some slender silky daisies. Suddenly he saw a bee alight on one of the daisies and the flower leaned over, swayed, shook, while the little bee clung and rocked. And as it flew away the petals fluttered as if joyfully.... Just for an instant Potts dropped into the world where this happened. He brought from it the timid smile with which he walked back to the car. But now everybody had disappeared except one young girl who stood beside the empty car reading.

At the tail of the procession came Potts in a cassock so much too large for him that it looked like a night-shirt and you felt that he ought to be carrying not a hymn and a prayer book but a candle. His voice was a very light plaintive tenor. It surprised everybody. It seemed to surprise him, too. But it was so plaintive that when he cried "for the wings, for the wings of a dove" the ladies in the congregation wanted to club together and buy him a pair.

Lino's nose quivered so pitifully, there was such a wistful, timid look in his eyes, that Potts' heart was wrung. But of course he would not show it. "Well," he said sternly, "I suppose you'd better come home." And he got up off the bench. Lino got up, too, but stood still, holding up a paw.

"But there's one thing," said Potts, turning and facing him squarely, "that we'd better be clear about before you do come. And it's this." He pointed his finger at Lino who started as though he expected to be shot. But he kept his bewildered wistful eyes upon his master. "Stop this pretence of being a fighting dog," said Potts more sternly than ever. "You're not a fighting dog. You're a watch dog. That's what you are. Very well. Stick to it. But it's this infernal boasting I can't stand. It's that that gets me."

In the moment's pause that followed while Lino and his master looked at each other it was curious how strong a resemblance was between them. Then Potts turned again and made for home.

And timidly, as though falling over his own paws, Lino followed after the humble little figure of his master....

78

Honeymoon

Katherine Mansfield

And when they came out of the lace shop there was their own driver and the cab they called their own cab waiting for them under a plane tree. What luck! Wasn't it luck? Fanny pressed her husband's arm. These things seemed always to be happening to them ever since they—came abroad. Didn't he think so too? But George stood on the pavement edge, lifted his stick, and gave a loud "Hi!" Fanny sometimes felt a little uncomfortable about the way George summoned cabs, but the drivers didn't seem to mind, so it must have been all right. Fat, good-natured, and smiling, they stuffed away the little newspaper they were reading, whipped the cotton cover off the horse, and were ready to obey.

"I say," George said as he helped Fanny in, "suppose we go and have tea at the place where the lobsters grow. Would you like to?"

"Most awfully," said Fanny, fervently, as she leaned back, wondering why the way George put things made them sound so very nice.

"R-right, *bien.*" He was beside her. "*Allay,*" he cried gaily, and off they went.

Off they went, spanking along lightly, under the green and gold shade of the plane trees, through the small streets that smelled of lemons and fresh coffee, past the fountain square where women, with water-pots lifted, stopped talking to gaze after them, round the corner past the café, with its pink and white umbrellas, green tables, and blue siphons, and so to the sea front. There a wind, light, warm, came flowing over the boundless sea. It touched George, and Fanny it seemed to linger over while they gazed at the dazzling water. And George said, "Jolly, isn't it?" And Fanny, looking dreamy, said, as she said at least twenty times a day since they—came abroad: "Isn't it extraordinary to think that here we are quite alone, away from everybody, with nobody to tell us to go home, or to—to order us about except ourselves?"

George had long since given up answering "Extraordinary!" As a rule he merely kissed her. But now he caught hold of her hand, stuffed it into his pocket, pressed her fingers, and said, "I used to keep a white mouse in my pocket when I was a kid."

"Did you?" said Fanny, who was intensely interested in everything George had ever done. "Were you very fond of white mice?"

"Fairly," said George, without conviction. He was looking at something, bobbing out there beyond the bathing steps. Suddenly he almost jumped in his seat. "Fanny!" he cried. "There's a chap out there bathing. Do you see? I'd no idea people had begun. I've been missing it all these days." George glared at the reddened face, the reddened arm, as though he could not look away. "At any rate," he muttered, "wild horses won't keep me from going in to-morrow."

Fanny's heart sank. She had heard for years of the frightful dangers of the Mediterranean. It was an absolute death-trap. Beautiful, treacherous Mediterranean. There it lay curled before them, its white, silky paws touching the stones and gone again.... But she'd made up her mind long before she was married that never would she be the kind of woman who interfered with her husband's pleasures, so all she said was, airily, "I suppose one has to be very up in the currents, doesn't one?"

"Oh, I don't know," said George. "People talk an awful lot of rot about the danger."

But now they were passing a high wall on the land side, covered with flowering heliotrope, and Fanny's little nose lifted. "Oh, George," she breathed. "The smell! The most divine...."

"Topping villa," said George. "Look, you can see it through the palms."

"Isn't it rather large?" said Fanny, who somehow could not look at any villa except as a possible habitation for herself and George.

"Well, you'd need a crowd of people if you stayed there long," replied George. "Deadly, otherwise. I say, it is ripping. I wonder who it belongs to." And he prodded the driver in the back.

The lazy, smiling driver, who had no idea, replied, as he always did on these occasions, that it was the property of a wealthy Spanish family.

"Masses of Spaniards on this coast," commented George, leaning back again, and they were silent until, as they rounded a bend, the big, bone-white hotel-restaurant came into view. Before it there was a small terrace built up against the sea, planted with umbrella palms, set out with tables, and at their approach, from the terrace, from the hotel, waiters came running to receive, to welcome, Fanny and George, to cut them off from any possible kind of escape.

"Outside?"

Oh, but of course they would sit outside. The sleek manager, who was marvellously like a fish in a frock coat, skimmed forward.

"Dis way, sir. Dis way, sir. I have a very nice little table," he gasped. "Just the little table for you, sir, over in de corner. Dis way."

So George, looking most dreadfully bored, and Fanny, trying to look as though she'd spent years of life threading her way through strangers, followed after.

"Here you are, sir. Here you will be very nice," coaxed the manager, taking the vase off the table, and putting it down again as if it were a fresh little bouquet out of the air. But George refused to sit down immediately. He saw through these fellows; he wasn't going to be done. These chaps were always out to rush you. So he put his hands in his pockets, and said to Fanny, very calmly, "This all right for you? Anywhere else you'd prefer? How about over there?" And he nodded to a table right over the other side.

What it was to be a man of the world! Fanny admired him deeply, but all she wanted to do was to sit down and look like everybody else.

"I—I like this," said she.

"Right," said George, hastily, and he sat down almost before Fanny, and said quickly, "Tea for two and chocolate éclairs."

"Very good, sir," said the manager, and his mouth opened and shut as though he was ready for another dive under the water. "You will not 'ave toasts to start with? We 'ave very nice toasts, sir."

"No," said George, shortly. "You don't want toast, do you, Fanny?"

"Oh, no, thank you, George," said Fanny, praying the manager would go.

"Or perhaps de lady might like to look at de live lobsters in de tank while de tea is coming?" And he grimaced and smirked and flicked his serviette like a fin.

George's face grew stony. He said "No" again, and Fanny bent over the table, unbuttoning her gloves. When she looked up the man was gone. George took off his hat, tossed it on to a chair, and pressed back his hair.

"Thank God," said he, "that's chap's gone. These foreign fellows bore me stiff. The only way to get rid of them is simply to shut up as you saw I did. Thank Heaven!" sighed George again, with so much emotion that if it hadn't been ridiculous Fanny might have imagined that he had been as frightened of the manager as she. As it was she felt a rush of love for George. His hands were on the table, brown, large hands that she knew so well. She longed to take one of them and squeeze it hard. But, to her astonishment, George did just that thing, leaning across the table, put his hand over hers, and said, without looking at her, "Fanny, darling Fanny."

"Oh, George!" It was in that heavenly moment that Fanny heard a *twing-twing-tootle-tootle*, and a light strumming. There's going to be music, she thought, but the music didn't matter just then. Nothing mattered except love. Faintly smiling she gazed into that faintly smiling face, and the feeling was so blissful that she felt inclined to say to George, "Let us stay here—where we are—at this little table. It's perfect, and the sea is perfect. Let us stay." But instead her eyes grew serious.

"Darling," said Fanny. "I want to ask you something fearfully important. Promise me you'll answer. Promise."

"I promise," said George, too solemn to be quite as serious as she.

"It's this." Fanny paused a moment, looked down, looked up again. "Do you feel," she said, softly, "that you really know me now? But really, really know *me*?"

It was too much for George. Know his Fanny? He gave a broad, childish grin. "I should jolly well think I do," he said, emphatically. "Why, what's up?"

Fanny felt he hadn't quite understood. She went on quickly: "What I mean is this. So often people, even when they love each other, don't seem to—to—it's so hard to say—know each other perfectly. They don't seem to want to. And I think that's awful. They misunderstand each other about the most important things of all." Fanny looked horrified. "George, we couldn't do that, could we? We never could."

"Couldn't be done," laughed George, and he was just going to tell her how much he liked her little nose, when the waiter arrived with the tea and the band struck up. It was a flute, a guitar, and a violin, and it played so gaily that Fanny felt if she wasn't careful even the cups and saucers might grow little wings and fly away. George absorbed three chocolate éclairs, Fanny two. The funny-tasting tea—"Lobster in the kettle," shouted George above the music—was nice all the same, and when the tray was pushed aside and George was smoking, Fanny felt bold enough to look at the other people. But it was the band grouped under one of the dark trees that fascinated her most. The fat man stroking the guitar was like a picture. The dark man playing the flute kept raising his eyebrows as though he was astonished at the sounds that came from it. The fiddler was in shadow.

The music stopped as suddenly as it had begun. It was then she noticed a tall old man with white hair standing beside the musicians. Strange she hadn't noticed him before. He wore a very high, glazed collar, a coat green at the seams, and shamefully shabby button boots. Was he another manager? He did not look like a manager, and yet he stood there gazing over the table as though thinking of something different and far away from all this. Who could he be?

Presently, as Fanny watched him, he touched the points of his collar with his fingers, coughed slightly, and half-turned to the band. It began to play again. Something boisterous, reckless, full of fire, full of passion, was tossed into the air, was tossed to that quiet figure, which clasped its hands, and still with that far-away look, began to sing.

"Good Lord!" said George. It seemed that everybody was equally astonished. Even the little children eating ices stared, with their spoons in the air.... Nothing was heard except a thin, faint voice, the memory of a voice, singing something in Spanish. It wavered, beat on, touched the high notes, fell again, seemed to implore, to entreat, to beg for something, and then the tune changed, and it was resigned, it bowed down, it knew it was denied.

Almost before the end a little child gave a squeak of laughter, but everybody was smiling—except Fanny and George. Is life like this too? thought Fanny. There are people like this. There is suffering. And she looked at that gorgeous sea, lapping the land as though it loved it, and the sky, bright with the brightness before evening. Had she and George the right to be so happy? Wasn't it cruel? There must be something else in life which made all these things possible. What was it? She turned to George.

But George had been feeling differently from Fanny. The poor old boy's voice was funny in a way, but, God, how it made you realize what a terrific thing it was to be at the beginning of everything, as they were, he and Fanny! George, too, gazed at the bright, breathing water, and his lips opened as if he could drink it. How fine it was! There was nothing like the sea for making a chap feel fit. And there sat Fanny, his Fanny, leaning forward, breathing so gently.

"Fanny!" George called to her.

As she turned to him something in her soft, wondering look made George feel that for two pins he would jump over the table and carry her off.

"I say," said George, rapidly, "let's go, shall we? Let's go back to the hotel. Come. Do, Fanny darling. Let's go now."

The band began to play. "Oh, God!" almost groaned George. "Let's go before the old codger begins squawking again."

And a moment later they were gone.

79

A Cup of Tea

Katherine Mansfield

Rosemary Fell was not exactly beautiful. No, you couldn't have called her beautiful. Pretty? Well, if you took her to pieces.... But why be so cruel as to take anyone to pieces? She was young, brilliant, extremely modern, exquisitely well dressed, amazingly well read in the newest of the new books, and her parties were the most delicious mixture of the really important people and...artists—quaint creatures, discoveries of hers, some of them too terrifying for words, but others quite presentable and amusing.

Rosemary had been married two years. She had a duck of a boy. No, not Peter—Michael. And her husband absolutely adored her. They were rich, really rich, not just comfortably well off, which is odious and stuffy and sounds like one's grandparents. But if Rosemary wanted to shop she would go to Paris as you and I would go to Bond Street. If she wanted to buy flowers, the car pulled up at that perfect shop in Regent Street, and Rosemary inside the shop just gazed in her dazzled, rather exotic way, and said: "I want those and those and those. Give me four bunches of those. And that jar of roses. Yes, I'll have all the roses in the jar. No, no lilac. I hate lilac. It's got no shape." The attendant bowed and put the lilac out of sight, as though this was only too true; lilac was dreadfully shapeless. "Give me those stumpy little tulips. Those red and white ones." And she was followed to the car by a thin shopgirl staggering under an immense white paper armful that looked like a baby in long clothes....

One winter afternoon she had been buying something in a little antique shop in Curzon Street. It was a shop she liked. For one thing, one usually had it to oneself. And then the man who kept it was ridiculously fond of serving her. He beamed whenever she came in. He clasped his hands; he was so gratified he could scarcely speak. Flattery, of course. All the same, there was something....

"You see, madam," he would explain in his low respectful tones, "I love my things. I would rather not part with them than sell them to someone who does not appreciate them, who has not that fine feeling which is so rare...." And, breathing deeply he unrolled a tiny square of blue velvet and pressed it on the glass counter with his pale finger-tips.

Today it was a little box. He had been keeping it for her. He had shown it to nobody as yet. An exquisite little enamel box with a glaze so fine it looked as though it had been baked in cream. On the lid a minute creature stood under a flowery tree, and a more minute creature still had her arms around his neck. Her hat, really no bigger than a geranium petal, hung from a branch; it had green ribbons. And there was a pink cloud like a watchful cherub floating above their heads. Rosemary took her hands out of her long gloves. She always took off her gloves to examine such things. Yes, she liked it very much. She loved it; it was a great duck. She must have it. And, turning the creamy box, opening and shutting it, she couldn't help noticing how charming her hands were against the blue velvet. The shopman, in some dim cavern of his mind, may have dared to think so too. For he took a pencil, leant over the counter, and his pale bloodless fingers crept timidly towards those rosy, flashing ones, as he murmured gently: "If I may venture to point out to madam, the flowers on the little lady's bodice."

"Charming!" Rosemary admired the flowers. But what was the price? For a moment the shopman did not seem to hear. Then a murmur reached her. "Twenty-eight guineas, madame."

"Twenty-eight guineas." Rosemary gave no sign. She laid the little box down; she buttoned her gloves again. Twenty-eight guineas. Even if one is rich.... She looked vague. She stared at a plump tea-kettle like a plump hen above the shopman's head, and her voice was dreamy as she answered: "Well, keep it for me—will you? I'll...."

But the shopman had already bowed as though keeping it for her was all any human being could ask. He would be willing, of course, to keep it for her for ever.

The discreet door shut with a click. She was outside on the step, gazing at the winter afternoon. Rain was falling, and with the rain it seemed the dark came too, spinning down like ashes. There was a cold bitter taste in the air, and the new-lighted lamps looked sad. Sad were the lights in the houses opposite. Dimly they burned as if regretting something. And people hurried by, hidden under their hateful umbrellas. Rosemary felt a strange pang. She pressed her muff to her breast; she wished she had the little box, too, to cling to. Of course, the car was there. She'd only to cross the pavement. But still she waited. There are moments, horrible moments in life, when one emerges from shelter and looks out, and it's awful. One oughtn't to give way to them. One ought to go home and have an extra-special tea. But at the very instant of thinking that, a young girl, thin, dark, shadowy—where had she come from?—was standing at Rosemary's elbow and a voice like a sigh, almost like a sob, breathed: "Madame, may I speak to you a moment?"

"Speak to me?" Rosemary turned. She saw a little battered creature with enormous eyes, someone quite young, no older than herself, who clutched at her coat-collar with reddened hands, and shivered as though she had just come out of the water.

"M-madame," stammered the voice. "Would you let me have the price of a cup of tea?"

"A cup of tea?" There was something simple, sincere in that voice; it wasn't in the least the voice of a beggar. "Then have you no money at all?" asked Rosemary.

"None, madam," came the answer.

"How extraordinary!" Rosemary peered through the dusk, and the girl gazed back at her. How more than extraordinary! And suddenly it seemed to Rosemary such an adventure. It was like something out of a novel by Dostoevsky, this meeting in the dusk. Supposing she took the girl home? Supposing she did do one of those things she was always reading about or seeing on the stage, what would happen? It would be thrilling. And she heard herself saying afterwards to the amazement of her friends: "I simply took her home with me," as she stepped forward and said to that dim person beside her: "Come home to tea with me."

The girl drew back startled. She even stopped shivering for a moment. Rosemary put out a hand and touched her arm. "I mean it," she said, smiling. And she felt how simple and kind her smile was. "Why won't you? Do. Come home with me now in my car and have tea."

"You—you don't mean it, madam," said the girl, and there was pain in her voice.

"But I do," cried Rosemary. "I want you to. To please me. Come along."

The girl put her fingers to her lips and her eyes devoured Rosemary. "You're—you're not taking me to the police station?" she stammered.

"The police station!" Rosemary laughed out. "Why should I be so cruel? No, I only want to make you warm and to hear—anything you care to tell me."

Hungry people are easily led. The footman held the door of the car open, and a moment later they were skimming through the dusk.

"There!" said Rosemary. She had a feeling of triumph as she slipped her hand through the velvet strap. She could have said, "Now I've got you," as she gazed at the little captive she had netted. But of course she meant it kindly. Oh, more than kindly. She was going to prove to this girl that—wonderful things did happen in life, that—fairy godmothers were real, that—rich people had hearts, and that women *were* sisters. She turned impulsively, saying: "Don't be frightened. After all, why shouldn't you come back with me? We're both women. If I'm the more fortunate, you ought to expect...."

But happily at that moment, for she didn't know how the sentence was going to end, the car stopped. The bell was rung, the door opened, and with a charming, protecting, almost embracing movement, Rosemary drew the other into the hall. Warmth, softness, light, a sweet scent, all those things so familiar to her she never even thought about them, she watched that other receive. It was fascinating. She was like the little rich girl in her nursery with all the cupboards to open, all the boxes to unpack.

"Come, come upstairs," said Rosemary, longing to begin to be generous. "Come up to my room." And, besides, she wanted to spare this poor little thing from being stared at by the servants; she decided as they mounted the stairs she would not even ring for Jeanne, but take off her things by herself. The great thing was to be natural!

And "There!" cried Rosemary again, as they reached her beautiful big bedroom with the curtains drawn, the fire leaping on her wonderful lacquer furniture, her gold cushions and the primrose and blue rugs.

The girl stood just inside the door; she seemed dazed. But Rosemary didn't mind that.

"Come and sit down," she cried, dragging her big chair up to the fire, "in this comfy chair. Come and get warm. You look so dreadfully cold."

"I daren't, madam," said the girl, and she edged backwards.

"Oh, please,"—Rosemary ran forward—"you mustn't be frightened, you mustn't, really. Sit down, and when I've taken off my things we shall go into the next room and have tea and be cosy. Why are you afraid?" And gently she half pushed the thin figure into its deep cradle.

But there was no answer. The girl stayed just as she had been put, with her hands by her sides and her mouth slightly open. To be quite sincere, she looked rather stupid. But Rosemary wouldn't acknowledge it. She leant over her, saying: "Won't you take off your hat? Your pretty hair is all wet. And one is so much more comfortable without a hat, isn't one?"

There was a whisper that sounded like "Very good, madam," and the crushed hat was taken off.

"Let me help you off with your coat, too," said Rosemary.

The girl stood up. But she held on to the chair with one hand and let Rosemary pull. It was quite an effort. The other scarcely helped her at all. She seemed to stagger like a child, and the thought came and went through Rosemary's mind, that if people wanted helping they must respond a little, just a little, otherwise it became very difficult indeed. And what was she to do with the coat now? She left it on the floor, and the hat too. She was just going to take a cigarette off the mantelpiece when the girl said quickly, but so lightly and strangely: "I'm very sorry, madam, but I'm going to faint. I shall go off, madam, if I don't have something."

"Good heavens, how thoughtless I am!" Rosemary rushed to the bell.

"Tea! Tea at once! And some brandy immediately!"

The maid was gone again, but the girl almost cried out. "No, I don't want no brandy. I never drink brandy. It's a cup of tea I want, madam." And she burst into tears.

It was a terrible and fascinating moment. Rosemary knelt beside her chair.

"Don't cry, poor little thing," she said. "Don't cry." And she gave the other her lace handkerchief. She really was touched beyond words. She put her arm round those thin, bird-like shoulders.

Now at last the other forgot to be shy, forgot everything except that they were both women, and gasped out: "I can't go on no longer like this. I can't bear it. I shall do away with myself. I can't bear no more."

"You shan't have to. I'll look after you. Don't cry any more. Don't you see what a good thing it was that you met me? We'll have tea and you'll tell me everything. And I shall arrange something. I promise. *Do* stop crying. It's so exhausting. Please!"

The other did stop just in time for Rosemary to get up before the tea came. She had the table placed between them. She plied the poor little creature with everything, all the sandwiches, all the bread and butter, and every time her cup was empty she filled it with tea, cream and sugar. People always said sugar was so nourishing. As for herself she didn't eat; she smoked and looked away tactfully so that the other should not be shy.

And really the effect of that slight meal was marvellous. When the tea-table was carried away a new being, a light, frail creature with tangled hair, dark lips, deep, lighted eyes, lay back in the big chair in a kind of sweet langour, looking at the blaze. Rosemary lit a fresh cigarette; it was time to begin.

"And when did you have your last meal?" she asked softly.

But at that moment the door-handle turned.

"Rosemary, may I come in?" It was Philip.

"Of course."

He came in. "Oh, I'm so sorry," he said, and stopped and stared.

"It's quite all right," said Rosemary smiling. "This is my friend, Miss——"

"Smith, madam," said the languid figure, who was strangely still and unafraid.

"Smith," said Rosemary. "We are going to have a little talk."

"Oh, yes," said Philip. "Quite," and his eye caught sight of the coat and hat on the floor. He came over to the fire and turned his back to it. "It's a beastly afternoon," he said curiously, still looking at that listless figure, looking at its hands and boots, and then at Rosemary again.

"Yes, isn't it?" said Rosemary enthusiastically. "Vile."

Philip smiled his charming smile. "As a matter of fact," said he, "I wanted you to come into the library for a moment. Would you? Will Miss Smith excuse us?"

The big eyes were raised to him, but Rosemary answered for her. "Of course she will." And they went out of the room together.

"I say," said Philip, when they were alone. "Explain. Who is she? What does it all mean?"

Rosemary, laughing, leaned against the door and said: "I picked her up in Curzon Street. Really. She's a real pick-up. She asked me for the price of a cup of tea, and I brought her home with me."

"But what on earth are you going to do with her?" cried Philip.

"Be nice to her," said Rosemary quickly. "Be frightfully nice to her. Look after her. I don't know how. We haven't talked yet. But show her—treat her—make her feel——"

"My darling girl," said Philip, "you're quite mad, you know. It simply can't be done."

"I knew you'd say that," retorted Rosemary. "Why not? I want to. Isn't that a reason? And besides, one's always reading about these things. I decided——"

"But," said Philip slowly, and he cut the end of a cigar, "she's so astonishingly pretty."

"Pretty?" Rosemary was so surprised that she blushed. "Do you think so? I—I hadn't thought about it."

"Good Lord!" Philip struck a match. "She's absolutely lovely. Look again, my child. I was bowled over when I came into your room just now. However...I think you're making a ghastly mistake. Sorry, darling, if I'm crude and all that. But let me know if Miss Smith is going to dine with us in time for me to look up *The Milliner's Gazette*."

"You absurd creature!" said Rosemary, and she went out of the library, but not back to her bedroom. She went to her writing-room and sat down at her desk. Pretty! Absolutely lovely! Bowled over! Her heart beat like a heavy bell. Pretty! Lovely! She drew her cheque book towards her. But no, cheques would be no use, of course. She opened a drawer and took out five pound notes, looked at them, put two back, and holding the three squeezed in her hand, she went back to her bedroom.

Half an hour later Philip was still in the library, when Rosemary came in.

"I only wanted to tell you," said she, and she leaned against the door again and looked at him with her dazzled exotic gaze, "Miss Smith won't dine with us tonight."

Philip put down the paper. "Oh, what's happened? Previous engagement?"

Rosemary came over and sat down on his knee. "She insisted on going," said she, "so I gave the poor little thing a present of money. I couldn't keep her against her will, could I?" she added softly.

Rosemary had just done her hair, darkened her eyes a little, and put on her pearls. She put up her hands and touched Philip's cheeks.

"Do you like me?" said she, and her tone, sweet, husky, troubled him.

"I like you awfully," he said, and he held her tighter. "Kiss me."

There was a pause.

Then Rosemary said dreamily, "I saw a fascinating little box today. It cost twenty-eight guineas. May I have it?"

Philip jumped her on his knee. "You may, little wasteful one," said he.

But that was not really what Rosemary wanted to say.

"Philip," she whispered, and she pressed his head against her bosom, "am I *pretty*?"

80

Taking the Veil

Katherine Mansfield

It seemed impossible that anyone should be unhappy on such a beautiful morning. Nobody was, decided Edna, except herself. The windows were flung wide in the houses. From within there came the sound of pianos, little hands chased after each other and ran away from each other, practising scales. The trees fluttered in the sunny gardens, all bright with spring flowers. Street boys whistled, a little dog barked; people passed by, walking so lightly, so swiftly, they looked as though they wanted to break into a run. Now she actually saw in the distance a parasol, peach-coloured, the first parasol of the year.

Perhaps even Edna did not look quite as unhappy as she felt. It is not easy to look tragic at eighteen, when you are extremely pretty, with the cheeks and lips and shining eyes of perfect health. Above all, when you are wearing a French blue frock and your new spring hat trimmed with cornflowers. True, she carried under her arm a book bound in horrid black leather. Perhaps the book provided a gloomy note, but only by accident; it was the ordinary Library binding. For Edna had made going to the Library an excuse for getting out of the house to think, to realise what had happened, to decide somehow what was to be done now.

An awful thing had happened. Quite suddenly, at the theatre last night, when she and Jimmy were seated side by side in the dress-circle, without a moment's warning—in fact, she had just finished a chocolate almond and passed the box to him again—she had fallen in love with an actor. But—fallen—in—love....

The feeling was unlike anything she had ever imagined before. It wasn't in the least pleasant. It was hardly thrilling. Unless you can call the most dreadful sensation of hopeless misery, despair, agony and wretchedness, thrilling. Combined with the certainty that if that actor met her on the pavement after, while Jimmy was fetching their cab, she would follow him to the ends of the earth, at a nod, at a sign, without giving another thought to Jimmy or her father and mother or her happy home and countless friends again....

The play had begun fairly cheerfully. That was at the chocolate almond stage. Then the hero had gone blind. Terrible moment! Edna had cried so much she had to borrow Jimmy's folded, smooth-feeling handkerchief as well. Not that crying mattered. Whole rows were in tears. Even the men blew their noses with a loud trumpeting noise and tried to peer at the program instead of looking at the stage. Jimmy, most mercifully dry-eyed—for what would she have done without his handkerchief?—squeezed her free hand, and whispered "Cheer up, darling girl!" And it was then she had taken a last chocolate almond to please him and passed the box again. Then, there had been that ghastly scene with the hero alone on the stage in a deserted room at twilight, with a band playing outside and the sound of cheering coming from the street. He had tried—ah! how painfully, how pitifully—to grope his way to the window. He had succeeded at last. There he stood holding the curtain while one beam of light, just one beam, shone full on his raised sightless face, and the band faded away into the distance....

It was—really, it was absolutely—oh, the most—it was simply—in fact, from that moment Edna knew that life could never be the same. She drew her hand away from Jimmy's, leaned back, and shut the chocolate box for ever. This at last was love!

Edna and Jimmy were engaged. She had had her hair up for a year and a half; they had been publicly engaged for a year. But they had known they were going to marry each other ever since they walked in the Botanical Gardens with their nurses, and sat on the grass with a wine biscuit and a piece of barley-sugar each for their tea. It was so much an accepted thing that Edna had worn a wonderfully good imitation of an engagement-ring out of a cracker all the time she was at school. And up till now they had been devoted to each other.

But now it was over. It was so completely over that Edna found it difficult to believe that Jimmy did not realize it too. She smiled wisely, sadly, as she turned into the gardens of the Convent of the Sacred Heart and mounted the path that led through them to Hill Street. How much better to know it now than to wait until after they were married! Now it was possible that Jimmy would get over it. No, it was no use deceiving herself; he would never get over it! His life was wrecked, was ruined; that was inevitable. But he was young.... Time, people said, Time might make a little, just a little difference. In forty years when he was an old man, he might be able to think of her calmly—perhaps. But she,—what did the future hold for her?

Edna had reached the top of the path. There under a new-leafed tree, hung with little bunches of white flowers, she sat down on a green bench and looked over the Convent flower-beds. In the one nearest to her there grew tender stocks, with a border of blue, shell-like pansies, with at one corner a clump of creamy freezias, their light spears of green criss-crossed over the flowers. The Convent pigeons were tumbling high in the air, and she could hear the voice of Sister Agnes who was giving a singing lesson. *Ah-me*, sounded the deep tones of the nun, and *Ah-me*, they were echoed....

If she did not marry Jimmy, of course she would marry nobody. The man she was in love with, the famous actor—Edna had far too much common-sense not to realize that would never be. It was very odd. She didn't even want it to be. Her love was too intense for that. It had to be endured, silently; it had to torment her. It was, she supposed, simply that kind of love.

"But, Edna!" cried Jimmy. "Can you never change? Can I never hope again?"

Oh, what sorrow to have to say it, but it must be said. "No, Jimmy, I will never change."

Edna bowed her head; and a little flower fell on her lap, and the voice of Sister Agnes cried suddenly *Ah-no*, and the echo came, *Ah-no*....

At that moment the future was revealed. Edna saw it all. She was astonished; it took her breath away at first. But, after all, what could be more natural? She would go into a convent.... Her father and mother do everything to dissuade her, in vain. As for Jimmy, his state of mind hardly bears thinking about. Why can't they understand? How can they add to her suffering like this? The world is cruel, terribly cruel! After a last scene when she gives away her jewellery and so on to her best friends—she so calm, they so broken-hearted—into a convent she goes. No, one moment. The very evening of her going is the actor's last evening at Port Willin. He receives by a strange messenger a box. It is full of white flowers. But there is no name, no card. Nothing? Yes, under the roses, wrapped in a white handkerchief, Edna's last photograph with, written underneath,

The world forgetting, by the world forgot

Edna sat very still under the trees; she clasped the black book in her fingers as though it were her missal. She takes the name of Sister Angela. Snip! Snip! All her lovely hair is cut off. Will she be allowed to send one curl to Jimmy? It is contrived somehow. And in a blue gown with a white head-band Sister Angela goes from the convent to the chapel, from the chapel to the convent with something unearthly in her look, in her sorrowful eyes, and in the gentle smile with which they greet the little children who run to her. A saint! She hears it whispered as she paces the chill, wax-smelling corridors. A saint! And visitors to the chapel are told of the nun whose voice is heard above the other voices, of her youth, her beauty, of her tragic, tragic love. "There is a man in this town whose life is ruined...."

A big bee, a golden furry fellow, crept into a freezia, and the delicate flower leaned over, swung, shook; and when the bee flew away it fluttered still as though it were laughing. Happy, careless flower!

Sister Angela looked at it and said, "Now it is winter." One night, lying in her icy cell she hears a cry. Some stray animal is out there in the garden, a kitten or a lamb or—well, whatever little animal might be there. Up rises the sleepless nun. All in white, shivering but fearless, she goes and brings it in. But next morning, when the bell rings for matins, she is found tossing in high fever...in delirium...and she never recovers. In three days all is over. The service has been said in the chapel, and she is buried in the corner of the cemetery reserved for the nuns, where there are plain little crosses of wood. Rest in Peace, Sister Angela....

Now it is evening. Two old people leaning on each other come slowly to the grave and kneel down sobbing, "Our daughter! Our only daughter!" Now there comes another. He is all in black; he comes slowly. But when he is there and lifts his black hat, Edna sees to her horror his hair is snow-white. Jimmy! Too late, too late! The tears are running down his face; he is crying *now*. Too late, too late! The wind shakes the leafless trees in the churchyard. He gives one awful bitter cry.

Edna's black book fell with a thud to the garden path. She jumped up, her heart beating. My darling! No, it's not too late. It's all been a mistake, a terrible dream. Oh, that white hair! How could she have done it? She has not done it. Oh, heavens! Oh, what happiness! She is free, young, and nobody knows her secret. Everything is still possible for her and Jimmy. The house they have planned may still be built, the little solemn boy with his hands behind his back watching them plant the standard roses may still be born. His baby sister.... But when Edna got as far as his baby sister, she stretched out her arms as though the little love came flying through the air to her, and gazing at the garden, at the white sprays on the tree, at those darling pigeons blue against the blue, and the Convent with its narrow windows, she realized that now at last for the first time in her life—she had never imagined any feeling like it before—she knew what it was to be in love, but—in—love!

81

The Fly

Katherine Mansfield

"Y'are very snug in here," piped old Mr. Woodifield, and he peered out of the great, green leather armchair by his friend the boss's desk as a baby peers out of its pram. His talk was over; it was time for him to be off. But he did not want to go. Since he had retired, since his…stroke, the wife and the girls kept him boxed up in the house every day of the week except Tuesday. On Tuesday he was dressed up and brushed and allowed to cut back to the City for the day. Though what he did there the wife and girls couldn't imagine. Made a nuisance of himself to his friends, they supposed.... Well, perhaps so. All the same, we cling to our last pleasures as the tree clings to its last leaves. So there sat old Woodifield, smoking a cigar and staring almost greedily at the boss, who rolled in his office chair, stout, rosy, five years older than he, and still going strong, still at the helm. It did one good to see him.

Wistfully, admiringly, the old voice added, "It's snug in here, upon my word!"

"Yes, it's comfortable enough," agreed the boss, and he flipped the *Financial Times* with a paper-knife. As a matter of fact he was proud of his room; he liked to have it admired, especially by old Woodifield. It gave him a feeling of deep, solid satisfaction to be planted there in the midst of it in full view of that frail old figure in the muffler.

"I've had it done up lately," he explained, as he had explained for the past—how many?—weeks. "New carpet," and he pointed to the bright red carpet with a pattern of large white rings. "New furniture," and he nodded towards the massive bookcase and the table with legs like twisted treacle. "Electric heating!" He waved almost exultantly towards the five transparent, pearly sausages glowing so softly in the tilted copper pan.

But he did not draw old Woodifield's attention to the photograph over the table of a grave-looking boy in uniform standing in one of those spectral photographers' parks with photographers' storm-clouds behind him. It was not new. It had been there for over six years.

"There was something I wanted to tell you," said old Woodifield, and his eyes grew dim remembering. "Now what was it? I had it in my mind when I started out this morning." His hands began to tremble, and patches of red showed above his beard.

Poor old chap, he's on his last pins, thought the boss. And, feeling kindly, he winked at the old man, and said jokingly, "I tell you what. I've got a little drop of something here that'll do you good before you go out into the cold again. It's beautiful stuff. It wouldn't hurt a child." He took a key off his watch-chain, unlocked a cupboard below his desk, and drew forth a dark, squat bottle. "That's the medicine," said he. "And the man from whom I got it told me on the strict Q.T. it came from the cellars at Windsor Cassel."

Old Woodifield's mouth fell open at the sight. He couldn't have looked more surprised if the boss had produced a rabbit.

"It's whisky, ain't it?" he piped, feebly.

The boss turned the bottle and lovingly showed him the label. Whisky it was.

"D'you know," said he, peering up at the boss wonderingly, "they won't let me touch it at home." And he looked as though he was going to cry.

"Ah, that's where we know a bit more than the ladies," cried the boss, swooping across for two tumblers that stood on the table with the water-bottle, and pouring a generous finger into each. "Drink it down. It'll do you good. And don't put any water with it. It's sacrilege to tamper with stuff like this. Ah!" He tossed off his, pulled out his handkerchief, hastily wiped his moustaches, and cocked an eye at old Woodifield, who was rolling his in his chaps.

The old man swallowed, was silent a moment, and then said faintly, "It's nutty!"

But it warmed him; it crept into his chill old brain—he remembered.

"That was it," he said, heaving himself out of his chair. "I thought you'd like to know. The girls were in Belgium last week having a look at poor Reggie's grave, and they happened to come across your boy's. They're quite near each other, it seems."

Old Woodifield paused, but the boss made no reply. Only a quiver in his eyelids showed that he heard.

"The girls were delighted with the way the place is kept," piped the old voice. "Beautifully looked after. Couldn't be better if they were at home. You've not been across, have yer?"

"No, no!" For various reasons the boss had not been across.

"There's miles of it," quavered old Woodifield, "and it's all as neat as a garden. Flowers growing on all the graves. Nice broad paths." It was plain from his voice how much he liked a nice broad path.

The pause came again. Then the old man brightened wonderfully. "D'you know what the hotel made the girls pay for a pot of jam?" he piped. "Ten francs! Robbery, I call it. It was a little pot, so Gertrude says, no bigger than a half-crown. And she hadn't taken more than a spoonful when they charged her ten francs. Gertrude brought the pot away with her to teach 'em a lesson. Quite right, too; it's trading on our feelings. They think because we're over there having a look around we're ready to pay anything. That's what it is." And he turned towards the door.

"Quite right, quite right!" cried the boss, though what was quite right he hadn't the least idea. He came round by his desk, followed the shuffling footsteps to the door, and saw the old fellow out. Woodifield was gone.

For a long moment the boss stayed, staring at nothing, while the grey-haired office messenger, watching him, dodged in and out of his cubby-hole like a dog that expects to be taken for a run. Then: "I'll see nobody for half an hour, Macey," said the boss. "Understand? Nobody at all."

"Very good, sir."

The door shut, the firm heavy steps recrossed the bright carpet, the fat body plumped down in the spring chair, and leaning forward, the boss covered his face with his hands. He wanted, he intended, he had arranged to weep....

It had been a terrible shock to him when old Woodifield sprang that remark upon him about the boy's grave. It was exactly as though the earth had opened and he had seen the boy lying there with Woodifield's girls staring down at him. For it was strange. Although over six years had passed away, the boss never thought of the boy except as lying unchanged, unblemished in his uniform, asleep for ever. "My son!"

groaned the boss. But no tears came yet. In the past, in the first months and even years after the boy's death, he had only to say those words to be overcome by such grief that nothing short of a violent fit of weeping could relieve him. Time, he had declared then, he had told everybody, could make no difference. Other men perhaps might recover, might live their loss down, but not he. How was it possible? His boy was an only son. Ever since his birth the boss had worked at building up this business for him; it had no other meaning if it was not for the boy. Life itself had come to have no other meaning. How on earth could he have slaved, denied himself, kept going all those years without the promise for ever before him of the boy's stepping into his shoes and carrying on where he left off?

And that promise had been so near being fulfilled. The boy had been in the office learning the ropes for a year before the war. Every morning they had started off together; they had come back by the same train. And what congratulations he had received as the boy's father! No wonder; he had taken to it marvellously. As to his popularity with the staff, every man jack of them down to old Macey couldn't make enough of the boy. And he wasn't in the least spoilt. No, he was just his bright, natural self, with the right word for everybody, with that boyish look and his habit of saying, "Simply splendid!"

But all that was over and done with as though it never had been. The day had come when Macey had handed him the telegram that brought the whole place crashing about his head. "Deeply regret to inform you...." And he had left the office a broken man, with his life in ruins.

Six years ago, six years.... How quickly time passed! It might have happened yesterday. The boss took his hands from his face; he was puzzled. Something seemed to be wrong with him. He wasn't feeling as he wanted to feel. He decided to get up and have a look at the boy's photograph. But it wasn't a favorite photograph of his; the expression was unnatural. It was cold, even stern-looking. The boy had never looked like that.

At that moment the boss noticed that a fly had fallen into his broad inkpot, and was trying feebly but desperately to clamber out again. Help! help! said those struggling legs. But the sides of the inkpot were wet and slippery; it fell back again and began to swim. The boss took up a pen, picked the fly out of the ink, and shook it on to a piece of blotting-paper. For a fraction of a second it lay still on the dark patch that oozed round it. Then the front legs waved, took hold, and, pulling its small sodden body up it began the immense task of cleaning the ink from its wings. Over and under, over and under, went a leg along a wing, as the stone goes over and under the scythe. Then there was a pause, while the fly, seeming to stand on the tips of its toes, tried to expand first one wing and then the other. It succeeded at last, and, sitting down, it began, like a minute cat, to clean its face. Now one could imagine that the little front legs rubbed against each other lightly, joyfully. The horrible danger was over; it had escaped; it was ready for life again.

But just then the boss had an idea. He plunged his pen back into the ink, leaned his thick wrist on the blotting paper, and as the fly tried its wings down came a great heavy blot. What would it make of that? What indeed! The little beggar seemed absolutely cowed, stunned, and afraid to move because of what would happen next. But then, as if painfully, it dragged itself forward. The front legs waved, caught hold, and, more slowly this time, the task began from the beginning.

He's a plucky little devil, thought the boss, and he felt a real admiration for the fly's courage. That was the way to tackle things; that was the right spirit. Never say die; it was only a question of.... But the fly had again finished its laborious task, and the boss had just time to refill his pen, to shake fair and square on the new-cleaned body yet another dark drop. What about it this time? A painful moment of suspense followed. But behold, the front legs were again waving; the boss felt a rush of relief. He leaned over the fly and said to it tenderly, "You artful little b...." And he actually had the brilliant notion of breathing on it to help the drying process. All the same, there was something timid and weak about its efforts now, and the boss decided that this time should be the last, as he dipped the pen into the inkpot.

It was. The last blot on the soaked blotting-paper, and the draggled fly lay in it and did not stir. The back legs were stuck to the body; the front legs were not to be seen.

"Come on," said the boss. "Look sharp!" And he stirred it with his pen—in vain. Nothing happened or was likely to happen. The fly was dead.

The boss lifted the corpse on the end of the paper-knife and flung it into the waste-paper basket. But such a grinding feeling of wretchedness seized him that he felt positively frightened. He started forward and pressed the bell for Macey.

"Bring me some fresh blotting-paper," he said, sternly, "and look sharp about it." And while the old dog padded away he fell to wondering what it was he had been thinking about before. What was it? It was.... He took out his handkerchief and passed it inside his collar. For the life of him he could not remember.

82

The Canary

Katherine Mansfield

... You see that big nail to the right of the front door? I can scarcely look at it even now and yet I could not bear to take it out. I should like to think it was there always even after my time. I sometimes hear the next people saying, "There must have been a cage hanging from there." And it comforts me; I feel he is not quite forgotten.

... You cannot imagine how wonderfully he sang. It was not like the singing of other canaries. And that isn't just my fancy. Often, from the window, I used to see people stop at the gate to listen, or they would lean over the fence by the mock-orange for quite a long time—carried away. I suppose it sounds absurd to you—it wouldn't if you had heard him—but it really seemed to me that he sang whole songs with a beginning and an end to them.

For instance, when I'd finished the house in the afternoon, and changed my blouse and brought my sewing on to the veranda here, he used to hop, hop, hop from one perch to another, tap against the bars as if to attract my attention, sip a little water just as a professional singer might, and then break into a song so exquisite that I had to put my needle down to listen to him. I can't describe it; I wish I could. But it was always the same, every afternoon, and I felt that I understood every note of it.

... I loved him. How I loved him! Perhaps it does not matter so very much what it is one loves in this world. But love something one must. Of course there was always my little house and the garden, but for some reason they were never enough. Flowers respond wonderfully, but they don't sympathize. Then I loved the evening star. Does that sound foolish? I used to go into the backyard, after sunset, and wait for it until it shone above the dark gum tree. I used to whisper "There you are, my darling." And just in that first moment it seemed to be shining for me alone. It seemed to understand this…something which is like longing, and yet it is not longing. Or regret—it is more like regret. And yet regret for what? I have much to be thankful for.

... But after he came into my life I forgot the evening star; I did not need it any more. But it was strange. When the Chinaman who came to the door with birds to sell held him up in his tiny cage, and instead of fluttering, fluttering, like the poor little goldfinches, he gave a faint, small chirp, I found myself saying, just as I had said to the star over the gum tree, "There you are, my darling." From that moment he was mine.

... It surprises me even now to remember how he and I shared each other's lives. The moment I came down in the morning and took the cloth off his cage he greeted me with a drowsy little note. I knew it meant "Missus! Missus!" Then I hung him on the nail outside while I got my three young men their breakfasts, and I never brought him in until we had the house to ourselves again. Then, when the washing-up was done, it was quite a little entertainment. I spread a newspaper over a corner of the table and when I put the cage on it he used to beat with his wings despairingly, as if he didn't know what was coming. "You're a regular little actor," I used to scold him. I scraped the tray, dusted it with fresh sand, filled his seed and water tins, tucked a piece of chickweed and half a chili between the bars. And I am perfectly certain he understood and appreciated every item of this little performance. You see by nature he was exquisitely neat. There was never a speck on his perch. And you'd only to see him enjoy his bath to realize he had a real small passion for cleanliness. His bath was put in last. And the moment it was in he positively leapt into it. First he fluttered one wing, then the other, then he ducked his head and dabbled his breast feathers. Drops of water were scattered all over the kitchen, but still he would not get out. I used to say to him, "Now that's quite enough. You're only showing off." And at last out he hopped and, standing on one leg, he began to peck himself dry. Finally he gave a shake, a flick, a twitter and he lifted his throat—Oh, I can hardly bear to recall it. I was always cleaning the knives at the time. And it almost seemed to me the knives sang too, as I rubbed them bright on the board.

... Company, you see—that was what he was. Perfect company. If you have lived alone you will realize how precious that is. Of course there were my three young men who came in to supper every evening, and sometimes stayed in the dining-room afterwards reading the paper. But I could not expect them to be interested in the little things that made my day. Why should they be? I was nothing to them. In fact, I overheard them one evening talking about me on the stairs as "the Scarecrow." No matter. It doesn't matter. Not in the least. I quite understand. They are young. Why should I mind? But I remember feeling so especially thankful that I was not quite alone that evening. I told him, after they had gone out. I said "Do you know what they call Missus?" And he put his head on one side and looked at me with his little bright eye until I could not help laughing. It seemed to amuse him.

... Have you kept birds? If you haven't all this must sound, perhaps, exaggerated. People have the idea that birds are heartless, cold little creatures, not like dogs or cats. My washerwoman used to say on Mondays when she wondered why I didn't keep "a nice fox terrier," "There's no comfort, Miss, in a canary." Untrue. Dreadfully untrue. I remember one night. I had had a very awful dream—dreams can be dreadfully cruel—even after I had woken up I could not get over it. So I put on my dressing-gown and went down to the kitchen for a glass of water. It was a winter night and raining hard. I suppose I was still half asleep, but through the kitchen window, that hadn't a blind, it seemed to me the dark was staring in, spying. And suddenly I felt it was unbearable that I had no one to whom I could say "I've had such a dreadful dream," or—or "Hide me from the dark." I even covered my face for a minute. And then there came a little "Sweet! Sweet!" His cage was on the table, and the cloth had slipped so that a chink of light shone through. "Sweet! Sweet!" said the darling little fellow again, softly, as much as to say, "I'm here, Missus! I'm here!" That was so beautifully comforting that I nearly cried.

... And now he's gone. I shall never have another bird, another pet of any kind. How could I? When I found him, lying on his back, with his eye dim and his claws wrung, when I realised that never again should I hear my darling sing, something seemed to die in me. My heart felt hollow, as if it was his cage. I shall get over it. Of course. I must. One can get over anything in time. And people always say I have a cheerful disposition. They are quite right. I thank my God I have.

... All the same, without being morbid, and giving way to—to memories and so on, I must confess that there does seem to me something sad in life. It is hard to say what it is. I don't mean the sorrow that we all know, like illness and poverty and death. No, it is something different. It is there, deep down, deep down, part of one, like one's breathing. However hard I work and tire myself I have only to stop to know it is there, waiting. I often wonder if everybody feels the same. One can never know. But isn't it extraordinary that under his sweet, joyful little singing it was just this sadness—ah, what is it?—that I heard?

83

The Wind Blows

Katherine Mansfield

Suddenly—dreadfully—she wakes up. What has happened? Something dreadful has happened. No—nothing has happened. It is only the wind shaking the house, rattling the windows, banging a piece of iron on the roof and making her bed tremble. Leaves flutter past the window, up and away; down in the avenue a whole newspaper wags in the air like a lost kite and falls, spiked on a pine tree. It is cold. Summer is over—it is autumn—everything is ugly. The carts rattle by, swinging from side to side; two Chinamen lollop along under their wooden yokes with the straining vegetable baskets—their pigtails and blue blouses fly out in the wind. A white dog on three legs yelps past the gate. It is all over! What is? Oh, everything! And she begins to plait her hair with shaking fingers, not daring to look in the glass. Mother is talking to grandmother in the hall.

"A perfect idiot! Imagine leaving anything out on the line in weather like this... Now my best little Teneriffe-work teacloth is simply in ribbons. *What* is that extraordinary smell? It's the porridge burning. Oh, heavens—this wind!"

She has a music lesson at ten o'clock. At the thought the minor movement of the Beethoven begins to play in her head, the trills long and terrible like little rolling drums... Marie Swainson runs into the garden next door to pick the "chrysanths" before they are ruined. Her skirt flies up above her waist; she tries to beat it down, to tuck it between her legs while she stoops, but it is no use—up it flies. All the trees and bushes beat about her. She picks as quickly as she can but she is quite distracted. She doesn't mind what she does—she pulls the plants up by the roots and bends and twists them, stamping her foot and swearing.

"For heaven's sake keep the front door shut! Go round to the back," shouts someone. And then she hears Bogey:

"Mother, you're wanted on the telephone. Telephone, Mother. It's the butcher."

How hideous life is—revolting, simply revolting... And now her hat-elastic's snapped. Of course it would. She'll wear her old tam and slip out the back way. But Mother has seen.

"Matilda. Matilda. Come back im-me-diately! What on earth have you got on your head? It looks like a tea cosy. And why have you got that mane of hair on your forehead."

"I can't come back. Mother. I'll be late for my lesson."

"Come back immediately!"

She won't. She won't. She hates Mother. "Go to hell," she shouts, running down the road.

In waves, in clouds, in big round whirls the dust comes stinging, and with it little bits of straw and chaff and manure. There is a loud roaring sound from the trees in the gardens, and standing at the bottom of the road outside Mr. Bullen's gate she can hear the sea sob: "Ah!... Ah!...Ah-h!" But Mr. Bullen's drawing-room is as quiet as a cave. The windows are closed, the blinds half pulled, and she is not late. The-girl-before-her has just started playing MacDowell's "To an Iceberg." Mr. Bullen looks over at her and half smiles.

"Sit down," he says. "Sit over there in the sofa corner, little lady."

How funny he is. He doesn't exactly laugh at you...but there is just something... Oh, how peaceful it is here. She likes this room. It smells of art serge and stale smoke and chrysanthemums...there is a big vase of them on the mantelpiece behind the pale photograph of Rubinstein...*à mon ami Robert Bullen...* Over the black glittering piano hangs "Solitude"—a dark tragic woman draped in white, sitting on a rock, her knees crossed, her chin on her hands.

"No, no!" says Mr. Bullen, and he leans over the other girl, put his arms over her shoulders and plays the passage for her. The stupid—she's blushing! How ridiculous!

Now the-girl-before-her has gone; the front door slams. Mr. Bullen comes back and walks up and down, very softly, waiting for her. What an extraordinary thing. Her fingers tremble so that she can't undo the knot in the music satchel. It's the wind... And her heart beats so hard she feels it must lift her blouse up and down. Mr. Bullen does not say a word. The shabby red piano seat is long enough for two people to sit side by side. Mr. Bullen sits down by her.

"Shall I begin with scales," she asks, squeezing her hands together. "I had some arpeggios, too."

But he does not answer. She doesn't believe he even hears...and then suddenly his fresh hand with the ring on it reaches over and opens Beethoven.

"Let's have a little of the old master," he says.

But why does he speak so kindly—so awfully kindly—and as though they had known each other for years and years and knew everything about each other.

He turns the page slowly. She watches his hand—it is a very nice hand and always looks as though it had just been washed.

"Here we are," says Mr. Bullen.

Oh, that kind voice—Oh, that minor movement. Here come the little drums...

"Shall I take the repeat?"

"Yes, dear child."

His voice is far, far too kind. The crotchets and quavers are dancing up and down the stave like little black boys on a fence. Why is he so... She will not cry—she has nothing to cry about...

"What is it, dear child?"

Mr. Bullen takes her hands. His shoulder is there—just by her head. She leans on it ever so little, her cheek against the springy tweed.

"Life is so dreadful," she murmurs, but she does not feel it's dreadful at all. He says something about "waiting" and "marking time" and "that rare thing, a woman," but she does not hear. It is so comfortable... for ever...

Suddenly the door opens and in pops Marie Swainson, hours before her time.

"Take the allegretto a little faster," says Mr. Bullen, and gets up and begins to walk up and down again.

"Sit in the sofa corner, little lady," he says to Marie.

The wind, the wind. It's frightening to be here in her room by herself. The bed, the mirror, the white jug and basin gleam like the sky outside. It's the bed that is frightening. There it lies, sound asleep... Does Mother imagine for one moment that she is going to darn all those stockings knotted up on the quilt like a coil of snakes? She's not. No, Mother. I do not see why I should… The wind—the wind! There's a funny smell of soot blowing down the chimney. Hasn't anyone written poems to the wind?…"I bring fresh flowers to the leaves and showers."…What nonsense.

"Is that you, Bogey?"

"Come for a walk round the esplanade, Matilda. I can't stand this any longer."

"Right-o. I'll put on my ulster. Isn't it an awful day!" Bogey's ulster is just like hers. Hooking the collar she looks at herself in the glass. Her face is white, they have the same excited eyes and hot lips. Ah, they know those two in the glass. Good-bye, dears; we shall be back soon.

"This is better, isn't it?"

"Hook on," says Bogey.

They cannot walk fast enough. Their heads bent, their legs just touching, they stride like one eager person through the town, down the asphalt zigzag where the fennel grows wild and on to the esplanade. It is dusky—just getting dusky. The wind is so strong that they have to fight their way through it, rocking like two old drunkards. All the poor little pahutukawas on the esplanade are bent to the ground.

"Come on! Come on! Let's get near."

Over by the breakwater the sea is very high. They pull off their hats and her hair blows across her mouth, tasting of salt. The sea is so high that the waves do not break at all; they thump against the rough stone wall and suck up the weedy, dripping steps. A fine spray skims from the water right across the esplanade. They are covered with drops; the inside of her mouth tastes wet and cold.

Bogey's voice is breaking. When he speaks he rushes up and down the scale. It's funny—it makes you laugh—and yet it just suits the day. The wind carries their voices—away fly the sentences like little narrow ribbons.

"Quicker! Quicker!"

It is getting very dark. In the harbour the coal hulks show two lights—one high on a mast, and one from the stern.

"Look, Bogey. Look over there."

A big black steamer with a long loop of smoke streaming, with the portholes lighted, with lights everywhere, is putting out to sea. The wind does not stop her; she cuts through the waves, making for the open gate between the pointed rocks that leads to…It's the light that makes her look so awfully beautiful and mysterious… *They* are on board leaning over the rail arm in arm.

"…Who are they?"

"…Brother and sister."

"Look, Bogey, there's the town. Doesn't it look small? There's the post office clock chiming for the last time. There's the esplanade where we walked that windy day. Do you remember? I cried at my music lesson that day—how many years ago! Good-bye, little island, good-bye… "

Now the dark stretches a wing over the tumbling water. They can't see those two any more. Good-bye, good-bye. Don't forget… But the ship is gone, now.

The wind—the wind.

84

Psychology

Katherine Mansfield

When she opened the door and saw him standing there she was more pleased than ever before, and he, too, as he followed her into the studio, seemed very very happy to have come.

"Not busy?"

"No. Just going to have tea."

"And you are not expecting anybody?"

"Nobody at all."

"Ah! That's good."

He laid aside his coat and hat gently, lingeringly, as though he had time and to spare for everything, or as though he were taking leave of them for ever, and came over to the fire and held out his hands to the quick, leaping flame.

Just for a moment both of them stood silent in that leaping light. Still, as it were, they tasted on their smiling lips the sweet shock of their greeting. Their secret selves whispered:

"Why should we speak? Isn't this enough?"

"More than enough. I never realized until this moment…"

"How good it is just to be with you… "

"Like this… "

"It's more than enough."

But suddenly he turned and looked at her and she moved quickly away.

"Have a cigarette? I'll put the kettle on. Are you longing for tea?"

"No. Not longing."

"Well, I am."

"Oh, you." He thumped the Armenian cushion and flung on to the *sommier.* "You're a perfect little Chinee."

"Yes, I am," she laughed. "I long for tea as strong men long for wine."

She lighted the lamp under its broad orange shade, pulled the curtains and drew up the tea table. Two birds sang in the kettle; the fire fluttered. He sat up clasping his knees. It was delightful—this business of having tea—and she always had delicious things to eat—little sharp sandwiches, short sweet almond fingers, and a dark, rich cake tasting of rum—but it was an interruption. He wanted it over, the table pushed away, their two chairs drawn up to the light, and the moment came when he took out his pipe, filled it, and said, pressing the tobacco tight into the bowl: "I have been thinking over what you said last time and it seems to me…"

Yes, that was what he waited for and so did she. Yes, while she shook the teapot hot and dry over the spirit flame she saw those other two, him, leaning back, taking his ease among the cushions, and her, curled up *en escargot* in the blue shell arm-chair. The picture was so clear and so minute it might have been painted on the blue teapot lid. And yet she couldn't hurry. She could almost have cried: "Give me time." She must have time in which to grow calm. She wanted time in which to free herself from all these familiar things with which she lived so vividly. For all these gay things round her were part of her—her offspring—and they knew it and made the largest, most vehement claims. But now they must go. They must be swept away, shooed away—like children, sent up the shadowy stairs, packed into bed and commanded to go to sleep—at once—without a murmur!

For the special thrilling quality of their friendship was in their complete surrender. Like two open cities in the midst of some vast plain their two minds lay open to each other. And it wasn't as if he rode into hers like a conqueror, armed to the eyebrows and seeing nothing but a gay silken flutter—nor did she enter his like a queen walking soft on petals. No, they were eager, serious travellers, absorbed in understanding what was to be seen and discovering what was hidden—making the most of this extraordinary absolute chance which made it possible for him to be utterly truthful to her and for her to be utterly sincere with him.

And the best of it was they were both of them old enough to enjoy their adventure to the full without any stupid emotional complication. Passion would have ruined everything; they quite saw that. Besides, all that sort of thing was over and done with for both of them—he was thirty-one, she was thirty—they had had their experiences, and very rich and varied they had been, but now was the time for harvest—harvest.

Weren't his novels to be very big novels indeed? And her plays. Who else had her exquisite sense of real English Comedy?...

Carefully she cut the cake into thick little wads and he reached across for a piece.

"Do realize how good it is," she implored. "Eat it imaginatively. Roll your eyes if you can and taste it on the breath. It's not a sandwich from the hatter's bag—it's the kind of cake that might have been mentioned in the Book of Genesis... And God said: 'Let there be cake. And there was cake. And God saw that it was good.'"

"You needn't entreat me," said he. "Really you needn't. It's a queer thing but I always do notice what I eat here and never anywhere else. I suppose it comes of living alone so long and always reading while I feed...my habit of looking upon food as just food...something that's there, at certain times...to be devoured...to be...not there." He laughed. "That shocks you. Doesn't it?"

"To the bone," said she.

"But—look here——" He pushed away his cup and began to speak very fast. "I simply haven't got any external life at all. I don't know the names of things a bit—trees and so on—and I never notice places or furniture or what people look like. One room is just like another to me—a place to sit and read or talk in—except," and here he paused, smiled in a strange naive way, and said, "except this studio." He looked round him and then at her; he laughed in his astonishment and pleasure. He was like a man who wakes up in a train to find that he has arrived, already, at the journey's end.

"Here's another queer thing. If I shut my eyes I can see this place down to every detail—every detail... Now I come to think of it—I've never realized this consciously before. Often when I am away from here I revisit it in spirit—wander about among your red chairs, stare at the bowl of fruit on the black table—and just touch, very lightly, that marvel of a sleeping boy's head."

He looked at it as he spoke. It stood on the corner of the mantelpiece; the head to one side down-drooping, the lips parted, as though in his sleep the little boy listened to some sweet sound...

"I love that little boy," he murmured. And then they both were silent.

A new silence came between them. Nothing in the least like the satisfactory pause that had followed their greetings—the "Well, here we are together again, and there's no reason why we shouldn't go on from just where we left off last time." That silence could be contained in the circle of warm, delightful fire and lamplight. How many times hadn't they flung something into it just for the fun of watching the ripples break on the easy shores. But into this unfamiliar pool the head of the little boy sleeping his timeless sleep dropped—and the ripples flowed away, away—boundlessly far—into deep glittering darkness.

And then both of them broke it. She said: "I must make up the fire," and he said: "I have been trying a new…" Both of them escaped. She made up the fire and put the table back, the blue chair was wheeled forward, she curled up and he lay back among the cushions. Quickly! Quickly! They must stop it from happening again.

"Well, I read the book you left last time."

"Oh, what do you think of it?"

They were off and all was as usual. But was it? Weren't they just a little too quick, too prompt with their replies, too ready to take each other up? Was this really anything more than a wonderfully good imitation of other occasions? His heart beat; her cheek burned and the stupid thing was she could not discover where exactly they were or what exactly was happening. She hadn't time to glance back. And just as she had got so far it happened again. They faltered, wavered, broke down, were silent. Again they were conscious of the boundless, questioning dark. Again, there they were—two hunters, bending over their fire, but hearing suddenly from the jungle beyond a shake of wind and a loud, questioning cry…

She lifted her head. "It's raining," she murmured. And her voice was like his when he had said: "I love that little boy."

Well. Why didn't they just give way to it—yield—and see what will happen then? But no. Vague and troubled though they were, they knew enough to realize their precious friendship was in danger. She was the one who would be destroyed—not they—and they'd be no party to that.

He got up, knocked out his pipe, ran his hand through his hair and said: "I have been wondering very much lately whether the novel of the future will be a psychological novel or not. How sure are you that psychology *qua* psychology has got anything to do with literature at all?"

"Do you mean you feel there's quite a chance that the mysterious non-existent creatures—the young writers of to-day—are trying simply to jump the psycho-analyst's claim?"

"Yes, I do. And I think it's because this generation is just wise enough to know that it is sick and to realize that its only chance of recovery is by going into its symptoms—making an exhaustive study of them—tracking them down—trying to get at the root of the trouble."

"But oh," she wailed. "What a dreadfully dismal outlook."

"Not at all," said he. "Look here..." On the talk went. And now it seemed they really had succeeded. She turned in her chair to look at him while she answered. Her smile said: "We have won." And he smiled back, confident: "Absolutely."

But the smile undid them. It lasted too long; it became a grin. They saw themselves as two little grinning puppets jigging away in nothingness.

"What have we been talking about?" thought he. He was so utterly bored he almost groaned.

"What a spectacle we have made of ourselves," thought she. And she saw him laboriously—oh, laboriously—laying out the grounds and herself running after, putting here a tree and there a flowery shrub and here a handful of glittering fish in a pool. They were silent this time from sheer dismay.

The clock struck six merry little pings and the fire made a soft flutter. What fools they were—heavy, stodgy, elderly—with positively upholstered minds.

And now the silence put a spell upon them like solemn music. It was anguish—anguish for her to bear it and he would die—he'd die if it were broken... And yet he longed to break it. Not by speech. At any rate not by their ordinary maddening chatter. There was another way for them to speak to each other, and in the new way he wanted to murmur: "Do you feel this too? Do you understand it at all?"...

Instead, to his horror, he heard himself say: "I must be off; I'm meeting Brand at six."

What devil made him say that instead of the other? She jumped—simply jumped out of her chair, and he heard her crying: "You must rush, then. He's so punctual. Why didn't you say so before?"

"You've hurt me; you've hurt me! We've failed!" said her secret self while she handed him his hat and stick, smiling gaily. She wouldn't give him a moment for another word, but ran along the passage and opened the big outer door.

Could they leave each other like this? How could they? He stood on the step and she just inside holding the door. It was not raining now.

"You've hurt me—hurt me," said her heart. "Why don't you go? No, don't go. Stay. No—go!" And she looked out upon the night.

She saw the beautiful fall of the steps, the dark garden ringed with glittering ivy, on the other side of the road the huge bare willows and above them the sky big and bright with stars. But of course he would see nothing of all this. He was superior to it all. He—with his wonderful "spiritual" vision!

She was right. He did see nothing at all. Misery! He'd missed it. It was too late to do anything now. Was it too late? Yes, it was. A cold snatch of hateful wind blew into the garden. Curse life! He heard her cry "au revoir" and the door slammed.

Running back into the studio she behaved so strangely. She ran up and down lifting her arms and crying: "Oh! Oh! How stupid! How imbecile! How stupid!" And then she flung herself down on the *sommier* thinking of nothing—just lying there in her rage. All was over. What was over? Oh—something was. And she'd never see him again—never. After a long long time (or perhaps ten minutes) had passed in that black gulf her bell rang a sharp quick jingle. It was he, of course. And equally, of course, she oughtn't to have paid the slightest attention to it but just let it go on ringing and ringing. She flew to answer.

On the doorstep there stood an elderly virgin, a pathetic creature who simply idolized her (heaven knows why) and had this habit of turning up and ringing the bell and then saying, when she opened the door: "My dear, send me away!" She never did. As a rule she asked her in and let her admire everything and accepted the bunch of slightly soiled looking flowers—more than graciously. But to-day…

"Oh, I am so sorry," she cried. "But I've got someone with me. We are working on some woodcuts. I'm hopelessly busy all evening."

"It doesn't matter. It doesn't matter at all, darling," said the good friend. "I was just passing and I thought I'd leave you some violets." She fumbled down among the ribs of a large old umbrella. "I put them down here. Such a good place to keep flowers out of the wind. Here they are," she said, shaking out a little dead bunch.

For a moment she did not take the violets. But while she stood just inside, holding the door, a strange thing happened… Again she saw the beautiful fall of the steps, the dark garden ringed with glittering ivy, the willows, the big bright sky. Again she felt the silence that was like a question. But this time she did not hesitate. She moved forward. Very softly and gently, as though fearful of making a ripple in that boundless pool of quiet she put her arms round her friend.

"My dear," murmured her happy friend, quite overcome by this gratitude. "They are really nothing. Just the simplest little thrippenny bunch."

But as she spoke she was enfolded—more tenderly, more beautifully embraced, held by such a sweet pressure and for so long that the poor dear's mind positively reeled and she just had the strength to quaver: "Then you really don't mind me too much?"

"Good night, my friend," whispered the other. "Come again soon."

"Oh, I will. I will."

This time she walked back to the studio slowly, and standing in the middle of the room with half-shut eyes she felt so light, so rested, as if she had woken up out of a childish sleep. Even the act of breathing was a joy…

The *sommier* was very untidy. All the cushions "like furious mountains" as she said; she put them in order before going over to the writing-table.

"I have been thinking over our talk about the psychological novel," she dashed off, "it really is intensely interesting."…And so on and so on.

At the end she wrote: "Good night, my friend. Come again soon."

85

Sun and Moon

Katherine Mansfield

In the afternoon the chairs came, a whole big cart full of little gold ones with their legs in the air. And then the flowers came. When you stared down from the balcony at the people carrying them the flower pots looked like funny awfully nice hats nodding up the path.

Moon thought they were hats. She said: "Look. There's a man wearing a palm on his head." But she never knew the difference between real things and not real ones.

There was nobody to look after Sun and Moon. Nurse was helping Annie alter Mother's dress which was much-too-long-and-tight-under-the-arms and Mother was running all over the house and telephoning Father to be sure not to forget things. She only had time to say: "Out of my way, children!"

They kept out of her way—at any rate Sun did. He did so hate being sent stumping back to the nursery. It didn't matter about Moon. If she got tangled in people's legs they only threw her up and shook her till she squeaked. But Sun was too heavy for that. He was so heavy that the fat man who came to dinner on Sundays used to say: "Now, young man, let's try to lift you." And then he'd put his thumbs under Sun's arms and groan and try and give it up at last saying: "He's a perfect little ton of bricks!"

Nearly all the furniture was taken out of the dining-room. The big piano was put in a corner and then there came a row of flower pots and then there came the goldy chairs. That was for the concert. When Sun looked in a white faced man sat at the piano—not playing, but banging at it and then looking inside. He had a bag of tools on the piano and he had stuck his hat on a statue against the wall. Sometimes he just started to play and then he jumped up again and looked inside. Sun hoped he wasn't the concert.

But of course the place to be in was the kitchen. There was a man helping in a cap like a blancmange, and their real cook, Minnie, was all red in the face and laughing. Not cross at all. She gave them each an almond finger and lifted them up on to the flour bin so that they could watch the wonderful things she and the man were making for supper. Cook brought in the things and he put them on dishes and trimmed them. Whole fishes, with their heads and eyes and tails still on, he sprinkled with red and green and yellow bits; he made squiggles all over the jellies, he stuck a collar on a ham and put a very thin sort of a fork in it; he dotted almonds and tiny round biscuits on the creams. And more and more things coming.

"Ah, but you haven't seen the ice pudding," said Cook. "Come along." Why was she being so nice, thought Sun as she gave them each a hand. And they looked into the refrigerator.

Oh! Oh! Oh! It was a little house. It was a little pink house with white snow on the roof and green windows and a brown door and stuck in the door there was a nut for a handle.

When Sun saw the nut he felt quite tired and had to lean against Cook.

"Let me touch it. Just let me put my finger on the roof," said Moon, dancing. She always wanted to touch all the food. Sun didn't.

"Now, my girl, look sharp with the table," said Cook as the housemaid came in.

"It's a picture, Min," said Nellie. "Come along and have a look." So they all went into the dining-room. Sun and Moon were almost frightened. They wouldn't go up to the table at first; they just stood at the door and made eyes at it.

It wasn't real night yet but the blinds were down in the dining-room and the lights turned on—and all the lights were red roses. Red ribbons and bunches of roses tied up the table at the corners. In the middle was a lake with rose petals floating on it.

"That's where the ice pudding is to be," said Cook.

Two silver lions with wings had fruit on their backs, and the salt cellars were tiny birds drinking out of basins.

And all the winking glasses and shining plates and sparkling knives and forks—and all the food. And the little red table napkins made into roses…

"Are people going to eat the food?" asked Sun.

"I should just think they were," laughed Cook, laughing with Nellie. Moon laughed, too; she always did the same as other people. But Sun didn't want to laugh. Round and round he walked with his hands behind his back. Perhaps he never would have stopped if Nurse hadn't called suddenly: "Now then, children. It's high time you were washed and dressed." And they were marched off to the nursery.

While they were being unbuttoned Mother looked in with a white thing over her shoulders; she was rubbing stuff on her face.

"I'll ring for them when I want them, Nurse, and then they can just come down and be seen and go back again," said she.

Sun was undressed, first nearly to his skin, and dressed again in a white shirt with red and white daisies speckled on it, breeches with strings at the sides and braces that came over, white socks and red shoes.

"Now you're in your Russian costume," said Nurse, flattening down his fringe.

"Am I?" said Sun.

"Yes. Sit quiet in that chair and watch your little sister."

Moon took ages. When she had her socks put on she pretended to fall back on the bed and waved her legs at Nurse as she always did, and every time Nurse tried to make her curls with a finger and a wet brush she turned round and asked Nurse to show her the photo of her brooch or something like that. But at last she was finished too. Her dress stuck out, with fur on it, all white; there was even fluffy stuff on the legs of her drawers. Her shoes were white with big blobs on them.

"There you are, my lamb," said Nurse. "And you look like a sweet little cherub of a picture of a powder-puff?" Nurse rushed to the door. "Ma'am, one moment."

Mother came in again with half her hair down.

"Oh," she cried. "What a picture!"

"Isn't she," said Nurse.

And Moon held out her skirts by the tips and dragged one of her feet. Sun didn't mind people not noticing him—much…

After that they played clean tidy games up at the table while Nurse stood at the door, and when the carriages began to come and the sound of laughter and voices and soft rustlings came from down below she whispered: "Now then, children, stay where you are." Moon kept jerking the table cloth so that it all hung down her side and Sun hadn't any—and then she pretended she didn't do it on purpose.

At last the bell rang. Nurse pounced at them with the hair brush, flattened his fringe, made her bow stand on end and joined their hands together.

"Down you go!" she whispered.

And down they went. Sun did feel silly holding Moon's hand like that but Moon seemed to like it. She swung her arm and the bell on her coral bracelet jingled.

At the drawing-room door stood Mother fanning herself with a black fan. The drawing-room was full of sweet smelling, silky, rustling ladies and men in black with funny tails on their coats—like beetles. Father was among them, talking very loud, and rattling something in his pocket.

"What a picture!" cried the ladies. "Oh, the ducks! Oh, the lambs! Oh, the sweets! Oh, the pets!"

All the people who couldn't get at Moon kissed Sun, and a skinny old lady with teeth that clicked said: "Such a serious little poppet," and rapped him on the head with something hard.

Sun looked to see if the same concert was there, but he was gone. Instead, a fat man with a pink head leaned over the piano talking to a girl who held a violin at her ear.

There was only one man that Sun really liked. He was a little grey man, with long grey whiskers, who walked about by himself. He came up to Sun and rolled his eyes in a very nice way and said: "Hullo, my lad." Then he went away. But soon he came back again and said: "Fond of dogs?" Sun said: "Yes." But then he went away again, and though Sun looked for him everywhere he couldn't find him. He thought perhaps he'd gone outside to fetch in a puppy.

"Good night, my precious babies," said Mother, folding them up in her bare arms. "Fly up to your little nest."

Then Moon went and made a silly of herself again. She put up her arms in front of everybody and said: "My Daddy must carry me."

But they seemed to like it, and Daddy swooped down and picked her up as he always did.

Nurse was in such a hurry to get them to bed that she even interrupted Sun over his prayers and said: "Get on with them, child, *do.*" And the moment after they were in bed and in the dark except for the nightlight in its little saucer.

"Are you asleep?" asked Moon.

"No," said Sun. "Are you?"

"No," said Moon.

A long while after Sun woke up again. There was a loud, loud noise of clapping from downstairs, like when it rains. He heard Moon turn over.

"Moon, are you awake?"

"Yes, are you."

"Yes. Well, let's go and look over the stairs."

They had just got settled on the top step when the drawing-room door opened and they heard the party cross over the hall into the dining-room. Then that door was shut; there was a noise of "pops" and laughing. Then that stopped and Sun saw them all walking round and round the lovely table with their hands behind their backs like he had done… Round and round they walked, looking and staring. The man with the grey whiskers liked the little house best. When he saw the nut for a handle he rolled his eyes like he did before and said to Sun: "Seen the nut?"

"Don't nod your head like that, Moon."

"I'm not nodding. It's you."

"It is not. I never nod my head."

"O-oh, you do. You're nodding it now."

"I'm not. I'm only showing you how not to do it."

When they woke up again they could only hear Father's voice very loud, and Mother, laughing away. Father came out of the dining-room, bounded up the stairs, and nearly fell over them.

"Hullo!" he said. "By Jove, Kitty, come and look at this."

Mother came out. "Oh, you naughty children," said she from the hall.

"Let's have 'em down and give 'em a bone," said Father. Sun had never seen him so jolly.

"No, certainly not," said Mother.

"Oh, my Daddy, do! Do have us down," said Moon.

"I'm hanged if I won't," cried Father. "I won't be bullied. Kitty—way there." And he caught them up, one under each arm.

Sun thought Mother would have been dreadfully cross. But she wasn't. She kept on laughing at Father.

"Oh, you dreadful boy!" said she. But she didn't mean Sun.

"Come on, kiddies. Come and have some pickings," said this jolly Father. But Moon stopped a minute.

"Mother—your dress is right off one side."

"Is it?" said Mother. And Father said "Yes" and pretended to bite her white shoulder, but she pushed him away.

And so they went back to the beautiful dining-room.

But—oh! oh! what had happened. The ribbons and the roses were all pulled untied. The little red table napkins lay on the floor, all the shining plates were dirty and all the winking glasses. The lovely food that the man had trimmed was all thrown about, and there were bones and bits and fruit peels and shells everywhere. There was even a bottle lying down with stuff coming out of it on to the cloth and nobody stood it up again.

And the little pink house with the snow roof and the green windows was broken—broken—half melted away in the centre of the table.

"Come on, Sun," said Father, pretending not to notice.

Moon lifted up her pyjama legs and shuffled up to the table and stood on a chair, squeaking away.

"Have a bit of this ice," said Father, smashing in some more of the roof.

Mother took a little plate and held it for him; she put her other arm round his neck.

"Daddy. Daddy," shrieked Moon. "The little handle's left. The little nut. Kin I eat it?" And she reached across and picked it out of the door and scrunched it up, biting hard and blinking.

"Here, my lad," said Father.

But Sun did not move from the door. Suddenly he put up his head and gave a loud wail.

"I think it's horrid—horrid—horrid!" he sobbed.

"There, you see!" said Mother. "You see!"

"Off with you," said Father, no longer jolly. "This moment. Off you go!"

And wailing loudly, Sun stumped off to the nursery.

86

Feuille d'Album

Katherine Mansfield

He really was an impossible person. Too shy altogether. With absolutely nothing to say for himself. And such a weight. Once he was in your studio he never knew when to go, but would sit on and on until you nearly screamed, and burned to throw something enormous after him when he did finally blush his way out—something like the tortoise stove. The strange thing was that at first sight he looked most interesting. Everybody agreed about that. You would drift into the café one evening and there you would see, sitting in a corner, with a glass of coffee in front of him, a thin, dark boy, wearing a blue jersey with a little grey flannel jacket buttoned over it. And somehow that blue jersey and the grey jacket with the sleeves that were too short gave him the air of a boy that has made up his mind to run away to sea. Who has run away, in fact, and will get up in a moment and sling a knotted handkerchief containing his nightshirt and his mother's picture on the end of a stick, and walk out into the night and be drowned... Stumble over the wharf edge on his way to the ship, even... He had black close-cropped hair, grey eyes with long lashes, white cheeks and a mouth pouting as though he were determined not to cry... How could one resist him? Oh, one's heart was wrung at sight. And, as if that were not enough, there was his trick of blushing... Whenever the waiter came near him he turned crimson—he might have been just out of prison and the waiter in the know...

"Who is he, my dear? Do you know?"

"Yes. His name is Ian French. Painter. Awfully clever, they say. Someone started by giving him a mother's tender care. She asked him how often he heard from home, whether he had enough blankets on his bed, how much milk he drank a day. But when she went round to his studio to give an eye to his socks, she rang and rang, and though she could have sworn she heard someone breathing inside, the door was not answered… Hopeless!"

Someone else decided that he ought to fall in love. She summoned him to her side, called him "boy," leaned over him so that he might smell the enchanting perfume of her hair, took his arm, told him how marvellous life could be if one only had the courage, and went round to his studio one evening and rang and rang… Hopeless.

"What the poor boy really wants is thoroughly rousing," said a third. So off they went to cafés and cabarets, little dances, places where you drank something that tasted like tinned apricot juice, but cost twenty-seven shillings a bottle and was called champagne, other places, too thrilling for words, where you sat in the most awful gloom, and where some one had always been shot the night before. But he did not turn a hair. Only once he got very drunk, but instead of blossoming forth, there he sat, stony, with two spots of red on his cheeks, like, my dear, yes, the dead image of that ragtime thing they were playing, like a "Broken Doll." But when she took him back to his studio he had quite recovered, and said "good night" to her in the street below, as though they had walked home from church together… Hopeless.

After heaven knows how many more attempts—for the spirit of kindness dies very hard in women—they gave him up. Of course, they were still perfectly charming, and asked him to their shows, and spoke to him in the café, but that was all. When one is an artist one has no time simply for people who won't respond. Has one?

"And besides I really think there must be something rather fishy somewhere…don't you? It can't all be as innocent as it looks! Why come to Paris if you want to be a daisy in the field? No, I'm not suspicious. But——"

He lived at the top of a tall mournful building overlooking the river. One of those buildings that look so romantic on rainy nights and moonlight nights, when the shutters are shut, and the heavy door, and the sign advertising "a little apartment to let immediately" gleams forlorn beyond words. One of those buildings that smell so unromantic all the year round, and where the concierge lives in a glass cage on the ground floor, wrapped up in a filthy shawl, stirring something in a saucepan and ladling out tit-bits to the swollen old dog lolling on a bead cushion… Perched up in the air the studio had a wonderful view. The two big windows faced the water; he could see the boats and the barges swinging up and down, and the fringe of an island planted with trees, like a round bouquet. The side window looked across to another house, shabbier still and smaller, and down below there was a flower market. You could see the tops of huge umbrellas, with frills of bright flowers escaping from them, booths covered with striped awning where they sold plants in boxes and clumps of wet gleaming palms in terra-cotta jars. Among the flowers the old women scuttled from side to side, like crabs. Really there was no need for him to go out. If he sat at the window until his white beard fell over the sill he still would have found something to draw...

How surprised those tender women would have been if they had managed to force the door. For he kept his studio as neat as a pin. Everything was arranged to form a pattern, a little "still life" as it were—the saucepans with their lids on the wall behind the gas stove, the bowl of eggs, milk jug and teapot on the shelf, the books and the lamp with the crinkly paper shade on the table. An Indian curtain that had a fringe of red leopards marching round it covered his bed by day, and on the wall beside the bed on a level with your eyes when you were lying down there was a small neatly printed notice: GET UP AT ONCE.

Every day was much the same. While the light was good he slaved at his painting, then cooked his meals and tidied up the place. And in the evenings he went off to the café, or sat at home reading or making out the most complicated list of expenses headed: "What I ought to be able to do it on," and ending with a sworn statement..."I swear not to exceed this amount for next month. Signed, Ian French."

Nothing very fishy about this; but those far-seeing women were quite right. It wasn't all.

One evening he was sitting at the side window eating some prunes and throwing the stones on to the tops of the huge umbrellas in the deserted flower market. It had been raining—the first real spring rain of the year had fallen—a bright spangle hung on everything, and the air smelled of buds and moist earth. Many voices sounding languid and content rang out in the dusky air, and the people who had come to close their windows and fasten the shutters leaned out instead. Down below in the market the trees were peppered with new green. What kind of trees were they? he wondered. And now came the lamplighter. He stared at the house across the way, the small, shabby house, and suddenly, as if in answer to his gaze, two wings of windows opened and a girl came out on to the tiny balcony carrying a pot of daffodils. She was a strangely thin girl in a dark pinafore, with a pink handkerchief tied over her hair. Her sleeves were rolled up almost to her shoulders and her slender arms shone against the dark stuff.

"Yes, it is quite warm enough. It will do them good," she said, putting down the pot and turning to some one in the room inside. As she turned she put her hands up to the handkerchief and tucked away some wisps of hair. She looked down at the deserted market and up at the sky, but where he sat there might have been a hollow in the air. She simply did not see the house opposite. And then she disappeared.

His heart fell out of the side window of his studio, and down to the balcony of the house opposite—buried itself in the pot of daffodils under the half-opened buds and spears of green… That room with the balcony was the sitting-room, and the one next door to it was the kitchen. He heard the clatter of the dishes as she washed up after supper, and then she came to the window, knocked a little mop against the ledge, and hung it on a nail to dry. She never sang or unbraided her hair, or held out her arms to the moon as young girls are supposed to do. And she always wore the same dark pinafore and the pink handkerchief over her hair… Whom did she live with? Nobody else came to those two windows, and yet she was always talking to some one in the room. Her mother, he decided, was an invalid. They took in sewing. The father was dead… He had been a journalist—very pale, with long moustaches, and a piece of black hair falling over his forehead.

By working all day they just made enough money to live on, but they never went out and they had no friends. Now when he sat down at his table he had to make an entirely new set of sworn statements… Not to go to the side window before a certain hour: signed, Ian French. Not to think about her until he had put away his painting things for the day: signed, Ian French.

It was quite simple. She was the only person he really wanted to know, because she was, he decided, the only other person alive who was just his age. He couldn't stand giggling girls, and he had no use for grown-up women… She was his age, she was—well, just like him. He sat in his dusky studio, tired, with one arm hanging over the back of his chair, staring in at her window and seeing himself in there with her. She had a violent temper; they quarrelled terribly at times, he and she. She had a way of stamping her foot and twisting her hands in her pinafore…furious. And she very rarely laughed. Only when she told him about an absurd little kitten she once had who used to roar and pretend to be a lion when it was given meat to eat. Things like that made her laugh… But as a rule they sat together very quietly; he, just as he was sitting now, and she with her hands folded in her lap and her feet tucked under, talking in low tones, or silent and tired after the day's work. Of course, she never asked him about his pictures, and of course he made the most wonderful drawings of her which she hated, because he made her so thin and so dark… But how could he get to know her? This might go on for years…

Then he discovered that once a week, in the evenings, she went out shopping. On two successive Thursdays she came to the window wearing an old-fashioned cape over the pinafore, and carrying a basket. From where he sat he could not see the door of her house, but on the next Thursday evening at the same time he snatched up his cap and ran down the stairs. There was a lovely pink light over everything. He saw it glowing in the river, and the people walking towards him had pink faces and pink hands.

He leaned against the side of his house waiting for her and he had no idea of what he was going to do or say. "Here she comes," said a voice in his head. She walked very quickly, with small, light steps; with one hand she carried the basket, with the other she kept the cape together… What could he do? He could only follow… First she went into the grocer's and spent a long time in there, and then she went into the butcher's where she had to wait her turn. Then she was an age at the draper's matching something, and then she went to the fruit shop and bought a lemon. As he watched her he knew more surely than ever he must get to know her, now. Her composure, her seriousness and her loneliness, the very way she walked as though she was eager to be done with this world of grown-ups all was so natural to him and so inevitable.

"Yes, she is always like that," he thought proudly. "We have nothing to do with these people."

But now she was on her way home and he was as far off as ever… She suddenly turned into the dairy and he saw her through the window buying an egg. She picked it out of the basket with such care—a brown one, a beautifully shaped one, the one he would have chosen. And when she came out of the dairy he went in after her. In a moment he was out again, and following her past his house across the flower market, dodging among the huge umbrellas and treading on the fallen flowers and the round marks where the pots had stood… Through her door he crept, and up the stairs after, taking care to tread in time with her so that she should not notice. Finally, she stopped on the landing, and took the key out of her purse. As she put it into the door he ran up and faced her.

Blushing more crimson than ever, but looking at her severely he said, almost angrily: "Excuse me, Mademoiselle, you dropped this."

And he handed her an egg.

87

A Dill Pickle

Katherine Mansfield

And then, after six years, she saw him again. He was seated at one of those little bamboo tables decorated with a Japanese vase of paper daffodils. There was a tall plate of fruit in front of him, and very carefully, in a way she recognized immediately as his "special" way, he was peeling an orange.

He must have felt that shock of recognition in her for he looked up and met her eyes. Incredible! He didn't know her! She smiled; he frowned. She came towards him. He closed his eyes an instant, but opening them his face lit up as though he had struck a match in a dark room. He laid down the orange and pushed back his chair, and she took her little warm hand out of her muff and gave it to him.

"Vera!" he exclaimed. "How strange. Really, for a moment I didn't know you. Won't you sit down? You've had lunch? Won't you have some coffee?"

She hesitated, but of course she meant to.

"Yes, I'd like some coffee." And she sat down opposite him.

"You've changed. You've changed very much," he said, staring at her with that eager, lighted look. "You look so well. I've never seen you look so well before."

"Really?" She raised her veil and unbuttoned her high fur collar. "I don't feel very well. I can't bear this weather, you know."

"Ah, no. You hate the cold… "

"Loathe it." She shuddered. "And the worst of it is that the older one grows…"

He interrupted her. "Excuse me," and tapped on the table for the waitress. "Please bring some coffee and cream." To her: "You are sure you won't eat anything? Some fruit, perhaps. The fruit here is very good."

"No, thanks. Nothing."

"Then that's settled." And smiling just a hint too broadly he took up the orange again. "You were saying—the older one grows——"

"The colder," she laughed. But she was thinking how well she remembered that trick of his—the trick of interrupting her—and of how it used to exasperate her six years ago. She used to feel then as though he, quite suddenly, in the middle of what she was saying, put his hand over her lips, turned from her, attended to something different, and then took his hand away, and with just the same slightly too broad smile, gave her his attention again... Now we are ready. That is settled.

"The colder!" He echoed her words, laughing too. "Ah, ah. You still say the same things. And there is another thing about you that is not changed at all—your beautiful voice—your beautiful way of speaking." Now he was very grave; he leaned towards her, and she smelled the warm, stinging scent of the orange peel. "You have only to say one word and I would know your voice among all other voices. I don't know what it is—I've often wondered—that makes your voice such a—haunting memory. Do you remember that first afternoon we spent together at Kew Gardens? You were so surprised because I did not know the names of any flowers. I am still just as ignorant for all your telling me. But whenever it is very fine and warm, and I see some bright colours—it's awfully strange—I hear your voice saying: 'Geranium, marigold and verbena.' And I feel those three words are all I recall of some forgotten, heavenly language... You remember that afternoon?"

"Oh, yes, very well." She drew a long, soft breath, as though the paper daffodils between them were almost too sweet to bear. Yet, what had remained in her mind of that particular afternoon was an absurd scene over the tea table. A great many people taking tea in a Chinese pagoda, and he behaving like a maniac about the wasps—waving them away, flapping at them with his straw hat, serious and infuriated out of all proportion to the occasion. How delighted the sniggering tea drinkers had been. And how she had suffered.

But now, as he spoke, that memory faded. His was the truer. Yes, it had been a wonderful afternoon, full of geranium and marigold and verbena, and—warm sunshine. Her thoughts lingered over the last two words as though she sang them.

In the warmth, as it were, another memory unfolded. She saw herself sitting on a lawn. He lay beside her, and suddenly, after a long silence, he rolled over and put his head in her lap.

"I wish," he said, in a low, troubled voice, "I wish that I had taken poison and were about to die—here now!"

At that moment a little girl in a white dress, holding a long, dripping water lily, dodged from behind a bush, stared at them, and dodged back again. But he did not see. She leaned over him.

"Ah, why do you say that? I could not say that."

But he gave a kind of soft moan, and taking her hand he held it to his cheek.

"Because I know I am going to love you too much—far too much. And I shall suffer so terribly. Vera, because you never, never will love me."

He was certainly far better looking now than he had been then. He had lost all that dreamy vagueness and indecision. Now he had the air of a man who has found his place in life, and fills it with a confidence and an assurance which was, to say the least, impressive. He must have made money, too. His clothes were admirable, and at that moment he pulled a Russian cigarette case out of his pocket.

"Won't you smoke?"

"Yes, I will." She hovered over them. "They look very good."

"I think they are. I get them made for me by a little man in St. James's Street. I don't smoke very much. I'm not like you—but when I do, they must be delicious, very fresh cigarettes. Smoking isn't a habit with me; it's a luxury—like perfume. Are you still so fond of perfumes? Ah, when I was in Russia..."

She broke in: "You've really been to Russia?"

"Oh, yes. I was there for over a year. Have you forgotten how we used to talk of going there?"

"No, I've not forgotten."

He gave a strange half laugh and leaned back in his chair. "Isn't it curious. I have really carried out all those journeys that we planned. Yes, I have been to all those places that we talked of, and stayed in them long enough to—as you used to say, 'air oneself' in them. In fact, I have spent the last three years of my life travelling all the time. Spain, Corsica, Siberia, Russia, Egypt. The only country left is China, and I mean to go there, too, when the war is over."

As he spoke, so lightly, tapping the end of his cigarette against the ash-tray, she felt the strange beast that had slumbered so long within her bosom stir, stretch itself, yawn, prick up its ears, and suddenly bound to its feet, and fix its longing, hungry stare upon those far away places. But all she said was, smiling gently: "How I envy you."

He accepted that. "It has been," he said, "very wonderful—especially Russia. Russia was all that we had imagined, and far, far more. I even spent some days on a river boat on the Volga. Do you remember that boatman's song that you used to play?"

"Yes." It began to play in her mind as she spoke.

"Do you ever play it now?"

"No, I've no piano."

He was amazed at that. "But what has become of your beautiful piano?"

She made a little grimace. "Sold. Ages ago."

"But you were so fond of music," he wondered.

"I've no time for it now," said she.

He let it go at that. "That river life," he went on, "is something quite special. After a day or two you cannot realize that you have ever known another. And it is not necessary to know the language—the life of the boat creates a bond between you and the people that's more than sufficient. You eat with them, pass the day with them, and in the evening there is that endless singing."

She shivered, hearing the boatman's song break out again loud and tragic, and seeing the boat floating on the darkening river with melancholy trees on either side… "Yes, I should like that," said she, stroking her muff.

"You'd like almost everything about Russian life," he said warmly. "It's so informal, so impulsive, so free without question. And then the peasants are so splendid. They are such human beings—yes, that is it. Even the man who drives your carriage has—has some real part in what is happening. I remember the evening a party of us, two friends of mine and the wife of one of them, went for a picnic by the Black Sea. We took supper and champagne and ate and drank on the grass. And while we were eating the coachman came up. 'Have a dill pickle,' he said. He wanted to share with us. That seemed to me so right, so—you know what I mean?"

And she seemed at that moment to be sitting on the grass beside the mysteriously Black Sea, black as velvet, and rippling against the banks in silent, velvet waves. She saw the carriage drawn up to one side of the road, and the little group on the grass, their faces and hands white in the moonlight. She saw the pale dress of the woman outspread and her folded parasol, lying on the grass like a huge pearl crochet hook. Apart from them, with his supper in a cloth on his knees, sat the coachman. "Have a dill pickle," said he, and although she was not certain what a dill pickle was, she saw the greenish glass jar with a red chili like a parrot's beak glimmering through. She sucked in her cheeks; the dill pickle was terribly sour...

"Yes, I know perfectly what you mean," she said.

In the pause that followed they looked at each other. In the past when they had looked at each other like that they had felt such a boundless understanding between them that their souls had, as it were, put their arms round each other and dropped into the same sea, content to be drowned, like mournful lovers. But now, the surprising thing was that it was he who held back. He who said:

"What a marvellous listener you are. When you look at me with those wild eyes I feel that I could tell you things that I would never breathe to another human being."

Was there just a hint of mockery in his voice or was it her fancy? She could not be sure.

"Before I met you," he said, "I had never spoken of myself to anybody. How well I remember one night, the night that I brought you the little Christmas tree, telling you all about my childhood. And of how I was so miserable that I ran away and lived under a cart in our yard for two days without being discovered. And you listened, and your eyes shone, and I felt that you had even made the little Christmas tree listen too, as in a fairy story."

But of that evening she had remembered a little pot of caviare. It had cost seven and sixpence. He could not get over it. Think of it—a tiny jar like that costing seven and sixpence. While she ate it he watched her, delighted and shocked.

"No, really, that is eating money. You could not get seven shillings into a little pot that size. Only think of the profit they must make... " And he had begun some immensely complicated calculations... But now good-bye to the caviare. The Christmas tree was on the table, and the little boy lay under the cart with his head pillowed on the yard dog.

"The dog was called Bosun," she cried delightedly.

But he did not follow. "Which dog? Had you a dog? I don't remember a dog at all."

"No, no. I mean the yard dog when you were a little boy." He laughed and snapped the cigarette case to.

"Was he? Do you know I had forgotten that. It seems such ages ago. I cannot believe that it is only six years. After I had recognized you to-day—I had to take such a leap—I had to take a leap over my whole life to get back to that time. I was such a kid then." He drummed on the table. "I've often thought how I must have bored you. And now I understand so perfectly why you wrote to me as you did—although at the time that letter nearly finished my life. I found it again the other day, and I couldn't help laughing as I read it. It was so clever—such a true picture of me." He glanced up. "You're not going?"

She had buttoned her collar again and drawn down her veil.

"Yes, I am afraid I must," she said, and managed a smile. Now she knew that he had been mocking.

"Ah, no, please," he pleaded. "Don't go just for a moment," and he caught up one of her gloves from the table and clutched at it as if that would hold her. "I see so few people to talk to nowadays, that I have turned into a sort of barbarian," he said. "Have I said something to hurt you?"

"Not a bit," she lied. But as she watched him draw her glove through his fingers, gently, gently, her anger really did die down, and besides, at the moment he looked more like himself of six years ago…

"What I really wanted then," he said softly, "was to be a sort of carpet—to make myself into a sort of carpet for you to walk on so that you need not be hurt by the sharp stones and the mud that you hated so. It was nothing more positive than that—nothing more selfish. Only I did desire, eventually, to turn into a magic carpet and carry you away to all those lands you longed to see."

As he spoke she lifted her head as though she drank something; the strange beast in her bosom began to purr…

"I felt that you were more lonely than anybody else in the world," he went on, "and yet, perhaps, that you were the only person in the world who was really, truly alive. Born out of your time," he murmured, stroking the glove, "fated."

Ah, God! What had she done! How had she dared to throw away

her happiness like this. This was the only man who had ever understood her. Was it too late? Could it be too late? *She* was that glove that he held in his fingers…

"And then the fact that you had no friends and never had made friends with people. How I understood that, for neither had I. Is it just the same now?"

"Yes," she breathed. "Just the same. I am as alone as ever."

"So am I," he laughed gently, "just the same."

Suddenly with a quick gesture he handed her back the glove and scraped his chair on the floor, "But what seemed to me so mysterious then is perfectly plain to me now. And to you, too, of course… It simply was that we were such egoists, so self-engrossed, so wrapped up in ourselves that we hadn't a corner in our hearts for anybody else. Do you know," he cried, naive and hearty, and dreadfully like another side of that old self again, "I began studying a Mind System when I was in Russia, and I found that we were not peculiar at all. It's quite a well known form of…"

She had gone. He sat there, thunder-struck, astounded beyond words… And then he asked the waitress for his bill.

"But the cream has not been touched," he said. "Please do not charge me for it."

88

Revelations

Katherine Mansfield

From eight o'clock in the morning until about half-past eleven Monica Tyrell suffered from her nerves, and suffered so terribly that these hours were—agonizing, simply. It was not as though she could control them. "Perhaps if I were ten years younger…" she would say. For now that she was thirty-three she had queer little way of referring to her age on all occasions, of looking at her friends with grave, childish eyes and saying: "Yes, I remember how twenty years ago…" or of drawing Ralph's attention to the girls—real girls—with lovely youthful arms and throats and swift hesitating movements who sat near them in restaurants. "Perhaps if I were ten years younger…"

"Why don't you get Marie to sit outside your door and absolutely forbid anybody to come near your room until you ring your bell?"

"Oh, if it were as simple as that!" She threw her little gloves down and pressed her eyelids with her fingers in the way he knew so well. "But in the first place I'd be so conscious of Marie sitting there, Marie shaking her finger at Rudd and Mrs. Moon, Marie as a kind of cross between a wardress and a nurse for mental cases! And then, there's the post. One can't get over the fact that the post comes, and once it has come, who—who—could wait until eleven for the letters?"

His eyes grew bright; he quickly, lightly clasped her. "*My* letters, darling?"

"Perhaps," she drawled, softly, and she drew her hand over his reddish hair, smiling too, but thinking: "Heavens! What a stupid thing to say!"

But this morning she had been awakened by one great slam of the front door. Bang. The flat shook. What was it? She jerked up in bed, clutching the eiderdown; her heart beat. What could it be? Then she heard voices in the passage. Marie knocked, and, as the door opened, with a sharp tearing rip out flew the blind and the curtains, stiffening, flapping, jerking. The tassel of the blind knocked—knocked against the window. "Eh-h, *voilà!*" cried Marie, setting down the tray and running. "*C'est le vent, Madame. C'est un vent insupportable.*"

Up rolled the blind; the window went up with a jerk; a whitey-greyish light filled the room. Monica caught a glimpse of a huge pale sky and a cloud like a torn shirt dragging across before she hid her eyes with her sleeve.

"Marie! the curtains! Quick, the curtains!" Monica fell back into the bed and then "Ring-ting-a-ping-ping, ring-ting-a-ping-ping." It was the telephone. The limit of her suffering was reached; she grew quite calm. "Go and see, Marie."

"It is Monsieur. To know if Madame will lunch at Princes' at one-thirty to-day." Yes, it was Monsieur himself. Yes, he had asked that the message be given to Madame immediately. Instead of replying, Monica put her cup down and asked Marie in a small wondering voice what time it was. It was half-past nine. She lay still and half closed her eyes. "Tell Monsieur I cannot come," she said gently. But as the door shut, anger—anger suddenly gripped her close, close, violent, half strangling her. How dared he? How dared Ralph do such a thing when he knew how agonizing her nerves were in the morning! Hadn't she explained and described and even—though lightly, of course; she couldn't say such a thing directly—given him to understand that this was the one unforgivable thing.

And then to choose this frightful windy morning. Did he think it was just a fad of hers, a little feminine folly to be laughed at and tossed aside? Why, only last night she had said: "Ah, but you must take me seriously, too." And he had replied: "My darling, you'll not believe me, but I know you infinitely better than you know yourself. Every delicate thought and feeling I bow to, I treasure. Yes, laugh! I love the way your lip lifts"—and he had leaned across the table—"I don't care who sees that I adore all of you. I'd be with you on mountain-top and have all the searchlights of the world play upon us."

"Heavens!" Monica almost clutched her head. Was it possible he had really said that? How incredible men were! And she had loved him—how could she have loved a man who talked like that. What had she been doing ever since that dinner party months ago, when he had seen her home and asked if he might come and "see again that slow Arabian smile"? Oh, what nonsense—what utter nonsense—and yet she remembered at the time a strange deep thrill unlike anything she had ever felt before.

"Coal! Coal! Coal! Old iron! Old iron! Old iron!" sounded from below. It was all over. Understand her? He had understood nothing. That ringing her up on a windy morning was immensely significant. Would he understand that? She could almost have laughed. "You rang me up when the person who understood me simply couldn't have." It was the end. And when Marie said: "Monsieur replied he would be in the vestibule in case Madame changed her mind," Monica said: "No, not verbena, Marie. Carnations. Two handfuls."

A wild white morning, a tearing, rocking wind. Monica sat down before the mirror. She was pale. The maid combed back her dark hair—combed it all back—and her face was like a mask, with pointed eyelids and dark red lips. As she stared at herself in the blueish shadowy glass she suddenly felt—oh, the strangest, most tremendous excitement filling her slowly, slowly, until she wanted to fling out her arms, to laugh, to scatter everything, to shock Marie, to cry: "I'm free. I'm free. I'm free as the wind." And now all this vibrating, trembling, exciting, flying world was hers. It was her kingdom. No, no, she belonged to nobody but Life.

"That will do, Marie," she stammered. "My hat, my coat, my bag. And now get me a taxi." Where was she going? Oh, anywhere. She could not stand this silent flat, noiseless Marie, this ghostly, quiet, feminine interior. She must be out; she must be driving quickly—anywhere, anywhere.

"The taxi is there, Madame." As she pressed open the big outer doors of the flats the wild wind caught her and floated her across the pavement. Where to? She got in, and smiling radiantly at the cross, cold-looking driver, she told him to take her to her hairdresser's. What would she have done without her hairdresser? Whenever Monica had nowhere else to go to or nothing on earth to do she drove there. She might just have her hair waved, and by that time she'd have thought out a plan. The cross, cold driver drove at a tremendous pace, and she let herself be hurled from side to side. She wished he would go faster and faster. Oh, to be free of Princes' at one-thirty, of being the tiny kitten in the swansdown basket, of being the Arabian, and the grave, delighted child and the little wild creature… "Never again," she cried aloud, clenching her small fist. But the cab had stopped, and the driver was standing holding the door open for her.

The hairdresser's shop was warm and glittering. It smelled of soap and burnt paper and wallflower brilliantine. There was Madame behind the counter, round, fat, white, her head like a powder-puff rolling on a black satin pin-cushion. Monica always had the feeling that they loved her in this shop and understood her—the real her—far better than many of her friends did. She was her real self here, and she and Madame had often talked—quite strangely—together. Then there was George who did her hair, young, dark, slender George. She was really fond of him.

But to-day—how curious! Madame hardly greeted her. Her face was whiter than ever, but rims of bright red showed round her blue bead eyes, and even the rings on her pudgy fingers did not flash. They were cold, dead, like chips of glass. When she called through the wall-telephone to George there was a note in her voice that had never been there before. But Monica would not believe this. No, she refused to. It was just her imagination. She sniffed greedily the warm, scented air, and passed behind the velvet curtain into the small cubicle.

Her hat and jacket were off and hanging from the peg, and still George did not come. This was the first time he had ever not been there to hold the chair for her, to take her hat and hang up her bag, dangling it in his fingers as though it were something he'd never seen before—something fairy. And how quiet the shop was! There was not a sound even from Madame. Only the wind blew, shaking the old house; the wind hooted, and the portraits of Ladies of the Pompadour Period looked down and smiled, cunning and sly. Monica wished she hadn't come. Oh, what a mistake to have come! Fatal. Fatal. Where was George? If he didn't appear the next moment she would go away. She took off the white kimono. She didn't want to look at herself any more. When she opened a big pot of cream on the glass shelf her fingers trembled. There was a tugging feeling at her heart as though her happiness—her marvellous happiness—were trying to get free.

"I'll go. I'll not stay." She took down her hat. But just at that moment steps sounded, and, looking in the mirror, she saw George bowing in the doorway. How queerly he smiled! It was the mirror of course. She turned round quickly. His lips curled back in a sort of grin, and—wasn't he unshaved?—he looked almost green in the face.

"Very sorry to have kept you waiting," he mumbled, sliding, gliding forward.

Oh, no, she wasn't going to stay. "I'm afraid," she began. But he had lighted the gas and laid the tongs across, and was holding out the kimono.

"It's a wind," he said. Monica submitted. She smelled his fresh young fingers pinning the jacket under her chin. "Yes, there is a wind," said she, sinking back into the chair. And silence fell. George took out the pins in his expert way. Her hair tumbled back, but he didn't hold it as he usually did, as though to feel how fine and soft and heavy it was. He didn't say it "was in a lovely condition." He let it fall, and, taking a brush out of a drawer, he coughed faintly, cleared his throat and said dully: "Yes, it's a pretty strong one, I should say it was."

She had no reply to make. The brush fell on her hair. Oh, oh, how mournful, how mournful! It fell quick and light, it fell like leaves; and then it fell heavy, tugging like the tugging at her heart. "That's enough," she cried, shaking herself free.

"Did I do it too much?" asked George. He crouched over the tongs. "I'm sorry." There came the smell of burnt paper—the smell she loved—and he swung the hot tongs round in his hand, staring before him. "I shouldn't be surprised if it rained." He took up a piece of her hair, when—she couldn't bear it any longer—she stopped him. She looked at him; she saw herself looking at him in the white kimono like a nun. "Is there something the matter here? Has something happened?" But George gave a half shrug and a grimace. "Oh, no, Madame. Just a little occurrence." And he took up the piece of hair again. But, oh, she wasn't deceived. That was it. Something awful had happened. The silence—really, the silence seemed to come drifting down like flakes of snow. She shivered. It was cold in the little cubicle, all cold and glittering. The nickel taps and jets and sprays looked somehow almost malignant. The wind rattled the window-frame; a piece of iron banged, and the young man went on changing the tongs, crouching over her. Oh, how terrifying Life was, thought Monica. How dreadful. It is the loneliness which is so appalling. We whirl along like leaves, and nobody knows—nobody cares where we fall, in what black river we float away. The tugging feeling seemed to rise into her throat. It ached, ached; she longed to cry. "That will do," she whispered. "Give me the pins." As he stood beside her, so submissive, so silent, she nearly dropped her arms and sobbed. She couldn't bear any more. Like a wooden man the gay young George still slid, glided, handed her her hat and veil, took the note, and brought back the change. She stuffed it into her bag. Where was she going now?

George took a brush. "There is a little powder on your coat," he murmured. He brushed it away. And then suddenly he raised himself and, looking at Monica, gave a strange wave with the brush and said: "The truth is, Madame, since you are an old customer—my little daughter died this morning. A first child"—and then his white face crumpled like paper, and he turned his back on her and began brushing the cotton kimono. "Oh, oh," Monica began to cry. She ran out of the shop into the taxi. The driver, looking furious, swung off the seat and slammed the door again. "Where to?"

"Princes'," she sobbed. And all the way there she saw nothing but a tiny wax doll with a feather of gold hair, lying meek, its tiny hands and feet crossed. And then just before she came to Princes' she saw a flower shop full of white flowers. Oh, what a perfect thought. Lilies-of-the-valley, and white pansies, double white violets and white velvet ribbon... From an unknown friend... From one who understands... For a Little Girl... She tapped against the window, but the driver did not hear; and, anyway, they were at Princes' already.

89

The Escape

Katherine Mansfield

It was his fault, wholly and solely his fault, that they had missed the train. What if the idiotic hotel people had refused to produce the bill? Wasn't that simply because he hadn't impressed upon the waiter at lunch that they must have it by two o'clock? Any other man would have sat there and refused to move until they handed it over. But no! His exquisite belief in human nature had allowed him to get up and expect one of those idiots to bring it to their room… And then, when the *voiture* did arrive, while they were still (Oh, Heavens!) waiting for change, why hadn't he seen to the arrangement of the boxes so that they could, at least, have started the moment the money had come? Had he expected her to go outside, to stand under the awning in the heat and point with her parasol? Very amusing picture of English domestic life. Even when the driver had been told how fast he had to drive he had paid no attention whatsoever—just smiled. "Oh," she groaned, "if she'd been a driver she couldn't have stopped smiling herself at the absurd, ridiculous way he was urged to hurry." And she sat back and imitated his voice: "*Allez, vite, vite*"—and begged the driver's pardon for troubling him…

And then the station—unforgettable—with the sight of the jaunty little train shuffling away and those hideous children waving from the windows. "Oh, why am I made to bear these things? Why am I exposed to them?…" The glare, the flies, while they waited, and he and the stationmaster put their heads together over the time-table, trying to find this other train, which, of course, they wouldn't catch. The people who'd gathered round, and the woman who'd held up that baby with that awful, awful head… "Oh, to care as I care—to feel as I feel, and never to be saved anything—never to know for one moment what it was to…to…"

Her voice had changed. It was shaking now—crying now. She

fumbled with her bag, and produced from its little maw a scented handkerchief. She put up her veil and, as though she were doing it for somebody else, pitifully, as though she were saying to somebody else: "I know, my darling," she pressed the handkerchief to her eyes.

The little bag, with its shiny, silvery jaws open, lay on her lap. He could see her powder-puff, her rouge stick, a bundle of letters, a phial of tiny black pills like seeds, a broken cigarette, a mirror, white ivory tablets with lists on them that had been heavily scored through. He thought: "In Egypt she would be buried with those things."

They had left the last of the houses, those small straggling houses with bits of broken pot flung among the flower-beds and half-naked hens scratching round the doorsteps. Now they were mounting a long steep road that wound round the hill and over into the next bay. The horses stumbled, pulling hard. Every five minutes, every two minutes the driver trailed the whip across them. His stout back was solid as wood; there were boils on his reddish neck, and he wore a new, a shining new straw hat…

There was a little wind, just enough wind to blow to satin the new leaves on the fruit trees, to stroke the fine grass, to turn to silver the smoky olives—just enough wind to start in front of the carriage a whirling, twirling snatch of dust that settled on their clothes like the finest ash. When she took out her powder-puff the powder came flying over them both.

"Oh, the dust," she breathed, "the disgusting, revolting dust." And she put down her veil and lay back as if overcome.

"Why don't you put up your parasol?" he suggested. It was on the front seat, and he leaned forward to hand it to her. At that she suddenly sat upright and blazed again.

"Please leave my parasol alone! I don't want my parasol! And anyone who was not utterly insensitive would know that I'm far, far too exhausted to hold up a parasol. And with a wind like this tugging at it… Put it down at once," she flashed, and then snatched the parasol from him, tossed it into the crumpled hood behind, and subsided, panting.

Another bend of the road, and down the hill there came a troop of little children, shrieking and giggling, little girls with sun-bleached hair, little boys in faded soldiers' caps. In their hands they carried flowers—any kind of flowers—grabbed by the head, and these they offered, running beside the carriage. Lilac, faded lilac, greeny-white snowballs, one arum lily, a handful of hyacinths. They thrust the flowers and their impish faces into the carriage; one even threw into her lap a bunch of marigolds. Poor little mice! He had his hand in his trouser pocket before her. "For Heaven's sake don't give them anything. Oh, how typical of you! Horrid little monkeys! Now they'll follow us all the way. Don't encourage them; you *would* encourage beggars"; and she hurled the bunch out of the carriage with, "Well, do it when I'm not there, please."

He saw the queer shock on the children's faces. They stopped running, lagged behind, and then they began to shout something, and went on shouting until the carriage had rounded yet another bend.

"Oh, how many more are there before the top of the hill is reached? The horses haven't trotted once. Surely it isn't necessary for them to walk the whole way."

"We shall be there in a minute now," he said, and took out his cigarette-case. At that she turned round towards him. She clasped her hands and held them against her breast; her dark eyes looked immense, imploring, behind her veil; her nostrils quivered, she bit her lip, and her head shook with a little nervous spasm. But when she spoke, her voice was quite weak and very, very calm.

"I want to ask you something. I want to beg something of you," she said. "I've asked you hundreds and hundreds of times before, but you've forgotten. It's such a little thing, but if you knew what it meant to me… " She pressed her hands together. "But you can't know. No human creature could know and be so cruel." And then, slowly, deliberately, gazing at him with those huge, sombre eyes: "I beg and implore you for the last time that when we are driving together you won't smoke. If you could imagine," she said, "the anguish I suffer when that smoke comes floating across my face… "

"Very well," he said. "I won't. I forgot." And he put the case back.

"Oh, no," said she, and almost began to laugh, and put the back of her hand across her eyes. "You couldn't have forgotten. Not that."

The wind came, blowing stronger. They were at the top of the hill. "Hoy-yip-yip-yip," cried the driver. They swung down the road that fell into a small valley, skirted the sea coast at the bottom of it, and then coiled over a gentle ridge on the other side. Now there were houses again, blue-shuttered against the heat, with bright burning gardens, with geranium carpets flung over the pinkish walls. The coast-line was dark; on the edge of the sea a white silky fringe just stirred. The carriage swung down the hill, bumped, shook. "Yi-ip," shouted the driver. She clutched the sides of the seat, she closed her eyes, and he knew she felt this was happening on purpose; this swinging and bumping, this was all done—and he was responsible for it, somehow—to spite her because she had asked if they couldn't go a little faster. But just as they reached the bottom of the valley there was one tremendous lurch. The carriage nearly overturned, and he saw her eyes blaze at him, and she positively hissed, "I suppose you are enjoying this?"

They went on. They reached the bottom of the valley. Suddenly she stood up. "*Cocher! Cocher! Arrêtez-vous!*" She turned round and looked into the crumpled hood behind. "I knew it," she exclaimed. "I knew it. I heard it fall, and so did you, at that last bump."

"What? Where?"

"My parasol. It's gone. The parasol that belonged to my mother. The parasol that I prize more than—more than…" She was simply beside herself. The driver turned round, his gay, broad face smiling.

"I, too, heard something," said he, simply and gaily. "But I thought as Monsieur and Madame said nothing…"

"There. You hear that. Then you must have heard it too. So *that* accounts for the extraordinary smile on your face…"

"Look here," he said, "it can't be gone. If it fell out it will be there still. Stay where you are. I'll fetch it."

But she saw through that. Oh, how she saw through it! "No, thank you." And she bent her spiteful, smiling eyes upon him, regardless of the driver. "I'll go myself. I'll walk back and find it, and trust you not to follow. For"—knowing the driver did not understand, she spoke softly, gently—"if I don't escape from you for a minute I shall go mad."

She stepped out of the carriage. "My bag." He handed it to her.

"Madame prefers…"

But the driver had already swung down from his seat, and was seated on the parapet reading a small newspaper. The horses stood with hanging heads. It was still. The man in the carriage stretched himself out, folded his arms. He felt the sun beat on his knees. His head was sunk on his breast. "Hish, hish," sounded from the sea. The wind sighed in the valley and was quiet. He felt himself, lying there, a hollow man, a parched, withered man, as it were, of ashes. And the sea sounded, "Hish, hish."

It was then that he saw the tree, that he was conscious of its presence just inside a garden gate. It was an immense tree with a round, thick silver stem and a great arc of copper leaves that gave back the light and yet were sombre. There was something beyond the tree—a whiteness, a softness, an opaque mass, half-hidden—with delicate pillars. As he looked at the tree he felt his breathing die away and he became part of the silence. It seemed to grow, it seemed to expand in the quivering heat until the great carved leaves hid the sky, and yet it was motionless. Then from within its depths or from beyond there came the sound of a woman's voice. A woman was singing. The warm untroubled voice floated upon the air, and it was all part of the silence as he was part of it. Suddenly, as the voice rose, soft, dreaming, gentle, he knew that it would come floating to him from the hidden leaves and his peace was shattered. What was happening to him? Something stirred in his breast. Something dark, something unbearable and dreadful pushed in his bosom, and like a great weed it floated, rocked…it was warm, stifling. He tried to struggle to tear at it, and at the same moment—all was over. Deep, deep, he sank into the silence, staring at the tree and waiting for the voice that came floating, falling, until he felt himself enfolded.

In the shaking corridor of the train. It was night. The train rushed and roared through the dark. He held on with both hands to the brass rail. The door of their carriage was open.

"Do not disturb yourself, Monsieur. He will come in and sit down when he wants to. He likes—he likes—it is his habit… *Oui, Madame, je suis un peu souffrante… Mes nerfs.* Oh, but my husband is never so happy as when he is travelling. He likes roughing it… My husband… My husband… "

The voices murmured, murmured. They were never still. But so great was his heavenly happiness as he stood there he wished he might live for ever.

90

A Nose for the King

John London

In the morning calm of Korea, when its peace and tranquility truly merited its ancient name, "Cho-sen," there lived a politician by name Yi Chin Ho. He was a man of parts, and—who shall say?—perhaps in no wise worse than politicians the world over. But, unlike his brethren in other lands, Yi Chin Ho was in jail. Not that he had inadvertently diverted to himself public moneys, but that he had inadvertently diverted too much. Excess is to be deplored in all things, even in grafting, and Yi Chin Ho's excess had brought him to most deplorable straits.

Ten thousand strings of cash he owed the government, and he lay in prison under sentence of death. There was one advantage to the situation—he had plenty of time in which to think. And he thought well. Then called he the jailer to him.

"Most worthy man, you see before you one most wretched," he began. "Yet all will be well with me if you will but let me go free for one short hour this night. And all will be well with you, for I shall see to your advancement through the years, and you shall come at length to the directorship of all the prisons of Cho-sen."

"How now?" demanded the jailer. "What foolishness is this? One short hour, and you but waiting for your head to be chopped off! And I, with an aged and much-to-be-respected mother, not to say anything of a wife and several children of tender years! Out upon you for the scoundrel that you are!"

"From the Sacred City to the ends of all the Eight Coasts there is no place for me to hide," Yi Chin Ho made reply. "I am a man of wisdom, but of what worth my wisdom here in prison? Were I free, well I know I could seek out and obtain the money wherewith to repay the government. I know of a nose that will save me from all my difficulties."

"A nose!" cried the jailer.

"A nose," said Yi Chin Ho. "A remarkable nose, if I may say so, a most remarkable nose."

The jailer threw up his hands despairingly. "Ah, what a wag you are, what a wag," he laughed. "To think that that very admirable wit of yours must go the way of the chopping-block!"

And so saying, he turned and went away. But in the end, being a man soft of head and heart, when the night was well along he permitted Yi Chin Ho to go.

Straight he went to the Governor, catching him alone and arousing him from his sleep.

"Yi Chin Ho, or I'm no Governor!" cried the Governor. "What do you here who should be in prison waiting on the chopping-block!"

"I pray your excellency to listen to me," said Yi Chin Ho, squatting on his hams by the bedside and lighting his pipe from the fire-box. "A dead man is without value. It is true, I am as a dead man, without value to the government, to your excellency, or to myself. But if, so to say, your excellency were to give me my freedom—"

"Impossible!" cried the Governor. "Besides, you are condemned to death."

"Your excellency well knows that if I can repay the ten thousand strings of cash, the government will pardon me," Yi Chin Ho went on. "So, as I say, if your excellency were to give me my freedom for a few days, being a man of understanding, I should then repay the government and be in position to be of service to your excellency. I should be in position to be of very great service to your excellency."

"Have you a plan whereby you hope to obtain this money?" asked the Governor.

"I have," said Yi Chin Ho.

"Then come with it to me to-morrow night; I would now sleep," said the Governor, taking up his snore where it had been interrupted.

On the following night, having again obtained leave of absence from the jailer, Yi Chin Ho presented himself at the Governor's bedside.

"Is it you, Yi Chin Ho?" asked the Governor. "And have you the plan?"

"It is I, your excellency," answered Yi Chin Ho, "and the plan is here."

"Speak," commanded the Governor.

"The plan is here," repeated Yi Chin Ho, "here in my hand."

The Governor sat up and opened his eyes, Yi Chin Ho proffered in his hand a sheet of paper. The Governor held it to the light.

"Nothing but a nose," said he.

"A bit pinched, so, and so, your excellency," said Yi Chin Ho.

"Yes, a bit pinched here and there, as you say," said the Governor.

"Withal it is an exceeding corpulent nose, thus, and so, all in one place, at the end," proceeded Yi Chin Ho. "Your excellency would seek far and wide and many a day for that nose and find it not."

"An unusual nose," admitted the Governor.

"There is a wart upon it," said Yi Chin Ho.

"A most unusual nose," said the Governor. "Never have I seen the like. But what do you with this nose, Yi Chin Ho!"

"I seek it whereby to repay the money to the government," said Yi Chin Ho. "I seek it to be of service to your excellency, and I seek it to save my own worthless head. Further, I seek your excellency's seal upon this picture of the nose."

And the Governor laughed and affixed the seal of state, and Yi Chin Ho departed. For a month and a day he traveled the King's Road which leads to the shore of the Eastern Sea; and there, one night, at the gate of the largest mansion of a wealthy city he knocked loudly for admittance.

"None other than the master of the house will I see," said he fiercely to the frightened servants. "I travel upon the King's business."

Straightway was he led to an inner room, where the master of the house was roused from his sleep and brought blinking before him.

"You are Pak Chung Chang, head man of this city," said Yi Chin Ho in tones that were all-accusing. "I am upon the King's business."

Pak Chung Chang trembled. Well he knew the King's business was ever a terrible business. His knees smote together, and he near fell to the floor.

"The hour is late," he quavered. "Were it not well to——"

"The King's business never waits!" thundered Yi Chin Ho. "Come apart with me, and swiftly. I have an affair of moment to discuss with you.

"It is the King's affair," he added with even greater fierceness; so that Pak Chung Chang's silver pipe dropped from his nerveless fingers and clattered on the floor.

"Know then," said Yi Chin Ho, when they had gone apart, "that the King is troubled with an affliction, a very terrible affliction. In that he failed to cure, the Court physician has had nothing else than his head chopped off. From all the Eight Provinces have the physicians come to wait upon the King. Wise consultation have they held, and they have decided that for a remedy for the King's affliction nothing else is required than a nose, a certain kind of nose, a very peculiar certain kind of nose.

"Then by none other was I summoned than his excellency the prime minister himself. He put a paper into my hand. Upon this paper was the very peculiar kind of nose drawn by the physicians of the Eight Provinces, with the seal of state upon it.

"'Go,' said his excellency the prime minister. 'Seek out this nose, for the King's affliction is sore. And wheresoever you find this nose upon the face of a man, strike it off forthright and bring it in all haste to the Court, for the King must be cured. Go, and come not back until your search is rewarded.'

"And so I departed upon my quest," said Yi Chin Ho. "I have sought out the remotest corners of the kingdom; I have traveled the Eight Highways, searched the Eight Provinces, and sailed the seas of the Eight Coasts. And here I am."

With a great flourish he drew a paper from his girdle, unrolled it with many snappings and cracklings, and thrust it before the face of Pak Chung Chang. Upon the paper was the picture of the nose.

Pak Chung Chang stared upon it with bulging eyes.

"Never have I beheld such a nose," he began.

"There is a wart upon it," said Yi Chin Ho.

"Never have I beheld——" Pak Chung Chang began again.

"Bring your father before me," Yi Chin Ho interrupted sternly.

"My ancient and very-much-to-be-respected ancestor sleeps," said Pak Chung Chang.

"Why dissemble?" demanded Yi Chin Ho. "You know it is your father's nose. Bring him before me that I may strike it off and be gone. Hurry, lest I make bad report of you."

"Mercy!" cried Pak Chung Chang, falling on his knees. "It is impossible! It is impossible! You cannot strike off my father's nose. He cannot go down without his nose to the grave. He will become a laughter and a byword, and all my days and nights will be filled with woe. O reflect! Report that you have seen no such nose in your travels. You, too, have a father."

Pak Chung Chang clasped Yi Chin Ho's knees and fell to weeping on his sandals.

"My heart softens strangely at your tears," said Yi Chin Ho. "I, too, know filial piety and regard. But—" He hesitated, then added, as though thinking aloud, "It is as much as my head is worth."

"How much is your head worth?" asked Pak Chung Chang in a thin, small voice.

"A not remarkable head," said Yi Chin Ho. "An absurdly unremarkable head! but, such is my great foolishness, I value it at nothing less than one hundred thousand strings of cash."

"So be it," said Pak Chung Chang, rising to his feet.

"I shall need horses to carry the treasure," said Yi Chin Ho, "and men to guard it well as I journey through the mountains. There are robbers abroad in the land."

"There are robbers abroad in the land," said Pak Chung Chang, sadly. "But it shall be as you wish, so long as my ancient and very-much-to-be-respected ancestor's nose abide in its appointed place."

"Say nothing to any man of this occurrence," said Yi Chin Ho, "else will other and more loyal servants than I be sent to strike off your father's nose."

And so Yi Chin Ho departed on his way through the mountains, blithe of heart and gay of song as he listened to the jingling bells of his treasure-laden ponies.

There is little more to tell. Yi Chin Ho prospered through the years. By his efforts the jailer attained at length to the directorship of all the prisons of Cho-sen; the Governor ultimately betook himself to the Sacred City to be prime minister to the King, while Yi Chin Ho became the King's boon companion and sat at table with him to the end of a round, fat life. But Pak Chung Chang fell into a melancholy, and ever after he shook his head sadly, with tears in his eyes, whenever he regarded the expensive nose of his ancient and very-much-to-be-respected ancestor.

91

The Young Girl

Katherine Mansfield

In her blue dress, with her cheeks lightly flushed, her blue, blue eyes, and her gold curls pinned up as though for the first time—pinned up to be out of the way for her flight—Mrs. Raddick's daughter might have just dropped from this radiant heaven. Mrs. Raddick's timid, faintly astonished, but deeply admiring glance looked as if she believed it, too; but the daughter didn't appear any too pleased—why should she?—to have alighted on the steps of the Casino. Indeed, she was bored—bored as though Heaven had been full of casinos with snuffy old saints for *croupiers* and crowns to play with.

"You don't mind taking Hennie?" said Mrs. Raddick. "Sure you don't? There's the car, and you'll have tea and we'll be back here on this step—right here—in an hour. You see, I want her to go in. She's not been before, and it's worth seeing. I feel it wouldn't be fair to her."

"Oh, shut up, mother," said she wearily. "Come along. Don't talk so much. And your bag's open; you'll be losing all your money again."

"I'm sorry, darling," said Mrs. Raddick.

"Oh, *do* come in! I want to make money," said the impatient voice. "It's all jolly well for you—but I'm broke!"

"Here—take fifty francs, darling, take a hundred!" I saw Mrs. Raddick pressing notes into her hand as they passed through the swing doors.

Hennie and I stood on the steps a minute, watching the people. He had a very broad, delighted smile.

"I say," he cried, "there's an English bulldog. Are they allowed to take dogs in there?"

"No, they're not."

"He's a ripping chap, isn't he? I wish I had one. They're such fun. They frighten people so, and they're never fierce with their—the people they belong to." Suddenly he squeezed my arm. "I say, *do* look at that old woman. Who is she? Why does she look like that? Is she a gambler?"

The ancient, withered creature, wearing a green satin dress, a black velvet cloak and a white hat with purple feathers, jerked slowly, slowly up the steps as though she were being drawn up on wires. She stared in front of her, she was laughing and nodding and cackling to herself; her claws clutched round what looked like a dirty boot-bag.

But just at that moment there was Mrs. Raddick again with—*her*—and another lady hovering in the background. Mrs. Raddick rushed at me. She was brightly flushed, gay, a different creature. She was like a woman who is saying "good-bye" to her friends on the station platform, with not a minute to spare before the train starts.

"Oh, you're here, still. Isn't that lucky! You've not gone. Isn't that fine! I've had the most dreadful time with—her," and she waved to her daughter, who stood absolutely still, disdainful, looking down, twiddling her foot on the step, miles away. "They won't let her in. I swore she was twenty-one. But they won't believe me. I showed the man my purse; I didn't dare to do more. But it was no use. He simply scoffed.... And now I've just met Mrs. MacEwen from New York, and she just won thirteen thousand in the *Salle Privée*—and she wants me to go back with her while the luck lasts. Of course I can't leave—her. But if you'd—"

At that "she" looked up; she simply withered her mother. "Why can't you leave me?" she said furiously. "What utter rot! How dare you make a scene like this? This is the last time I'll come out with you. You really are too awful for words." She looked her mother up and down. "Calm yourself," she said superbly.

Mrs. Raddick was desperate, just desperate. She was "wild" to go back with Mrs. MacEwen, but at the same time....

I seized my courage. "Would you—do you care to come to tea with—us?"

"Yes, yes, she'll be delighted. That's just what I wanted, isn't it, darling? Mrs. MacEwen... I'll be back here in an hour... or less... I'll—"

Mrs. R. dashed up the steps. I saw her bag was open again.

So we three were left. But really it wasn't my fault. Hennie looked crushed to the earth, too. When the car was there she wrapped her dark coat round her—to escape contamination. Even her little feet looked as though they scorned to carry her down the steps to us.

"I am so awfully sorry," I murmured as the car started.

"Oh, I don't *mind*," said she. "I don't *want* to look twenty-one. Who would—if they were seventeen! It's"—and she gave a faint shudder—"the stupidity I loathe, and being stared at by old fat men. Beasts!"

Hennie gave her a quick look and then peered out of the window.

We drew up before an immense palace of pink-and-white marble with orange-trees outside the doors in gold-and-black tubs.

"Would you care to go in?" I suggested.

She hesitated, glanced, bit her lip, and resigned herself. "Oh well, there seems nowhere else," said she. "Get out, Hennie."

I went first—to find the table, of course—she followed. But the worst of it was having her little brother, who was only twelve, with us. That was the last, final straw—having that child, trailing at her heels.

There was one table. It had pink carnations and pink plates with little blue tea-napkins for sails.

"Shall we sit here?"

She put her hand wearily on the back of a white wicker chair.

"We may as well. Why not?" said she.

Hennie squeezed past her and wriggled on to a stool at the end. He felt awfully out of it. She didn't even take her gloves off. She lowered her eyes and drummed on the table. When a faint violin sounded she winced and bit her lip again. Silence.

The waitress appeared. I hardly dared to ask her. "Tea—coffee? China tea—or iced tea with lemon?"

Really she didn't mind. It was all the same to her. She didn't really want anything. Hennie whispered, "Chocolate!"

But just as the waitress turned away she cried out carelessly, "Oh, you may as well bring me a chocolate, too."

While we waited she took out a little, gold powder-box with a mirror in the lid, shook the poor little puff as though she loathed it, and dabbed her lovely nose.

"Hennie," she said, "take those flowers away." She pointed with her puff to the carnations, and I heard her murmur, "I can't bear flowers on a table." They had evidently been giving her intense pain, for she positively closed her eyes as I moved them away.

The waitress came back with the chocolate and the tea. She put the big, frothing cups before them and pushed across my clear glass. Hennie buried his nose, emerged, with, for one dreadful moment, a little trembling blob of cream on the tip. But he hastily wiped it off like a little gentleman. I wondered if I should dare draw her attention to her cup. She didn't notice it—didn't see it—until suddenly, quite by chance, she took a sip. I watched anxiously; she faintly shuddered.

"Dreadfully sweet!" said she.

A tiny boy with a head like a raisin and a chocolate body came round with a tray of pastries—row upon row of little freaks, little inspirations, little melting dreams. He offered them to her. "Oh, I'm not at all hungry. Take them away."

He offered them to Hennie. Hennie gave me a swift look—it must have been satisfactory—for he took a chocolate cream, a coffee éclair, a meringue stuffed with chestnut and a tiny horn filled with fresh strawberries. She could hardly bear to watch him. But just as the boy swerved away she held up her plate.

"Oh well, give me *one*," said she.

The silver tongs dropped one, two, three—and a cherry tartlet. "I don't know why you're giving me all these," she said, and nearly smiled. "I shan't eat them; I couldn't!"

I felt much more comfortable. I sipped my tea, leaned back, and even asked if I might smoke. At that she paused, the fork in her hand, opened her eyes, and really did smile. "Of course," said she. "I always expect people to."

But at that moment a tragedy happened to Hennie. He speared his pastry horn too hard, and it flew in two, and one half spilled on the table. Ghastly affair! He turned crimson. Even his ears flared, and one ashamed hand crept across the table to take what was left of the body away.

"You *utter* little beast!" said she.

Good heavens! I had to fly to the rescue. I cried hastily, "Will you be abroad long?"

But she had already forgotten Hennie. I was forgotten, too. She was trying to remember something.... She was miles away.

"I—don't—know," she said slowly, from that far place.

"I suppose you prefer it to London. It's more—more—"

When I didn't go on she came back and looked at me, very puzzled. "More—?"

"*Enfin*—gayer," I cried, waving my cigarette.

But that took a whole cake to consider. Even then, "Oh well, that depends!" was all she could safely say.

Hennie had finished. He was still very warm.

I seized the butterfly list off the table. "I say—what about an ice, Hennie? What about tangerine and ginger? No, something cooler. What about a fresh pineapple cream?"

Hennie strongly approved. The waitress had her eye on us. The order was taken when she looked up from her crumbs.

"Did you say tangerine and ginger? I like ginger. You can bring me one." And then quickly, "I wish that orchestra wouldn't play things from the year One. We were dancing to that all last Christmas. It's too sickening!"

But it was a charming air. Now that I noticed it, it warmed me.

"I think this is rather a nice place, don't you, Hennie?" I said.

Hennie said: "Ripping!" He meant to say it very low, but it came out very high in a kind of squeak.

Nice? This place? Nice? For the first time she stared about her, trying to see what there was.... She blinked; her lovely eyes wondered. A very good-looking elderly man stared back at her through a monocle on a black ribbon. But him she simply couldn't see. There was a hole in the air where he was. She looked through and through him.

Finally the little flat spoons lay still on the glass plates. Hennie looked rather exhausted, but she pulled on her white gloves again. She had some trouble with her diamond wrist-watch; it got in her way. She tugged at it—tried to break the stupid little thing—it wouldn't break. Finally, she had to drag her glove over. I saw, after that, she couldn't stand this place a moment longer, and, indeed, she jumped up and turned away while I went through the vulgar act of paying for the tea.

And then we were outside again. It had grown dusky. The sky was sprinkled with small stars; the big lamps glowed. While we waited for the car to come up she stood on the step, just as before, twiddling her foot, looking down.

Hennie bounded forward to open the door and she got in and sank back with—oh—such a sigh!

"Tell him," she gasped, "to drive as fast as he can."

Hennie grinned at his friend the chauffeur. "*Allie veet!*" said he. Then he composed himself and sat on the small seat facing us.

The gold powder-box came out again. Again the poor little puff was shaken; again there was that swift, deadly-secret glance between her and the mirror.

We tore through the black-and-gold town like a pair of scissors tearing through brocade. Hennie had great difficulty not to look as though he were hanging on to something.

And when we reached the Casino, of course Mrs. Raddick wasn't there. There wasn't a sign of her on the steps—not a sign.

"Will you stay in the car while I go and look?"

But no—she wouldn't do that. Good heavens, no! Hennie could stay. She couldn't bear sitting in a car. She'd wait on the steps.

"But I scarcely like to leave you," I murmured. "I'd very much rather not leave you here."

At that she threw back her coat; she turned and faced me; her lips parted. "Good heavens—why! I—I don't mind it a bit. I—I like waiting." And suddenly her cheeks crimsoned, her eyes grew dark—for a moment I thought she was going to cry. "L—let me, please," she stammered, in a warm, eager voice. "I like it. I love waiting! Really—really I do! I'm always waiting—in all kinds of places...."

Her dark coat fell open, and her white throat—all her soft young body in the blue dress—was like a flower that is just emerging from its dark bud.

92

An Empty Frame

George Egerton

It was a simple, pretty little frame, such as you may buy at any sale cheaply; its ribbed wood, aspinalled white, with an inner frame of pale-blue plush; its one noticeable feature that it was empty. And yet it stood on the middle of the bedroom mantelboard.

It was not a luxurious room; none of the furniture matched. It was a typical boarding-house bedroom.

Any one preserving the child habit of endowing inanimate objects with human attributes might fancy that the flickering flames of the fire took a pleasure in bringing into relief the bright bits in its dinginess; for they played over the silver-backed brushes and the cut-glass perfume bottles on the dressing-table, flicked the bright beads on the toes of coquettish small shoes and the steel clasps of a travelling bag in the corner, imparting a casual air of comfort such as the touch of certain dainty women lends to a common room.

A woman enters,—a woman wondrously soft and swift in all her movements. She seems to reach a place without your seeing how; no motion of elbow or knee betrays her. Her fingers glide swiftly down the buttons of her gown; in a second she has freed herself from its ensheathing; garment after garment falls from her, until she stands almost free. She gets into nightdress and loose woollen dressing-gown, and slips her naked feet into fur-lined slippers, with a movement that is somehow the expression of an intense nervous relief from a thrall. Everything she does is done so swiftly that you see the result rather than the working out of each action.

She sinks into a chair before the fire, and clasping her hands behind her head, peers into the glowing embers. The firelight, lower than her face, touches it cruelly; picks out and accentuates as remorselessly as a rival woman the autographs past emotions have traced on its surface; deepens the hollows of her delicate thoughtful temples and the double furrow between her clever irregular eyebrows. Her face is more characteristic than beautiful. Nine men would pass it, the tenth sell his immortal soul for it. The chin is strong, the curve of jaw determined; there is a little full place under the chin's sharp point. The eyes tell you little; they are keen and inquiring, and probe others' thoughts rather than reveal their own. The whole face is one of peculiar strength and self-reliance. The mouth is its contradiction; the passionate curve of the upper-lip with its mobile corners, and the tender little under-lip that shelters timidly under it, are encouraging promises against its strength.

The paleness of some strong feeling tinges her face; a slight trembling runs through her frame. Her inner soul-struggle is acting as a strong developing fluid upon a highly sensitized plate; anger, scorn, pity, contempt chase one another like shadows across her face. Her eyes rest upon the empty frame, and the plain white space becomes alive to her. Her mind's eye fills it with a picture it once held in its dainty embrace,—a rare head among the rarest heads of men, with its crest of hair tossed back from the great brow, its proud poise and the impress of grand, confident, compelling genius that reveals itself, one scarce knows how; with the brute possibility of an untamed, natural man lurking about the mouth and powerful throat. She feels the subduing smile of eyes that never failed to make her weak as a child under their gaze, and tame as a hungry bird. She stretches out her hands with a pitiful little movement, and then, remembering, lets them drop, and locks them until the knuckles stand out whitely. She shuts her eyes, and one tear after the other starts from beneath her lids, trickles down her cheeks, and drops with a splash into her lap. She does not sob, only cries quietly; and she sees, as if she held the letter in her hand, the words that decided her fate:—

> "You love me; I know it, you other half of me. You want me to complete your life, as I you, you good, sweet woman; you slight, weak thing, with your strong will and your grand, great heart; you witch, with a soul of clean white fire. I kiss your hands,—such little hands! I never saw the like; slim child-hands, with a touch as cool and as soft as a snow-flake! You dear one, come to me; I want you, now, always. Be with me, work with me, share with me, live with me, my equal as a creature; above

me, as my queen of women! I love you, I worship you; but you know my views. I cannot, I will not bind myself to you by any legal or religious tie. I must be free and unfettered to follow that which I believe right for me. If you come to me in all trust, I can and will give myself to you in all good faith,—yours as much as you will, forever! I will kneel to you; why should I always desire to kneel to you? It is not that I stand in awe of you, or that I ever feel a need to kneel at all; but always to you, and to you alone. Come! I will crouch at your feet and swear myself to you!"

And she had replied "No!" and in her loneliness of spirit married him who seemed to need her most out of those who admired her.

The door opens, and he comes in. He looks inquiringly at her, touches her hair half hesitatingly, and then stands with his hands thrust in his pockets and gnaws his mustache.

"Are you angry, little woman?"

"No," very quietly; "why should I be?"

She closes her eyes again, and after five minutes' silence he begins to undress. He does it very slowly, looking perplexedly at her. When he has finished, he stands with his back to the fire, an unlovely object in sleeping suit.

"Would you like to read her letter?"

She shakes her head.

"I suppose I ought to have sent her back her letters before, you know. She hadn't heard I was married."

"Yes," she interjects, "it would have been better to start with a clean bill; but why talk about it?"

He looks at her awhile, then gets into bed and watches her from behind the pages of the "Field." It seems unusually quiet. His watch that he has left in his waistcoat pocket, thrown across the back of a chair, seems to fill the whole room with a nervous tick.

He tosses the paper on to the floor. She looks up as it falls, rises, turns off the gas-jet, sinks back into her old position, and stares into the fire. He gets up, goes over, and kneels down next her.

"I am awfully sorry you are put out, old girl. I saw you were when I answered you like that; but I couldn't help feeling a bit cut up, you know. She wrote such an awfully nice letter, you know, wished—"

"You all sorts of happiness," with a snap, "and hopes you'll meet in a better world?"

He rises to his feet and stares at her in dumb amazement. How could she know? She smiles with a touch of malicious satisfaction, as she sees the effect of her chance shot.

"It's a pity, isn't it, that you both have to wait so long?"

He imagines he sees light, and blunders ahead like an honest man.

"I wouldn't have sent those things back now if I had thought you cared. By Jove, it never entered my head that you'd be jealous!"

"Jealous?" She is on her feet like a red white flash. "I, jealous of her?" Each word is emphasized. "I couldn't be jealous of her, *Nur die Dummen sind bescheiden*! Why, the girl isn't fit to tie my shoe-strings!"

This is too much; he feels he must protest.

"You don't know her," feebly. "She is an awfully nice girl!"

"Nice girl! I don't doubt it; and she will be an awfully nice woman, and under each and every circumstance of life she will behave like an awfully nice person. Jealous! Do you think I cried because I was jealous? Good God, no! I cried because I was sorry, fearfully sorry, for myself. She"—with a fine thin contempt—"would have suited you better than I. Jealous! no, only sorry. Sorry because any nice average girl of her type, who would model her frocks out of the 'Lady's Pictorial,' gush over that dear Mr. Irving, paint milking-stools, try poker-work, or any other fashionable fad, would have done you just as well. And I"—with a catch of voice—"with a great man might have made a great woman; and now those who know and understand me [bitterly] think of me as a great failure."

She finishes wearily; the fire dies out of eyes and voice. She adds half aloud, as if to herself,—

"I don't think I quite realized this until I saw how you took that letter. I was watching your face as you read it; and the fact that you could put her on the same level, that if it had not been for a mistake she would have suited you as well, made me realize, don't you see? that I would have done some one else better!"

He is looking at her in utter bewilderment, and she smiles as she notes his expression; she touches his cheek gently, and leans her head against his arm.

"There it's all right, boy! Don't mind me. I have a bit of a complex nature; you couldn't understand me if you tried to, and better not try!"

She has slipped, while speaking, her warm bare foot out of her slipper, and is rubbing it gently over his chilled ones.

"You are cold, better go back to bed; I shall go too!"

She stands a moment quietly as he turns to obey, and then takes the frame, and kneeling down puts it gently into the hollowed red heart of the fire. It crackles crisply, and little tongues of flame shoot up; and she gets into bed by their light.

When the fire has burnt out, and he is sleeping like a child with his curly head on her breast, she falls asleep too, and dreams that she is sitting on a fiery globe rolling away into space; that her head is wedged in a huge frame, the top of her head touches its top, the sides its sides, and it keeps growing larger and larger, and her head with it, until she seems to be sitting inside her own head, and the inside is one vast hollow.

93

One Summer Night

Ambrose Bierce

The fact that Henry Armstrong was buried did not seem to him to prove that he was dead: he had always been a hard man to convince. That he really was buried, the testimony of his senses compelled him to admit. His posture—flat upon his back, with his hands crossed upon his stomach and tied with something that he easily broke without profitably altering the situation—the strict confinement of his entire person, the black darkness and profound silence, made a body of evidence impossible to controvert and he accepted it without cavil.

But dead—no; he was only very, very ill. He had, withal, the invalid's apathy and did not greatly concern himself about the uncommon fate that had been allotted to him. No philosopher was he—just a plain, commonplace person gifted, for the time being, with a pathological indifference: the organ that he feared consequences with was torpid. So, with no particular apprehension for his immediate future, he fell asleep and all was peace with Henry Armstrong.

But something was going on overhead. It was a dark summer night, shot through with infrequent shimmers of lightning silently firing a cloud lying low in the west and portending a storm. These brief, stammering illuminations brought out with ghastly distinctness the monuments and headstones of the cemetery and seemed to set them dancing. It was not a night in which any credible witness was likely to be straying about a cemetery, so the three men who were there, digging into the grave of Henry Armstrong, felt reasonably secure.

Two of them were young students from a medical college a few miles away; the third was a gigantic negro known as Jess. For many years Jess had been employed about the cemetery as a man-of-all-work and it was his favorite pleasantry that he knew "every soul in the place." From the nature of what he was now doing it was inferable that the place was not so populous as its register may have shown it to be.

Outside the wall, at the part of the grounds farthest from the public road, were a horse and a light wagon, waiting.

The work of excavation was not difficult: the earth with which the grave had been loosely filled a few hours before offered little resistance and was soon thrown out. Removal of the casket from its box was less easy, but it was taken out, for it was a perquisite of Jess, who carefully unscrewed the cover and laid it aside, exposing the body in black trousers and white shirt. At that instant the air sprang to flame, a cracking shock of thunder shook the stunned world and Henry Armstrong tranquilly sat up. With inarticulate cries the men fled in terror, each in a different direction. For nothing on earth could two of them have been persuaded to return. But Jess was of another breed.

In the gray of the morning the two students, pallid and haggard from anxiety and with the terror of their adventure still beating tumultuously in their blood, met at the medical college.

"You saw it?" cried one.

"God! yes—what are we to do?"

They went around to the rear of the building, where they saw a horse, attached to a light wagon, hitched to a gatepost near the door of the dissecting-room. Mechanically they entered the room. On a bench in the obscurity sat the negro Jess. He rose, grinning, all eyes and teeth.

"I'm waiting for my pay," he said.

Stretched naked on a long table lay the body of Henry Armstrong, the head defiled with blood and clay from a blow with a spade.

94

Monday or Tuesday

Virginia Woolf

Lazy and indifferent, shaking space easily from his wings, knowing his way, the heron passes over the church beneath the sky. White and distant, absorbed in itself, endlessly the sky covers and uncovers, moves and remains. A lake? Blot the shores of it out! A mountain? Oh, perfect—the sun gold on its slopes. Down that falls. Ferns then, or white feathers, for ever and ever——

Desiring truth, awaiting it, laboriously distilling a few words, for ever desiring—(a cry starts to the left, another to the right. Wheels strike divergently. Omnibuses conglomerate in conflict)—for ever desiring—(the clock asseverates with twelve distinct strokes that it is midday; light sheds gold scales; children swarm)—for ever desiring truth. Red is the dome; coins hang on the trees; smoke trails from the chimneys; bark, shout, cry "Iron for sale"—and truth?

Radiating to a point men's feet and women's feet, black or gold-encrusted—(This foggy weather—Sugar? No, thank you—The commonwealth of the future)—the firelight darting and making the room red, save for the black figures and their bright eyes, while outside a van discharges, Miss Thingummy drinks tea at her desk, and plate-glass preserves fur coats——

Flaunted, leaf-light, drifting at corners, blown across the wheels, silver-splashed, home or not home, gathered, scattered, squandered in separate scales, swept up, down, torn, sunk, assembled—and truth?

Now to recollect by the fireside on the white square of marble. From ivory depths words rising shed their blackness, blossom and penetrate. Fallen the book; in the flame, in the smoke, in the momentary sparks—or now voyaging, the marble square pendant, minarets beneath and the Indian seas, while space rushes blue and stars glint—truth? or now, content with closeness?

Lazy and indifferent the heron returns; the sky veils her stars; then bares them.

95

The String Quartet

Virginia Woolf

Well, here we are, and if you cast your eye over the room you will see that Tubes and trams and omnibuses, private carriages not a few, even, I venture to believe, landaus with bays in them, have been busy at it, weaving threads from one end of London to the other. Yet I begin to have my doubts—

If indeed it's true, as they're saying, that Regent Street is up, and the Treaty signed, and the weather not cold for the time of year, and even at that rent not a flat to be had, and the worst of influenza its after effects; if I bethink me of having forgotten to write about the leak in the larder, and left my glove in the train; if the ties of blood require me, leaning forward, to accept cordially the hand which is perhaps offered hesitatingly—

"Seven years since we met!"

"The last time in Venice."

"And where are you living now?"

"Well, the late afternoon suits me the best, though, if it weren't asking too much——"

"But I knew you at once!"

"Still, the war made a break——"

If the mind's shot through by such little arrows, and—for human society compels it—no sooner is one launched than another presses forward; if this engenders heat and in addition they've turned on the electric light; if saying one thing does, in so many cases, leave behind it a need to improve and revise, stirring besides regrets, pleasures, vanities, and desires—if it's all the facts I mean, and the hats, the fur boas, the gentlemen's swallow-tail coats, and pearl tie-pins that come to the surface—what chance is there?

Of what? It becomes every minute more difficult to say why, in spite of everything, I sit here believing I can't now say what, or even remember the last time it happened.

"Did you see the procession?"

"The King looked cold."

"No, no, no. But what was it?"

"She's bought a house at Malmesbury."

"How lucky to find one!"

On the contrary, it seems to me pretty sure that she, whoever she may be, is damned, since it's all a matter of flats and hats and sea gulls, or so it seems to be for a hundred people sitting here well dressed, walled in, furred, replete. Not that I can boast, since I too sit passive on a gilt chair, only turning the earth above a buried memory, as we all do, for there are signs, if I'm not mistaken, that we're all recalling something, furtively seeking something. Why fidget? Why so anxious about the sit of cloaks; and gloves—whether to button or unbutton? Then watch that elderly face against the dark canvas, a moment ago urbane and flushed; now taciturn and sad, as if in shadow. Was it the sound of the second violin tuning in the ante-room? Here they come; four black figures, carrying instruments, and seat themselves facing the white squares under the downpour of light; rest the tips of their bows on the music stand; with a simultaneous movement lift them; lightly poise them, and, looking across at the player opposite, the first violin counts one, two, three——

Flourish, spring, burgeon, burst! The pear tree on the top of the mountain. Fountains jet; drops descend. But the waters of the Rhone flow swift and deep, race under the arches, and sweep the trailing water leaves, washing shadows over the silver fish, the spotted fish rushed down by the swift waters, now swept into an eddy where—it's difficult this—conglomeration of fish all in a pool; leaping, splashing, scraping sharp fins; and such a boil of current that the yellow pebbles are churned round and round, round and round—free now, rushing downwards, or even somehow ascending in exquisite spirals into the air; curled like thin shavings from under a plane; up and up.... How lovely goodness is in those who, stepping lightly, go smiling through the world! Also in jolly old fishwives, squatted under arches, obscene old women, how deeply they laugh and shake and rollick, when they walk, from side to side, hum, hah!

"That's an early Mozart, of course——"

"But the tune, like all his tunes, makes one despair—I mean hope. What do I mean? That's the worst of music! I want to dance, laugh, eat pink cakes, yellow cakes, drink thin, sharp wine. Or an indecent story, now—I could relish that. The older one grows the more one likes indecency. Hah, hah! I'm laughing. What at? You said nothing, nor did the old gentleman opposite.... But suppose—suppose—Hush!"

The melancholy river bears us on. When the moon comes through the trailing willow boughs, I see your face, I hear your voice and the bird singing as we pass the osier bed. What are you whispering? Sorrow, sorrow. Joy, joy. Woven together, like reeds in moonlight. Woven together, inextricably commingled, bound in pain and strewn in sorrow—crash!

The boat sinks. Rising, the figures ascend, but now leaf thin, tapering to a dusky wraith, which, fiery tipped, draws its twofold passion from my heart. For me it sings, unseals my sorrow, thaws compassion, floods with love the sunless world, nor, ceasing, abates its tenderness but deftly, subtly, weaves in and out until in this pattern, this consummation, the cleft ones unify; soar, sob, sink to rest, sorrow and joy.

Why then grieve? Ask what? Remain unsatisfied? I say all's been settled; yes; laid to rest under a coverlet of rose leaves, falling. Falling. Ah, but they cease. One rose leaf, falling from an enormous height, like a little parachute dropped from an invisible balloon, turns, flutters waveringly. It won't reach us.

"No, no. I noticed nothing. That's the worst of music—these silly dreams. The second violin was late, you say?"

"There's old Mrs. Munro, feeling her way out—blinder each year, poor woman—on this slippery floor."

Eyeless old age, grey-headed Sphinx.... There she stands on the pavement, beckoning, so sternly, the red omnibus.

"How lovely! How well they play! How—how—how!"

The tongue is but a clapper. Simplicity itself. The feathers in the hat next me are bright and pleasing as a child's rattle. The leaf on the plane-tree flashes green through the chink in the curtain. Very strange, very exciting.

"How—how—how!" Hush!

These are the lovers on the grass.

"If, madam, you will take my hand——"

"Sir, I would trust you with my heart. Moreover, we have left our bodies in the banqueting hall. Those on the turf are the shadows of our souls."

"Then these are the embraces of our souls." The lemons nod assent. The swan pushes from the bank and floats dreaming into mid stream.

"But to return. He followed me down the corridor, and, as we turned the corner, trod on the lace of my petticoat. What could I do but cry 'Ah!' and stop to finger it? At which he drew his sword, made passes as if he were stabbing something to death, and cried, 'Mad! Mad! Mad!' Whereupon I screamed, and the Prince, who was writing in the large vellum book in the oriel window, came out in his velvet skull-cap and furred slippers, snatched a rapier from the wall—the King of Spain's gift, you know—on which I escaped, flinging on this cloak to hide the ravages to my skirt—to hide.... But listen! the horns!"

The gentleman replies so fast to the lady, and she runs up the scale with such witty exchange of compliment now culminating in a sob of passion, that the words are indistinguishable though the meaning is plain enough—love, laughter, flight, pursuit, celestial bliss—all floated out on the gayest ripple of tender endearment—until the sound of the silver horns, at first far distant, gradually sounds more and more distinctly, as if seneschals were saluting the dawn or proclaiming ominously the escape of the lovers.... The green garden, moonlit pool, lemons, lovers, and fish are all dissolved in the opal sky, across which, as the horns are joined by trumpets and supported by clarions there rise white arches firmly planted on marble pillars.... Tramp and trumpeting. Clang and clangour. Firm establishment. Fast foundations. March of myriads. Confusion and chaos trod to earth. But this city to which we travel has neither stone nor marble; hangs enduring; stands unshakable; nor does a face, nor does a flag greet or welcome. Leave then to perish your hope; droop in the desert my joy; naked advance. Bare are the pillars; auspicious to none; casting no shade; resplendent; severe. Back then I fall, eager no more, desiring only to go, find the street, mark the buildings, greet the applewoman, say to the maid who opens the door: A starry night.

"Good night, good night. You go this way?"

"Alas. I go that."

96

Kew Gardens

Virginia Woolf

From the oval-shaped flower-bed there rose perhaps a hundred stalks spreading into heart-shaped or tongue-shaped leaves half way up and unfurling at the tip red or blue or yellow petals marked with spots of colour raised upon the surface; and from the red, blue or yellow gloom of the throat emerged a straight bar, rough with gold dust and slightly clubbed at the end. The petals were voluminous enough to be stirred by the summer breeze, and when they moved, the red, blue and yellow lights passed one over the other, staining an inch of the brown earth beneath with a spot of the most intricate colour. The light fell either upon the smooth, grey back of a pebble, or, the shell of a snail with its brown, circular veins, or falling into a raindrop, it expanded with such intensity of red, blue and yellow the thin walls of water that one expected them to burst and disappear. Instead, the drop was left in a second silver grey once more, and the light now settled upon the flesh of a leaf, revealing the branching thread of fibre beneath the surface, and again it moved on and spread its illumination in the vast green spaces beneath the dome of the heart-shaped and tongue-shaped leaves. Then the breeze stirred rather more briskly overhead and the colour was flashed into the air above, into the eyes of the men and women who walk in Kew Gardens in July.

The figures of these men and women straggled past the flower-bed with a curiously irregular movement not unlike that of the white and blue butterflies who crossed the turf in zig-zag flights from bed to bed. The man was about six inches in front of the woman, strolling carelessly, while she bore on with greater purpose, only turning her head now and then to see that the children were not too far behind. The man kept this distance in front of the woman purposely, though perhaps unconsciously, for he wished to go on with his thoughts.

"Fifteen years ago I came here with Lily," he thought. "We sat somewhere over there by a lake and I begged her to marry me all through the hot afternoon. How the dragonfly kept circling round us: how clearly I see the dragonfly and her shoe with the square silver buckle at the toe. All the time I spoke I saw her shoe and when it moved impatiently I knew without looking up what she was going to say: the whole of her seemed to be in her shoe. And my love, my desire, were in the dragonfly; for some reason I thought that if it settled there, on that leaf, the broad one with the red flower in the middle of it, if the dragonfly settled on the leaf she would say "Yes" at once. But the dragonfly went round and round: it never settled anywhere—of course not, happily not, or I shouldn't be walking here with Eleanor and the children—Tell me, Eleanor. D'you ever think of the past?"

"Why do you ask, Simon?"

"Because I've been thinking of the past. I've been thinking of Lily, the woman I might have married.... Well, why are you silent? Do you mind my thinking of the past?"

"Why should I mind, Simon? Doesn't one always think of the past, in a garden with men and women lying under the trees? Aren't they one's past, all that remains of it, those men and women, those ghosts lying under the trees,...one's happiness, one's reality?"

"For me, a square silver shoe buckle and a dragonfly—"

"For me, a kiss. Imagine six little girls sitting before their easels twenty years ago, down by the side of a lake, painting the water-lilies, the first red water-lilies I'd ever seen. And suddenly a kiss, there on the back of my neck. And my hand shook all the afternoon so that I couldn't paint. I took out my watch and marked the hour when I would allow myself to think of the kiss for five minutes only—it was so precious—the kiss of an old grey-haired woman with a wart on her nose, the mother of all my kisses all my life. Come, Caroline, come, Hubert."

They walked on past the flower-bed, now walking four abreast, and soon diminished in size among the trees and looked half transparent as the sunlight and shade swam over their backs in large trembling irregular patches.

In the oval flower bed the snail, whose shell had been stained red, blue, and yellow for the space of two minutes or so, now appeared to be moving very slightly in its shell, and next began to labour over the crumbs of loose earth which broke away and rolled down as it passed over them. It appeared to have a definite goal in front of it, differing in this respect from the singular high stepping angular green insect who attempted to cross in front of it, and waited for a second with its antennæ trembling as if in deliberation, and then stepped off as rapidly and strangely in the opposite direction. Brown cliffs with deep green lakes in the hollows, flat, blade-like trees that waved from root to tip, round boulders of grey stone, vast crumpled surfaces of a thin crackling texture—all these objects lay across the snail's progress between one stalk and another to his goal. Before he had decided whether to circumvent the arched tent of a dead leaf or to breast it there came past the bed the feet of other human beings.

This time they were both men. The younger of the two wore an expression of perhaps unnatural calm; he raised his eyes and fixed them very steadily in front of him while his companion spoke, and directly his companion had done speaking he looked on the ground again and sometimes opened his lips only after a long pause and sometimes did not open them at all. The elder man had a curiously uneven and shaky method of walking, jerking his hand forward and throwing up his head abruptly, rather in the manner of an impatient carriage horse tired of waiting outside a house; but in the man these gestures were irresolute and pointless. He talked almost incessantly; he smiled to himself and again began to talk, as if the smile had been an answer. He was talking about spirits—the spirits of the dead, who, according to him, were even now telling him all sorts of odd things about their experiences in Heaven.

"Heaven was known to the ancients as Thessaly, William, and now, with this war, the spirit matter is rolling between the hills like thunder." He paused, seemed to listen, smiled, jerked his head and continued:—

"You have a small electric battery and a piece of rubber to insulate the wire—isolate?—insulate?—well, we'll skip the details, no good going into details that wouldn't be understood—and in short the little machine stands in any convenient position by the head of the bed, we will say, on a neat mahogany stand. All arrangements being properly fixed by workmen under my direction, the widow applies her ear and summons the spirit by sign as agreed. Women! Widows! Women in black——"

Here he seemed to have caught sight of a woman's dress in the distance, which in the shade looked a purple black. He took off his hat, placed his hand upon his heart, and hurried towards her muttering and gesticulating feverishly. But William caught him by the sleeve and touched a flower with the tip of his walking-stick in order to divert the old man's attention. After looking at it for a moment in some confusion the old man bent his ear to it and seemed to answer a voice speaking from it, for he began talking about the forests of Uruguay which he had visited hundreds of years ago in company with the most beautiful young woman in Europe. He could be heard murmuring about forests of Uruguay blanketed with the wax petals of tropical roses, nightingales, sea beaches, mermaids, and women drowned at sea, as he suffered himself to be moved on by William, upon whose face the look of stoical patience grew slowly deeper and deeper.

Following his steps so closely as to be slightly puzzled by his gestures came two elderly women of the lower middle class, one stout and ponderous, the other rosy cheeked and nimble. Like most people of their station they were frankly fascinated by any signs of eccentricity betokening a disordered brain, especially in the well-to-do; but they were too far off to be certain whether the gestures were merely eccentric or genuinely mad. After they had scrutinised the old man's back in silence for a moment and given each other a queer, sly look, they went on energetically piecing together their very complicated dialogue:

"Nell, Bert, Lot, Cess, Phil, Pa, he says, I says, she says, I says, I says, I says——"

"My Bert, Sis, Bill, Grandad, the old man, sugar,
Sugar, flour, kippers, greens,
Sugar, sugar, sugar."

The ponderous woman looked through the pattern of falling words at the flowers standing cool, firm, and upright in the earth, with a curious expression. She saw them as a sleeper waking from a heavy sleep sees a brass candlestick reflecting the light in an unfamiliar way, and closes his eyes and opens them, and seeing the brass candlestick again, finally starts broad awake and stares at the candlestick with all his powers. So the heavy woman came to a standstill opposite the oval-shaped flower bed, and ceased even to pretend to listen to what the other woman was saying. She stood there letting the words fall over her, swaying the top part of her body slowly backwards and forwards, looking at the flowers. Then she suggested that they should find a seat and have their tea.

The snail had now considered every possible method of reaching his goal without going round the dead leaf or climbing over it. Let alone the effort needed for climbing a leaf, he was doubtful whether the thin texture which vibrated with such an alarming crackle when touched even by the tip of his horns would bear his weight; and this determined him finally to creep beneath it, for there was a point where the leaf curved high enough from the ground to admit him. He had just inserted his head in the opening and was taking stock of the high brown roof and was getting used to the cool brown light when two other people came past outside on the turf. This time they were both young, a young man and a young woman. They were both in the prime of youth, or even in that season which precedes the prime of youth, the season before the smooth pink folds of the flower have burst their gummy case, when the wings of the butterfly, though fully grown, are motionless in the sun.

"Lucky it isn't Friday," he observed.

"Why? D'you believe in luck?"

"They make you pay sixpence on Friday."

"What's sixpence anyway? Isn't it worth sixpence?"

"What's 'it'—what do you mean by 'it'?"

"O, anything—I mean—you know what I mean."

Long pauses came between each of these remarks; they were uttered in toneless and monotonous voices. The couple stood still on the edge of the flower bed, and together pressed the end of her parasol deep down into the soft earth. The action and the fact that his hand rested on the top of hers expressed their feelings in a strange way, as these short insignificant words also expressed something, words with short wings for their heavy body of meaning, inadequate to carry them far and thus alighting awkwardly upon the very common objects that surrounded them, and were to their inexperienced touch so massive; but who knows (so they thought as they pressed the parasol into the earth) what precipices aren't concealed in them, or what slopes of ice don't shine in the sun on the other side? Who knows? Who has ever seen this before? Even when she wondered what sort of tea they gave you at Kew, he felt that something loomed up behind her words, and stood vast and solid behind them; and the mist very slowly rose and uncovered—O, Heavens, what were those shapes?—little white tables, and waitresses who looked first at her and then at him; and there was a bill that he would pay with a real two shilling piece, and it was real, all real, he assured himself, fingering the coin in his pocket, real to everyone except to him and to her; even to him it began to seem real; and then—but it was too exciting to stand and think any longer, and he pulled the parasol out of the earth with a jerk and was impatient to find the place where one had tea with other people, like other people.

"Come along, Trissie; it's time we had our tea."

"Wherever *does* one have one's tea?" she asked with the oddest thrill of excitement in her voice, looking vaguely round and letting herself be drawn on down the grass path, trailing her parasol, turning her head this way and that way, forgetting her tea, wishing to go down there and then down there, remembering orchids and cranes among wild flowers, a Chinese pagoda and a crimson crested bird; but he bore her on.

Thus one couple after another with much the same irregular and aimless movement passed the flower-bed and were enveloped in layer after layer of green blue vapour, in which at first their bodies had substance and a dash of colour, but later both substance and colour dissolved in the green-blue atmosphere. How hot it was! So hot that even the thrush chose to hop, like a mechanical bird, in the shadow of the flowers, with long pauses between one movement and the next; instead of rambling vaguely the white butterflies danced one above another, making with their white shifting flakes the outline of a shattered marble column above the tallest flowers; the glass roofs of the palm house shone as if a whole market full of shiny green umbrellas had opened in the sun; and in the drone of the aeroplane the voice of the summer sky murmured its fierce soul. Yellow and black, pink and snow white, shapes of all these colours, men, women, and children were spotted for a second upon the horizon, and then, seeing the breadth of yellow that lay upon the grass, they wavered and sought shade beneath the trees, dissolving like drops of water in the yellow and green atmosphere, staining it faintly with red and blue. It seemed as if all gross and heavy bodies had sunk down in the heat motionless and lay huddled upon the ground, but their voices went wavering from them as if they were flames lolling from the thick waxen bodies of candles. Voices. Yes, voices. Wordless voices, breaking the silence suddenly with such depth of contentment, such passion of desire, or, in the voices of children, such freshness of surprise; breaking the silence? But there was no silence; all the time the motor omnibuses were turning their wheels and changing their gear; like a vast nest of Chinese boxes all of wrought steel turning ceaselessly one within another the city murmured; on the top of which the voices cried aloud and the petals of myriads of flowers flashed their colours into the air.

97

The Mark on the Wall

Virginia Woolf

Perhaps it was the middle of January in the present year that I first looked up and saw the mark on the wall. In order to fix a date it is necessary to remember what one saw. So now I think of the fire; the steady film of yellow light upon the page of my book; the three chrysanthemums in the round glass bowl on the mantelpiece. Yes, it must have been the winter time, and we had just finished our tea, for I remember that I was smoking a cigarette when I looked up and saw the mark on the wall for the first time. I looked up through the smoke of my cigarette and my eye lodged for a moment upon the burning coals, and that old fancy of the crimson flag flapping from the castle tower came into my mind, and I thought of the cavalcade of red knights riding up the side of the black rock. Rather to my relief the sight of the mark interrupted the fancy, for it is an old fancy, an automatic fancy, made as a child perhaps. The mark was a small round mark, black upon the white wall, about six or seven inches above the mantelpiece.

How readily our thoughts swarm upon a new object, lifting it a little way, as ants carry a blade of straw so feverishly, and then leave it.... If that mark was made by a nail, it can't have been for a picture, it must have been for a miniature—the miniature of a lady with white powdered curls, powder-dusted cheeks, and lips like red carnations. A fraud of course, for the people who had this house before us would have chosen pictures in that way—an old picture for an old room. That is the sort of people they were—very interesting people, and I think of them so often, in such queer places, because one will never see them again, never know what happened next. They wanted to leave this house because they wanted to change their style of furniture, so he said, and he was in process of saying that in his opinion art should have ideas behind it when we were torn asunder, as one is torn from the old lady about to pour out tea and the young man about to hit the tennis ball in the back garden of the suburban villa as one rushes past in the train.

But as for that mark, I'm not sure about it; I don't believe it was made by a nail after all; it's too big, too round, for that. I might get up, but if I got up and looked at it, ten to one I shouldn't be able to say for certain; because once a thing's done, no one ever knows how it happened. Oh! dear me, the mystery of life; The inaccuracy of thought! The ignorance of humanity! To show how very little control of our possessions we have—what an accidental affair this living is after all our civilization—let me just count over a few of the things lost in one lifetime, beginning, for that seems always the most mysterious of losses—what cat would gnaw, what rat would nibble—three pale blue canisters of book-binding tools? Then there were the bird cages, the iron hoops, the steel skates, the Queen Anne coal-scuttle, the bagatelle board, the hand organ—all gone, and jewels, too. Opals and emeralds, they lie about the roots of turnips. What a scraping paring affair it is to be sure! The wonder is that I've any clothes on my back, that I sit surrounded by solid furniture at this moment. Why, if one wants to compare life to anything, one must liken it to being blown through the Tube at fifty miles an hour—landing at the other end without a single hairpin in one's hair! Shot out at the feet of God entirely naked! Tumbling head over heels in the asphodel meadows like brown paper parcels pitched down a shoot in the post office! With one's hair flying back like the tail of a race-horse. Yes, that seems to express the rapidity of life, the perpetual waste and repair; all so casual, all so haphazard....

But after life. The slow pulling down of thick green stalks so that the cup of the flower, as it turns over, deluges one with purple and red light. Why, after all, should one not be born there as one is born here, helpless, speechless, unable to focus one's eyesight, groping at the roots of the grass, at the toes of the Giants? As for saying which are trees, and which are men and women, or whether there are such things, that one won't be in a condition to do for fifty years or so. There will be nothing but spaces of light and dark, intersected by thick stalks, and rather higher up perhaps, rose-shaped blots of an indistinct colour—dim pinks and blues—which will, as time goes on, become more definite, become—I don't know what....

And yet that mark on the wall is not a hole at all. It may even be caused by some round black substance, such as a small rose leaf, left over from the summer, and I, not being a very vigilant housekeeper—look at the dust on the mantelpiece, for example, the dust which, so they say, buried Troy three times over, only fragments of pots utterly refusing annihilation, as one can believe.

The tree outside the window taps very gently on the pane.... I want to think quietly, calmly, spaciously, never to be interrupted, never to have to rise from my chair, to slip easily from one thing to another, without any sense of hostility, or obstacle. I want to sink deeper and deeper, away from the surface, with its hard separate facts. To steady myself, let me catch hold of the first idea that passes.... Shakespeare.... Well, he will do as well as another. A man who sat himself solidly in an arm-chair, and looked into the fire, so—A shower of ideas fell perpetually from some very high Heaven down through his mind. He leant his forehead on his hand, and people, looking in through the open door,—for this scene is supposed to take place on a summer's evening—But how dull this is, this historical fiction! It doesn't interest me at all. I wish I could hit upon a pleasant track of thought, a track indirectly reflecting credit upon myself, for those are the pleasantest thoughts, and very frequent even in the minds of modest mouse-coloured people, who believe genuinely that they dislike to hear their own praises. They are not thoughts directly praising oneself; that is the beauty of them; they are thoughts like this:

"And then I came into the room. They were discussing botany. I said how I'd seen a flower growing on a dust heap on the site of an old house in Kingsway. The seed, I said, must have been sown in the reign of Charles the First. What flowers grew in the reign of Charles the First?" I asked—(but I don't remember the answer). Tall flowers with purple tassels to them perhaps. And so it goes on. All the time I'm dressing up the figure of myself in my own mind, lovingly, stealthily, not openly adoring it, for if I did that, I should catch myself out, and stretch my hand at once for a book in self-protection. Indeed, it is curious how instinctively one protects the image of oneself from idolatry or any other handling that could make it ridiculous, or too unlike the original to be believed in any longer. Or is it not so very curious after all? It is a matter of great importance. Suppose the looking glass smashes, the image disappears, and the romantic figure with the green of forest depths all about it is there no longer, but only that shell of a person which is seen by other people—what an airless, shallow, bald, prominent world it becomes! A world not to be lived in. As we face each other in omnibuses and underground railways we are looking into the mirror; that accounts for the vagueness, the gleam of glassiness, in our eyes. And the novelists in future will realize more and more the importance of these reflections, for of course there is not one reflection but an almost infinite number; those are the depths they will explore, those the phantoms they will pursue, leaving the description of reality more and more out of their stories, taking a knowledge of it for granted, as the Greeks did and Shakespeare perhaps—but these generalizations are very worthless. The military sound of the word is enough. It recalls leading articles, cabinet ministers—a whole class of things indeed which as a child one thought the thing itself, the standard thing, the real thing, from which one could not depart save at the risk of nameless damnation. Generalizations bring back somehow Sunday in London, Sunday afternoon walks, Sunday luncheons, and also ways of speaking of the dead, clothes, and habits—like the habit of sitting all together in one room until a certain hour, although nobody liked it. There was a rule for everything. The rule for tablecloths at that particular period was that they should be made of tapestry with little yellow compartments marked upon them, such as you may see in photographs of the carpets in the corridors of the royal palaces. Tablecloths of a different kind were not real tablecloths. How shocking, and yet how wonderful it was to discover that these real things, Sunday luncheons, Sunday walks, country houses, and tablecloths were not entirely real, were indeed half phantoms, and the damnation which visited the disbeliever in them was only a sense of illegitimate freedom. What now takes the place of those things I wonder, those real standard things? Men perhaps, should you be a woman; the masculine point of view which governs our lives, which sets the standard, which establishes Whitaker's Table of Precedency, which has become, I suppose, since the war half a phantom to many men and women, which soon, one may hope, will be laughed into the dustbin where the phantoms go, the mahogany sideboards and the Landseer prints, Gods and Devils, Hell and so forth, leaving us all with an intoxicating sense of illegitimate freedom—if freedom exists....

In certain lights that mark on the wall seems actually to project from the wall. Nor is it entirely circular. I cannot be sure, but it seems to cast a perceptible shadow, suggesting that if I ran my finger down that strip of the wall it would, at a certain point, mount and descend a small tumulus, a smooth tumulus like those barrows on the South Downs which are, they say, either tombs or camps. Of the two I should prefer them to be tombs, desiring melancholy like most English people, and finding it natural at the end of a walk to think of the bones stretched beneath the turf.... There must be some book about it. Some antiquary must have dug up those bones and given them a name.... What sort of a man is an antiquary, I wonder? Retired Colonels for the most part, I daresay, leading parties of aged labourers to the top here, examining clods of earth and stone, and getting into correspondence with the neighbouring clergy, which, being opened at breakfast time, gives them a feeling of importance, and the comparison of arrow-heads necessitates cross-country journeys to the county towns, an agreeable necessity both to them and to their elderly wives, who wish to make plum jam or to clean out the study, and have every reason for keeping that great question of the camp or the tomb in perpetual suspension, while the Colonel himself feels agreeably philosophic in accumulating evidence on both sides of the question. It is true that he does finally incline to believe in the camp; and, being opposed, indites a pamphlet which he is about to read at the quarterly meeting of the local society when a stroke lays him low, and his last conscious thoughts are not of wife or child, but of the camp and that arrowhead there, which is now in the case at the local museum, together with the foot of a Chinese murderess, a handful of Elizabethan nails, a great many Tudor clay pipes, a piece of Roman pottery, and the wine-glass that Nelson drank out of—proving I really don't know what.

No, no, nothing is proved, nothing is known. And if I were to get up at this very moment and ascertain that the mark on the wall is really—what shall we say?—the head of a gigantic old nail, driven in two hundred years ago, which has now, owing to the patient attrition of many generations of housemaids, revealed its head above the coat of paint, and is taking its first view of modern life in the sight of a white-walled fire-lit room, what should I gain?—Knowledge? Matter for further speculation? I can think sitting still as well as standing up. And what is knowledge? What are our learned men save the descendants of witches and hermits who crouched in caves and in woods brewing herbs, interrogating shrew-mice and writing down the language of the stars? And the less we honour them as our superstitions dwindle and our respect for beauty and health of mind increases.... Yes, one could imagine a very pleasant world. A quiet, spacious world, with the flowers so red and blue in the open fields. A world without professors or specialists or house-keepers with the profiles of policemen, a world which one could slice with one's thought as a fish slices the water with his fin, grazing the stems of the water-lilies, hanging suspended over nests of white sea eggs.... How peaceful it is down here, rooted in the centre of the world and gazing up through the grey waters, with their sudden gleams of light, and their reflections—if it were not for Whitaker's Almanack—if it were not for the Table of Precedency!

I must jump up and see for myself what that mark on the wall really is—a nail, a rose-leaf, a crack in the wood?

Here is nature once more at her old game of self-preservation. This train of thought, she perceives, is threatening mere waste of energy, even some collision with reality, for who will ever be able to lift a finger against Whitaker's Table of Precedency? The Archbishop of Canterbury is followed by the Lord High Chancellor; the Lord High Chancellor is followed by the Archbishop of York. Everybody follows somebody, such is the philosophy of Whitaker; and the great thing is to know who follows whom. Whitaker knows, and let that, so Nature counsels, comfort you, instead of enraging you; and if you can't be comforted, if you must shatter this hour of peace, think of the mark on the wall.

I understand Nature's game—her prompting to take action as a way of ending any thought that threatens to excite or to pain. Hence, I suppose, comes our slight contempt for men of action—men, we assume, who don't think. Still, there's no harm in putting a full stop to one's disagreeable thoughts by looking at a mark on the wall.

Indeed, now that I have fixed my eyes upon it, I feel that I have grasped a plank in the sea; I feel a satisfying sense of reality which at once turns the two Archbishops and the Lord High Chancellor to the shadows of shades. Here is something definite, something real. Thus, waking from a midnight dream of horror, one hastily turns on the light and lies quiescent, worshipping the chest of drawers, worshipping solidity, worshipping reality, worshipping the impersonal world which is a proof of some existence other than ours. That is what one wants to be sure of.... Wood is a pleasant thing to think about. It comes from a tree; and trees grow, and we don't know how they grow. For years and years they grow, without paying any attention to us, in meadows, in forests, and by the side of rivers—all things one likes to think about. The cows swish their tails beneath them on hot afternoons; they paint rivers so green that when a moorhen dives one expects to see its feathers all green when it comes up again. I like to think of the fish balanced against the stream like flags blown out; and of water-beetles slowly raising domes of mud upon the bed of the river. I like to think of the tree itself: first the close dry sensation of being wood; then the grinding of the storm; then the slow, delicious ooze of sap. I like to think of it, too, on winter's nights standing in the empty field with all leaves close-furled, nothing tender exposed to the iron bullets of the moon, a naked mast upon an earth that goes tumbling, tumbling, all night long. The song of birds must sound very loud and strange in June; and how cold the feet of insects must feel upon it, as they make laborious progresses up the creases of the bark, or sun themselves upon the thin green awning of the leaves, and look straight in front of them with diamond-cut red eyes.... One by one the fibres snap beneath the immense cold pressure of the earth, then the last storm comes and, falling, the highest branches drive deep into the ground again. Even so, life isn't done with; there are a million patient, watchful lives still for a tree, all over the world, in bedrooms, in ships, on the pavement, lining rooms, where men and women sit after tea, smoking cigarettes. It is full of peaceful thoughts, happy thoughts, this tree. I should like to take each one separately—but something is getting in the way.... Where was I? What has it all been about? A tree? A river? The Downs? Whitaker's Almanack? The fields of asphodel? I can't remember a thing. Everything's moving, falling, slipping, vanishing.... There is a vast upheaval of matter. Someone is standing over me and saying—

"I'm going out to buy a newspaper."

"Yes?"

"Though it's no good buying newspapers.... Nothing ever happens. Curse this war; God damn this war!... All the same, I don't see why we should have a snail on our wall."

Ah, the mark on the wall! It was a snail.

98

Chit-chat from Andalusia

Florence Marryat

A couple of springs ago, business compelling some friends of mine to cross over into Spain, I gladly accepted the cordial invitation they extended to me to visit with them that 'splendid realm of old romance.'

Our destination was Utrera, a small town situated between Seville and Xeres, and lying in the midst of those vast plains so often mentioned in the *Conquest of Granada*.

I confess that I was rather disappointed to find how hurriedly we passed through Madrid and Seville, and I longed to be permitted to linger for a little space within their walls; but ours was not entirely a party of pleasure, and a diversion was soon created in my thoughts by our arrival at Utrera, which, from a distance, presented a most Oriental appearance. The houses, many of which are built in the Moorish fashion and dazzlingly white, stand out clearly defined against the deep blue southern sky; the tall tower of Santiago, with little perhaps but its unusual height to recommend it to a stranger's notice, has, nevertheless, an imposing appearance; and even a palm tree, which, solitary and alone, rears its stately head in the centre of the town, puts in its claim for adding in no small degree to the effect of the whole picture. Notwithstanding, with all the combined advantages of white houses, tall towers, solitary palm trees and romantic situations, I would advise no one who is not a traveller at heart or intent upon his worldly profit to fix his residence in this primitive little Andalusian town.

We first took up our quarters at the posada, with the intention of remaining there during our stay, but were soon obliged to abandon the idea, for, though the best inn in Utrera, it was most uncomfortable, and noisy beyond description.

We began to look about us, therefore, and were soon installed in a small but beautifully clean and cool-looking house in a street leading out of the plaza, and found no reason to be discontented with our abode. It boasted of a pleasant patio (or inner courtyard) and a wide verandah or gallery, into which our rooms opened. As the days grew warmer (and very warm indeed they grew after a while) this patio was our greatest comfort; for, following the example of our neighbours, we had it covered with an awning, and spent the greater part of the day, seated with our books or work, beside its mimic fountain. But if we gained in material comfort by exchanging the noisy and dirty posada for apartments of our own, we had also drawn down upon ourselves the burden of housekeeping, which we found in Spain to be no sinecure. Some friends who had resided a few months in the town, and acquired a fair knowledge of the language, manners, and customs of the natives of Utrera, volunteered to send us a maid, warranted honest and a tolerable proficient in the art of cookery. But she proved a care-full blessing. To give her her due, she possessed one good quality, and we found by experience that it was about the only one she or her sisterhood could boast of: she was very fond of water. The floors of our new house were formed of stone, partially covered by strips of matting which were easily removed; and we soon lived in a perpetual swamp. Antonia was always both ready and willing to 'clean up,' and never seemed happier than when dashing water in all directions, or brushing away vigorously at the matting with her little short-handled broom.

By the way, I wonder why Spanish women prefer to bend double over their sweeping, instead of adopting our easier method of performing the same operation? In vain did I strive to convince Antonia of the advantages attendant on the use of a broom with a long handle: she only smiled, shook her head, and went obstinately on her weary way.

The water for our own consumption was drawn daily from the Moorish aqueduct just outside the town, and brought to us by the aguador, an old fellow who wore a rusty black velvet turban hat stuck full of cigarettes, besides having one always in his mouth. He would pour the water from his wooden barrels into a large butt which stood in the kitchen; but as we discovered that he (together with all who felt so inclined) dipped his glass, with the fingers that held it, into the reservoir whenever he wished to quench his thirst, we speedily invested in a filter.

We soon found that it was utterly impossible to infuse any ideas of cookery or housework into the head of the fair Antonia. If we showed her how to lay the tablecloth and place the dishes, she eyed us with surprise, bordering on contempt, that ladies should perform such menial offices; and the next day all our instructions were as though they had never been. It was the same with everything, until we decided that it was far less trouble to wait on ourselves, and our life at Utrera resolved itself into a picnic without an end.

Nevertheless, when we arose one morning to find that Antonia (wearied perhaps of English suggestions) had quietly walked off and left us to shift entirely for ourselves, we felt inclined to think that we had undervalued her. But she had received her wages on the day before, and we learned afterward that under those circumstances it is a common thing for Spanish servants to quit their places without any warning, and return home for a while to live at their ease on the produce of their labour.

Our next attendant was Pepa, a bright, dark-eyed girl, who always looked so picturesque, with a spray of starry jessamine or scarlet verbena coquettishly placed in her black hair, that it was impossible not to overlook her misdemeanours. She had such an arch way of tossing her head and shaking her long gold earrings that there was no resisting her; and indeed Pepa was but too well aware of the fact herself, and made the best use of her knowledge.

But the dinners were still our *bêtes noirs*, and in these, notwithstanding all her prettiness, she could help us little better than her predecessor. The meat which we procured was simply uneatable, but happily animal food is little needed in those southern climes, and we had plenty of game. Hares, partridges, and wild ducks were most abundant; and a woman used constantly to call on us with live quails for sale, which she would despatch by sticking one of their own feathers into their brains.

Of course, everything was more or less spoiled which we entrusted to the tender mercies of our handmaid; but fortunately there were no epicures amongst us, and we generally received the goods the gods provided with contentment if not gratitude, and had many resources to turn to in order to eke out a distasteful meal. The bread was excellent, and we always had an abundance of oranges, chestnuts, melons, and pomegranates; so that, under the circumstances, we were not to be pitied.

But one day Pepa, disheartened by her repeated failures, begged to be allowed to serve us a Spanish dinner, after tasting which, she affirmed, we should never desire to eat any other; and having received the permission of her mistress, she set to work, and at the usual hour triumphantly placed the national dish of 'puchero' upon the table. We gathered round it rather doubtfully, but after the first timid trial pronounced it 'not so bad, though rather rich.' It seemed to contain a little of everything—beef, lard, garlic, garbanzos (or small, hard beans), lettuce, pepper, potatoes, and I know not what besides; and the mixture had been kept simmering in an earthenware pot for hours. The next dish served by Pepa was 'gaspacho,' or a Spanish salad, which is mixed quite differently from an English one, and to most tastes not so palatable. And then she placed before us a large dish of rice, profusely sprinkled with cinnamon, and various small cakes fried in oil; and Pepa's Spanish dinner (which, by the way, was only a sample, I suppose, of the most ordinary national fare) was concluded.

We were thankful that it had been sufficiently good to enable us to praise it enough to give her satisfaction, though we were compelled to adopt more than one ruse in order, without hurting her feelings, to escape having the same feast repeated every day.

There are not many 'lions' in Utrera, but, such as they are, of course we visited them. The principal one perhaps is in the vaults beneath the church of Santiago, but we were scarcely prepared for the ghastly spectacle which met our gaze there. It appears that, many years ago, while digging for some purpose round the church, the workmen found several bodies, which, owing to some peculiar quality of the soil in which they had been buried, were in a wonderful state of preservation; and, by order of the authorities, they were placed in upright positions against the walls of the church vaults. The old sacristan, who acted as our cicerone, pointed out the bodies to us with his lighted torch, and directed our attention especially to one, evidently that of a very stout woman, which had still a jacket and skirt clinging to it. Strange to say, the bodies were all clothed, although in most cases it had become difficult to distinguish the garments from the remains, for all seemed to partake of the same hue and texture. It is a humbling sight to look upon the dead after they have turned again to their dust, and with but a semblance of the human frame left clinging to them, as though in mockery of our mortality. We could not bear to see the idlers who had followed our party down into the vaults jeering at the appearance of these poor carcases, and touching them in a careless and irreverent manner. Had we had our way, they should all have been tenderly consigned again to the bosom of their mother earth, and we experienced a strange sensation of relief as we turned our backs upon them and emerged once more into the open air.

The principal object of a stroll in Utrera is a visit to the Church of Consolation, which stands on the outskirts of the town, at the end of a long walk bordered with lines of olive trees. At intervals along the way benches are placed, and here on Sundays and feast-days the inhabitants congregate as they come to and from the church. The latter is an interesting edifice, though its architecture is unpretending enough.

Its nave is lofty, and on the whitewashed walls hang hundreds of little waxen and silver limbs, and effigies, with articles of children's clothing and an endless assortment of plaited tails of hair. These are all offerings made to 'Our Lady of Consolation,' in fulfilment of vows or as tokens of thanksgiving for recovery from sickness; and there is something very touching in the idea of these women giving up their most cherished possessions (for every one knows how justly proud the Spanish are of their magnificent hair) as tributes of gratitude to her from whom they have received the favours.

The walls near the western door of the Church of Consolation are hung with innumerable pictures, each bearing so strong a resemblance to the other, both in style and subject, that they might have been drawn by the same hand. As works of art they are valueless, for even the rules of perspective are ignored in a most comical manner, and with slight variations they all represent the same subject. On one hand is an invalid man, woman or child, as the case may be, and on the other a kneeling figure imploring aid for them of the 'Virgin of Consolation,' who is also portrayed appearing to the suppliant, and encircled by a golden halo. Beneath the painting is inscribed the name of the patient, the nature of his disease, and the date of his recovery.

At the back of the church is a large garden belonging to one of the richest proprietors in the neighbourhood of Utrera, and as the midday heat became more oppressive it was a favourite haunt of ours during the cool of the evening, when the air was laden with the perfume of orange blossoms and other sweet-smelling flowers. The owners of the garden permitted it to grow wild, but that circumstance only enhanced its beauty. The orange trees were laden with golden fruit, of which we were courteously invited to gather as much as we pleased. But our visits to this charming retreat were necessarily short, for, as in most southern latitudes, there was scarcely any twilight in Utrera, and it always seemed as though the ringing of the Angelus were a signal for the nights immediately to set in. But what glorious nights they were! The dingy oil-lamps in the streets (for gas is an innovation which had not yet found its way there) were little needed, as the sky always seemed to be one bright blaze of beautiful stars.

The cemetery at Utrera is a quiet spot, surrounded by a high white wall and thickly planted with cypress trees, which give it a most solemn and melancholy appearance. They have the custom there (I am not sure it is not prevalent in other parts of Spain) of burying the dead in recesses in the walls, which are built expressly of an immense thickness; the coffins are shoved into these large pigeon-holes, and the opening is closed with a marble slab, which bears the inscription usual in such cases, somewhat after the fashion of open-air catacombs. But little respect seemed to be shown to the dead.

One day I met some children bearing a bier, upon which was stretched the corpse of a little girl clothed in white garments, and with a wreath of flowers placed upon the placid brow. The children, apparently quite unaware of the reverence due to their sacred burden, carelessly laughed and chatted as they bore it along the highway, sometimes sitting down to rest, and then hurrying forward with unseemly haste, as though to make up for lost time. A tall man, wrapped in a huge cloak, and who evidently belonged to the little *cortège*, followed at a distance, but he too performed the duty at his leisure, and seemed to find nothing extraordinary or out of the way in the children's want of decorum.

With the exception of periodical visits to the Church of Consolation before mentioned, the people of Utrera rarely seemed to leave their houses. To walk for the sake of walking is an idea which finds little favour with a Spanish lady, and my friends and myself were looked upon as very strange beings for taking so much exercise and caring to explore the surrounding country.

But to our English taste it was pleasant to stroll up the Cadiz road until we reached a small mound situated thereon, which was belted with shady trees and amply provided with stone seats. This elevation commanded the view of a vast extent of country, with the grand frowning hills of the Sierra Nevada in the far distance, which the gorgeous sunsets always invested with a strange, unearthly beauty. The intense solitude of the scene, too, was not without its own peculiar charm. At intervals the silence would be broken by the approach of a picturesque-looking peasant bestriding a mule, the silvery jangle of whose bells had been heard in the calm atmosphere for some time before he made his personal appearance. These muleteers never failed to interrupt the monotonous chants they are so fond of singing, to wish us a friendly 'Buenas tardes' ('Good evening') while proceeding on their way, and then we would listen to the sound of the mule's bells and the low rich voice of his master until both died away in the distance, and the scene resumed its normal condition of undisturbed tranquility.

We made an expedition once, by the new railroad, to Moron, a very old town perched on an almost perpendicular rock and visible for miles distant. The heat was intense, but we toiled manfully up the steep and execrably-paved street from the station, and, weary and footsore, were thankful to find ourselves within the cool walls of the fine old church. It possesses some valuable Murillos—one of which, representing the head of our Blessed Lord, is especially beautiful. The altar-rails, screen and reredos are all richly gilt, and the sacristan, taking us into the vestry, unlocked several massively carved chests, which disclosed some valuable plate and precious stones; referring to which, he boasted, with pardonable pride, that Utrera could not produce anything half so handsome. And indeed the inhabitants of Moron may well congratulate themselves on these treasures having escaped the grasp of the French during the war, for the sacristan related to us how everything had been hidden away and miraculously preserved from the hands of the spoiler.

But my chit-chat is drawing to a close. It was not without a certain regret that we bade farewell to Utrera, for during the whole of our stay there we had experienced nothing but kindness from all with whom we had come in contact, and the memory of our sojourn in that little out-of-the-way Andalusian town, if not fraught with brilliant recollections, will, at all events take its rank with that portion of the past which has been too peaceful to rise up again to trouble us. And it were well if we could say the same for every part of our storm-ridden lives.

99

How to Fight the Devil

Harriet Beecher Stowe

"Look here, boys," said Sam, "don't you want to go with me up to the Devil's Den this arternoon?"

"Where is the Devil's Den," said I, with a little awe.

"Wal, it's a longer tramp than I've ever took ye. It's clear up past the pickerel pond, and beyond old Skunk John's pasture-lot. It's a 'mazin' good place for raspberries; shouldn't wonder if we should get two, three quarts there. Great rocks there higher'n yer head; kinder solemn, 'tis."

This was a delightful and seductive account, and we arranged for a walk that very afternoon.

In almost every New-England village the personality of Satan has been acknowledged by calling by his name some particular rock or cave, or other natural object whose singularity would seem to suggest a more than mortal occupancy. "The Devil's Punchbowl," "The Devil's Wash-bowl," "The Devil's Kettle," "The Devil's Pulpit," and "The Devil's Den," have been designations that marked places or objects of some striking natural peculiarity. Often these are found in the midst of the most beautiful and romantic scenery, and the sinister name seems to have no effect in lessening its attractions. To me, the very idea of going to the Devil's Den was full of a pleasing horror. When a boy, I always lived in the shadowy edge of that line which divides spirit land from mortal life, and it was my delight to walk among its half lights and shadows. The old graveyard where, side by side, mouldered the remains of Indian sachems and the ancients of English blood, was my favorite haunt. I loved to sit on the graves while the evening mists arose from them, and to fancy cloudy forms waving and beckoning. To me, this spirit land was my only refuge from the dry details of a hard, prosaic life. The schoolroom—with its hard seats rudely fashioned from slabs of rough wood, with its clumsy desks, hacked and ink-stained, with its unintelligible textbooks and its unsympathetic teacher—was to me a prison out of whose weary windows I watched the pomp and glory of nature,—the free birds singing, the clouds sailing, the trees waving and whispering,—and longed, as earnestly as ever did the Psalmist, to flee far away, and wander in the wilderness.

Hence, no joy of after life—nothing that the world has now to give—can equal that joyous sense of freedom and full possession which came over me on Saturday afternoons, when I started off on a tramp with the world all before me,—the mighty, unexplored world of mysteries and possibilities, bounded only by the horizon. Ignorant alike of all science, neither botanist nor naturalist, I was studying at firsthand all that lore out of which science is made. Every plant and flower had a familiar face to me, and said something to my imagination. I knew where each was to be found, its time of coming and going, and met them year after year as returning friends.

So it was with joyous freedom that we boys ram bled off with Sam this afternoon, intent to find the Devil's Den. It was a ledge of granite rocks rising in the midst of a grove of pines and white birches. The ground was yellow and slippery with the fallen needles of the pines of other days, and the glistening white stems of the birches shone through the shadows like ivory pillars. Underneath the great granite ledges, all sorts of roots and plants grappled and kept foothold; and whole armies of wild raspberries matured their fruit, rounder and juicier for growing in the shade.

In one place yawned a great rift, or cavern, as if the rocks had been violently twisted and wrenched apart, and a mighty bowlder lodging in the rift had roofed it over, making a cavern of most seductive darkness and depth. This was the Devil's Den; and after we had picked our pail full of berries, we sat down there to rest.

"Sam, do you suppose the Devil ever was here?" said I. "What do they call this his den for?"

"Massy, child! that 'are was in old witch times. There used to be witch meetins' held here, and awful doins'; they used to have witch sabba' days and witch sacraments, and sell their souls to the old boy."

"What should they want to do that for?"

"Wal, sure enough; what was it for? I can't make out that the Devil ever gin 'em any thing, any on 'em. They warn't no richer, nor didn't get no more'n this world than the rest; and they was took and hung; and then ef they went to torment after that, they hed a pretty bad bargain on't, I say."

"Well, people don't do such things any more, do they?" said I.

"No," said Sam. "Since the gret fuss and row-de-dow about it, it's kind o' died out; but there's those, I s'pose, that hez dealins' with the old boy. Folks du say that old Ketury was a witch, and that, ef't ben in old times, she'd a hed her neck stretched; but she lived and died in peace."

"But do you think," said I, now proposing the question that lay nearest my heart, "that the Devil can hurt us?"

"That depends consid'able on how you take him," said Sam. "Ye see, come to a straight out-an'-out fight with him, he 'll git the better on yer."

"But," said I, "Christian did fight Apollyon, and got him down too."

I had no more doubt in those days that this was an historic fact than I had of the existence of Romulus and Remus and the wolf.

"Wal, that 'ere warn't jest like real things: they say that 'ere's an allegory. But I 'll tell ye how old Sarah Bunganuck fit the Devil, when he 'peared to her. Ye see, old Sarah she was one of the converted Injuns, and a good old critter she was too; worked hard, and got her livin' honest. She made baskets, and she made brooms, and she used to pick young wintergreen and tie it up in bunches, and dig sassafras and ginsing to make beer; and she got her a little bit o' land, right alongside o' Old Black Hoss John's white-birch wood-lot.

"Now, I've heerd some o' these 'ere modern ministers that come down from Cambridge college, and are larnt about every thing in creation, they say there ain't no devil, and the reason on't is, 'cause there can't be none. These 'ere fellers is so sort o' green!—they don't mean no harm, but they don't know nothin' about nobody that does. If they'd ha' known old Black Hoss John, they'd ha' been putty sure there was a devil. He was jest the crossest, ugliest critter that ever ye see, and he was ugly jest for the sake o' ugliness. He couldn't bear to let the boys pick huckleberries in his paster lots, when he didn't pick 'em himself; and he was allers jawin' me 'cause I would go trout-fishin' in one o' his pasters. Jest ez if the trout that swims warn't, the Lord's, and jest ez much mine as his. He grudged every critter every thing; and if he'd ha' hed his will and way, every bird would ha' fell down dead that picked up a worm on his grounds. He was jest as nippin' as a black frost. Old Black Hoss didn't git drunk in a regerlar way, like Uncle Eph and Toddy Whitney, and the rest o' them boys. But he jest sot at home, a-soakin' on cider, till he was crosser'n a bear with a sore head. Old Black Hoss hed a special spite agin old Sarah. He said she was an old witch and an old thief, and that she stole things off'n his grounds, when everybody knew that she was a regerlar church-member, and as decent an old critter as there was goin'. As to her stealin', she didn't do nothin' but pick huckleberries and grapes, and git chesnuts and wannuts, and butternuts, and them 'ere wild things that's the Lord's, grow on whose land they will, and is free to all. I've hearn 'em tell that, over in the old country, the poor was kept under so, that they couldn't shoot a bird, nor ketch a fish, nor gather no nuts, nor do nothin' to keep from starvin', 'cause the quality folks they thought they owned every thing, 'way-down to the middle of the earth and clear up to the stars. We never hed no sech doin's this side of the water, thank the Lord! We've allers been free to have the chesnuts and the wannuts and the grapes and the huckleberries and the strawberries, ef we could git 'em, and ketch fish when and where we was a mind to. Lordy massy! your grandthur's old Cesar, he used to call the pond his pork-pot. He'd jest go down and throw in a line and ketch his dinner. Wal, Old Black Hoss he know'd the law was so, and he couldn't do nothin' agin her by law; but he sarved her out every mean trick he could think of. He used to go and stan' and lean over her garden-gate and jaw at her an hour at a time; but old Sarah she had the Injun in her; she didn't run to talk much: she used to jest keep on with her weedin and her work, jest's if he warn't there, and that made Old Black Hoss madder'n ever; and he thought he'd try and frighten her off'n the ground, by makin' on her believe he was the Devil. So one time, when he'd been killin' a beef critter, they took off the skin with the horns and all on; and Old Black Hoss he says to Toddy and Eph and Loker, 'You jest come up tonight, and see how I'll frighten old Sarah Bunganuck.'

"Wal, Toddy and Eph and Loker, they hedn't no better to do, and they thought they'd jest go round and see. Ye see 'twas a moonlight night, and old Sarah—she was an industrious critter—she was cuttin' white-birch brush for brooms in the paster-lot.

"Wal, Old Black Hoss he wrapped the critter's skin round him, with the horns on his head, and come and stood by the fence, and begun to roar and make a noise.

"Old Sarah she kept right on with her work, cuttin' her brush and pilin' on't up, and jest let him roar. Wal, Old Black Hoss felt putty foolish, 'specially ez the fellers were waitin' to see how she took it. So he calls out in a grum voice,—

"'Woman, don't yer know who I be?"

"'No,' says she quite quiet, 'I don't know who yer be.'

"'Wal, I'm the Devil,' sez he.

"'Ye be?' says old Sarah. 'Poor old critter, how I pity ye!' and she never gin him another word, but jest bundled up her broom-stuff, and took it on her back and walked off, and Old Black Hoss he stood there mighty foolish with his skin and horns; and so he had the laugh agin him, 'cause Eph and Loker they went and told the story down to the tavern, and he felt awful cheap to think old Sarah had got the upper hands on him.

"Wal, ye see, boys, that 'ere's jest the way to fight the Devil. Jest keep straight on with what ye're doin', and don't ye mind him, and he can't do nothin' to ye."

100

The McWilliamses and the Burglar Alarm

Mark Twain

The conversation drifted smoothly and pleasantly along from weather to crops, from crops to literature, from literature to scandal, from scandal to religion; then took a random jump, and landed on the subject of burglar alarms. And now for the first time Mr. McWilliams showed feeling. Whenever I perceive this sign on this man's dial, I comprehend it, and lapse into silence, and give him opportunity to unload his heart. Said he, with but ill-controlled emotion:

"I do not go one single cent on burglar alarms, Mr. Twain—not a single cent—and I will tell you why. When we were finishing our house, we found we had a little cash left over, on account of the plumber not knowing it. I was for enlightening the heathen with it, for I was always unaccountably down on the heathen somehow; but Mrs. McWilliams said no, let's have a burglar alarm. I agreed to this compromise. I will explain that whenever I want a thing, and Mrs. McWilliams wants another thing, and we decide upon the thing that Mrs. McWilliams wants—as we always do—she calls that a compromise. Very well: the man came up from New York and put in the alarm, and charged three hundred and twenty-five dollars for it, and said we could sleep without uneasiness now. So we did for awhile—say a month. Then one night we smelled smoke, and I was advised to get up and see what the matter was. I lit a candle, and started toward the stairs, and met a burglar coming out of a room with a basket of tinware, which he had mistaken for solid silver in the dark. He was smoking a pipe. I said, 'My friend, we do not allow smoking in this room.' He said he was a stranger, and could not be expected to know the rules of the house: said he had been in many houses just as good as this one, and it had never been objected to before. He added that as far as his experience went, such rules had never been considered to apply to burglars, anyway.

"I said: 'Smoke along, then, if it is the custom, though I think that the conceding of a privilege to a burglar which is denied to a bishop is a conspicuous sign of the looseness of the times. But waiving all that, what business have you to be entering this house in this furtive and clandestine way, without ringing the burglar alarm?'

"He looked confused and ashamed, and said, with embarrassment: 'I beg a thousand pardons. I did not know you had a burglar alarm, else I would have rung it. I beg you will not mention it where my parents may hear of it, for they are old and feeble, and such a seemingly wanton breach of the hallowed conventionalities of our Christian civilization might all too rudely sunder the frail bridge which hangs darkling between the pale and evanescent present and the solemn great deeps of the eternities. May I trouble you for a match?'

"I said: 'Your sentiments do you honor, but if you will allow me to say it, metaphor is not your best hold. Spare your thigh; this kind light only on the box, and seldom there, in fact, if my experience may be trusted. But to return to business: how did you get in here?'

"'Through a second-story window.'

"It was even so. I redeemed the tinware at pawnbroker's rates, less cost of advertising, bade the burglar good-night, closed the window after him, and retired to headquarters to report. Next morning we sent for the burglar-alarm man, and he came up and explained that the reason the alarm did not 'go off' was that no part of the house but the first floor was attached to the alarm. This was simply idiotic; one might as well have no armor on at all in battle as to have it only on his legs. The expert now put the whole second story on the alarm, charged three hundred dollars for it, and went his way. By and by, one night, I found a burglar in the third story, about to start down a ladder with a lot of miscellaneous property. My first impulse was to crack his head with a billiard cue; but my second was to refrain from this attention, because he was between me and the cue rack. The second impulse was plainly the soundest, so I refrained, and proceeded to compromise. I redeemed the property at former rates, after deducting ten per cent. for use of ladder, it being my ladder, and, next day we sent down for the expert once more, and had the third story attached to the alarm, for three hundred dollars.

"By this time the 'annunciator' had grown to formidable dimensions. It had forty-seven tags on it, marked with the names of the various rooms and chimneys, and it occupied the space of an ordinary wardrobe. The gong was the size of a wash-bowl, and was placed above the head of our bed. There was a wire from the house to the coachman's quarters in the stable, and a noble gong alongside his pillow.

"We should have been comfortable now but for one defect. Every morning at five the cook opened the kitchen door, in the way of business, and rip went that gong! The first time this happened I thought the last day was come sure. I didn't think it in bed—no, but out of it—for the first effect of that frightful gong is to hurl you across the house, and slam you against the wall, and then curl you up, and squirm you like a spider on a stove lid, till somebody shuts the kitchen door. In solid fact, there is no clamor that is even remotely comparable to the dire clamor which that gong makes. Well, this catastrophe happened every morning regularly at five o'clock, and lost us three hours sleep; for, mind you, when that thing wakes you, it doesn't merely wake you in spots; it wakes you all over, conscience and all, and you are good for eighteen hours of wide-awakeness subsequently—eighteen hours of the very most inconceivable wide-awakeness that you ever experienced in your life. A stranger died on our hands one time, and we vacated and left him in our room overnight. Did that stranger wait for the general judgment? No, sir; he got up at five the next morning in the most prompt and unostentatious way. I knew he would; I knew it mighty well. He collected his life-insurance, and lived happy ever after, for there was plenty of proof as to the perfect squareness of his death.

"Well, we were gradually fading toward a better land, on account of the daily loss of sleep; so we finally had the expert up again, and he ran a wire to the outside of the door, and placed a switch there, whereby Thomas, the butler, always made one little mistake—he switched the alarm off at night when he went to bed, and switched it on again at daybreak in the morning, just in time for the cook to open the kitchen door, and enable that gong to slam us across the house, sometimes breaking a window with one or the other of us. At the end of a week we recognized that this switch business was a delusion and a snare. We also discovered that a band of burglars had been lodging in the house the whole time—not exactly to steal, for there wasn't much left now, but to hide from the police, for they were hot pressed, and they shrewdly judged that the detectives would never think of a tribe of burglars taking sanctuary in a house notoriously protected by the most imposing and elaborate burglar alarm in America.

"Sent down for the expert again, and this time he struck a most dazzling idea—he fixed the thing so that opening the kitchen door would take off the alarm. It was a noble idea, and he charged accordingly. But you already foresee the result. I switched on the alarm every night at bed-time, no longer trusting on Thomas's frail memory; and as soon as the lights were out the burglars walked in at the kitchen door, thus taking the alarm off without waiting for the cook to do it in the morning. You see how aggravatingly we were situated. For months we couldn't have any company. Not a spare bed in the house; all occupied by burglars.

"Finally, I got up a cure of my own. The expert answered the call, and ran another ground wire to the stable, and established a switch there, so that the coachman could put on and take off the alarm. That worked first rate, and a season of peace ensued, during which we got to inviting company once more and enjoying life.

"But by and by the irrepressible alarm invented a new kink. One winter's night we were flung out of bed by the sudden music of that awful gong, and when we hobbled to the annunciator, turned up the gas, and saw the word 'Nursery' exposed, Mrs. McWilliams fainted dead away, and I came precious near doing the same thing myself. I seized my shotgun, and stood timing the coachman whilst that appalling buzzing went on. I knew that his gong had flung him out, too, and that he would be along with his gun as soon as he could jump into his clothes. When I judged that the time was ripe, I crept to the room next the nursery, glanced through the window, and saw the dim outline of the coachman in the yard below, standing at present-arms and waiting for a chance. Then I hopped into the nursery and fired, and in the same instant the coachman fired at the red flash of my gun. Both of us were successful; I crippled a nurse, and he shot off all my back hair. We turned up the gas, and telephoned for a surgeon. There was not a sign of a burglar, and no window had been raised. One glass was absent, but that was where the coachman's charge had come through. Here was a fine mystery—a burglar alarm 'going off' at midnight of its own accord, and not a burglar in the neighborhood!

"The expert answered the usual call, and explained that it was a 'False alarm.' Said it was easily fixed. So he overhauled the nursery window, charged a remunerative figure for it, and departed.

"What we suffered from false alarms for the next three years no stylographic pen can describe. During the next three months I always flew with my gun to the room indicated, and the coachman always sallied forth with his battery to support me. But there was never anything to shoot at—windows all tight and secure. We always sent down for the expert next day, and he fixed those particular windows so they would keep quiet a week or so, and always remembered to send us a bill about like this:

Wire	$2.15
Nipple	.75
Two hours' labor	1.50
Wax	.47
Tape	.34
Screws	.15
Recharging battery	.98
Three hours' labor	2.25
String	.02
Lard	.66
Pond's Extract	1.25
Springs at 50	2.00
Railroad fares	7.25
	19.77

"At length a perfectly natural thing came about—after we had answered three or four hundred false alarms—to wit, we stopped answering them. Yes, I simply rose up calmly, when slammed across the house by the alarm, calmly inspected the annunciator, took note of the room indicated; and then calmly disconnected that room from the alarm, and went back to bed as if nothing had happened. Moreover, I left that room off permanently, and did not send for the expert. Well, it goes without saying that in the course of time all the rooms were taken off, and the entire machine was out of service.

"It was at this unprotected time that the heaviest calamity of all happened. The burglars walked in one night and carried off the burglar alarm! yes, sir, every hide and hair of it: ripped it out, tooth and nail; springs, bells, gongs, battery, and all; they took a hundred and fifty miles of copper wire; they just cleaned her out, bag and baggage, and never left us a vestige of her to swear at—swear by, I mean.

"We had a time of it to get her back; but we accomplished it finally, for money. The alarm firm said that what we needed now was to have her put in right—with their new patent springs in the windows to make false alarms impossible, and their new patent clock attached to take off and put on the alarm morning and night without human assistance. That seemed a good scheme. They promised to have the whole thing finished in ten days. They began work, and we left for the summer. They worked a couple of days; then they left for the summer. After which the burglars moved in, and began their summer vacation. When we returned in the fall, the house was as empty as a beer closet in premises where painters have been at work. We refurnished, and then sent down to hurry up the expert. He came up and finished the job, and said: 'Now this clock is set to put on the alarm every night at 10, and take it off every morning at 5:45. All you've got to do is to wind her up every week, and then leave her alone—she will take care of the alarm herself.'

"After that we had a most tranquil season during three months. The bill was prodigious, of course, and I had said I would not pay it until the new machinery had proved itself to be flawless. The time stipulated was three months. So I paid the bill, and the very next day the alarm went to buzzing like ten thousand bee swarms at ten o'clock in the morning. I turned the hands around twelve hours, according to instructions, and this took off the alarm; but there was another hitch at night, and I had to set her ahead twelve hours once more to get her to put the alarm on again. That sort of nonsense went on a week or two, then the expert came up and put in a new clock. He came up every three months during the next three years, and put in a new clock. But it was always a failure. His clocks all had the same perverse defect: they would put the alarm on in the daytime, and they would not put it on at night; and if you forced it on yourself, they would take it off again the minute your back was turned.

"Now there is the history of that burglar alarm—everything just as it happened; nothing extenuated, and naught set down in malice. Yes, sir,—and when I had slept nine years with burglars, and maintained an expensive burglar alarm the whole time, for their protection, not mine, and at my sole cost—for not a d—-d cent could I ever get THEM to contribute—I just said to Mrs. McWilliams that I had had enough of that kind of pie; so with her full consent I took the whole thing out and traded it off for a dog, and shot the dog. I don't know what you think about it, Mr. Twain; but I think those things are made solely in the interest of the burglars. Yes, sir, a burglar alarm combines in its person all that is objectionable about a fire, a riot, and a harem, and at the same time had none of the compensating advantages, of one sort or another, that customarily belong with that combination. Good-by: I get off here."